Bearslayer

Book One of the Hereward Saga

Dennis Freeman-Wright

me and some thought my appearance 'odd'. When other children wanted to taunt me, they often shouted 'spooky eyes', but name calling never bothered me. I did notice that my mother and Uncle Brand's eyes were blue, whereas my father's eyes were grey, this just confirmed to me that I belonged to both of them.

We continued our horseplay for some time until Feng ambled down from the hall. "Young master Heri, if your ma sees you like this there will be trouble; you'd best be getting cleaned up and ready for church." Reluctantly I parted from my friends and returned to my small place in the hall where I kept my personal belongings. Looking myself up and down I realised that I had to do a complete change of clothing or my mother would explode so I stripped off and donned my best breeches and tunic. I used my prized possession, my ivory comb to compose my hair. Like all true northerners, Danes, Norwegians, and us Angles I valued my carved whalebone comb; after straightening out my hair I tied it back with a leather strip so that I looked less unkempt.

Just as I had finished composing myself my mother exited her bower together with Hilda her maid dressed in a fine woollen dress with an embroidered over-tabard. Her hair was coiled around her head leaving her swanlike neck exposed. I knew she was truly beautiful and understood why my father loved her.

"Well, Heri for once you have tidied yourself up, you must promise me to remember to keep an acceptable hygienic standard in your father's hall. Come." I followed my mother out of the hall; of course, our farm did not have a church, the nearest one being at Bourne but with my uncle being present there was no way that mass would not be said. The whole farm population gathered at the major oak that grew between the farm yard and the stream. The tree was enormous and all the residents of the farm could shelter beneath its spreading branches.

We dutifully listened as my uncle intoned a lengthy prayer to the almighty, I did not understand a lot of it but when he had finished, we all shouted a rousing "Amen". We then sang a hymn and again I was not sure of all the words so I suppose I sounded like a strangled cat squeaking inanity. My uncle had a finely wrought goblet for the Eucharist, which he filled from a leather flask he carried with him and he had a box of strange wafer biscuits that I had tasted before; they tasted bland and were most unappetising and I could not believe they came from the flesh of Christ, but what do I know? Wynter asserted that when my uncle was at the farm his mam baked them from just flour and water. I queued with most everyone else to take the Eucharist, I had made my confession the day before and as usual it centred on my lack of smart appearance and the need to set an example to the other members of our small community. The wine was thin and watery but refreshing and after the final hymn and prayers I was more positive about my future and determined to make my mother proud of me. My birthday was celebrated with a small feast.

The following day Abbot Brand mounted his old mule and I my small pony, the animal I loved second only to my dog Boy. My pony had been gifted to me by my father and had come from some moor over in the west. It was a beautiful chestnut coloured mare with a lighter mane and tail. I felt I was getting a little too big for her but as I was small for my age perhaps this was wishful thinking. I called her Beda after my mother's maid because they both had wide arses. This was a source of amusement for my friends and I but we kept the joke to ourselves as I am sure my mother would not have seen the funny side and I am sure Beda would not.

The weather was overcast but the rain held off as we made our way westwards towards Stamford and the track west. My dog Boy roamed widely ahead of us enjoying the discovery of new smells and spores. In late spring the ground was drying out and the journey only took four days across the border of the Danelagh at Haverberg and then following the valley of the River Avon to Coventry. Coventry was built on low lying ground on both sides of the river Sherbourne but it was on the south side of the river that my father's hall was situated together with a mess of building works I later learnt was to be a monastery.

Our entourage dismounted at the entrance to the earl's great hall, it was much larger than the hall in Bourne and was the biggest building I had ever seen. It even appeared to have more than one entrance with small doors at either end of the building. The main door was in its usual place along the side of the hall facing south away from the chill north winds of our English winters. I thought the extra doors were likely to make the place much draughtier than a normal hall and also make the place harder to guard, but I could see that having extra exits reduced the likelihood of a successful hall burning like in the Fall of the Niflungs.

"Come on Heri." My uncle gruffly motioned me towards the guarded entrance. I had the presence of mind to tie Boy to one of the porch posts before I ascended two wooden steps, which I saw were designed to keep rainwater from the hall and stood before the two huscarls. Both warriors were encased in mail coats to their mid-thigh. They wore nasal helmets with coifs that hid most of their faces. Large round shields were slung on their backs and they both held angon spears a foot or so taller than they were. They looked suitably fierce.

"Who wishes entrance to the Lord of Mercia?" one of the warriors boomed from within his coif. Taking a deep breath and before Uncle Brand could interpose.

"I am Hereward Leofricson of Bourne, son of the Earl and he has sent for me." I replied. The two huscarls exchanged glances and the same huscarl who had previously challenged me responded, "Then enter little lord the earl is inside."

I passed through the wide doors noticing the intricate carvings around the supports and lintel; although they displayed the usual Anglian love of intertwined foliage and writhing serpents, I noticed there was a profusion of Christian crosses, pascal lambs and other motifs. I stepped boldly into the hall, or so I hoped; for although I was fond of my father, he was distant in that I rarely met him and was not sure what to expect. My uncle Brand placed his hand reassuringly on my shoulder and guided me forward. As in all mead halls large or small the layout was similar; there were long trestle tables running the length of the hall, they had been pushed back to allow a wide space to walk in the centre of the hall north to south. The floor was covered in matted rushes and in the centre of the hall was a long fire pit and in late spring embers still glowed. The wooden walls of the hall were covered in woollen hangings with various pictures depicted on them but at that time I did not notice what they were. Unlike the hall in Bourne, which had a thatched roof this hall had a wooden ceiling with carved and ornamental beams. There were some men lounging on the benches at the trestle tables, mostly off-duty huscarls I guessed and a few young girls were moving around carrying large pots of beer or mead for the men's pleasure.

Looking to the south end of the hall I saw the raised platform where I expected my father to be sitting, I immediately saw that there were four people sitting on wooden chairs on the dais. Walking steadily towards them I realised that of the three people seated around my father, one was a woman, one a young man and the last an unmistakable priest of some sort. Ignoring all of them I kept my eyes locked on my father until I halted directly in front of him.

My uncle spoke first, "My lord Earl, at your command I have brought young Hereward from Bourne." I thought to myself, he could have said "I have brought your son", but the tension in the hall was apparent so I was still. After a long pause when I felt that I was being examined and appraised by all on the dais my father spoke.

"Welcome to Coventry young Hereward." His voice was melodious and betrayed his west country origins; my uncle had explained that my father was hereditary Ealdorman of the Hwicce, a territory further to the south west than Mercia and less influenced by the Danish colonisation in the east of Mercia. My father was Earl of Mercia by right of his marriage to his lawful wife Godgifu and by the authority of a previous King of England, Knut the Mighty. Even seated my father was an authoritative figure; his hair was long and flowing in the Anglian manner, it remained loose and unbraided but his full beard was neatly combed. He looked tall when seated but I knew, like me, he was of only medium height. He wore rich dark green robes with red embroidered trims and his trousers appeared to be gartered with gold bands. Across his knees, as was the custom, he held a jewelled sheathed ring sword. I knew he was about fifty years of age and no longer a young man and I realised I was a son of his middle years.

My father launched into what was obviously a carefully prepared introduction. "Hereward, I have summoned you to my court so that you may be educated to a level to suit your station. It is my intention that you will play a role in Mercia when you reach man's estate. Obviously at your age it cannot be certain what your future contribution will be in supporting the earldom be it secular or temporal but you will be given the appropriate training whatever. I have appointed tutors for your martial development and my lady wife has appointed Brother Herluin here for your spiritual education and letters." My father indicated the priestly figure seated on a stool to his right. I looked across briefly to see a scowling, dark visaged man of middle years dressed in black and white robes. His jet-black hair was neatly tonsured and his clawlike fingers clutched a wooden rosary with a pendant cross affixed. He looked far from happy and I wondered what I had done to upset him.

My father continued, "Before I release you to your tutors' I must first introduce you to my wife Godgifu, Lady of the Mercians and to my eldest son Aelfgar." I turned my head slightly to take in my father's lawful wife for the first time and gasped in astonishment! Even at my tender age I knew true beauty and I also knew that I beheld it for the first time in my life. I had thought my mother was beautiful and I knew my father loved her but next to this goddess every other woman I had seen paled into insignificance. Godgifu's hair was a brilliant burnished golden waterfall, even when it was bound and plaited. The plaits of her hair fell from her head to the floor when seated. She had confined her hair in a gold headband with a fabric net head-covering sprinkled with sparkling stones leaving her face unhindered. Her face was a marvel to behold, smooth with a creamy complexion, arched eyebrows above sky blue eyes and long lashes that confounded her hair by being dark and long. Her neck was swan-like; many beautiful women are likened to having a swan-like neck but in Godgifu's case it was true. Her large and swollen breasts were encompassed in rich shiny blue fabric that accentuated every curve, they were truly bountiful and must be the envy of every other female. Her form otherwise was slender; I suspected that when she stood, she was taller than my father. From beneath the hem of her robe a dainty foot peeped out clad in gold slippers that matched her glorious hair. Although no longer a maid her beauty was timeless, I was told later that she was past forty years of age, which I did not believe.

The lady spoke to me but I really did not take in what she said so dazed and bemused was I. Whilst talking her face was stern, hostile even, if such a face could express such negative expressions. I was entranced and completely mesmerised by Lady Godgifu's beauty and totally missed the trail of conversation that followed. After some time, I realised that the other person on the dais was addressing me and I could see from the expression on his face that he was amused and clearly understood how my mind had been captured.

His conversation started to register when he said "….. and eventually you may become my squire in the French manner." Blinking I dragged my attention away from the Lady Godgifu's face to the younger man sitting to her right. I thought young but this was relative to the age of my father, the man was probably about twenty-five years of age and in the prime of his life. He had sandy hair, slightly dishevelled and a freckled face; if he was the eldest son of my father and the Lady of Mercia, he did not resemble them in any way being the lesser of either of their noble attractions; but he was tall, I could see that, tall and thin.

"Father let me take young Hereward away and show him around, this all must be very strange to him and I would put him at ease." The man spoke to my father and this confirmed him to be Aelfgar my older step-brother. After my father gave a nod of consent my older brother stepped down from the dais grabbed my shoulder and escorted me out of the hall through a back entrance; my uncle remained.

As we left the hall, I heard the Lady Godgifu speak "What is the matter with his eyes?" I did not hear anymore. Aelfgar sat me down at a bench near a horse paddock at the back of the hall.

"Well Hereward I can see you were smitten by my mother." I blushed and looked embarrassed and Aelfgar laughed. "Don't be embarrassed about your reaction to my mother, all men act the same way from young boys like you to old men who can barely walk." I now looked shocked. "My mother has that effect on men but do not be deceived. She is no love goddess like Freya and what is more she does not particularly like men, let me explain. My mother was only twelve when she was forcibly married off to an evil man called Edric Streona, one of the late King Aethelred's cronies. Edric did the king's dirty work, assassinations, that sort of thing. When the king made Edric the Ealdorman of the Mercians he even gave his own daughter to him as wife but Edric was unfaithful to Aethelred and betrayed him to Knut the Dane who became the English King. So, Edric repudiated Aethelred's daughter and forcibly married my mother who as I said was the Mercian heiress the daughter of Ealdormen Aelfhelm. It did not do Edric any good though because Knut soon executed him as he did not trust traitors. King Knut made our father the new ealdorman or earl as he is being called now. Our father was the hereditary ealdormen of the Hwicce and so Knut advised him to marry my mother as well; so, within a few years she was married twice and I was born when she was fifteen. Apart from the abuse she had received from Edric my birth was apparently a frightful affair when she nearly died." I was mesmerised by all this, another part of the jigsaw that made up the relationship between my own mother and my father the earl. "After that, well my mother vowed to have no more children and dedicate herself to God and the church. Of course, because of her position she could not become a nun but she shuns men. I know why my father visits your mother and I understand but strangely my mother does not, she expects Leofric to remain celibate like her and that is why she hates your mother and she hates you." Aelfric finished with a wry smile.

"That's a lot to take in I know but I will help you through this." Aelfgar smiled more openly and added "Meanwhile I have an absolute brute of a huscarl named Fridleaf who is going to teach you to be a real warrior."

1052 – The Youth

I was angry, furious, yet again I had been insulted and abused by my step-mother and that bastard Norman priest, Herluin; the insidious sniping was always worst when my father was away. After a morning of stormy exchanges, I fled Coventry and ended up sitting in an inn on the road to Warwick.

I was now fifteen summers and had been under Herluin's tutelage for nearly five years. Much had happened in those years but I had been left out of any part of it. My father had been involved in the national affairs down in Wessex with the king, Edward the Mild, trying to stiffen his spine against the Godwinsons and the Normans. My father and Siward, Earl of Northumbria had managed to have Godwin and his sons outlawed and they were currently raiding the south coast of Wessex, when the weather permitted. The King still kept his Norman friends close. My half-brother Aelfgar had, more or less taken, over the military side of ruling the earldom for my father and was spending a lot of time in the west rebuffing the incursions of Welsh raiders.

Me, I was sent to school. Some of my education was not at all bad. The housecarl Fridleaf was a superlative teacher when it came to combat. He toughened me up, I was covered in layers of muscle. He taught me how to use every conceivable weapon, how to ride, how to shoot with bow and arrow and how to survive in the wilderness. I did not grow that tall but I knew he was proud of me.

I did not become my brother's squire in the Norman-French manner. This was because my step-mother had other ideas. She routinely pressed my father about not doing enough for the church although she seemed to be endowing churches and monasteries every other month. She persistently kept suggesting I should be trained and enter holy orders even though anyone could see I was unsuited for such a life. My father prevaricated knowing my martial inclination but unwilling to go against his wife's wishes. This left me in limbo and I freely admit I was going mad with frustration.

To make things worse I was still infatuated by my step-mother. In the last few years, growing into manhood I became aware of my sexuality. Uncontrolled erections, masturbation in the dark of my closet and worse, sexual fantasies about my step-mother. Other women and girls paled in comparison to her and I found it hard to have any interest in other females. I found myself following her around, spying on her, I yearned to see her naked. Of course, she saw right through me and despised me accordingly; her 'squint-eyed peeper' she called me to her confidante, Herluin the priest.

Spurred on by my behaviour, Herluin excelled in his punishments; cold baths, whippings, enforced fasting and prayers. I was the subject of all punishments that would not be noticed by my father or Aelfgar. I, of course was, in no position to complain about my treatment. I remained at the ville in Coventry whilst my father perambulated around Mercia exercising his authority or was down in Winchester or London at the king's court, and even sneaking off to Bourne to see my mother, without me.

The Welsh were raiding in Herefordshire and although the county was not considered to be in Mercia or he Hwicce, Aelfgar had mustered a host to guard our south western border and go to the aid of the Earl of Hereford if need arose. I desperately wanted to be with him but knew that Godgifu would prevent it.

My real torment, however was meted out by Brother Herluin; every day I would have to submit to his lessons, which mainly consisted of homilies on the lives of the saints and reading and learning Latin from various religious books. He would deride every error I made with insulting and snide remarks the worst always referring to my bastard status or my 'devil's eyes'. He seemed to have no understanding of the nature of handfast marriage considering it a sin. Once when I pointed out that the great King Knut had had more than two wives, he ranted on about the heathen Dane being nothing more than a viking who undoubtably burned in hell. His method of correction was to switch me with a birch rod usually on the back but sometimes on the knuckles. He was always suggesting that I should wear a novice's habit and refrain from carrying my hunting knife at my belt; needless to say, I always resisted these strictures. In my earlier years it seemed to please him immensely when the beatings made my eyes brim with tears, which I always held back refusing to cry in front of him. Later as my body toughened and my frame expanded the beatings did not bother me much at all physically but the humiliation and insults festered worse.

I had to admit that not all his lessons were intolerable, I became adept at reading and enjoyed reading those parts of the Bible where the judges of old fought and defeated the enemies of the Hebrews. There were other books in my father's library written by Roman and Greek writers from times long past. I devoured the books on warfare and military strategies and even took to borrowing the books to read alone in the woods when time allowed.

I had no friends; boys of my own age were kept from me by Godgifu and my only release from my prison was my strange relationship with Brother Martin. Like me Brother Martin seemed to be the lowest of the low in the church hierarchy. He spent most of his time labouring and cleaning up after other priests and monks, this meant he spent a lot of time in the stables where we first met. Martin would tell me stories that I had never heard before, wonderful tales of heroes and adventures; tales of a warrior king of the Britons called Arthur and a hero of the Franks called Hrodland. They slew dragons and monsters, rescued fair ladies and according to Martin, Arthur defeated and drove out the Angles from England. This was patent nonsense of course as the Angles ruled the island, not the Britons, who we call Welsh. Still the stories were fascinating and allowed me to escape from the strictures that surrounded me.

The other reason I was thankful for Brother Martin was because of Boy. Although the Earl's hall was home to several hunting hounds belonging to my father, the Lady Godgifu refused to let Boy into the hall and insisted it should be 'put down' or at least returned to Bourne. Brother Martin removed the offensive animal from sight and looked after Boy for me.

I had been sitting outside the inn drinking steadily for some time and as I was unused to large quantities of ale, I was somewhat tipsy. To my surprise down the road mounted on a magnificent bay mare, all glossy coat and jingling expensive harness came Brother Herluin. He quickly spotted me and walked his horse over to my bench.

"Well, what have we here; a drunken rogue unfit for polite society, what do you think our Lady Godgifu will say when she hears about this?" Herluin sneered.

"Well, the only way she will hear about this will be if you tell her and I am sure you will embellish the tale suitably to make a simple drink at a tavern sound like the feast of Belshazzar." I retorted. I could see that my response had infuriated Herluin and without thought he lifted his riding crop and brought it down upon my head.

"You heathen miscreant, I will have you cast out for this." Herluin roared.

At first, I was momentarily stunned and then my fury boiled over, I leapt up and grabbed the horse's reins pulling them towards me. This had the desired effect as the horse was prevented from rearing back, I grabbed Herluin's expensive furred robe, which he habitually wore over his habit and pulled him headlong from the saddle. Herluin was much lighter than I had imagined and he flew past my shoulder and landed prone on top of the wooden trestle table. Groggily he rolled over and I could see that his face was covered in blood where is nose had smashed against the wooden board.

"You bastard boy, I will have you whipped for this." Herluin hissed. This remark only added to my fury; the word 'whipped' reminded me of all the times Herluin had administered the rod on my back. I picked up the riding crop that lay on the ground and grabbed hold of the priest's shoulder and rolled him back onto his stomach. I then commenced to beat his buttock's as hard as I could. After several minutes I regained my senses and realised that I had probably gone too far; Herluin was blubbering, tears running down his face so I rolled him over and searched his garments for a piece of cloth to wipe his face. My hand found a pocket within his expensive robe and inside I felt a hard object, pulling it out I was astonished to find my whalebone comb, which I had lost some months before, or so I supposed. I now realised Herluin had stolen it.

"You bloody thief; call yourself a man of God, you are no more than a miscreant yourself." I shouted in his ear. I placed my comb in my pouch and for good measure I kicked the priest on his sore buttocks. It then came to me that making the foul priest walk back to Coventry would be most appropriate, so I caught the horse, mounted, and rode away.

I cantered the horse back to the stables in Coventry noting that the stable boy gave me a funny look when he saw the horse I was riding. Not knowing quite what to do I went to see Fridleaf my war-master and related the whole tale to him. His face grew more concerned as the tale unfolded.

"Young master Hereward you have done a foolish thing, the Lady will take Herluin's side in this and your father isn't here to protect you." Fridleaf concluded gravely.

"Should I flee?" I responded despairingly; I realised what Fridleaf had said was true and I was in big trouble.

"You are the Earl's son so that is out of the question, you must face your fate, the Lady would not dare act against you without the Earl's agreement.

I waited in the hall with trepidation knowing that a summons would eventually come but I was not expecting the armed retainers that were sent to fetch me. Two huscarls covered from neck to mid-calf in padded ring mail gambesons, with their heads covered by coifs and helmets and carrying round shields and spears marched into the hall and flanked me.

"Right lad, the Lady wants to see you." There was no point in protesting so they led me away from the hall into Lady Godgifu's bower.

The Earl's wife sat on a chair arrayed with cushions and surrounded by her ladies-in-waiting. However, the group of women were flanked by two huscarls on each side and of course standing behind Godgifu and whispering in her ear was the toad Herluin. The countess glared at me and made the sign of the cross before her as if a devil was approaching her. Herluin mimicked her action, his face was too bruised for his usual sneer to show.

"Well, boy, you have gone too far this time, sacrilege, an assault on the body of a man of God and theft from Holy Church." Godgifu spoke seemly in despair at my outrageous conduct.

"That is not true." I shouted, "He struck me first, on the head, without provocation and he stole my comb. Yes, I retaliated but he deserved it."

"You were drunk and beat a defenceless priest." She added.

"No, I was not drunk, I had been drinking, yes but that is not a crime. He had no right to admonish me." I responded forcefully, the two huscarls moved nearer to me.

"I do not want to hear more; you do not seem to understand that Herluin is a man of God not to be treated with violence. You will be taken to the King in Winchester for his justice to be administered."

The huscarls ushered me away and I was taken to a small room with no windows or other means of exit. Clearly it was assumed I would run away if allowed. The day had not turned out as I had expected and to make matters worse no one bothered to feed me.

The next day Lady Godgifu set off with an entourage of warriors and her household ladies and of course Herluin who sat rather uncomfortably on his recovered horse; I was placed on a small horse without a saddle and my feet were tied beneath the horse's girth, my hands were also tied behind my back. For the second day I was denied food and water. I was flanked by the two huscarls so that I had no chance to escape not that I wanted to. I knew that my father was with the king and I believed that he would see justice done in my favour.

The journey to Winchester took two weeks, Lady Godgifu travelled sedately and ensured she stayed at religious houses each night. Eventually on the third day of my captivity I was given some stale bread and hard cheese with a jug of water; the huscarls were clearly bored with this leisurely journey, as was I. Eventually we reached Winchester, which was the favoured capital of the English Kings, deep in their original home territory of Wessex. I was placed in a room in a large house, which I assumed was my father's town house when he was attending the King. Within a very short time my father entered the room, he looked very upset, and I knew I had let him down.

"Hereward, boy, what have you done?"

"Father, I have behaved like a man, not a slave to be abused." I responded, "If I have acted unwisely, it is because I was

21

provoked and treated below my station. I have been starved and shackled; am I not an earl's son? If I am, I should be treated with respect not beaten relentlessly; if I am not then cast me out, let me return to my mother or live the life of a free viking."

Exasperated Leofric outlined the realities, "That is your uncle Brand speaking, you are not your ancestor Palna-Toki the Jomsviking and you are not even your great-grandfather who died fighting for Byrhtnoth at Maldon against Olaf Tryggvason and Tall Thorkell. England is a different place now under the rule of Edward the Mild; for a start he is excessively pious, just like your step-mother and any assaults on the church however well justified will be dealt with harshly. I have spent a great deal of effort weakening the power of the Godwinson's only to have that fool king pardon them. They are even now here in Winchester and they will take every opportunity to weaken me. They will see your misdemeanour as a means to strike against me."

"What is the worst they can do to me?" I had been thinking about this for some time on the journey south.

"Well, I won't lie, there is the death penalty for sacrilege but beating a priest and a Norman at that should not get much support from the lords despite what the King and his bishops may think and my name still counts for something." Leofric adjudged, "No, I think it will be a fine and a penance but you are right I must ship you back to your mother as my original idea of bringing you into my household clearly will not work."

I could see that my father was disappointed, disappointed with me and that somehow, I had let him down. The prospect of returning to the Danelagh, to my own real kin did not dismay me so much. I was never going to be more than a captain in my brother Aelfgar's retinue if I stayed in Mercia and at least I would be free to make my own decisions if only my father would gift me my mother's lands in Bourne when she died. I did not say this as I was not about to disappoint my father still further.

It was the next day that I was brought before the king. Normally I would be overawed by being in the King's presence and the presence of the great lords but this was not the time to let my mind wander. My father had already informed me who would be there, centrally, of course, sat King Edward the Mild, he was an aged but noble looking man with long flowing locks of light auburn, although he looked careworn. He was wearing a light crown, a gold circlet across his brow, which fitted well and left his hair above uncovered. For the rest he wore a long robe of emerald green with a red trim cinched at the waist by a chain belt of gold lozenges held together by wire links. Each lozenge had a semi-precious stone set in it. The ensemble was topped by a red cloak with gold edging. The king also wore purple leather boots, which I understood was a sign of royalty. I was shocked in that he did not hold a sword of justice but rather nervously fingered a gold cross hanging from a chain around his neck.

Next to the King on a smaller seat sat his wife, Queen Edith the daughter of Earl Godwin, she was much younger than the king with a pinched face and troubled look about her. She too was richly apparelled and wore a slim gold circlet about her black braided hair. The royal couple were flanked upon both sides by church prelates, but I was relieved to see that there were only two. First, there was the newly appointed Archbishop of Canterbury, Stigand, a tall thin cadaverous man, middle aged and reputably in the Godwinson's camp. Stigand was vastly experienced having served three previous kings, Knut, and his sons Harald and Harthaknut. Apparently on Earl Godwin's reinstatement three of the Norman bishops appointed by the king had fled the country and the Normans were no longer in the ascendant in England. The second bishop standing beside the queen was Leofric, Bishop of Exeter, my father had indicated that he was some far out relative of our family. He had a jovial face and the simplest pallium I had ever seen being just a stout vine rod. Both bishops, especially Stigand were magnificently attired.

On both sides of the wooden beamed hall sat in rows were many of the lords of England but with nobles from Wessex being in the majority There was obviously two parties, on the one side sat Earl Godwin of Wessex, now an elderly man but without doubt the most powerful person in the kingdom. He was probably about the same age as the king and similarly attired. He was flanked by his sons, Harold Godwinson, Earl of East Anglia and Tostig Godwinson. There were also a number of Wessex thegns in support. Both the Godwinsons were in martial attire but with empty scabbards as their swords were not permitted in the King's presence.

On the other side of the hall sat my father and next to him a giant of a warrior who could only be Siward, Earl of Northumbria the son of a Danish viking who could reputedly transform into a bear at will. Hence Siward was called Bjornson, bear's son. To make himself look even larger he wore a huge white bearskin, which presumably had been taken from one of the giant mythical white bears that dwell on the northern ice. Like all north men he wore his hair carefully braided but shaved his chin leaving a drooping moustache making him look even fiercer; also, on my father's side of the hall were some jarls from the Danelagh.

The archbishop raised his hand for quiet and the nobles settled down to listen to his introductory statement. "We now come to a grave matter, a charge of sacrilege. The youth before us is one Hereward Leofricson who was under the religious tutelage of Brother Herluin of Coventry. He is charged with assault on the said priest and stealing church property. I need not remind you that this is a grave offence."

The king spoke, "Archbishop, who are the accusers of this boy let us hear their testimony."

"My lord, the accusers are Brother Herluin, obviously, and that very pious lady Godgifu, Countess of Mercia and the wife of Earl Leofric here present."

"Then proceed with the witness's archbishop." The king waved his hand but before the first witness was brought forward Earl Godwin spoke up.

"My lord king, may I ask a question, a point of clarification?" The earl rose from his seat to command the room.

The king frowned but responded. "Of course, what is the confusion here?"

"My lord, as I understand it this youth is called Hereward Leofricson, and by that I understand that he is the son of Earl Leofric and his wife, Lady Godgifu." He paused for effect and continued, "Now I know that the lady is very pious but surely she is not planning to have her son tried for sacrilege and theft against a Norman priest." Earl Godwin emphasized the word Norman with some relish. "Perhaps the Earl of Mercia can enlighten us on what is going on in his household?"

I must admit I was not sure if the earl was speaking up for me or just trying to embarrass my father. My father stood when the king raised his eyebrows in his direction.

"My lord king, it is true that Hereward is my son, but he is not the Lady Godgifu's son; sadly, my wife has taken against the boy although any sin is clearly mine. The boy is generally of excellent disposition but has not responded well to Brother Herluin's tuition."

The king's face registered disapproval, "That point has been clarified but the serious charge still remains, we will hear the witnesses."

I had to sit biting my tongue whilst first Brother Herluin related a pack of lies about me and the incident, even my bone comb was declared a relic that Herluin had confiscated from me when he found out I had taken it from a church in the Danelagh; and then my step-mother confirmed and supported Brother Herluin's account pointing out that it was impossible for a man in holy orders to lie. I noted that Archbishop Stigand looked sceptical at this statement but the King nodded his head sagely in support of such pious logic.

There was no one to speak for me but the King did permit me to make a statement in my defence. I related all the events as I saw them and pointed out that as an earl's son, I should not have been abused by the priest the way he had. I also pointed out that the lie about the comb could be easily disproved by sending for my uncle Brand and my mother who could confirm that it was a gift to me and not a holy relic. Much to my relief my father stood and confirmed that he knew the comb was a gift and not a holy relic.

I was taken away whilst the king and his councillors deliberated on my fate. The bitterness I now felt towards my step-mother and the priest was deep and abiding; if ever I had the opportunity, I would have my revenge but first I had to survive. Finally, and after what seemed a very long time I was brought back into the king's hall. The archbishop raised his hand and the muttering and noise subsided.

"It is the decree on the King and his Council that you, Hereward Leofricson, be outlawed from this land for the crime of sacrilege, namely the assault on a church servant in holy orders, Brother Herluin, for one full year." The archbishop paused for effect, "Be warned, if found within the bounds of this kingdom after a week hence any man is free to kill you without redress." Stigand glanced at the Godwinsons when he said this. "On the subject of the comb being a relic or not, this has not been clearly established and the said article will be held by the King's Reeve for investigation. Finally, Brother Herluin, as a Norman priest, is no longer welcome in England and he shall depart from Dover also within the week."

Earl Godwin was smiling at my father maliciously but rather surprisingly Earl Harald Godwinson spoke up, "This is a sad day for England when a stout lad, a potential warrior and protector of the realm, is outlawed on the say so of a snivelling Norman priest. I know that if I had been beaten by a priest, I would have defended myself vigorously also. My lord you and England will regret this decision."

I was ushered out of the hall and back to my room, my small prison cell, shortly thereafter I was joined by my father. "My wife has had her day and Earl Godwin ensured her victory. Of course, this was not aimed at you, it was directed at me. She wanted you dead but the king would never agree to that, as a pawn in the game none cared much for your future but they all wanted to hurt me. I am sorry Hereward; I had hoped to be able to send you home to your mother but it is not to be, it helped that the bishops were not much agitated over a Norman priest being harmed, but our overly pious king and my wife were relentless. You have a week to clear the English borders so there is no chance that you can go east to Bourne and your mother. From Winchester the quickest way to leave England is by boat from Southampton or to head west to Bristol and Wales. I am sorry my son that I could not protect you." My father looked downcast.

I had little time to consider my position but I had quickly determined that I would become a sell-sword, some sort of a hero, like Beowulf and win renown, I was a callow youth what did I know of the world?

"Don't worry about me, father, I will get by, but I do need some weapons and a horse would greatly help a speedy farewell from England's shores."

My father was, as always, good with practical matters a good, well-balanced sword was found for me, nothing too fancy but with a good edge. I was also given a chainmail hauberk that belonged to one of my father's huscarls that fitted tolerably well. I declined a hunting spear, which I considered would get in the way and opted to take a bow and a full quiver of arrows as in this way I could keep a replenished larder. Finally, a small axe and a dagger completed my equipment. With some relish my father also confiscated Brother Herluin's horse as it actually belonged to the earldom rather than the priest so I was reunited with the beautiful bay mare for the time being.

I was determined to set out very early the next morning so I declined to feast with my father's retainer's and settled for a muted farewell assuring him that I would write or communicate in some manner with him and my mother. Before he quit my room, he pressed a purse of coins into my hand, quite a heavy purse.

"Buy a new comb with this and remember what your mother requires of you, keep clean and wash regularly." We both laughed at this quip as it was so true. "I will see you in a year's time, God willing." My father added.

The next morning just as the sun was lightening the darkness somewhat, I went to the stables to fetch my new horse. I saddled her and was delighted to find that someone had left me a shield in the stall. It was a large round buckler made of linden wood with a red painted face. Painted on the surface in black was the symbol of the Mercian knot. I did not know the origin of this symbol but I loved its symmetry; all the Mercian huscarls carried similar shields and my father's banner also displayed the knot. I was not completely cast out, the shield displayed to the world my origins. Hanging next to the shield on the stall hook was a leather bag full of food.

"Which way to go?" I thought as I walked my mare down the road from the king's palace. There were four gates to Winchester, north, south, east, and west. The eastern road eventually led to London and Canterbury still deep within the king's control. North led back into Mercia and although I suspected my father would try and protect me, I knew my step-mother would have me killed at the first opportunity and as the

27

lady of the Mercians through whose rights to the earldom my father partially held his position there were many thegns and huscarls who would do her bidding against the wishes of my father. The southern gate led to the coast at Southampton water, one of the realm's main sea ports; I knew it was only some fifteen or twenty miles and I could be there before noon but I also knew that Earl Godwin had tight control of the south coast and a large fleet of ships that he had recently been raiding and wasting the Isle of Wight with was somewhere out there, so although there may be many ships available to depart from England I may just be putting myself into the hands of my father's enemies. That left west, it was a long ride to the west coast and the nearest port with any decent shipping was Bristol. Bristol was about a hundred miles or so and I had one week to reach there, find a ship, and leave the country. I could just do it especially if I outrode the news of my banishment. I was not sure who the lord was in the Bristol area but I knew it was not Godwin or one of his sons so it had to be the safer option. I nudged the horse to a trot and headed for the west gate. There were a few peasants up and about and the sentries at the gate saw me leave.

Once free of the town I rode due west at a canter on the old Roman road towards Sarum or Salisbury as it was beginning to be called, I knew that I had to climb up onto the downs north of that place towards the old Roman town of Bath but I was not sure of the exact route and intended to ask directions at Sarum. It suddenly occurred to me that I had retained a lot of information from the years of tuition I had received from Brother Herluin and from the books he had permitted me to read. So those tormented years were not all wasted.

I had been moving steadily along the road for a couple of hours and must have been at least ten miles from Winchester, there were few other people moving along it and most of those were heading towards Winchester not away from it, when I became aware that I was being followed. There was little cover to hide behind as the Roman road still had all its original features with the road being higher than the surrounding meadows. I decided to stop and confront the person. To my amazement I could see that as the tracker approached, he was on foot and running at a fast pace that would eventually have meant he would have overtaken me even though I was mounted and he was not. I placed my mare four square across the road as I was no longer sure he was actually following me or just in a hurry to go elsewhere.

The man looked quite grotesque, he appeared to be wearing a monk's habit but he had tied up the hem under his crotch to give his legs room to stretch out. His feet were quite bare and filthy. He had a dark complexion but was clean shaven as one would expect if he was a monk, but I saw no sign of a tonsure as he had a hood pulled well over his face. He was stick thin and his long legs were stringy, reminding me of the herons I used to see as a boy in the fens of the Danelagh. He was certainly older than me, maybe by five years.

"Hold there, Martin." I shouted, for it was my storyteller from Coventry. "Whence the haste that causes you to outrun a horse?"

Martin cast himself down on the ground panting like a dog. It took him several minutes to recover his breath until he gasped. "Hereward Leofricson the outlaw?"

"What if I am, and what is it to you?" I replied.

"Then know that an ambush is being prepared for thee and I would warn you." The strange fellow panted.

Alerted to danger I became more direct, "What do you know of an ambush and how does anyone know the direction I have taken this morning?"

"That's a lot of questions young lord, give me time to recover, running is my game but ten long miles even on the flat takes time to recover from."

"Here drink this." I threw him a leather water bag I was carrying on my saddle; he uncorked it and took a long drink.

After a few minutes the scarecrow of a man leapt to his feet. "Until this morning I was a lay-brother at the Coventry minster and I accompanied the Lady Godgifu's entourage to Winchester. Last night before compline I overheard a discussion in the minster between a certain lady and the Bishop of Exeter. The bishop was assuring the lady that arrangements had been set in place to intercept a certain outlaw on whichever road he left Winchester from this morning."

I interrupted, "The Bishop of Exeter is a relative of mine, or at least of my father; he was all smiles yesterday why would he wish me ill?"

"Young lord, a man goes where he is paid to go and although he may be a relative of your father, he owes his position to the lady. Your life is forfeit in a week or tomorrow." Martin opined soberly.

I had to give this some thought; if I was to be ambushed on the road how far away from Winchester would it be; how could I know for sure this man, Martin, was telling the truth? "Why have you come to tell me this, if what you say is true then your own life is now at risk." I probed.

"My young lord, like you I have been oppressed by priests most of my life. I was not serving at the minster by my will but because the local abbot deemed it appropriate for a vagabond to give righteous service rather than roam free. I was beaten every day for no particular reason; fed the slops with the pigs. The only gain I made by living at the minster was sneaking into the library and reading books, I love books lord, I love what knowledge is in them."

"You can read?" I responded in some astonishment.

"My life has been varied and I have had opportunities despite my present condition; but why have I come to warn you, lord?" Martin looked at me lopsided. "I see a hero within you, a great viking warrior, valiant but rash also. You need someone to watch your back in a fight and ensure you are not murdered in your sleep. I seek the adventure that you will bring, let me serve you and I will do so faithfully. You were the only one who was interested in my stories and empathised with the heroes of old."

I was somewhat taken aback by this but under the circumstances I had to accept the offer, I clearly needed help and this Martin fellow might just tip the scales in my favour. "I accept your offer of service Martin; my prospects are grim you may regret this." Martin went down on his knees in front of me and held his hands forward as in prayer. I had seen huscarls and thegns swear fealty to my father so I knew what was expected. I dismounted and I placed my hands around his and Martin swore his oath.

"Hereward Leofricson, Mercian lord, I swear that I will be your man, I promise on my faith that I will in the future be faithful to you, never cause you harm and will observe my homage to you completely against all persons in good faith and without deceit."

"Well, I cannot offer you land or wealth, as yet, but who knows what tomorrow may bring. However, I will give you, arms, as is fitting between a fighting man and his servant." I went to my horse and pulled my hand axe from the bundle tied behind the saddle.

"Here, Martin, my gift to you, this was given to me by my father the Earl of Mercia and it is a noble weapon, use it well in my service." Martin gleefully took the axe and stroked its iron head; he seemed well pleased with it.

"Little axe, I see the valknut runes on your blade, you are blessed by the Norns and will serve your master well." Martin stroked the axe head and crooned over it.

"That's the Mercian knot, Martin."

"Same thing, master, it represents the means by which the threefold sacrifices are made to Odin." I looked at the axe markings with renewed interest.

"One more thing master." Martin's face looked sad.

"What is it?"

"The Lady, she had your dog, Boy, drowned in the mill pond outside the great hall in Coventry the day before we left. They whipped me when I protested."

I boiled up in fury but soon realised how fruitless this was and how impotent I was. There would be a time for revenge; I kept my grief inside. Turning to more practical matters I pondered our next move. If there were men waiting ahead of us waiting in ambush, they would certainly be somewhere along the old Roman road to Sarum and I was puzzled as to how the Bishop of Exeter could forewarn them. Perhaps he had dozens of men spread out around Winchester for every eventuality but if this was the case, they would be spread thin and I may not have to confront many of them or I might even be able to slip through the net.

"Martin, the ambushers will almost certainly be more numerous along the main highway so I propose to head north and pass Sarum on the downs to the north."

"That makes sense, master, we should head directly towards Amesbury and the Giant's Dance and pass over the river Avon higher up than you originally intended."

"Can you keep up if I ride between a trot and a canter?" I asked.

"Over rough ground I will have no difficulty in keeping up lord."

"Good let us depart."

We left the highway and travelled north west across meadows interspersed with woodland. Here and there were flocks of sheep grazing on the lush grass and solitary shepherds watched us warily. The land slowly rose onto the downs, a plateau type landscape where trees became sparser but travelling was distinctly easier. Clouds sailed majestically across the sky from west to east with brilliant blue heavens in between. It was a warm day. Here and there were old tracks leading in the general direction we wanted to go.

Martin panted, "There is a track that runs due west from Amesbury to the Giants Dance and that will take us over the Avon water." We skirted Amesbury and hit the track, which possibly had been a Roman road heading west, and it was not long before we saw the Giants Dance. Everyone in England knew of the Giants Dance but few in Mercia had visited it. For Christians it was a place of evil and had been part of the landscape since time began. Many thought it was a pagan temple made by the Devil himself, others said it was raised up by the arch wizard Merlin, or so Martin avowed. As we neared the site the huge stone structure left me gasping, it was much larger than the minster in Winchester, which was the largest building I had seen. People said the king was building a huge minster in London that may be bigger than this but I did not know that for sure. This monolith appeared to be half ruined, some of the stones seemed cast down.

As we neared the structure my mare's ears pricked up and twitched; danger!

"Martin, something has unsettled my horse."

"I feel it to, master; perhaps it is just this evil place?"

Nothing of the kind, from behind the stone arches several men appeared. They all carried spears and some had swords at their belts, others axes. None wore mail, the best they had were leather jerkins with studs or rings stitched on for greater protection. Not huscarls then, hired ruffians to do the assassin's work. The ambushers spread out denying us passage. I could of course turn and gallop away but that would leave Martin vulnerable, although I expected he could run faster than my mare and the assassins.

They were about two hundred paces away, "I count ten men master." Martin sounded eager. This was it, my first fight for real, now my skills would be tested and Beada's and Fridleaf's teaching evaluated. I slid from my horse; English warriors fought on foot although I had heard that in Normandy warriors fight from horseback. I had not been trained to do that and I was not sure it was possible anyway.

"One thing Martin, they all have spears and they possibly expected me to have a spear to, but I am sure they did not anticipate I would have my bow." I pulled the bow stave from the strapping behind the mare's saddle and quickly strung it. The arrow case was also attached to the saddle. "Martin hold my horse's head and keep her still." I pulled the first arrow from the case and nocked it and without thought drew and let fly. None of the approaching men wore jerkins that could withstand the shaft shot from a heavy Danish longbow, they may as well have been naked, and none carried shields. My first arrow took a man cleanly into his mid-chest, with a strangled scream he fell back onto the grass. Before he had fallen, I had shot a second shaft that pierced another man's shoulder. He dropped his spear and knelt on the ground groaning. The other men now realised the danger they were in and started to run towards Martin and I but they had at least a hundred and twenty paces to cover. They crouched down as they ran but this did not stop me launching arrow after arrow at them. My targets became larger and easier to hit as they neared us and by the time they were too near for me to risk another shot there were only three uninjured assailants.

I dropped my bow and pulled out my sword and pulled the shield from its hook on the saddle. I took up a guard stance with my shield pushed forward and my sword high as I had been trained to do. From my right I felt Martin standing behind my horse with his axe in his hand. I was worried that the ambusher that was making for Martin might spear my horse but I could not do anything about it as the other two slowed and cautiously approached me now that the risk of being shot by an arrow had been removed. They extended their spears ready to jab at me when an opportunity arose. It was clear that if I moved against one attacker it would leave me exposed to a thrust from the other.

The three of us warily circled around waiting for an opportunity to strike when suddenly my horse squealed and bolted between my assailants and me. I kept my concentration and as the horse cleared one assailant but was still in the way of the second one, I sprang forward and chopped off the head of his spear. This made him jump back desperately clutching a useless stump of wood and presumably feeling very vulnerable and as my mare cleared the second assassin, I neatly chopped off his spear head as well.

Now the combat turned in my favour, one assailant had a scramaseax, a short sword with a one-edged blade and the other had an axe. I outreached them with my sword. I shuffled forwards holding my shield out, eventually the man with the axe foolishly tried to smash my shield or possibly he was trying to hook it away. Instead, I caught the impact on the boss turning it aside in front of the other attacker and then I lunged forward shoving the sword point into the man's throat. The assailant fell back clutching his throat and as he did so I stepped forward and swung around to batter away the thrust the other man was making with his scramaseax. I then back handed my sword across his throat and he to fell away, blood arcing across the grass.

I looked around to see Martin standing watching me, the other assailant was lying on the ground with his head smashed in but I could see that Martin's axe was unbloodied. Martin smiled.

"Your mare took a dislike to being poked and kicked the man's head in." he explained. I could see my mare was standing someway off in the meadow and having calmed down was now eating grass.

"Come on, let's see to this lot." I urged. We moved along the trail of bodies that littered the ground between where we had fought and the upright stones. Most of the men were only injured and incapacitated by the arrows, it is actually rare for someone to be killed instantaneously by an arrow. Martin stroked his axe blade across each of the men's throats as we reached them but the penultimate ambusher, the one with the arrow in his shoulder, was trying to limp away by the time we reached him. I knocked him down and was infuriated with myself as my arrow that was still sticking out of his shoulder snapped. What a waste, the man screamed as the arrow tore his shoulder muscle again making more blood flow down his tunic.

"How did you know I was coming this way?" I demanded. He ignored me, which prompted Martin to grab the arrow and yank it viciously.

"Yarrgh! Alright don't; lots of us were paid to lay ambush at all points around Winchester, far enough out for the King not to get wind of our purpose. It was chance that you came our way."

"Who paid you?" I prompted. Martin gripped the arrow stump again.

"I don't know, our leader made the deal and he is on the Roman road this side of Sarum." The would-be assassin panted in pain.

I nodded and Martin drew his axe blade across the man's neck. He gurgled out his life in a welter of frothy blood. As I walked over to retrieve my mare I started to shake. I had never killed a man before but fortunately I felt no fear whilst in combat. I had put pay to nine men, killing two in hand-to-hand combat. True they were not huscarls, experienced warriors, but I had survived.

My mare was still trembling but I calmed her down speaking gently and breathing into her nostrils. I checked her limbs, chest and flanks and could find no injuries. Eventually I spotted a tiny puncture wound in her rump and realized that it was Martin who had made her bolt by jabbing her with the spike on the reverse side of his axe blade head. I did not know whether to laugh at his ingenuity of be angered at his callous treatment of my prized horse, however as the result of his actions allowed me to kill two attackers, I shrugged it off. They were very valuable, so I retrieved all the undamaged arrows from my victims intending to re-sharpen the points and check the fletching's over the next few evenings.

"Come on we need to leave this evil place before any more of these hired killers turn up." I concluded.

We entered Bristol two days later after an uneventful journey from the Giants Dance. We did have the presence of mind to search the dead men before we left them but it did not provide us with any material gains except a few lumps of hack silver and a very good dagger. Martin's main benefit was to discard his habit and re-clothe himself in various items of clothing from the dead bodies. He now sported a grubby woollen tunic and a leather jerkin; his ensemble was completed by a pair of tight trousers that only fitted to just below his knees. None of the ambushers' shoes came near to fitting his long claw-like feet so he was still shoeless.

I paid for a room at a dockside inn that was lousy with fleas and smelled badly of urine. I am sure it had been built over an open sewer. This accommodation did allow us to sleep out of the inclement weather that had blown in from the west with stormy showers and dark scudding clouds. It also meant that we were out of sight if anyone was still searching for me.

After a night of restless sleep, filled with visions of a beautiful naked Godgifu trying to slide a dagger into my groin I gained consciousness; I needed to take stock of my position. It was now the fourth day of my outlawry and I had three more days before I was fair game to be killed if I was still in England. Not that any potential assassins cared a jot about my seven days grace. The weather suggested that we might not claim passage on a ship leaving any day soon. The only other alternatives were to travel further west into Cornwall where the English law was often ignored, of travel further north west into south Wales where the English law did not apply at all and I would be clearly outside England. The advantage of the latter course was that I could possibly link up with my older brother Aelfgar who spent most of his time rebuffing Welsh raids into Mercia and often retaliating by raiding into Wales.

I offered to buy Martin a horse but he declined preferring to walk or run and truth be told he never seemed to lag or tire. Obviously, he could not keep up with a galloping horse but he stayed comfortably close at a canter or trot and seemed to be able to keep up this sort of pace all day.

Without delay I opted to ride north into Wales. All I knew about Wales was that the dominant king who my brother and my father had been fighting for years was called Gryffudd ap Llywelyn and he was the king of north Wales but had been gradually exerting his control over the whole of Wales. Only this year he had led a devastating raid into Herefordshire allied with Sweyn Godwinson, whilst the Godwinsons, father and sons were exiled, and five years ago he had defeated the Mercian forces led by my brother at the battle of Rhyd-y-groes. There was another king in south Wales, also called Gryffudd who had successfully resisted Gryffudd ap Llywelyn and his territory was called Gwent or Glamorgan, or something like that and it would be his territory I would be entering.

We headed towards the banks of the river Severn, which turned out to be a mighty river just like the rivers Trent and Ouse; rivers that I was familiar with in Mercia and the Danelagh that could not be crossed easily. There was no way to immediately cross so we were obliged to head north along its bank until we came to the first fording place. Eventually after we had travelled about twenty miles the river turned west and formed a great horseshoe bend. We had been informed by other travellers that there was an old ford at the apex of the bend and by the end of the day we reached the ford. The crossing had been staked out but we decided that it would be safer to pass over in the morning rather than missing our footing in the poor light.

We slept out in the open, screened from the river by a large thicket and a stand of trees. In the morning when we rose, I could see armed men at the ford.

"Martin, I think we have more assassins awaiting us."

"I can see only three men, master. Easy for a hero like you."

I glanced at my companion to see if he was being sarcastic."

"I'll shoot a couple if I can, we do not need to tarry this side of the river."

"I do not believe the Lady Godgifu cares which side of the river you are on when you are slain."

"Come on." Martin led my horse whilst I held my strung bow with an arrow on the string. We walked clear of the thicket boldly

37

and walked across the meadow towards the ferry. We were noticed almost immediately and rather than waiting for us the three men ran off along the riverbank.

"Cowards." I concluded.

"Nay, they go for help, there must be more of them nearby." Martin cautioned.

With two more days before my outlawry became official Martin and I crossed the old ford. I knew that Herefordshire lay north west of us so we turned direct west to head into Wales. Sweyn Godwinson had been the earl of this part of the country but since the Godwinsons' outlawry his earldom seemed to have lapsed and I had no idea who was the law in the land. I was hoping that my brother was active in the area but I could not count on it so I needed to be in Wales proper by the following day and I did not doubt that Godgifu's assassins would be after us.

The land to our right was becoming more rugged and the hills were rising and the area was heavily forested; I knew that the river Wye was somewhere ahead and was the likely border between the two countries. Eventually after another long day's journey we descended into the valley of the Wye where it joined another river at a small, mean looking settlement. This settlement accommodated a wooden fort with a watchtower dominating the wooden bridge over the river. On the bridge there were two guards, but a rough bothy at the far end of the bridge suggested additional guards to be called upon when needed.

One of the guards at the nearer end of the bridge held up his hand and waved us to a halt. He spoke a string of words that were totally incomprehensible that I naturally assumed was Welsh.

"I am sorry but I have no Welsh, does anyone speak English?" The guard scowled but before he could reply Martin chipped in with a long monologue in Welsh. After a lengthy discussion the guard eventually waved us over the bridge.

"I didn't know you could speak Welsh, Martin." I queried.

"My mother was Welsh and I spoke their tongue from my cradle." Martin replied.

"I seem to know nothing much about you and yet you know everything about me, we must discuss your early life sometime."

I suggested, "However, for the time being what did you say to the guards to get us into this place?"

"This place is called the mouth of the Monnow, which is the name of the river that joins the Wye here." Martin explained. "As to why they let us through I was honest and told them we had been outlawed in England and was seeking to serve as mercenaries to a Welsh lord."

"Well, I don't really want to do that, linking up with my brother or continuing on to Ireland is much more to my liking." I responded.

"Once we pass through here, we can head north west and as long as we don't drift back into England by accident we should end up in mid-Wales at a place where we may hear of the whereabouts of your brother; but I think that we had better continue claiming we are outlaws and mercenaries seeking to fight against the English just to prevent our throats being cut." Martin suggested.

After spending some time in the settlement at the mouth of the river Monnow we set off west into the interior of Wales. Although the land was fertile it was only sparsely populated and was gently undulating rather than mountainous as I was given to expect, although eventually we observed the hills of Brecon rising to our left. After a couple of days of travelling north west we considered we were due west of Hereford and we needed to ascertain some information regarding the whereabouts of my brother.

At a small hovel we were told that there was a considerable army about five miles to the north and that the farmer had seen men foraging in close proximity to his home. We decided to risk riding towards the assembly and within four miles we were accosted by a band of wild looking hillmen on shaggy ponies. Again, Martin had a long and animated discussion in Welsh; I did not like the way the Welshmen kept eyeing my mare as it was clearly a target for looters. However, from their body language I guessed that Martin had convinced them of our friendly disposition.

"We are in luck, King Gryffudd, the one ruling north Wales, is camped ahead of us and is in discussions with none other than your brother, Aelfgar" The band of foragers rode off leaving one of their number to lead us to their camp.

We rode down into a sheltered valley that was crowded with tents. The larger tents were clearly Mercian but the numbers of Welsh and Angles appeared about even. By a small stream was a larger farmstead and it was to this obvious meeting point that we were taken. The armies' leaders were sitting on conveniently large tree trunks facing each other and I spotted my brother immediately as he dominated the surroundings with his usually assured personality and physical height. However, the man opposite him looked equally impressive. Probably about the same age as my brother he was, unlike his unkempt warriors, attired in gleaming mail and purple-coloured breeches and a purple cloak; he obviously thought he was an emperor! This was Gryffudd ap Llywelyn, King of north Wales and it was well known he aspired to be king of all Wales. Surprisingly he was beardless, which I discovered later was a trait of the Welsh princes. He was not as good looking as Aelfgar but he was not ugly either; a strong face, a hard face but clearly someone men would follow. Aelfgar looked up.

"Hereward, by God it's you!" I grinned and slid from my mare; we embraced.

"Hello brother, well met." I turned and bowed to the Welsh king.

"Lord Gryffudd, may I introduce my brother Hereward Leofricson, who like many an Englishman as fallen foul of our King's ire and is currently an outlaw."

The Welsh king nodded at me clearly unimpressed as he wanted to continue is negotiations with Aelfgar. I slipped into the background as the discussions my arrival had interrupted continued. It was not until much later in the day that I had the opportunity to talk with my brother in his tent.

"Well Hereward, what have you done? I hear you have been outlawed for sacrilege no less, which I find astonishing for one of your lack of interest in all things spiritual." Aelfgar did look concerned so I answered as soberly as I could.

"I was pushed beyond my endurance by the priest Herluin who repeatedly beat me and then stole from me. I struck him and for that I was outlawed by the king at the instigation of your mother." I did not mention that she had tried to have me waylaid and killed.

"Yes well, King Edward would take a dim view of such action as he is a noted supporter of holy church." Aelfgar ignored the jibe against his mother.

"You cannot stay with me, but you are lucky. King Gryffudd and I have come to an accommodation, we have made a treaty, a peace treaty and mutual support treaty between Mercia and Wales. I have agreed that my daughter, Ealdgyth, is to marry Gryffudd next year when she is old enough to cement the pact and you can be useful to me in this matter. Consider staying with Gryffudd, help fight his wars, keep an eye on what is going on here for me and I will try and get your outlawry rescinded before the year is out."

I considered this proposal, to be honest I was not much bothered by my outlawry, which now that I was out of England laid lightly on me. However, I did not want to disappoint my brother by rejecting his offer and I did want to support him. "I will do as you ask brother but, only for a short time, until Ealdgyth is safely ensconced as queen here." I affirmed.

"Good, I will speak to Gryffudd about this."

So, it was decided, when my brother departed back to Mercia, I stayed on in Gryffudd's household as a mercenary warrior, a huscarl would be too polite a term. Martin and I bunked in with the other companions of the Welsh king. Gryffudd did not make his way back to his main palace in north Wales as it transpired that he was planning another foray into Brecon against his namesake Gryffudd of south Wales; very confusing.

Martin and I practiced our arms training together and I occasionally had a bout with a Welsh warrior. They were lightly armed and nimble and could dance around me waiting for an opening. Using the tried and tested method of English combat by keeping my larger shield forward and covering my body and moving to face the rapidly circling Welshmen I invariably landed the killing blow without harm to myself. My superior mail and helmet protected me from javelin thrust or sword slash if I was too slow to block an attack. I could see why the Welsh never managed to be consistently successful in their wars with the English shield wall.

Gryffudd moved his motley army south towards a place called Brecon, which was apparently an important stronghold but as we neared the crossing point of the river Wye, we came across the men of south Wales holding the ford. Gryffudd ap Llywelyn did not feel inclined to force the ford as his army was small consisting of only about five hundred men and the south Welsh force did not seem much smaller, maybe even larger. So, our force dug in on an escarpment above the ford awaiting, I know not what? Interestingly a series of duels developed between champions from both sides on our side of the ford in the lush meadow from which the southern Welsh had long since driven off their sheep.

Martin and I watched these duels with interest and they very much reminded me of the duel between David and Goliath. Lightly armed warriors would square up to each other and cast javelins before rushing at each other with swords and their small shields, targes. Few wore serious armour, an occasional leather helmet and jacket adorned with studs. The outcome of these duels rarely ended in a kill, lots of pointless blows were struck and much loud shouting and insults thrown before the protagonists withdrew each claiming a moral victory.

I determined to spoil this carnival by taking my turn. I ambled down to the meadow as another desultory melee came to an end. I found a firm relatively flat area that had been grazed down to short grass by sheep and stood facing the ford. I presented my shield bearing the Mercian knot emblem towards the enemy camp and as I expected this caused some commotion as the southern Welsh warriors realised there was a hated Englishman challenging them. A heated argument ensued as it appeared several warriors wanted the opportunity to fight me. I hoped I would be able to fight more than one but I had to be patient as they sorted themselves out.

The honour eventually went to a tall, thick-set opponent probably ten years older than me. I noted that he was better dressed than most and did sport a leather helmet. However, his arms were the same as all the others and he defended himself with a small round leather targe, which had a wicked spike thrusting out from its boss. It also looked like the small shield had a metal rim to prevent it being hacked to pieces. The fighter carried two javelins and was armed with a sword strapped to his thigh. The warrior approached me, he started shouting but obviously I could not understand him as my Welsh was still very rudimentary. I reacted by slamming my sword hilt against my shield and shouting the English war chant, "Ut! Ut! Ut!"

I was armed in my usual fashion with a mail coat that reached to my knees, below them leather boots that had iron plates stitched into them to prevent leg wounds. My shield was a large round English oak board with an iron rim and bronze domed boss. I held it forward covering my torso inviting blows to my legs or head only. I had a steel helmet in the viking fashion with a nasal guard and I had chosen not to use javelins but as he neared, I held my sword high ready to deliver a telling blow where possible.

At fifteen paces the man put all his strength and weight into a javelin throw. The missile flew deadly accurately towards the upper rim of my shield. I crouched and slightly inclined my shield and the javelin struck and careened off above my head. My assailant had not taken the opportunity to charge whilst the javelin was in flight so I resumed my stance, shield to the fore, whilst he danced around me trying to deliver a telling throw with his second javelin. Having observed previous duels, I knew this could continue in this fashion for some time so I started to edge forward and close on my assailant. I did this by moving one leg forward slowly to ensure I had a firm stance. As expected, my opponent retreated, all the time shouting intelligible taunts. I then took a risk to precipitate the close combat; I lowered my shield slightly, sufficient to expose my throat and upper chest. My opponent quickly cast his second javelin but as I was anticipating this I easily twisted to the side and the javelin passed by. My attacker rushed forward immediately he had released his javelin pulling out his sword as he did so. I swung my shield back into place and crouched to render his small targe ineffectual. I felt his sword impact on my shield rim above my head whilst I was in the process of sweeping my sword in a circular arc across the man's shins. My blow completely severed his left leg and bit into the calf of his other leg and the man howling in agony collapsed onto my shield and slid onto the floor. I rose up and slashed down with my sword and nearly severed his head cutting short the screams of pain.

There was a great roar from both behind me and in front of me as this was the first time anyone had been killed in any of the duels. I was barely breaking sweat so I stood my ground and several of the south Welsh rushed forward. However, someone in authority pulled them back and eventually a second protagonist approached me across the ford. This man was even older than the first, maybe thirty-five or forty and had greying hair. He too was unarmoured and he did not even carry a shield but he was armed with a sword in his right hand and a small axe in his left. The southern Welsh started chanting.

"Cynan, Cynan, Cynan." I assumed that this was the man's name. Maybe a noted warrior, which made me cautious.

I took up my defensive position and watched the man approach. Without a pause he walked right up to me and without breaking stride he raised his axe and hooked it over my shield rim. I braced but was unable to prevent my shield being pulled down slightly. The warrior had raised his sword in anticipation of a stab at my exposed throat. The sword flashed forward and I was barely able to deflect it with my own sword. His sword point scrapped along my left shoulder but did not break the links of my mail. I backhanded my sword towards his face but he ducked and drew his sword back for another strike. As the sword point rushed at me again, I managed to parry it with my sword but at the same time he unhooked his axe with the intention of chopping into my exposed flank. With my shield in play again I pushed forward and rammed the shield rim into his face. I felt the axe handle hit my side but clearly my forward momentum had meant the blade missed me. With the blow to his face my assailant staggered back and with my sword free and already raised I brought it down on my attacker's left wrist and severed it cleanly, the hand and axe falling to the trampled grass.

The Welsh warrior groaned but still had the presence of mind to raise the stump of his severed arm to jet the spurting blood towards my face. I knew I had to maintain momentum and pressed the man back with my shield eventually bowling him over onto his back. I was covered in his blood but relatively unharmed though somewhat bruised. The older warrior now down was unable to regain his feet and was slowly fading through loss of blood. He was a brave and wily advisory and I did not have any appetite to kill him.

He spoke to me and although I did not understand him, I deduced that he would prefer to die rather than slowly fade away or live maimed and humiliated. I nodded and neatly pierced his throat with my sword. He died instantly. Again, there were cries of outrage from the southern Welsh and I had to raise my shield as stones started to fall around me. Should I retreat now or stand my ground I thought. Making up my mind for me a man on a small Welsh pony splashed across the ford. In broken English he shouted as he rode up.

"Who are you that tramples on our customs?"

I was puzzled, "What customs?" I demanded.

"It is customary for our warriors to demonstrate their skills in combat before a fight, the skill is to show that you could kill your enemy but choose not to. You have abused this time-honoured custom by killing two of our best men."

I was bewildered but had the presence of mind to retort, "Those two men knew I was a Mercian and that any fight between me and them was not a fancy show. They were trying to kill me and I killed them; and if they were two of your best men you should flee now before any further fighting ensues."

"No! We will settle this now, we two in single combat."

I smiled, "Nothing would please me more, I am Hereward Leofricson, son of the Earl of Mercia, brother to Aelfgar, Earl of East Anglia who you will be familiar with."

"I am Iestyn ap Rhydderch brother to King Gryffudd of Deheubarth and it is fitting that I should slay one such as you, you filthy Sassenach."

The young prince, for he could not have been any older than me slid off his pony and unhooked his shield and javelin. He was undoubtably better equipped than the two previous Welshmen I had killed. He had a chainmail shirt that reached to below his waist and a leather helmet banded by metal strips. His shield was larger too, but still not as large as mine. He set himself to cast his javelin at me and I took up my usual stance. He edged around me until he was on rising ground with the ford to my back and then he hurled his javelin with all his strength. He was lightning quick and I had no chance of avoiding the projectile. It hit the top rim of my shield and the point passed clean through towards my face. As I anticipated Prince Iestyn rushed after his javelin with his sword raised. There was no way I could hold my shield up so in desperation I threw it forward, fortunately it fell between us and stopped my attacker in his tracks. I gripped my sword with both hands and gave a mighty swipe at him. He could not avoid it and he held his shield out in defence. My sword cut into the shield and sliced clean through it cleaving it into two useless pieces. Fortunately for the prince I missed his hand so he dropped his shield unharmed.

I pulled out my hand axe from my belt and we circled each other looking for an opening. Tentatively we both probed with our swords. The duel finally came to a ridiculous end when Iestyn fell over my discarded shield. I leapt forward with the intention of denying him the chance of regaining his feet; he fended me off with his sword whilst he squirmed backwards on his back. Eventually in frustration I chopped down onto his ankle and took his foot off; this distracted him and I thrust my sword into his groin. He died mewling like child.

I knew it was time to quit the field, the southern Welsh were clearly furious with the loss of their king's brother and they started rushing across the ford towards me. With little dignity I ran back to our camp. The north Welsh warriors were all assembled in a shield wall of sorts at the edge of camp as they had been watching my duels, and were prepared to repel an assault on their lines. The southern Welsh chased up the slope after me and were met be a hail of javelins that hit many of them, wounding most, killing some and within a heartbeat they were tumbling back towards the ford in disarray followed by the jeers of the northern army.

King Gryffudd ordered the men forward and we tramped down the slope in a loose formation towards the ford. Such was the turmoil in the enemies ranks that they immediately fled at our approach and by the time we waded across the ford the enemy was nowhere to be seen.

"What do you think of that Martin, strange way to fight a war." I commented.

"It only takes one determined warrior to decide a melee, my lord, and this case you were that man." Martin seemed inordinately pleased.

The north Welsh warriors dispersed when they crossed the ford and set off to plunder anything and anywhere, they could find. This seemed foolish to me as we had not really defeated the opposing army, which could still be lurking nearby. However, King Gryffudd seems very pleased as apparently it never was his intention to mount a full-scale invasion of the south on this occasion and after several days of plundering the area our little army retreated north disbanding on the way.

The small nucleus of King Gryffudd's household troop stayed with the king as we journeyed north into Powys, which I knew was one of the northern principalities that Gryffudd came from. We were heading for his stronghold of Mathrafal, which from what I could make out was about fifteen miles west of Shrewsbury, which was a fortified burh of us Mercians.

Martin informed me that King Gryffudd was to meet my brother at Mathrafal where the marriage of my niece, Ealdgyth, with the king was to take place. It did seem rather odd to me that my father and brother would ally themselves with our traditional enemies and I was not sure I could see why they would do so. The only reason I could come up with was that they wanted to create a line of resistance against the Godwinsons who were all powerful in the south from the Severn in the west to East Anglia in the east. My father had a good relationship with the Anglo-Danes in the five boroughs of Lincoln, Stamford, Derby, Nottingham, and Leicester. I was not so sure of his relationship with Earl Siward of Northumbria but I knew Northumbria traditionally opposed Wessex. The old territory of the Hwicce had become a debatable area, although it was the traditional home of my father's family and his ancestors had been Ealdormen of the Hwicce before they became Earls of Mercia; the Godwinsons had now seized control over the southern part leaving only Herefordshire outside of their control. I assumed that either Gryffudd or my father would wish to control this area.

We arrived at Mathrafal, the royal enclosure of the north Welsh king and it was definitely the grandest settlement I had yet seen in Wales. I was informed by Martin, who seemed to know everything, that the Welsh Kingdom of Powys used to have its capital at Shrewsbury, which they called Pengwern but they lost it to the Mercians generations ago. On arrival at the king's hall preparations were immediately put in place for a feast to celebrate the victory, if you could call it that, over the southern Welsh. I was apparently the hero of the hour having defeated the enemy army single handed, as it was loudly declaimed to anyone who was prepared to listen to King Gryffudd's bard. Martin explained that the bard had composed a poem in my honour that was to be sung at the feast. This amused me for at sixteen years old I did not feel like a hero although I did consider I had made a good start towards making a name for myself.

The actual feast itself was not much different than the feasts in Mercia, probably less solemn as the priests seemed merrier and did not prolong their prayers unduly. I made a fool of myself getting roaring drunk but this only seemed to amuse my host. Martin stayed sober and watched my back. When the bard took up his place near the heath fire everyone quietened down. The Welsh certainly respected their bards more than their priests and I liked that. The bard had a wonderful voice, somewhat effeminate and high toned; of course, I could not understand a word of it, for although I had mastered rudimentary conversation by this time, the singing voice was much harder to follow. When the bard had finished everyone roared their approval and applauded., so I did likewise.

Martin whispered, "Hereward, that was a praise song to you, so you must reward the bard." Fortunately, I had my wallet with me that still contained most of the silver my father had given me; I fumbled around and took out a large silver brooch that had not been broken down into hack silver. It had a writhing dragon motif embossed on it with ruby insets for eyes. It was worth the price of a good horse and was probably far too much for the praise song but Martin seemed pleased when he saw what I proposed to give the bard. I stepped over to the man making sure I did not trip over the deerhounds and handed him the brooch. The whole hall erupted in cheers. And they started repeatedly chanting "Wahardd, wahardd."

I stumbled back to my bench, "What are they shouting, Martin?"

"They are shouting – Outlaw, outlaw. I am afraid it is their name for you as they cannot begin to pronounce Hereward." I laughed; outlaw indeed. Later in the room allotted to me I asked Martin about the praise song.

"Apparently, you are Gwalchmai returned. If my memory serves me aright Gwalchmai was one of Arthur's warriors and fought in the wars after the Romans had left these isles; a great champion by all accounts."

"Who is, was Arthur?" I asked innocently.

Martin spluttered into the ale he was drinking and after coughing he managed to compose himself and explain, "Arthur was the champion of the British who fought against the Saxons and Angles when they first came to Britain many generations ago. He defeated them many times and eventually pushed most of them back into the sea or accepted them under his rule."

"Well, how is it that we Angles are here and ruling the island if this Arthur defeated us?" I queried, much amused by Martin's animated description of this Welsh paragon.

"Well like all great rulers Arthur had to contend with the jealousy of his own people and eventually he was killed by some of his own followers. After that there was no one to stop the Angles and Saxons coming back, which they did; and the Britons, who you call Welsh are now living in the far west of the island and are, as ever, divided into contending principalities." Martin explained in some detail.

"This Gryffudd seems hell bent on unifying all the Welsh, maybe he will become a threat to us English in time?" I mused.

After nearly a month of waiting with nothing much to do but feast and train, my brother and his entourage eventually arrived at Mathrafal. The king met Aelfgar at the settlement gates as a mark of honour and obviously I was there also. My brother had a mounted troop of some one hundred retainers and huscarls. There was also a wagon that appeared to be conveying several ladies who I took to be my niece's maids and by the look of one of them her aged nurse as well. However, Aelfgar's daughter was not in the wagon, she was riding a delicate piebald pony with a beautiful embroidered saddlecloth and a red leather saddle. Ribbons were tied into the pony's luxuriant tail and mane, which cascaded nearly to the ground. This was an enchanting sight but

49

was as nothing compared to the beast's rider. My niece, Ealdgyth, was a true beauty, although still only about thirteen or fourteen she had shed the puppy fat that I remembered from my early years in Coventry. Her hair hung in golden braids down to her knees as she sat on her pony. Around her forehead were woven garlands of flowers in colours that complimented her hair and complexion. Her body was slender, encased in a sky-blue dress, showing little sign of approaching maturity. However, my main image was of her grandmother, Godgifu; Ealdgyth was Godgifu written in miniature, perhaps as Godgifu must have appeared when she was a young girl. I felt my member stiffen; what was it with me, why did I only have sexual thoughts for my hated step-mother and her kin?

King Gryffudd grunted in appreciation at the delicate morsel that was about to be placed in his bed. Aelfgar had requested that Gryffudd restrained himself for perhaps a year before deflowering his young wife but somehow, I doubted that he could be that patient. Ealdgyth spotted me in the crowd, a welcome familiar face, and waved and smiled, a smile that lit up the assemblage. The Welsh folk started to cheer in appreciation of the honour that was being bestowed upon them and their king.

The leading Mercians entered the Welsh king's hall whilst the remainder set up a tented pavilion outside the settlement. Refreshments were offered to the Mercian lords whilst Aelfgar and Gryffudd discussed the forthcoming marriage arrangements and Aelfgar introduced Eadgyth to her betrothed. After sometime Aelfgar acknowledged me and beckoned me over.

"Hello brother, I understand you have made an impression since we were last together."

I grinned, "I do intend to make a name for myself as I am unlikely to have status by any other means."

"Well, be careful, I don't want you getting killed needlessly just so you can show off." Aelfgar retorted.

"I understand, but may I be impertinent." I plunged in, "I do not really understand why you are wedding your daughter to the Welsh king? It does not make a lot of sense to me."

Aelfgar gave a grim smile. "You have been too young to understand what is going on in England. Essentially there is a power struggle between the Godwinsons and the other magnates.

As you do know the Godwinsons were outlawed recently, mainly at the instigation on my father and Earl Siward but they neatly turned the tables on us when they raided the south coast like vikings and frightened the king into reinstating them. Whilst they were outlaws, the King gave me East Anglia the eastern counties where Harold Godwinson had been earl. Now that the Godwinsons are back, Harold has been given back East Anglia and I have been effectively demoted. Our father needs to strengthen our position against the Godwinsons and needs to pacify Mercia's western border quickly. Seeking an accord with Gryffudd is the quickest and most effective way of achieving this. I am afraid that my daughter, like many a nobleman's offspring is a hostage to fortune and circumstances. and right now, we need this alliance. Your strong showing against the southern Welsh did us no harm at all and if you are up for it, I am sure there will be another foray south."

Shortly after this conversation I sought out my niece and reacquainted myself. She was cautious with me as she had been much influenced by her grandmother, the Lady Godgifu but as I was a familiar face in a sea of Welsh she soon thawed and we were laughing about old reminiscences before long. She had heard of my exploits and expressed admiration and this made me exceedingly conceited and pleased with myself. I really wanted to carry her off and deflower her but she was not for me and I could not dishonour my brother so.

The marriage took place at the entrance to the King's chapel two days after the Mercians' arrival. It was a magnificent affair that in typical Welsh fashion was dominated by the bards' poems and songs, in fact it turned into something of a bardic contest especially where extolling the beauty of the bride was concerned. I could see that Martin was enjoying it immensely but I had to admit I found the continuous feasting wearisome despite the fact that there was many a pretty girl throwing themselves at me. I suppose I was not really mature enough to appreciate female company and my head was filled with thoughts of martial activity.

The only interruption to the round of feasting and sports was another attempt upon my life. This time a man who had come in the entourage of my niece tried to stab me in the back while I was bathing in the river, only for Martin to restrain him and draw his axe across the would be assassin's throat. Eadgyth was distraught, claiming that she did not know the man or how he came to be with her retinue. Aelfgar suspected that he had been placed there by his mother in another attempt to assassinate me. Gryffudd had little interest in the death of an Englishman and the affair was soon forgotten.

Eventually Aelfgar and his Mercians took their leave and my niece was left to her new life with only her maidens for company. I made a point of presenting myself to her on a regular basis to be pleasant and to ensure she was not being abused by her new husband. We agreed to learn the Welsh language together and as I had a head start in that direction, I did not find this too stressful especially as Martin undertook to be our tutor along with Eadgyth's new Welsh father confessor, a rather benign monk answering to the name Antony. In this way the rest of the year passed uneventfully. Unlike eastern Mercia and the Danelagh, Wales was excessively cold and wet, with snow blanketing the ground for nearly two months. The Christmas and New Year festivities tended to be localised affairs as movement was restricted by the weather and I became increasingly irritable by this forced inactivity. I was pretty sure that Gryffudd consummated his marriage over the festive period from the changes in Eadgyth's mannerisms. Gryffudd also displayed a more covetous side of his nature towards his wife and little things like the way he placed his hand on her shoulder and caressed her neck confirmed their intimacy. I admit to being very jealous of Gryffudd's good fortune and I often dreamed of being between Eadgyth's legs ploughing her furrow. Well at least it diverted my mind from her grandmother.

I could see that Eadgyth was quite comfortable with her changed circumstances and she was taking an increased share of the responsibilities of running her husband's household; I felt that now was the time to move on.

1053 – The Outlaw

It was immediately after Christmas that I received a message from my brother Aelfgar, it was in the spoken word rather than a letter and I had the impression there was some secrecy about it. The messenger was one of Aelfgar's huscarls. In effect Aelfgar wanted me to journey into south Wales, seek out and kill Rhys the eldest son of Gryffudd, the king whose army I had fought the previous year. Apparently, this Rhys had been raiding almost continuously into England and had infuriated King Edward. Numerous attempts had been made by the Godwinsons and others to counter him but all had failed.

I discussed this with Martin and we both agreed that this was a very dangerous adventure that was unlikely to turn out well for us. Martin knew I was impetuous by nature and anticipated that I would undertake this mission so he suggested that we travel in disguise rather than boldly ride south as I would have done without sage guidance. I reluctantly agreed and without warning to anyone in Mathrafal, including the king or Queen Eadgyth, we slipped away the day after the New Year.

We travelled south more or less on the route we had used when we came north in the previous year. I rode a hill pony and Martin, of course, trotted along beside me. We assumed that this Rhys would be somewhere near the English border so we decided to retrace our steps to the settlement at the mouth of the River Monnow. After ten days hard travelling through snow, we eventually reached the settlement. I reluctantly released my pony so that we both appeared as lowly travellers, our weapons carefully concealed beneath our voluminous cloaks. Martin did most of the talking and we gained entrance to the village easily, mainly because the sentry was too cold and disinterested to bother scrutinising us. We knew that we would soon be spotted as outsiders, especially at this time of the year so I determined to be bold and we asked the priest at the small church for the whereabouts of Lord Rhys as we had a message for him from his father the king. His response was very positive.

"Lord Rhys has a leman he keeps in the settlement, a woman he captured from the English, he visits her here whenever he feels disposed to, so rather than go wandering off looking for his current camp I would suggest it is in your best interests to wait here and he will turn up withal." The look on the priest's face showed he clearly disapproved of the prince's fornication. We thanked the priest and gave alms, which pleased him. Our next problem was where to wait out the prince's arrival. With snow on the ground, we could not go far but to stay in the settlement was to invite scrutiny so we moved up onto the hillside and made a small shelter in the woods. We desperately hoped the Welsh prince would turn up soon as we were not sure how many days we could survive, in such inhospitable a shelter. We did allow ourselves a fire when it snowed as the smoke would not be seen. For the next three days Martin sneaked back into the settlement to see if Lord Rhys had arrived but on the fourth day with a clear sky, we saw a group of four riders enter the village from the south.

"I think we are in luck Martin. Who else would be out and about on a day like this other than a man wanting a woman?"

"Woman is the root of all evil, quoth the bishop, as he lay his head in his leman's lap." Smirked my servant.

Carefully we marked into which hall the men entered and where their horses were stabled. I intended to wait for darkness to descend before attacking the hall but by mid-day a blizzard had blown in from the west. Martin and I stumbled through the deepening snow down into the settlement neatly avoiding the guards as we had learnt to do over the last three days. We sneaked around the back of the hall the men had entered earlier.

"We must confirm it is Rhys in there before we attack." Whispered Martin.

"Yes, but how?" I countered.

"I could pretend to be a messenger from the priest saying he has a message from Rhys's father the King."

"That might work but I favour a more direct action. There is probably only four or five men in there, let's just go in and kill them all." I decided.

"Impetuous." Martin pointed out.

"Decisive." I responded.

I selected an axe and a short sword, a Saxon scramaseax with a heavy single blade; ideal for close quarter fighting.

"Come on." I walked around the side of the hall and mounted the entrance step. Huddled in the doorway was a guard who did not even lift his head as I thrust the seax into his neck. He toppled over and I kicked him off the porch. I listened at the door before lifting the latch and I pushed my way in. Inside standing either side of the hearth fire were two huscarls, well Welsh warriors, warming their hands around cups of some beverage. They looked up when I entered and it was moments before they realised that I was not the guard. I stepped forward across the hall as they scattered to pick up their weapons. I caught up with one before he could clutch his spear leaning against the wall and smashed my axe into his unprotected skull. He fell in a silent heap across the bench near the wall and the wall hangings were covered in blood. The other warrior made it to his spear but it was next to useless in the hall as it was too long to be easily levelled and Martin caught him and drove a dagger into his back.

As we looked at each other a curtain at the end of the hall was thrust aside and a tall rangy man came into the main hall only half dressed carrying a sword. He yelled something in Welsh, which in my excitement I was unable to understand.

"Is this Rhys, Martin?" I thundered careless of discovery.

"Yes, I believe it is." Martin responded. I moved forward across the hall, ten paces, to within the sword range of the prince.

"I killed your uncle last year." I stated boldly, but in English.

"Hereward Evil-Eye the outlaw." He snarled back in broken English. I was pleased he knew me.

"Die." He screamed as he lunged at me, sword extended.

I had deliberately provoked him and made him angry. He was skilful but his lunge was an angry rush. I sidestepped nimbly and brought my seax down on his wrist chopping it clean through. I would not have been able to achieve this if he had been armoured with wrist guards and in his anger, he had forgotten to be cautious. As he stood looking at the stump of his hand pumping fountains of blood, I brought my axe down on his neck and it cut into his shoulder bone and on through into his chest. He sank to the ground dead.

"We need the head for proof." Martin said as he came up to my side. Just then a fourth man peaked around the curtain. He looked at the carnage around the hall and started to scream an alarm when he gasped and went white; he staggered forward clutching at his back and as he twisted around in pain, I could see that he had a dagger lodged between his shoulder blades, eventually he too fell to the floor. From behind the curtain appeared a young woman clutching a sheet to her naked body. She looked around until she saw the body of her captor, Rhys.

"Is he dead?" she asked in English.

"If he isn't, he soon will be," I responded. I gave Martin my axe and he efficiently chopped at the Welshman's neck until it separated from his body.

"Martin, find a sack, we need to take the head." I instructed my servant.

"Take me with you." The young woman pleaded.

"We must flee through the snow; how would you survive. Anyway, who are you?" I queried.

"My name is Winfled and I am the daughter of a wealthy merchant from Gloucester. That horrible man kidnapped me when he raided the outskirts of Gloucester. I was staying on one of my father's farms when he took me; he has kept me here for over a year. I cannot stay, my father would pay much to have me returned."

I looked at Martin, "What do you think?"

"She may be killed if she remains here, or she may be passed on to another man to be used." Martin considered, "Maybe she considers death a better prospect. Let us take her, she is young, she may survive."

"Right, we will fire the building, that will give us time. You, Winfled, get some clothes on, warm clothes with trousers, no long skirts."

The weather outside was still snowing a blizzard and in fact only minutes had passed since we had stormed the hall. Martin found a sack in which to deposit Rhys' head, whilst I sought out food to take with us on our journey north. Winfled returned bundled up in warm clothes and a fur trimmed hat.

"Martin, you take Winfled and go to the stables, I'll set light to the hall."

After Martin and the girl had left the hall, I quickly took the burning logs from the central fire and laid them against the wooden walls of the hall. I piled the dried rushes from the floor onto the burning logs to assist the conflagration. Some of the rushes were damp from being trampled on and I made sure some of these were on the fires as well to encourage smoke to hide our escape. I left the hall with the door open to encourage a draft to kindle the fire. The space before the hall was deserted owing to the snow blizzard whistling down the street. I bent my head into the storm and followed Martin to the stable where we had seen the horses being led to. I ducked under the stable lintel into darkness and immediately stumbled over something.

"Watch out, master. The man guarding the horses has been most inconsiderate, he fell over and blocked the entrance when I cut his throat." As my eyes adjusted to the dim interior of the stable, I could make out Martin saddling a horse, whilst Winfled struggled with another horse's bridle. I could see that I had stumbled over the prone body of another Welsh warrior, who had obviously been left behind to guard the horses. I quickly assisted Martin to saddle up all four horses, we could always do with a spare and leaving a horse behind would only assist any pursuit. As we led the horses out, I could hear some shouts of alarm and I could see that smoke was now billowing from the hall roof.

"Come on, quick." I prompted as we mounted. The settlement guards had run towards the burning hall leaving the western gate unguarded and open and we took the opportunity to spur the horses at a reckless canter through the gate. As I looked back the hall suddenly caught alight with a 'whoosh' as the thatched roof dried to critical point and the whole edifice went up in a sheet of flame. Everyone would be too busy preventing the fire spreading to the other huts and houses to pursue us.

We rode north west as fast as the horses could flounder through the snow. We had no idea if we were on a road or not but we assumed that if we kept out of the woods and followed the river, we would eventually re-enter Powys in a couple of days. Our progress was frustratingly slow and Martin, who hated horses, quickly slid off his mount and proceeded on foot. He actually seemed to move easier through the snow than the horses did, I had no idea how, just another peculiarity about the man.

We knew we had not travelled far by nightfall but we could not move forward in the dark and the blizzard so we sought a place to shelter. Eventually we decided to dismount and lead our horses into a nearby wood. We walked on until the trees closed around us and their foliage was so dense that the snow failed to reach the floor. We found a space between several massive trees where we could tether the horses and build a fire, safe in the knowledge that it would not be seen from more than a few paces away. The wind fallen branches on the ground were sufficiently dry to ignite easily and we were soon huddled around the fire's warmth.

"The blizzard will make it impossible for any pursuers to track us." Martin smiled as he explored his parcel of food. Some slightly damp bread appeared with a lump of hard cheese, he offered some around and we all broke off bits to chew.

"Winfled, are there many men in Monnow who would want to avenge Rhys?" I asked.

Winfled looked slightly embarrassed and her face flushed, "I cannot tell, I was tied up most of the time, tied to the bed. I was never let out of the hall.

Without thought I said, "What not even to wash and relieve yourself?"

Winfled burst into tears and I realised I had stepped over a line that must remain ever drawn regarding her time as a captive. Eventually we all three fell asleep, I should have insisted on one of us keeping guard but we were all too exhausted for any of us to remain awake.

When dawn broke there were thin beams of sunlight filtering through the leafy canopy. The blizzard had ceased. The fire had burnt out, we did not linger but quickly led our horses out of the wood and resumed our journey north into Powys. Martin had the presence of mind to scoop handfuls of snow into the sack which held Rhys' head to prevent it rotting, that and the cold would suffice until I could send it on to my brother. Eventually we reached Mathrafal without mishap and I was immediately summoned to the king's presence.

"Where have you been, Hereward, we have been concerned for you?" Gryffudd sat on his throne with my niece Eadgyth, his queen beside him. I explained what my brother had asked of me and what I had done to execute that request. I offered to show him the head of Rhys but with his queen beside him Gryffudd declined.

"This is a great benefit to me, as well as to King Edward the Mild, although perhaps not so mild to want Prince Rhys' head." He sniggered. I apologised for sneaking away but I explained that I was not sure if there were people within Powys who might want to warn Rhys or his father about further attacks from Powys. I also requested that someone should be sent to my brother with the decomposing head, so that it could be presented to King Edward without my part in its separation from the rest of his body becoming generally known.

"I will certainly have the head conveyed to Aelfgar but I want Gryffudd to know that his son was slain by a warrior from Powys." Gryffudd smirked.

After some celebrations, I managed to request that Eadgyth take Winfled into her service as I privately thought that the young girl's father might not be so pleased to have a ruined daughter returned to him. My niece readily agreed as she was quite horrified when I related what had happened to the girl.

Later I heard that Aelfgar presented Rhys' head to King Edward at Gloucester, much to the Godwinsons annoyance and it was not long afterwards that I received another message from my brother, which read.

"Wales is no longer safe for you. The Godwinsons know you are there and so does my mother. I suggest you leave immediately and go to either Dublin or Orkney."

It was a timely reminder as Martin and I were alert to another assassination attempt when a man tried to slide a dagger into my back one evening on my way to the king's hall. Martin buried his axe into the assassin's skull for his pains and my chainmail deflected the thrust and I was only scratched. English coins were in the bastard's wallet bearing the old king Aethelred's head. A sure sign the man had been paid for his services in England; Godgifu's arm was long and spiteful.

Spring 1054 – The Bearslayer

I sat on the cross bench in the great hall at Thurso, Martin sat beside me. Only that morning we had been welcomed and accepted by Thorkell Fosterer the administrator or crowner of the Orkneys for Jarl Thorfinn the Mighty.

Following my brother's timely warning I had left Wales in the late autumn of the previous year. King Gryffudd was sorry to have me leave as I was a useful supplement to his warband, not least because I had killed two of his principal opponent's family, a brother, and a son. He loaded me with gifts, fortunately of the portable variety so I was able to travel in style. I rode north within King Gryffudd's kingdom of Gwynedd to the island of Anglesey where Martin and I bought passage in a merchant ship bound for Dublin, that great viking entrepot. Regrettably I had to leave my beautiful mare in the care of King Gryffudd's steward, hoping that one day I would be reunited with her.

Ivar Haraldson was King of Dublin and he was a relative of King Gryffudd of Gwynedd, and Powys and so I was welcomed. However, all was not well in Dublin, King Ivar was only ruling on the whim of the Irish High King and King of Leinster, Diarmait mac Máel na mBó who had installed him recently after driving out the previous king. Seeing no prospects of staying on in Dublin I enquired where I could find suitable employment for a warrior and the answer was Scotland.

Martin and I bought passage north to the isles, which were then under the control of Thorfinn, Jarl of Orkney and king of most of Scotland. Apparently, many years ago Thorfinn had killed the previous Scottish king, someone called Duncan Mac Crinan and had taken most of Scotland under his rule. Duncan and Thorfinn were half-brothers, both sons of a daughter of Malcolm King of Scots who was king before Duncan. Princess Bethoc had been married to Crinan the ruler of Atholl and before that had been married to Sigurd Jarl of Orkney. Her son by Earl Sigurd, Thorfinn was brought up at the Scottish court rather than with his father in Orkney; and because the Scots did not appreciate his Norse name of Thorfinn they called him

MacBethoc, shortened to MacBeth. When Jarl Sigurd was killed at the celebrated battle of Clontarf in 1014 the King of Scots hastily married Bethoc to Crinan Mormaer of Atholl and the western Isles and it was their son Duncan who the King of Scots decided would succeed him. Confusingly, as both half-brothers were sons of Bethoc, they could equally be called MacBeth, but as Crinan was a good Gael it was more acceptable for Duncan to be referred to as Mac Crinan, whilst for a time Thorfinn was fostered out to Princess Donada, Bethoc's sister who was married to Findleah Mormaer of Moray. When Thorfinn MacBeth's father died his three older half-brothers in Orkney shared out the islands between them leaving nothing for Thorfinn, but his grandfather the King of Scots made him Earl of Caithness, the northern province of Alba. Over the years Thorfinn acquired more and more of the isles until he was not only Earl of Caithness but also the sole Jarl of Orkney. Thorfinn also married the heiress of the province of Moray, a royal princess called Grouch, which meant he controlled more of Scotland than his half-brother. Inevitably civil war arose and Thorfinn MacBeth killed his half-brother and became king of Scots.

King Duncan's two sons escaped the fate of their father and fled to England; they were very young and not in a position to oppose their uncle's seizure of power in Scotland. Besides according to Scottish law, he had just as much right to be king as they had. The Scots were mainly quiescent but still insisted on referring to Thorfinn as King MacBeth. King Thorfinn MacBeth ruled well and wisely for many years but as he was getting older the sons of Duncan were becoming warriors with the intention of wresting the crown of the Scots away from him. War was coming and Scotland was a suitable place for Martin and I to find martial employment.

Thorkell Fosterer walked over to the table we were sitting at and spoke. "My boy has decided that he will not use the Orkney men to fight his Scottish war but he is not averse to employing mercenaries. I want you to take three ship loads of warriors that have assembled here from Iceland, Dublin, and Norway down to join the king in Perth." Thorkell always referred to the King as 'my boy' in consideration of the fact that whilst he was the youthful Earl of Caithness, he had relied of Thorkell to keep him alive and successful against the actions of his older brothers.

"What forces will we be facing in Scotland, Fosterer?" I asked.

"The late King Duncan had two sons, Malcolm, and Donald Ban; they have been in the English king's court these many years but the report is that the English king has sent them north to Earl Siward Bjornson of Northumbria who he has commanded to assist them to take Scotland away from 'my boy', Thorfinn."

"So that means there will be the Northumbrian host, any dispossessed from Scotland and any mercenaries looking for loot they can acquire." I summarised.

"That is about it," Thorkell responded, "'My boy will have the men of Moray where his step-father Findleah was Mormaer, and the men of Caithness and Sudrland who he can rely upon. Various pirates from the isles and some Norman refugees from the Saxon court. The Gallowegians will be side-lined and not much use. The Scots and Angles in the south, Fife, Lothian, Fortrenn, anyone south of the Tay are not to be relied upon." Most of these places meant nothing to me but I knew the south of Scotland was more densely populated than the north. "Oh! And by the way, you might want to know that Earl Godwin of Wessex has died and his son Harold is now Earl of Wessex and your brother has been reinstated as Earl of East Anglia." This was Thorkell's parting shot but really these happenings down in England made little impression on me.

The next day I went down to the beach to look over the ships I would be taking south. Although I fancied myself as a viking, I had not much experience of ships as the Danes in the Danelagh had become settled over the past hundred years and the Mercians were even less inclined to go sailing. Fortunately, each of the three ships, which were knarrs, that is ocean going cargo ships that the earl used for trading with Norway, Denmark and Flanders were piloted by experienced ships captains. They were all roughly the same size, maybe fifty feet in length with a beam of fifteen feet. They were shorter than the raiding snekkjas and drakkers and relied more on sail power than oars. They would be crewed by volunteers from Caithness and carry extra warriors; all in all, maybe a hundred and fifty men in the three ships.

It was while I was at the wooden jetty that I spotted a smaller sailing boat heading towards where I was standing. It had clearly come across from Hoy, the nearest of the Orkney islands. As it slid into its berth, I could see sitting in the centre of the boat a young girl, she was wrapped in furs as it was still early spring but I could see she was very beautiful. The rowers jumped out of the boat and tied up to the nearest staves and the girl stood and sedately stepped out of the boat right next to me.

"Who are you?" she demanded looking straight at me. I felt compelled to answer politely.

"I am Hereward Leofricson from Mercia in England and I have agreed to aid Jarl Thorfinn in his forthcoming struggle with Siward Bjornson of Northumbria."

"That is good and will you kill Asbjorn Siwardson for me?" she smiled sweetly.

"I assume Asbjorn Siwardson is Earl Siward's son, why do you want him dead?" I responded.

"Because he has sworn to take me as his concubine when he kills my father, Jarl Thorfinn." She retorted.

"You are Jarl Thorfinn's daughter?"

"Yes, did I not say so?" She ended the conversation by abruptly walking away towards Thurso followed by four huscarls to ensure her safety.

Later I learnt that her name was Ingibiorg and she was Thorfinn's only daughter, although he had two sons Paul and Erland who were still staying on the Orkneys. Apparently, they would have no claim to the throne of the Scots as Thorfinn's stepson, a man named Lulach had a stronger claim. I did not try and understand this.

I found Ingibiorg entrancing and unashamedly paid court to her in the few days I had before I sailed for Perth. Even though I had promised both my mother and father to always keep clean and smart I took extra care around Ingibiorg. I washed in the sea every day wore my best clothing and fastidiously combed my hair until my hair hung around my shoulders in waves of white blond tresses. She and I were of a similar age and I obviously had more appeal than the older men around her. We got on well together, she teased me about my wispy fair beard and it was her suggestion that I adopted the Hebridean practice of shaving and growing a moustache with long droopy ends. However, with my fair hair this persona was not very effective and my attempts at a beard or moustache were so unsuccessful I eventually abandoned the idea and shaved my upper lip. I dallied with her, when I could and even managed a kiss when Thorkell Fosterer was absent. She clearly enjoyed my advances but as a princess she was well capable of controlling my ardour. In less than a week I had to leave and she was returning to the Orkneys.

The weather was improving as our three knarrs rounded Duncansby Head and turned south before a stiff north westerly that filled the sails and pushed us through the sea's troughs at a shuddering pace. Fortunately, I found the experience exhilarating and felt no sea sickness. I feared to be sea sick in front of the hardened sailors from the north. Martin was equally comfortable on the waves as were the Icelanders and Norwegians, not so some of the men of Caithness and Sudrland who like me were no seamen. In one day, we made good time and put into a bay that the pilot on my ship called Dornoch; we 'hove to' for the night in calm waters and cooked on the beach. We were still well inside King Thorfinn MacBeth's territories with no fear of enemies.

The following day progress was much harder, we had to sail due east against the prevailing wind, which meant we had to tack through most of the next forty miles until we rounded the high headland at the eastern most point of Moray. With the wind now in our favour the ships captains elected to sail on through the night, south west towards Angus, one of the subdivisions of Scotland, north of Perth. It was about mid-day on the following day that we entered the mouth of the River Tay, which led up to the settlement of Perth. Apparently, the River Tay separated the lands of Thorfinn MacBeth to the north from the lands to the south over which he had uncertain control. For this reason, the ships' pilot steered to the north shore to ensure they were not interfered with by potential enemies. Eventually we reached the stronghold of Perth, which is a fortified town on the south bank of the River Tay. The ships were tied up along a series of wooden jetties and together with the leaders of the various groups that made up my small army I made my way, as directed, to the king's hall. The hall was unlike the traditional halls of my Anglian kin in the south, which were long halls, this one was round with a main entrance facing south and two small doorways to the east and west. We were challenged at the doorway by two huscarls dressed like Orkney vikings who handled their axes with dexterity; we were allowed in after I had identified to them that we were the leaders of a contingent of warriors from the north. Inside the fire burned in the hearth at the centre of the hall; the support pillars around the hall sides had been used to create a number of private cubicles in which sat various warriors, some with women and others with male companions. On the north side of the hall alone on a raised dais sat the king.

I had been told by Thorkell Fosterer that Thorfinn MacBeth's wives were dead. Apparently, he had two wives, the first was Ingibiorg daughter of some jarl from Denmark by which he had two sons, Paul and Erland who were still in Orkney and one daughter, my sweet Ingibiorg named after her mother, and the second wife was a woman called Gruoch the daughter of a Scottish prince whose first husband Thorfinn had killed in Moray with a hall burning. Thorfinn MacBeth had married this Gruoch by force to strengthen his claim to Moray for although Thorfinn MacBeth was a foster-son of a previous Mormaer of Moray, Gruoch's first husband was another Mormaer of Moray from a collateral line. I found this all very confusing but on consideration it was not much different from the convoluted arrangements for the rulers of Mercia. Anyway, both wives were deceased and this was taken as a diminishing of Thorfinn MacBeth's rights in Scotland, and especially Moray, but apparently not Orkney. Gruoch's son from her first marriage, a young man called Lulach was now hereditary Mormaer of Moray.

As I approached the high seat, I could see that the king was a tall dark man, very ugly, with stern features. He was middle aged and had been ruling Scotland, or as the Scots called it Alba for many years. His reign was considered just and he managed the country well. To achieve this, he had killed his cousin Ragnald Brusison and the previous King of the Scots, Duncan, and although he ruled fairly in Alba, he had for many years led viking raids into England and Ireland. For this reason, he had made a pilgrimage to Rome some years before to have his sins absolved.

I approached the king and saluted him. "And you are?" he grated in a harsh voice.

"Lord King, I am Hereward Leofricson of Mercia and I bring one hundred and fifty men from Orkney to fight for you."

"One hundred and fifty men, not nearly enough, cannot Thorkell do better than that?" the king huffed.

"I have only led these men south and I am not privy to your foster-father's planning, but he was unhappy that you would not call on the Orkney men to fight; but these are good men, from Iceland, Ireland, and Norway." I responded feeling somewhat disappointed by the king's reaction.

"I do not doubt it Hereward Leofricson." The king paused. "Are you the Hereward Evil Eye, the Outlaw who killed the Welsh king's son last year?"

"I have that honour, it was in a fair fight, and with any luck I will kill Asbjorn Siwardson on the request of your daughter." I bragged somewhat.

Thorfinn MacBeth laughed. "My daughter stirring the pot again, only last year she was eager to marry the young bear." I was a bit put out at this as Ingibiorg had given no hint of this formal marital possibility.

"Look, young man. I have been the king, in Alba, for many years and at the same time before that I have been Jarl of Orkney since I was a boy. I have maintained my position not just by fighting but by diplomacy, something you apparently know nothing about. In my time I have had to come to terms with Knut the Mighty, King of the North, the present kings of Denmark, and Norway and the various rulers of Dublin, Mann, and the Isles. I had a good relationship with Northumbria before Siward was made jarl and I have tried to have a decent relationship with him but to no avail. Now the milksop king of England has taken the cause of my predecessor's sons to heart and has asked Siward to assist them to usurp my throne. They are gathering an army to attack me and mine and for that reason I have been left with no option but to fight."

I was very interested in his explanation for his current predicament but to be honest I could not see how he could succeed if he could not put a strong army into the field.

"The Orkney men want to fight, lord King." I responded.

"I know they do but the Orkneys are not part of Alba, as jarl there I am a vassal of the king of Norway. If I fail as king here in Alba, I do not want the Orkneys to suffer, it is my home. If I lose Alba my sons retain the Orkneys, they will never be kings in Alba anyway, they have no right." Thorfinn MacBeth looked pensive. "Over the years I conquered most of Alba by force, seven mormaerships or earldoms, as you English name them. By right I am mormaer of Caithness and Sudrland, I gained control of Ross and Moray by marriage and by killing the previous mormaer Gillecomgain. I gained control of the Hebrides and Isles, Galloway, Angus, Fortrenn and the Levenach. I killed Crinan of Atholl and laid the land beneath my feet. My control of the southern land that until recently belonged to Northumbria has always been tenuous. Siward wants them back and Duncan's sons would give them to him if I could be killed. I would leave Alba to my step-son Lulach but I am afraid he lacks a martial character" The kings homily trailed off and I could see he was mulling over his difficulties.

After a while I discharged myself and stepped back from his presence. I needed to find an army marshal who would accommodate the men in preparation for the forthcoming war. I was concerned that the king seemed distracted, he was not at all as I had imagined the great viking leader to be. Eventually I found a military captain called Ewen O'Beolan Lord of Ross who was acting as the king's marshal. He allocated the men I had brought with me to a camp on an area called the North Inch, which was a wide meadow along the riverside. This area already had a significant number of tents erected to accommodate the king's supporters from across Alba, or Scotland as we English call it. There was already a large number of islanders from the west and many of the men that had sailed south with me joined them. The same applied to the Caithness and Sudrland men. This left a small nucleus of Icelanders who opted to stay with me as a co-leader with their leading man a skald called Thordolf Arnorson. There were about thirty Icelanders, one shipload who needed a link man between them and the Scots leadership; they considered I would be a useful go-between.

To be useful I suggested to the Icelanders that we should practice a cohesive battle formation. We were all familiar with the shield wall and the battle snout so we practiced for several days to ensure we worked efficiently as a unit. More of the king's supporters came into the camp over the following days and the army swelled to what I thought was reasonable numbers. I was concerned about the quality of these warriors for although they were suitably fierce and would no doubt be formidable in hand-to-hand combat, they seemed very ill-disciplined. Most of the army consisted of highlanders from the north, places called Lochaber, Moray, and Ross. There were also men from the western seaboard, lands called Argyll and Cowall. They were all lightly armed, no armour just swords, spears, and axes with small round shields, targes with wicked spikes jutting out from their bosses. There were some men from the eastern towns in the areas called the Garioch, Angus and the Mearns. They were clad in equipment more like the southern Angles; larger shields and good solid spears, some had helmets. I was particularly interested in a group of mounted warriors that turned out to be Normans that had ridden north when King Edward the Mild had expelled the Normans from England at the insistence of the Godwinsons.

These Normans I knew were descended from vikings that had invaded the Loire and Seine river lands in France after they had been expelled from England by Alfred, King of Wessex many years ago. Led by a Norwegian named Gangu Hrolf, or Walking Hrolf, they established control of an area along the north coast of France that they called Normandy. The king of France was compelled to accept their presence and made this Hrolf the first duke of Normandy. The Normans remained a thorn in the side of all their neighbours and exchanging their ships for horses became very effective mounted warriors. King Edward the Mild of England's mother was a Norman princess and he had a deep affection for that race and welcomed many of them into England. Not surprisingly the English thegns hated the Normans and were pleased when the Godwinsons had them expelled.

So here in Scotland there was a small nucleus of refugee Normans, about forty of them led by two brothers. They had apparently been part of the force led by Eustace Count of Boulogne who had quarrelled with Earl Godwin over an incident at Dover. Why they had not returned to Normandy or Flanders I never found out. I could not understand their language as they spoke French not the Danish or Norwegians dialects I had expected; but I was interested in their fighting methods. They practiced on the open meadow called the North Inch near our camp. They all rode large horses, much larger than my mare and the highland garrons in Scotland. They had high cantled saddles and they rode with straight legs braced in long strapped stirrups. They all wore full chain mail armour down to their knees, coifs that protected their necks and faces and nasal helms like my own. They had kite shaped shields that protected their left leg and all had a sword and a long lance sporting a pennant. The formations they practiced seems to be of two types; advancing together in a long line held tight and straight by supreme discipline and at an order they all hurled their lances forward together and drew their swords. They practiced this manoeuvre time and time again. The second drill they practiced was to charge in a wedge formation with the two brothers at the head of the wedge; by this method I assumed they intended to break through a shield wall, like the infantry battle boar snout. It cheered me to see that at least one other unit of the Scottish army, beside my Icelanders, were practicing a disciplined approach to the forthcoming conflict.

After three weeks of waiting the king called a war counsel and I was invited even though I only ordered a small contingent. The king's hall was crowded with his supporters and I had enough Gaelic by now to understand their names and some of what was being said. I would have preferred the king to speak in Nordic but as he was not in the Orkneys and his subjects were mainly Scots he was obviously obliged to speak in Gaelic, which was the language he was raised in at the Scots king's court before he went back to Caithness and the Isles. There were at least two dozen clan chiefs present, I was not sure who were mormaers, that is sub-kings, and who were thegns but they seemed to represent a large swathe of Alba north of the highland line and to the west. Any warriors from Ireland or Caithness and Sudrland were more or less multi-lingual so the only groups that had difficulty following the discussions were the two Norman brothers and I. King MacBeth, for so everyone referred to him by this name at the meeting, explained the latest developments.

"My spies and scouts have informed me that Earl Siward of Northumbria has set out from Bamburgh with a force of some two thousand huscarls and fyrdmen, he has crossed the River Tweed and is heading north presumably towards the waist of Scotland at Stirling. At least one of the sons of Duncan is with him, Malcolm the older of the two, and it is assumed that part of the force is made up of huscarls gifted to Malcolm by King Edward and there may be some dissident Scots." MacBeth saw the smiles around the hall and raised his hand. "Yes, two thousand is not of great concern but that is not all. It is understood that Earl Siward's son Asbjorn is leading a fleet of ships along the coast supporting the land army. There are five ships laden with warriors and by my reckoning that could be anywhere between another three hundred to five hundred men. Lastly there is another force marching from Carlisle over the Tweed watershed presumably to join up with Siward near Stirling. Altogether a force of some three thousand is arrayed against us." The king concluded.

The clan chiefs started discussing the information between themselves and the volume of voices escalated considerably. I could see that there was some consternation as the forces arrayed against us were formidable and equal in size to our own. What also concerned me was that the king had made no mention of the MacDubh, Mormaer of Fife and the men of Atholl who had a hereditary kinship to King Duncan's sons. This meant there was a potential further addition to Siward's army numbering hundreds.

I sidled over to the King and spoke quietly. "If you had some of your Orcadian longships here you could demolish the support fleet easily."

MacBeth glared at me, "You know why I will not do that; besides it is too late now."

"Siward's fleet can outflank you if you march south to fight his Northumbrian army before he joins up with the Cumbrian host so you really have no choice to but stay here and surrender the whole of the south of Scotland to Siward and this Malcolm." I concluded.

"I realise that and intend to fortify the Tay crossings." MacBeth responded.

"That still will not stop Asbjorn's fleet outflanking you. In my opinion you may as well attack Siward before he joins up his forces anyway. It gives you a better chance of winning." I responded.

MacBeth looked long and hard at me and I knew he would not do as I advised. It was not because I was young and inexperienced; he knew I was right but I had not considered his supporters.

"There is no way that my followers will march south and leave their lands to be ravaged by Asbjorn and maybe the Atholl men as well. No, we have to remain near the highland line and prevent any incursions into my followers' territories. The battle must be fought here or near here." Looking at the clan chiefs I could see that what he had said was a truth that could not be changed.

It was estimated that it would take Earl Siward about eight weeks to reach Perth, while his small fleet crawled along the coast putting in at every available port so as not to outpace the land army. This gave our army plenty of time to prepare and fortunately allowed a further few hundred of MacBeth's supporters to trickle in from further afield. I felt that we should not just let the Northumbrians advance unchallenged but I knew little of the country between Perth and the advancing army and no one else seemed much bothered. Nevertheless, I felt I had to try, so I approached the king once more.

"My lord, I know you have spies out watching the approach of the Northumbrian army but we could do more than this. Let me approach the Normans and ask them if they would accompany me and harass the enemy as they approach. The Norman contingent is small and they cannot affect the outcome of any battle but they are highly mobile and can discomfort the enemy foragers and deny sustenance to Siward's men. It will also encourage our troops to see we are positively and actively resisting the invasion."

MacBeth considered this proposal for some time. "You are right, it will not make any difference in the long run so ask the Normans and do it, if they agree. Maybe then you will stop pestering me." MacBeth grimaced mirthlessly. I believed he was fey and he felt his fate was set but that was not going to stop me fighting. I found the Normans out on the meadows training as was their wont and hailed their two leaders.

"Do you understand Norse or English?" I asked in both Norse and English.

"We can speak some English as we were on the Welsh marches for over a year before we were forced to leave." Clearly the brother who spoke was the elder. Both brothers were dark haired and clean shaven as I understood was quite normal in their own country.

"I am Hereward Leofricson an outlaw from England and I have a proposal for you."

"We know who you are, you slew King Gryffudd's brother and son a year back. I am Turstan and this is my brother Ivo, we to are outlaws from Normandy for rebelling against our bastard duke. Our father and three of our brothers are dead, killed by the duke's men, our lands forfeit, we had hoped to receive lands in England but now our hope is for land in this Scotland. What is your proposal?"

"King MacBeth has agreed for your troop to harass the approaching Northumbrian army and discomfort them if you can. I do not see this as particularly hazardous as you are all well mounted and can avoid serious conflict at will. What do you say" I explained.

The two brothers drew off and had an animated discussion and then relayed the message to some of their colleagues. The brother Turstan walked his horse back to me. "Can we keep the loot we take?" I had not discussed this issue with MacBeth but as I did not want to lose the opportunity to fight, I decided to lie.

"Yes, within reason, apart from any important prisoners the loot would be all yours. I would wish to accompany you but I am not looking for material gain either."

The discussions between the Normans continued with the final decision being that they would undertake this role and ride out the following day. "What mount do you have.?" The younger brother Ivo questioned.

"None, I had to leave my mount in Wales when I sailed north, I have been ship bound ever since." I replied.

"We will lend you a destrier; can you ride well?" was the laconic response.

"Not as well as you Normans but I can keep up." I retorted stoutly. They laughed and Turstan responded, "We'll see, meet us at our camp at daybreak tomorrow."

Martin was annoyed that he could not accompany me on the planned raid, but he would not ride so he had to remain behind. The Normans gave me a large but apparently docile grey mare with a heavy wooden saddle with leather covering. I would not call the horse nimble but I suspect it was formidable in a charge. The Norman troop, which they called a conroi, set out in a column of twos and headed out south towards Stirling. The Normans had ridden through the lands of southern Scotland when they came north so had a better idea than I of the terrain ahead. The plan was to ride south west to Stirling, which was still in MacBeth's control, stay there one night and then ride east towards Dun Edyn, which was probably not in MacBeth's control and then scout carefully forward from there. All went according to plan until we rounded the shoulder of the rock stack the fortress of Dun Edyn was built upon. From the elevated ground we could see that there were several ships berthed along the waterside of the town's port area that we assumed were the English fleet. Five of these ships were clearly large knarrs, ideal to be utilised as transport ships.

I sidled up to the Norman leaders and addressed them. "If that is the Northumbrian fleet, I cannot see what benefit there is in them berthing here; it must be only temporary as they are much more likely to bypass Fife and land in the Tay. I think, if they have been shadowing the Northumbrian land army it must not be far from here"

The Norman brothers agreed, "The Northumbrians must be either east or south of here and not far away. We need to wait here and send out scouts to locate the army."

The Normans were very businesslike and within the hour several scouts, in pairs, radiated out from our bivouac. We waited patiently watching the ships, there was some movement between the ships and the shore but it mainly appeared to consist of the transference of stores. By the evening two scouts had returned from the south reporting that they had spotted forage parties in villages ten miles to the south but no sign of the main Northumbrian host.

"I expect that the Northumbrians are approaching from the east after following the flat coastal plain for ease of movement." The younger brother, Ivo, concluded.

"We will wait for more scouts to come in." Turstan decided, stoically determined.

During the night more scouts returned from the east. It was confirmed that the Northumbrian army was marching towards Dun Edyn from the east and were about two days march away at a place the locals called Dunbar. The scouts had avoided several foraging parties ahead of the main Northumbrian host with ease as they were all afoot. The Norman brothers decided to rest the night where we were and move on in the morning. Out of politeness Turstan asked me how I thought they should approach the morrows conflict. I had thought about this but I knew that I could make a fool of myself if I suggested something completely inappropriate for the Norman methods of combat.

"I have watched your training methods, advancing in line, and charging in wedge and can see the benefits of these two methods of attack but I had hoped we could catch our enemies whilst they are foraging and most likely in loose formation in villages or farmsteads. If the terrain is right, we could surround the foragers and close on them from all sides, massacre them." I suggested.

Turstan and Ivo smiled, "Not bad, for a novice, we will certainly surround them but when we charge only one side of our troop will charge. What we do not want is for our forces to meet in the middle and collide with each other, that would be a mess and a terrible damage to horse flesh. If any of the foragers run before us, they will be held by our encirclement and disposed of.

This was exactly what happened. At dawn we rode south searching for foraging bands of Northumbrians and eventually one of our scouts returned and informed us that there was a farmstead ahead that was being ransacked by a band of Northumbrians, all on foot; and the best news was they had no sentries out. We moved slowly forward through low scrub until we saw the undergrowth clearing ahead; at that point Turstan motioned for an encirclement and the Norman cavalry split and encircled the farmstead. Within moments the encirclement was complete and Ivo clasped his horn and raised it to his lips. At a nod from his brother a mournful lowing emitted from the horn

74

and Turstan bellowed "Diex Aie" and spurred his horse forward, his conroi measured their pace with Turstan's mount all yelling together and my horse was carried along with the rush, well trained and needing no spur from me. About fifteen Normans charged forward out of the shrubbery straight for the farmstead. The heads of the foragers all spun around towards the approaching horsemen in shock. I could see that there was maybe twenty or thirty of the Northumbrians so the odds were even.

Within moments the Normans ploughed into the loosely dispersed Northumbrians. I saw Turstan's lance pass clean through the body of the nearest man who was holding a goose by the neck and had not even had time to drop it and draw his sword. Almost immediately the rest of the foragers turned and ran; before they had run twenty strides half of the fleeing men had been speared. I had drawn my sword and caught a running man on the back of his neck and took his head clean off leaving his upright body spouting fountains of blood. I was so excited I was even yelling "Diex Aie" like the Normans. I saw the Normans on the far side of the farmstead, they had spread out and were herding the foremost of the fleeing Northumbrians back towards the farm, any of the foragers that seemed likely to burst through the net the Normans mercilessly stabbed with their lances. In no time at all the few Northumbrians that were left alive were herded into the pig pen, five men.

"Well, that went well." I smiled at Ivo who was busy wiping blood off the spiked head of a rather wicked looking mace.

"Not even worked up a sweat, the bastards could have tried a bit harder." He grumbled.

"Well, there's more." I laughed in return.

Turstan, all business called on his men, none of whom had been scratched, to search the farmstead for anything of value. It occurred to me that here were poor Scots on no particular side in the conflict being plundered by both sides but I soon realised that the farmer and his wife would not object as they were found inside the farm, dead. It was obvious that the wife had been raped and had her throat cut, there was a young boy too, maybe ten years old and he had been sodomised, emasculated, and then had probably bled to death. The Northumbrians had already taken everything of value from the farm so more was found on the dead bodies of the foragers than in the farm. The Normans took the weapons, any decent clothing not ruined by wounds and blood and any hacksilver, armbands, and trinkets they could find. The farm animals, a slaughtered pig, two dead geese and a collection of eggs and vegetables went into the Normans' saddlebags to supplement our diet.

"What about the prisoners?" I asked Turstan.

"I don't think they have anything useful to tell us and we cannot sell them, so." He left the question unanswered but it was obvious what he intended. Within moments Ivo was directing the Normans to strip the Northumbrians who immediately guessed what was happening. The Normans efficiently tied the Northumbrians to the pig pen fence. Ivo drew his sword and hacked into the first Northumbrian's neck cracking the shoulder bone and severing the man's spine. He flopped down, twitching and jerking. The other Northumbrians started screaming or crying depending on their disposition but Ivo ruthlessly hacked into each of the prisoners' necks with sufficient force to ensure death came swiftly.

"Leave them as they are as a message for whoever finds them." Turstan ordered, "Come on, mount up."

We moved on and attacked two more foraging parties that day, both groups smaller than the first one, with the same results. The Normans only received superficial wounds due to their heavy mail and padded armour. I was most impressed by the Normans' military skills, which was clearly far more sophisticated than anything I had seen so far in England, Wales, Ireland, or Scotland. That night we pulled back west from the area likely to be searched by any Northumbrian scouts. Turstan and Ivo sat with me at the campfire, they clearly were dissatisfied with the days results.

"We gained almost nothing of wealth today, just a few bits of hack silver, no coin, nothing." Ivo rumbled.

"We must change our tactics and attack the Northumbrians where we can gain from our actions." Turstan added.

I thought about this for a while. "There must be some coin that Siward needs to pay his mercenaries and the Wessex huscarls that have come north with Malcolm but it will be in the baggage at the rear of the army and that could be as far back as three or four miles behind the Northumbrian advance guard. To attack it would be a much greater risk, you may lose some men, although I am sure you can outrun any pursuit."

Turstan and Ivo discussed the possibility. "We have decided to try this tomorrow."

Early the next morning the troop was mounted and trotted away east giving the advancing Northumbrian army a wide berth to the north. It took most of the morning to clear the advancing enemy before it was deemed safe to veer north towards where we thought the baggage train might be.

Turstan never let the troop advance anywhere without outlying scouts and it was one of these that located the wagons that were clearly part of the Northumbrian army's baggage train. A detailed scrutiny from a convenient nearby copse of trees established that the group of wagons numbered twelve with maybe fifty guards, all on foot. A quick discussion determined that the Normans would charge the wagons obliquely from the rear allowing the Normans to use their lances and swords freely and without hindrance. I pointed out that this tactic would not endanger the Northumbrian guards on the other side of the wagons and that perhaps we should split the force so that some of the Normans could attack them. Ivo laughed.

Turstan responded, "No it is difficult to attack shield side to the enemy as we would not be able to effectively swing our swords or level our lances. We think the other guards will run." I shrugged; I could see it was a weakness but had to accept their assessment of the situation. Once more the Normans horn blared out and the conroi of horsemen burst from the copse forming into a tight wedge. They aimed for the rear of the wagons attacking obliquely, spearing some of the guards and bowling over others by the force of the impact. Not being competent to charge in the wedge I cantered my horse behind the Normans and was lucky enough to down two guards who had run from the other side of the wagons after the Normans had passed. It took only moments for the Normans to clear the guards from their side of the wagons; when they cleared the front wagon they swung around and galloped down the other side of the wagon train but as Turstan had anticipated the Northumbrian guards, who were probably only untrained fyrd men were running away as fast as they could.

The waggoneers were still sitting on the driving seats looking on in amazement but as the Normans closed in, they too quickly leapt from their platforms and ran. Some of the Normans gave chase. lazily lopping heads as they cantered after the fleeing Northumbrians.

"Come back you fools." Ivo shouted, "Loot the wagons, that's what were here for." I reflected that looting was not what we were harassing the enemy for, but I also had to admit the Normans were hardly likely to risk their lives without the chance of gain.

Most of the Normans dismounted and started to ransack the wagons. They were loaded mostly with foodstuff and some weapons but eventually there was a shout of delight as one of the Normans found two chests filled with hacksilver and coin. Ivo and Turstan rode over and supervised the removal of the silver to bags that could be carried on the horses. I was more concerned with not being ambushed in return, so I rode to the head of the wagons looking west to see if any of the Northumbrians had raised the alarm. After what seemed to be only a few moments but was probably longer I espied a troop of mounted Northumbrian huscarls. There was maybe fifty of them riding much smaller horses than the Norman destriers but as they clearly outnumbered our conroi I spurred back to Turstan and yelled, "Time to go." I pointed in the direction of the returning Northumbrians. Turstan nodded and yelled at his men. The Norman troop quickly remounted and rode back the way we had come.

"The Northumbrians will pause at the wagons to assess their losses; this will give us some time to get away." Ivo yelled as we thundered south. I was not sure if there ever was any pursuit as we never saw any Northumbrians as we made our way back west towards Dun Edyn. The Normans were very happy with their loot and I persuaded them to take out two more foraging parties before it was decided to return to Perth. I was not sure if our raid had delayed Siward at all for it seemed that his army had halted at Dun Edyn to regroup anyway. After three more days we made it back to the Scottish army at Perth none the worse for our exertions, especially with no loss of life or horses. I was immensely impressed with the way the Normans handled themselves, their fighting ability and techniques, and their expertise in fighting from horseback, which was almost unheard of in England, although Martin would have me believe that the legendary Arthur did just that.

King MacBeth had not been idle while we were away and the Scots had erected a series of earthworks along the crossings of the River Tay. Clearly the king intended to deny the Northumbrians a foothold on the north bank of the river and make the enemy fight with their backs to the water, a very vulnerable position to be in. I was still unsure that this would work because I could not see why Siward would not outflank these defences by landing men from his fleet behind the enemy lines. I raised this issue again with the King and he acknowledged that this may, probably would, happen, but the flanking force would not be sufficient in number to unlock his defences.

Martin had been waiting patiently for my return, chiding me for the risks I had taken without him. Clearly, he did not mind me fighting but wanted to be there every time. The Icelanders were impressed with the Normans' success and loot, pointing out that these Normans came from the same root stock as they did, Scandinavia.

After more weeks of inaction, we learnt from MacBeth's scouts that Earl Siward and his Northumbrian army had resumed their march and had reached Stirling, the strategic gateway to the north. The Northumbrian army had been joined by the troops from Cumbria led by Gospatrick. On MacBeth's orders the town had been evacuated but the fort on top of the rock was being held by trusted troops. The Northumbrian army was only two or three day's march from Perth and the River Tay crossings and the army was on high alert. King MacBeth called another meeting of the army leaders and when all were assembled in his hall, he outlined his plans.

"As you all know I intend to contest the fords across the river. My intention is to frustrate Siward's attempt to move his army north of the river and the main battle will be fought here. However, I anticipate that he will try and outflank my army by landing troops from his fleet behind us on the north shore of the Tay estuary, probably somewhere near Invergowrie. I will have a smaller force watching for this landing with the intention of delaying their advance towards Perth long enough to prevent them having any influence on the outcome of the main battle. This force will be small but sufficient to delay the flanking move, leaving my main army at Perth large enough to overwhelm Siward." MacBeth's grim visage was stern but positive and gave off an aura of confidence. I thought that his strategy was high risk with many opportunities for it to go wrong but equally I could see that at this point there was no choice to adopt other more elaborate defences, much less an attacking strategy.

"Who is going to lead the force chosen to oppose the Northumbrian fleet?" MaelPedair Mormaer of Angus, and the Mearns asked the question I most wanted to have answered.

"As the landing will almost certainly take place in your territory, I would ask you to undertake this task." King MaBeth acknowledged the pointed question. I could see that MaelPedair was young for the task, as young as I and I anticipated what would come next.

"Your forces from Angus and the Mearns will be supplemented by the Normans who are skilled in the ways of warfare and I would ask you to be guided by Turstan their leader."

MaelPedair was obviously delighted that he had his own force acting independently but I suspect he was less pleased to have the Normans foisted upon him. I realised that this was a prudent move as the Norman horse would be much less effective holding a line on the River Tay fords. MacBeth detailed the deployment of the main force, which without the forces of the Mormaership of Angus and the Mearns numbered some two thousand, outnumbered by Siward's Northumbrians and Cumbrians by about five hundred, which I considered insignificant given that the Northumbrians had to contest the river fords and defences of the Scots.

I had already scouted the banks of the River Tay around Perth and there was no doubt that it would be a complicated river to defend and to cross. The river was quite wide at this point and was nearly tidal up to the town. The highest ford upriver was near Scone and MacBeth had built a fortified ditch and rampart about fifty paces back from the ford. The ditch curved around to enclose the ford in a horseshoe killing ground and I was reasonably confident this ford defence could withstand anything thrown at it. Nearer to the town itself there were two possible crossings, both very difficult fords but one of these crossings had been supplemented by a wooden bridge that spanned across stone supports that I understood were built by the Romans; again, MacBeth had blocked this approach by an extensive earthwork and to my mind effectively. The other area of weakness, further downstream from Perth was where the river split into two and flowed around a low-lying island. This island could be gained by wading across the larger western channel at many points and the island was nearly a mile long. The eastern channel was no barrier at all. Rather than try and defend the whole length of the island MacBeth had decided to place a strong force centrally on the island to repel any attacks when and where they developed. This would be more open fighting and for that reason he chose the better armed, and in my opinion, the most formidable warriors for this role; the Icelanders, Dublin vikings and the Gall-Gaedhil from the western islands. The bridge earthworks were to be manned by MacBeth's highlanders who were lightly armed, some with mail but most just with a small shields, swords, and daggers.

Thordolf Arnorson with the Icelanders and Martin and I took up our position on the island the next morning and we were joined by the Dubliners and Islanders within the hour. We numbered about three hundred with the bulk of the Scots army facing the fords nearer Perth and I understood about two hundred men marched west to cover the Scone ford led by the Mormaer of Strathearn who had nobly given up most of his own men to MacBeth in the centre host. MaelPedair Mormaer of Angus and the Mearns had already taken his five hundred men east to watch for the Northumbrian fleet. Later in the day we saw the Northumbrian army moving into the town of Perth. The fortress on a rise above the river remained manned by the Scots and for the time being the English host ignored them. MacBeth had long since ordered an evacuation of the town so there was no killing, just a systematic and controlled looting of anything that had been left behind by the citizens, whilst a heavily contingent of Northumbrian huscarls quietly watched the fords.

By early evening I observed a group of horsemen riding along the opposite bank of the river assessing our defences. I could see the giant figure of Siward Bjornson Earl of Northumbria dwarfing his horse and wearing his distinctive white bearskin cloak. I had no idea who the other English riders were but I assumed that Siward's kin would be with him, and maybe Gospatrick of Cumbria. I also assumed that at least one of the exiled princes, sons of the late unlamented King Duncan would also be present, probably Malcolm. The Northumbrians were clearly in no hurry and it was obvious that any serious attack across the river would not materialise until the morning. I suggested to the leaders of each contingent, the Icelanders under Thordolf, the Dubliners and Hebrideans under a warrior called Eachmarchach Ragnaldson, who had apparently once been King of Dublin to stand down and make themselves comfortable. I ensured that there were sufficient sentries watching the river crossings so that we were not surprised in the night.

I spent some time in the evening with Eachmarchach who turned out to be a charming and entertaining fellow probably about the same age as King MacBeth. It transpired that Eachmarchach and MacBeth were the best of friends and used to spend every summer in their youths raiding down the west coast of England and Wales and all around the coast of Ireland. Eachmarchach insisted on referring to MacBeth as Thorfinn as for most of their time together they both saw themselves as viking chieftains rather than kings. I returned to the sentry outposts several times throughout the night to ensure their vigilance and whilst I snatched some sleep Martin kept watch.

I roused the warriors just before dawn, which was as well as the Northumbrians could be seen mustering on the far bank of the river and it was obvious that they intended to attempt a crossing at first light. The Icelanders, Dubliners and Hebrideans were all of Scandinavian stock and were equipped accordingly. Most had chainmail shirts and segmented helmets with a nasal guard. Some of the helmets had a mail neck guard and one or two had an old-fashioned face protector covering the top half of the face. All of the warriors had either a Dane axe or sword and I had ensured that each man was armed with a spear from King MacBeth's arsenal. Every man also had an oval wooden shield faced with leather and bound with an iron re-enforcing strip. One or two of the better armed men had leather boots with protective vertical iron strips sewn onto them to protect from slashes to the legs. The group I was with were generally much better equipped than the rest of the Scottish army.

Although Scotland, Ireland, the Isles, and Iceland were nominally Christian I noticed a number of warriors with Thor's hammer amulets around their necks. I had a wooden crucifix around my neck; this had been given to me by my uncle Brand but I had no clear inclination towards Christianity as my experiences with my step-mother and her pratting monks had soured any feelings I had in that direction. My shield still sported the Mercian Knot emblem of which I was inordinately proud; the Islemen tended to display a drawing of a black galley on their shields, or a black raven, presumably for Odin. Surprisingly Eachmarchach displayed a painted white cross on his shield. I was the only warrior in the line with a kite shaped shield, similar to the Norman shields. I had learnt that a shield of this design gave better protection for the legs in a melee or shield wall as it did for the mounted Normans in a charge.

I shouted, "Form the line, shield wall." As discussed earlier the northern warriors formed into a three-line shield wall with one hundred warriors in each line. The front line carried javelins and swords, the second line carried spears and axes and the third line also had spears and a mixture of swords and axes; all of us had a smaller scramaseax in our belts for close quarter fighting. The Icelanders were all in the first row on the right-hand side of the line and I placed myself on the extreme end of the line guarding the right end man's sword side; Martin was with me protecting my back.

The Northumbrians had come down to the riverbank and were tentatively testing the water depth at various points to determine the best approach to the island. I could see that Earl Siward was not with the attacking party, the obvious leader was a much younger man in shimmering silver mail and a scarlet cloak he sat astride a horse at the rear of his lines exhorting is men to advance.

When the lead huscarls had ascertained that an advance across a broad front could be achieved the advancing host spread out along the river bank. There were many more of them than us, perhaps six hundred and they too formed a loose shield wall in three lines. Although my mind was focussed on the advancing enemy, I became dimly aware of the sound of battle off to my right and realised that the fight at the Perth bridge had already begun.

The Northumbrians slowly waded into the river along a wide front that overlapped our own lines. The river was perhaps fifty paces wide at the intended point of conflict. The Northumbrians were spread across a width of two hundred paces, overlapping our line by fifty paces either end. I had brought my bow with me and I started to fire arrows off immediately. The front rank of the Northumbrians was heavily armoured like ourselves but I expected some of my shots to be lucky and within the first twenty paces or so I had manged to hit one huscarl in his unprotected face. I hoped his scream would unnerve his comrades. At twenty-five paces, the deepest part of the river, when the huscarls were chest high in the water they hit our little surprise. In preparation for the impending fight, we had sunk sharpened stakes into the river bed along sections of the passable areas in the river. Shouts of alarm were emitted from our enemies as they blundered into the sharp stakes. I knew that the stakes were unlikely to seriously hurt anyone but they did cause considerable confusion as the Northumbrians either tried to pull the stakes free from the river bed or tried to find a way around them.

I knew that the enemy's confusion would allow me to have some clearer shots and within a few moments I had downed at least four huscarls with arrows to their necks, faces or under arms where their mail protection allowed gaps. As intended the stakes forced the Northumbrians into access channels through the ford, making them press together. This tactic meant that the huscarls could only attack us in four places along the two hundred paces front they had originally intended to attack along. Eachmarchach gave the prearranged horn blown signal and our shield wall split into four groups of seventy-five on a twenty-five-man front facing each of the oncoming Northumbrian wedges seeking to emerge from the river. At fifteen paces our front rank all hurled javelins at the struggling attackers. Still up to their thighs in the river, the Northumbrian front line lacked the ability or agility to dodge the volley of missiles and many of the huscarls were hit, others caught the javelins on their shields but once the javelins were embedded in the shields the huscarls struggled to hold them up in a defensive barrier and the shield wall faltered. It was a testament to their courage and resolution that the Northumbrian huscarls struggled on to reach our waiting line. With our shield wall intact, they faced an impenetrable barrier bristling with spears held high by our second rank. Without the need for orders our front rank went to work, those with axes tried to hook them over their opponents shields and pull them down thus exposing their attacker to a spear thrust from his supporting spearman in the second line. In this way many of the Northumbrians were wounded and fell back adding more to the loss of cohesion of the enemy shield wall.

At the extreme right flank of the Icelanders, I could see that they had brought the enemy attack to a standstill and the opposing Northumbrians could not get a purchase on the muddy river bottom to push back at us. The Icelanders' Dane axes were reducing the Northumbrian huscarl's shield to tinder leaving them vulnerable and with no choice but to fall back,

As I was on the shield side of the Northumbrians, I was less than effective so I leapt forward into the shallows and took a swipe at the enemy line anchor man's leg. My sword bit into the back of his leg just below the knee and he immediately collapsed screaming. Leaving him to Martin's axe I stepped passed the wounded warrior and did the same to the next man who did not even see my attack. He too collapsed and the man behind him tried to turn to confront me only to receive a spear thrust into his unprotected side. In this manner the enemy attack line collapsed and the Northumbrians pulled back towards midstream. This was a slow process as those that foolishly turned away were immediately speared in their backs. The sensible huscarls covered themselves with their shields and edged back into the deeper water.

Of the hundred and fifty or so enemy warriors that had attacked us probably thirty or forty lay dead or dying in the shallows. The blood ran in rivulets down the river and I wondered if MaelPedair's force would see the red flow further down the river towards the sea.

I looked along the island bank and could see that the other groups had also repelled the attackers in their killing grounds. Assuming that they had been as successful as we had been the enemy losses may have been as many as one hundred, a sixth of their force. I was not even tired after the first melee and was pleased with the ease we had repelled the attackers. Thorfinn MacBeth's plans were working well for us. I could still hear the fighting off to the west indicating that the fight half a mile to our right was continuing.

The Northumbrians, to their credit, came at use twice more, but with the same result and with increased losses on their part and negligible deaths on ours. Now I was tired and we seemed to have been fighting all day but the sun told me that it was still before mid-day. The Northumbrian host, now much depleted, moved off west to the jeering of the Icelanders. With nothing else to do, we dragged the dead Northumbrians into a barrier along the edge of the river bank so that the enemy would have to climb over their own dead if they returned to the attack. Leaving the Icelanders and Hebrideans watching the ford I decided to go and see what was happening at the bridge of Perth and inform Thorfinn of our situation. Martin and I jogged west along the river bank.

The fight before Perth soon came into view. Thorfinn had broken the bridge at the last moment denying Siward's army an easy passage. Streams of Northumbrians were wading across the river to be met by screaming Scots at the designated killing grounds. The areas within the barricades were slick with mud and blood and although much better equipped than the Scots the Northumbrians could make little headway. Thorfinn had the invading army successfully contained.

Asking the whereabouts of King MacBeth along the barricade line I was directed to the centre where I soon saw the King dressed in full mail standing on the lip of the barricade with a large flag waving above his head displaying a black boar. He bore a long shield similar to mine and hefted a large Dane axe; I clambered up beside him.

"What are you doing here?" he demanded roughly. Looking at me I could see his face was covered with gore and the axe head, handle and his right hand were also bloodied.

"I have come to report; the attacks on the island to the east have been repelled easily and the Northumbrian contingent has withdrawn. Is there anything we should be doing other than sitting on our arses?" I smiled but he did not relax.

"Do you think it would be safe to withdraw some of the men and support MaelPedair?" he queried.

"I think it would be safe to do so; instead of three hundred, I think half that number could hold the island now that Siward knows how hard it is to attack it."

"Good, then leave Eachmarchach on the island and take the Icelanders and a contingent of Islemen and move east to support MaelPedair. We are doing well here too and I cannot see Siward breaking through unless he can outflank us."

Martin and I jogged back to the island and relayed Thorfinn MacBeth's instructions to Eachmarchach and Thordolf Arnorson. Thordolf assembled his crew and Eachmarchach selected another hundred men from the Hebrides, warriors known as Gall-Gaedhil, a hard mercenary lot who favoured the Dane axe. My first command set off at a trot, eastwards along the north bank of the Tay. It was some fifteen to twenty miles to where the Mormaer MaelPedair was awaiting any seaborne landing and I knew it would take most of the rest of the day to reach him but I had already realised that this battle was not going to be resolved in one day. The river was calm and clear to our right with the weak sunlight shimmering on the rippling current. The country was fair and lush meadowland with several muddy rivulets working their way down towards the Tay river bank that slowed my troop down occasionally.

After a steady march for a full watch, I spotted ships in the river ahead, six in all, and they were clearly crossing from the south bank of the river. At the point where they were crossing the river was about a mile and a half wide. Their crossing point was still about another half watch march from our current position even if we trotted but I did not want us to arrive exhausted and it would clearly be dusk by the time we arrived. Unless disaster had already struck, and it did not appear so as the ships had not landed yet then our arrival for tomorrow's conflict would be timely.

We doggedly marched on and as we neared the crossing point, I became aware of two things; one, the ships were heavily laden with warriors, and two there were sounds of battle ahead, so some of the enemy force had already landed on the north bank of the river. Thorfinn MacBeth had suggested that Asbjorn Siwardson was leading a force of three hundred to five hundred seaborne invaders but if these men had already landed on the north bank and the six ships I could no longer see were carrying more of the enemy from the south bank of the river, Fife; then tomorrow MaelPedair could be facing anywhere up to a thousand of the enemy with only five hundred men from Angus and the Mearns! My one hundred and fifty men could make all the difference.

As dusk fell, we stumbled into the rear of MaelPedair's force. The fighting had obviously stopped with both sides drawing back to rest and recuperate. I walked through our lines of warriors and it was obvious they were weary and bloodied. Many were wounded and if the invaders could have summoned enough energy to attack now, they would just walk straight over them. I found Mormaer MaelPedair at the sparse line of trees that signalled the incline of the land into the river valley. Even in the dark I could see that we were at least a mile from the river bank and the dim outlines of the now grounded ships.

"My lord Mormaer, King MacBeth has sent me with one hundred and fifty men to support your resistance to the seaborne flanking movement, how goes it?" I introduced myself and enquired of the situation. MaelPedair was sat upon a fallen tree trunk, he was covered in gore some of which was his own as one of his men was bandaging up a cut to the Mormaer's arm and he already had a dirty rag of a bandage wrapped around his shin. He looked at me sullenly and with no thankfulness in his look for my troop's timely arrival.

"More betrayal, that bastard MacDubh of Fife is supporting Malcolm MacCrinan and Asbjorn Siwardson. The Northumbrians landed just before midday and I did not think there was more than three hundred of them at first. Although they were well armoured and better disciplined than my own warriors, we held them back successfully for nearly a full watch but during that time the ships that had conveyed them here had crossed over to the south bank of the river and taken on another full complement of Fife men with their Mormaer MacDubh who joined Asbjorn by early afternoon and with double their numbers they started to push us back from the river. Just before dusk when the fighting broke off another shipload of Fife clansmen came over and so they must be nearly a thousand strong on their beach head. I have lost over a hundred men and some of my clansmen are deserting, and those Normans were no use at all either" MaelPedair sounded bitter and angry, as well he might, for although I did not know it at the time his young wife was the daughter of the MacDubh Mormaer of Fife.

"We can regroup in the morning." Was all I could think of saying. I was concerned that MaelPedair was losing the will to fight on and that a real threat of our main force being outflanked could result.

I returned to my troop and appraised them of the situation, I then sought out the most robust Icelander I could find and sent him back to King Thorfinn MacBeth with a message detailing the situation and the likelihood of the Northumbrians and Fife men breaking out from their beach head in the morning. After I had organised a place for my troop to rest before the forthcoming fight, I sought out Turstan the Norman. I found the Norman force separate and isolated from the rest of MaelPedair's force but strategically placed on the Angus men's right flank near the river and low-lying flat land, ideal for a conroi charge, or so I thought.

Turstan and his brother Ivo were sardonic about the situation. "He hasn't a clue how to place or use mounted warriors. He actually expected us to charge the enemy shield wall whilst it was still intact and in fact in much better order than our own lines. If the Northumbrians had horsemen, they could have swept this ill-led group of ill-disciplined farmers away in a trice." Ivo opined.

"Were going to be defeated tomorrow, even with your reinforcements and it will be us who will have to hold back the enemy when our men are routed." Turstan observed and I could only agree with him.

"The Icelanders and Hebrideans will form a shield wall and hold back the Northumbrians as long as we can tomorrow." I announced. "If you can keep our flanks, we may delay the enemy most of the day and this will give Thorfinn MacBeth time to redeploy, although I have no idea if he has any fall-back plan."

Turstan and Ivo nodded and I returned to my group to get what rest I could. Strangely impending fights never bothered me like most other men. I do not know if I am just too stupid to imagine the worst possible outcome to a fight, or whether I am what people define as courageous, which is a form of stupidity, I suppose, but I had now been in two major conflicts, one in Wales and today's fight on the island and terror never took hold of me. I did not count single combats or small melees that require a different kind of bravado. I decided I was more akin to the Norman professional mercenaries, perhaps I was on the road to becoming a hard-bitten fighting man who just becomes used to the tension and consequences of continuous conflict. I noticed that Martin never appeared bothered by impending conflict either. I could see that many of the Icelanders were nervous and a lot of the local Mearns and Angus men were plainly terrified of the forthcoming battle.

I slept fitfully, concerned about the tactical situation and how to oppose the overwhelming force arrayed against us. When I finally fully woke, I could see that many of our men had sneaked away in the night. MaelPedair sought me out, he was distraught.

"What can we do, I can never prevent the Northumbrians from marching on Perth with the few men I have left."

"Yes, that is true, but we can delay them and allow MacBeth to come up with an alternative strategy before he is outflanked and trapped. I imagine he will pull back, retreat if you like, to somewhere he can hold against a larger united Northumbrian force. You are reasonably local do you know of anywhere he might retire to?" I asked.

MaelPedair calmed himself and thought out the possibilities. "There are a number of fortified places north of Perth, there is Kinnoul Hill, and Kinnaird, and further north there is Dunsinane Hill; all are fortified." MaelPedair suggested.

"I have passed Kinnoul and Kinnaird when I sailed up the Tay, both are too near Perth to be effective as a place to make a stand and MacBeth's army would still be trapped between the two enclosing Northumbrian forces. I do not know this Dunsinane, MacBeth must make the decision and let us know.

He should already be aware of our situation and we may hear from him this morning." I responded as positively as I could. "Now let us marshal our forces. I noticed that there is a muddy stream that flows down into the Tay about three hundred paces behind our right flank. I suggest we draw up our forces behind this stream in a tight shield wall. My Icelanders will hold the left flank on the rising ground and the Normans can prevent us being outflanked. To get passed your force on the right the Northumbrians would have to re-embark on their ships but this would take some time and that is what we want."

MaelPedair and I marshalled the line, two lines deep, over a length of five hundred paces, only four hundred men and one hundred and fifty were Icelanders and Hebrideans. Over one hundred of the Angus and Mearns men had fled in the night. To our advantage the weather had worsened and a slight drizzle of rain was falling. This would make the enemy advance more difficult and the stream crossing muddier; even better the rain was from the west and into the faces of the enemy. The Icelanders shield wall was as formidable as it could be, with larger round wooden shields overlapping and full mail shirts and iron helmets; the Albans to our right were not as formidable with much smaller leather targes that failed to cover the whole torso leaving them vulnerable to spear casts and arrows. Few had mail shirts and hardly any had helmets; they were fast and mobile skirmishers using javelins and small axes but that would not help in a stubborn fight for ground in the shield wall.

The Northumbrians took their time assembling their own shield wall; this again was to our advantage, clearly their leader or leaders had not grasped the need for urgency. When their line was finally in place I noticed that like us there were two distinct groups. In front of the Icelanders were a long line of Albans similarly armed to the Angus men on our side. These I assumed to be the Fife clansmen. There were upwards of six hundreds of them and they outflanked us by at least twenty paces. Facing MaelPedair's clansmen were a tight core of three hundred Northumbrians, all with large round shields, helmets, and mail shirts. There favoured weapon was the spear and these would outreach MaelPedair's warriors' weapons.

A tall heavy built young man wearing a white bearskin was at the forefront of the Northumbrians exhorting them to fight well. He wore magnificent armour with an ornate full-faced helmet covered in scroll work. I assumed this was Asbjorn Siwardson of the line of Danish chieftains claiming descent from the fairy bear. I idly wondered if the fairy bear was that Danish hero Bodvarr Bjarki, whom the Angles called Beowulf, who could shape change into a bear in battle. If so, a truly magnificent pedigree to match my own.

MaelPedair was screaming at his own men to stand and fight like heroes when the bulls' horns sounded the advance and the Northumbrians moved forward at a steady pace.

I shouted across the field to MaelPedair. "Hold the line and don't let your men throw their javelins until the enemy reaches the stream." I hope he heard me.

As the enemy approached once more the few Icelanders who carried bows started peppering the enemy. Unlike the battle the day before the approaching Fife men were more vulnerable to the arrows raining down on them and several fell with arrows in their faces or parts of their torsos not covered by their small shields. The Fife men clambered down the slight slope into the muddy stream and at this point I shouted to go forward and the shield wall moved as one, three paces onto the Fife men as they tried to extricate themselves from the stream up our bank. Some were slipping as our shields impacted on them and countless clansmen went down into the stream. Killing them was easy, spearing them like fish in a barrel, their own axes and spears sliding harmlessly off our heavy shields. Within moments at least twenty of the enemy warriors were down dead and dying, the stream red with blood and mud. Other Fife men were slipping and floundering in the stream trying to extricate themselves before they too were speared. I stepped back out of the melee to see what was happening elsewhere. Amazingly MaelPedair's men were holding the Northumbrian huscarls at the stream. Fortunately, the muddy ditch was proving as much of an obstacle to the armoured attackers as the Alban clansmen. However, all was not well on our left flank; the Fife clansmen that had overlapped our line in the advance had crossed the ditch and swung around to attack the end of our shield wall. Upwards of forty Fife clansmen had surrounded the few Icelanders at the end of our line who had formed a small circle to hold them off and prevent the shield wall from collapsing.

Suddenly I felt the ground tremble and saw the small Norman conroi surge forward at a slow gallop from two hundred paces in our rear. Iron men on massive frenzied war horses. Huge clods of mud were thrown up by the iron shod hooves; the wide dilated nostrils and bared teeth of the destriers was enough to panic the bravest warriors. They hit the rear of the Fife men like a thunderbolt, their horses lashing out with their hooves and lunging with snapping teeth, whilst the riders speared the Fife men either in the back or if an enemy warrior was lucky enough to turn and face the charge, with a lance that simply went straight through the leather targe and impaled him through the torso. In a trice the Fife men turned and fled, all six hundreds of them, although now there were considerably less. The twenty or thirty of the Fife clansmen that we had accounted for were as nothing to those ridden down by the Norman charge. I was amazed that a few horsemen could create such havoc, they pursued the running Fife men back along the meadow lopping unprotected heads or smashing brains in with maces. The iron shod hooves of the Norman destriers crunched through the spines of fallen Albans leaving a bloody red path of death and destruction.

Martin pulled on my arm, "Lord, now is the time to outflank the Northumbrians." He nodded to our right; many of the Northumbrian huscarls were in the muddy stream struggling to gain a purchase on our side. There were three hundred of them being held by a similar number of our clansmen but we had one hundred and twenty Icelanders and Hebrideans and it was our turn to attack.

I struggled through the mud and drizzle to Thordolf Arnorson, "It's our turn now." I indicated to the exposed flank of the Northumbrians. Thordolf nodded. Together we marshalled the host and waded through the stream and up the opposite side, which was slippery with blood and gore and dead Fife men.

"Swine array." Thordolf screamed. The descendants of vikings immediately responded by forming into a rough wedge with Thordolf and I at its apex. Horns sounded our charge and we stumbled forward as best we could. The Northumbrians were exposed as we attacked their right-hand side where no shields protected them. Thordolf and I hit the end of the Northumbrian line hard, we both downed our first opponents who were blissfully unaware of our approach as they struggled with MaelPedair's clansmen to their front. Thordolf brained his opponent with an axe blow that dented the poor man's helmet making the rivets snap. The blow crushed the man's skull and he dropped like a stone. I slid my sword into the kidneys of my opponent bursting the links of his mail. He screamed and twisted around pulling the sword out of the wound, this allowed me to smash my shield into his face and I simultaneously hacked at his knee, which being unarmoured severed from his body. He fell and I moved on to the next opponent who was more ready for me. He turned towards me only to receive a wound from the clansman he had been fighting moments before. Our wedge started to wrap around the rear of the Northumbrian huscarls striking at their exposed backs. Not surprisingly the Northumbrians began to fall back covering themselves with their shields. The enemy shield wall was bowing backwards as we attacked their wing and the movement was contagious and the whole line started to give way. At the same time Martin informed me that the Normans were cantering back to the battle having routed the whole Fife contingent. The enemy line was starting to resemble a half circle backing up against the River Tay. They had effectively reformed their shield wall and few of MaelPedair's men or the Icelanders were keen on a final assault against an unbroken line of shields. Why die when the battle is nearly won? Asbjorn Siwardson held the centre of the line with his imposing presence. I found MaelPedair exhorting his men into making a final assault.

"You are wasting your time, lord." I remarked. "None of these men will risk their lives at the end of a fight, they all want to live to tell the tale." MaelPedair was clearly frustrated, just to rub salt in his wounds I observed, "I think the Normans earned their pay, don't you." He looked at me searchingly and so I mollified him by admitting, "But they won't attack an unbroken shield wall either."

"What are we to do?" MaelPedair asked.

"I have an idea, something I learnt in Wales." I strode out of the Alban line towards the Northumbrians;

No, I did not stroll, I swaggered and shouted. "Ut, Ut, Ut!" I screamed the Anglian war cry in the face of my own far out kinsmen.

"I am Hereward Leofricson, Earl's son, Prince Slayer, Wave Rider, Evil Eye, and I have sworn to kill Asbjorn Siwardson. Fight me man to man or forever be called nithing." Well 'wave rider' was going a bit far, but I had killed my share of Welsh princes and I was sure Earl Siward's son would not refuse such a challenge. Asbjorn stepped out from the enemy shield wall. He was much taller than I and looked impressive in his gilded mail and heavy white bear cloak. He lifted the face mask on his helmet so that I could see his face. He was very handsome with blond wavy hair, long flowing moustaches, and a ruddy face, even more so after the days exertions; a true Viking warrior.

"Hereward Leofricson, yes, I remember you, a snivelling boy who my father arranged to have outlawed at the milksop king's court. Are you really an Earl's son, can Leofric get it up anymore, I heard he isn't boning Godgifu and what a waste that is."

I laughed, "At least my father isn't fucking polar bears; is it true you have hairy ears or just a hairy arse?"

"Alright, let's not play around, this isn't a holmgang, no rules and to the death." Asbjorn snarled. He fronted is shield, which unsurprisingly had a white bear painted on a black field, and drew his sword. I too fronted my kite shaped shield and held my sword high. We circled slowly, weighing each other up; I was surprised he had not discarded his heavy bears cloak as it would surely slow him up. The ground was soddened, and slippery, as the rain continued to fall in a cold drizzle. Asbjorn had closed his helmet face again and I assumed that his vision was impaired by this, although the eye holes were large. The metal worked face on the iron plate was fascinating and resembled my imagined likeness of Thor with a flowing brass moustache. It was mesmerising and I nearly missed the message in Asbjorn's eyes preceding his first attack. He thrust forward his shield and swept his sword in a broad arc towards my left knee. With a traditional oval shield his blow would have connected with my leg but having a longer kite shaped shield, the sword bit into the lower part of the shield giving me time to leap back out of his reach. He moved on me quickly trying to prevent me from making a good defence and any counter blows. I kept catching his blows on my shield; the blows were heavy and were numbing my arm, he was very strong. As I anticipated, he was slower than I, although not by much. I kept dancing to my right, his left, around his shield side and out of his helmeted line of vision. This gave me time to return a few blows, most landed on his shield but I did manage to land a blow on his shoulder but my sword bounced off his bearskin cloak and now I realised why he still wore it. Asbjorn, in turn, started revolving to his left to keep me in sight, but he stood still so as to keep a firm purchase on the muddy ground. My manoeuvre was the riskier as I was dancing over slimy mud and I suppose it was unsurprising that eventually I slipped. My feet shot from under me and I fell back onto my bottom, fortunately I kept hold of both shield and sword. Asbjorn was on me like a falling raptor, trying to spear me with the point of his sword. I felt a blinding pain in my thigh, where one of his jabs hit home. My mail had rucked up as I fell and exposed my leggings to mid-thigh and that was where the point of his sword penetrated the muscle. I squirmed backwards and blindly I hit out with my sword in retaliation and was lucky enough to catch Asbjorn's foot as he stepped forward. My sword sliced through the leather boot below his iron shin guard, maybe I had sliced off one or two of his toes. Asbjorn hopped backwards cursing and this gave me time to clamber up onto my unsteady feet. My leg hurt like the devil but it held my weight. I fronted my shield and awaited his next move; we were both wounded and bleeding and I was covered in mud but nothing fatal to either of us. I could dimly hear the shouts and chanting of both armies as they watched the spectacle.

Asbjorn limped towards me and I found I still had no difficulty in moving away from him and to his left. He was slower now and my very next blow disabled him further. I took two quick paces to my right and brought my sword round the back of Asbjorn's left leg and sliced through his tendons. It did not take his leg off but he lost control of it and was reduced to hopping on his one good leg. Blood coursed down his leg and I could see his boot filling with a crimson flood. Asbjorn managed to remain standing and for a while we remained slashing at each other slowly reducing our shields to matchwood. I felt Asbjorn's sword bite into my shield arm and knew that my shield was past protecting me and I had to do something urgently. Relying on what speed I still had I jumped into Asbjorn's swinging sword arc and punched him with all my remaining strength with my iron shield boss, pain shot up my arm but despite his strength and because he only had one leg to support himself, he was hurled backwards and fell onto his back, but he too, like me managed to keep his sword and shield. Not wishing to approach his blade I took the wisest course and slashed at his good leg and this time I was fortunate enough to bite deep into his knee. He screamed and I knew he could not now rise. I danced around him, forcing my wounded leg to move, he kept the remains of his shield across his torso trying to protect himself from any fatal blow but this allowed me free rein to land sword blows on his legs and helmet. He was now floundering and both armies had gone quiet waiting for the fatal blow. I waited until the time was right and stamped down on his sword pushing it down into the mud. I raised my sword and slashed off his hand at the wrist, bravely but quite feebly he raised his mutilated wrist trying to aim the fountaining blood towards me, a fighting warrior and true viking to the last. I avoided the blood and pushed aside the shield and thrust my sword into his chest breaking the mail and slicing through his ribcage to his heart. His eyes dimmed and his body relaxed in death.

I staggered back and raised my arms in triumph, the Albans and Icelanders cheered, I held the pose whilst the rain washed the blood from my mail. After a brief pause, I shouted.

"Who now speaks for the Northumbrians?"

An elderly man stepped forward and walked across the mud towards me, I readied myself in case he decided I was now an easy target.

"I am MacDubh, the Mormaer of Fife, I speak for both the Northumbrians and what remains of my host." His grizzled countenance showed weary acceptance of the situation.

"Well listen MacDubh, your army is defeated and is unfit to fight on, however we would lose to many of our own men if we chose to exterminate you, so go now, get in your ships and sail back to Fife and we will not harm you further."

MacDubh considered the situation for a brief moment and then shrugged and nodded. "What about Lord Siward's son?" MacDubh indicated the corpse.

"Take his body back to his father, he fought and died nobly like a true viking. The only item I will take is his bearskin." I bent and unpinned the long ornate brooches and pulled off the bearskin cloak. I turned and limped back up the muddy slope towards my compatriots. I held up the bearskin for all to see. They cheered and the Icelanders started to chant, "Asbjornbana! Asbjornbana! Bearslayer, bearslayer, bearslayer. Martin came down to greet me grinning from ear to ear. He took the cloak.

"I'll clean it, and you need to get those wounds seen to."

MaelPedair also walked out of the host. "Well done, we have beaten them but why are you letting them go?" he asked, clearly frustrated.

"They are not going to surrender and even if they did, we cannot corral them and guard them with the numbers we have. I suspect MacBeth will need us back at Perth very soon so we cannot linger here." I explained. We were all exhausted so we drew back from the field of blood and tended to our wounds. I asked Turstan and Ivo to ride back to Perth with their Normans as soon as they were able and report to Thorfinn MacBeth. Unbelievably they had only lost two of their number in the charge and once again I was impressed by the effectiveness of using cavalry in battle.

The Northumbrians and Fife men slowly drifted back to the ships and embarked with Asbjorn's corpse carried on a stretcher made from two spear shafts and cloaks. I was sure some would cross back to Fife; others would sail up the Tay hoping to join with Earl Siward's forces. Either way, they were a spent force and they would dishearten the main Northumbrian host rather than enhance it.

I could not see any way that our small army could be persuaded to march back to Perth before the next morning and truth to tell my body ached and was sore from my wounds; more wounds than I realised. Martin insisted upon washing the wounds thoroughly with clear water obtained further upstream and then binding them with clean rags, where he obtained them from, I had no idea. We rested where we lay, near the battlefield, watching the enemy leave. When they had finally embarked MaelPedair had all his men stand down except for a few unlucky sentries. I slept.

It was after midnight when Martin roughly shook me awake. "Hereward, Lord, there's news from Perth."

I came awake slowly and my wounds and bruises hurt when I moved. "What is it?" I grumbled as I clawed my mind out of the fog of a deep sleep.

"There's a messenger from the King, he is with MaelPedair at this moment." Martin explained.

I crawled from my blanket and without donning any mail I buckled on my sword and stumbled after Martin. "Don't you ever sleep, Martin?" I moaned.

"That's not my lot, lord."

I followed Martin to a smouldering fire that several men were huddled around. MaelPedair looked up. "Hereward, this is Fergus, he's newly come from the King with serious news." MaelPedair quickly explained that whilst we were fighting Asbjorn's ship borne invasion Thorfinn MacBeth had continued to repel Earl Siward's attempt to cross the river at Perth. However, late in the afternoon a report had reached the King that a large body of men were closing upon his rear coming from the direction of Dunkeld down the Tay's north bank through Birnham Wood. With his flank turned the King had been left with no choice but to pull back from the Tay defences and retreat north east. Some of the Northumbrians had managed to cross the river and were in pursuit of the King's forces and a running fight had developed between the forces from Dunkeld and Siward's forces combined, and MacBeth's rearguard.

"We must march to the King's aid." MaelPedair announced forcefully.

"I agree," I responded "but where are we to march to?" Turning to the messenger, I asked pointedly, "Where is MacBeth heading, has he a plan?"

"The King asked you to meet him at Dunsinane, that's a fortress."

"I know," cutting him off, "I have heard of the place, MaelPedair, how long will it take for us to reach this Dunsinane from here?"

"It is about six miles from here, flat but rising ground; if we rouse the men, we could be there in well before noon." MaelPedair calculated.

"That's good, not too far and no need to wake the men yet, let them sleep. We need to arrive at Dunsinane fresh for an anticipated battle tomorrow morning. Let them have another full watch sleep and then a quick march to arrive as timely reinforcements." I suggested.

Everyone agreed to that, pleased that the men's sleep would be uninterrupted; before I returned to my blanket, I asked the messenger if there was any more information regarding the new enemy force from Dunkeld.

"Malcolm Mac Duncan the exile is the grandson of Crinan who was Mormaer of Atholl, and Dunkeld is the gateway to Atholl. The King assumes that the enemy are Atholl men and Lochaber clans led by Flannchu Mac Bannchu the Thegn of Lochaber. King MacBeth slew both Crinan and Bannchu in battle some years back. By report there was at least five hundred of them marching down the Tay valley."

"MacBeth has is fair share of enemies." I noted wryly. I went back to my blanket, which was now cold and unwelcoming but I was too tired to protest and slipped into another restless sleep.

Martin was already up when I finally awoke and he had found me another shield, this time an oval shield with a white bear on it; obviously picked up from the battlefield. Thordolf Arnorson had assembled the Icelanders and Hebrideans and he seemed in a jovial mood, Martin said it was because he was composing a poem about some bearslayer or other. I sighed, well this was what I wanted, fame as a warrior, but I had to admit the bruises and cuts would make anyone think twice about such a fancy.

The army straggled off following MaelPedair and his closest companions who knew the way to Dunsinane intimately. Thordolf's Icelanders brought up the rear, sweeping up any stragglers and herding them on to Dunsinane. Scouts were sent out ahead to ensure we were not going to run into any of Siward's Northumbrians or the new force from the north. I could see everything was being done properly so I concentrated in placing one foot before the other and dragged myself along with the rest of the Icelanders. Initially I had wrapped myself in the white bearskin I had taken as a trophy from the dead Asbjorn but after a while its weight became burdensome and I discarded it with the comment to Martin that it needed to be cut down so that it fitted across my shoulders only to provide protection from blows, the rest of the bearskin I would use as a sleeping blanket. Martin shouldered the weight.

The morning air was cold and brisk but seasonal, it looked like rain but it thankfully held off. Meadows and woods stretched before us and after an hour or so I could discern rising ground and the suggestion of a fortified hill some three miles ahead of us. As we neared, I listened for sounds of conflict but could hear none. The scouts returned to inform us that MacBeth was indeed ensconced in the fortress and a large army was encamped beyond it. Obviously the two enemy forces had combined and would mass for an attack in due course but first it looked like we would be able to slip into Dunsinane if that is what Thorfinn Macbeth wished?

We approached the fortress from the south east and were not visible to the enemy. I suggested to MaelPedair that we should halt and send a messenger to MacBeth asking for orders as he may not want us in the fortress. The messenger was duly sent off and we all hunkered down in some pleasant meadow land that was reasonably dry to await orders.

Thordolf and Martin sat with me. "What do you think?" I asked Thordolf.

"Well, things have not worked out quite as we had hoped, as mercenaries we fight for loot and reward but pickings look meagre at the moment. On the other hand, we have been very successful in our endeavours so far, with little loss of life, so we still may come out of this as winners. As for you, I think you fight for renown and you have surely succeeded in gaining such fame. Your victory over Asbjorn Siwardson is the talk of the men and will be passed on throughout the length and breadth of Alba, England, and Iceland."

I grunted, "That may be true, but I was thinking more of the conflict that still lies before us."

Martin interrupted, "There isn't much to say about that until we learn more of Thorfinn MacBeth's situation. The recognised practice is that any force manning a fortress should be able to successfully hold it against a much larger besieging force, so unless the Albans were badly mauled yesterday, we might be able to hold off the Northumbrians."

"Yes, I see that Martin but how long can the Northumbrians maintain themselves here and for that matter how long can Thorfinn MacBeth hold out in the hill fort, especially if it is not provisioned to withstand a siege?" I responded. I turned and saw a large force of Alban warriors trotting towards the camp, clearly these were sent by Thorfinn MacBeth as our messenger was with them. The leaders of the group ran up to MaelPedair so I joined the group to hear what they had to say.

"Well met and timely met MaelPedair. I am Feradach one of the Kings hearth companions. The King has sent me to explain the situation. Yesterday after fighting most of the morning MacBeth became aware of a force approaching from the north. It was about five hundred strong and we later learnt it was led by Malcolm Mac Duncan himself, he had apparently slipped away from the Cumbrian force he was leading with Gospatrick and made his way secretly to his grandfather's old mormaership of Atholl. He was accompanied by Flannchu the son of the old Thegn of Lochaber, who has returned from exile in Wales, and between them they raised the force in our rear. As previously arranged, the King ordered our army to pull back north east to Dunsinane; as we withdrew the Atholl force attacked our left flank but we fought them off and kept retreating. However, the delay allowed some of the Northumbrians to cross the river and march on our rear. For most of the afternoon and until the light faded, we fought a running battle with both enemy bodies and we suffered badly. At one point we were pressed so hard we did not think we would make it but even as we were breaking the Normans charged the Northumbrians and broke them. The Normans saved us, they charged like madmen into the enemy's loose ranks and cut down dozens of them and we escaped."

I interrupted, "And the Normans?"

Feradach looked sheepish, "We ran, but the Normans sacrificed themselves to save us, they were surrounded and cut down one by one."

Thordolf and I exchanged looks, "That's one lot of mercenaries who didn't make a profit from this, God rest them, but they were valiant men." I mourned.

"Well, how many men does the King have in Dunsinane?" demanded MaelPedair.

"The king still has some fifteen hundred men, too many for the fortress to comfortably hold so he does not want you to join him. He sends me and this force of three hundred and suggests that we could undertake our own flanking attack if the circumstances present themselves." Feradach responded.

"By my calculation the Northumbrians still outnumber us by maybe five hundred to a thousand, which is nowhere near enough to assault the fortress or even construct siege lines." I stated thoughtfully.

"There is more." Feradach added, "The King would like the Icelanders and Hebrideans to join him in Dunsinane as they are more heavily armoured and can provide a stouter resistance to an assault."

So Thorfinn MacBeth was swapping three hundred Albans for just over a hundred Icelanders and Hebrideans. Thordolf assembled the men and we cautiously continued our approach to the hill fortress. The Northumbrians had made no attempt to surround the hill so our march was unchallenged and we eventually entered the east gate of the fortress through a winding approach path up the steep incline. The fortress was basically a wooden stockade with stout untrimmed stakes twice the height of a man set in the turf rampart and bound together with withies. A fighting platform had been constructed around the perimeter of the fort wide enough for one fighting man and for another to pass behind. Access to the fighting platform was by wooden ladders. Inside the fortress was half a dozen wattle and daub huts of a size to accommodate maybe twenty men each, at a push; but there were large areas that were available to house cattle. Even then, the area was crowded with warriors, many wounded, some obviously dying.

I could see the King and Eachmarchach standing on the stockade platform above the eastern gate and so I made my way over with Thordolf. The ladder at this point was stout and wide, although still green wood, allowing two men to ascend at the same time. From the platform the land fell away before the gate displaying a wide panoramic view of the south west approach to the fortress and the enemy encampment. There were a few small tents but many of the Northumbrians were bivouacked in the open and most uncomfortable they must be. There were clearly more of them than

103

us, but not that many more. Close scrutiny revealed that there were actually three camps, slightly separate from each other.

"My lord king, here we are, as requested; what is your command?" I addressed Thorfinn MacBeth who at that moment was gazing out over the enemy encampment thoughtfully, his ugly black visaged face was blank and masked not giving any emotion away. He turned and looked down upon me and Thordolf.

"Thank you for coming, you mercenaries are serving me well, better than most." I took this to be an oblique reference to the Normans and kept silent.

"What can you see?" Thorfinn waved away over the battlements towards the enemy force.

"I can see three groups, one flying the flag of the white bear for Siward, one flying the black boar of Ben Gulban for Alba, which you also display, so that must be Malcom Mac Duncan and the third a cat, I think, which must be the clans from Atholl and Lochaber. Is this significant?"

Thorfinn ever looking thoughtful responded, "Yes, I think it does. In the fighting at the river yesterday I fought a young man leading the enemy host and slew him. I understand that this was Earl Siward's nephew another Siward. I also understand that you killed Earl Siward's son yesterday. Together the loss of his son and nephew are a grievous loss to an old man and I think the fight has gone out of him. When the enemy forces chased us yesterday the fighting was mainly done by the Cumbrians led by Gospatrick and the forces from Atholl and Lochaber led by Malcolm and Flannchu. It was only when we were safely ensconced here in Dunsinane that the Northumbrians arrived and they have shown no warlike movement since."

I considered and responded, "If your reading of the situation is correct then without Northumbrian support the Cumbrians and Albans cannot circumvallate the fortress and their numbers are only equal to our own."

"My thoughts also, and if MaelPedair's men can weaken their supply line from Perth, Siward just might pack up and go back to Northumbria." We watched the enemy all day and there were no aggressive movements; the next day they had all gone.

Autumn 1054 – The Exile

We waited a further day and then we started to shadow the enemy forces. Earl Siward and his Northumbrian host marched straight through Perth and set fire to it. Later reports said that young Malcolm was furious with Earl Siward for destroying a town he considered his by right. After the Northumbrians had moved on, we entered the ruins of Perth and relieved the garrison of the fortress. Although the Northumbrians devastated the Lothians on their march south it was obvious that Thorfinn MacBeth could no longer control any part of Alba south of Perth especially as the enemy lands of Fife lay to the east. Thorfinn MacBeth could still maintain control of Galloway and the Levenach through his viking fleet from the Orkneys but all the central lowland of Scotland would henceforth be disputed territory. Even in the highlands Thorfinn MacBeth had the problem of Atholl and Lochaber to resolve before he could stabilise his rule.

We later learnt that Malcolm had not returned to the court of King Edward the Mild but had ensconced himself at Carlisle calling himself Prince of Cumbria. For a time, King Thorfinn MacBeth kept his small army at Scone the inaugural seat of the Kings of Alba. Eachmarchach led his Hebridean gall-gaedhil across country to the Levenach to collect his longships that he had left at Dunbarton. MaelPedair stayed with the king but the Icelanders clearly wanted to be gone. To my delight and a little embarrassment Thordolf performed a poem in the hall the night before the Icelanders were to sail. The lay was a 'praise song' in my honour, which he had entitled 'Bearslayer' and recounted my fight against Asbjorn Siwardson. Martin appeared even more pleased than I was as he clearly saw it as vindication of his decision to associate himself with me.

The Icelanders were suitably rewarded for their service by Thorfinn MacBeth, both with silver and goods; the king also made a free gift of the knarr they were to sail home in. The departure of the Icelanders and Hebrideans could no longer hide the fact that Thorfinn MacBeth had been badly mauled at Perth and Dunsinane. Without his mercenary supporters and with his own Albans wishing to return to their homes to harvest their crops it was obvious that he could not maintain his position at Scone, he had to retreat north; additionally, it was important for him to return to the Orkneys to stabilise his control of the north. A month after the battle the king called me into his presence.

"Well Hereward Bearslayer," this term made the king smile wryly, "You have exceeded my expectations and I can see that, as young as you are, you have a wise head on your shoulders. I would like to offer you a permanent place in my retinue, perhaps as a thegn in Moray or Ross." Thorfinn paused looking sad. "Realistically, however I don't think my time as King of Alba has long to run." I started to protest but Thorfinn gave his habitual frown and stayed my remonstrations with a wave of his hand. "I am not foolish and I can see quite clearly that I cannot hold on to Alba. The Lothians are firmly under the heel of Earl Siward; Cumbria, Fife and Atholl are against me, which means I have no means of controlling any lands south of the Grampians. Angus and the Mearns will fall away from me despite MaelPedair's wish to support me." Thorfinn fell silent and pensive for a while before continuing. "Whilst I was married to Grouch her position as a descendent of Alban kings helped to cement my claim to the throne for despite the fact that I was the grandson of King Malcolm, just like Duncan, I was never accepted because of my Norse heritage, whereas her pedigree was impeccable. Her son Lulach has a claim to the throne but my sons by Ingiborg, my first wife, only have a claim to Orkney. Eventually I will be displaced by the young Malcolm Mac Duncan who people are now calling Canmore or Big Chief a sure sign of things to come; also, there is his brother Donald Ban; who knows what he is up to? I will just become Thorfinn again, or they will kill me so I will not offer you a place as a thegn. I will reward you mightily but you can forget any idea of marrying my daughter Ingiborg she is not for you."

I felt downcast at that last statement, especially as I felt I had earned her esteem and gratitude by slaying Asbjorn. Later I discussed the situation with Martin. My outlawry had now expired as the one year had long passed so I could return to England and I longed to see my mother. However, reaching the Danelagh would be difficult as I would have to pass through or passed Northumbria with a very hostile Earl Siward; or down through Cumbria with an equally hostile Prince Malcolm. Martin felt that we only had two choices; we could either sail to Denmark and make our way down the Flemish coast and across to the Danelagh, or we could travel west to the Hebrides and sail down to Mann and Wales. I pointed out that the second choice still left the whole breadth of England between us in Wales and my mother, not to mention the malevolent Lady Godgifu. We decided on the first course of action, mainly because it appealed to my sense of adventure.

I bade my farewell to King Thorfinn MacBeth, wishing him well in his future endeavours. He was a truly noble king although to his Alban subjects, he had appeared harsh through conquest; but he had ruled wisely and well, giving the people of Alba many years of peace and prosperity.

Martin and I made our way east to the port of Dundee seeking a trading ship to Denmark. The town had its fair share of Danish merchants and so it was without difficulty that we obtained a passage on a merchant knarr heading for Hamburg, which I considered near enough to Denmark as not to matter. We set out in the latter days of the year just before it would be unwise to make a deep-sea voyage but with a blue sky and a mild south-easterly wind that carried us gracefully across the bleak North Sea due east straight for Denmark. The captain was hopeful of a quick and safe passage; I knew the captain intended to strike the Jutland peninsula and then sail south down the coast to Hamburg. I hoped he would put in at some point along the Danish coast so that Martin and I could disembark. The weather, however did not behave, one day out of Dundee and the wind died and we were virtually becalmed. It became increasingly hotter and humid, and the captain predicted an autumn thunderstorm. The crew manned the four long sweeps that the knarr was fitted out with and tried to make some headway but the Jutland coast was not in sight and if a thunderstorm was imminent there would be no way to avoid it.

The captain ordered everything to be lashed down as a precaution and it was not long afterwards that we noticed a bank of clouds rolling up out of the north. I had not noticed the wind change but there was a noticeable steady blow from the north and the captain half raised the sail to achieve some movement. We gradually picked up speed as the clouds built up behind us turning from a chilly grey to an ominous black. The waves increased in depth and force and then the storm hit. The ship was hurled around like a toy in a millstream. The captain threw a bucket at me and shouted for me to bale. Martin grabbed another wooden pail and acted likewise. The waves cascaded over the stern of the ship and deluged the deck, bailing seemed pointless but it was the only action, ineffectual as it was, we could do to combat the climatic assault on the ship. For our own safety Martin and I lashed ourselves to the mast, it was chaos.

Whilst we were bailing the captain and his crew were rigging a storm drogue from an old sail, which they threw over the stern of the knarr to slow the boat down and stabilise her. This action immediately minimised the force of the waves arching over the stern of the knarr. After this the knarr wallowed for what seemed like many hours doggedly weathering the storm. Rain lashed down onto the deck minimising visibility until it felt we were descending into the dark pits of hell. The helmsman resolutely stayed at his post holding the knarr stable running before the wind and waves, After what seemed an eternity the rest of us were overwhelmed by fatigue and ceased bailing but it did not seem to make any difference anyway; thoroughly saturated we all crept under what canvass shelter we could find and sat out the storm.

Martin nudged me warily. "Here, eat, drink." He offered me some soggy bread and hard cheese and although I did not feel like eating, I knew that if I did not, I would not be strong enough to help the others save the ship. I looked around and saw that the storm was abating and the sky was clearing somewhat. The knarr was in a poor shape, half submerged and wallowing in the now lazy waves. I started to bale again as did the rest of the crew. No one had been lost overboard except the ship's cat; the captain gave me a surly look as if I had caused him to lose his feline ratter. The thought crossed my mind that the storm and the half-submerged state of the knarr would have caused the evacuation of the old tub by rats more efficiently than any cat.

"It looks like we have survived the storm but where are we."

Martin looked up from bailing, "There is land over there." He pointed east. I stood up and gazed where he was pointing and could clearly see a long low-lying spit of land. The captain had seen it also and was in deep conversation with the helmsman. I clambered over the chaotic mess of ropes, oars and cargo that had been thrown around the deck and approached the captain.

"Is that the coast of Denmark?" I queried.

"Hard to tell, it could be any coastline from the Skagen to the mouth of the Rhine estuary, but as we were being blown south throughout the storm, I would guess we are well passed Denmark and are maybe near Hamburg as the land is still to the east. If the land was to the south we could be along the Frisian coastline. The land turns south again after that towards Flanders. Who knows?"

"What your saying is that we could be anywhere along maybe five hundred miles of coastline. What do you intend to do?" I replied sardonically.

"We can only sail slowly into the coast looking for a safe landing place. We need to unload what is left of the cargo and repair the ship in the best way we can. The wadding between the strakes has been mostly compromised and we are leaking in many places, it can be repaired but my fear is that if we land in the wrong place the local inhabitants may try and take my ship and the cargo." I nodded and returned to Martin who was diligently collecting our belongings. I was concerned about my mail and weapons, he about the hack silver. Fortunately, most was still intact as they had been lashed down well. I reminded myself that the weapons must be cleaned to prevent rust when we finally made landfall.

The knarr slowly neared the coast, a bleak line of sand dunes and scrubland with no sign of life, neither animal nor human. More animated discussion took place at the helm and again I went over to the captain.

"Well, you know something of our whereabouts?" I demanded.

"Yes, yes, I am sure we are entering the mouth of the Rhine, we are much further south and west than I originally thought, the storm must have sucked us into the funnel of the channel between Flanders and Kent. We are lucky we were not thrown onto the sandbanks of the Frisian Isles. Our destination, Hamburg lies over a hundred miles north east of here."

"How do you know where we are?" I asked puzzled by his positivity.

The helmsman chipped in. "The colour of the water at the mouth of the Rhine estuary is significantly different to the open sea and there is nowhere on this coast like it. I am positive about where we are."

The helmsman steered the ship slowly to the mouth of a small river, which the knarr could comfortably sail into. The captain announced that this was a small river near the Rhine called the Rottar where we could lay up and sort out the ship. Apparently, this area was part of the County of Holland ruled by a man called Floris who the captain thought was a fair and just ruler who encouraged trade and would be unlikely to impound his ship.

I went away to discuss the situation with Martin, it was clear that we were not going to make landfall in Denmark or Hamburg and as our objective was to return to England and Bourne in particular, I could see no reason why we should stay with the knarr. The problem was we were effectively stranded in the middle of nowhere; the coast of Holland was sparsely populated and most ports were inland along the various rivers. The coast was low lying and swampy and difficult to traverse. The more prosperous and populated County of Flanders was on the other side of the Rhine estuary and it was far more likely that we would get passage to England from there. How to get there? Eventually we decided to leave the knarr, bidding farewell to the captain and crew and wishing them better luck for the future and set off along the south bank of the River Rottar. We very soon became mired in mud and swampy marshland and became covered in slime. Each step caused our boots to sink into the mire with a slimy squelch and the sucking sound as we pulled our feet from the mud was as unpleasant as it was tiring. Our heavy chest of silver did not help. It soon became obvious that we could not traverse this land on foot and that the only sensible method of travel was by boat. Thankfully after days of very slow progress and depletion of our food supply we came across a few hovels on the riverbank with, most importantly, a skiff lazily drifting against its mooring stake.

The peasants were fearful of us and ran off so I left a ridiculous amount of hacksilver, enough to purchase five replacement skiffs and we loaded up the boat and pushed off. I would have liked to pay for a guide to the nearest town but it was clear that the peasants were not going to return whilst we tarried at their domicile. Martin and I poled our way along the river, which turned out to be a labyrinthine number of streams that split and merged along its route. It was still tidal so we had our work cut out to make way but by staying near the south bank we found that we could successfully pole our way along. By always heading east and south we assumed that eventually we would reach 'civilisation', and we did but only after several weeks living on fish. The river channel we chose to go down narrowed into a more manageable stream without a strong current and after poling down this channel we eventually spilled out into a wide river that we deduced was the main channel of the Rhine. Discarding our poles, we used the crude paddles in the skiff to make our way across the river to the south bank, which I assumed was Flanders; Flanders and civilisation. The strong current of the enormous river carried us back west towards its mouth and we must have been driven west by over a mile before we landed on the south bank. Fortunately, the riverine area was alive with fish, eels and sea birds and we had no difficulty in staying alive; cooking the carcasses was more difficult than catching the live creatures. The whole area reminded me of the fens to the south east of my home in Bourne, as I was too young to join hunting expeditions before I was conveyed to Coventry, I only heard second hand of the teeming harvest of seafood and birds of the air in the fenlands of Lincolnshire and East Anglia but this reminded me very much of the stories related to me by my uncle.

There were villages on the south bank of the river and this was because the land was less swampy and slightly higher and drier. we coasted slowly along for three days until we came to a large farm where we dragged the skiff up onto the muddy bank. Several men came down to the shore all armed with some farm implement that could be used as a rudimentary weapon. Martin and I held our palms out showing we meant no harm and we were eventually surrounded by four curious Flemings.

"We are travellers trying to reach Ghent or Lille." I explained in English. I knew that the Flemish language and our own Anglian tongue were very similar and I hoped they would understand what I was saying. The four men looked slightly puzzled. "We are looking for shelter for a night and can pay." I added. Eventually the eldest of the four spoke very slowly in a dialect that I could just about understand.

"You are welcome to stay the night. We are poor farmers and fishermen but we always extend hospitality to honest travellers." He emphasized the word 'honest'. I held out my hand and we shook in agreement. Martin did likewise and then we shook hands all round.

"I am Hereward Leofricson from Mercia in England and this is my man, Martin." I announced slowly.

"Good, I am Jan Jansen and these are three of my four sons. Welcome to Tonnekreek, my farm."

Although isolated the farm was quite large and had obviously grown as Jan Jansen's family had grown. Apart from the main farmhouse, which was constructed mainly of turf sods and wattle and daub, there were three smaller dwellings all within a fenced compound. The farmer's sons had mostly married local girls and the family had expanded. There were two large barns and several smaller constructions housing pigs, chickens, and geese and two old plough horses of considerable size. There was very little wood in these constructions, which reflected the surrounding marshland and low-lying river plain where good wood was sparse but willow for the wattle and daub plentiful. Jan's wife was a good solid woman with massive breasts and fleshy biceps. She was very jovial and it was quite obvious that she was the real master of the house. We were welcomed inside the main farm house with a piping hot bowl of stew laced with vegetables and various produce from the sea, mussels, fish and possibly crab. It was quite delicious. The extended family crowded in ogling the unexpected travellers. It was obvious we were military men, testified by our arms and armour and several young boys surrounded us staring wide eyed at our equipment. When the impromptu meal was finished and we were furnished with a passable ale Jan Jansen cleared his throat and to the expectation of his family spoke.

"I can see you are not from around here, neither Flemish nor Frisian, can you tell us your story?" This was not an unusual request to travelling strangers and it was how solitary settlements learned what was happening in the outside world and I saw no reason not to indulge them.

"My name is Hereward Leofricson and I am from Mercia in the island of the English over the sea and this is Martin my companion in arms." I went on to explain our adventures in Wales and Alba and our desire to return to Mercia from any decent harbour along the Flemish coast. My story started something of a discussion of where best for us to travel to. After some lengthy debate Jan informed us that we should aim for Antwerp, which was a reasonably large town with a port that regularly traded with England. The next question surprised me.

"We see you have a skiff; this will not be of any assistance to you in travelling to Antwerp." It was an obvious observation and was clearly leading to a negotiation. I was reluctant to give it away for free.

"I would trade the skiff for one of your horses as I imagine it will be a long walk to Antwerp." I knew Martin would not thank me for the gift of a horse to ride, so I determined on bartering for one horse, this was of great benefit for Jan and his family as I had noticed that the two horses in the paddock were old and knackered. Nevertheless, Jan prevaricated declaring that without two horses how could the family plough their fields. I doubted that the two horses in tandem had the strength to plough a garden, let alone a field but I went along with the negotiations for the fun of it pointing out that an additional skiff would enable his sons to increase their harvest from the river. The upshot of these negotiations was that I could choose which horse I wanted for an additional piece of hack silver and the family received the skiff, which in my opinion was in pretty poor shape anyway. Martin pulled a long face and I suspected that in this part of the world the hack silver would buy them a much younger and more useful nag.

Despite this Martin and I were housed royally in an adjacent hut with warm blankets for bedding, the children were much taken with my polar bear skin when I wrapped it around me before sleep. I believe it was from this time on that the story started to spread that I had slain a real gigantic bear rather than Asbjorn Siwardson. I guess this was a much more enjoyable tale for the romantic minded!

The following morning torrential rain had set in and I was reluctant to set off anywhere. I did examine the two horses, they were very large, which I was informed was the norm in Flanders, both were black with white markings and they were truly knackered. Both were mares with little to choose between them but clearly one was lame so I chose the other one. One of the children solemnly informed me that the horse was called Buttercup. The family had no saddle or harness and I suspected the horses had long since forgotten how to pull a plough. However, it proved unnecessary to test the horse's stamina that day as the rain continued remorselessly. In fact, it rained non-stop for the next two weeks. Jan and his family seemed quite happy to allow us to remain with them through the onset of winter and in fact we ended remaining with them throughout Yule enjoying the rustic festivities. We were too near the coast to expect much snow but it was not until mid-January before Martin and I decided to make the dash for Antwerp.

I threw my polar bear skin over the mare's back hoping the weight would not cause it to collapse and used some old rope to fashion a rein. I thanked Jan and his wife for their hospitality and gave them more silver in payment for our extended lodgings; I also wished them well before carefully clambering onto the mare's back. The horse grunted in surprise at my weight but nevertheless stood stock still, maybe it could not move? Waving goodbye, I gave the mare a gentle kick and as I was beginning to suspect would happen it elicited no response. Jan started to look embarrassed but Martin grabbed the horse's mane and gave a prolonged pull at which the mare started to amble forwards; and so, we proceeded.

The track to Antwerp ran straight across low lying moorland and shrubland with some well wooded areas away from the river. Buttercup kept up a stoical plod that clearly frustrated Martin, and I acknowledged that I could walk twice as fast but refused to put aside my dignity and besides, apart from me, Buttercup was also carrying all our kit. There was nowhere to shelter each night so we slept where we could find cover and our appearance suffered accordingly.

It was thirty or so miles to Antwerp and we reached the city in six days. It was the second largest town I had ever seen, more solid than Winchester and less squalid than Dublin, which was larger. It exuded prosperity and was dominated by a large church with a spire that rose above the surrounding flat countryside. It had a stockade wall around the town and we were stopped by the town guards at the open gate. They were clearly amused by our down and out appearance and the corpse like gait of old Buttercup. Laughing they waved us in to the town and I found it annoying that they did not consider us a threat in any way and unworthy of interrogation. Martin asked a passing priest in Latin if there was a reasonable inn that we could stay at. The priest eyed us suspiciously clearly wondering how we could afford a 'reasonable' inn and then indicated we should make for a hostelry named the "Porridge Bowl" opposite the church; he made a vague gesture to the church spire and hurried on.

We plodded on until we came to the square fronting the church main entrance and there, we spotted the inn, a substantial two storey wooden structure painted white between the support beams. A large wooden bowl hung on a scaffold above the door. Martin went in to negotiate our stay whilst I unpacked Buttercup. What should I do with the old mare now? A brief thought of her being served up in tomorrow's stew made me feel guilty but it was clear that she was not worth anything. I looked around and seeing the church I had an idea. I dragged Buttercup over to the church door and accosted another priest as he emerged from within.

"Stay, sir priest." I requested in passable Latin. "I have here a gentle mare, past her working life on the farm but she may still serve God. Does the Bishop or whoever leads your congregation here in Antwerp need a gentle beast to convey him around?"

The priest scowled at me and looked poor Buttercup up and down. "Our church is under the control of Deacon Paul and he does not have the funds to purchase a sorry nag like this." The priest made to move on but I stepped in front of him.

"You misunderstand me, sir priest. I offer this mare as a free gift to the church and to Deacon Paul. I want nothing from him or your church other than your goodwill, of course."

The priest's demeanour changed abruptly and smiling avariciously he took the makeshift bridle. "Bless you my son for this thoughtful gift to God and Deacon Paul. The priest smartly disappeared around the side of the church dragging the exhausted Buttercup behind. I retraced my steps to the inn smiling to myself with my opinion of the acolytes of holy church confirmed.

Martin was waiting at the door. "Found Buttercup a good home I take it?" he queried.

"I hope so, either that or the priests will be dining on horse stew for the rest of the week." I opined. The inn was clean and warm and Martin had acquired us a decent room on the first floor with a window no less that could be closed with wooden shutters. The room had two cots, luxury indeed after the last few nights and after a good meal we opted to get a good rest before we made enquiries of ships sailing in the morning.

Rising late Martin and I sat outside the inn munching on some delicious fresh bread and soft cheese when we were presented with an astounding sight. From the side of the church in procession came none other than Buttercup arrayed in magnificent regalia, red leather bridle and harness and a tooled red leather saddle with high cantles before and behind the rider. The mare's rump was covered by an embroidered blanket that was adorned with stitched panels of Christ crucified. It looked remarkably like an altar cloth. Bestride Buttercup, it could only be the Deacon Paul, another sour looking priest, but managing in this instance to look inordinately pleased with himself. He too was dressed to impress with an embroidered cassock and over cloak and carrying on his right hand an elaborate crozier. Fortunately, the Deacon Paul was stick thin and unlikely to collapse the old nag with his weight. The deacon was followed by a train of priests chanting some psalm or other and Buttercup was being led by a young pageboy, of course.

The procession wound its way around the square and stopped in front of Martin and I, we stood with due deference.

"You are the stranger you gifted this fine mare to the church of our Lord?" the deacon asked.

"Yes, your excellency." I responded, deliberately addressing the deacon with a term far above his station. This elicited a beam of pleasure from his cadaverous face.

"And who may you be my son?" he responded genially.

"I am Hereward Leofricson, younger son of the Earl of Mercia in England. I was recently shipwrecked and I am trying to make my way back to England, which is why I am here in Antwerp."

"In that case I may be able to help you, a pursuivant lord is currently here in Antwerp meeting his factor who deals with the wool trade to England. He is Gilbert, Lord of Ghent and if anyone can return you to England he can." The deacon sniffed and I realised that this was his expression of pleasure at being so knowledgeable and obliging.

"Your excellency, I am forever in your debt; may I enquire where I would find this Gilbert, Lord of Ghent?

"Of course, you will find him at the Wool Merchant Guildhall." The deacon indicated a large three storied building across the square from the inn, not so far.

I gave a low bow of appreciation and without another word the deacon directed his young page boy to lead on and the procession moved on to wherever the deacon was going to lord it over the town members. Plodding on stoically I swear Buttercup gave me a sly grin, if such was possible from the equine species. Martin and I returned to our room to make ourselves look as presentable as possible; I had had my clothes cleaned by the landlord's wife and even my polar bear shoulder cape looked pristine. Martin always kept my weapons clean and sharp and so we set off for the Wool Merchant Guildhall full of hope.

The guildhall was a very imposing building with blackened beams supporting a mud brick infill facia with several inset window frames with glass panes, it was a tribute to the town's trading wealth. I knew from my time at home with my mother and again with my father that wide areas of east Mercia and the Danelagh produced good quality sheep and wool that was sold off to traders from Flanders. There was no bar to our entry so Martin and I strolled into the ground floor reception area that was quite full of the merchant class; well-dressed but sober individuals. I cast around to recognise a great lord amongst these traders to no avail. Martin made enquiries and was informed that Lord Gilbert was on the first floor with his factor. We climbed the stairs and was finally opposed by a man-at-arms.

"Lord Gilbert is having a meeting on this floor, no one is admitted." The guard growled in a low voice.

"I seek a word with your lord, I am a noble from England." I responded loud enough for all to hear, as I hoped my statement pricked the Lord of Ghent's interest and I heard a barked instruction to permit my access. The guard stood aside and I ascended the last few steps onto the wooden floor. There was a stout wooden table in the centre of the room, obviously for guild meetings and this was surrounded by carved chairs, one of which was occupied.

Gilbert, Lord of Ghent was a large man, a very large man. Not tall but wide of girth and broad of shoulder. He was dark visaged with bushy black eyebrows and a bristling beard almost hiding a bull like neck. His clothing was not much different than the merchants except in their quality. Black velvet and black beaver pelt collar. His sleeveless over tabard was heavy wool weave. It was the jewellery that set him above everyone else. A magnificent gold chain adorned his shoulders and chest. His fingers were covered in at least three gold rings on each hand and from a wide black leather belt hung a bejewelled dagger glinting with precious stones. Next to the chair upon which the Lord of Ghent reposed stood a much smaller man with a sallow complexion. He wore much plainer homespun clothing and carried a large bundle of parchments; the factor.

I bowed low, "Good morning my lord." I started but was interrupted abruptly.

"Who are you to dare to walk in on me as to a war?" the Lord of Ghent demanded in a harsh guttural voice.

"Why as to who I am, I am Hereward Leofricson, son of the Earl of Mercia in England; as to my apparel I always travel to war and am ever prepared for it."

"Hereward Leofricson, the outlaw, known as the Bearslayer?"

"You have heard of me, I am flattered but I am not an outlaw, my year banishment ceased some months back and I am seeking to return to England, the Danelagh to be precise as I have a wish to see my beloved mother and I was hoping you could guide me in this matter."

To my surprise the Lord of Ghent burst out laughing and it was some moments before he could calm sufficiently to respond to my announcement. "Well as to providing guidance I certainly can. If you return to England, you will hang as sure as Woden did on Yggdrassil for you are still an outlaw and banished from England in perpetuity." The Lord of Ghent noted the confusion on my face and laughed again. "Hubert, get the Bearslayer a drink." He indicated to his factor. "Hereward, sit and I will relate to you what you obviously are totally unaware of." I sat down at the table, whilst Martin guarded the stair eyeing the man-at-arms and the factor equally.

"I will start from the battles you fought in Scotland. Shortly after he returned home from there Earl Siward died of a broken heart." Gilbert of Ghent pointed at me. "Your fault, you killed his son and his nephew died in the battle too, so I heard."

"It was a fair fight, a holmgang, no dishonour there." I expostulated.

"Maybe not, but old King Edward didn't see it like that and when the new Earl of Northumbria called for your trial and punishment, egged on by the Northumbrian thegns, it was a forgone conclusion what the outcome would be even though your brother Aelfgar spoke up for you."

"What did Aelfgar say?" I asked.

"Aelfgar pointed out that it was a fair fight and that under the obligation of service you had with the King of Scots you would be expected to fight for him and you were doing no wrong. For all his outspokenness all Aelfgar succeeded in doing was getting himself outlawed too, even though everyone but the Godwinsons could see he had done no wrong."

"My brother, outlawed?" I gasped, "What did my father say to all this?"

"It would seem your father was somewhat isolated; his major ally Siward lies dead and he is surrounded by Godwinsons. I did not tell you that the new Earl of Northumbria is Tostig Godwinson and that Earl Godwin has also died and Harold his son is Earl of Wessex and another Godwinson, cannot remember which, is now Earl of East Anglia in place of your brother." The Lord of Ghent almost looked jovial about it all.

I am sure I looked stunned, "So I am banished from England for life." I stated, not a question, my plans were is disarray.

"My lord, do you know where my brother is?" I asked ruefully.

Gilbert raised an eyebrow to his factor and the obsequious factor responded. "It is rumoured that he has fled across the border into Wales."

Of course, I thought, he would have gone to his brother-in-law's stronghold in Powys. The marriage of his daughter to Gryffudd was fortuitous after all.

"I need to go to my brother." I stated.

"Don't be over hasty, I could use a warrior like you." Gilbert of Ghent interceded. "My cousin Robert, has been ordered to wage war against certain lords in Flanders and requires my help. He needs tried and tested warriors and warband leaders and you would fill the role nicely." The Lord of Ghent smiled mirthlessly; here was a man who was a schemer looking to advance himself at every opportunity and using mercenaries was one way of reducing the risk to himself in the process.

"My lord, your offer in generous and under any other circumstances I would readily accept but first I must support my brother, especially if he has unjustly been outlawed because of me."

The Lord of Ghent shrugged, "Well maybe next year then, I am sure our little war will drag on until then."

It seemed that the Lord of Ghent held no animosity after I had declined his invitation and was helpful enough to arrange a passage to England. There were obvious dangers in landing on English shores but no traffic was sailing straight to Wales or Ireland. The best I could hope for was a set down in a westerly port and the ship was coasting along the English coastline as far as Exeter so there was every chance Martin and I could slip across the border into Cornwall without notice.

Summer 1055 – Aelfgar

The king's hall in Dublin was crowded, Martin had remained outside in the clean air but I was at the council meeting supporting my brother. To say the meeting was complicated was an understatement, the king of Dublin was an Irishman, Murchad Mac Diarmait, Diarmait was the King of Leinster and also termed the high king of Ireland or Ard Righ Erinn, with opposition, which I suppose meant he was not really the high king at all but liked to pretend he was. However, Diarmait had taken control of Dublin from the traditional viking rulers, in fact from Eachmarchach my old friend from Alba where we had fought at Perth together. The Irish certainly did not prefer to live in towns but as Dublin, a major trading centre, was too important to leave to an underling to manage Dairmait had appointed his son Murchad to be king in-situ.

Murchad was still a young man little older than I, he had a coterie of older Irish nobles surrounding him providing advice and he clearly did not like this situation. On the other hand, there was a powerful group of Irish vikings of Scandinavian extraction whose views had to be considered and the two opposing camps were obvious. I could see that both Murchad and my brother were playing these two groups off against each other to achieve a mutual advantage.

I had made my way to Wales earlier in the spring only to find that my brother, on the advice of his brother-in-law Gryffudd, King of Powys, had moved on to Dublin. The purpose of this move was to recruit a viking fleet to attack the coastline of England. Gryffudd's mother was apparently an Irish princess and he had close allies in Leinster. Martin and I had no difficulty in gaining conveyance to Dublin where I rejoined my brother. Our meeting was friendly but confusing to me. First, I wanted to know why and how he had been outlawed because of me; it made no sense. His response was illuminating.

"Brother, you were just an excuse to get at me, although to be honest I did not expect you to kill Asbjorn Siwardson, the son of your father's and my greatest ally." I was about to protest but Aelfgar pre-empted this.

"King Edward is getting on in years and it is obvious he will have no direct heir, the Godwinsons are manoeuvring to gain power in England presumably to control the new king whomsoever that may be, or to seek the throne for themselves. When Earl Godwin died and his elder son Harald was made Earl of Wessex and at the same time Earl Siward died, Harald lost no time engineering his brother Tostig's elevation to the Earldom of Northumbria. Your father opposed this move claiming that our family had closer ties to the old Northumbrian line of rulers and suggested that I should be the Earl thereof. King Edward wavered and it was at this juncture that Tostig, to curry favour with the Northumbrian nobles, brought up your slaying of Asbjorn, which I naturally opposed. The Godwinson's and their supporters howled me down and it is a testament to their power and the King's weakness that they gained my outlawry."

Still feeling I was unjustly blamed, I tried to be constructive. "Brother, I may have caused you problems and weakened your position at court but I could not in all honour act any other way."

Aelfgar laughed, "Yes, I know, you always had a sense of the dramatic, believing in the romance of the saga stories and now you have lived through one of their favourite dichotomies where the warrior is forced to decide between honouring two conflicting loyalties. Was MacBeth a good choice?"

Caught off balance by the last challenging question I responded truthfully, "Thorfinn MacBeth was the best lord anyone could have, a noble man and a great king." This response sobered my brother to the reality of England under King Edward the Mild. "What is your intention?" I asked.

"I have been well schooled on that score. I intend to follow the Godwinsons example, raise a viking fleet and raid the coast of England. I have also persuaded by brother-in-law Gryffudd to invade Herefordshire where King Edward's brother-in-law Ralph of Mantes has been newly made earl. Another half Norman sycophant."

The counsel in the king's hall was another in the developing discussions on the aid and profitability to be gained for King Murchad for the raiding venture my brother proposed.

"My Leinster lords are lukewarm about a venture that may possibly damage their trade with the English ports, especially Bristol." Murchad observed for the third time that day.

"I understand my lord but I have no intention of raiding near Bristol, although I do not wish for my purpose to become general knowledge," Aelfgar looked around to ensure only the King and I were in hearing, "I intend to raid the English south coast, as did the Godwinsons two years back; and I will only do that after the raid into Hereford this summer."

Murchad considered, "And you say I will receive a third of the plunder?"

"Yes indeed, a third to you, a third to me and a third for the vikings I recruit; what say you?" Aelfgar urged. "There will be gold and slaves, girl slaves, again what say you?"

Murchad licked is lips, the thought of young girl slaves clearly was enticing. "Well, it is true that although my Leinster lords are reluctant in this matter, my Dublin vikings are literally drooling at the prospect and will rid me of the most troublesome of my subjects for a season."

Murchad looked around at the sea of expectant faces, bearded and clean-shaven Irish faces and the frowning faces of the viking kin with their drooping moustaches and plaited hair. He nodded and stretched out his hand. Aelfgar took it and they sealed their agreement with a cup of heady wine.

After the king's decision had been made known to the lords Aelfgar approached the leading Dublin chiefs and arranged to meet them to outline his plans. This second meeting of the day took place down in the wharfs along the Liffey River side in a hostelry entitled 'The Draft of Loki" a name clearly intending to be meaningless to all but Scandinavians. The spokesman for the ships' captains was named Asketil and he started on a sour note.

"Since the blasted Irish have taken control here trade is not what it was. The lousy Christian priests complain to Murchad about our slave trade and we are not allowed to raid into the interior for slaves anymore." Asketil surreptitiously fingered a Thor's hammer amulet hung around his neck. "Not that I am not as good a Christian as the next man you understand."

Aelfgar came straight to the point. "I need a fleet of longships to raid the coast of England, not Wales or Mercia, mainly Wessex and taking slaves and plunder from another country other than Ireland is perfectly acceptable to your king." The crowd of captains looked pleased, but Asketil still prevaricated.

"I will be honest, at this time of year only about ten ships are available for raiding, Many of the crews are out in knarr's already trading and are unavailable to man the snekkjas."

Aelfgar was urgent, too urgent I thought. "I will take that ten but I need more."

Asketil leaned in and said more quietly, "I know where you can get another ten, maybe more."

"Where?" Aelfgar had lowered his voice accordingly.

"As you know Murchad is currently king of Dublin but the previous Norse king is not far away, on the Isle of Mann to be precise. He would help for a price."

"You mean Eachmarchach." I interrupted.

Asketil looked over at me. "Ah! Bearslayer is it. You fought in Alba with Eachmarchach and Jarl Thorfinn, you will know his worth."

I looked at my brother, "It's true Eachmarchach would be an asset to any raiding fleet but surely Murchad would take a dim view of it?"

"He would, if he knew." Interjected Asketil raising his bushy eyebrows.

My brother tensed, "Can you arrange it?" Asketil nodded. "Then it is settled then; how soon can we sail.?"

"Two weeks." Asketil asserted.

Later I felt compelled to point out to my brother that to be ready in two weeks meant that Asketil and Eachmarchach must have already have been in communication about this possibility and that the end game for them might not be the same as ours.

"Little brother, I care not, as long as I can strike at the Godwinsons and am in England before my father dies so that I can rightfully take my place as the Earl of Mercia."

"My father's health is poor?" I queried.

"No, he is quite robust for his age, but don't forget he is quite old, well over fifty years and cannot be expected to live longer for my convenience."

It was with some trepidation that I set off in Asketil's snekkja, a sleek raiding ship, with twenty oars to each side and a carved bull's head on the prow. Aelfgar watched with delight as a score of longships swung into line behind us as we made our way out of the Liffey estuary and sailed due east towards Wales. A swift crossing with a favourable south easterly wind saw us off the coast of Anglesey by mid-day on the second day of sailing at precisely the point where Asketil had arranged for us to meet our ally and fellow marauder, Eachmarchach King of Mann and the Sudreys, at one point a sub-king to Thorfinn Earl of Orkney and King of Alba but now semi-independent due to Thorfinn's weakened position.

Swinging in close to Asketil's snekkja Eachmarchach leaned out from the prow of his own dragon ship and shouted across.

"Well met Bearslayer we fight together again. I take the tall man beside you to be Earl Aelfgar, hail to you, my lord. Where is that seadog Asketil?" Asketil came strolling down from the stern, shouting jovially.

"Hail, lord king, we have missed you."

"Not for much longer, I hope." Eachmarchach shouted back. "There is a quiet beach near here where we can stretch our legs and discuss tactics, follow me in."

Eachmarchach led the now enlarged fleet, eighteen longships and two knarrs west about the island and into a broad bay with a gently sloping beach wide enough for all the ships to pull up on to. Asketil informed me that this was known as Trearddur Bay by the locals who would not bother such a large assemblage of vikings. Eachmarchach's crew were already collecting driftwood for fires and spreading out canvass sails for tenting as we congregated for an evening of planning and a good meal. I introduced Eachmarchach formally to my brother and just like everyone else Aelfgar found Eachmarchach's cheeky irreverence and smiling demeanour infectious and relaxing. By the time the meal was over everyone was on good terms.

Eachmarchach by way of beginning the serious discussions of the evening said. "Well, we are viking raiders and know our business, but Lord Aelfgar, you aren't so how do you propose to organise this campaign?"

"Blunt but perceptive Eachmarchach; you are right I am no viking raider and I do not intend to be but I do need the raids to be in my name. How say you?"

"I do not care if the Emperor of Constantinople is blamed for the raids as long as me and mine get plenty of plunder. The isles I rule are poor and I need to supplement my income from more wealthy neighbours." Eachmarchach was ever practical.

"This is the way of it then. I intend to leave the fleet here and travel to Powys and link up with my brother-in-law King Gryffudd. From there I will raid into England and attempt to confront the new Earl of Hereford and defeat him and devastate Herefordshire before the Godwinsons can bring up overwhelming forces against me at which point I will retreat. I want you and Asketil, in my name, to raid the south coast of England, a large part of which is under the direct control of Harald Godwinson, Earl of Wessex. I warn you he has his own warships so you must take care; it is not part of my plan for you to be bettered.

Eachmarchach considered this plan, "I like this, I promise not to loot church property, too much, or kill priests, unless they fight back. It will take a clever Saxon sailor to outsmart my Gall-Gaedhil viking rovers and I will ensure there is sufficient plunder for Murchad so that he does not accuse you of defrauding him of his share. Can I take the Bearslayer with me?"

"No, I need Hereward with me, I recognise he has a talent for warfare but I do want you to take my uncle Godwine with you." My brother indicated to a man sitting next to him, presumably a cousin of my step-mother Godgifu. I felt a distinct itch between my shoulder blades when he looked at me. "Although ten years older than me he does look a lot like me, unlike Hereward who is too singular in his looks to pass for me or anyone else. It will be Godwine's role to fool King Edward and the Godwinsons into thinking I am with you until it is too late for them to intervene decisively in Herefordshire." Clearly my brother had thought it all out and this explained why my curious uncle was with us, and yes, he did look somewhat like Aelfgar.

"Well, that's a shame." Eachmarchach boomed jovially. "I was hoping Hereward would come with me, he has a talent for killing people, no mistake."

"One more thing, you have eighteen longships, snekkjas, with about forty crew to each, that is over seven hundred warriors. I need fifty to accompany me so all your ships will sail three men light."

"No matter, I am told Cornish monks make good rowers, we'll manage." Eachmarchach grinned his infectious grin. The rest of the plans were hammered out and it was suggested that there would be a likely rendezvous back at Trearddur Bay in early autumn.

The next morning Eachmarchach and Asketil unbeached their ships and sailed away south for a summer's plundering. Before midday a party of riders appeared over the sand dunes with a small herd of ponies for Aelfgar, myself and our large retinue. This proved to be the Lord of Aberffraw, a chieftain of King Gryffudd's who had arranged for our swift passage to Mathrafal, the stronghold of the King of Powys.

A week's solid riding saw us at the King's gate with Martin complaining every step of the way for having to ride. A quick glance to the surrounding meadows confirmed that the king's army was assembling, there being already two or three hundred warriors in weathered tents. We quickly threaded our way to the king's hall where Aelfgar's daughter, Aeldgyth was overjoyed to see us, it was notable that she was heavy with child and so there was congratulations all round when Gryffudd appeared.

It was Aelfgar's intention to set off as soon as possible towards Hereford and Gryffudd confirmed that another two days would see most of his warriors from the north congregate at Mathrafal, more would join the army as they marched south. It was anticipated that by the time we neared Herefordshire the army would be some six hundred strong and capable of ravaging Herefordshire thoroughly.

Aelfgar made it clear to me that I was in charge of our viking contingent as he was too busy; I welcomed this prospect as I was at a loose end when not travelling. I congregated the Dubliners on the meadow outside the King's stronghold and inspected them. They were not as well equipped as the Icelanders I had led in Alba but they all had serviceable weapons, shields, and helmets. They had swords or axes and daggers but no spears as these were generally of little use in sea warfare. I took them through the routine drills, shield wall and battle-snout; I was pleased to see they all had a good strong longbow that they were skilled in using from the deck of their ships when fighting at sea. I let them know that they would be the elite fighters in the assembling army and that I would ensure their share of the loot reflected their status. They cheered and seemed very happy with their lot.

We set off from Mathrafal at the height of summer and for a change it was not raining. The army on the advice of King Gryffudd skirted the hill country of County Salop west about and made our way along the valley of the River Lugg deliberately swinging west away from Leominster, where King Gryffudd had fought with the English a couple of years previously. More Welshmen joined the army as we marched and the number swelled to about six hundred passable warriors as we neared the border with England. We camped ten miles north of Hereford intending to attack the town in the morning. I had had a few conversations with Martin and some of the more prominent Dublin vikings about what I thought we could expect to meet by way or resistance from Earl Ralph. My main concern was that as Earl Ralph was a Norman, I assumed he may well have a conroi of Norman horsed warriors or 'miles' as they often called themselves. I had seen what a small group of horsed Norman warriors could do to disorganised infantry at Perth and to be frank the Welsh were no better organised than the Scots were.

Naturally the Dubliners were of the opinion that a stout shield wall would stop the horsed warriors but I was not so sure, neither was Martin, although he added that with the right terrain a shield wall could perhaps hold a horsed charge but he could not see how foot warriors could attack horsed warriors out in open ground. Being ever pragmatic Martin's solution was to shoot the horses with arrows, he never liked horses. I agreed that this might work if there were enough archers, but what was to stop the horsed warriors riding down the archers?

"Woods, ditches, fences." Martin enumerated.

"Yes, I agree but all you have listed indicate a defensive action; how do we attack them?" I argued.

"An ambush." Martin decided.

"Well, I like that but it still is not an offensive attack in open terrain." I countered. "We need to choose our ground so that the horsed warriors are hindered whilst they charge, say like across marshy ground, that would slow them down and lay them open to men on foot bringing them down with spears or even large Dane axes."

"Well, it probably won't be our decision Earl Aelfgar and King Gryffudd will decide how we go about this tomorrow." Olaf, one of the Dubliners stated pointedly. Time to sleep I thought.

Early the next morning our army continued down the track to Hereford. I did not like the way it was strung out along the road with no scouts out ahead or to our flanks and said so to Aelfgar. After a brief discussion with King Gryffudd, Aelfgar suggested I should send some scouts forward. I sent Martin off smartish and then organised three small bands of four men, two of the groups were to fan out on our flanks and the third was to follow Martin forward. The objective was to know if any enemies were near us on our flanks or ahead within at least a mile. Within the hour a couple of the Dubliners came running back from the south, sent by Martin, there was an army of Normans and Saxons astride the road south to Hereford behind a small village on rising ground. I gave orders to call in my flanking men and suggested to Aelfgar that our army should advance in a shield wall, to ensure we were not attacked whilst in column. This rearrangement of our order caused some confusion so whilst it was being undertaken, I jogged forward to see the enemy for myself. I found Martin near the village in a stand of trees completely invisible to the enemy force.

"What's to do Martin?" I asked.

"There is an army of English and Normans marching up the road from Hereford, they are strung out across the road, the Norman horsed warriors are riding along the road in column, two by two, and the Saxon huscarls and fyrdmen are walking either side of the road and making hard work of it." Martin grinned he was clearly delighted by what he had seen. "This village is called Weobley and just to the north on the rising moorland it becomes very marshy; but the marshy land is within an arrow flight of the road. If we are quick a good place for an ambush I would say." Martin pointed in the direction of some slightly rising moorland.

Not one for indecision I told Martin to run back to the column and bring up my Scandinavian archers. Moving out of the copse

I walked around the village onto the slightly rising ground and was delighted when I found myself squelching through boggy ground. The road, or track was to the east of the bog, slightly raised and offering a wonderful target for archers. Whilst I was reconnoitring the area my brother came trotting up, shadowed by a dozen of his huscarls.

"I understand you are splitting our forces and bringing your Dubliners here, why?" Aelfgar enquired.

As briefly as I could I explained what I had in mind, "This is a good place to ambush the English and Normans. I want you to take the Welsh and your Mercian huscarls into the village and barricade yourselves against a cavalry charge. Earl Ralph has set his army unwisely his horsed Normans have the comfort of the road whilst his infantry is struggling along in the ditches and tussocks either side. I intend to ambush his line of approach to the village with archers in the bog. One half of his men will be rendered useless by being on the other side of his horse and his infantry on our side of the road will be sitting ducks for our archery. They will try to attack us but will fail to reach us through the mire. Then the Normans, mounted, will try and they too will be bogged down, that is when you will charge from the village and roll them back to Hereford."

Aelfgar looked at me in some surprise, "You have learnt a lot about fighting then. Alright, we will do as you say." Aelfgar and his men trotted back towards our advancing army passing my fifty Dublin vikings coming the other way. I explained what I wanted and the archers spread out in a line along the side of the road but at least fifty short paces into the bog. They crouched down, as instructed, becoming almost invisible in the low shrubbery and gorse. I could see Gryffudd's forces come up to the village of Weobley startling the villagers who had been going about their everyday chores. A sudden exodus of these said villagers became manifest as they urgently straggled out of the village northwards away from the likely scene of the forthcoming carnage. The army did what it could to erect barricades with the items lying around in the village and some enterprising souls brought out tables and beds from the cottages to enhance the defences. This was a hurried exercise as the English army very soon appeared along the road.

There was clearly a large number of English huscarls and fyrdmen and although they were strung out over at least a mile disappearing into the distance behind the vanguard. I calculated that there must be at least a thousand foot, with five hundred each side of the road and thirty of forty Norman horsed warriors, two abreast stretching back two hundred paces in the van; I could see no horsemen further back. The Welsh were outnumbered nearly two to one.

As soon as the English saw the entrenched Welshmen there was a discernible whoop of delight from the Norman horsemen. Horns were sounded as if to a hunt and several of the horsemen surged forward as if they intended to expel the Welsh army from the village all on their own. Obviously wiser heads took control and called back the eager horsemen. Given the terrain I was hopeful that the English would move forward past my ambush point before deploying into line. I noted that all the horsemen were heavily armoured, reminiscent of the Normans I was familiar with from Alba. I had no doubt that if they caught the Welsh out in the open, they would inflict fearful damage with their lances and maces.

Apart from an order for a group of huscarls on foot to form up ahead of the horsed warriors the English formation remained the same and it moved forward again steadily. I allowed the vanguard to pass our ambush point and watched as they were preparing to deploy into line for the standard shield wall. By now my men in the bog had been spotted by several of the Normans who were shouting and pointing in our direction, but this meant nothing as the trap had already been sprung. I stood up and shouted.

"Rise up, shoot."

My fifty Dublin Norse all stood and nocked their arrows. The huscarls and fyrdmen on our side of the track had started to remove their shields from their backs and place them in their left hand, those that had shields that is, many of the fyrdmen had no shields and only spears for a weapons; initially many of the warriors wore their shield facing away from us.

The first volley of arrows, although ragged, could hardly miss a target. Fifty missiles and nearly fifty hits. It is hard to kill an enemy outright with an arrow unless you are very skilled but they are very effective at disabling an opponent and rendering them 'hors de combat'. Our side of the English column was thrown into instant chaos. Screams and cries from the wounded overbore any immediate shouts for order. The second volley of arrows followed directly, not as effective as the first as some arrows were hitting already wounded fyrdmen and two arrows in the same man was invariably a waste of one arrow; nevertheless at least another twenty of the enemy foot were disabled. The tail end of the Norman horsemen had become acutely aware that they were under attack and were trying to turn their horses and re-establish control. I tried a long shot and as luck would have it struck a Norman horse in the rump. The horse immediately became unmanageable and started to rear and tried to bolt but the crowd of men around him made this impossible although the horse did force the nearest men on foot to scatter away causing more chaos. Finally, a lead huscarl called for the remaining infantry to charge us, it had become clear that there was only a few of us and well within charging distance. The huscarl formed a rudimentary shield wall of just a few men and started out across the tussocks and mossy grass towards us; additionally, from further back along the track another leader, probably a thegn, had arranged a group of thirty of more warriors to move off the track and charge our left flank. I had anticipated these moves and my archers concentrated on the two attacking groups.

The small group approaching our line where I was were equipped with shields and therefore less prone to be wounded by an arrow storm. I had chosen a small group of ten of my best archers to concentrate on piercing their legs but I anticipated a close quarter fight. The rest of the archers around me continued to pepper the ranks of the English still hanging back around the road.

The archers on our left flank were much better placed as their attackers were mostly lightly armoured fyrdmen led by one heavily armoured thegn. By concentrating their archery against the unarmoured fyrdmen they quickly disposed of this attack for as their injuries accumulated, they lost their nerve and turned and fled.

The small group facing me reached the bog and this slowed them down considerably making it much easier to shoot effectively against them. Slowly they were shot down until none remained standing, although most were only wounded.

My archers had expended maybe half of their arrows by this point, at least I had, and without having to physically repulse any attackers. It would appear than none of the enemy were archers, fortunately, or if they were, they were not in the van. Our devastation of the English foot had exposed the rear of the Norman horse who had now managed to turn and trot back down the track. Seeing the failure of the foot to attack us and still not understanding the nature of the terrain they spilled over the edge of the track towards us at their best canter. Cries of 'Dex Aie' split the air as at least ten Normans charged us. Twenty paces from the track they hit the bog; one horse went down in a mud hole his foreleg smashed, another of the Norman's horse received an arrow deep into its chest as it too slewed forward into the mud screaming. Both riders were catapulted forward towards our line but probably never survived the impact with the muddy turf as they did not move or attempt to rise. The remaining riders pulled frantically on their reins to prevent their steeds having a similar fated to their comrades; this did not prevent two more riders slithering into the bog with their horse's front legs buried deep in the mire. I stopped my archers peppering them with arrows as they were being wasted against their wooden kite-shaped shields and reinforced armour. I shot both horses to be sure they were out of the fight.

"Martin, sound the charge." As instructed Martin, who was carrying a large bull's horn, raised it to his lips and blew a mournful blast; the signal for the Welsh army to charge. Within seconds the Welsh warriors leapt out from behind their unrequired barricades and ran towards the English vanguard who were milling about in confusion. Without being in a shield wall, the English van knew it would be overlapped, overwhelmed, and killed and to a man, they turned and fled.

I could hear the Norman horsed warriors on the road screaming for the foot soldiers to hold, stand turn and fight, but to no avail. The horses were still milling around in confusion and terror, the occasional arrow found a mark to an equine rump or neck where it was exposed to my Dubliners who still had the odd arrow in their quivers. As the Welsh and Mercians neared the Normans, they too, fled along the road back to Hereford.

"Come on." I shouted as loud as possible and waved my men forward. We struggled through the marshy moor towards the road. The Welsh streamed passed us in pursuit of the enemy and it looked like we would be the at the rear of the rush to Hereford.

I knew we were still a good eight or nine miles from Hereford and so I instructed my Dubliners to slow down to a steady jog as we did not want to arrive at the gates of the town worn out. So, we trotted along the road at a steady pace. We soon started to pass dead Englishmen, most stabbed in the back or smashed down by a blow to the back of the head. Welshmen were stopping to loot the dead but we kept to a steady pace and soon we were passing Welshmen sitting by the roadside recovering from their mad dash at the enemy.

"Follow on behind us and try and keep up." Martin yelled in his best Welsh dialect. After about four miles Aelfgar and King Gryffudd caught us up, trotting along on the familiar small Welsh hill ponies.

"Hail Heri!" Aelfgar yelled as he passed us, "That was a rare ambush, I've never seen an enemy run so fast."

Gryffudd laughed, "Brother, you should have been with us when Hereward slew the southern Welsh prince, they ran even faster." The horsed troop quickly passed by and I anticipated that they would be at the gates of Hereford a good quarter watch before us. I only hoped that the Welsh would not fall into an ambush in turn. After another good quarter watch my troop and I arrived at the gate of Hereford. To my surprise the wooden gates stood wide open and from the noise emanating from the town it was clear that the Welsh were sacking the place.

"Come on lads, you're missing the fun." I shouted and with a mighty roar the Vikings rushed the gate. "Martin, go to the south gate and make sure that there is no armed resistance, I'll find my brother and the King." Martin nodded and ran off around the outer wall, this surprised me but on second thoughts I realised that rather than getting lost in the town running around the outer defences would ensure Martin would not get lost and would avoid trouble.

I marched through the north gate, which I understood was referred to as the Wydmarsh Gate, perhaps if Earl Ralph had heeded that name, he may have been better prepared. The first few streets were deserted suggesting that the inhabitants had had a short time to run before the Welsh spilled through the undefended gate. I headed towards the obvious centre of the town, which was the tower of the church dedicated to St Ethelberht, some miracle working king of old. There were streets off to my left and right and I could hear screams coming from both sides, women's screams. I was old enough to know what that meant, especially after talking to Winflaed after I had rescued her from Prince Rhys. It did occur to me that I was eighteen years old and had never had a woman but I was not sure I had the stomach for rape and the only woman I desired was Godgifu, my step-mother. I would have forced her, for sure.

I eventually came to the square in front of the church and to my surprise there were a dozen or so monks defending the minster door and preventing the Welsh rabble from entering. I walked up to where my brother and King Gryffudd sat on their ponies.

"What's to do?" I queried.

"These monks will not let my men plunder the church, they call us heathen, which is a joke considering we were Christian before these English monks' pagan forefathers crawled out of their German bog five hundred years ago. Begging your pardon, Lord Aelfgar." King Gryffudd chortled. At that point a huge monk wielding a large iron candle holder brained a Welshman who crept too near, splattering the poor man's brains across the cobbles.

"This will not do; we could be counter-attacked at any time and your army is in disarray. You probably have no scouts out to the south." I countered rather abruptly.

"My brother is ever watchful." Aelfgar observed, "The truth is these Welsh are nervous about attacking men of the cloth and the sack of the town is stalling."

"I will resolve this." I stated. I strode forward and pushed passed the reluctant Welsh warriors. "Make way, I say."

The Welshmen fell back, I heard muttering, "It's the Bearslayer." "Evil eye." "Wahardd! Wahardd!"

135

I stood forth from the crowd and faced the monks. "Lay down your arms and you will live. These Welsh warriors will not dishonour the church; yes, they will plunder it but the sacred ornaments will go into churches in Wales, no doubt where some of them came from in the first place." Of course, I did not believe this, I knew Gryffudd would have his share but much of the loot would be chopped up for hack silver and exchangeable goods by needy warriors. Unfortunately, the monks did not believe me either.

"Bugger off boy." The large monk spat out at me. Of course! Well, this monk was not to know that I disliked priests and monks intensely, apart from my uncle Brand and that I already had a track record of attacking such. I stepped up to the monk and before he had any opportunity to raise his makeshift club, I rammed my sword clean through his unarmoured stomach. The monk looked at me in puzzlement and stupidly mouthed silent curses as he lost his will to stand and silently slid off my sword onto the cobbles.

The rest of the monks howled in protest but the flood gates had been opened and the Welsh warriors rushed forward and overwhelmed them. I flurry of stabs and clubbing and a dozen monks lay dead at the church door and the raiders flowed over them into the dark interior of the house of God.

"Jesus, Mary, Hereward, I can't believe you did that, you killed a monk, a man of God." Aelfgar looked pale.

I turned on him in anger, "Well somebody had to do it, and I am the outlaw, remember."

Martin came running up and saluted me. I nodded acknowledgement.

"The timid earl hasn't stopped running and there isn't an English army this side of Gloucester."

King Gryffudd overheard and smiled thinly. "Loot the town and then burn it." He shouted and hell came to Hereford.

It had been two days since the storming of Hereford by the Welsh and vikings, the Welsh had run riot killing indiscriminately and burning the houses and eventually the minister church. All had burned merrily to the screams of the violated women. When the minster burned more monks or priests appeared from hiding and ran for their lives with the excited

Welsh behind them, several monks were caught near the sacred well and the looters considered it hilarious to throw the monks alive down the well. The 'game' expanded to throwing others down the well, women, and children, even King Gryffudd considered this act excessive and ordered a stop. My vikings were far more prosaic; whilst the Welsh warriors killed, maimed, and violated, the Dublin warriors had an eye on gain. They rounded up large groups of prisoners, mainly women and children but also healthy men, chained them together and guarded them from more abuse. They even prevented the Welsh killing the women after they had raped them so that they could be sold in the Dublin slave market. Other vikings systematically looted the houses for silver and any other precious items such as tools, good clothing, and jewellery of lesser worth. They even found carts to convey the loot back to their ships.

I rounded up as many of the Welsh as I could and I sat on the edge of St Ethelberht's Well in the space between the church and the castle. I addressed the bedraggled Welshmen surrounding me. "I think it would be best if we retrieve the dead bodies from the well and bury them. If the English find them down there, they will be minded to retaliate on your families in kind. If they find a row of neatly buried monks, women, and children they will not bother digging them up and the atrocities we have committed will be less vivid. Now, who is going to climb down the well?" The Welsh reluctantly followed my suggestion.

King Gryffudd and Aelfgar had invited me to their deliberations on what to do next. I was conscious that as far as Aelfgar was concerned this whole debacle was to force King Edward the Mild to rescind his outlawry, whereas I was not sure what Gryffudd wanted to gain from this foray, other than to oblige his brother-in-law.

"I think we should stay here and wait to see what response Edward will make to our challenge." Aelfgar asserted.

"We need to secure the loot, the slaves and silver." Gryffudd was very firm on this but tempered this with, "What do you think Bearslayer?"

"Gloucester is about thirty miles from here and is a major town on the Wessex border. Any resistance to our presence will materialise from there and not to our eastern flank, where lies

Mercia. The resistance will come from Harald Godwinson who is King Edward's Magister Militum, or Master of his Soldiers. Earl Ralph the Timid will have reached Gloucester the day we took Hereford, two days ago. Harald and King Edward in Winchester will probably know what we have done by now and by all accounts Harald Godwinson is no slouch. I anticipate that he will start to muster an army and move on Gloucester immediately, which means he will have some sort of an army assembled within a week. If you leave Hereford and retreat back into Wales, he may not follow but he will not consider reinstating Aelfgar to his earldom in East Anglia. So, a sizeable force must remain to challenge him but in a position of strength that the Godwinson will not want to assault. I suggest we fortify the bridge and ford across the river south of the town and dare him to attack us. Meanwhile we send out the vikings raiding to show we are not running from the English."

Aelfgar looked pleased that I was thinking of his reinstatement, "How long do you think we have got before the Wessex army arrives?"

"I would guess Godwinson would have a force he considers adequate to attack us in ten days, but he may be bold and have a smaller force before the ford in seven. If he did that and it was a real war, I would attack him whilst he is weak but with a small force he may choose to parley and that is what we want, is it not?" I explained, then I added to their surprise, "I sent Martin south yesterday to watch Gloucester and we will have at least two days warning of the English approach."

Aelfgar laughed, "Ever the wakeful then Hereward."

And so, I took control of both the 'clean up' operation of Hereford and the defence of the ford whilst my brother, King Gryffudd and his lords feasted in the castle. A grizzled Welshman from the mountains of Snowdonia volunteered to be roped down to the well bottom and the laborious task of pulling up the bodies began. I arranged a group of men to dig graves, not a long pit but individual graves with a wooden cross for each one; there would be no evidence to tell tales of the atrocities committed on the residents of Hereford. Of course, this could not conceal the blackened shells of the houses and church minster, whereas mostly the walls of the town and the castle survived. I also took the precaution of sending most of our prisoners and portable plunder north into Powys to ensure we did not lose it if our fortunes changed. Ever wakeful indeed.

The castle was an interesting assembly in wood that I had never seen before but it had been described to me by the Normans I had met and fought alongside in Scotland. It was what the Normans called a motte and bailey. It appeared to be a large natural mound with some additional earthworks to make the hill or motte larger and flat on top. Access to the hilltop was by a series of wide dugout steps with tree planks to stop the steps degrading. On top of the motte a wooden fortress had been erected; vertical piles bound together with withies and nailed boards. The interior of the wooden wall had a walkway around the top so that defenders could fire down onto attackers. At the centre of the wooden circular fort was a wooden tower, three storeys high. All was easily defended especially as the wood was green and would not fire easily. Obviously, it kept the Normans safe inside and allowed them to sally out and attack the surrounding area. Such a strong point was quite novel in England but it was of no account if the holders of the castle were not prepared to defend it like timid Earl Ralph.

My brother and King Gryffudd were ensconced in the wooden tower or 'keep' spending much of the day drinking and abusing captured women. I found this peculiarly satisfying as it left me in control without censure or stricture, I realised I did not react well to orders from others, especially when those orders were quite often pointless or plain wrong-headed. The defence of the river crossing was progressing well, with King Thorfinn MacBeth as my tutor in this method of defence I soon had the Welsh planting sharpened wooden stakes in the river up and down the ford and bridge area. The bridge itself was wooden, although there were stone supports showing in the river further downstream, indicating the old Roman bridge long since crumbled to ruin. I decided to leave the bridge intact but introduced metal caltrops across the planks and laid heavy logs at our end of the bridge as a barrier. The bridge could become a trap and a killing zone. I also erected a wooden wall, chest high along the river bank for the defenders to man, and shelter behind if attacked.

Of course, there was always the possibility that the English army might advance on the east side of the River Wye rendering all my defensive works redundant, but this would mean Godwinson entering the old territory of the Hwicce, the traditional homeland of my father Leofric's family and I was counting on Godwinson avoiding bringing my father into this little war.

To support my strategy, I sent my fifty vikings south towards Gloucester with orders to raid farms and villages on the west side of the River Wye, burn and harry. The destruction of the area would entice the English to advance along this route. Fortunately, I was proved right as after two weeks Martin brought news that a large English army was marching out of Gloucester, displaying the Dragon of Wessex and the Fighting Man, the personal banner of the Godwinsons. Additional scouts brought the news that the enemy army numbered upwards of two thousand and apart from the few Normans they were all on foot. My Norse band straggled in shortly afterwards with a string of captives and portable loot.

There was the inevitable war counsel held in the castle keep and I noted many concerned faces on my arrival. King Gryffudd opened the discussion, pointedly looking at me. "Well Hereward, we have done as you suggest and built defences at the ford but the army coming against us is many times larger than ours. We will not stand a chance if we remain here."

I could see many of the Welsh lords and Aelfgar's Mercian thegns were nodding in agreement. "Not so, my lord King. To attack the ford successfully Harald Godwinson would need at least three, maybe four thousand men and even then, it would be folly as he would lose many men in a head on attack. I understand that he is a wise tactician and he will immediately see the strength of our position and seek other means to gain his objective. The logical alternative would be for him to march back along the Wye to the next suitable ford and outflank us, by which time we would be well away. No, we only have to hold our nerve and we will prevail and gain our objectives." I looked meaningfully at my brother.

"I agree with my brother, we must be bold and not run before the Wessex men or we will lose what we have gained. Hereward has described to me the fight at the ford at Perth in Alba and how a much smaller army held the Northumbrians at bay. Anything Scots can do Welshmen can." Aelfgar added appealing to the Welsh sense of vanity. The debate continued for some time but clearly King Gryffudd, whose decision was final was much in favour of holding his ground. There was little doubt that if he came out of this raid favourably it would much strengthen his bid to become king of all Wales. Finally, this decided the issue.

"We stay and fight." The King grinned mirthlessly.

After a delay of several days the English army finally assembled across the river. It was truly quite a large army, probably bigger than the scouts had estimated but that in itself presented the Godwinson with problems. Feeding his warriors and keeping the fyrdmen from deserting back to their farms after they had been away for over two weeks already was going to be a problem. The Godwinson would also know that his fyrdmen would be worse than useless attacking a redoubt across a river and that he could only rely on his huscarls, maybe three hundred of his personal bodyguard and a hundred or so that were supplied to Earl Ralph. The professional warriors were truly magnificent fighters but they too would suffer in this type of fight and he would not want to lose so many good men. The English army camped well back from the ford and wooden bridge and settled in for the night and of course, being near Wales, it started to rain.

After an uncomfortable night for the English and a relatively comfortable night for the Welsh I was not surprised when a herald approached the south end of the bridge and asked for a parley. I agreed that King Gryffudd and Aelfgar would meet Harald Godwinson and Earl Ralph on the bridge and after some negotiations relating to bodyguards and armament it was agreed. I accompanied my brother as one of the guards, dressed as a viking mercenary. Earl Harald and Earl Ralph walked onto the bridge from the south side with four bodyguards. King Gryffudd and my brother walked onto the bridge from the north side with four bodyguards, myself included. None of us carried missile weapons, only daggers or scramaseax. I had a nasal helmet on that partially hid my features.

"Good morning, Earl Harald, how can we help you?" began King Gryffudd mildly. Earl Harald Godwinson was a tall man with dark hair and a long sweeping moustache in the Danish fashion. His powerful arms were bare of mail and they bulged with muscles. He was half Dane and his family had supported King Knut the Mighty before changing their allegiance to Edward the Mild. Beside him in heavy mail stood a much shorter man who could only be Earl Ralph of Hereford, a much reduced, Hereford.

Earl Harald smiled broadly. "I am puzzled to know why the King of North Wales would wish to attack our town of Hereford, King Edward has, not to my knowledge, ever been aggressive towards you or your kingdom. Whereas you have had a long running feud with the Mercians and if I am not mistaken, a scion of the Mercian earls stands alongside you?"

That was nicely done, I thought. Try and break up the opposition, divide and conquer.

"Aelfgar is my beloved father-in-law and our differences have been resolved amicably. Who else would he come to but to me when he has been treated so shabbily and unjustly by the English king?" King Gryffudd countered.

"Ah! True. Aelfgar's banishment was unjust I acknowledge that. Are you suggesting that your little invasion is purely to assist Aelfgar to regain his rights?" The Godwinson was all smiles, like a wolf.

"Of course, it damn well is!" spluttered King Gryffudd.

"Well in that case all can be resolved. If I agree to intercede of Lord Aelfgar's behalf with the King and the Witanagemot and have him reinstated as Earl of the East Angles, will you retreat back into Wales?"

With somewhat of a surprised look on his face King Gryffudd responded, "Yes, of course I would."

"And what say you, Aelfgar?" Harald directed his question to my brother.

"I wish to be reinstated but I would seek reassurances that the King and your brother Earl Tostig will be reconciled with me."

"With the king there is no problem, alas my brother is headstrong and not easily controlled but he is running on his own fate in Northumbria and you do not need to worry unduly about him." Harald smiled again and held out his hand, "Do we have an agreement then?"

"There is the matter of my brother, Hereward." Aelfgar responded, I winced, so near and now he was spoiling the negotiation.

Harald looked thoughtful and looked directly at me. "When your brother was initially outlawed, I said England would come to regret it, alas this proved to be true. Your brother is now a noted reiver and killer of men. In fact, he is everything that King Edward abhors. I would never be able to convince our ruler that the Bearslayer is pardoned. I understand that he leads a crew of Dublin Norse, he and his crew cannot ever be brought into the law whilst our present king lives. Even his father, Earl Leofric supports this view."

I should have been deflated by this explanation of my situation but strangely I was not. A life as a law-abiding thegn working a farm did not appeal to me at all.

"One last thing; nothing can be done to rectify the destruction meted out on Hereford but I assume that you have enslaved many of the villagers and townsfolk and I would wish them liberated. I would be prepared to pay a reasonable gelt for them." Harald I could see was tense and clearly this was a major issue that he had introduced as an aside.

"I will release all the captives for a price Earl Harald but you must know that the vikings that accompanied us have since left with some of the captives and I cannot liberate them for you." King Gryffudd looked uncomfortable as my presence showed that clearly one viking was still present.

My brother interceded, "Earl Harald, I will be meeting our fleet at Chester after the campaign and I will undertake to liberate as many of the captives as I can."

"Can I have the Bearslayer's assurance on this matter?" Again, the Godwinson looked directly at me and so did Aelfgar. I felt obliged to speak.

"Earl Harald, I am not a friend of your house and certainly not of your brother Tostig, but know this, I am here to assist my brother and although I am a poor man, I will do everything in my power to help my brother keep his promise."

"It was you who set the ambush that defeated Earl Ralph and this," he scanned the defences to Hereford, "You did this?"

"Yes."

The Godwinson looked at me long and hard, we measured each other and neither of us found the other wanting.

"So be it." Earl Harald nodded at the King and the newly reinstated Earl of the East Angles and abruptly turned on his heel and walked off the bridge.

Autumn 1055 - *Ottar*

The weather was turbulent in the Irish Sea and I could see that the Norsemen clearly did not wish to be afloat at this time of the year but the rendezvous with my brother had been set and payment was not to be forgone. The eighteen Norse longships with the two knarrs lay in the estuary of the River Dee, neither in English Mercia nor in north Wales. In addition, there were three captured English merchant vessels that I understood were filled with plunder from the ports and villages along the south coast of England, Plunder taken from Land's End to the Isle of Wight. I had reunited my Dublin Norse with their crew mates who were jubilant when they saw the additional loot and captives from Hereford. Having no troop of men to lead I sat in Eachmarchach longship near the prow with Martin whilst the two groups of vikings squabbled over the plunder. It was clear that Asketil and the Dubliners wanted the slaves to sell in their thriving entrepot, walking profit. On the other hand, Eachmarchach only needed slaves to work on the farms of his men from Galloway and Mann, and of course a few women to keep him warm at night. The negotiations were amicable enough with much of the portable loot and half of the silver going to Eachmarchach's men and most of the slaves allocated to Asketil's crews. I knew that my brother would want to offer silver for many of Asketil's captives and I wondered how the Norseman would respond to this. A meeting had been arranged for the following day outside the walls of Chester. I could not attend, as an outlaw in England anyone could lawfully kill me, or try to. I was informed that my father would be attending the meeting along with Aelfgar the now reinstated Earl of the East Angles.

Eachmarchach and Asketil were, however, arguing over a female captive. I had not seen her but apparently, she was a beauty; Eachmarchach wanted her for himself but Asketil saw a huge profit in selling her in Dublin, possibly even to the Irish King himself. Things were getting heated so I decided to intervene.

"Eachmarchach, Asketil, this bickering over a woman is unseemly when you have so much and expect more from my brother. What is it about this woman that has created this animosity between you?"

"I captured this girl in a raid on a settlement in Cornwall, she is beautiful and I want her." Eachmarchach explained.

"Bearslayer, this girl is a chieftain's daughter, a Dublin Norseman called Aleif, who I know well, is her father; he rules a small settlement of Dublin Norsemen who left Dublin when Eachmarchach was expelled. I would sell her back to her father, unharmed, for a honourable price. Yes, she is a beauty, which would be reason enough for Eachmarchach to want her but there is more to it than that. This girl is betrothed to Eachmarchach's nephew who is the current King of Veðrafjǫrðr and Eachmarchach has a grudge against him." Asketil explained.

"Is this true?" I asked Eachmarchach.

"I should, by rights, be king of Dublin and Veðrafjǫrðr, not just Mann and a few stinking isles up north curtesy of Thorfinn." Eachmarchach muttered sullenly, "It's the fault of that Brian Borumhe, ever since Clontarf the Irish won't behave themselves."

"Eachmarchach, alienating other Norsemen, your natural allies, won't get you back Dublin." I pointed out. "There are plenty of beautiful women to bed let Asketil return the girl to her father with a request that he helps you regain Dublin." I suggested.

Asketil nodded vigorously adding. "My lord, you know I support your return, let's all pool our resources and plan to retake Dublin from the Irish."

Eachmarchach eventually agreed after more discussion and argument. Afterwards I wanted to see what all the wrangling was about and asked where this beauty was being held. Eachmarchach indicated to one of the captured English merchant vessels. The next day after Eachmarchach and Asketil with their bodyguards and chieftains left for Chester I rowed across to the merchant ship to see this remarkable captive. The captain of the vessel looked at me in a surly manner but as he knew who I was he did not try and stop me.

"Where is this chieftain's daughter that is causing all the trouble?" The captain indicated to a group of captive women at the stern of the boat. I scrambled over piles of sacks and boxes filled with plunder until I reached the stern platform, seated around were a dozen or so women, huddled against the wind with blankets that kept their features and shapes well concealed; probably a wise precaution with all the lusty Norsemen around.

"Which one of you is Aleif's daughter?" I demanded.

A very young and delicate face emerged from under the blankets, she was quite dark, long black hair woven into two long plaits with red ribbons. She had the look of the Irish about her and I assumed that Aleif had had the usual mixed marriage with an Irish woman. As she emerged from the blanket it was obvious, she was very small and very young, maybe twelve or thirteen, her small budding breasts barely showed under her bodice.

"What's your name?" I demanded again.

"Hild, Sunhild." Barely a whisper.

"I have spoken to King Eachmarchach and Asketil the Dublin chief and it has been agreed that you will be returned to your father unharmed or more probably you will be sent direct to Veðrafjǫrðr where I understand your betrothed is king. I will make sure the crew on this boat know this and any harm that comes to you will be regretted. You understand?"

"Yes." Another whisper.

"Good." I turned to go.

"Wait." She managed a louder voice, "What of my nurse?"

I looked over the sorry group. "Your nurse is with you?"

"Yes, this is Una."

From under the blankets climbed another young woman. I had been expecting an old woman, well past her prime but was stunned to see a real Irish beauty. Luxurious long red her, loose and tangled, a creamy complexion with a hint of freckles and large languid green eyes. She was much taller than her charge, taller than me if truth be told with a full figure and wide hips.

"I am Una." she said in a low sultry voice. I saw that her well-made woollen dress had been torn at the shoulder and she was displaying a smattering of blueish bruises across her cheek and exposed arms.

"You have been taken, by them?" I indicated over my shoulder to the crew.

"No, by their king, as a trade for not touching my ward."

I reached out and touched her cheek; she did not flinch away. "Eachmarchach wasn't gentle then?"

She did not answer but I could see the challenge in her eyes. I turned to Sunhild Aleifsdatter, "I will do what I can, no promises."

As I rowed back to Eachmarchach snekkja I realised that I wanted her, Una I meant; this came as a shock as I had reconciled myself to being mostly immune to women's charms. I thought my feelings through, she was not at all like Godgifu, my passion, nor like Aelfgar's daughter, my Godgifu in miniature. She was provocative, a challenge, maybe that was it, I always found it difficult not to accept a challenge.

Martin noted the change in me but said nothing. It was not until mid-day on the following day that Eachmarchach and Asketil returned to the fleet. They seemed in high good humour and I could see that Aelfgar and another were in the longship with them. They swung alongside our ship and they all leapt over. The fourth, elderly man staggered as he stepped onto our ship's top strake and I caught and steadied him.

"Hello father." I stepped back giving him room to steady himself, he was quickly followed by my brother Aelfgar. Leofric looked very old and tired. His hair was grey and his once robust body was slightly bowed. He reached out and took hold of Aelfgar's arm for support. Leofric looked me up and down and I realised I did not much care for his appraisal.

"Hereward, I needed to see you one last time." Well, that was a way to start a conversation, did he mean I was going to die, or that he was going to die?

"I am here." I sounded wooden, detached, what could I offer him?

"You have become a great warrior, so young, I wish your path had been different."

I could not resist my response. "Well, you had the power to direct my future and chose this for me." My father looked sad but I could not comfort him, all I could offer was. "My fate is my own, I tread the swan's path joyfully and call no man my master."

"But you have killed so many men and you broke Siward's heart, my friend."

"That old plunderer had no business invading Alba where King Thorfinn MacBeth is my friend."

"But you can never return to England, never see your mother or little brother." Leofric opined.

"What little brother, I have no brother except Aelfgar and he spends almost as much time an outlaw as I do." I responded.

"Shortly after you left your mother fell pregnant again, a child of my old age, she now has another son, named after me, Leofric."

"Well make sure he is well cared for or your saintly wife, Godgifu, will take all from him and my mother when you die."

"Of course, I have made arrangements for both him and you. Your brother Aelfgar will hold land for you until better times when you can reclaim your rights. Three farms around Bourne have been made over to your mother and young Leofric. I have filed these charters with the church, your uncle Brand, and the Abbot at Peterborough."

"Well, I doubt I will come into my own again whilst King Edward the Mild, the straw king, is alive and God alone knows what will happen to England when he dies, as he will." I felt like a prophet of old.

"All will be well, we have sent out to divers lands in the east to find the off-spring of the King's brother, the Ironside, then we will have a true Aetheling heir to the throne." Explained my father.

I laughed, "Harald Godwinson permitting you mean. Look for an early death for any Aethelings returning to England. Like father like son. I hear Earl Godwin choked and died of his bread when swearing he had nothing to do with the death of the King's brother Alfred." Leofric looked crushed.

"Look father, I love my brother Aelfgar and will support him too, whatever, as I have done times past. I will never stand against Mercians or the good men of the Danelagh. For Northumbrians and Wessex men I care nothing. My life for the foreseeable future lies elsewhere." I held out my hand in friendship, I could not embrace him. He took my hand in both hands, he was close to tears, and I did not want to unman him, in

148

his time he had been a great earl but like many a great man his wife brought him down. He turned and gestured to Aelfgar, who came forward with a bundle.

"Father wanted you to have these." Aelfgar pulled from the sack a beautiful sword in a leather-bound scabbard. The hilt was made of ivory, probably from a narwhal's tusk, the cross guard was short like the Scandinavians used, rather than the longer type favoured by the Normans and the hilt was mounted with a rare red crystal. The leather along the length of the scabbard had been tooled into writhing serpents and so had the belt that was designed to be slung across the shoulder. Following the sword was a large wooden shield in the kite shape favoured by the Normans. Painted onto the parchment face were two designs, at the top was the Mercian knot, my favourite motif, yellow on black and at the bottom an upright white polar bear on a red background. Lastly Aelfgar withdrew a helmet of the early Anglian type, a segmented helm held together by metal bands all embossed with hunted animals, stags, bears, boars. The helmet had a neck guard of mail and a half face mask in the shape of the god Odin with is two ravens for eyebrows. There was also mail to cover the lower face. The war gear was a wonder to behold and I was at a loss.

"Father, forgive my surliness, these gifts are truly magnificent and any son would be proud to own them. I will wear them with pride and let everyone know I bear the badges of Mercia." I stepped forward and embraced my father. "Don't worry about me, I will do great things, some good, some bad, some very bad." I laughed, I was thinking about when I killed the monk in Hereford, it was fortunate he did not know about that, that is unless Aelfgar told him. "I will always fight for Mercia and the Danelagh."

"You remind me of my elder brother, Norman, the one killed by Knut before you were borne, he too was a valiant warrior who lived his life precariously. I was never his equal. The sword is, was, his, he named it Dragon's Breath" There was still sadness in his voice. "I must go now, thank you for helping Aelfgar back to his earldom."

He will not keep it, I thought, Harald Godwinson will expel him before long. My father and Aelfgar left, I had said my farewells to Aelfgar and informed him that I would probably be in Ireland or Wales if he needed my help in the future.

It appeared that the dealings between Aelfgar and the Norsemen had gone well. With the help of our father Aelfgar had stumped up enough gelt to buy most of the captives from Hereford and even some taken from the south coast of England thus fulfilling their promise to Harald Godwinson. Both Eachmarchach and the Dubliners had mostly silver and trade goods rather than slaves, which were much easier to transport across the sea. No one cared too much about the captives taken from Cornwall so Aleif's daughter and her nurse Una were still aboard the captured English ship.

I approached Eachmarchach and Asketil. "You have reached an equitable arrangement with my brother; I trust you were paid well for your services?"

"Better than we had hoped, we should be able to raise a sizeable force to retake Dublin." Eachmarchach enthused. "Also, I have a surprise for you Hereward. "Look yonder." Eachmarchach pointed across the channel to the rest of the fleet.

I was puzzled. "You will have to do better than that, I have seen the fleet every day this past month."

"Then you will know the longship *'Ottar'* well." Eachmarchach smiled. "It's yours."

"What, how?"

"As I said the negotiations went better than I hoped, your father bought the ship for a ridiculous amount of silver and then announced he was giving it to a wastrel like you." Eachmarchach laughed. I had mixed emotions, shame being uppermost, my father loved me despite my actions and clearly did this in the face of his wife's disapproval.

"How will I crew it?" Again, Eachmarchach and Asketil both laughed.

"I am sure that half a hundred young fellows will be gagging to sail with a fighter like you. The crew already on her will sail for Dublin with Asketil and from there the world is your oyster." Eachmarchach looked pleased with himself.

"One last thing then." I added, "I too have received a substantial amount of treasure from King Gryffudd and my brother and I would like to offer you both a gift for your true support in our little war with the English and also in token of your generous decision to allow Sunhild Aleifsdatter and her nurse to return to her father." I proffered two magnificent silver arm rings and two thin wired and bound Welsh gold torcs, a pair each.

Asketil gasped with delight. "My wife will love the torc as a necklace, she'll let me swive her from now until Easter next for this."

Eachmarchach was a little less enthusiastic but nevertheless accepted the gifts. "Sunhild and her nurse, I don't remember the agreement covered the nurse." He paused, "Hey Ho, what is the difference, she was a good fuck but any port in a storm will do I always say. She is yours and welcome but I warn you she does scratch." His laughter died away as he strode back to the helm to get his fleet underway.

Yule 1055 – The Holmgang

I sat near the doorway of the hall looking out towards the Liffey and my snekkja as it sat drifting lazily in the current. Martin had insisted it was not to be tied up against the wharf in case we had to flee precipitously from the town. He was more cautious than I for I had no real reason to think that the Irish king would have any ill-will towards me, that is unless he considered me to be in the camp of Eachmarchach the previous expelled viking ruler of the town. He certainly held that view of Asketil for immediately we climbed onto the wooden dockside Asketil was seized by the king's guards.

The Irish King had agreed to the Dublin Norse assisting my brother in raiding England and clearly understood a sizeable portion of the loot would come to him. Asketil had become too forceful and the Irish king did not trust him, I knew with good reason the king was right. I had an uncomfortable audience with the king. He turned out to be very young and excitable, his name was Murchad Mac Diarmait and he had been installed as king in Dublin by his father the dominant Irish king in the area, a man named Diarmait Mac Mael na mBo, meaning something like 'the son of the bald cattle stealer'. Dairmait was King of Leinster, which was the south eastern part of Ireland wherein Dublin, Veðrafjǫrðr, and Vicklo, that is most of the Norse settlements in Ireland lay. These new towns founded by the vikings had made King Dairmait very wealthy through trade and he more and more wanted to tightly control them, hence the establishment of his son in Dublin.

"I remember you came with your brother to hire mercenaries to ravage England, why have you come back here?" the young king demanded.

"Lord king, the raid was a success and my brother has been reinstated to his earldom in England. I on the other hand am a wolf's head in England and could not return with him so I had little choice but either to stay in Wales or return here. As it happens, I had an additional reason to return to Dublin as I must return a chieftain's daughter to her betrothed the King of

152

Veðrafjǫrðr." I added as an afterward, "I trust your portion of the gelt brought back by Asketil met with your approval."

The young king became very agitated at the mention of Asketil. "Asketil is a rogue and a traitor who intended to keep the gelt and fund a rebellion together with the ex-king of Dublin, Eachmarchach. Asketil is already dead, I had him hanged this morning, you can see his body hanging over the town's sea gate if you want."

"I know nothing of a proposed rebellion." I lied smoothly, "I have fought beside Eachmarchach in Alba and England, I did not know he was ever a king in Ireland."

"Well, he was and the only reason he still lives is because he is protected by Thorfinn Jarl of Orkney and the Isles."

"None of this has anything to do with me, tis true I am a sell sword, a mercenary but I have no interest in Ireland or Dublin."

"Good, will you fight for me?" the young king leant forward eagerly.

"That depends who you are fighting, I will not fight my kin unless attacked by them and I will not fight Jarl Thorfinn who I count my friend. Any Irish chieftain is fair game though."

"Is it true you killed a white bear with your bare hands, I see the white bear skin around your shoulders."

I laughed, "People say so, but the truth is less magical, I slew Asbjorn Siwardson of Northumbria a descendent of the fairy bear and yes, he did have hairy ears just like a bear."

A sly look came over King Murchad's face as he changed tack, "This chieftain's daughter, she is the daughter of Aleif of Marazion in Cornwall?"

"I understand she is." I responded, wondering where this line of questioning was going.

"Aleif is a Dublin Norseman who fled when my father took the town, he is a supporter of Eachmarchach."

"I do not know about that; I have never met him or her betrothed at Veðrafjǫrðr. I only interceded on her behalf because I felt she was too young to be abused by Eachmarchach or Asketil."

"That was very gallant of you, perhaps I should take her off your hands." Murchad sneered childishly.

"You would be no better than Eachmarchach then." I riposted hoping that this would be the comment that would restrain him.

Murchad's face became suffused with anger but he managed to restrain himself somewhat. "I am not really interested in this girl myself but I have an uncle, a bastard uncle, who likes to fuck virgin girls and boys. He is a great warrior and very skilled, let us have a wager. You will fight my uncle for the girl, if you win the girl is yours and you are free to go, if my uncle wins, he gets to fuck the girl front and back. The fight will be to the death so you will not be going anywhere. How does that suit you?"

"I am sure your father never made you king in Dublin to act in this manner, but I can see I have no choice. Do we fight a holmgang?" I responded.

"Yes, yes, let us make it a viking holmgang. My Norse subjects will appreciate that." Murchad laughed and clapped his hands together in glee. "You will not object if my bodyguard keeps you close until the fight I trust?" Murchad indicated to his guards who closed around me. I was kept in a small room at the back of the king's hall. Holmgangs are usually held three of four days after a challenge but this was hardly usual. I was permitted to send for my armour and weapons and was gratified when Martin turned up with them.

"Well Martin I have walked into a right mess here. The last place we should be is in Dublin apparently."

Martin did not look particularly concerned. "This is what you were born for, battle fame, what the Normans call chivalry. King Murchad's men have taken Sunhild and Una into their custody. I have kept our crew on board the *Ottar* and the king has not bothered us as yet.

"What can you tell me about my opponent?" I asked.

"I have not seen him, apparently, he lives in a rath, or fortress, inland some ten miles and will be here tomorrow, which is when the fight will be. His name is Gluniairn, which means Iron-Knee in the Gaelic. I imagine this is a nickname rather than his real name but apparently, he is a famous reiver who has been banished from his brother's court for countless controversies, murders, rapes, and the like."

"Charming." I responded, "Where will the holmgang be held is there an island near here?"

"Apparently not, there are islands further out into the estuary but that would be too far for the crowd to go, and there will be a vast crowd to be sure. No, Murchad intends to stake out the hazel rods on some flat ground outside the wall." Martin explained.

"Right, I am sure that Murchad will not play by the rules but I want the sword Dragon's Breath, my father gifted me and want my mail ready but I doubt we will use any, the fight will be 'baresark'. My father's shield I will not use as I do not want it damaged but I am sure that the three shields I will be supplied with will be defective." I smiled at Martin hoping I looked confident, which I was not.

"You will conquer." Was Martin's parting shot.

The following day I was led out of the hall by the king's men and on through the town. A large crowd had assembled outside the wall on the west side of the town, an area called 'The Green'. Apparently, it had been given out that the duel was to be held over a girl, which we both coveted. No mention of who she was but it had been explained to the townsfolk that I was some viking rover. The hazel rods had been staked out in the traditional fashion with only limited room for manoeuvre, ropes had been tied between each rod and if either of the combatants touched these ropes, they would be deemed forfeit. Martin stood on one side of the area holding three round wooden shields. I looked across to the other side of the holmgang arena and saw my opponent. He was undoubtably the largest man I had ever seen, taller than Thorfinn MacBeth and whereas the Alban king was thin, this Gluniairn was bulky, a mass of muscles. His upper torso was bare and covered in tattoos so that his body looked mostly blue. I noted that there were some scars and I took comfort from this, he had been hit in the past so he could be hit again. His hair hung loose and unkempt like a Pict or Finn and it partially covered his face, which was also covered in tattoos. He was an ugly brute.

His only clothing was some woven trews tied tight around the calf and then I noticed his 'iron knee'. On his right knee he had an iron cap fitted with a wicked spike standing proud from its centre. Clearly this was the genesis of his nickname and of course his wearing of this unusual weapon was not strictly acceptable within the rules of holmgang. However, I had been left in my war

155

boots that had metal bands stitched in them to protect from leg cuts so I deemed that a fair exchange.

I entered the hazel ring and realised Gluniairn towered over me by well over a foot. King Murchad entered the arena, all smiles.

"For your entertainment you are privileged to observe a match between my uncle the renowned Gluniairn and this young viking known as the Bearslayer. Iron Knee against the Bearslayer. The Irish cheered Gluniairn but I noticed that the majority of the crowd, Dubliners of Danish and Norwegian origin remained silent, sullen almost. Clearly the Irish rule in Dublin was not popular with the locals and I decided to exploit this situation. I shouted to the crowd,

> *"Outlaw and viking am I,*
> *Lordless and landless,*
> *Through land and sea, I fare,*
> *Soft is my elf locks, hard my sword edge,*
> *Wakeful men call me,*
> *In Alba I slew the fairy bear,*
> *Took his white fur coat,*
> *At my sword stroke I felled him,*
> *Wolf of the holmgang,*
> *Splinterer of the wooden wall,*
> *Iron knees won't help him.*
> *Dragon's Breath will seek him out"*

I paraded around the ring, disclaiming my worth and the Norse of Dublin warmed to my courage, a courage I was not sure I had against this monster.

"Skall to the stranger." "Skall to the young viking." The crowd cried in my favour.

Obviously, this did not please King Murchad who sidled up to me. "Crow all you like Bearslayer, but my uncle will kneel on your neck with his iron knee and your bones will crack."

The hulking Gluniairn stood menacingly saying nothing, I noticed he was chewing something, slowly masticating until tiny droplets of foam started to dribble from the sides of his mouth.

"My lord," Martin shouted from the edge of the ring, "He is chewing the berserker mushroom, take care." It was well known in the north that many of the so called 'berserkers' chewed hallucinogenic mushrooms that gave them increased strength and agility. Berserkers were notoriously hard to kill, even maiming them and wounding them rarely slowed them down.

Three wooden shield boards were placed against the hazel rods behind me, where Martin was in support ready to pass the shields forward as necessary and I was allowed to keep my sword, the sword that my father had given me. I examined the shield boards and could see that they were old and worn and in particular that they had no iron rim strengtheners. However, I took heart from the fact that they depicted black ravens on their faces. Perhaps they were remnants of the 'Great Army' led by the sons of Ragnar Lodbrok.

"High flies the ravens,
Huginn and Muninn,
The sons of Lodbrok the Irish feared,
When the wings beat take heart,
Northmen victorious."

Gluniairn's shields looked in better shape than mine and they did have iron bands around the rims. Well, I did not expect a fair fight but the odds were stacking up. I took up my first shield and faced my opponent. In a holmgang there are strict rules and there was normally an agreement on who should strike first but no instructions were given and the fight was suddenly precipitated when Murchad screamed.

"Begin, kill him uncle." Gluniairn came alive, he thundered across the arena at breakneck speed swinging his sword overhead, presumably with the intention of splitting me in two from poll to crotch. Before I had time to raise my shield in defence his sword came swinging down. I twisted to the side and his sword caught on my shield rim and went through it like paper, almost half of my shield fell away. By the rules of holmgang I should have been permitted to discard this shield and take up another but I realised the rules counted for nothing. Gluniairn pressed me relentlessly with a back hand swing that again caught in my shield. He punched forward with his shield allowing me no time to riposte with my own sword and I staggered backwards nearly falling. He tugged backwards with his sword trying to release it from my shield and such was the strength of his tug I lost my grip on the shield, this surprised me as my grip was usually sure but I then realised that it was the shield grip that had snapped, probably due to woodworm. Gluniairn screamed with frustration as he stood trying to shake off my useless shield from his sword blade. This gave me the opportunity to run over to Martin and grab another shield. As I turned to face him Gluniairn was all over me, he brought his sword down on my head with the shield still attached like a huge ungainly club. I dodged and ducked but the shield caught me on the side of the head and on my left shoulder sending me sprawling on the ground. Although dazed I had enough presence of mind to cover my torso with my shield hoping he would not chop at my legs. In his fury Gluniairn stood over me and thrashed down with his sword with my old shield still attached. It hit square onto my second shield and it felt like the hammers of hell smashing into my body. The shield attached to his sword splintered into a hundred pieces but my shield remained intact with me relatively unharmed underneath. In desperation I thrust out my sword and felt it connect with something. Gluniairn screamed again but it did not sound like it was because he was in pain so I assumed I had not harmed him. Nevertheless, I had time to role away, dazed as I was and forced myself to my knees before he came at me again. This time because I was so far beneath him, he had to stand back to make a swing at me. I anticipated another overhead pounding and it duly came with massive force onto my upturned shield, He did not seem to distinguish between me and my shield and he kept pounding uselessly on my shield board. I knew that eventually this shield would break too, but the few moments respite allowed me to think and I delivered a swipe at his unprotected left leg. My sword point connected, only an inch but it sliced into his calf just below his knee. Again, he appeared to show no signs of injury so I rolled away again and this time I managed to get to my feet however unsteady before he came after me.

As I stood the force of the crowds cheering, screaming, groaning assailed my ears. I danced away from the giant and this time he did not immediately follow me. He stared menacingly at the crowd who immediately fell silent. I could see that blood was streaming down both of Gluniairn's legs so I had had some effect on him. I also realised I was bleeding from several cuts and there was definitely a stickiness about my left ear. The ogre of a man turned towards me again and this time approached me in a lumbering gait, shield, and sword to the fore. I danced away to my right, his left, keeping us, shield to shield, and masking my movements. With a bellow he swung his sword wide in an arc, which I knew would lodge in my shield. I stepped into the arc of the blow and rammed my sword point first into the giant's thigh. I felt the sword point slide in remorselessly until it hit bone but at that point Gluniairn's sword slammed into my shield and I was thrown sideways back onto the floor. I slid a couple of paces across the ground and nearly collided with the hazel rods. My shield had exploded into shivers and I had a deep cut behind my left arm bicep. I flexed my left fist and was assured nothing was broken but I was bleeding badly. Strangely this wound, bad as it was, seemed to galvanise me and I jumped to my feet ready to defend myself.

Gluniairn stood before me with blood sheeting down both legs, he was losing blood quickly, I believe that when he smashed me away my sword point had twisted in the wound and severed an artery. His eyes were bloodshot and wild, I do not think he felt any pain. Suddenly he threw away his shield and rushed at me, at least he thought he rushed at me, his legs would not respond to his demands and a rush became a stumble. He reached out to grapple with me and to save myself from a sword cut I was compelled to step within his arms so that his sword swung harmlessly behind me. I drove my sword as hard as I could into his stomach trying to twist the blade up towards his heart. Gluniairn's arms enfolded me and tightened. He started to squeeze me in a relentless attempt to crush my body. Try as I might I could not bust free, his strength was overwhelming and I could feel myself weakening, my eyesight blurring. He was going to crush me to death. He had lifted me off my feet and our faces were aligned. I could see into his sightless eyes, his pupils dilated by the drug he had consumed. He could already be dead but he was still killing me. Vainly I rammed my head into his face with what little strength I had left. I tried again, no response, what could I do, repetitively I butted his face with mine unto all I could see was blood. I kept on head butting him until I lost consciousness.

Eventually I fought my way out of the miasma of insensibility, I tried to open my eyes but something was stopping my eyelids from working. I tried to move but I could not. I knew I was not dead because I hurt too much. I felt pain in all my limbs and my face throbbed. I lay on my back and was too tired to emit even a groan. I must have fallen asleep or lost consciousness again eventually I was awoken again by the feel of cool water on my face. The damp cloth gently bathed my eyelids and I could feel the encrusted blood loosening its grip and finally I found I could open my eyes.

"Martin." I croaked.

"Yes, master. I am here and you may live if I can repair these wounds." Martin was working to clean up my naked torso. Many scratches and abrasions hurt like the fires of hell but they were as nothing to the two or three deeper wounds, one to my left arm, one to my skull and another to my chest where Martin assured me only a few ribs were broken.

"Did that mad bastard die?" I croaked.

"He did and just to make sure his own brother put a blackthorn stake through his heart just to keep him that way." Martin quipped.

"His brother?" I gasped, what brother?

"Save that, my lord. You need rest while I sew up these wounds. Drink this it will help." Martin proffered me a flask of some stinking concoction that I would normally spit out but I was suddenly overcome by a tremendous thirst and swallowed it all down. I drifted off into a deep sleep.

Martin's time in the monastery was not wasted as he was a superior physician for after several days of recuperation, I was able to stand and hobble about. The cut in my arm throbbed and I had to wear a sling to keep the weight off the tendons whilst they healed. My ribs had knitted together well and were just a dull ache as long as I did not aggravate them. I had a swelling on the side of my face the size of an egg and a splitting headache but as long as I moved my head slowly, I could manage. I

160

challenged Martin for an explanation of our circumstances at the first opportunity and he was delighted to inform me that our situation was for the better. Apparently as Gluniairn and I lay on the floor of the holmgang arena Murchad was all for killing me but the crown of Dubliners shouted him down and were so aggressive that he and his bodyguard felt intimidated. The situation was likely to come to blows when up rode none other than King Diarmait, Murchad's father, demanding to know what was going on.

Martin explained further. "It turned out that King Diarmait was already on his way to Dublin because he had become disturbed by rumours of the way his son was behaving. Dublin is very important to the King of Leinster and the last thing he wanted was his son messing things up with the locals. Apparently, King Diarmait was not on good terms with his berserk half-brother Gluniairn either. The foul ogre had become somewhat of an embarrassment to him as he went around raping nuns and killing merchants and when he found out his son had attached himself to his errant uncle he decided on a visit."

So, it would seem that I had unwittingly done the King of Leinster a favour as killing your own half-brother never looks good, whatever the circumstances.

"What of Aleif's daughter, and Una?" I asked.

"They are held close by King Diarmaid but I don't think he means them harm." Martin responded.

"I need to speak to the King as soon as he will grant me an audience." I muttered. Martin gave me a quizzical look, probably wondering why I was overly concerned about another man's woman. Later that day I hobbled into the King's hall and sat at the nearest trestle table to the door. I could just see the high seat through the smoke of the fire, whereat sat King Diarmait Mael na mBo, King of Leinster and next to him his snivelling son Murchad. I could also see young Sunhild seated at the top table looking down pensively into her goblet. No sign of Una. A serving maid came and gave Martin and I a hunk of bread and bowl of stew each. The bread was newly baked, as one would expect in a king's hall and the stew was delicious soaked into the bread. I realised that I was famished and that my appetite was returning. I would soon have to resume light training to prevent my muscles wasting through neglect. The king's herald came slowly down the hall to stand before me.

"The king, my master, wishes to talk to you." The herald as was the nature of such beings preened himself and displayed his fine clothes. I sat in my worn shirt, the tears and rips had been repaired by Martin, but the blood stains still showed faintly despite the hard washing it had been subject to. My sailor's pants were clean but faded and only my boots and belt showed my possible worth. Nevertheless, like all true vikings I had spent some time washing and combing my hair so that it cascaded in blonde clean tresses. Like all in the hall I was unharmed, many had left their weapons outside but Martin and I had left ours in our room. Although I did know Martin always kept his small axe in his shirt. I arose and hobbled down to the high seat and stood before the King of Leinster.

"You are he who people call the Bearslayer?" the King enquired in a deep melodious voice. He was a regal looking man, dressed magnificently. Like his father Mael na mBo he was nearly bald, obviously a family trait, but this was neatly hidden by a gold circlet atop of a velvet cap. Despite the loss of head hair, he was hirsute with a quite splendid flowing beard of red hair.

"I am Hereward Leofricson, a son of Earl Leofric of Mercia in England and brother to Earl Aelfgar of the East Angles. I am called by the name Bearslayer but I am often referred to as the outlaw as I have been outside of the law in England this past three years now."

"And what do you do with yourself, other than kill people at will? The king enquired again, mildly.

"I have spent much of my time fighting for my friends and kin. For my friend I cite Earl Thorfinn of Orkney, sometimes called King MacBeth of Alba. For my kin I have fought for my brother Aelfgar and for my cousin-in-law Gryffudd, King of North Wales. I rarely pick fights heedlessly or unprovoked."

"But you fought my half-brother, Gluniairn." Not a question but an affirmation.

"I had little choice in the matter," I glanced over at Murchad who sat sulkily sipping his drink.

The King of Leinster looked thoughtful, then continued, "I have heard from those who know, that is those who have fought alongside you in Wales and Alba, that you are something of a master of war, a tactician as the Romans name them."

"I usually see things clearly in battle, tis true, but I am sure I have just been lucky at times, or my opponents have been overconfident or foolish." I answered as honestly as I could without bragging Martin smiled at that, knowing how hard I found it to be modest.

"Would you fight for me?" the king leant forward eager for a positive answer.

"I have provisos, I will not fight against my kin or friends but other than that I would fight for you." I replied.

"Good, I will hold you to that, but not now. I can see that you need time to recover from your fight with my obnoxious unlamented half-brother. Yule is nearly upon us and I would welcome you to my court in my rath at Fearns."

"My lord, I would ask after the daughter of Aleif, that Sunhild who I have vowed to return to her betrothed in Veðrafjǫrðr." Martin sighed, why did I always have to push things too far?

"Ah! Sunhild, a sweet little thing, a bit too young for my taste. I hold her safe and she will accompany us to Fearns. I certainly would not trust her with my foolish son." The king glanced across at Murchad. "I will be leaving another of my brothers, a reliable one, with my son to ensure my rule in Dublin is wiser and calmer. Rest assured that Sunhild will come to no harm; the rule of Veðrafjǫrðr is in my remit as well as Dublin. It is important that the viking adventurers work for the benefit of Ireland, not against it. I do not mind the odd raid east over sea or even in the north, Ulster, or Connaught, but they must be under my direction. Young Ragnald of Veðrafjǫrðr is compliant enough, unlike that wolf Eachmarchach who had to be chased out of Dublin. If Ragnald receives his bride from me that will make him more my client and less in the grip of Aleif." The king leaned down and offered me his goblet of wine.

"Drink." I took a long draught and saw that there was a gold arm ring lodged in the cup. "Skall to the viking." The king shouted.

Yule in the rath at Fearns was a joyous affair not least because Sunhild was joined to Ragnald in matrimony and I finally lost my virginity. King Dairmait Mael na mBo was not slow in informing Ragnald of Veðrafjǫrðr that he had his betrothed in his custody and invited him to the Yule feast. Ragnald arrived hotfoot and eager to comply with his overlord's invitation. The Veðrafjǫrðr Norse were not what they were and trading was their main interest; Ragnald's father had built up a solid economic base in Veðrafjǫrðr and Ragnald was not the young warrior to disrupt it. Dairmait was clearly pleased with Ragnald's compliance and suggested an immediate Yule wedding.

Ragnald sought me out and thanked me effusively for saving his betrothed from dishonour; although Ragnald had not met Sunhild before the betrothal, he had now and was clearly smitten. He offered me a treasure for my services, which I gallantly refused much to Martin's horror.

Martin had sailed my snekkja *Ottar* from Dublin down to Veðrafjǫrðr and then rejoined me at Fearns and whilst away had commandeered Una to see to my welfare. She was efficient at tending my wounds and with various poultices ensured none went bad. I found I was very shy with her, which was not like me but I realised I had no idea how to behave with women. She recommended I rode on a docile pony rather than ride in a wagon that would probably shake my bones and do more damage. She walked alongside my pony and gradually I learned how to talk with a woman, other than my mother or niece.

"Una, how did you come to be in Cornwall, when clearly you are Irish?" I asked.

"I was in a handfast marriage with one of Aleif's chieftains, a half-Irish, half-Norse trader, he was much older than I and actually he bought me from my father, a minor king in Ossory. When Aleif fled to Cornwall my husband sailed in his knarr with him and took me along. My husband went trading south overseas and never came back, after two years Aleif suggested I would be a good nurse for his daughter, he took my husband's farm so I had no choice."

"You are the daughter of a king?" I was astonished.

Una laughed, "You are obviously not familiar with Irish customs, every rath has its king, and every tribe has its tribal king, every part of Erinn has its over-king and every one of the over-kings strives to be Ard Righ Erinn, the high king; me being a daughter of a rath king is at best a minor chieftain's daughter in your polity." I joined in her laughter, it warmed me. We gossiped about many subjects, she was particularly interested in my white bearskin shoulder protector and wanted to know about the white polar bears from which it came. I related to her how King Knut the Mighty had had twelve such bear skins, which he displayed in some church or other. She was interested in how Asbjorn Siwardson was connected to bears so I explained the history of Siward Bjorn and how his father was said to have been born from a bear and a princess. I then explained that what this really meant was that the family descended from the bear clan in Oster Gotland that could trace their ancestry all the way back to a great hero called Bodvarr Biarki, or 'Battle Bear', also known to the English as Beowulf, many centuries ago.

She wanted to know why I was an outlaw in England; this question led to a lengthy discourse of English politics. I thought she would be scandalised when I explained I had an aversion to the Christian church but she seemed quite amused and I gathered that the Irish did not see the Catholic church in England and in Rome as a true Christian community.

I found it much harder to talk about lighter subjects, trivialities to me but I found she had a great store of knowledge about trees and plants and nature in general. She seemed to know the names of every type of bird of the air and every type of tree and plant and what they were good for. I felt humbled by my lack of knowledge and realised that although I had absorbed everything I could read or learn about warlike practices and had neglected many, many things. She was older than me, maybe by as much as ten years. She was a voluptuous woman, not a girl and I realised that appealed to me. I wanted her physically but had no idea how to go about it.

The road to Fearns from Dublin skirted the Sléibhte Chill mountain to the west of Vicklo and followed the coast through two smaller Norse settlements at Vicklo and Arklow. The distance was not much less than eighty miles and took over a week to traverse. After three days sitting on the docile pony, I decided that walking would be better for my battered body as I needed to strengthen it and loosen tightening wounds. Una did not object to this; her time was divided between me and Sunhild. Sunhild rode with the king at the head of the column while I trailed along in the rear. I did sleep in the cart though, as the ground was cold and wet, fortunately there was no snow. Apparently, it rarely snowed in Ireland but it rained all the time.

By the fifth day we started to climb up from the coast, west into rolling hills south of Arklow. I was feeling much better and slung my sword and shield over my shoulder to increase the weight my body supported. Although tired by the end of the day I was not worn out and happily sat around a large fire listening to one of the Irish bards, or Ollamhain, or Filidhe, I think the Irish call them. He had a small harp that he nestled in to his hip and as he sang, he played wonderful supportive chords mimicking feelings, sounds of horses and even the weather. It was quite entrancing although I did not understand a word of it. Una sat down beside me and explained what the song or poem was all about. Apparently, many years ago there was a warrior band that defended all Ireland against the vikings. This band was called the Fianna and was led by a great hero Fionn Mac Cumhal. There were many great heroes in the Fianna but the most handsome was Dairmait O'Duine. Fionn was betrothed to a princess called Grainne but she fell in love with Diarmait and they ran away together. Una explained that the song was about the pursuit of Dairmait and Grainne around all Ireland; I realised I could hear the baying of the hounds and the drumming of horses' hooves in the music. The tune had a tragic feel to it and I suspected even before Una explained it that the ending was tragic death and sadness.

"The bard is very good." I commented to Una as the crowd's cheers and applause died down.

"He should be, he is King Dairmait's personal filidhe and accounted the best in Ireland."

I went to the cart to sleep very contented that night and Una returned to her charge. I awoke in the silent of the night instinctively making a grab for my dagger. My hand collided with an arm and a hand that was covering the hilt of my dagger.

"I don't want you to stab me with this sharp weapon, I was thinking of a blunter one." The husky voice in the dark was female, there was a fragrance of wild flowers.

"Una!" I exclaimed.

"Shhsh, don't talk." Una moved beside me, removing the dagger, and placing it above my head where it would harm no one. I had removed my shirt earlier as I preferred to sleep cool and Una's hand caressed my chest and it provocatively slid down my torso and fumbled with the string of my trousers under the white bearskin. I rolled onto my back, this allowed me to use both hands and I clasped her shoulders and drew her towards me.

"I like your clean chin." She murmured, "I hate hairy men with their rough beards." Her hand loosened my drawstring and she slid her fingers down over my abdomen and grasped my erect shaft. I gasped in shock, no one had ever touched me there before, I thought my member would burst, explode.

"You hardly have any hair down there either, this is wonderful, your body is like a Greek god or Baldur of the Shining Limbs." She whispered. I could feel that Una was only wearing a thin shift, she must have partly disrobed before she climbed into the cart. I reached down and found her hip and ran my hand down her leg until I reached the rucked-up hem of her shift. I grasped the hem and felt Una sway away from my body allowing me to lift the shift clear of her torso and under her armpits. She settled down again against me and I could feel the complete nakedness of her against my body. Smooth and sweet my hands roamed across her, cupping her breasts, gently rubbing her taut nipples, and finally cupping her loins, caressing the silky hair between her legs. She was very aroused; I could tell from the excessive wetness between her legs. She was clinging to me gasping and moaning.

"I know you haven't done this before but don't fret, it will be quick but I want it, I want it now." She hissed. I forced her back and spread her legs with my own. I felt a slight twinge from my ribs but this did not dampen my ardour. Instinctively I tried to align my throbbing member with her vulva; in the dark this involved some guesswork but almost immediately I felt her hand grasp my member and pull it towards her. I felt the bulbous end touch something wet and warm.

"Yes, yes, push." She whispered. I pushed, none too gently but this did not seem to matter as my appendage slipped into her vagina inexorably. I felt like I was going to explode, her vaginal walls closed upon me tight but rippling. I had the uncontrollable urge to ram her like I had seen dogs do, vigorously, forcefully. Her voice was urging me on but my mind had lost clarity, my body was consuming me like fire. I was jerking uncontrollably until suddenly I was on a higher plane; my mind cleared the pistoning motion of my loins was magically rhythmical and I could feel something frighteningly tight building up in my ball sack. I could not have stopped if I had wanted to, but...

"Spurt, come in me now." Una's voice caressed my ear. I exploded, the heat from my testicles coalesced into a molten jet of fluid that rushed up the shaft of my penis and shot out in violent jets deep into Una's womb. I tried to keep thrusting but the intensity of my first orgasm was such that I felt I was falling away, losing control, becoming weaker by the moment.

"Ssshh! There my brave lover; you have conquered, you have taken your first woman. You are a full man now." Una soothed me and gripped me with her legs entwinned about my torso. Her womanly parts still rhythmically massaged my shaft, not letting me slip out. I could feel rippling sensations as the internal walls of her vagina clenched and unclenched against me. Miraculously I could feel my member regaining some hardness and I started to match her rhythm.

"Yes, yes, take me again." Una mewled in ecstasy providing with an immediate fillip. We went on to make love three times during the night and I eventually helped her to achieve a climax. I learnt a lot that night.

Our bouts of love making were repeated the following nights as we neared Fearns. Rather than setting back my recuperation it seemed to invigorate me and aided the healing process. Martin was amazed at my good health when we were reunited at Yule. For my part I noticed, when I had time to ponder that my regular assignations with Una had completely wiped out my obsession with my mother-in- law, Godgifu. Maybe this was part of 'growing up', I was only eighteen, soon to be nineteen and although I had seen enough fighting for a lifetime the more mundane aspects of life had passed me by.

So, Yule passed in a whirl of celebration and sex. Was I in love? It certainly felt like it, Martin, who had come up from Veðrafjǫrðr where he had berthed my *Ottar*, said nothing but he could see I was distracted? It never occurred to me that we should marry, I suppose my inherent prejudices, me being an earl's son, an earl who ruled a third of England and area equal to the size of all Ireland and Una being a daughter of a village chieftain. I suppose if I had thought about it at all I expected to marry to my station, an earl's daughter no less. Yet I could have made her a handfast wife, as is the way of the pagan vikings and my father but this often is prompted by a liaison resulting from a pregnancy and Una never became pregnant.

Yule eventually passed and King Ragnald of Veðrafjǫrðr and his new bride, Sunhild made to leave. Everything came to a head quickly. Sunhild wanted Una to accompany her to Veðrafjǫrðr, I was in two minds whether to follow when a messenger from King Gryffudd arrived asking for my help in another flare up with the English. I was torn, fighting was my trade and if I settled in Veðrafjǫrðr, I would become just another merchant or local chief. This was not appealing to me and Una knew this. The upshot was that I decided to go to Wales but promised Una I would then come to Veðrafjǫrðr and perhaps help the King of Leinster in his wars. We all travelled down to Veðrafjǫrðr for I needed to collect my ship and crew and in the few days left to us we made love fervently.

In no time at all, however, I was at sea. I had no trouble raising a warlike crew from Veðrafjǫrðr, all wanted to sail with the Bearslayer and it was well known those that did were amply rewarded. I had a new sailing master, Egil, an old rogue who used to sail with Ragnald's father and who wanted to recapture his youth before taking the 'swan's path' to Valhalla. He certainly was not a Christian but then again, I was not sure that I was. My snekkja *Ottar* was made of good Irish oak and was built probably before Eachmarchach was expelled from Dublin, it was maybe twenty years old. It was a twenty bencher so I needed forty rowers, substitutes, and additional warriors, plus the sailing master and a couple of rigging lads; a crew of upwards of fifty-three. I managed to sail with sixty on board, with a real bonus of an apprentice sailing master in Egil's son Eystein.

To leave Veðrafjǫrðr we coasted down the River Suir for a few miles before we entered the River Bannow heading south to the sea. When we hit the tidal flow in the Bannow we had to man the oars to pass the Hook so that we could turn towards England and Wales. We sailed east along the coast from Veðrafjǫrðr, as it was early in the year, not quite spring, with late winter storms still prevalent, we kept close to shore with the intention of beaching at night and running for shelter at the first sign of a squall. We were in luck with a constant if robust south-easterly, the wind that tended to push us towards the shore and the helmsman had to fight the wind to keep us off the beach but when we saw the cairn on the south-east headland of Ireland pass us by with the open sea ahead, we made a run for Wales hoping the wind would not change or increase.

I was still new to the sea and it was exhilarating flying across the waves at a quite unimaginable speed, certainly as fast, if not faster than a horse could gallop. The one hundred miles of so distance between the two islands were quickly traversed and we made it from the foot of Ireland to the Bar of the River Mawddach in one day in the daylight hours, and at this time of the year that was no mean feat. Crossing the sandy bar, we rowed into the wide estuary of the river. Egil, who had raided in this area many years before informed me that the river was navigable for a snekkja up to a place called Llanelltyd, where we would have to leave the boat. I was not worried about this as we were well within Powys, Gryffudd's kingdom, and well away from Hereford where trouble was likely to be looked for. The longship would be safe with a small guard whilst we raided further east.

A suitable anchorage was found in the centre of the river with the boat pegged to a sand bar. We would have to wade off, maybe swim a little but it would help safeguard the snekkja until we returned. Egil who preferred fighting at sea and had already fallen in love with *Ottar* chose to stay with the rigging lads and two other warriors, the least agile of the crew. The rest of the crew, Martin and I set off south along the river bank to the nearest sizeable Welsh fortress, which I knew was called Dolgellau. I informed the chief of this place of the presence of my snekkja and how it should not be attacked whilst I was off supporting his king. Fortunately, the chief, a jovial fellow by the name of

Hywel, knew of me and considered it a great honour to protect my boat. He wanted to wine and dine my crew and I but I was not too sure of the urgency of my mission so declined and hurried on. My band of warriors had to traverse the southern foothill passes of the mighty mountainous massif of Gwynedd heading towards Y Trallwng and thence on to Mathrafal. It was still late-winter and the upper slopes were covered in snow, we kept as low down the hillsides as possible to speed our journey but still had to contend with the rain and enumerable swollen streams.

We straggled into Mathrafal near the end of March as the weather was picking up. We were warmly welcomed by both King Gryffudd and his wife, my niece, Eadgyth. I was invited to see their new daughter, a petite infant called Nesta. Gryffudd already had two grown up sons so he revelled in his new daughter. Eventually I had the opportunity to raise the question uppermost in my mind. "You have summoned me and I am here, what is the threat, who is your enemy this time?"

Gryffudd looked slightly uncomfortable, "After Hereford, after your brother and your vikings left my chieftains in the south kept raiding into England. Not only into Hereford, a prospect that would not have concerned me but east into the Hwicce, your father's old lands."

"Has my father retaliated?" I asked perturbed by this turn of events.

"No, he has been very circumspect. He sent a herald requesting that I control my chiefs and warned me that his writ does not run in the Hwicce anymore. Apparently, Harald Godwinson has appointed a shire reeve to supervise Herefordshire whilst Earl Ralph is ailing and abed in Gloucester, a man called Elnoth and he has appointed your father's cousin, a Godwine Leofricson, as Alderman of the Hwicce.

"So, you're saying that the English intend to retaliate into your territory." I concluded.

"It may be so. In addition to these appointments Bishop Athelstan of Hereford died a few weeks back and Earl Harald arranged for his mass-priest to be appointed in his place. This new Bishop, Leofgar is apparently very militant and wears mail over his cassock. Even if Reeve Elnoth and Godwine Leofricson are not inclined to attack Powys it would appear that Bishop

Leofgar will, in revenge for the burning of Hereford's church and the massacre of the monks."

I thought about my relationship with my family, I would not fight my father but I did not know this relative, this Godwine Leofricson, at all. The other two magnates were unknown to me also. "We must be ready, it would be unwise to pre-empt any attack with a counter raid as we do not want to bring all the English forces into play, especially my father. I suggest we place scouts on all our approaches and set contingency plans for any attack. We must lure the English into a disadvantageous position and then repulse them." I was already working out various possibilities in my mind.

"Good, I knew I could count on you. They will never win against your fighting ability. My men will follow you more eagerly than they will follow me, they will feel assured of victory." Gryffudd looked satisfied, pleased his machinations had worked out.

"One thing though." I added, "This likely little war must have a better resolution than the last one. Aelfgar was restored to his earldom last time but a lasting treaty should have been concluded between the English King and yourself so that raiding stops." Gryffudd considered this, could he achieve this, was it possible for him to control his wild chieftains; raiding was very profitable and had been going on for years, centuries even. "Edward the Mild would have to recognise you as king of all Wales." I added, and that clinched it.

Spring 1056 - Powys

I had scouts out all around the southern perimeter of Powys; not only watching the approaches from Herefordshire but the roads west from the rest of the Hwicce, mainly Worcestershire. I envisaged a flanking movement from Ludlow or Worcester towards Leominster and on into Powys by-passing the northern road from Hereford, flanking the site where we had fought Earl Ralph the previous year. A strike north-west across the Shropshire hills was equally a possibility, a thrust directly at Mathrafal. I believed that a direct attack west from Shrewsbury was most unlikely as that town was solidly within my father's control.

Martin was chief scout, he excelled at this type of work and he coordinated those Welshmen chosen to infiltrate the English towns and watch the fords of the River Lugg. I had no intention of being surprised. I knew that any raid into Powys would be an English affair as the Norman chivalry would not follow an English leader. Any host would therefore be mainly on foot, a nucleus of huscarls and the local fyrd. I was therefore keen to improve the quality of my Welsh warriors with a regime of training. I arranged for small bands of men to be sent to me from each settlement in Southern Powys to undergo two weeks of stiff training in infantry formations and use of various weapons. Few Welsh warriors had mail and at best had leather jackets with metal plates as strengtheners. For hunting they favoured light javelins and slings, much as the Irish. I made sure that all the men had a shield as there would be no chance at all withstanding the English shield wall without one. Each group was shown how to make a shield and sent home to make one for everyone in their settlement who were to be summoned to repel the anticipated raid. There were hardly any swords but most men had a long vicious dagger and a wood axe. I set my vikings to train the Welsh on the use of an axe in the shield wall. The art of axe work in a shield wall is to hook the opponents shield and expose them by pulling the shield down. The javelin men could then pierce the enemy successfully. The fighting line was intended to be a row of shield men with axes and a row of javelin men behind. Slingers on the flanks.

Training these men also helped me to regain my own physical fitness. I found that I was somewhat depressed by my circumstances, my life seemed to have become one long bout of fighting my own people for a king and people I had no real affinity with. I concluded that I was missing Una badly and for the first time in my life I was thinking about and caring for someone else other than myself. Perhaps being a hero was not all it was made out to be?

I had noticed when I was staying in Mathrafal previously that there was a group of Norsemen from Ireland that had settled west of Chester at the time of Alfred the Wessex King. The descendants of these warrior settlers were adept with the northern longbow for fighting from ship deck. I asked Gryffudd if he could persuade a group of these men to join us for together with my Irish Norse this would provide us with a formidable missile advantage. I was delighted when a band of these settlers arrived three weeks later led by Asmund Asmunderson a descendent of the original Norse settlers. There was only two score of them but each one had a large viking longbow and a full kit, mail, shield, sword and helmet, a match for any English huscarl. They were paid mercenaries to be sure but so was I, and I had more confidence in their ability than the Welsh hillmen.

Eventually eight days before midsummer the scouts came in reporting that the English were on the move. Martin's scouts reported that there was a large body of men moving west from the Hwicce, Worcester to be precise, moving towards Leominster and the crossing of the River Lugg there. Estimates indicated that there was upwards of six hundred warriors, all on foot with the usual mixture of huscarls and fyrd. Presumably these men were being led by Godwine Leofricson, my possible cousin, I suppose.

At the same time and obviously coordinated, another army had marched out of Hereford, or the ruins of the town, west towards the border at the River Wye. Obviously the two armies intended split the Welsh defenders preventing a combined Welsh army capable of defeating the main thrust into southern Powys. The army from Hereford was bigger than the army from the

Hwicce, maybe twice the size, again all foot. This army was led by the shire reeve, Elnoth, but also with an ecclesiastical coterie displaying a huge wooden cross carried on a cart and a high cleric, probably the Bishop of Hereford, riding a caparisoned horse wearing a mixture of canonical robes and armour. Together these two armies would number nearly two thousand men, mostly fyrdmen but with a nucleus of maybe four hundred huscarls, a formidable army indeed. I would be lucky if I could muster three hundred Welshmen, and together with the Norsemen, I had around just under four hundred men at my disposal.

King Gryffudd would, of course, march down from Mathrafal with many more warriors but it would take time for them to arrive and I did not want to give the English the pleasure of plundering the countryside, whilst the totality of King Gryffudd's forces assembled.

I gathered my lead men, the officers, of my small army. This included Martin, my chief scout, Asmund Asmunderson, leader of the Cheshire Vikings, Egil Eysteinson leading my ship's crew, and two Welsh chieftains, Owain from Llanandras, and Iestyn from Tref-y-clawdd, a small community further north. These last two were the recognized leaders in the area of southern Powys, they were related to King Gryffudd in some way and were noted warriors. Our camp was approximately two miles east of Llanandras in a lush meadow beside the River Lugg, I was sure the English had no idea where we were. Everyone assembled beneath a large oak tree as my mean tent that I shared with Martin could not accommodate more than the two of us.

"You all know the English are on their way. I do not intend to allow them to ravage southern Powys before Gryffudd arrives. If their two forces manage to combine, we will not be able to contain them so my intention is to keep the two forces apart." I looked at the faces of my men, all older than me, or most of them anyway. Nevertheless, they looked resolute, which was encouraging.

"How can we, so few, achieve this?" Owain of Llanandras asked; his settlement lay right in the path of the army moving west from Leominster.

"The army moving west from Leominster intends to cross the River Lugg somewhere east of Llanandras. I do not intend to allow them that route. We must persuade the forces under Godwine Leofricson to stay north of the river and advance along the north bank into Wales on a route that will keep them separated from the Hereford army. Meanwhile we must also slow the army west from Hereford so that we have time to destroy the English north of the Lugg."

"Yes, but how?" persisted Owain of Llanandras, he really was as young as I was.

"Part of our army will find a defensive site to hold the English advance from Hereford in the same way we stopped them before we burnt Hereford. Either a river ford or suitable defendable hill. The other part of our army will find a place on the River Lugg to prevent their crossing, probably in or near Llanandros. When they cannot cross and move on towards Wales on the north side of the river, we will then harry them to oblivion."

"There must be something I haven't seen; both our small detachments will still be heavily outnumbered; how can our force at the river harry their much larger force?" Thus, spoke young Egil Eysteinson.

"Horses." I responded. Egil still looked puzzled.

"None of the English hosts have horses in any numbers and I have seen how a few well managed horsed warriors can cause havoc that far outweighs their numbers. We do not have Norman knights but the Cheshire vikings rode down here and if we can muster another fifty of so hill ponies to mount my crew, we will have upwards of seventy archers that can decimate Godwine Leofricson's warriors before they even get close. If we can take down over two hundred of them, they will turn tail and run, nothing surer."

A heated discussion followed, debating the sanity of my plans, but it soon devolved into an argument into how and where. Young Owain was explaining that the River Lugg was not a wide river and that it meandered rather aimlessly. There was a ford at Llanandros, the main ford but there were also other spots where the river could be crossed. Nevertheless, he thought the ford could be held. The route of the southern Hereford army was less easy to predict, it appeared they were heading due west avoiding

176

the old battle ground at Weobley, which everyone agreed was too near Hereford for our men to successfully reach and fortify again. To cross into Wales proper, they had to cross the Wye at one of several fords; the likeliest being at Hay or Glasbury, or they might turn north. There was a dearth of high ground or suitable fortresses to dig in to. Iestyn from Tref-y-clawdd was of the opinion that the best and only way to stop them was at the fords.

The other issue was one of timing it was about twenty miles from Worcester to Leominster and a further ten miles from Leominster to Llanandros, so that it was likely that an army on foot would take two or three days to reach the Welsh border.

From Hereford to Hay on Wye was about twenty miles, but with a larger army moving slower, it too would also arrive in the area in about two or three days. This was a problem; how could we slow the southern army down? I did not want to fight both armies on the same day if I could help it.

Like any good general, and I hoped I was one, I had to be prepared to change my plans. The southern army had to be harassed and slowed down considerably so I decided to halve my horsed force, sending thirty archers south to harry the flanks of the southern army. I exchanged them for thirty Welsh javelin throwers who were also adept as slingers. We needed to move quickly; I decided I was needed with the southern force as they had to face the larger enemy army. Egil and Martin went with the troop to Llanandros to throw up a defensive barrier at the ford.

I moved my force south sending out scouts to find the vanguard of the Hereford force with the intention of harassing them even before they approached the fords into Wales. It was almost the same distance from Llanandros to Hay as it was from Hereford to Hay but I intentionally moved fast, leaving the foot behind to make their way independently to the Hay ford, and racing ahead to intercept the English.

We managed to intercept the English about five miles from Hay late on the second day, they were making camp in a broad meadow, which was easily fortified. They had just erected their tents, those that had shelters, that is, and settled down to eat supper, fires were soon burning and the smell of fresh meat began to permeate the air. The leaders of the English did have enough sense to place sentries, but in my opinion not nearly enough.

I decided that our harassment of the enemy would start as soon as darkness fell. A night attack is no place for horses, so I instructed Asmund Asmunderson to take the mounted javelin men to the far side of the English encampment and cut down any fleeing enemy. I then spread out my archers and slingers in a line. Quietly I gave instructions making sure everyone understood their role in the attack. I gave the word to go and they all sped away into the darkness but their silhouettes were clear to me against the fires of the enemy encampment. Silently the slingers crept forward and took out the sentries. A quiet whirring sound and the whoosh of the stone was all that could be heard. The noise of the falling sentry made much more noise but even this did not stir the camp, fortunately there was a strong wind that deadened their falls.

Within moments a young Welsh slinger ran back from the English camp with the embers from one of the dying fires. My archers had prepared several arrows each, tying strips of cloth to the arrow heads ready to light. Without instruction the slinger walked down the line of archers allowing each man to light his fire arrow, when all the archers had a lit arrow, they fired a ragged volley at the tents in the English camp. They then repeated the process as the young Welsh slinger retraced his steps back along the line of archers. Another volley of fire arrows fell on the tents. Very slowly the arrows smouldered, would they catch? Faint noises of alarm started to permeate the enemy camp, clearly the arrows penetrating the tent skins must have alarmed or woke some of the resting men. Suddenly one of the tents sprouted flames, which quickly engulfed the tent. The wind assisted the flames and one after another, tents on our side of the enemy encampment burst into flames. Within moments men started to tumble out of the burning tents and were quickly met by the deadly accuracy of the Norsemen's arrows and the bone breaking impacts of the Welsh slingers. Chaos ensued.

I decided to participate as I had brought my war bow with me and started shooting along with my men. It was simply a case of shooting at silhouettes. I quickly loosed six or seven shafts, each one finding a mark. In the dark it was impossible to tell if any of the shots were fatal but the screams and cries assured me that we were damaging the enemy. Initially, after the first few volleys it was noticeable that those tumbling from the tents were fleeing away from the edge of the encampment towards the centre, away from danger. After a few minutes the perimeter of the camp was deserted and the firing from my men died down from a lack of targets. There was shouting and a loud cacophony of noise emitting from the interior if the camp and it was obvious that a counter attack would be erupting from the camp shortly.

"Right lads, time to pull back disappear into the wood and rendezvous where we agreed," I shouted both in Welsh and Norse. There was no misunderstanding and my men melted back into the woods and individually skirted the enemy camp to liaise with our mounted troop. A quarter watch or so later most of the men had assembled together with Asmund's horsemen on the other side of the enemy encampment. The camp was still in an uproar but most of the noise came from the other side of the camp. I found Asmund, "How is it here?"

"We have had nothing to do, no one has come this way. I was sorely tempted to attack the camp from this side as the sentries rushed off when you attacked but I decided not to as it would then have revealed our rendezvous point."

"Good, I want you and the rest of the horsed warriors to attack and harry their rear guard in the morning. I think we may have put pay to maybe fifty of them with arrows and slings and we destroyed a lot of tents." I responded, quite satisfied with the night's work.

Some of our stragglers came in over the next hour and reported that they had difficulty circling the enemy encampment as quite a few fyrdmen were fleeing the camp back towards Hereford and they had to kill some of them to force a passage. This development was exactly what I was hoping for.

However, fate is inexorable and early the next morning the heavens opened to a deluge. The rain soon plastered us in mud and we floundered around. My scouts came in to inform me that the Hereford force had stayed in camp. They had flung up a miserable encampment from what was left of their burnt equipment and dug in for the duration of the bad weather. I prayed that it would be several days of bad weather. I immediately mounted my Welsh hill pony and rode north, leaving Asmund Asmunderson and Iestyn in charge. It was probably only just over twenty miles to Llanandros but it still took me a full watch to reach the ford in the torrid conditions. I was challenged by a picket set by Martin, a very good precaution in this weather as an outflanking manoeuvre would not be seen in such poor visibility; I was then directed to the leadership position.

Falling off my pony, I wearily asked, "What is the situation here?"

Martin smiled, "Good day master. If you observe the ford it has swollen to twice its normal height in the last hour. Most of our men are fortifying this side of the ford but I have Egil with twenty men on the other side of the river in case we need a flanking attack when the enemy arrive. However, my scouts tell me that the force from Worcester has settled in to Leominster sheltering from the rain and are hardly likely to move until the weather improves."

"Circumstances change Martin and we must change with them. It looks like there will be no action here at the ford for the next two, maybe three days, so we must force a resolution with the Hereford force. I will take the rest of the horsed archers, it is a pity Egil and his men are on the other side of the ford and we cannot get them back, but no matter; and I will take the thirty javelin-armed Welsh to bolster my force. Somehow, I intend to flank the Hereford army with my lighter infantry and harry their flanks and rear; demoralise them before the army you face leaves Leominster. Hopefully I will be back in a couple of days to support you." I sounded confident but I was not.

I rounded up the men I was taking with me and got as many mounted as I could and rode back to my little force in the south. The rain persisted and it was an uncomfortable ride, particularly for those left on foot that were hanging on to their comrades' stirrups. I arrived back from whence I started that day as dusk approached, with my men straggling in behind me, but still had time to call my chiefs to a war council. We sheltered under a large tree, the canopy of leaves giving the best possible cover under the circumstances. I looked around at my bedraggled men and laughed.

"You all look like drowned rats and I imagine the English are no better off; but we are Welsh and vikings and we are better than them. While they cower in their tents from the rain, we will show them that rain is nothing to a mountain Welshman or sea roving viking." They smiled at that; it amused them to think we were better than the opposition. "Early on the morrow I intend to leave all the infantry at Hay to hold the ford, and all the archers. You will be the holding ford in case the enemy advance but I do not intend that to happen." I had their attention now. "All the horse and the slingers will come with me; we will make our way across the drowned land between us and the enemy and flank them. I want to attack their right flank and rear. I do not intend to close with them, we will harass them with javelins and sling stones. In this weather the archers are virtually useless anyway as the rain will eventually ruin their bow strings, but javelins and sling stones will still be deadly. Any questions?"

"Why just the right flank?" Iestyn queried.

"Good question. I want the untrained fyrdmen to feel they can flee away east or south. It means we are attacking the non-shield side of their army and besides many of the fyrdmen will not have shields." I explained.

"What if they do continue to advance against my archers?" Asmund looked thoughtful, perhaps not liking the odds.

"As I said your bows will eventually become useless in this weather, so I want you to resist, but not put yourselves at risk. If the huscarls come at you in force, fall back." Asmund nodded, obviously pleased that he was not being asked to sacrifice his men needlessly.

"No more questions? Right try and rest, possibly sleep, we move before dawn."

Having worked out in my mind what needed to be done I realised that my little army would need to circle around the English army again as we were now on the wrong side to launch the attack that I intended. This did not particularly bother me because assuming that the English moved forward, I would simply lead my men across the ruins of their encampment attacking the English both from the rear and their right flank. I needed to give my men the best opportunity to inflict damage to the enemy without endangering lives.

The men led by Iestyn moved west before dawn to beat the English to the Hay ford, I marshalled my men, partook of a breakfast of cold meats, hard cheese, and bread, and moved up to the treeline to observe the English break camp. The English camp looked a sorry affair, perhaps a third of the tents were burnt or damaged, some fires were burning, despite the rain, to prepare a hot meal for the huscarls, the fyrdmen looked dispirited, hungry, wet, and cold. Even in the dawn light I could see a few fyrdmen slipping away east to their homes. We had perhaps reduced the enemy numbers by two hundred, but they still outnumbered my horsemen by twenty to one. They were so disorganised that I felt we could attack immediately.

"Right lads, we are going to ride right across the rear of the camp, as we go, I want each one of you to ride in close and throw a javelin, make it count, if we can kill or maim twenty or thirty fyrdmen, three times that number will desert and run home to Hereford."

I raised my own javelins, three, and kicked my pony forward, he objected so I kicked harder and he resentfully broke into a trot, then a canter. We all emerged from the tree line together but quickly formed into a loose line, I led. We cantered towards the enemy encampment heading towards the eastern perimeter. Cries of alarm soon rent the air and men started running for their shields and spears. I looked to see if any of the huscarls were present trying to marshal the fyrdmen but there were none apparent. My pony was determined not to go faster than a canter but it really did not matter as none of the English foot men could keep up with us in the atrocious conditions. As I cantered towards the tents most of the fyrdmen turned and ran into the centre of the encampment and I became concerned that there would be no one to kill. However, as luck would have it a huscarl arrived on the scene screaming for the fyrdmen to stand and face us. He did not call for a shield wall because he could see that most of the fyrdmen did not have a shield. He pushed and pulled the fyrdmen into a line, spears levelled at us but of course we had no intention of charging a hedge of spears. I rode up to the line of men who all looked fearful, and with good cause. I rose in my stirrups and threw my first javelin at the line. I made sure I aimed at a man without a shield and was satisfied when the javelin took the man in his shoulder. He dropped his spear, screaming and fell back. I rode on and a succession of riders behind me repeated the exercise. When I reached the far side of the English encampment I reined in and looked back; fifty javelins thrown and maybe thirty casualties in the fyrdmen's ranks. We were not being followed; my men milled around me and I ordered them into the nearby tree line to wait and observe events. I could see more huscarls arrive at the eastern perimeter of the camp, heavily armoured with shields, spears, and helmets, many with mail. Javelins would do little damage to these professional warriors. The huscarls bullied and shoved the huscarls into some order. Tents were pulled down and loaded onto wagons and after a very long time the army started to move west towards Hay.

I arranged a rolling attack where my horsemen cantered in an arc, riding in from the rear of the English column, throwing a javelin and then riding away north to come back in a loop to attack again. As the English saw my cavalry approach they stopped and formed a wall of spears as directed by huscarls interspersed along the column. This slowed down the English advance considerably and with every pass and javelin shower a few more fyrdmen fell dead or wounded. Once or twice a couple of English huscarls, perhaps braver than most, ran out from the defending line in an effort to come to grips with a horseman, but my riders simply swerved away out of reach. More fyrdmen, quite openly now, were detaching themselves from the main body of the English and were fleeing back east, we let them go. I also noticed that the English column was gradually edging away from us, moving south west, rather than, directly west in an unconscious effort to be further away from the javelin storm. And still it rained. It took the English all day to travel the few miles to the ford at Hay. The river Wye was shallow and the current was rapid in places but could be easily crossed six abreast. I rode ahead to the ford and splashed through to join with Asmund.

The Cheshire vikings had thrown up a defensive barrier of felled logs about one hundred paces long right up against the river bank. It could be flanked easily enough and would not stop a determined attack but it was better than nothing and looked more robust than it really was.

"Hail, Hereward, how is it with you?" Asmund looked out from the log barrier as I walked my horse along its length.

183

"Well enough, we have lost, not a one, just a few lamed ponies, and the English are sore wounded. Best is that many fyrdmen are running for Hereford and I anticipate that by the morrow the English army will have halved. All our horses are blown though and need a good day's rest before further action."

"Good, I have welcome news, as well. When I arrived here, I found upwards of two hundred Welshmen ready to defend the ford, most have spears and shields so all together we can muster nearly four hundred men if the English try and push across the ford."

"Then we will try and hold the ford; dig in, put your archers and slingers on the wings and funnel the enemy into the barricade if you can. I will return to the horse and continue to harass their right flank. I will try and join you at dawn tomorrow."

I splashed back across the ford and joined my men on the north flank of the English army. We were close enough to see the English leaders congregated in the van of their troops under a huge wooden cross fitted onto a cart pulled by two large horses. They could see the ford slightly below their position and they could observe the defences and the numbers holding the ford. It looked like a heated debate was going on. Eventually the English army moved off the road into a meadow area on the south side of the track on slightly rising ground. A good choice, I thought, at least it will be less sodden.

When dusk fell the rain eased slightly. My men still had some javelins left from the bundles we had brought with us as reserves. I decided we would still harass the English through the night leaving our horses to rest. We did this by creeping up and throwing the javelins indiscriminately at the remaining tents. The javelins easily sliced through the woollen and hide covers and dropped into the interior of the tents; this meant that even if we did not injure anyone the occupants had to sleep, if they could, in armour with their shields above them. Not once did they counter-attack. After midnight we had run out of projectiles and so I had to call off the attacks. My men were as exhausted as the English, so we hunkered down where we could and tried to sleep. I set a watch and tried to sleep as well. I slept fitfully with erotic images of Una interspersed with imaginary duels with giants and bears. I awoke abruptly for no other reason than I knew something was not right. I clambered up and stretched my stiff limbs. I listened but could not identify any specific concern. Then I realised the silence was the issue other than the sounds of my immediate companions the night out there, beyond our camp, was still.

I made my way to the edge of the wood we were sheltering within and found a sentry slumbering. I kicked him and he awoke terrified and apologetic. "Don't." I said tersely, "just fetch the other sentries, who are probably asleep too."

The enemy camp still had some fires burning and I could see one or two sentries, but something was not right. The camp was too quiet and then I realised that the cross on the cart, which had been set up on a rise in the centre of the camp was not there. I drew my sword and started running towards the English camp. I was soon running between the tents towards the nearest fire where I could see a sentry silhouetted. As I approached, he did not move or seem to hear me. I took his head, below his helmet; it bounced away. Straw. The sentry was a dummy and so were most of the others. Had the English fled back to Hereford? No, I did not think they had given up yet so they were planning something.

I was soon joined by most of my small troop, they had caught a live sentry who revealed that he had been left behind to keep the fires going whilst the army slipped away. "Away, away where?" I demanded. The sentry shrugged. I hit him and left him in not doubt about his fate if he refused to tell me all he knew. Eventually I was satisfied that he really did not know what the English leaders were planning, all he could reveal was that the English army had slipped away south in the night.

"Get the horses and join me at the ford and don't forget to bring my horse too" I instructed my men. I could not let the English sentry go, too risky, so I slit his throat with my seax. I then ran down to the ford where I hoped that the sentries would be awake and not under attack.

They heard me splashing through the ford so I shouted. "I am Hereward Leofricson and I'm coming in, don't shoot."

Asmund Asmunderson was sleeping against the barricade and was soon with me, helping me over the wooden logs. "What's happened?" he asked rubbing his eyes.

"The English have slipped away south, is there a local man here?" I shouted.

"I live in Hay, my name is Owain." A small wiry man came out of the dark.

"Well, Owain from Hay, what's to the south of here, is there another ford?" I asked anxiously.

"Yes, my lord there is another ford at Glasbury about four miles from here."

"We must beat them to the ford to prevent them crossing." Asmund interjected.

"Wait." I said, "Owain, what is the way like from here to Glasbury, can we catch the English they have maybe an hour or two head start,"

Owain thought for a moment and then said, "The Wye meanders between Hay and Glasbury and you do not get there by following the river. From here to Glasbury is actually marginally quicker on the English side of the river but the ford is confusing to those who are not familiar with it. There is an island in the river and some people unwittingly cross to the island thinking they are right across the river. The ford is at the south end of the island and is quite narrow. I think you could beat the English to Glasbury on the Welsh side of the river if you rode but I do not think you could arrive there before they do if you go on foot."

I had to think quickly but still make the right decision. If we set off now the horsed warriors could be in position to contest the ford but would be in insufficient numbers to prevent a crossing. "Right, this is what we are going to do. Asmund you are to take all the horsed warriors and ride on the Welsh side of the river to Glasbury and parade along the river bank. This will not stop the English but will ensure that they send over their best huscarls to push you away so that the whole English army can cross. Meanwhile I will take everyone else and follow the English on their side of the river. I intend to come up upon them when they are half way across the ford with their army split in two and at their most vulnerable. We will attack and annihilate them."

I insisted that we move immediately, Hay was abandoned and all the warriors that were previously manning the barricade crossed the ford and marched into the night behind me. I had

Owain and other local men lead the way. I heard, rather than saw, Asmund lead out the horsed warriors south across the river, I prayed they would beat the English to the ford.

A night march is always the stuff of nightmares but we were lucky, we soon stumbled onto the track of the English army who had already trampled down the bracken either side of the track marking our way. The air was fresh after the rain, but the ground was still sodden, and walking was difficult, but this would be the same for the English and I comforted myself with the knowledge that the Welsh were accustomed to the wet weather and muddy conditions. After a half a watch, we came across a group of English stragglers, fyrdmen who had dropped out intending to go home. They were quickly dealt with but not before they told us how far we were behind the English column. With the knowledge that we were only half a watch behind the English and coming up fast I ordered a more leisurely pace. I did not want to arrive at the ford before the English started to cross.

Dawn was approaching and I could discern streaks of cobalt blue across the eastern sky. It should be at this point that the English intended to debouch onto the meadows before the ford and I hoped be faced with the viking archers who had ridden ahead to hold the ford. Resisting the urge to run I deliberately kept the column at a leisurely pace but I did send forward more scouts as I really wished to know what was about. I had a thirst for information. After about another quarter watch, several scouts came in at once. It was definite, horsemen were milling about on the far side of the ford and firing arrows at some English huscarls that were testing the crossing of the ford. The main English army were massed above the ford, the cart with the wooden cross could clearly be seen. We were about a mile behind. Again, there was an overwhelming urge to run to the battle but I supressed this desire and kept up our leisurely pace. My warriors were going to arrive refreshed and ready for combat, I wished our ambush to be complete.

Eventually, I could hear the sound of fighting ahead, there was cheering and I imagined this was from the English fyrd when they saw their professional huscarls forcing the ford. I just hoped that Asmund had not let any of our horsed warriors become closely engaged. Our path led over a small rise in the ground and my scouts warned me that this would expose our presence to the English. I halted our army and moved them from column into line so that they spread out along the approach to the ridge. I cautiously walked up the slope and peeped over the rise. Everything was as I had hoped. There were about eight hundred Englishmen, those that had not been killed or fled; they were massed at the ford and perhaps a third were already on the far side in Wales. I could see by their orderly ranks that the van was made up of most of the huscarls, maybe two and half hundred; leaving the rest of the professional warriors on the English side of the river to supervise the six hundred or so fyrdmen. The fyrdmen clustered about the cart with the wooden cross in no order, as if to find safety from their religious icon. I could see a man in religious vestments standing in the cart exhorting the crowd; probably their bishop. With odds at two to one in their favour I felt confident, best odds we have had so far in this sorry war. I moved back slowly from the hill crest and turned to address my men.

"Welshmen, you are now going to strike a blow to your hated enemies. They are not expecting you and their best men are on the other side of the river. These fyrdmen are farmers and labourers, not warriors, some do not even have proper weapons. You are going to charge over this rise and hit them whilst they are facing the ford, do not shout, keep quite the surprise will be greater and we will kill more of them." The irony of this address was not lost on me, here I was helping the Welsh to kill my own people, or maybe not. I saw myself as an Anglo-Dane from the Danelagh, these men before us were Saxons from Wessex, who generally disliked us Danish settlers. I had more of an affinity with the vikings from Dublin and Cheshire.

I signalled the throng forward and we crested the rise like a wave flowing against the beach. We had maybe four hundred long paces to run and I kept ahead of my men and set the pace, a steady trot rather than a mad dash. No one noticed us for the first hundred paces and then several men turned as they caught movement in the side of their eyes. Cries of alarm went up and faces turned towards us, we had covered another hundred paces by then. Many of the fyrdmen turned towards us but still many had not even noticed us as they were fixated on the action at the ford. Time to wake them up, I filled my lungs and shouted.

"Powys!" A roar went up behind me as hundreds of voices shouted, "Powys!"

Every head turned now and panic set in. As with all armies the nervous and downright cowardly were at the rear and were suddenly faced with a charging horde of Welshmen. Before a stroke had been struck, they turned to flee, but to where? They were neatly trapped between the ford and our line. Another hundred paces were gone and we swept onto them; at the last moment we increased our pace and hit their line with great force.

All the Welshmen carried small round shields, targes, they were useful in deflecting attacks but were not good in a steady shield wall. As many of the English fyrdmen had no shields and only spears the Welsh warriors used the shield to deflect any half-hearted thrusts with the English spears and closed on their prey. Many English fyrdmen were struck down immediately by axe blow or spear thrust and the blood sprayed out across the line causing more panic and fear. Scores of the English were turning to flee pushing against their comrades in a wild bid to get clear of the melee, many died with spear thrusts to their backs. Some tried to surrender holding open hands high in token of their willingness to be taken captive.

I did see one large and formidable English huscarl stride forward and strike down a Welsh spearman with his Dane axe. The rest of the Welsh quickly gave this man a wide berth, no one wants to die needlessly. I decided that I was the only warrior on our side with a chance of opposing this warrior so I moved through the throng shouting a challenge. He saw me and heard me at the same time. He banged his shield with his axe and shouted his war cry; my war cry, "Ut! Ut! Ut!" I returned the compliment, which puzzled him. However, before we could close a sling shot hit his helmet making it ring like Coventry church bell. The huscarl staggered, almost fell, but pushed himself upright, at that moment another sling shot hit his helmet and this time he did collapse. I could see the huge dent in the side of his helmet where the strengthener bands had sprung apart with the force of the projectile. These Welsh slingers were not to be underestimated.

The whole of the English army was pushing away from our assault, running away from the ford and towards woodland further south. They were fleeing past the cart supporting the wooden cross and the church prelate was exhorting them to stay and fight the heathen Welsh. That made me laugh, I knew that the Welsh had been good Christians for many hundreds of years before the Angles and Saxons had come to these shores. The priests are all liars. Around the cross were a group of huscarls clearly intent on defending both the cross and the prelate. I did not want these professionals to decimate the lighter Welsh warriors so I moved across and ordered the Welsh back leaving the defenders in a circle of trodden grass.

Staying well back from their swords and axes I swept the scene to ascertain how the attack was developing. To a man the fyrdmen had fled south towards the woodlands clearly hoping for concealment and an opportunity to flee back east. There was a tightly knit group of huscarls surrounding the cross cart, maybe fifteen and there were some two hundred huscarls on the other side of the ford. A sizeable number of my Welsh warriors, slingers amongst them, had ranged themselves on this side of the ford preventing the huscarls retreat; these huscarls were still being bombarded with arrows from Asmund's men.

I spread my arms and called for the Welshmen to fall back, I did not want them to die needlessly on the swords and axes of the huscarls. The circle around the huscarls and their cart widened and the fighting ceased. I stepped forward.

"Listen to me." I shouted. "Do not die needlessly, you have lost and your fyrdmen have fled away. I am Hereward Leofricson the Outlaw and I guarantee that if you lay down your arms, I will let you walk away back to Hereford."

The huscarls remain silent and guarded, but the prelate on the cart screamed with rage and shouted back at me. "Foul traitor, priest killer, apostate. You and these heathen barbarians will burn in the fires of hell, each and every one of you. The Lord Jesus Christ is at our right hand and he will smite you down." The prelate ranted on for some time making the Welsh warriors restless and angry. I was not surprised when a Welsh warrior stepped forward and cast a javelin that struck the priest square in the chest. There was a look of shock on the church man's face as

190

he looked down and saw the javelin protruding from his chest. He had been thrown back against the cross. There were cries of consternation mixed with cheers and jeers from the Welsh. The huscarls tightened their shield wall defence, one of them shouted out.

"You have attacked the holy bishop, Leofgar of Hereford, tis a mortal sin."

I held up my hands again and shouted for calm. "Bishop Leofgar, if he was a truly holy man should not have been on the field of battle. Bishop Leofgar, if he truly was a holy man should not have insulted the Welsh and incited them to murder. Bishop Leofgar was a fool and will die a fool's death." While I shouted, I could see the bishop slowly sliding down the wooden cross, leaving a smear of blood along the cross face. A true martyr's death, I thought. His face was pale and he clearly was not long for this world.

"You huscarls are not comitatus to the bishop and are not oath bound to die with him. My offer stands, you can leave now and no harm will come to you; do not die for this fool." I pleaded.

The same huscarl replied, "Our lord is Reeve Elnoth who is on the other side of the river, will you let us join him?"

"No, I will not, but I will offer him the same terms, if he will have them." I replied. I was quite desperate to keep the death toll of my Welshmen down.

"You may pass across the ford and speak to Reeve Elnoth." I indicated the way through the Welsh throng. The huscarl did not lack courage and he boldly walked through the close crowd of the Welshmen surrounding the cart. I watched him as he walked down the slope to the ford. He was escorted by a small group of my vikings so that he did not get killed.

We all waited tense and ready for the battle to renew but it was not the English huscarl that returned. A young Welsh slinger ran up the slope and saluted me. "My lord, the Reeve Elnoth is already dead with an arrow through his throat, from the bow of Lord Asmund himself. Elnoth's huscarls are set to die with their lord and the huscarl who went down with your message has refused to leave his lord's corpse and will die there."

I cursed my luck, but I still was not going to let the body count rise. "Draw back let the surrounded huscarls have an avenue of escape east." I shouted. "We go to the ford to kill the rest of the English."

The Welsh flowed around the remaining huscarls and moved off down the slope towards the ford. The fourteen remaining huscarls were left with a dilemma, by their oath they should attack us and die to a man with their lord but the fire had gone out of their veins and the courage to follow us down the slope was lacking. The small group moved away east seeking home. There were about a hundred and fifty huscarls left alive on the west side of the Glasbury ford and we outnumbered them but they were professional killers and would take a heavy toll on us, especially the lightly armed Welsh. I therefore decided on a cautious war of attrition. The huscarls could not escape and although they were heavily armoured would eventually fall to a sustained missile attack. Throughout the rest of the day, they were bombarded with arrows, javelins, and stones, by dusk they had lost half of their force to injury or death. I called for their surrender but they refused, staying true to their oath. By nightfall the fighting stopped and the Welsh pulled back leaving the way open east. The opportunity was irresistible and I could see huscarls fleeing away in ones and twos throughout the night.

Early the next morning I could see maybe two score of the huscarls were left and most of these had waded back across the ford to the east side. I ordered the way left open for a retreat to Hereford and kept the Welshmen back from any further fighting. I sent a message across the ford, avoiding the English requesting Asmund Asmunderson to ride with all speed to Llanandros, or wherever our northern force may be. My attention had switched to the threat from the Worcester force led by Godwine Leofricson, my kinsman.

When the English huscarls realised that they were not being attacked they no longer had the will to resist and the final few carrying their wounded limped off east. We had won against overwhelming odds and the English army from Hereford never even made it into Powys. The local Welsh were ecstatic, looting the corpses. I instructed the local chiefs to bury or burn the dead with honours, but did not linger. I promptly led the nucleus of my Welsh fighting force back north as fast a pace as they could manage. We had not passed the ford at Hay before a rider came in from Martin with information. Now the rain had stopped the English had moved out of Leominster and were approaching Llanandros north of the river; the Welsh were holding the ford and Egil and his small viking raiding party were harassing the enemy.

Although the circumstances had changed, I still felt it would be to our benefit if we kept the English moving north west as it would mean King Gryffudd would have less ground to cover before we could join and destroy the English. I rode ahead of the Welsh infantry and ran Martin and Asmund to ground west of Llanandros overlooking the River Lugg. Martin was relieved to see me, especially as I had left him with very few men a few days before. He was less relieved when he realised that I had travelled ahead of my men and the foot would take at least a day to come up. "Well, Martin, we have had good viking weather luck and this has allowed us to repel the southern English army before this one has even entered Wales."

Martin gave me a sour look, he obviously did not relish a leadership role, especially one with hardly any men. "It is even better master. Whilst we have been waiting for the English to come up are force has been supplemented by over three hundred Welsh farmers from roundabout here. When your men finally arrive, we may have as many as six hundred men at our disposal, good odds I think."

"More like five hundred men, Martin. The battle at the ford of Glasbury was not without casualties on our side and I had to leave the wounded at the battle site. The one truth I have learnt is that the Welsh, lightly armed as they are, cannot withstand the English huscarls." I responded.

"And the English fyrdmen are worse than useless too." Asmund came up leading his horse. We clasped hands.

"Well met, Asmund; you held the ford as Glasbury like a true hero and I hear you struck down the Shire Reeve Elnoth with your own hand." I praised him, as he deserved.

"My own arrow, I am afraid. No hero sword clash but he died nevertheless." Asmund smiled ruefully.

"Well down to business, Martin where are the English?" I became all business like.

"Their movements are mysterious to say the least, they left Leominster yesterday and marched along the south side of the river Lugg, but when they reached Lye, they crossed the ford there and have been moving northwest towards a place called Tref-y-clawdd, which means 'place near or on the dyke' and that must be on the old dyke King Offa of Mercia built to keep out the Welsh from his kingdom. So, they are still in England." Martin observed.

"Mmmm, maybe they were only intended as a diversion to draw King Gryffudd away from the southern army." I mulled this over.

"They will not know that the southern army is destroyed yet." Asmund observed.

"This is true Asmund so we have a decision to make, do we want to inform them of the disaster that befell their Hereford army and let them run away, or do we want to engage with them and give them a bloody nose?" I posed the question.

"Fighting with them in England makes us the aggressors." Martin pointed out.

"True, Martin, but I am pretty sure now that they will not enter Wales willingly, they are only making a demonstration." I responded.

"What is to be done then?" Asmund interjected.

"I believe it is in King Gryffudd's interest for this army to be given a bloody nose. We need to lure them into the debatable land north of Tref-y-clawdd, the heavily wooded area the English refer to as the Shropshire Forest. The Welsh are specialists at ambush and lightning strikes, much better than when they are asked to stand in a shield wall. If we fight them there both sides will claim the other side invaded and the morality will be lost." I concluded.

"How can we lure them on?" Asmund queried.

"Lure might be the wrong word, press them, more like. If we follow on their heels' they are unlikely to turn on us unless they become desperate. When they reach Offa's Dyke and see King Gryffudd's army before them they will move north east to avoid our overwhelming numbers surrounding them. They will enter the forest area and then we can strike." I elaborated.

Asmund and Martin acquiesced with my plan and the next morning, we moved out and crossed the Lugg, with some difficulty as it was still swollen after the rain and the fords were high. I directed our horsed warriors under Asmund to ride ahead and close on the rear of the English army cutting off stragglers and ensuring supplies were kept limited. The archers' quivers had been replenished and they were able to shower the English rear guard from time to time inflicting a few casualties but keeping the enemy compact and moving the way we wanted them to go. It was only a day's march from the Lugg fords to Tref-y-clawdd and we had a shorter march than the English so we came up to them shortly after noon. I had sent off several scouts to try and locate King Gryffudd and his host and one of the scouts came back by noon to inform me that he had found the King's army at Llangunllo only five miles west of Tref-y-clawdd and that he and his army were marching east to intercept the English. The King's army numbered over five hundred so we were going to outnumber the enemy considerably; a nice change of fortune.

I now decided to move my men slightly to the east to leave an open corridor, an escape route, for the English either north or north-east into the forest. My scouts observed the English crossing the River Teme and moving off north east presumably towards Caer Caradoc the other side of the forest. I sent word for King Gryffudd to follow on over the ford and attack the English rear-guard. Meanwhile I took my host across another ford over the Teme further east of Tref-y-clawdd and raced to intercept the English vanguard.

The ground was uneven and wooded with dense shrubbery in places, my scouts reported that the English were up ahead making their way across country threading through scrub land and copses. There was no way they could form a shield wall as the country was insufficiently open and to make matters worse it began to rain again. It was no terrain for horses so I sent my few cavalry east about to prevent the English fleeing home. I gave the word to charge the enemy in as compact a formation as possible and to try not to engage with the heavily armoured huscarls. This message was passed along the line quietly so not as alert the English of our presence.

I raised the battle cry, "Cymry" and "Powys", the Welsh warriors roared and surged forward bursting from the shrubbery and racing across the uneven scrub towards the enemy ranks. The English were clearly startled by this unexpected attack. I could see that there were few huscarls with the vanguard, presumably because they had been sent back to bolster the rear guard against King Gryffudd's attack.

"Javelins." I screamed as we came within killing distance of our foe. The Welsh warriors threw their light javelins with dexterity and as we attacked the English from their spear side many of the fyrdmen fell to the rain of missiles because they were unarmoured. Within a few heart beats we were amongst the English fyrdmen and I started to lay about with my sword. Most of the fyrdmen were timid and pulled back offering their spear points towards us as a defence. It was easy to lop off the spear heads, many of which were just fire hardened points, leaving the amateur warriors defenceless. I found it easier to cut arms and legs, disabling rather than killing my opponents, it caused more chaos, screaming and confusion than a clean death. I broke the line quite easily and the English backed off ready to run. One of the few huscarls came at me intent of stopping a major cause of the English indiscipline. I fronted my shield and prepared for a more realistic duel. However, this was not to be as a sling stone hit the huscarls helmet with a hefty thwack, the helmet's strengthener bands sprang apart on impact and the side of the helmet caved in. The huscarl swayed and then toppled over and the Welsh skirmishers flooded over him. The speed of our attack overwhelmed the enemy who soon turned and fled north faster than I could imagine. Fear lent their feet wings.

"Stop! Stop!" I shouted as loud as possible and then remembered to shout in Welsh. I indicated that our attack should swing left towards the main array of the English, which I hoped would now be caught in a pincer movement between ourselves and King Gryffudd's main army. Many of my men ran to recover their javelins, making sure at the same time that their original targets were dispatched with a quick dagger slash to an exposed throat. The element of surprise had now gone and I could see that the main army of Godwine Leofricson had formed a shield wall but only twenty huscarls wide, pitiful really; the undergrowth did not allow natural tactical deployment. I could hear sound of battle up ahead and knew that King Gryffudd had engaged the rear guard of the English. Even if the huscarls, well trained as they were, held, the remaining fyrdmen were likely to break at any time and I determined on a forceful frontal assault.

"Charge, kill the English!" I yelled, again forgetting to shout in Welsh, but the warriors around me needed no translation as they surged forward. I ran with them surrounded by my Dublin Norsemen. We formed a shield wall as we ran with deadly Dane axes ready to pull down the enemy shields. I noticed to my right a flag displaying the Mercian Knot, a badge only carried before a scion of the Mercian leadership, a badge I had the right to carry through my father. The old warrior beneath this banner must be Godwine Leofricson, probably my great-uncle or a cousin once removed, or something, although I had never met him. The two front ranks came together with a loud and furious clash. Shield boards smashed into each other as warriors tried to push their opponents back. Wily vikings stopped short of the impact zone and lashed out with their axes to hook over their enemies shields to pull them down. The Norse working in tandem with a Welsh javelin thrower opened up the English line to a shower of javelins that pierced mailed bodies rather than shields. Many huscarls were wounded, some died, the shield wall buckled. I edged to my right, towards Godwine but a burly huscarl placed himself between me and my target. He was armed with an axe which he hefted and brought down with force onto the top rim of my shield. The impact forced my shield arm down exposing me to an attack on my undefended torso but, as is often the case, his axe was jammed in my shield where it had split the iron band rim. He tried to cover himself with his shield while he tugged trying to dislodge his axe but I used the obvious counter in these circumstances and swept my sword low and cut off his foot above the ankle but below his leg defence plates. He toppled to my right leaving a space for me to step into. I knew the huscarl would be finished off by the men behind me so I advanced on Godwine Leofricson.

I could see his eyes behind his nasal and mail coif and they looked old, he was maybe as old as my father. "Live, surrender and you may live; we are kin" I called out.

"You are no kin to me Welshman." He bellowed back. He clearly had no idea who I was and now was not the time to enlighten

197

him. I fronted what remained of my shield and he saw the Mercian knot proudly displayed.

"You dare carry the Mercian shield, what are you a traitor?" he shouted. Without giving me the opportunity to answer he lunged forward with his sword but I easily parried the thrust with my shield and when he then tried another swipe from right to left across my body I stepped within the arc of his sword and smashed my shield into his, sending him sprawling on the gorse.

"I am Hereward Leofricson and in honour of my father I don't want to kill you, now get up and go back to the Hwicce and leave the Welsh in peace." I shouted.

Struggling to his feet he spluttered through the blood streaming from his nose, which sprayed through his mail ventail.

"Foul traitor, you are no kin of mine and the Lady Godgifu would amply reward me for your death." Godwine rushed forward with his sword extended presumably with the intention of running me through but in all honesty his rush was feeble and I had no trouble in brushing his sword thrust to one side with my shield. His statement of intent and the mention of my step-mother's name angered me and without thought I rammed my sword into his abdomen, breaking his mail and forcing the blade clear through his body until its point exited from his back. I could feel the blade grate on his spine as he wriggled and writhed feebly trying to pull back. I lifted my foot as he sank down and with the sole of my boot pushed him off the sword blade. Godwine fell on his back, blood pooling out from the exit wound.

"Kin slayer, rot in hell." Godwine feebly gasped out the curse as his voice faded. Kin slayer, another epithet to my roll of fame, or shame, whichever way you looked at it. I just hoped that Godwine and my father were not close and that this would not weaken my father's position in England. I looked around at the ongoing melee and was pleased to see that the Welsh had carried the day. The English were fleeing the field in complete disorder. I saw a small group of English huscarls in a tight shield wall slowly edging away from the fighting. They were still formidable and I was pleased to see that the Welsh were avoiding them and concentrating on easier pickings. Hundreds of the English fyrdmen were dead, their lack of defensive armour meant that the fatal attrition rate was high. I assumed that most of the huscarls were not the sworn men of my dead relative or they would have been expected to die with him. The two Welsh armies, my small one and the King's much larger host, came together threw up their arms and cheered their victory. King Gryffudd spied me supervising the rounding up of many of the English fyrdmen who failed to flee before they were caught.

"Bearslayer, you have done it again, with a war leader like you how can I fail." It was a statement not a question so I did not feel impelled to answer. I smiled weakly and Gryffudd continued. "The English will not wish to challenge me again and I am now free to exert my will on all Wales." King Gryffudd could not hide his satisfaction, I was not so sure that Harald Godwinson would take this lying down, as it were.

"Each farm will have an English slave to pull the plough and save our good Welsh ponies the hardship." He laughed. It took the rest of the day to bring order to the chaos of the battlefield, many weapons were collected, shields and helmets, which would greatly enhance the Welsh ability to defend their land. I made sure that my crewmen and Asmund's Cheshire Norsemen gained their share of the battlefield loot, armbands, gold rings and the huscarl swords and axes. Gryffudd paid my men well, as a ring giver should. Much of this wealth was distributed through me as the Dublin Norse leader, thereby enhancing my authority and prestige.

That night before the impromptu feast I drew King Gryffudd aside. "Lord King, I must inform you that I have to leave your service as soon as may be." Gryffudd looked concerned, perhaps an acknowledgement of how useful I had become to his martial activities.

"But why?" he did show some bewilderment.

"I killed Godwine Leofricson of the Hwicce with my own hand, he was far out kin to me, probably a cousin of my father who may not take this slaying well, neither may my brother Aelfgar for all I know. You cannot afford to alienate my family for my sake, so I must take the blame and make myself scarce."

King Gryffudd understood, kin slaying was not to be taken lightly; rather than return with the king to Mathrafal I determined that I would retrace my steps straight back to my snekkja and sail to Ireland.

Autumn 1056 - Iverk

I sat athwart my sea chest in the well of my snekkja, *Ottar* plaiting a rope intended to be used in the rigging. I was performing this task in an absent-minded way, my mind clearly on other matters. I had been in Veðrafjǫrðr for three weeks, since my return from Wales and I should have been planning my future but I found myself to be very lethargic.

I had arrived back in Veðrafjǫrðr walking up to King Ragnald's hall with most of my crew carrying gifts for the king, Sunhild and Una. The king and his wife met me joyfully and with enthusiasm for my gifts from the raid into England, but Una was not there. I made discreet enquiries with Sunhild who informed me that shortly after I had left for Wales Una's husband had miraculously returned from his long trading venture, a venture that had turned into a disaster, the loss of his ship and enslavement by pagan devils that ruled a country far to the south called Andalucía. After more than a year Una's husband managed to escape and return to Cornwall where Alief had lent him a ship to retrieve his wife from Ireland. Una had dutifully returned to Cornwall with her husband. I was quite downcast by this turn of events believing that Una preferred me rather than her husband. I harboured ideas of rescuing her, of killing her unwanted husband. I became morose and surly and stayed on board *Ottar* rather than alienate my friend with my bad temper. I was eventually called upon by a local monk; he was very clean and despite his poor apparel, neat and tidy.

"Good morrow, sir. You are he they refer to as the Bearslayer, one Hereward Leofricson?" he queried light-heartedly, by way of an introduction.

"What is that to thee?" I responded sulkily.

"I have been charged with a missive from the lady called Una, she who used to be Queen Sunhild's nurse. I wrote it down for her in Latin, if you cannot read, I can read it for you."

"I can read, let me see it." I responded eagerly.

The letter was written in a neat script on none too expensive vellum.

My beloved Hereward

Against all hope my husband has returned to me and as you will now know I have returned home with him. Please understand I love my husband; he has been good to me and I cannot desert him on my honour. I know you understand honour. I will always remember my time with you and cherish it, you will become a great man, I know, and there would be no part for me to play in your life. Think on me kindly my beautiful lover as I will you.

Una.

I sat looking at the letter having read it several time, the monk spoke but I struggled to follow what he was saying.

"Lord, the lady Una is a honourable and upright person, she knew she was committing a grave sin by cleaving to you but she was unable to stop herself. The Lord has forgiven her transgression and she has returned to her rightful husband. You should consider asking for the Lord's forgiveness too."

Fury at this monk's admonition of my supposed sin boiled over within me and I back-handed him across his cheek sending him sprawling to the floor. He scrambled up and scuttled away as fast as his robes allowed. And so, I sat upon my ship athwart my sea chest plaiting ropes, my anger and self-pity consuming me.

Several men clambered aboard; I noticed that Martin had brought King Ragnald. "Hereward, brother, I grieve for your sour mood and would lighten your brow. Martin tells me that nothing more than war gladdens your heart and I have enough to satisfy anyone." Ragnald looked suitably concerned.

This pricked my interest. "What say you, are you threatened?"

"I have a long-standing border conflict with Fergus O'Brodair Lord of Iverk and he has raided my lands this very day and carried off cattle and women." Ragnald opined. Martin smiled as he knew this would galvanise me and take my mind off my supposed loss.

"Where is Iverk.? I asked.

"It is the land north of Veðrafjǫrðr. Fergus holds several small raths and can command maybe a hundred men." Ragnald explained.

"You can command many more men than that, why do you not destroy him?" I countered.

"Two reasons, first, we are both oath bound to King Diarmait Mael na mBo so a war between us would not be looked upon kindly, and secondly, my Norsemen are traders with no interest in the Irish hinterland and frankly couldn't care less if a few of my Irish kerns and their wives are seized and are unwilling to react to a call to arms to protect them" Listening to Ragnald's explanation I realised that he was quite a weak descendent of his ferocious viking forebears.

"I will take my crew and retrieve your Irish for you, can you send someone with me as a guide?" I decided to overcome my lethargy in the only way I knew how, violent action, blood, and death.

"Yes, I have a retainer, an old viking who yearns for action, he will surely help." Ragnald confirmed.

Less than a quarter watch later Martin had assembled my crew and we had been joined by a disreputable old man with only one leg, the other leg having been replaced by an ivory stump.

"This is Eystein Whaleleg, he was a warrior of my father's household and knows Egil your helmsman; he can lead you to Fergus of Iverk's rath." Ragnald added by way of an introduction.

The old Viking sized me up and his face cracked into a toothless smile. "I see Odin's ravens follow you, to the hall of the slain we will go. Aagh."

"Is he quite mad?" I asked Ragnvald.

"Maybe, but he knows the way to Iverk." The king replied.

I had the crew cast off and we rowed the *Ottar* upstream. Veðrafjǫrðr lay on the River Suir within its tidal reach but the river was navigable further upstream where Iverk lay. We were able to make swift progress upriver despite the down current and I was comfortable in the knowledge that we were travelling much faster than the raiders could retreat with the stolen cattle and captives. Even allowing for the meanderings of the river it was only about ten miles to where the nearest rath belonging to Fergus Lord of Iverk lay. We tied up on an island in the middle of the river at a place called Fiodh Dúin after two-or-three quarter watches, leaving Egil and the ship's boys to watch *Ottar*. The rath was on the north east side of the river and we swam and waded from the ship to the shore. I took fifty of my crew with Eystein Egilson, who obligingly carried Eystein Whaleleg on his shoulder across the river. We assembled on the bank of the river and shook ourselves dry.

"The rath is over yonder." Eystein indicated towards rising ground hidden by woods to the north east.

"The track from Veðrafjǫrðr is only a hundred paces or so over there." This time Eystein pointed due east. "It may be that the raiders haven't made it this far yet."

"Let's go and see." I decided. We moved off across the river meadow and within a short walk we came to the north, south track. It was obvious that no large herd of cattle had passed this way for some time so I assumed that we had gotten ahead of the raiders. "Martin, take two lads and scout south along the road, make sure no one sees you. Egil, send two men up towards the rath, we do not want to be surprised by an attack from that quarter." I ordered. The rest of my men spread themselves out either side of the track in any available concealment, mainly scrub and bushes. We all sat down to wait; waiting being the normal course of any campaign. Predicably it started to rain but this would assist our concealment.

After about another quarter watch, one of Martin's scouts came back up the trail and I whistled him over. "The Iverk men are coming up the trail, maybe a quarter to half a watch behind, Martin is keeping an eye on them." He informed me panting from his exertion.

"How many?" I queried.

"There are about forty warriors, two dozen cattle and maybe a dozen or so women, some with children." The scout appeared pleased he had remembered the numbers.

"Good, well done, take a rest now." I passed the information along to the concealed crewmen, who mostly relaxed when they understood that the odds were fairly even and that they had superior weapons and the element of surprise. At least ten of the Norse had brought along their longbows to improve the ambush.

The time passed slowly, as it always does, when expecting a fight. Finally, Martin and the other scout came in. Martin crawled up next to me. "Master, they are two hundred paces out but the cattle are moving slowly. They have no scouts out ahead but three or four men to the rear in case they are pursued. They have stopped a couple of times to rape women; this has delayed their progress."

"A mean bunch then." I observed. Finally, the raiders could be heard; lowing, protesting cattle and crying captives. There were a few hoarse shouts from the raiders as they drove the walking plunder into view along the track. As the track was not particularly wide the cattle were being driven along two at a time with the captives behind. Some of the women were nearly naked clutching shreds of clothing around their bodies. The raiders were therefore strung out and totally unprepared for our ambush.

When the raiders column had passed me by and reached the last of my concealed warriors, I gave a shrill whistle and a dozen arrows winged into the line. At least half a dozen raiders were hit with the inevitable screaming, alarm, and panic. My men and I leapt up and ran towards the column. I looked for the leader of the raiding party but could not see anyone obviously in authority. My first opponent could not have been more than twelve or thirteen. He had been driving the cattle with a stick and turned to me with a startled and terrified look on his face. He wore a simple brat, the over cloak the Irish traditionally covered themselves with. The bottom edge of his brat appeared to have recent semen stains on it and I assumed he had expended his virginity on one of the female slaves earlier that morning. As he stood there looking at me in astonishment, I decapitated him. His body remained upright for a few moments with blood fountaining from his severed neck before he collapsed. I looked around to see that my heavily armoured men had made short work of the Irish raiders. Some of the Irish at the rear of the column had run off south as fast as their legs would carry them and there was no way my mailed Norsemen would catch them. Two or three Irish raiders at the head of the column ran for the rath but Egil's scouts intercepted them. One of the Irish escaped by running back along the track towards me; I noticed that he had a sword and small shield so I assumed he was the leader of the band.

"Hold fast if you want to live." I shouted. With a frantic expression and wild eyes, he ran at me, or maybe he was trying to run past me. I stuck out my boot and tripped him. He hit the ground at speed and slid a couple of paces before I had the opportunity to place my booted foot in the small of his back. He was gibbering with fright after I had kicked his sword away and turned him over. I placed the point of my sword at his throat.

"Name?" I demanded.

"Muircheartaich, brother of Fergus." He stuttered.

"Oh! Good a useful hostage for Ragnald that will help keep your brother in check. Martin, tie him up and we need to get these kine out of here quickly before the Irish in the rath become aware of us." My crew rounded up the cattle and turned them around, prodding and goading them back toward Veðrafjǫrðr. I instructed Martin to return to the *Ottar* with the captives and have Egil drift the snekkja back to Veðrafjǫrðr on the current whilst the crew and I guard the cattle and herd them south.

I saw the mast of the *Ottar* drifting south within short order with the rescued women and children aboard. The cattle were a different proposition and I was notified by one of my scouts that there was a sally from the Irish rath that would come up to us within moments. He estimated around two dozen warriors. As the Irish eventually came screaming down the track they saw a dozen of my Norsemen form a small shield wall in front of the cattle. Seeing that they outnumbered my men two to one they increased their pace and ran at the shield wall. It was then that the rest of my Norsemen rose up from the scrub either side of them and shot arrows into their unarmoured sides. At least six of the enemy fell and the rest seeing that they were outnumbered turned and retreated as fast as they had advanced. Only one of the enemy stood resolute shouting for the Irish to stand and fight. I strode over to him and fronted my shield.

"I am Hereward Leofricson, who are you?" I shouted.

The man was furious, he was wearing a mail shirt, which suggested some wealth and held a sword and small shield, a targe. He was the only Irishman who had a helmet on, an interesting one at that. It looked to be bronze or brass, a beaten dome around which a gold crown or circlet had been affixed. He was tall and wiry, dark of hair, with a cleft lip that gave him the appearance of having a continual snarl. "I am Fergus O'Brodair Lord of Iverk and you are trespassing on my land." He shouted, with some venom.

"I think we are returning the compliment and we have your brother as captive to prove it." I smiled menacingly. This confused the O'Brodair and gave him pause. "I will not kill you but remember if you or yours attack Veðrafjǫrðr again your brother will be castrated and hung from the town gate. Now go, flee back to your stinking rath."

The O'Brodair looked at me with anger, weighing up the odds of killing me but with my crew surrounding him he had little chance of escaping alive. He shrugged and hurried away toward his rath. It took the rest of the day to herd the cattle back to Veðrafjǫrðr. I had no idea which farms the cattle belonged to or whether the owners were alive or dead, so we drove them back to the town gates where King Ragnald awaited us.

"The Bearslayer victorious again, what of Fergus?" Ragnald asked anxiously.

"Fergus lives and now that you hold his brother as a hostage, he may leave you alone. His warriors are much depleted and I have lost none of mine."

"I must reward you for you have removed a difficulty from me in a way I could not have hoped for." Ragnald smiled.

"It is of no matter you have helped me remove a burden from my soul and I am ready to resume my life. I have decided to return to Fearns and offer my services to King Diarmait Mael na mBo."

"Yes, a wise move, I hear he is about to embark on a war with Munster." Ragnald responded with alacrity; I suspected he would be pleased to see me leave as I was probably having an unsettling effect on is younger warriors.

Once I had decided to leave, I became businesslike and informed my crew of my intentions. Most wanted to remain with me but a few Veðrafjǫrðr men had no wish to move from their base at Veðrafjǫrðr. and chose to remain at home. These places were quickly filled by those younger warriors that Ragnald was, no doubt, pleased to see the back of. I had so many recruits that I overloaded my snekkja to accommodate as many as I could take; I knew I would need them in the forthcoming war.

I said my farewells to King Ragnald and Sunhild who was pleasantly showing signs of her first pregnancy, a bit young perhaps but not unusual. I had decided to sail my snekkja around the coast to Veisafjǫrðr and sail into Loch Garman. I understood from local warriors that the River Slaney running into Loch Garman from the north was navigable nearly all the way to Fearns and that the river rarely narrowed down to less than twenty paces. My snekkja could be sailed stern first I was not unduly worried as long as there was sufficient draft beneath the keel; as it transpired, we managed to row *Ottar* up river to a place called Inis Córthaidh only a few miles west of Fearns. I left the snekkja moored up to a small islet in the river with Egil in charge, typical viking caution, I loved my boat. I took half of my crew and walked the short distance to Fearns. The King of Leinster's rath was the largest Irish fortress I had seen and unlike the smaller ones had a stone foundation with a wooden stake wall built on top as a parapet. The rath was surrounded with a typical ditch that had filled up over time with brackish water. I had spent the previous Yule feast here when Ragnald was married to Sunhild so I knew my way about. I directed my men to a nearby hostelry and Martin and I went up to the king's round house. The round house was the largest in the town but was dwarfed by the adjacent church, which again had substantial stone foundations with a wooden superstructure. Like all the kings in Ireland Diarmait Mael na mBo was deeply religious, with several saints in is ancestry.

Martin and I were challenged at the door to the king's rath by two guards but both were known to me and I to them so this was a perfunctory process. We were permitted into the interior of the smoky king's hall minus our weapons. Like most of the Irish halls the perimeter was sectioned off into booths that could be curtained off for privacy or left open as the occupant preferred. There were two obvious entrances opposite each other and the King's booth was always to the right side of the hall. King Diarmait Mael na mBo sat before it on a raised dais in a carved chair, or maybe it was a throne. He had a wand in his left hand and a sword near his right hand, propped against his chair arm. He still looked suitably regal but when he saw me, he smiled expansively and beckoned me forward.

"Well met, Bearslayer. Are you coming to serve?" The king made a gesture to a young woman nearby who promptly proffered Martin and I goblets full of mead. Heady stuff.

"Lord, I would gladly fight for you, given the fight is worthy and the rewards for my men are plentiful. My ship and crew lie nearby."

"Good, I plan to attack Munster in the new year and assert my hegemony over the upstart Dal gCais. Your men will counter any Limerick Vikings they may bring to the fray, I will give you leave to recruit in Dublin and the other viking ports in Leinster." The king invited me to sit with him at the evening feast and in the days leading up to Yule his campaign was formed. I found the culture of the Irish fascinating; it was so unlike anything in England or Wales for that matter, although there were similarities with the kin groupings in Alba. Ireland was broadly divided into five provinces or kingdoms, Leinster in the south east, Munster in the south west, Ulster in the north east, Connaught in the north west and in the centre Midhe, the middle kingdom. All the kings of the provinces vied to be the Ard Righ Erinn or High King. Traditionally the high kingship tended to be with the ruling families of Ulster descended from an ancient king called Niall of the Nine Hostages and the northern kings were sometimes challenged by the Kings of Leinster in the south. However, all this changed when about three generations previously a powerful warrior from northern Munster called Brian Borumhe, a prince of the Dal gCais tribe, developed a strong army and gradually exerted his control over Munster and then Leinster. He persistently raided into Connaught, Midhe and Ulster until they recognised his authority as Ard Righ. His reign culminated in the great battle of Clontarf just outside Dublin between on the one side the vikings and the Leinster kings and on the other Brian Borumhe's Munster army. Although Brian was killed in the battle the vikings and Leinster men were soundly defeated. The high kingship temporarily returned to the Ulster kings but Munster remained a powerful force.

The interesting result of this power struggle was that the viking settlements were weakened and the Leinster King was able to take control of them. The subsequent wealth the Leinster king acquired through these trading ports enabled him to challenge for the high kingship. Dairmait had allied himself with the King of Ulster and this had enabled him to control Dublin on Leinster's northern border. He had now recently allied himself with a claimant to the Munster crown called Toirdelbach, a nephew of the current king, and with his support he aimed to bring down the son of Brian Borumhe, King Donnchad of Munster, and claim the undisputed high kingship for himself.

Yule in Fearns was a merry affair but I spent most of my time planning the forthcoming campaign. King Brian Borumhe had tamed the Limerick vikings and had introduced many of the viking military features into his army. The Munster elite warriors now favoured the Dane axe and wore mail so that they were a much more formidable prospect than other Irish fighting units. Additionally, many of the old Munster king's campaigns had involved using the Limerick viking fleet to transport his army up the River Shannon, the gateway to the heartland of Ireland, providing much needed mobility. In my view the key to Brian Borumhe's success was the Limerick fleet and it needed to be neutralised to ensure Leinster's success in the forthcoming war.

In the wet aftermath of Yule when most people lay a bed recovering from the exhausting revelry, I approached King Dairmait with my idea. Suppled with a brimming cup of ale I broached the subject. "Lord King, I have an idea that will greatly increase the success of your forthcoming war with Munster."

King Dairmaid leant forward in his seat, all ears, so I explained my strategy.

Spring & Summer 1057 – Limerick

The wind was a brisk north westerly, blowing down the Irish Sea through the narrow channel between Kintyre in Alba and the coast of Ulster. I stood on the foredeck of my snekkja, *Ottar,* looking back at the line of ships coming about from the mouth of the Liffey passed Dun Laoghaire. One by one oars were shipped and spars were raised allowing the sails to be unfurled and catch the wind. Ten snekkjas were sailing in line following me down the coast to Vicklo, Arklo and beyond. I had convinced King Diarmait that the way to defeat Donnchad of Munster was to attack Limerick by sea and neutralize the viking fleet. To this end I had spent the last month in Dublin persuading the viking merchants to support such a venture. I appealed to their greed, I suggested that they may then have more influence in Munster and I encouraged their animosity against the Ui Ivar, the old viking ruling family of Limerick, although it no longer existed. The threats from King Diarmait's despicable son Murchad also helped, I could not help but think some of the Dublin traders joined my force simply to get away from him. Ten snekkjas plus *Ottar* meant upwards of five hundred warriors and I had the hope, the prospect of gleaning more ships from Vicklo, Arklo and even maybe Veðrafjǫrðr. Egil and the crew were happy to be on the water, rather than wasting their lives in town, especially with the prospects of plunder to be had.

The journey down the coat of Leinster was a joy with good fresh winds that bowled us along. It was a shame to put in at the smaller viking trading settlements of Vicklo and Arklo especially as it enhanced my force by only four ships and those quite small. My fleet entered Loch Garman on the third day of sailing to be met by another four long ships intent on joining my enterprise. I already knew they would be waiting as I had secured their support when my snekkja had left its berth on the Slaney after the Fearn Yule feast to sail around to Dublin. With a force of nineteen snekkjas and a thousand warriors I was assured I had enough force to damage Limerick's fleet. The next day we continued our journey with the weather still holding and rounded the headland south of Rosslare into the ocean swell. The prevailing north westerlies permitted us to maintain a steady course along Ireland's southern shore until we turned into the Barrow estuary and headed for Veðrafjǫrðr. I left the fleet in the sheltered mouth of the estuary and had the crew row *Ottar* up to the wharfs at Veðrafjǫrðr. King Ragnald came down to the wharf to great me, my *Ottar* being well known in the town.

"Greeting's brother, you look well, better than I saw you last." Ragnald waved and gave a welcoming smile. "What are you up to, are you still in Mael na mBo's service?"

"I am indeed and would speak to you about just that." I replied.

"Well come into the hall and Sunhild will provide food and drink. You must also be introduced to the new ruler of Veðrafjǫrðr, my son Ivarr." Ragnald patted me on the back as I alighted from my boat, he was clearly in a cheery mood.

"Congratulations on becoming a father." I responded.

We entered the hall where I was met by a blossoming Sunhild carrying a rosy cheeked infant that took one look at me and started to bawl. Everyone laughed at my embarrassment; food and drink were passed around and I sat with Ragnald and explained my business. I could see that he was reluctant to have any part in the expedition but he could see that there could be economic benefits to Veðrafjǫrðr if the Limerick vikings were reduced.

"I am far out kin to the Hy Ivar and would not feel comfortable warring against them, although I have no such compulsion with regards the Dal gCais and the other Irish Munster clans. I will put it to my chiefs and if any wish to join your expedition I will not prevent them." Ragnald decided.

To be honest this was what I suspected he would do. His viking family were no longer the raiders and adventurers of the past. My crew and I were feasted in the hall that night and Ragnald and I spoke to the chieftains about my intentions. None of the ships' captains we willing to join such an adventure but there were upwards of twenty youths who were keen to join me and I was pleased to make room for them on my slightly overcrowded ships. I returned to my fleet the next day and because the wind had increased in strength overnight, we lay in the estuary for a couple of days for the slight storm to blow over. It is not good for vikings to lay about in idleness although this is not an uncommon occurrence so I organised games between the crews, oar-walking and snekkja racing, and the like to keep them occupied. I was slightly concerned that someone from Veðrafjǫrðr may decide to ride across country to warn the Dal gCais chieftains of my intent, but it was a long way overland and I could afford two days delay.

When the wind finally reduced it had shifted around to a mild north westerly coming offshore. My fleet left the estuary of the River Barrow and tacked up the south coast at a much slower pace using oar power to come about with each tack. In this way my fleet made its way passed Cobh and other smaller Norse settlements, which were within Munster. We sailed about a mile offshore so we would not be immediately observable. I was worried that when we made the south western tip of Ireland and had to tack north, we would be fighting against a head wind making our approach to Limerick very difficult and wearing. My fears were alleviated somewhat as we approached Carn Uí Néid where the towering cliffs of the jagged peninsulas jutted out into the sparkling Atlantic. As we cleared the headland the wind died to a gentle breeze and although it meant rowing northward it was not impossible.

It had taken us a week to sail from Dublin passed Cobh and a further day to reach the end of Ireland. We still had a stiff row north passed enumerable beetling cliffs and jagged rocky peninsulas to reach the mouth of the Shannon and the passage to Limerick and after that the Shannon estuary up to Limerick was another day's row with the help of the wind if we were lucky. We had to be lucky, I wanted the element of surprise.

Limerick was built on a peninsula formed by a wide bend in the river, which was not untypical of the original viking long ports. For nearly two hundred years the town was ruled by the Hy Ivarr, the descendants of the first viking raider to establish a base there. Apparently, there was ample space in the river both upstream and downstream of the town for ships to berth. There was a constant stream of shipping up and down the river and out to sea and it was vital that we prevented an early warning to the town that we were approaching. I intended to approach in the darkness and arrive at dawn but this needed careful handling and I was in the hands of the local Irish Norse who had previously visited the trading centre.

The weather held and we made the wide estuary of the mighty River Shannon as dusk was falling. I was assured that most sea traders would anchor close to shore in the estuary at night, rather than run aground. My fleet kept in line behind *Ottar* allowing us to mark the way with a small stern lantern. We entered the mouth of the river and as we felt the wind move around to our larboard side, we hoisted a half sail and moved smoothly into the centre of the river.

Eystein Whaleleg, who was still with me, had taken up point at the bow post and was scanning the waters ahead claimed to know the river like the back of his hand. Our sail set gave us sufficient forward way so that the men could rest; it was essential that they recovered from their long row before we attacked the long port. We passed several trading vessels moored up and we left them alone, for now, as they could not warn Limerick before we attacked. There was a crescent moon and a clear sky; this was good for the last leg of our journey but less fortuitous for launching our attack on the town. I could discern strands of dawn light up before us, and Eystein reassured me that Limerick lay directly ahead.

I signalled back to the following longships to spread out across the river, I had already instructed them to attack every vessel in the river; destroying the town's fleet was more important than attacking the town. My fleet made the last turn of the river and the strand of Limerick was exposed to our view. At least fifteen ships were moored up at a wooden jetty, they were all knarrs, trading vessels. In the river itself I counted a dozen snekkjas swinging in the current. Beyond that I saw more boats pulled up on the river bank before the river bend hid anything else.

Everything seemed quiet, no observable person had stirred from their slumber and I saw no guards on the town wall, an earthen embankment with wooden palings. The timing of the attack was perfect. As previously instructed, Egil swung *Ottar* close to the right bank so that we would pass across the sterns of the berthed knarrs.

213

Martin had retrieved the burning lantern from the stern post now it was no longer needed and was passing along a group of my crew that had been selected to torch the enemy ships. They all held wooded batons with rags soaked in whale oil wrapped around their torch heads. Each man lit his torch from the lantern flame. Egil brought our boat up to the sterns of the knarrs in a smooth glide and as we passed each moored knarr two burning brands were thrown into the waist of each ship. My men were trying to hit the furled sails, which with luck would catch quickly and be difficult to quench. Two additional snekkjas followed *Ottar* astern and the incendiary process was repeated. *Ottar* had not cleared the last of the trading vessels before flames licked up from the first.

The rest of my fleet had singled out snekkjas moored in the river and had moved alongside to board them. I would have liked to burn these longships, as well, but the Dublin Norse were scandalised by my suggestion. After much discussion and argument, I had to disavow my original intention and agree that the snekkjas should be captured, if possible, but I insisted the trading vessels should be burnt to cripple the Munster economy.

My Norsemen moved their boats effortlessly alongside the still dormant vessels and warriors slipped over the top strakes, hand axes at the ready. From the dearth of noise, it appeared that most of the moored longships only had skeleton crews while most of the warriors were in the town. I smiled as the Limerick vikings would be impotent without their shipping.

Egil manoeuvred *Ottar* passed the burning knarrs towards the ships beached on the shingle beyond; the following longships copied our course. It was impossible to pass close to the beached ships without the risk of running aground so throwing burning brands into them was not an option. However, Martin had foreseen this and had prepared fire arrows. Each warrior with a bow lit a fire arrow and fired into one of the beached ships; the following longships copied our assault and the beached ships soon caught fire. Having neutralised the boats tied up to the shore I signalled to the following snekkjas to fan out and attack any enemy shipping in the river. Egil steered *Ottar* to the bend of the river upstream from the jetty, and as the further reaches of the river came into view, I could see that there was still more shipping in the river and against another jetty.

"Martin, sound a horn we must attack these other ships and destroy them." I shouted.

"It will alert the town, master." Martin called back. I looked back at the burning enemy ships.

"That won't matter soon." I could already hear shouts of alarm.

Martin placed a bull's horn to his lips and blew a long low blast; viking heads turned toward us from most of our ships and I waved frantically. I knew it would be hard to persuade the Norsemen to abandon their captured ships but I hoped there would be enough to be effective. The three snekkjas that had supported us in the burning of the boats swung back in line, rowing after us. It took time for my fleet to disengage but at least five other snekkjas started rowing in our direction. Nine ships would have to do.

Shouts were now being heard from the town and men were seen running down to the water's edge. They started shouting impotently. Some grabbed buckets and started to fight the fires on the burning ships but it was far too late for that.

Eystein shouted the time to my rowers and Egil steered *Ottar* forwards to engage with the nearest enemy ship. It was a low sleek but small snekkja drifting at anchor in the current twenty paces from the shore. A single face peeped over the sheer strake with a look of shock. As *Ottar* glided in I leaped from the foredeck and landed square in the well of the enemy snekkja. Without thought I brought my sword down of the horrified face of the guard. It was only a boy but his head split nevertheless. Blood fountained. I looked around and saw there was no one else aboard. Two vikings had followed me.

"Use your axes, sink it." I shouted and turned and jumped back onto *Ottar* before it had swept passed. We managed to bring destruction upon two more snekkjas moored in the river in the same fashion before the rest of my longships joined us in the general mayhem.

Towns people were now scrambling down to the docked knarrs on the upstream part of the town and I doubted that we could destroy these boats without taking casualties of our own.

215

Within a quarter of a watch, we visited destruction on the river's moored shipping. There were a few ships hauled up on the shore but none of the townspeople were brave enough to push them into the stream and offer battle. They all stood impotent on the beach and wharves watching their livelihoods being destroyed. By noon I called off my sea wolves and directed *Ottar* back towards the open sea; my fleet disengaged slowly and I was not surprised to see that each snekkja was towing a captured ship, mostly snekkjas, but the odd knarr also. I fine haul of plunder to gladden the heart of any viking. My fleet made its way down towards the river mouth with the strong current. I could see that my crew were disgruntled by the fact that they had no plunder to show for leading the assault but I remembered the moored-up traders I had spotted on the way into the river overnight. Before we had reached the sea the ships boy up on the spar shouted that there was a large knarr ahead coming towards us obviously unaware of the recent attack on Limerick.

"Right lads!" I called them all to attention. "This is your prize, not only the ship but the cargo. Rowers, make way she is ours for the taking." We closed on the knarr fast, its crew were rightly alarmed at seeing a sizeable fleet bearing down upon it from what they considered to be a friendly port. The knarr's sheer strake was much higher that our snekkjas but the Norsemen were familiar with assaulting such a ship. They knew that the knarrs crew rarely exceeded ten or twelve and the crews were not heavily armed. It was true that there were usually a few archers on board but they were nullified by prudently raising your shield boards and ensuring that the snekkja's helmsman, old Egil, was well covered.

The knarr keeled over as it turned tightly around in an attempt to flee. The captain of the knarr quickly decided that their only chance of escape was to head for the distant shore but as the river estuary had widened out considerably there was no chance that the knarr would ground before we caught up with it. The knarr's four long sweeps came out in a vain attempt to speed it along but our snekkja was cutting through the water like a salmon as we raced up to its stern. A couple of desultory arrows hit our deck to no effect and with that we swept alongside the labouring trading vessel. Three of my crew threw iron grappling hooks over the side of the knarr whilst my archers scanned the enemy's sheer strake for foolish heads to pop up. Standing on *Ottar's* sheer strake I hooked a small axe up over the knarr's side placed my foot on its hull and pulled myself up, as my head cleared the knarr's sheer strake an enemy crewman ran at me with a spear levelled. I swung my sword and deflected the spear and I pulled myself over the side of the knarr. I fell onto the deck and rolled clear hoping to avoid an attacker until I could stand. Coming to a crouch I looked around and saw that my recent attacker had been stabbed by another of my crew. I could only see the knarr's crewmen on the stern platform surrounding the tiller. They had formed a small shield wall with large wooden shields and small working axes. They could not be skewered with arrows so I concluded that it was their best defensive option.

My men piled on to the knarr deck looking round for resistance. "Hold!" I shouted. The crew gave me their attention and formed up facing the enemy. I moved forward to the shield wall.

"Who speaks for you, who is your captain?" I shouted.

"A grizzled sailor standing next to the tiller shouted back. "I am, what's to do?"

"We have your ship but I have no interest in killing you or your crew. Surrender and I will let you go free at our next landfall."

"We are legitimate traders bound for Limerick, why do you, coming from Limerick wish to rob us?" The captain shouted back.

"We are not from Limerick and have just raided the town on behalf of King Diarmait Mael na mBo of Leinster; you are fair game for us, that is your fate." I responded. "Surrender now."

After a brief deliberation the captain of the knarr instructed his crew to lay down their weapons. They all looked relieved as I imagined they did not want to die so pointlessly. My crew were inordinately pleased as they now had equivalent loot with the rest of the crews in the fleet. The rest of the fleet had come up and crowded around.

I shouted across instructions to the skippers to sort out their crews and provide each of the captured boats with skeleton crews as it would not be possible to tow the captured ships in the open sea. We had to sail at the speed of the slowest knarr as I had no intention of losing wealth gained, but fortunately the wind was still from the north west and we sailed comfortably south and east. We arrived back in the long port of Dublin as summer blossomed, the last part of the journey spoilt by squally rain delivered by a soft north wind, which meant a long row up the east coast of Leinster. We had dropped off the Loch Garman, Arklo and Vicklo crews and their captured ships on the way. I was pleased to see King Diarmait Mael na mBo on the jetty, he had taken the time to walk down to the shore to greet me, a mark of respect I hoped. I would certainly wish to deal with him rather than his obnoxious son.

Of course, he would want his share of the loot, a couple of ships should do it. Several of the captured trading vessels and cargo on board that would be shared out on the beach. I had marooned the captive crew on a beach near Cobh on the Irish south coast but was surprised to find several slaves incarcerated in the small hold of the knarr along with jars of wine and metalware. The slaves were all women and amazingly they were all a black brown in colour. Where they had been captured or bought, I had no idea and had failed to ask the marooned captain. One of my Dublin Norse informed me that they probably came from Andalucia, a part of Hispania or from the coast of Maroc; apparently these were lands far to the south of England, and Ireland across the sea. I knew from my Latin education that these lands had been part of the ancient Roman Empire. There had been coloured slaves in Dublin before in the time of the sons of Ragnar Lodbrog, the vikings called them 'blue men'. Some of my crew wanted to have sex with them as a novelty, others thought nothing but bad luck would come from intimacy with such devil women. I decided that I would test the truth and permitted an older crew member answering to the ubiquitous name of Stump to couple with one of the women. Naturally he chose one who had big breasts but as they all appeared ugly to me, I was not sure if she was beautiful by their tribe's standards.

She was laid naked on the deck in the belly of the ship surrounded by the non-rowing crew members. Stump had no compunction about raping the woman in front of all of us and his endeavours were encouraged by the cheering crew. Surprisingly the woman did not appear put out by Stump's endeavours and even appeared to caress and encourage him to greater exertions. Under these circumstances it was not long before Stump grunted out his juices into the moaning woman.

The shout went up, "Too quick Stump." I laughed as it was clear that Stump wanted more.

"No, that's it." I shouted, "If they are devil women Stump has done enough to either die or seed the woman. You will have to wait until we reach Dublin to get a turn. Put them back in the knarr's hold."

In anticipation of such unusual carnal delights, I am sure the crew rowed all the harder.

Alighting from my snekkja onto the wooden jetty I saluted King Diarmait. "Well met, my lord. The Limerick fleet has been mostly destroyed, we have captured over a dozen ships, snekkjas and knarrs both." I indicated to the enlarged fleet berthing along the river front.

"Splendid, Munster is open to attack and I will be King of Leth Moga before the year is out."

That night the king held a great feast for my fleet's captains and helmsmen. The king and I distributed the loot evenly throughout the crews but each ship's captain was allowed to keep and or sell their captured ship to the benefit of his crew. Finally, I called upon Stump.

"Stump, stand forth." I cried. The shambling Norseman made his way to the King's table looking somewhat downcast. "Well Stump, tell us, was the blue woman a devil or a sidhe fairy woman to give otherworldly bliss to a man?"

The feasters cheered. They shouted, "Yes, tell us Stump, how good was she?"

"She was a she-devil; I haven't stopped itching since we mated." Stump muttered.

"Louder Stump, was fucking the blue woman worth it?" I shouted.

"No, no, she has given me crabs." The crowd of men screamed with laughter.

"I think Stump needs a good bath." Shouted Martin, ever the analyst.

"To the river with Stump." Shouted the throng. Stump was grabbed by the excited feasters and hoisted onto their shoulders and marched out of the king's hall heading for the river.

The king laughed with everyone else but soon became serious, it was clear he wanted to talk about the rest of the years campaigning.

"Bearslayer, I conceive that Munster will be heavily defended even without the Dal gCais lack of a fleet to transport their army up and down the Shannon rapidly. I have taken steps to strengthen our position. I have allied with Ossory my neighbouring kingdom in Leinster and have made an alliance with a claimant to the Munster throne who is also allied to Connaught. Munster will be invaded from all points within the month. I intend to move through Ossory against Cashel the stronghold of the Eoghanachta, the rival clan of Munster who I hope will not contend our advance over much. This should open up the approach to Limerick and the Dal gCais capital at Kincora further up the Shannon by land. A campaign I intend to accomplish next year."

"And what role would you wish me to play, lord?" I responded.

"Nothing this year, you have done enough. I will want my viking fleet to assail the Shannon next year to prevent the Dal gCais moving east from Limerick." Diarmait smiled with satisfaction, "Maybe you would wish to dally with a dusky she-devil awhile?"

"I think not, to be honest I am not sure what is to be done with them. The crews now think they are tainted so they are not worth much." I responded.

"I will buy them," Diarmait smiled craftily, "I have a mind to give them as gifts to the kings in the north.

How malicious, I thought, nevertheless an outbreak of sexual diseases amongst the rulers of Ulster and Connaught had its amusing side.

"I accept your offer, lord." I announced with alacrity.

The rest of the summer passed in a hazy sunshine. King Diarmait went off to war and the Norse merchants dispersed. I decided to take my snekkja *Ottar* to the Isle of Mann and on to the Hebrides more out of sheer pleasure than anything else. On

Mann I renewed my acquaintance with Eachmarchach Ragnaldson, who at the time was King of Mann, the Rhinns of Galloway and some of the Alban Isles. I had first met him whilst assisting King Thorfinn MacBeth repel the English invasion of Alba three years previously and he had assisted in the raids on England to help my brother regain his Earldom. I found him entertaining and exuberant, he always took adversity lightly and he had had a surfeit of adversity having been previously expelled as King of Dublin by Diarmait. However, he was now in his fifties and feeling his age and quickly commandeered me to collect taxes for him from his northern possessions. This translated into a meandering sail around the southern Hebridean isles, Kintyre, Islay, Jura, Arran, and the Rhinns of Galloway. None of these areas were particularly prosperous and the taxes were meagre, but the scenery was quite breathtaking even for a reiver like me to appreciate. I was accompanied back to Mann with a knarr, captained by a chief from Islay, loaded with goods, taxes in kind, even some livestock. Nevertheless, this still pleased Eachmarchach and his Mann chieftains who did not appear particularly wealthy themselves.

The night of our arrival was the inevitable feast, it was mid-August and the days were beginning to shorten so Eachmarchach had his hall lit with fires in iron brackets on stands away from the walls to prevent a hall burning. I sat next to Eachmarchach in the middle of the cross table and he handed me a cup of ale.

"I have news, Bearslayer, ill news." Eachmarcach started.

"So have I, are we talking the same ill news?" I answered. Eachmarcach looked puzzled.

"You have heard of the death of your sire, Leofric, whilst you were north in the Alban isles?"

I looked stunned; I had not expected this, I knew my father was aged but he did not look at death's door when I had last seen him at Chester. "No, no, that is not the news I have. My father dying is ill news and I will grieve. I was not close to him but I respected him greatly. This is a lot to take in. What of my brother, have you heard of his circumstances?"

"Yes, he has come into his inheritance, he is now Earl of Mercia, supported by his mother, the Lady Godgifu and his brother-in-law King Gryffudd of North Wales."

That at least was some good news, my brother was now in a much stronger position than he had been in East Anglia and almost an equal to Harald Godwinson of Wessex. Eachmarchach sat silently whilst I considered the ramifications of my father's death. Eventually I returned to my original ill news.

"Eachmarchach, I learnt in Galloway that Thorfinn MacBeth had been surprised and killed at Lumphanan, north of the Mounth, by Malcolm MacCrinan who is now King of Alba, although Lulach, MacBeth's step-son has also declared himself King of Alba up in Moray."

Eachmarchach looked crestfallen, "That is bad news, Thorfinn and I have been friends and allies since Knut Sweynson's days and I will have a hard time keeping my lands in Alba against Malcolm."

"Malcolm may have his hands full with Harald Godwinson's brother Tostig who King Edward the Mild, or should I say Earl Harald, has made Earl of Northumbria, to the detriment of the hereditary lords of Bamburgh, the Edulfings. Tostig is a wolf and not to be trusted on Alba's southern border." I added.

For Eachmarchach and I the feast started and ended in sadness, my father, and a friend both passed beyond the river.

I stayed on in Mann for a few more weeks at something of a loss, apart from renewing my mercenary activities in Ireland my future looked bleak, at least to me. My followers may see me as a great warlord but I did not see fighting petty wars in Ireland as any advancement of my status or a sensible direction for the future.

More news filtered through from the wider world. Thorfinn MacBeth's vivacious daughter Ingibiorg had been forcibly married by Malcolm, King of Alba, who was now calling himself Canmore, or great chief, and he had wisely left Thorfinn's sons Paul and Erland as joint rulers of the Orkneys, especially as their overlord was the King of Norway. They obviously had not felt strong enough to oppose Malcolm and as they had no claim on the Alban throne the Orkney vikings were not inclined to support any such aspiration.

Not surprisingly, in England, Harald Godwinson had taken the Earldom of East Anglia back into his family's control, giving it to a younger brother, Gyrth, meaning that my brother's Mercia was surrounded by Godwinson earldoms; it did not look good for my brother in the long run.

By September, with my crew muttering, I sailed back to Dublin with meagre profit, just enough to keep the crew from mutiny but as I could not find a legitimate enemy to fight, I remained sanguine. However, I had decided that I must move further afield as I had no wish to become inveigled in the interminable Irish wars for the rest of my life.

I found Dublin quiet, counting its trading season's profits, the news from Fearns was that Diarmait Mael na mBo had led a successful invasion of eastern Munster, defeated the Munster army, and pushed them back towards Limerick; his plans were coming to fruition. I had no choice but to winter over in Dublin and I knew that I would lose a substantial number of my crew over this period as success breeds renown but since my raid on Limerick my success had been in short supply. I missed Una and was losing confidence. Martin had struck up a friendship with a Dublin trader and was spending more and more time at the wharfs. Yule was a muted affair accompanied with the usual squally rain and even the occasional flurry of snow. I had no joy in the feasting.

Spring 1058 – The Norwegians

I was galvanised by the news, action at last. A message arrived from King Gryffudd, now king of all Wales. Aelfgar, my brother had been banished yet again and another massive raid into England was planned and this time with the support of the Norwegians. Apparently, Magnus Haraldson, the King of Norway's son was sailing to the Orkneys to ensure the young Earls of Orkney, Paul and Erland gave due homage to their overlord, his father and he was to be persuaded to assist in the raid on England by my brother. I did not relish fighting yet another war on the English, Welsh border but the prospect of fighting alongside the Norwegian vikings was appealing and likely to restore my fortunes. I resolved to sail to the Orkneys and meet up with Magnus Haraldson as soon as the sailing season set in. I announced my plans to my crew, or what was left of them, Egil, his son and half a dozen others and started to prepare my snekkja, *Ottar* for sea. Many of the Dublin Norse had lost their affinity with their northern brethren and were not willing to participate in any activity that might damage their trade. I eventually left Dublin with a skeleton crew determined to supplement them from enthusiastic youngsters on Mann or in the Hebrides, Eachmarchach's lands. As the weather turned, I prepared to sail on the morning tide; suddenly Martin clambered onto *Ottar.*

"Time to leave, master." He stated.

"Martin, I haven't seen you in weeks, since Yule in fact, and now you clamber aboard and say it's time to leave." I demanded, quite bewildered.

"If we don't leave now, I'm a dead man, master." Martin responded and from his manner I could tell he was deadly serious.

"Egil!" I shouted. Egil came stumbling over, clearly just awoken. "Cast off now and move into the middle of the river." I ordered.

"But all the crew isn't here?"

"No matter, they will find a way to join us or they will be left behind." My look brooked no delay.

Several of the crew pushed the snekkja from the jetty out into the Liffey and we dropped an anchor stone a hundred paces out from the shore. Several of the crew hurriedly leapt aboard.

"Now Martin, what's this all about?" I demanded somewhat exasperated.

"Master, I have slain King Diarmait's chief supporter in Dublin. When the King's son finds out I will be hunted down and killed."

"But why have you done this?" I was no clearer as to why Martin had acted in such an uncharacteristic way.

"Well, the night will be long so I will explain all." Martin calmed himself and smiled grimly. "As you know I have spent my youth in monastic communities in England but before that I lived in servitude with my mother. She was Welsh but had been taken into slavery by the Irish Dublin vikings; she was sold to an Irish merchant trader in Dublin who used her as a whore, his bed warmer, thus I was born. The merchant treated my mother abominably, beating her when he was drunk, abusing her without restraint. She protected me the best she could but eventually he beat her to death and sold me to an Irish monastery who regularly bought slaves' freedom. I was trained and educated at that monastery and eventually accompanied a sainted abbot to England where I became incarcerated in your step-mothers foundation in Coventry, another form of slavery. Just before Yule this same merchant, my father, returned to Dublin; I recognised him immediately. My time for retribution had come, I immediately started to ingratiate myself into his confidence and circle of business acquaintances. I did not want to just assassinate him in the street, I wanted to confront him and make it known to him why I was killing him. He was guarded well; he even had a couple of huscarls loaned to him by the King's son. Anyway, your precipitous decision to leave Dublin meant I had to bring my plans forward. I managed to corner him in his warehouse tonight and confront him with my identity and then I put my axe through his brain, unfortunately I had to kill his two huscarls in my escape. That is my story, I am at your mercy master."

This was a lot to digest but there was only one answer. "Martin, you are my only trusted friend and I love you like a brother. Any obligations I have to King Diarmait is nothing compared to you." We embraced and I felt I had someone that was truly family for the first time ever.

When dawn broke, we set sail down the Liffey estuary with what crew I had aboard. Fortunately, there was no sign of pursuit as with the skeleton crew we could not have fought off an attack. Once clear of the river we set a course for Mann. There was a stiff westerly bringing squally rain that leadened the sail but we raced along and once clear of the coast I knew there was not a boat that could catch us. From the estuary of the Liffey to the southernmost point of Mann was approximately seventy to eighty miles and I hoped to make landfall before dusk. I intended to sail up the west coast of the island to Peel Island where I hoped to find King Eachmarchach in residence. The island had a convenient sheltered bay, housed a defensive peel tower, and a church dedicated to St Patrick. It was one of the main fortresses on the island and used by Eachmarchach when trading with Ireland, but since he had been ousted from Dublin his trade had mainly been with the O'Neil clans of Ulster. Egil slipped *Ottar* into the bay after dusk but the lights from the isle and villages along the bay enabled us to run our keel up onto the shingle and make the boat fast. I left the snekkja in Egil's care and with Martin, Eystein and four others of my crew made my way along the bay towards the chieftain's hall.

The hall was ablaze with light from many braziers and I could hear roistering in the hall. The door was unguarded and ajar. The heat from the interior was like a blast from a blacksmith's furnace. I entered cautiously not knowing what to expect. My men and I were not noticed as we made our way down the hall towards the high seat. The Manx Norse were carousing and, in their cups, many women, I was not sure if they were slaves or servants, were in a state of undress. Some of the women were being mounted in full view of the hall, it was a regular Bacchanalian orgy. I reached the high seat and observed Eachmarchach lolling on his carved throne in a state of semi-dress, his eyes closed. A naked woman was kneeling before him with is manhood engulfed in her mouth. Next to Eachmarchach a younger man was sitting on a stool with a young girl sitting on his knee. The young man had his hand down her blouse fondling her breast and kissing her neck, she appeared to be enjoying his attentions.

Eachmarcach slowly opened his eyes and smiled lazily. "Well, Bearslayer, welcome to my hall, what do you here?" The question was interspersed with gasps of pleasure resulting from the ministrations of the kneeling woman.

"Eachmarchach, a child could set fire to this hall and there would be such a hall burning as not seen since Njal was burnt in Iceland." I responded. Eachmarchach giggled at this and promptly orgasmed into the woman's mouth.

"By Freya's tits, I needed that." He exclaimed hoarsely. "Just got back from Orkney, that son of Harald Hardrada is only a young sprig, full of himself."

"That's why I am here, tidy yourself up and we need to talk." I countered rather brusquely. I left the hall and returned to my ship, I preferred not to be so exposed as Eachmarchach and his companions were, in all senses of the word. The next day, Eachmarchach came down the beach walking rather unsteadily, the younger man I had seen next to him at the feast was with him; he looked rather sick too.

"Well met Bearslayer, bit of a night last night, don't remember much of it though." I nodded to the younger man, probably about my age and raised my eyebrow by way of a query. "Oh aye, this is my son Solmund, until recently he has been with my wife Affrica in Kintyre and I have cut him a bit of slack lately. His wife is a terrible prude, she is an Irish princess of the O'Neill of Ulster, reinforces my hold on the Isles."

I nodded at the young man. "That wasn't his wife last night then?"

"What, oh! No, it will not do him any harm to sow some wild oats." Eachmarchach laughed, but I was not sure he had any idea what he was referring to.

"You said you have just returned from Orkney after meeting with Magnus Haraldson." I prompted.

"Yes, I have a difficult relationship with my superiors." Eachmarchach used the term derisively. "As you know when I was expelled from Dublin, I was given Mann, Kintyre, and the southern isles to rule on behalf of Thorfinn, but Thorfinn himself was a subject of the King of Norway. That hard bastard Harald of Norway has sent his son Magnus west to secure the Orkneys and I was summoned to Dingwall to give my allegiance. Well Magnus is but a boy but he has some of King Harald's forecastle men with him, men who were with Hardrada down in Miklegard fighting the Saracens and they have seen a few things and are not fools. Paul and Erland are in close ward and do as the Norwegians see fit. I swiftly gave reassurances of my loyalty, not least to escape alive from Dingwall and get back here where I deem it is safe. I picked up my son on the way as I have no intention of him being made a hostage for my good faith." Eachmarchach finished lamely and I could see that he was a spent force and no longer the man who had fought beside Thorfinn MacBeth in Alba.

"I have received information that Magnus intends to sail south and assist my brother raiding in England. Aelfgar has been outlawed again." I ended lamely.

"That means he may come here." Eachmarcach looked alarmed.

"I will go to the Orkneys and persuade the Norwegians to attack down the east side of England, Northumbria and East Anglia, lands controlled by the Godwinsons." I countered.

Eachmarchach's face lightened, "Would you, that would be good; that would be very good."

"One thing, I need a crew; I sailed from Dublin in haste, not to return. I need forty good men. I will sail with the Norwegians so there will be loot."

Eachmarchach quicky found me a crew but I could see that they were made up of the scum of the island, brigands, and wastrels but as I was considered such myself, I suppose I could not complain; surprisingly Stump was one of them. Nevertheless, I was able to sail on within two days and made for Kintyre. As I sailed through the isles, I managed to pick up six more small snekkjas, the locals called them birlinns. Raiding always had an appeal to the islemen as they were mostly poor, half Irish, half Norwegian, called Gall-Gaedhil. I was therefore able to make a reasonable showing when I sailed into Kirkwall Bay. Kirkwall was bustling with shipping. I knew that the two earls of Orkney commanded dozens of snekkjas and knarrs but in addition to these there were a dozen larger snekkja and a huge drakkar, king's ships from Norway.

Martin and I made our way up to the earls' hall, two heavily armoured huscarls held the door; they were in full mail shirts, down to mid-thigh, nasal guard helmets with an additional chainmail coif that hid their faces. Both guards had placed their shields against the stone wall of the hall and held large Dane axes with extended hafts for two-handed strikes. The shields were emblazoned with rampant lions holding axes, the emblem of the Norwegian King. There was no question who was in control here.

"Who goes?" the huscarl on the left uttered a guttural challenge.

"I am Hereward Leofricson, brother to Aelfgar, Earl of Mercia in England and I would speak to Magnus Haraldson and the young Orkney earls."

"Wait." Commanded the huscarl, he went inside the hall and the other huscarl moved across to bar our way. We waited some time but not so long as to be insulted when the huscarl returned and ushered us in. We were met inside by a herald in some finery, in fact, a glance around the hall showed that he was the only man unarmoured.

"Follow me, my lord." He obviously had no knowledge of my status and assumed that I was an ambassador for my brother. He led us to the high seat where a young man maybe six or seven years younger than I sat in state with a large sword across his knee in traditional fashion. To one side sat the two young Orkney earls, Paul, and Erland who I knew slightly and to the prince's right stood a large man with a long beard that flowed down his chest, braided with ribbons and finger bones. This I assumed was the young princes' 'minder' and adviser, the real leader of the expedition from Norway.

The herald introduced me, "My lords, this is Hereward Leofricson, brother of Earl Aelfgar of Mercia in England, he has six snekkjas in the Sound." I bowed low to the Norwegian prince; this was not the time to act independently.

It was not the young prince who responded but the older man. "I am Eystein Orri, King Harald's councillor and guardian of the young prince here, what is it you want?"

"I have come to offer my services to the prince, I understand he is contemplating a raid on England to support my brother Earl Aelfgar in his dispute with Earl Harald Godwinson." I explained.

"It is true that your brother has sent an embassy to the prince and his representatives are still here, however, they have not made a good case for this raid upon England. At the moment my king has no quarrel with England."

"I would not agree with that assessment, may I speak with the embassy and ascertain what their proposal is?"

Eystein Orri shrugged, "I do not see why not and if you can come up with a better offer than theirs, I would say my prince would be interested."

I was directed to an adjacent hall where Aelfgar's representatives were housed, it was unguarded and I walked straight in. Two young men sat near the fire, both with drinking horns to hand and in deep discussion. They looked like twins, both with blonde braided hair tied back with a hairband and both dressed similarly in tunics and hose, the only difference was that one's apparel was russet red and the others was white, well off-white, or as white as it could be.

"You are my brother's emissaries?" I demanded, both heads swung towards me together and in unison they exclaimed.

"Cousin!"

Cousin, I thought, how am I, their cousin? "Who are you?" They both stood.

"I am Siward the White and this is my brother Siward the Red, we are the sons of Maelswegn, Shire Reeve of Lincoln, your uncle and brother of Abbot Brand and your mother."

"I don't remember meeting you before." I responded somewhat perplexed.

"You were sent to stay with your father before we could meet, but uncle Brand has told us all about you. Hereward the Outlaw, wolfs head, Bearslayer, priest killer, viking!"

I dismissed all the adulation. "My mother, uncle Brand, are they well?"

"Yes, your mother lives quietly near Bourne with your younger brother. Uncle Brand moves around the Danelagh doing good works and resides in Ely." I was fascinated as to how the two young men spoke together, filling in each other's phrases as if they knew what would be spoken by each other in advance.

"Why did your father call you both by the same name? It is very confusing."

They laughed and obviously it was a question they were continuously asked. "Our father had decided on the name for his first-born son, Siward, but he did not anticipate twins, I was born slightly before my brother and was nice and pink, my brother, smaller and more frail was quite white for a time, so he called me red and him white." Siward the Red explained.

"Siward the Red and Siward the White." His brother added grinning. After prolonged introductions and small talk, I brought the conversation round to the reason why they were in the Orkneys.

"Your brother chose us to come to see Prince Magnus because we were visiting him at Chester when he was outlawed. We were on our way to find you in Ireland and he gave us a ship and asked us to come here. I do not think he wanted to jeopardise any of his Mercian thegns and the Godwinsons tend to leave the Danelagh alone."

"What proposal were you to place before Magnus?" I queried.

"Aelfgar wanted the Norwegians to raid down the west coast of England in the same way King Eachmarchach did last time, but they don't seem very interested." Siward the Red explained.

"I'm not surprised, the west coast of England holds no prospects for the vikings, Cumbria is poor, Wales is an ally of Aelfgar and that means a long voyage south to the Cornish peninsula before the plundering is worthwhile and to top that, as you say, Eachmarchach looted that land and the English south coast recently." I summarised the flaws in the proposal. "No, Aelfgar should have realised that this plan is flawed and unlikely to appeal to the Norwegians. Something must be proposed that will make Harald Godwinson take notice and I have just the answer." I smiled calculatingly.

The next day I asked for an audience with Prince Magnus but was unsurprised when I was ushered in to the presence of Eystein

Orri in a small cubicle off the great hall. "Magnus is off hawking with the earls, I will decide on our planning, what do you propose, Bearslayer?"

So, he knew something of my background, that might help, I launched into my plan. "The way I see it Prince Magnus has been sent overseas west to learn and become a warrior like his father. The Orkneys have been easily cowed and brought back under the control of the Norwegian crown now that Jarl Thorfinn is dead, but that has not advanced Prince Magnus' education one jot. What you need is a successful raid preferably against opponents that are perceived to be unfriends of the Norwegian crown. There are four obvious choices; one, King Malcolm Canmore of Alba who previously allied himself with old Sigurd Digre the Danish Jarl of Northumberland and is no friend of Norway; two, the English Earldom of Northumbria presently ruled by Tostig Godwinson, related in marriage to the Danish crown; three the Norse towns in Ireland or finally, four raid Wales. I would suggest that a raid down the east coast of Alba and Northumbria would be most profitable and give the prince the best opportunity to partake of some reasonable fighting. There are rich pickings along the east coast and it is much easier to return to Norway this year, whereas a raid down the west way would mean a winter over here and a return next year and besides Wales and Scotland are poor and the ports in Ireland already hold some allegiance to Norway"

Eystein Orri stroked his luxurious beard and looked thoughtful, eventually he smiled. "Your reputation is well earned, for such a youngster and I like your proposal; as you know my king has been warring with Denmark for years and he is well aware of the close relationship between Sweyn Estridson, the upstart, and the English Godwinsons. To strike at Tostig Godwinson would please King Harald greatly and I have seen that by doing this, it would assist your brother's cause somewhat even if it does not appear that we are helping him and his Welsh allies directly." He smiled again, showing a yellowing broken set of teeth that had clearly been smashed in some early encounter. "You and your little fleet will be joining us?"

I was not sure if this was an order or a question but, "I wouldn't miss it for anything."

Later the two Siward's were jubilant, "How did you manage to change their minds, cousin?"

"Eystein Orri is an old warrior who has seen a bit in his time and understands military strategy. By switching the vikings advance from west to east it all became clear to him that there was profit in it both for him and his king." I elucidated. "You must both return to Aelfgar and explain the change in strategy. A viking raid on the Northumbrian coast simultaneously with increased aggression from Wales will cause Harald Godwinson to become anxious and seek to reach a resolution with my brother."

"But cousin, we want to stay with you, to go viking." They looked crestfallen.

I laughed, "Duty first, honour my brother. Together we will rescue him from his impasse, but you must tell him from me that he must be more circumspect in future or Harald Godwinson will swallow him up. I will not be around to offer my help as I intend to sail with the Norwegians or offer my services in Flanders. I have had my fill of Ireland and Wales."

It took two days to provision and equip the Norwegian drakkars and snekkjas for the raid, the ships were not over filled in anticipation of needing space for plunder. The weather was kind and our fleet of twenty warships cleared the north eastern promontory of Caithness by mid-day. The kind weather however did not include a favourable wind, which was consistently blowing from the south, but only mildly. There would be no raiding in the north of Alba, an area that was mostly colonised by Norwegians and, which had been ruled by Jarl Thorfinn and his father Jarl Sigurd the Stout for many years. Shouting across to Eystein Orri, I suggested we raided Fife and the wealthy church lands at Kilrymont, the holy church of St. Andrew. This suggestion was pleasing to Eystein Orri who knew of my reputation for burning churches. On the third day, after long days of rowing, we coasted passed the estuary of the River Tay with the broad peninsula of the ancient kingdom of Fife ahead of us. From my previous sojourn in Alba, I knew that there was a suitable landing place in the mouth of the River Eden just north of the ecclesiastical town. The river estuary was a maze of shifting sandbanks but we took time to negotiate them safely and ran the ships up on a beautiful white sandy beach that was overlooked by steep sandhills. Eystein Orri wisely left a large troop of warriors to guard the fleet and led eight hundred men over the rough gorse sandhills towards the town. The settlement was just over a mile south on the coast; it would be considered remote for all but seafarers such as ourselves. There was a church with a tall tower of stone and around the church were several large buildings that I took to be monastic buildings. The secular town was spread around it and there were no defensive earthworks.

Before we had approached too near, Eystein Orri passed the word that the town was not to be fired as that would warn other settlements further south of our approach. Portable loot was to be taken and no more than one or two women for each boat. No longer than half a watch was to be spent plundering before a return to the ships was required. The vikings favoured controlled looting rather than wanton destruction. The Norwegians spread out in a wide arc to envelope the town; within a quarter of a mile from the settlement we were spotted by a shepherd boy who abandoned his sheep and ran towards the settlement.

"Rush the town now!" shouted Eystein Orri; the bulls horns sounded and the vikings increased their pace. The sooner we were among the houses the greater the surprise would be. My crews had held together as a unified band until we reached the outlying cottages but as no resistance materialised, I instructed them to fan out and loot, but to stay in small groups to give support to each other in case of any counter attacks. I kept *Ottar's* crew with me and ran towards the small fort near the church and monastic complex, if any attempt to stop us did come it would be from the fort. I could hear the screams emanating from the cottages and I knew the looting had started. I was concerned that my crew was the only organised group left to counter any warriors that may sally from the fort and shouted that a shield wall may need to be formed at a moment's notice. We cleared the sprawling settlement and approached the ecclesiastical compound and the adjacent fort; as we did the wooden gates of the fort opened and a score of Alban warriors spilled out. They were regimented and all carried a shield and a spear but there was no obvious leader. My men set up a defiant roar and the Albans faltered. After some hesitation they turned and scurried back into the fort and pushed the gates shut. I laughed at such timidity, but on reflection I considered that the whole garrison was no greater than a couple of dozen and they could see that there were hundreds of vikings plundering the settlement. Eystein Orri came lumbering up with Prince Magnus in tow.

"I will secure the fort, my lord. The monastery and church are yours." I smiled, monks were a good introduction for the young prince, little chance of coming to grief. Eystein Orri nodded and led the prince and his troop towards the church.

My crew and I kept a sharp eye on the fort whilst the vikings plundered the settlement. I noted they were well disciplined and kept to Eystein Orri's timetable; the Norwegians were soon carrying loot back to the ships, church silver plate, alter cloths, carved woodwork prized from benches and chairs and metal candlestick, brass, and iron. More prosaically some carried sacks of flour and other vegetable, staples from the monastery's gardens. I did not enquire regarding the state of the monks, alive or dead. After the vikings had cleared the church and monastery, I ordered my crew to fall back through the village. We passed a few plunderers still preoccupied raping women and my men dragged them off and made them fall back with us. I saw few bodies and was relieved that most of the prince's men did not feel the need for gratuitous violence. By mid-day we had all assembled back at the fleet, Eystein Orri called me over.

"That went well Bearslayer, did not lose a man and the young prince bloodied his sword and his manhood, there was a sweet nun is the church, just right for a young boy. He obviously enjoyed himself as he insisted, she was brought along with us; Hardrada will be proud of him." Eystein stroked his beard thoughtfully. "You did well, guarding against the fort and protecting the strandhog, it was noted by the prince and that taught him a lesson in how not to let your guard down. You and your crew will be rewarded from the plunder when it is shared."

"Thank you, my lord. That will please my crew."

The vikings loaded the ships and shared out the few women prisoners who would be well used, no doubt. By dusk our fleet had rounded the eastern point of Fife and entered the more sheltered waters of the Forth, an ideal location to hold up overnight. Eystein Orri took the precaution of spreading a few snekkjas across the mouth of the Firth estuary to waylay any merchant shipping and keep our presence a secret from the heavily populated areas along the banks of the River Forth further west. My crew settled down to sleep with just a single night sentry at the helm who I checked throughout the night. It was a pretty dark night, cloudy with some light rain. The quiet of the night was disturbed occasionally by the crying of women being abused. The crew slept having eaten well on stolen cold meats, dried fish, cheese, and fresh bread; plenty of ale too.

The next morning, early, we raised sails and coasted down the eastern seaboard of Lothian. The coast of Lothian does not offer many places to run a snekkja in for a quick raid, with beetling cliffs and a rugged coast line, but where the coast allowed Eystein Orri sent in one or two of his dragon ships to raid a village. The fortified strongholds of Dunbar and Berwick were too strong to attack without incurring loss, which brought us the Northumbrian border, where I wanted the real plundering and ravaging to begin. Inevitably, like all good viking raids on England, Lindisfarne monastery was our first port of call. The fleet sheltered in the lee of the Farne Islands whilst Eystein Orri, the prince, and his crew went ashore. I went along as I was mildly interested in St Cuthbert's shrine and abode. The monastery was quite shabby and run down, it had been raided so many times that there was nothing of any value and I was informed that St Cuthbert's relics were long gone. The old impressive stronghold of Bamburgh could be seen to the south; the old royal residence of the kings and earls of Bernicia. I informed Eystein Orri that the current earl of Northumbria might even be in residence.

The following day I was instructed by Prince Magnus, obviously at Eystein Orri's instigation, to seek information from the coastal settlements to the south of Bamburgh. I knew of a fishing village to the south of Bamburgh and I decided to take all my longships and run them up on the long sandy beach south of the village headland. I left half of the crews with the ships with ample sentries to the north so as I was not to be surprised by a sally from Bamburgh. With such arrangements in place, I strolled into the fishing village with a dozen of my crew, whilst the rest, some two hundred men circled the settlement to ensure no one could flee.

I found a rickety old inn that had seen many better days with some sawn logs judiciously placed outside for customers who found the reek inside objectionable. I instructed a crewman to drag the landlord out, together with a horn of ale and some bread and cheese. Within moments the landlord tumbled out of the tavern wringing his hands on a grubby apron.

"Good day, master. It is a pleasure to serve you, please accept the hospitality of my humble establishment, free, or course."

"Sit with me, I would talk with you." A doxy brought out some hard bread and even harder cheese and a brimming tankard. I took a sip.

"By Mimir's well, what is this, a rare vintage?" I smacked my lips savouring the smooth sweet drink.

"Tis a honey mead drink, my lord, a speciality of the area." The landlord informed me ingratiatingly.

"What is your name, innkeeper?" I demanded.

"Tis Edwy, sir, Edwy Edison."

"Tell me innkeeper, is the earl up in yon fortress?" I enquired.

"Which earl would that be sir, the old one or the new one?" the landlord stammered.

"I mean Tostig Godwinson, is there another one?"

"Well sir, there is the old earl of Bernicia who no longer has the favour of the English, he is up yonder." He indicated towards Bamburgh. "Then there is the new Saxon earl, him you mentioned, he is down in Deira, at York. They do not get on much, in fact, nobody gets on much with the new one, I understand the thegns are not too pleased with his high and mighty ways."

I discussed the state of the crops, how business was going, the weather, the landlord's family and learnt a great deal about the state of Northumbria. I enjoyed the mead and paid him for a couple of barrels and returned to the fleet as they coasted up to the settlement.

I reported to Eystein Orri and his young prince. "To be effective we need to raid further south in what is called Deira. I would suggest we attack Scarborough, Filey, and Bridlington and the villages in the Holdr's Ness. Apparently, these are all

237

wealthy settlements, attacking these settlements will greatly annoy and upset Earl Tostig; he does not much care for the poor north."

I persuaded Eystein Orri that this was the best course and the two barrels of mead helped.

We continued down the east coast of Northumbria, raided where it was likely some plunder was available, until we came to the large estuary of the River Tyne, sometimes considered to be the border between Bernicia and Deira. The viking fleet entered the river and the snekkjas ran up the muddy banks on both sides of the river with vikings spilling out and plundering in earnest. Loot started coming back to the ships in large quantities, some of it, like live cows and horses, quite unsuitable to convey. Once more my crews acted as look outs, covering the flanks of the vikings assaults to ensure we were not surprised by any relief force led by Tostig Godwinson. After three days the vikings were forced to have a giant strandhog on the river bank, slaughtering the cattle and horses, which, of course, they could not take with them. From the Tyne south the vikings now fired the settlements and farms, killing the men and taking selected girls and boys as slaves. The same method of raiding was repeated in the valley of the River Wear and the valley of the River Tees. I became concerned that the longships were overloaded already and the vikings would choose to turn back before any pressure was put on Tostig Godwinson.

Our fleet was preparing to put to sea when I was informed by one of my scouts that a herald was approaching from the west. I notified Eystein Orri and a small boat was sent across to the mud bank to convey the herald to the prince's snekkja. I made sure I was present at the interview.

"I come from Earl Tostig of Northumbria and he would treat with you, he would wish to know what terms he can offer you to leave?"

"What is your name herald?" Eystein Orri handing the herald a horn of mead.

"I am Gamel Ormson of the Holdr's Ness." The herald responded.

"The Holdr's Ness, I am sure you do not wish us to sail any further south Gamel of Holdr's Ness." Eystein Orri chortled. Gamel looked suitably discomforted.

"A gelt?" Prince Magnus chipped in. "Isn't that what we want foster father?"

"Yes, a gelt herald. We want five thousand pounds worth of silver." Eystein Orri demanded.

I almost choked, this was a very small sum compared to the gelt's paid in the past and I anticipated that Tostig would have been prepared to pay much more.

The herald kept his face straight and replied. "I will relate your proposal to the Earl, my lord and return tomorrow." I whispered in Eystein Orri's ear and he smiled and nodded.

"Herald, if Earl Tostig is so nearby, we would seal our agreement man to man. Tell your earl we will meet on the South Gare at noon." Eystein Orri added, "We will bring twenty men and one small snekkja and he will bring the same, and the silver." The herald left, leaving Eystein Orri jubilant. "Five thousand pounds of silver and a fleet laden with plunder, King Harald will be pleased." Eystein turned to me, "Why did you want the face-to-face meeting with Tostig?"

"He is not popular with his subjects, my lord, and if they see him grovelling before you it will damage his reputation still further. Trouble in Northumbria and on the Welsh border will persuade Harald Godwinson, the true ruler of England, that reinstating my brother will ease his problems. Indulge me in this I can do nothing more for my brother."

"You're a staunch companion Bearslayer and you have asked little of me and given good service; this is the least I can do in return."

The next day, at noon, the English party descended the steep sand dunes to the white sands of the South Gare. The silver was transported on mules as a wagon could never make it through the loose sand. True to the agreement Earl Tostig was accompanied by twenty men, twenty heavily armed huscarls. Eystein Orri had brought a small birlinn, one of my Hebridean ships to the beach with the agreed twenty vikings of which I was one. The rest of the fleet stood off the headland in a calm swell, they could reach the shore in the blink of an eye, in case Tostig contemplated treachery. Tostig rode up on a mettlesome black horse, all his huscarls were horsed likewise, leading the pack mules. I had taken the precaution of arming myself with my bow; a horse finds it hard to run with an arrow in its chest.

"Good day to you Earl Tostig," exclaimed Eystein Orri, "May I introduce Prince Magnus, the son of King Harald Hardrada."

Tostig was a dark haired and black visage man, given to scowling, unlike his charming brother. Harsh would be a good description. He was tall though, taller than his brother, he was magnificently dressed in black velvet with fur trims and gold thread. The hilt of his sword glistened with jewels, an unwise display and temptation in the presence of vikings.

"I would have preferred it if the royal prince had chosen another place to gain his experience." Tostig was terse almost insulting; not the way to handle vikings, especially Norwegians.

"It is perceived that your grip on your earldom is somewhat slack, what better time to attack when an earl's men will not support him." Eystein Orri provided the studied insult I was looking for.

"I have had to make representation to my brother for this gelt, it is not what I would have wished." Very unwise to reveal that, I thought, but it confirmed my understanding of the situation in Northumbria.

"We will leave and relieve you of the embarrassment, and relieve you of the silver. Nothing personal, my lord earl." The Norwegians started removing the silver and loading it on the boat, I kept watch with my bow at the ready. I saw one of Tostig's huscarls sidle his horse up to him and mutter something. Tostig looked my way.

"You, I would talk with you." Tostig pointed a finger at me. I walked over cautiously. "My huscarl recognises you with the long blonde flowing locks and the odd coloured eyes. You are Hereward Leofricson the Outlaw, who slew Siward's son."

I grinned provocatively, "Well you gained an earldom from that slaying, Godwinson."

"I should slay you; you are outside of the law in England and in England you are."

"True but if you try, I will kill that beautiful black mare you are riding and then you will look even more foolish than you already are." I flexed my bow. "And besides, if I tell Eystein that your derisory five thousand pounds of silver is half of what you were prepared to pay, the vikings will raid and burn the English east coast all summer."

"My brother is negotiating with Aelfgar over in Wales because of this viking raid. It was all your doing, wasn't it?" Tostig snarled.

"I'm just a viking outlaw, I don't play politics with great lords like you." I deliberately insulted him in front of his guards. Tostig wheeled his horse away and rode off towards the sand dunes.

"Couldn't wait for me to say, thank you then?" Eystein Orri trudged across the sand and joined me as the Northumbrians wheeled away and rode after their master. "Come on, it's all there, genuine silver and all loaded."

The Norwegian fleet immediately set sail north for Orkney taking advantage of the prevailing southern winds. It was fortunate that the weather was so kind as the snekkjas, unsuitable for trading, were burdened down to the sheer strakes with plunder. I debated on whether I should return to the Orkneys; I had no reason to return there. Obviously my Hebrideans would wish to return but my crew on *Ottar* had no allegiance to anything or anyone but silver. Reality, however, compelled me to find a base where my crew and I could safely store our plunder. I discussed this with my crew and after a wide discussion it was agreed that the best place to store wealth safely was in Flanders. The Count of Flanders, Baldwin, the fifth of his name, known as the Pious and Debonair was well known for creating a welcoming haven for any of the world's misfits, outlaws and pirates. He had great influence across Europe, he was married to the daughter of the King of France, and his daughter was married to Duke William the Bastard of Normandy, and his half-sister Judith was married to Tostig Godwinson, no less, and the Count was himself a powerful noble in the German Empire. He would turn a blind eye to any raiding and plundering I may decide upon as long as he made a profit. Additionally, I had already been offered employment by Gilbert of Ghent, a relative of the Count.

I informed Eystein Orri of my decision and he was genuinely sorry to see me leave, he assured me that there would be a place for me at King Harald Hardrada's court; and plenty of fighting, of course. I knew that the fighting referred to was with the Danes and as I was a half Dane by birth and a native of the Danelagh, I did not feel comfortable with that. I bade my farewell and thanks to the Hebridean crews and reminded them to give their king, Eachmarchach his share of the plunder, as was his due. Then, as the viking fleet heeled over to larboard to catch the wind, I commanded my crew to man their oars and turn south into the wind.

It was approximately four hundred miles south east to Flanders from Northumbria and by sailing slightly east of our intended course we could catch the wind somewhat and raise a half sail to assist our manual endeavours. I anticipated that it would take a dozen days unless a more favourable wind came up.

Autumn 1058 – Guines

I had left *Ottar* pulled up on the beach as near as possible to the old town of Bruges; as usual Egil had insisted upon staying with the ship and cleaning the hull and re-caulking her and applying a fresh coat of tar to the lower strakes. I knew he would happily spend the winter pottering around the ship until he was satisfied that she was as seaworthy as could possibly be. Several of the older crew members elected to stay and help with the much overdue repair work, including old Eystein Whaleleg who had chosen to stay with me. Before the rest of us left we hastily erected a small hall for the remaining crew to live in, we located this on the edge of the large fishing village that went by the name Bruges by the Sea. There was an inn and a few doxies that would keep the crew entertained throughout the winter.

Before setting off to Bruges I assembled the crew and distributed the plunder we had gained in the summer's campaign. Each man had a bag of silver with a few jewels, weapons and armour, and the other items of worth they had gained were considered personal possessions and every crew member was very well armed. The one slave girl that had been allocated to the *Ottar* was left with the ship. I wanted to get away from the fishing village before some of the less sensible crew members spent their loot on prostitutes and ale. I had the problem of conveying my share of the plunder, the captains share and my previous wealth, as it was far too much for me to carry myself, even if Martin shared the burden. However, I was fortunate enough to be able to purchase an old mule from the village that could bear both mine and Martin's wealth.

My arrival in Bruges had no impact as it was a bustling commercial town. Obviously, it was noted that a viking crew of sixty warriors had entered the town and this information had been passed to the town ruler so it came has no surprise when I was summoned to the town fortress. The fortress of Bruges was a stone castle built in the way of the Romans; indeed, it may well have been built on Roman foundations. Still, it was a formidable structure with a stout wooden gate and partly surrounded by water. Martin and I were ushered through the gate and into the fort; even the interior buildings were stone foundations with elaborate wooden superstructures with carved painted gables. The walkways were cobbled stone and quite dry with no mud. I wondered how the horses managed on them.

I was led into the stone keep and traipsed up two storeys to a hall with a blazing fire in a stone carved fireplace; something I had not seen before. The walls were covered in woollen hangings with pictures sewn into them, I perceived they were hunting scenes, very pretty. Seated by the fire sat an old grizzled warrior, he wore mail with a half coat over the mail. He wore high leather riding boots with metal plates stitched onto them. He was clean shaven with a trim moustache and close-cropped hair, a fashion I knew was popular with the Normans to the south of Flanders. Opposite the man sat a much younger woman who seemed absorbed in embroidery.

"Who are you?" he demanded brusquely.

I bowed courteously, "Good day, my lord; I am Hereward Leofricson, brother to the Earl of Mercia in England."

The man eased somewhat when he realised, he was addressing a noble. "Oh! Right, I am Bauldran, Castellan of Bruges and this is my lady wife, Dedda. May I inquire what you are doing here?"

"My lady, it is a pleasure to meet you." I bowed again, "My lord castellan, I have come to Flanders seeking service. The last time I was here Lord Gilbert of Ghent suggested that there was profit for mercenaries fighting against Flanders enemies. Alas at the moment I am outlawed from my own country and lands. My ship is at the fishing village near here and I would locate Gilbert or the Count of Flanders."

The Lady Dedda looked up from her embroidery, "You are he who men call the Bearslayer?" She was very beautiful her hair was hidden by a wimple but it was her eyes that commanded attention. Large, sapphire blue with dark, long lashes and fine arched eyebrows. Her complexion was olive coloured, suggesting an origin in the south of France, or even Italy or Spain. Her gown could not hide the fullness of her breasts or her slim waist. Her rosebud mouth was impossibly cherry red and I wondered if she coloured them in some way.

"I am sometimes named the Bearslayer, also called the outlaw for such is my lot." I responded hoarsely, conscious that her beauty had affected me.

The castellan intervened, "Come have a drink of our fine Flemish wine, Ghent is not many miles from here and I will provide you with horses, meanwhile you can regale my wife and I with your adventures."

I talked with the castellan and his wife for some time, I tried to avoid talking about my life and persistently steered the conversation towards the political situation in Flanders. I learnt that Count Baldwin had secured his borders, which were not particularly natural with most of his neighbours, but that he always had a running sore of a relationship with the people to his northern border and to various smaller counts within Flanders itself, smaller counts who persistently attempted to assert their independence.

I stayed with the castellan a few days but left before I cuckolded him with his wife. It was obvious she would have obliged me but my, perhaps misguided, honour prevented me from putting horns on my host. As promised, Bauldran provided me with several horses, not enough for all my crew but several took turns in riding to ease the walk after so many months at sea. Martin naturally walked. It took two days to reach Ghent, staying at an inn on the way for one flea-ridden night's sleep. Naturally Gilbert Lord of Ghent was not present, off somewhere on the count's business, but I found reasonable accommodation for my men and I decided to wait having nothing better to do. My men were soon in the flesh pots of the town and were quite happy. Eventually Gilbert returned to his town and when he heard I was waiting on him he soon requested my presence.

"Well, Bearslayer, I take it that you want service with my master the Count?" The gruff black visaged trader cum noble smiled grimly at me.

"I have a viking crew that needs entertainment before they wear the whores of your town to a frazzle." I responded with alacrity.

"Good. I have just returned from Lille where my good lord Baldwin is in residence. He has recently quarrelled with the Count of Guines, a small place on the coast south of here. He has appointed his son Robert to lead a force of soldiers to bring the count to heel. Your men will join him; he will like you; he likes vikings, fancies himself one, he does. Come, sup with me Bearslayer."

Several days later my men and I set out together with a force of one hundred men supplied by Gilbert of Ghent. Surprisingly Gilbert did not accompany us, placing the whole band under my command. His men had a nominal leader called Gerold who understood he had to defer to me. I always liked an independent command but I felt slightly nervous as I had thirty horsed warriors under my command, something I was not used to, as I had only ever observed a conroi of Norman horse operating in Alba and had only used Welsh ponies as speedier transport for my archers. I was instructed to march to a town called St. Omer where I was to liaise with the Lord Robert, a younger son of the Flemish Count. Travelling across country this was a distance of about eighty English miles and it took us just short of a week. From St Omer the town of Guines was about twenty miles to the north towards the coast and it was from St Omer that the combined army of the Flemings was going to advance.

St Omer proved to be a very attractive little town with a stone wall around it and the inevitable church, which was dedicated to a St Audemar, from whom the town was named. The town houses were often two storeys, overhanging the streets and some had small railed balconies from which pretty ladies were draped ogling the passing traffic. These ladies were revealing quite some flesh, their draperies hanging loose off their shoulders. I assumed that they were whores, prostitutes for hire. It seemed to me that these types of women were a lot more prevalent in Flanders than in my islands. They were certainly a lot cleaner and comelier than those I had observed in Wales and Ireland. I had been mostly too young to remember what they had looked like in England. I could see my men were getting quite excited and I only hoped that the Lord Robert, son of Count Baldwin had already arrived or they would be all penniless anon.

As it turned out the Lord Robert had not yet arrived and I was obliged to beg accommodation and supplies from the castellan of St Omer for myself and my men. We were tented in the castle grounds; an area called the baillie. The castle itself was more a squat stone tower with three floors towering over the town, I was not invited to sup with the castellan, perhaps he did not trust me or my rather rough looking men. The castellan informed me, through Gerold that Lord Robert was due to arrive in St Omer in about a week's time. I did not want my men to be idle so I arranged a series of training exercises, which also enabled me to observe Gerold putting the mounted conroi through military manoeuvres. I had seen the Normans in Alba advance in line and wedge and appreciated their mobility, what I wanted to observe more closely was the use of their lances. These lances were quite light, much lighter than a foot warrior's spear, it could be used overhead in a downward thrust, useful against infantry, or it could be used underhanded, levelled against other horsemen; by this grip it was very dextrous and could be reversed or used across the horse's neck to the shield side of the horseman. Of course, a nimble warrior on foot with a sword or axe could sever the lance point rendering the weapon relatively useless but each mounted warrior also had a sword or mace as a secondary weapon. All the mounted warriors had a kite shaped shield covering his left side protecting his torso and just as importantly his left leg. They also had full body armour, either chain mail or lamellar armour, which usually consisted of overlapping plates of metal or leather, making them look like they were wearing a fish scale shirt. My mail was much lighter and more flexible than the lamellar armour, which was obviously less expensive and less time consuming to make. I rode with the conroi and managed to keep up, I was only an average horseman but my men from Ghent were not the best either. The foot soldiers from Ghent were also put through exercises with my viking crew; it was immediately apparent that their version of the shield wall was not as tight and disciplined as my crew's. The situation improved after a couple of days training and a few bashed heads. If the Guines Count had a decent conroi of his own then a stout shield wall would be essential.

Not being familiar with the area, I also decided upon a reconnoitre of the land between St Omer and Guines. The distance between these two towns was only about twenty miles and a swift advance into the rebel territory could be achieved in one or two days. I sent Martin off with a score of vikings to scour the area between us and Guines and to especially locate any places where our troops could be ambushed in our anticipated advance.

Within three days Martin had returned and informed me that the approach to Guines was mostly flat land, similar to the Danelagh, in England but heavily forested with ample places for ambush from woods along the flanks of the road. Just over half way to Guines the fortified village of Ardres lay, again encircled by woods. Martin believed Ardres was a forward outpost of Guines, intended to prevent a direct advance on Guines. It looked well-fortified and there were quite a few mounted warriors practicing in the meadows outside the walls.

As anticipated, I noticed that my viking crew were dissipating their wealth in the fleshpots of St Omer and I was relieved when the Flemish army arrived from Lille. I was summoned to a council of war later that same day. The son of the Flemish Count had set up a pavilion outside the town with his army camped around him. I was directed to the largest tented pavilion I had seen by far. It was draped with heraldic banners, something that the Flemish were inordinately fond of, and fluttering banners on lances were rammed into the ground around the tent. I noticed that most of the banners bore lions, a riot of colour. The guards at the entrance to the pavilion were also elaborately clad. In addition to their mail both sentries bore shields with black lions painted upon them. Their nasal helms were adorned with goose feathers and their voluminous cloaks also displayed embroidered lions, stitched in gold. Their lances had pennons attached in black and gold bars. They ignored me as I swept passed them, so either they were well briefed or incompetent, I looked at Martin who raised an eyebrow. The interior of the tent was crowded with many elaborately dressed nobles; Flanders was clearly a wealthy country. Their coats were of the finest wool with embroidered cuffs and hems. Most of the nobles wore their hair long and curled, like me, although unlike me most had dark locks. Some of the nobles had their hair shorn short in the Norman fashion, all were clean shaven, which made my vikings moustachioed faces a novelty. They all wore their swords and daggers in the presence of the Count's son, this certainly would not be allowed in Wales or Leinster, as there it was a sure way to lose your throne.

A table was placed in the centre of the tent and behind it stood the son of the Count, Robert. I would guess he was maybe five years older than I, tall slim and handsome. His brown hair flowed to his shoulders and was held back by a gold circlet across his brow. He had thick eyebrows that gave him a serious aspect, that is until he smiled. His teeth were perfect and white, I suspected he was very vain about his appearance. He was more richly dressed than all his nobles, lots of gold thread and bejewelled fingers. How he held a sword with all those rings on I could not imagine. All heads turned as Martin and I stepped into the tent. We certainly brought the tone of the place down. My mail was serviceable but worn. It had been repaired several times. The only item of my apparel that was pristine was my white bear shoulder protector, which Martin washed religiously. Oh! And of course, my weapons, my sword, Serpents Breath, and my scramaseax were the best that could be acquired, gifts from my late father.

A herald or constable, or somebody, stepped forward. "You are in the presence of Robert, son of Baldwin, Count of Flanders, give due obeisance and identify yourself."

Obeisance! I nodded at Robert and introduced myself. "I am Hereward Leofricson, battle leader for Ghent, I bring one hundred and forty warriors, thirty horsed, seventy Ghent militia and my forty vikings."

"Vikings!" the count's son shouted excitedly. "We have some vikings fighting for us, that is excellent, I must see them."

"Later my lord, first we must establish our course of action." This contribution was made by an elderly man standing next to Lord Robert. He was also splendidly dressed with yet another lion embroidered onto his tunic.

Directing his comments to me, Lord Robert responded. "My uncle Herman has no time for the romance of the vikings and he has been foisted upon me by my father to ensure I do nothing foolish. Viking Hereward, may I introduce my uncle Herman von Gleiberg, scion of the house of Luxemburg." I nodded, trying to show some respect, and settled back intending to listen to the discussion on strategy that was to follow. I was somewhat surprised to find out that this amounted to nothing more than deciding on a date and place of combat. I shared a glance with Martin apparently our reconnaissance was pointless as the Flemings imagined that they could advance without risk to a site where a battle would take place. Eventually it was decided that the battle site would be in the meadows south of Ardres. I felt I had to speak.

"My lord, nobles of Flanders, my men have scouted the land between here and Guines and although the road is straight and dry, easily traversed, there are woods on either side from which ambuscades can be set. To advance to Ardres, which is well fortified, without securing our flanks would be dangerous."

The nobles looked at me with astonished expressions on their faces.

"Ambuscades!" Herman von Gleiberg retorted, "That would be completely against the rules of chivalry, totally unacceptable. The Count of Guines would be a pariah in Flanders, France, and Germany if he entertained such a vile deception." All around the table the nobles muttered and I immediately understood I had made a social error.

"I must apologies, my lords, vikings rarely behave with such social niceties so I tend to see risk where none exist." I backtracked hastily. The rest of the meeting was a discussion, or even an argument, on the places each lord thought he had a right to in the battle array. It was clear that there would be little central control in the forthcoming battle. Afterwards a herald was sent off to Guines to challenge the count to meet face to face at the chosen field of battle outside of Ardres, ten days hence.

My vikings found the whole exercise amusing but we continued to train the Ghent militia to ensure we fought as an efficient unit. The march to Ardres was leisurely, what could be achieved in one or two days took eight days. The supply train was expansive and my vikings could not remember when they had eaten so well on campaign. I became concerned about the lack of scouts and guards, both when camped and on the march and cautiously sent out several of my viking scouts who were already familiar with the terrain to keep us safe. Amazingly they reported no one was monitoring our advance.

When we arrived at Ardres we were met by a herald from the Count of Guines informing Lord Robert that ten days was insufficient for him to assemble his retainers and asked for a delay of a further week before the battle took place; and Lord Robert agreed! This was undoubtably the strangest warfare I had ever come across but it did remind me of my first campaign in Wales when the whole exercise was treated like a game. Confirmation of this view was reinforced when challenges started being issued between nobles from Ardres and our army to partake in single combat between the lines until the Count of Guines and his army came up.

The servants of the nobles erected their tented pavilions and the foot soldiers and militia set up what small tents they had. My vikings only had flimsy individual seal skin shelters held up by a sword or spear, but fortunately the late summer, autumn weather was mild and dry. On the second day since our arrival, we went through the lines to watch the individual combats. All these duels were on horseback and only the nobles took part. They mainly happened one at a time so that the other lords could admire their skill in handling their horses and their weapons and occasionally two or three combats occurred at the same time, when the various combatants became over excited. The dualists always declaimed their names and ancestry, if they had any, before the onset, then they rode at each other and tried to strike their opponent on the shield. If they managed to unhorse their opponent it was considered a victory and the defeated combatant was taken as a prisoner to be ransomed, usually within a day. This entertainment went on for three days before I decided enough was enough.

I went over to Lord Robert's pavilion and entered without any announcement. The count's son and his uncle were dining at a trestle table; wine in glass goblets, pheasant, venison and pig, the smell of fresh bread permeated the tent.

"My lord, I ask a boon." I spoke precipitously.

"Ah! My viking." Robert sounded in good spirits. "What would you ask of me?"

"I would go out and fight one of these nobles from Ardres. The viking way." I announced.

Herman von Gleiberg smiled maliciously. "That would be entertaining, do you ride?"

"Oh! I have sat on a horse before but vikings and Danes from the Danelagh prefer to fight on foot."

"I've heard that a viking can decapitate a horse with one blow of his axe; is that true?" Lord Robert exclaimed excitedly.

"My lord, it may well be true but, to be honest, I have not seen this done myself." I added.

The upshot of the conversation was that it was agreed I should issue a challenge but it was emphasized that I had to make this challenge providing my lineage, citing that I was the son of a count from England. I instructed Martin to declaim my challenge on the meadow in front of Ardres and await a reply. Within the hour Martin returned to Lord Robert's pavilion.

"Speak up Martin, do I have a challenger?" I demanded. Both Lord Robert and Herman von Gleiberg leaned forward in anticipation.

"Yes, master Hereward. The announcement of your lineage caused a stir and there was some debate on who should accept your challenge. Eventually I was informed that one, Hoibricht of Guines, accepted your challenge and will meet you in the meadow in one hour."

"Hoibricht, why that is the Count of Guines' grandson, a noted fighter, he must be one of the leaders of the garrison at Ardres." Herman von Gleiberg explained.

From that point on, the next hour was all bustle. I returned to my men and fully armed myself, I then asked around for a sharp Dane axe, which I borrowed from a young mountain of a Dublin man named Eric. He informed me that the axe was named 'Headtaker', which I informed him was very apt for what I had in mind. Martin chided me for not removing my woollen cloak but I insisted I would keep in on for the time being. I eventually rode out onto the meadow before Ardres making sure that I arrived before my opponent; I wanted no suggestion that I was slow at coming to the war play.

Hoibricht rode out of the gate from Ardres on a magnificent black horse, a stallion by the look of it, hardly manageable, I thought. I was riding my Flemish horse that I had been riding since Ghent, serviceable but certainly not a warhorse. Hoibricht rode up to me waving his lance with a pennon fluttering near its very sharp looking point. "I am Hoibricht of Guines, I have defeated thirty chevaliers in single combat and never been unhorsed, you will go the same way." He paused, puzzled, "Where is your lance?"

I responded.

> *"Hereward Leofricson, Earl's son am I,*
> *Bearslayer, kin slayer, priests' bane,*
> *War leader of the Welsh and Irish*
> *Viking marauder, sea rover, outlaw"*

"Are you frightened of a man without a lance? Do you fear a Dane axe?" I slipped from my saddle onto the ground and slapped the horse away. "Come let us dance the dance of death." I wore my nasal helm and it was hard for him to see my face but he had on an open-faced helm and I could see the uncertainty on his shaven face. I fronted my shield towards my opponent but kept my axe shaft held in my shield hand whilst I casually unpinned my cloak with my right.

"Come on! Are you fighting or not?" I shouted and just to annoy him I started chanting the English war cry. "Ut! Ut! Ut!"

Hoibricht kicked his stallion into a wide canter to gain distance between us for his charge, to counter this I ran forward to reduce the distance between us. He faced me and dug his spurs into the stallion's flanks, the horse reared and came down galloping; but the distance was too short between us for the horse to gain real momentum. Hoibricht raised his spear in an over hand action intending to bring it down upon my upturned shield but at this point I swung my cloak around and waved it up into the face of his horse. Startled the horse shied away from me before Hoibricht could control and counter the move. Hoibricht's lance lost all direction as he strained with his reins to bring the agitated stallion under control. I moved in and taking the Dane axe in both hands I lifted it high and brought it down on the horse's neck with all my strength. I felt the blade bite into the spinal column and pass straight through into the muscle tissue beneath. I thought I had failed when the blade seemed to slow whilst passing through the muscle and meat of the horse's neck but with a final pull back the blade cut through the last tissues and skin and exited beneath the head. The stallion's head fell forward free of the rest of the animal's torso, blood fountained out in a great torrent covering me in gore. Hoibricht fell forward into the pool of blood spreading on the ground before what was left of his steed. I stepped onto his lance to ensure he could not use it and rolled him over with my axe head.

"Well, that did not turn out to well for you, did it." I panted. "Shame about the horse, wasn't his fight after all."

Hoibricht was dazed but not unduly hurt, he spluttered, "You killed my horse, you barbarian!"

I laughed, "Where I come from you would be dead along with it; but I suppose I should observe the niceties, so come along now." I reached down and dragged him up and pulled him towards the Flemish camp.

"So, you are the grandson of the Count of Guines; you should fetch a petty penny, which will please my men as I share my plunder with them." Naturally Herman von Gleiberg disapproved of my naked aggression but my vikings and the rest of the common soldiery cheered my exploit. Lord Robert was beside himself with glee, his pet viking had beheaded a horse with a single blow of his axe, a feat befitting the saga stories. Martin just smiled that knowing smile. Me, it took three baths to wash the horse blood from my war gear and clothing. Eric went around showing off his axe to anyone prepared to give him a free drink for his tale. Naturally Lord Robert entertained Hoibricht royally and that individual soon regained his sangfroid. Robert gave me guidance in establishing Hoibricht's ransom size, as I had no idea of the worth of Flemish nobles. I also was given to understand that the horse Hoibricht rode into battle was forfeit as well but as I had no idea what to do with a horse carcase, I magnanimously informed him that he could keep his horse. I did confiscate his arms and armour though because they could usefully be shared out amongst my crew, many of whom would gladly improve the quality of their war gear. Although my dual with Hoibricht was the talk of the camp I was a bit downcast when I saw Hoibricht without his armour; he was young and slight and I found it hard to believe he was a renown warrior. Thankfully the Count of Guines and his army appeared the next day and Hoibricht was ransomed, to my relief. Discussions between the heralds took place and it was agreed that the battle would take place the next day at dawn.

That evening in Lord Robert's pavilion a party atmosphere was the order of the day, nobles drank Rhenish wine with cheeses and fresh bread and German sausage and onions, the place reeked. The discussion was solely centred on the order of battle for the morning. Noble vied against noble for the right to lead the van, or the place of honour with the Flemish banner. None of this bothered me overmuch, as a mercenary I would fight where I was placed and ensure I earned my fee. Finally, I gathered that the whole army would be lined up with the van on right wing and rear guard on the left and Lord Robert in the centre with his uncle. Each noble would assemble his own conroi of horsed warriors about him with his foot militia in a loose shield wall. I consulted with Herman von Gleiberg and was not surprised when he indicated that my vikings and Ghent militia were to be placed in the rear of the line as a reserve.

I returned to my men and explained to as many of them as possible what was required of us. The vikings smirked but the Ghent militia were relieved. I knew that my vikings believed that they were the deadliest warriors on the field and to be placed in the reserve was an insult but a convenient one. I then instructed everyone to get some rest as it would be an early start. How wrong I was.

I assembled my men just before dawn and ensured they ate a light breakfast. I led the men out to our assigned position only to find none of the other battles of our army assembled. They were not just not assembling they were just crawling out of their bed rolls. What part of dawn did they not understand? Thankfully the enemy army seemed just as dilatory in assembling their battle lines and half of the morning was wasted in breaking fast and assembling for the fray. I had long since ordered my men to stand down and they spent part of the morning lazing on the trampled grass.

Finally, as noon approached the battle lines were formed, a riot of colourful pennants, shining mail, colourful cloaks, and painted shields. Heralds from both sides rode up and down setting the lines, until they were satisfied. Finally, on the

255

instructions of Herman von Gleiberg, our heralds sounded bronze trumpets, shrill and strident, making the horses skittish; the principal herald gorgeous in a multi-quartered tabard of red and gold rode forward and issued a formal challenge to the Count of Guines, or submit forthwith to the high and pursuivant Lord of Flanders. I would have laughed loud and long if after all the messing about the Count of Guines agreed to submit but fortunately this was not to be; in just as haughty tones as our herald, the Count of Guines' herald told us to 'fuck off', or words to that effect.

After the lines were finally set as the herald's wished, a quiet lull swept over the field; the quiet before the storm. At a prearranged signal, from where I did not see, the trumpets blew and the mounted chevaliers spurred their horses forward towards the enemy. The infantry lines, both sides, walked forward, a hedge of spears. The distance between the two armies rapidly diminished, galloping horsemen can cover a few hundred paces in seconds and the two armies crashed together with an ear-splitting crash of metal, wood, and flesh. I could observe many dexterous manipulations of lance and shield but truth be told fighting in a melee with a lance against another horseman similarly accoutred was rather ineffectual. The lance was more deadly when riding down foot soldiers and I found it unsurprising when most of the mounted warriors had discarded their lances for sword, mace, or axe. These types of weapons were much more deadly in smashing wooden shields to splinters or breaking the reinforced bands of all but the best helmets.

Lord Robert and Herman von Gleiberg had charged with the rest of the mounted warriors and I could not see any of the Flemish nobles that were not in the forefront of the battle. This seemed an utter folly to me as it was clear that there was no one left in control of the Flemish forces. Any change in fortunes requiring any part of the army to manoeuvre, either to flank or to a point where our forces were getting the worst of it could not be made swiftly and decisively. In fact, the only person left on our side in this battle who could make any decisive decisions was me! It was obvious that this sort of fight was likely to be lengthy in duration; individual fights to the death, very messy. The infantry lines came together in separated clumps of individuals, avoiding the swirling duals of the horsemen, the rearing and kicking horses. The foot soldiers had lost all cohesion and prodded ineffectually at each other and totally ignoring the mounted nobles who presumably were so far above them, both physically and metaphorically as to be untouchable.

The only compensation to this riot of indiscipline was that the Guinois seemed just as poorly led and lacking in tactics. Despite the Flemish county being larger and more populous than little Guines the two armies seemed more or less the same size, although the Guinois clearly had less mounted warriors. The melee continued for some hours with many of the mounted nobles riding from the conflict to quench their thirst; I concluded that this method of fighting was not going to produce a decisive outcome. The field had been churned up and the foot soldiers were finding it hard to move about. I decided that the fighting would peter out shortly as it became more difficult to move about and I was not inclined to intervene. My Norsemen had lost interest and were sitting around snacking and drinking, their contempt for the proceedings palpable.

Suddenly a cry went up, the melee intensified around Lord Robert's standard. "The count's son is in trouble master" Martin called out. Losing a paymaster is not the act of a wise mercenary, I had to do something.

"I'll go get him, Ghent conroi, mount up and follow me." I shouted. I hoisted myself onto the horse I had been using to get about, as a leader should, and kicked it towards the battle. The Ghent horsemen mounted up and followed.

"Form a wedge on me." I shouted. I drew my sword and concentrated on moving my horse up to full speed. Not having far to travel and not being the best of horsemen, I was only at a canter as I burst into the melee knocking the unsuspecting Flemish foot soldiers aside but my steady approach had allowed my men to form solidly behind me. I came upon the wall of Guinois warriors clustered around the still waving Flemish banner; not wishing to hit a solid rump of another warhorse my mount slid into a gap between two of my enemies' mounts colliding with the stirrups and legs of both riders throwing them sideways. I lashed out backhanded with my sword and connected with the neck and shoulder of my unsuspecting adversary on my right who promptly fell away off his horse. With a continuing forward slash, I managed to hit the right arm of my adversary to my left; his mail broke and I saw blood. He dropped his lance and tried to pull away, this gave my horse sufficient space to push through and I collided with the next ring of our enemies that had surrounded the Flemish Lord Robert. I jabbed my sword into the rump of the next rider's horse, which reared in agony and tried to bolt forward. There was nowhere for the horse to go so it conveniently reared back allowing me to stand in my stirrups and bring my blade down onto the unfortunate rider's helmet. The helmet split asunder and I pulled the blade back slicing the stunned enemy's skull. The impact of my sword was sufficient to ensure the rider rolled back off his horse beneath its flailing hooves.

My men had forced the enemy horsemen apart the, unlooked for, organised impact scattering our adversaries. Forcing my horse forward by kicking wildly at its flanks I came up against a small group of Flemish nobles afoot surrounding their leaders. Several of the Guines nobles, in desperation, had dismounted and tried to beat down the shields of their enemies with axes and maces, I set about them in the same way my men and I had dispatched the mounted Guines nobles. I had no compulsion about striking men in the back, they died quicker and easier. Two strenuous downward strokes laid the two attackers in front of me low in the blink of an eye. They thought their own men protected their backs; they were wrong.

"Come, my lord; time to leave the field." I gasped, swinging down from my saddle, I offered Lord Robert my mount. The young lord was covered in blood and his sword was slimy from tip to hilt, clearly, he had had his share of combat but fortunately he did not seem hurt.

"I cannot leave my uncle, Herman." I looked down and saw Herman von Gleiberg sitting propped up against a dead charger, he had a lance through his shoulder that must have wedged in his shoulder blade. He looked pale and had lost much blood but whether or not the puddle of blood he sat in was all his I had no way of knowing.

I looked around and with some relief I saw that Martin and Eystein Egilson had brought up my crew and the Ghent militia in a good ordered shield wall and were gradually clearing away the disorganised units between us.

"Your men can carry him to the rear, I will hold back the enemy for you." I informed Robert. Gerold was beside me. "Gerold, escort Lord Robert and his remaining nobles to the rear." I turned and shouted to the *Ottar* crew. "Vikings, on me." Martin saw me and waved his axe.

The shield wall advanced over the few bodies scattered on the ground and formed up either side of me. We opened ranks and let Gerold lead the Lord Robert and his party back and as the ground cleared before us it revealed the disorganised ranks of the Guinois.

"Right lads! Let us show these bastards what a shipload of vikings can do. Keep the shield wall firm, two lines, axes to the fore." My crew knew what to do and the Ghent militia had been trained hard by example. Our line advanced into the enemy who naturally bunched together to oppose us. We clashed shields and, in the time-honoured way, my vikings hooked their axes over their opponents shields and pulled them down. The Ghent militia in the second rank darted their spears forward and the enemy started to die in earnest. One of my vikings leapt out of the ranks and sank his axe into an opponent head, splitting it in two. He screamed, "I give thee to Odin!" I did not approve of his indiscipline but one look at him was to freeze your blood and unsurprisingly the Guinois before him turned and fled as one. So, after a few moments hard fighting the enemy was defeated and fled to Ardres with my men in pursuit cutting down those not quick enough to escape our axes; so very few wounded made it into Ardres, only the fleet of foot.

Across the messy meadow I came across none other than Hoibricht trying to stem the rout. I gave him due respect for his bravery but. "Hoibricht, were not duelling today, run now before it's too late." I smiled and held my sword up for him to see the blood.

"No tricks today, Norseman and there are no horses left to kill. Try me." Hoibricht shouted.

"Tch, tch! That is not polite calling me a Norseman, I will answer to Mercian or Dane, viking or reiver, but I am not a Norseman."

Hoibricht came at me but cautiously, he was clearly learning from previous mistakes. He had a sword and shield and so did I so we were equally matched; of course, he was taller than I, but many are, I was broader and harder to knock down. He thrust his sword forward at my eyes but I parried the thrust easily with my sword; my parry turned into a back-handed slice to his neck, which he had to jump back to avoid. We circled and before long we were surrounded by my men, forming an arena for us to fight within. We exchanged blows and parries seeking an advantage or opening but none came. I stepped back.

"Look Hoibricht, I have nothing against you, I am fighting for money not glory and I have no reason to want you dead. Why do not you just go home." I offered. This caused a look of fury on his face and he leapt at me swinging his sword in a wide arc clearly intending to take my head from my shoulders. I had no difficulty in deflecting this blow with my shield and as he had taken the precaution of covering himself with his shield, I calmly stabbed him in the left foot. The point of my sword went in cleanly through his boot, his foot, and the sole of the boot and with some force and carried on into the soil beneath. Holbricht howled in pain and tried to withdraw his foot but as I was still holding my sword and pressing down, he could not. I took a risk and let go of my sword and quickly drew my scramaseax from behind me where it was strapped to my belt. With my shield held above me I deftly leant in and severed Holbricht tendons behind his left knee. He wobbled and collapsed back onto the ground, his leg twisted and contorted because my sword was holding his foot at an awkward angle. Mercifully for him I sheathed my scramaseax and withdrew my sword from his foot. Another scream of pain; warily I kicked away his sword, turned to Martin and spoke.

"Looks like Hoibricht is coming with us, again." Eystein laughed and the men cheered. Checking I could see that most of the Guinois had made it back to Ardres and the gates slammed shut.

Later, back in camp, I asked to see my viking warrior who had started the rout. I knew his name was Gautrek, he shambled up looking a bit dazed. "Are you alright Gautrek?" I inquired.

"He is always a bit fuddled after a fight, after the battle madness takes him." Eystein remarked. Gautrek grunted and looked sheepish.

"Well, Gautrek, you scared them shitless and turned the tide of battle and for that I thank you with all honour." I unwound a gold armband from my sword arm and handed it to him. My viking crew cheered.

"Skoll! To the ring giver!" they shouted swords aloft.

"Come on lads." I shouted back, "Time for a drink."

We all strolled back to the Flemish camp where wounds were being tended and cauldrons of stew were being prepared. Plenty of horse meat to go around. I went to Lord Robert's pavilion and walked in unannounced. Herman von Gleiberg was lying on a fabric camp bed with a chirurgeon or surgeon bent over him. The man held a sharp knife and was about to cut out the head of the lance embedded in the wounded noble's shoulder.

"I trust that knife has been cauterised?" I interrupted. The surgeon unbent and turned to me. He was an elderly man with a long grey beard that he had encased in a fine gauze scarf, presumably to prevent it getting in the way of his ministrations. His face was lined and darker coloured than most. He wore long woollen robes in striped colours that were long and flowing. His head was covered with a wound scarf. I noticed he had a chain around his neck and from this hung a pointed star.

"Sir, I am Salman Ben Isaac of Salamanca, I have been taught in the very best medical academies and have been practicing medicine and surgery for over twenty years. I can assure you that the knife has been cleaned in pure spirits and heated in the fire. In addition, all of my surgical instruments have been treated in the same way." Having completely dismissed my comment he turned again to the patient. "The lance has penetrated cleanly and sliced through the leather shoulder protection, with luck none of the underlying fabric will have penetrated the wound and I will be able to extract it with pincers without undue problems; that is assuming that the lance point has not severed any major internal arteries. Fortunately, my patient is unconscious and will not feel the pain as severely as if he was awake."

Whereupon the surgeon made a clean deep incision either side of the lance, widening the hole within which the lance head was embedded. Using a pair of bronze tongues Salman Ben Isaac gripped the remaining shaft of the lance near the chest and pulled with all his strength. The lance head came free with a disturbing sucking sound followed by a fountain of blood that spread across the injured von Gleiberg chest. Very swiftly the surgeon placed a large wad of linen onto the wound and pressed down holding the wound together. The unconscious man groaned. "I will have to clean and sew the wound immediately to prevent infection, I would ask you all to leave the tent while I do this; it will take time." The physician huffed.

I immediately left the pavilion and was shortly joined by the Lord Robert and his entourage. "You rescued me, out there Hereward Leofricson, you have my thanks." Robert began, I cut him off.

"It's bad business to lose one's paymaster, can't make a living that way." I smiled whilst saying this and fortunately he saw the funny side of my observation.

"Ah! I would expect nothing more from a viking. Tell me, what did you think of our battle today?"

I pondered whether he wanted the truth. "Well, my lord, in truth the battle was a chaotic mess with no plan or direction. Are all wars fought like this in Europe?" Robert looked troubled and thoughtful all at the same time and it took him some time to collect his thoughts before he replied.

"This has been bothering me for some time; as you know my uncle was sent with me to advise on the conduct of this campaign and he insisted that it be fought in the time-honoured way; hence the challenge and battle on the agreed day. It is true that for many years battles and campaigns have been fought between the descendants of Charlemagne in such a stylised way but the great emperor never fought in this manner and the vikings of the north and nomads from the east have never fought in this manner and we have had to adapt our fighting methods to counter them, and yet. And yet, we still fight each other in what is obviously a silly way. I have noticed that Count William from Normandy, my sister's husband, in the south has thrown off this tactic and has adopted various stratagems to defeat his enemies successfully."

"My lord, the English have never fought in this manner, maybe because we have been fighting the Norwegians and Danes for as long as you have. Now we are all mixed up, English, Saxon, Danes, Norwegians, and we use what tactics and strategies seem good to us. I looked at what happened today and, quite frankly, an English army would have decimated you, or the Count of Guines army and I dread to think what an army of vikings would do to you. However, I have also seen Norman's mounted on well trained horses that could smash any army with their discipline and tactics and I think that must be the future for mainland armies that use horses as their main assault weapon."

"I like the way you think and I want you to stay with me and help me. Will you do that for me Hereward?"

"Are there any bears in Flanders, my lord?"

"No, we killed them all a long time ago."

"Well in that case a bit of campaigning in Flanders is nothing to worry over, so as long as the rewards are good, I'm your man." I laughed at his puzzled expression.

The next morning Robert received a herald from the Count of Guines suing for peace and agreeing to paying homage to the Count of Flanders. Apparently, the count was distraught about his missing grandson, Hoibricht and I was magnanimous enough to send him back to his grandfather before the second ransom was agreed. Without my asking Salman Ben Isaac the physician had cleaned and stitched his wounds; Hoibricht would always limp but would walk with a leg brace successfully enough and his disability would not hinder his riding skills.

I went in search of the old man to offer payment for his services and was directed to a two wheeled carriage that was wedged flat by props under the carriage pole. There were wooden steps to the rear of the carriage and it even had a door. Chairs were set outside on the grass around a folding wooden table; all very neat and ordered. I rapped on the door; I heard movement inside and moments later the door creaked open and Salman peered out.

"Sir Salman, I would have a word."

"Ah! Yes, you are one of the young men from the Count's pavilion, the one concerned with the hygiene of my surgical instruments. What can I do for you?"

"You treated one of my prisoners yesterday and I have come to pay you for your services."

"I do not charge for my services." The physician replied as he descended the wooden steps to the ground and carefully shut the door.

"Everyone charges for services; how can you live if you don't have an income?" I responded, puzzled.

The physician chuckled, "You are quite right, I do receive an income from the Count of Flanders himself, which covers my expenses and allows me a modest living. In return I treat anyone and everyone, in the service of the great count, without additional charges."

"That's extraordinarily honest of you; a lesser man would take advantage of the opportunity to get paid twice."

"Although prevalent thinking would suggest otherwise Jews do not practice such deceptions." The surgeon explained.

"You are a Jew?"

"I thought that was obvious, does it surprise you?"

"Well, I have never met a Jew before only read about them in the Bible and been preached about how wicked you all are for killing Jesus Christ."

"And do you believe that?"

"I hated the priest who preached those homilies and if I ever meet him again, I will kill him, I have killed other priests and monks so I am not a Christian paragon." I concluded.

"It is not wise to mock God." The Jew replied.

"Oh! I do not mock God, only those who use his name to make profit, the priests, the monks, all of them. I have only met one good Christian and that is my uncle Brand. I understand from my lessons that many Christians in the east cannot even decide if Jesus Christ is part of God, or something else."

"Ah! Constantinople, the city of all sins. Of course, we Jews have no such illusions, for us Jesus was a man, just like Moses and Abraham. He was undoubtably a great prophet and teacher, but just a man."

"But didn't he claim to be the son of God?"

"We are all sons of God, every last one of us, Jews, Christians, Muslims, even the ones you call pagans, the followers of many gods." Salman responded. "There is only one God and he has many names."

"You mean if I worship any god, I am worshipping the same God?" I thought I might catch him out here.

"It is not the name of God that is important, it is how you worship him."

"And how should a man worship God?"

"With righteousness and truth." Salman smiled and knew what was coming next.

"And what is righteousness and truth?" I responded.

"There is only one righteousness and your Christ said it and many other Jewish rabbis have said it. Do not unto others you would not have done unto you."

"Oh! One of the commandments then."

"No, the commandment, it covers the truth of all the others."

The door of the carriage opened and an angelic face peered out. Ivory skin, large almond eyes, rimmed with kohl, long shiny black tresses covered in a veil of net with pearls stitched therein. Lips, lips the colour of cherries. I caught my breath and Salman Ben Isaac turned to look where I was gazing.

"Ah! Rebecca, we have a visitor, bring a glass of sherbet." The dazzling beauty descended the steps carrying a goblet made of glass. Glass! I had only seen a glass object once and this was a goblet owned by my hated step-mother, Godgifu. This lovely vision offered this treasure to me. I took the glass goblet carefully and thanked her.

"This is my daughter, Rebecca. She is my only child and is also my student. She has defter hands than I and her stitching of wounds is a wonder to behold."

I was mesmerised by the sway of her hips as she returned to the carriage. I sipped the sweet cordial, it was not to my taste, but I drank it out of courtesy. The presence of the girl had made me thoughtful.

"Salman, let me speak plain, your daughter is very beautiful and because of that she is in great danger in a camp full of, how shall I put this, a camp full of lustful, unchristian men who would like nothing more than to rape her. This is truth." I looked suitably uncomfortable when I said this.

"I have Count Baldwin's protection." The surgeon stated showing little concern.

"Count Baldwin's protection will count for nothing with many of these men." I waved my hand in the direction of the camp. "Many of them will see a Jewess as fair game."

"We have been safe thus far and the young Lord Robert has been most attentive to our welfare."

"I bet he has." I responded ruefully. I could imagine what Robert thought of the lovely Rebecca. "Nevertheless, if you have problems of any sort, I am in your debt, do not hesitate to ask for my assistance." I announced. I found the old man affable and interesting and decided I would speak with him again. I returned to my camp and informed Martin of my visit to Salman ben Isaac. I knew Martin would be interested in his medical skills and would want to meet the Jew.

Lord Robert met with the Count of Guines to ratify the agreement and accept homage on behalf of his father, the Count of Flanders. Afterwards it was agreed that I would take the militia I was leading back to Ghent and then meet Lord Robert at Lille, where his father was currently in residence.

Spring 1059 – Countess Judith

Lille in the spring was a handsome place, a mixture of hard stone walls, timber framed houses and whitewash, with slate roofed houses. Many of the houses had small gardens growing a profusion of root vegetables and apple trees. It was a walled city, a bygone from the days of the Northmen raids. There were at least two large churches and probably several smaller ones I had not noticed. The Count of Flanders had a stone palace with a stout gate flanked by two strong rectangular stone towers; a rare sight indeed and I had seen nothing like it since the old Roman fort at Chester.

After returning the Ghent militia to their home town I had become concerned about the inactivity of my crew. Hanging about Lille would not be good for them and so I had sent them back to my ship *Ottar* near Bruges. I had a considerable amount of plunder at the ship and it was not good to have it lying about idle. I decided that I needed to use it to extend my wealth, both for my crews benefit and mine. I instructed Martin to go with Eystein Egilson and together with my ship master Egil to search out and purchase a knarr for trading. It seemed to me that when I did not need all my crew for fighting having a second ship for trading would keep them busy.

Martin was reluctant to leave me but there was no one I could rely upon more than him to handle finances, just as there was no one more able than Egil to select a fine sea going knarr and go trading. I left for Lille with just two of the crew, those two being the best horsemen in my troop, Beornwulf and Gauti. I would never be the best horseman in the world but by familiarisation I was becoming competent. We rode south to Lille by an old Roman road that was thronged with traffic, clearly Flanders was a wealthy country. I found that I particularly liked the landscape, as it reminded me of my home in the Danelagh. The land was low lying, flat and fertile, particularly suited for sheep, I almost expected to ride around a corner and see my mother's farm spread out before me. Lille was situated in the south of Flanders, almost on the border with Normandy and near to France. This was a convenience to the Count as he was married to the daughter of the King of France and was heavily involved in the affairs of France as its king was aging.

I arrived in Lille for the Christmas celebrations, which although were not as riotous as those in Orkney and Ireland were nevertheless sumptuous. The palace's great hall could easily house a hundred or so of the great and the good for a feast and I was lucky enough to be invited, as I was in the retinue of the Count's youngest son. On arrival in Lille, I had presented myself to Robert who seemed delighted to see me again and he housed me in a substantial room in his town house as he was staying in his father's palace. Rather than letting my two guard's bunk in a tavern they slept in my room as it was far bigger than I was used to anyway; they still slipped off to a local tavern whenever the opportunity arose.

In due course I was introduced to Robert's father Count Baldwin of Flanders, fifth of his name, called the debonaire, whatever that meant, some French word. He was an elderly man and had been ruling many years. He had gradually expanded his territory and influence until he was one of the most powerful of men in north western Europe. I met him in a side room to the great hall where he did most of his business, he was soberly, yet magnificently dressed with a few well-placed jewels around his shoulders on a gold chain of office. He wore a velvet cap with a pearl brooch appended, which I suspect was because he was balding and wanted to appear younger. In attendance on the aged count was his eldest son, another Baldwin who was much older than his younger brother Robert. This Baldwin gave the impression of the count in miniature and he was also balding. Both were not tall men, my height, whereas Robert towered over us, Robert introduced me.

"Father, may I introduce Hereward Leofricson, brother to the Earl of Mercia in England, a noted warrior and battle leader." Count Baldwin gave me a searching look.

"Good day my lord, it is an honour to meet you." I spoke as formally as I could.

"You are the battle leader that gave the Welsh and Irish kings their victories? I cannot pronounce their names." Count Baldwin queried.

"I did fight for Gryffudd, King of Wales and Diarmait King of Leinster with some success, yes." I responded.

"Ah! The Bearslayer and outlaw, a noted reiver and pirate and enemy of Tostig." The younger Baldwin chipped in, trying not to stare at my parti-coloured eyes.

Sensing antagonism, I responded, "I understood many outlaws were welcome in Flanders?"

Robert interceded, "Father, Hereward is my pet viking, I would use him in our ongoing disputes with Scheldtmerland, he has a viking longship." I was not too happy at being referred to as a 'pet' viking but let it go for the time being.

The count looked thoughtful. "Leofricson, you are familiar with our dispute with Scheldtmerland?"

When in doubt, honesty is the best response. "My lord, I have no idea where Scheldtmerland is, let alone what dispute you have with the inhabitants." Robert looked slightly crestfallen and his older brother smirked.

"Scheldtmerland consists of the islands at the mouth of the river Scheldt, the inhabitants are notorious for ignoring their obligations and submission to Flanders, just like the Count of Guines. The islands are low lying, marshy and difficult to access and their inhabitants have repeatedly refused to submit to me, their natural lord." Count Baldwin explained. This explanation piqued my interest; a low-lying riverine area consisting of a number of islands was an ideal place to raid with my *Ottar*; I could probably do more damage to the inhabitants than a large army of horse and foot with no means of accessing the islands.

"I know where you mean now." I replied. "The area at the mouth of the River Scheldt is a large estuary dotted with islands, some large, some small, I sailed passed its mouth on the way to Flanders last year, we Anglo-Danes from the Danelagh call it Zealand. Back in the days of the Great Heathen Army, the viking leader Hastein wintered over in a fortified camp on one of the islands."

"I have been trying, or rather my son has been trying," the Count looked across at his namesake, who looked uncomfortable, "to assert my control over that area of Flanders for some years without success, what do you say?"

269

"My lord, as you know I am a paid mercenary and my talent is having a record of successful strategies and tactics that provide my paymasters' with the results they desire. I am familiar with the landscape and difficulties of such an area, which is not unlike where I was born, I know the people will be stubborn and brave but I believe I have the means to pressurise the inhabitants of these islands to accept your authority."

"Good, I will give you a year to prove your worth, the details of your remuneration will be agreed with my son Baldwin." The Count smiled for the first time and held out his hand, which I took giving a firm handshake in the way of the Danelagh. Robert was less than pleased.

"Father, the Bearslayer is my battle leader and I should be the one to lead the new campaign in Scheldtmerland, Baldwin has had his chance."

"I am the paymaster Robert and I decide, you have had a successful campaign against the Count of Guisnes, now let your brother have his opportunity to learn from a master." Count Baldwin countered. A master! I preened inside; I was being recognised as a proven war leader it was important that I should not fail now.

Count Baldwin's eldest son was not an easy man to get on with; he was taciturn and defensive. He was aware that he was not as talented as his father nor as flamboyant and well-loved as his younger brother Robert. He certainly was not of the warrior class and I suspected he secretly abhorred the idea of fighting and bloodshed. His close advisors reflected this attitude, a clutch of priests and merchants who always had an eye on trade or enlarging church lands. Apparently, the people loved him but the nobles were less enthusiastic. Baldwin was already the Count of Hainaut by his marriage to Richilde, Countess of Hainaut. This marriage was devised by his father and it had caused a war with the Holy Roman Emperor, which the counts, father, and son, had won, so that when he eventually succeeded his father as Count of Flanders, he would be a mighty lord indeed.

Discussing warlike preparations for the forthcoming campaign in the River Scheldt estuary was therefore difficult. Baldwin certainly did not wish it to be an expensive drain on the resources of Flanders. He did not want to commit a large army to the assault on the islands. In the end he enthusiastically agreed to my proposals, proposals that I had intended to be adopted all along.

Simply I intended to replicate the strategy adopted by the Great Heathen Army from two hundred years previously. After the Great Heathen Army had been expelled from Wessex by King Alfred and his son Edward, the Danes led by Hastein had crossed over to mainland Europe and ravaged France and the low countries. Using their standard tactics, they had established certain fortified encampments, usually at the mouths of major rivers or on islands that enabled them to raid along the river valleys and winter over where they could not be assaulted by the land-based armies of the old Frankish empire. I would find a site on one of the islands in the Scheldt estuary and build a fortified camp from where I intended to terrorise the inhabitants by longship until they submitted.

Obviously my one snekkja and my anticipated knarr would not convey enough men onto whichever island I chose as my base, so I either had to acquire more ships or ferry men to the intended encampment. I sent Beornwulf back to Bruges to liaise with Egil, Eystein and Martin and inform them regarding the forthcoming campaign. I then settled down to enjoy Yule and the turning of the year at the Flemish court. Yule was a more formal and religious affair than in the British Isles where a great deal of ale and mead is consumed with many boisterous games, songs, and celebrations. There were several large and formal feasts that gave me the opportunity to meet some of the principal lords of Flanders and its surrounding territories. The lords of Alost, Mons and Lens were present and interested in meeting me and my old employer Gilbert of Ghent renewed his acquaintance and took great pleasure in proclaiming his role in introducing me into the politics of Flanders and the success at Ardres.

I found the entertainment boring, the Flemish and French minstrels, as they were called, sang melodious songs with none of the vim and verve of the Nordic skalds. Even the tumblers and conjurers were demur in their performances, no innuendo or sexual suggestiveness, no sly insults to the great and good. Equally the food was not particularly to my taste, unlike the solid English fare, roasted meats, root vegetables and bread with tasty gravy, washed down with ale; the Flemings seemed hell bent on introducing as many fancy additions to the meal as possible. A riot of tastes and colour was presented before any eating took place. Roast boar and deer, peacock and swan were all cooked and then redressed in their skins and feathers to look almost lifelike and paraded around the banqueting hall, smothered in glazed spices imported from the east, to ecstatic applause. An infinite variety of pastries, sausages, and sweetmeats, together with fruits festooned the platters. The good honest tastes of the meat were lost under honey and wines. The ladies of the court cooed over sugared nuts and jellies, which turned my stomach. Instead of ale the Flemings preferred wines from France that were sweet and heady. I did not mind the wine, especially the Rhenish blends that tasted tarter and fresher but I found I could not handle them like ale and frequently ended up the worse for over indulging until I realised, they were not to be swilled down like ale but sipped decorously. I admit the bread was usually fresher and crustier than at home, but it became stale and hard after a single day, but as there was copious amounts, the Flemings did not seem to mind this at all.

Even more astonishing was the knives; like most warriors I always carry a small knife and spoon in my belt wallet. I was particularly proud of my set as the knife had a whalebone handle and the spoon was carved completely from whalebone with a fine rune name of Bragi carved into the handle, Bragi being a Norse god with a ravenous appetite. In the court at Lille the countess had acquired a huge set of pewter knives, enough for all the guests at the banqueting tables. Each place therefore was provided with a knife for cutting meats and a napkin; opulence indeed. Unlike my knife I noticed that all the knives provided had blunted ends, no doubt to prevent drunken quarrels turning murderous.

The one banquet that I did find interesting was held the day before the turning of the year when Count Baldwin had invited chosen foreign guests; the guests included none other than his son-in-law, William, the Duke of Normandy, and his brother-in-law Tostig Godwinson, Earl of Northumbria. Tostig Godwinson arrived in Lille first, he had been married to Count Baldwin's sister Judith for some nine or ten years. They had made the short crossing from Dover to Calais the day before, so clearly Tostig had not been in his Earldom of Northumbria for several days if not weeks. He rode into Lille on horses provided by the Count of Flanders with a retinue of huscarls and ladies-in-waiting to his wife. It was inevitable that we would meet and I decided it would be safer, for both of us, if we met in the company of Count Baldwin's sons. I made sure I was present in Baldwin of Hainaut's retinue when Tostig and his wife met her father and mother formally in the great hall.

Now that Tostig held the earldom of Northumbria he was a magnate of equal status with his father-in-law, more lands but less wealth, and had to be received as such. There was much embracing and cheek kissing; Judith was particularly pleased to see her brother. Tostig was cheerful and jovial and made much of his nephews, Baldwin of Hainhaut and Lord Robert, it was whilst he was shaking the hand of Baldwin of Hainaut that he noticed me. Initially he said nothing to me, indeed ignored me but later in the reception he sidled over.

"Well fancy seeing you here, Leofricson." Tostig smiled evilly. "Every outlaw and vagabond turns up on the shores of Flanders eventually but my good brother-in-law is scraping the bottom of the barrel with you."

"Good-day to you too, my lord of Northumbria, I seem to remember that you fled here when you were outlawed a few years back, if I get a sister of the Count to wife like you, I will consider that a good investment of my time." I responded.

"You will stay an outlaw for ever, Bearslayer, the Godwinsons rule England now." Tostig sneered.

"The Godwinsons don't rule Mercia and you will never be accepted in the north." I knew that he was little liked in Northumbria and the youngest child of Siward Bjornson was still alive.

"Just stay out of my way, dog." Tostig swung around and stormed off, I noticed that Robert had observed our little spat but I knew he would not share this with either his father or brother.

Tostig's wife Judith was a totally different animal; she was blousy and blonde with a voluptuous figure, comfortable breasts, and a roving eye. She was aware of who I was and eyed me provocatively, she had recently given birth, to a girl, I believe and her figure was still matronly. The way she tucked in to the viands provided at the reception suggested that she would struggle to recover her figure quickly. Nevertheless, her Junoesque physique attracted men like flies to a dead carcass, or should that be like bears to honey? I warned Gauti, my single huscarl or guard to watch my back whenever any of Tostig's men were in the vicinity.

The day before the feast Duke William of Normandy and his retinue rode into Lille. The difference in the appearance and demeanour of the Normans, from both the Flemings and Earl Tostig's followers was immediately apparent and impressive. The duke and his wife rode in the forefront of his mesnie. William was a large man in his prime, musclebound, and solid. He was the only Norman not wearing mail; he wore a long dark green surcoat with a split at front and back to permit comfortable riding. He had stout leather boots lodged into the horse's iron stirrups, upon which he wore brutal looking spurs. The duke was bare headed, dark haired, displaying a strange bowl-shaped haircut and shaved chin. He had a stern face, strong with a malleable mouth and square jaw. He clearly had to shave regularly to maintain this appearance. His horse was a massive black warhorse with a white blaze on his forehead, the muscles in the horse's hind quarters were impressive and powerful. His wife, Matilda, was mounted on a diminutive white palfrey, well it looked small next to the duke's massive horse. She was dressed elegantly in a blue gown with an overcoat to match with fur trims. She was quite beautiful, exquisite, which I suppose was expected of princesses and duchesses but usually was not always translated into reality. It was said that the duke loved her and was faithful, which is unusual in princes' but perhaps that was because of his bastard status. She wore a tiny coronet above a fine linen headdress pinned to her blonde hair; glossy tresses woven into long plaits with red ribbons.

Behind the ducal pair rode the duke's guard, rank upon rank of mailed horsemen four abreast. Each rank consisted of two nobles and their gonfalonier or pennon bearer. The mailed horsemen were all dressed remarkably similar, mailed, and hooded hauberks with a nasal helm atop; their faces obscured. The only exception to this severe mode of dress was their kite shaped shields and their banners. Every shield bore a different design or motive, I recognised dragons, lions, wolf heads, crosses, and many abstract symbols in all colours the banners waving at the ends of their gonfalonier's lances matched. Each rider, including the duke had a sword strapped to his belt. I estimated forty horsemen, suggesting that the duke was bringing twenty of his nobles with him, either he was very sure of his power or he dare not leave them back in Normandy to meddle and possibly rebel?

Count Baldwin received the duke even more warmly than he had Earl Tostig. The Norman military power was renowned in all Europe. The Norman Duke had put down many rebellions by his warlike barons from early youth, he had repelled his liege lord the King of France on several occasions and had won conflicts with Anjou, Maine, and Brittany. Norman mercenaries had carved out principalities in southern Italy and were the most feared fighters on the continent. For Baldwin to have cordial relations with the aggressive dukedom on his southern borders was a necessity.

There were other dignitaries from the surrounding counties but no one of such consequence as Duke William. Apparently, the Normans were mad about hunting in any form, the Duchess Matilda particularly liked hawking and the duke preferred hunting deer and boar. A series of hunts were organised for the two days following the feast and a lot of politicking would be done throughout. I chose to join a hunt in a forest area a quarter-watch ride to the east of Lille, both Tostig and Duke William were present and were being guided by Count Baldwin of Hainhaut and Lord Robert. Both the earl and the duke were accompanied by a dozen or so of their retinues and as Tostig was there I took the precaution of having Gauti watch my back. Everyone was armed with bows as it was intended to bring down deer so I took along my large viking bow. The nobles were placed along a ditch on the east side of a wood as the chief forester intended to drive the deer that way using a long line of beaters. I stood a few paces from Lord Robert and beyond him stood Tostig and one of his senior huscarls. To my right the Normans lords were strung out along the ditch, with the Norman duke several positions down from me. I noticed that the Normans were handling smaller flat bows, at least a foot shorter than mine, these were more suitable in wooded areas where long shots were rarely needed. I saw that Tostig and his companion had the longer viking self-bows, like mine.

After a while I could hear the beaters hallooing and thrashing the bushes, it sounded like someone had a drum that was being beaten rhythmically. I realised that with the ditch in front of us the deer would either swerve to left or right or leap the ditch and burst out into the open in panic. The danger, of course, was that an archer in his excitement may swing around to shoot a deer as it leapt the ditch and if he missed the projectile would fly parallel with the ditch towards the other hunters strung out either side – fatal. I deliberately took several paces back from the ditch, hoping to minimise the possibility of being skewered by mistake, or by being shot by Tostig, intentionally.

The sounds of the beaters grew louder and nearer and before long and without warning a large stag burst from cover to my right directly in front of Duke William. The well-trained Norman lords knew not to shoot before their lord did and Duke William swiftly drew his bow and shot an arrow deep into the stag's chest. The beast somersaulted over as it lost its footing and the duke coolly shot a second arrow into the stags heaving flank, stilling its death throws. From the corner of my eye, I saw a doe burst out of the bracken in front of me and without thinking I drew and released, placing an arrow neatly into her chest behind her right foreleg. The missile went straight to the heart and the deer collapsed in a heap. Several deer were now streaming from the undergrowth; I nocked another arrow but allowed the other hunters to shoot and make their kills. As I suspected some arrows flitted passed my front, which could have proved injurious if I had been standing further forward. After what must have been only a few moments the rush of the herd died down and everyone started to babble loudly and excitedly, extolling their own ability and success. Without warning a large, nay huge, stag burst from the foliage, clearly, he objected to being driven and was the last of the herd to leave cover. No one was ready for this and few had their arrows nocked and so luckily for the stag it passed through the line of hunters and fled away in great bounds. As it passed Lord Robert he cursed and nocked an arrow, he shot after the stag but it was already out of effective killing range for his short flat bow. Several other hunters loosed off missiles but all dropped short of their intended target. I placed one of my war arrows on the nock and drew to full stretch, flight to the ear, and calmed myself. I imagined where the stag would be when my arrow arrived and loosed. The shot was well over one hundred and fifty paces but the heavy barbed iron head fell true into the spine of the stag, punching into the vertebrae and severing the spinal cord. The stag crashed to the ground, legs flailing, bravely it tried to rise but failed and fell back. I relaxed and smiled inwardly, a show of martial skill in front of employers was always a good ploy.

"Good shot, I don't think I have ever seen a shot that good; may I see your bow?" I turned and saw the Norman duke approaching surrounded by his lords. Without thinking I handed the bow over to the duke who carefully examined it. "This is much longer and has a greater pulling power than the bows we use in Normandy?" It was a query and I responded.

"This is a viking longbow we use aboard ship, my lord. It is not really suitable for hunting and is best when the field of fire is flat and clear, my ancestors developed such for sea battles." I explained.

"Your ancestors, and you are?" the duke smiled like creased granite.

"I am from the Danelagh in England, my lord. I am named Hereward Leofricson."

"Ah! The Danes, your ancestors and mine are of the same stock. Many of my Norman lord's ancestors came from Denmark and my own ancestor Ganger Hrolf came from Norway." The duke mused and then added. "But you sell yourself short, you are he they call the Bearslayer, outlawed son to the late Earl of Mercia, are you not?"

I shrugged, there was no point in denying it as I had no idea how I stood in the eyes of the Norman Duke. "I am lodged with the Count of Hainhaut for the moment." I confirmed.

"Ah! Yes, the war against the Zealanders," It was clear that the Norman duke knew most everything.

"In the spring, my lord when the Scheldt floods recede."

277

"Interesting, I suspect our solemn friend the Count of Hainhaut, my good brother-in-law, will have more success now you are involved. I would like to talk more with you before I leave perhaps you should come and meet my wife, the duchess at dusk today and we can continue our conversation." The duke walked away to see to his kill, Gauti had already started to divest my doe of her innards before the carcass was conveyed back to the town. Lord Robert came over, excited as usual to congratulate me on the shot that killed the king stag and naturally, I gifted the carcass to him.

Not wishing to offend such a powerful lord as the Norman duke, I presented myself at his chamber before compline when we would sit down for our evening banquet. I had changed into a rather drab over tunic to my standard sailor leggings and boots. I had tied the waist with an expensive tooled leather belt with inter-twinned writhing snakes in the Gaelic style from which I hung my satchel purse and a suitably large dagger. The tunic was trimmed with Gaelic weave, this time interlocking dragons, a riot of tortuous loops, whirls, and knots. My only indication of rank was a Mercian knot stitched to my left breast in gold thread.

I was ushered into the duke's chamber by a mailed guard and saw the duke, already clad for the feast standing in front of a large fire with a goblet of wine in his hand. Sitting beside him was the duchess, this time clad in a green over gown, split to show the red under shift. Her hair was uncovered and seasonal flowers wove into her honey blonde hair. Again, I was smitten by her beauty, she stood and offered me her hand; I bowed and kissed the beringed fingers. Her white hands were small and delicate, as I straightened, I realised she was quite small, maybe five foot and a few inches, I good height for someone of my stature. The duke towered over her.

"Good evening, Lord Hereward, I am glad to meet you." Her voice was low and husky, very attractive in a woman. I could see the duke was still smitten, even though she had born him several children.

"Well met, my lady, but I think Lord Hereward is a bit exalted a title for someone like me." I responded.

"What should I call you then, not Bearslayer surely?" she smiled warmly, clearly amused.

"I would be honoured to be referred to just as Hereward." I replied.

"La! How appropriate but Hereward will not do, in our bastardised French we would call a Hereward, Howard, and Howard you shall be. Come sit with us and tell us all about your adventures." The duchess had a way of drawing people out and had soon wheedled out of me much of my life.

"Dear Howard, I suspect you are being modest, how you have fought in all those Welsh, Scottish and Irish wars without achieving any personal success and merit is quite unbelievable. I am sure you are quite the hero, no?" She purred. I had already realised that she was interrogating me on her husband's behalf; he sat quietly listening.

He did eventually interrupt. "Tell me Howard, what is your opinion of Harald Godwinson?"

Dangerous water; I ruminated on a tactful reply, and failed. "Harald Godwinson is an enemy of my house and one day there will be a reckoning between him and me. The same applies to his brother Tostig who is married to your aunt, my lady."

The duke grimaced, or possibly smiled, "Is this a blood feud?"

Obviously, the Duke was well aware of the consequences of an English blood feud. "No, my lord, not a blood feud; under other circumstances I could like Harald well but for the past three generations the houses of Mercia and Wessex have contended against each other to influence the English kings for the good governance of the realm. The Godwinsons are over mighty and take upon themselves regal powers; in so doing they have worked against the interests of my brother the Earl of Mercia, and the jarls of the Danelagh."

"Your English king, Edward, is aged and childless, who, in your opinion, will be king after he has died?" Matilda interrupted.

"It is not for the likes of me to know, my lady, but the order of kingship in England is quite straight forward. The Witenagemot, that is the tribal leaders, proclaim who is to be king; they will almost certainly choose someone from the blood royal."

"And who is of the blood royal of England?" the duchess prompted.

"Well, it used to be the Aethelings of Wessex, but it could also include someone of the Scyldings of Denmark, since Sweyn Forkbeard and his son Knut the Mighty seized the throne. I understand there is an infant Aetheling still alive after the Godwinsons murdered the adults but I do not know if there are any Scyldings in the male line in Denmark."

"The last two kings of England were sons of my aunt Emma." The duke added. I understood immediately what he was implying.

"My lord duke, I am not aware that the crown of England has ever passed through the female line." I asserted.

"Hummph!" was all the comment this statement elicited from the duke.

The conversation changed abruptly. "Howard, I understand that whilst in Scotland you became acquainted with some Norman mercenaries fighting for, who was it now. Ah! King MacBeth, that is it."

"Yes, and stout fighters they were, all dead I am afraid." I responded.

"How is it that they all died?" the duke queried.

"They gave their lives for MacBeth, which is not what a mercenary should do, of course. They were greatly outnumbered but slew many more of the enemy before they died." I remembered my fallen comrades with some sadness and affection. I refrained from informing the duke that if there had been more mounted Normans the outcome would have been entirely different.

The meeting remained cordial and ended with a parting shot from Duke William. "If the opportunity came to fight Harald Godwinson and restore the power of Mercia, would you take it?"

"Only if my outlawry was rescinded, I hold the English law inviolate, even if I don't agree with the decisions the king gives." I bowed and left the duke and duchess' chamber.

The feast that followed was not particularly memorable other than the fact that Tostig became obnoxiously drunk and started boasting about how he intended to destroy the Welsh and Scots. It was clear that the Normans considered drunkenness to be the height of bad manners and the Countess Judith was suitably embarrassed by her husband's behaviour. I was thankful that I stayed reasonably sober, which was not my wont under normal circumstances but I did feel as though I was under intense scrutiny by the Normans present. I was approached by one of the Normans at the feast, one William Fitz Osbern; apparently, he was a steward to the duke and a near relative. He was blunt and to the point.

"Are you acquainted with my brother Osbern; he is a chaplain at the English court?"

"I am afraid I have had very little by way of dealings with King Edward's court, except to be outlawed." I responded, perhaps too peevishly.

"Well, there is another Norman you may have been acquainted with, a distant relative of mine who died two years back, Ralph de Mantes, your king elevated him to the Earldom of Hereford."

"Yes, I knew of him, we crossed swords a couple of time, but I only saw his back when he ran away from the battle." I knew this would antagonise the Norman but I could not help it.

Fitz Osbern snarled angrily through his whiskers, "If we ever meet on the field of battle, you can be sure I won't be running away."

He was taller than me, but that was not unusual; I looked him up and down casually. "If I understand you correctly your name suggests a bear in your family, I seem to run into bears quite a lot and not to their benefit, which is why I am called the Bearslayer."

"Mark me well, Bearslayer, when we meet again it will go ill with you." Fitz Osbern swung on his heel and stomped off.

It was clearly time for me to leave and as I made my way to the great hall's exit, I was amused to see Tostig being carried out, totally insensible. His robes were stained with red wine and I could smell the reek of vomit from four paces away. I paused to let the carriers pass by, careful not to step in any of the leftover slime on the rush matting.

"Hello, are you leaving as well?" I turned to the direction of a husky female voice and was confronted by none other than Tostig's wife, the Lady Judith. Her gown had accidently slid from one shoulder giving a tantalising glimpse of her swollen breasts. She held the front of her crimson gown in a clenched fist under her chest thereby showing her diaphanous white under dress and her tiny feet peeping out in beautifully embroidered shoes. Her hair, still in long blonde plaits had been wound in coils either side of her head, a look that reminded me of those rams with curved horns. Her face was flushed, she had obviously been drinking too, but clearly not as much as her husband.

"My lady, I find the wine too heavy for my taste and I plan on leaving Lille soon to campaign in Scheldtmerland." I responded bowing slightly.

"La! As you can see, I am abandoned by my husband, I am sure you would not wish me to wander this palace alone, perhaps you could escort me to my chambers?" Her eyes were bright with anticipation.

The thought of cuckolding Tostig Godwinson was at the forefront of my mind so I extended my arm and she slid hers around me bicep, squeezing it provocatively. Obviously, I had no idea where she was leading me and it crossed my mind that I could well be led into a trap. The corridors, however were brightly lit, even the stairwell. I was sure Tostig was genuinely drunk and insensible so I went along with the situation. We eventually came to a strong wooden door which Judith leaned back against and pulled me towards her. I could feel her hands fumbling with my hose; she was not familiar with Norse pants that were much looser than the tighter woollen hose worn by both the English and Flemish. She could find no way through them, even though she could feel my hard member bulging out.

"Come in, come in and come in me. I want you in me." She panted heavily.

"Your husband is within; unconscious or not, it won't do." I whispered whilst I squeezed her large soft breast.

"No, no. he is not within, this is an extra chamber I have, my old room from when I grew up here. Only I have a key, look." She fumbled with her girdle belt from which hung a wallet; she extracted a key and promptly unlocked the door. Pushing it open a small chamber was revealed only illuminated by the taper bracketed on the corridor wall behind us.

She pulled me in and shut the door but beforehand retrieved the key and relocked the door from the inside.

"We are alone and cannot be disturbed now." She whispered. As my eyes accustomed themselves to the dim interior of the room, I could see a small bed that was obviously previously of use to a child and was inadequate to support two adults. There was a large deerskin carpet on the floor and I decided that would have to do. I removed my cloak and laid it on top of the deerskin. "I love your strange eyes." She purred. "They are so wild; would you take me by force?" She hissed. I had the presence of mind not to damage her apparel. I lifted her dress over her head revealing a fine linen shift that did nothing to hid the voluptuous contours of her body. I held her from me and stoked her breast through the material. She moaned in anticipation, flapping ineffectually at my belt. There were thin laces cross-threaded holding her bodice together, with my free hand I unlaced them and pulled them apart. In this manner, I was able to pull her shift free of her shoulders and down over her breasts until it fell free only to be caught by her wide hips. In the dim light she looked like an ethereal ghost; her breasts were magnificent, large, full with nipples like ripe raspberries. I gripped the teats, no squeezed them, eliciting another more pained moan. I pulled her towards me and kissed her forcefully on her rosy full lips. Her mouth parted and a tiny pointed tongue probed my mouth urgently.

I pushed her down to the floor and stood over her whilst I slowly undid my belt and divested myself of my tunic. Even in the darkness she could clearly see my scars on my chest and shoulders and this seem to excite her even more. Without my belt to support them my voluminous sailor's trousers fell to my boot tops exposing my rampant manhood. Stepping back, I pulled off my armoured boots.

Although I wanted her badly, my experiences with Una had taught me to appreciate a woman's body and to try and reciprocate the pleasure of sex with a partner. I wanted an ally in the Godwinson camp and the Lady Judith just might be the answer. I knelt down between her legs and I know she expected me to ram my member straight into her; but I snuggled down between her thighs and gave her slit a long slow lustful lick with my tongue, whilst I played with her sensitive pink nipples. She shuddered and groaned again grabbing at my hair and pushing my face into her sex. I proceeded to work on her opening with

283

my tongue, prizing her lips apart and searching for her secret spot. She was surprisingly hairless, perhaps because of her blonde hair, and her secretions were copious. I flicked her special place with my tongue and gently bit it with my teeth; it was much larger than Una's love spot and my ministrations made her buck and writhe, but fortunately she muffled her screams and moans.

I slowly worked my way up her bountiful body; her abdomen was still soft and flabby from her recent childbirth, with a slight roll of fat beneath her navel. Her breasts were large and soft, falling slightly either side of her chest, her nipples were large and I wondered if she was still breast feeding. I kissed her mouth and she clung to me shuddering. I eased myself into her but in truth there was no need as she was so wet. I slowly started to move into her and she started to make animal grunts and thrust back at me. She was as tall as I and so could reach around and clasp my buttocks, her nails dug into my muscles and entreated me to move faster and harder.

"Fuck me! Do it hard." She cried. I increased my pace and started to ram hard at her groin. I knew that at this pace I would not last long but I tried to hold back as long as I could. When I came the intensity was explosive, I was elated when she orgasmed with me. It was obviously what she desperately wanted.

"Oh! God. Oh! God, I'm coming. Yes." She had entered a world of her own and I knew she would be floating around in it for some time.

I cuddled her and whispered that I wanted her again and I would take her by force if she refused me. This excited her even more and her orgasm crashed again and she released a flood of fluid; my legs were soaked from my groin to my knees. I continued to kiss her and fondle her and bring her back to the real world, and then when she was sensible again, I took her again, for longer the second time. She was a woman who loved sex, a wanton. Maybe a watch had passed before we had done, we lay with my cloak around us, keeping warm from the winter chill.

"A fire would be nice." I suggested.

"What, my lover, am I not hot enough for you?" She purred.

"Your cunt is hotter than the gates of hell but I would gladly burn my cock trying to get in." I responded.

She laughed throatily. "God, I needed a good fuck and I knew as soon as I saw your evil eyes that you were the one."

"I am your husbands sworn enemy, you know."

"Of course, I know, that is what made it even better than I had hoped it would be. My husband is an ignorant Saxon, a fool and so, so boring in bed." She laughed. "I am surprised though, I didn't think you would be so good at the foreplay; where did you learn that, your mother?"

Judith did not see my hesitation when she mentioned my mother, as I immediately thought of Godgifu, my step-mother, who I had lusted after for years. "I learnt it from the Irish." I explained.

"Well good for them, I must try an Irishman next time."

"We have been here a while you will be missed." I suggested.

"I probably won't be, but you are right, we must sneak back to our dreary lives." Judith sat up. "Good God, I am encrusted in juices, yours, and mine both, I need to get clean before I return to Tostig's bed.

"I think my buttocks are bleeding, your nails are sharp." I winced as I stood.

We both dressed and Judith carefully opened the door a crack and peeped out. Nothing was moving and the palace was silent. She turned and pressed her lips to mine. "We will do this again, promise?" She sounded desperate. I assured her that we would continue where we left off at the first possible opportunity. She slipped out, I followed and she locked the door.

I made my way back to my chamber where Gauti was still awake and clearly worried about my whereabouts. I assured him I was safe and apologised for losing contact with him, I winked and he realised I had been with a lady. The following day the Normans left Lille to return to the border; I received a nod from the duke and a scowl from Fitz Osbern; I had a feeling I would see them again.

Tostig Godwinson and his wife stayed on in Lille for a further week before returning to England and at this time of the year the short sea voyage could be tricky and delay their departure for many days. Judith and I managed to make love twice more, once when Tostig was with the Count of Hainhaut hunting and once again after Tostig over imbibed the wine at the table. Both sessions were exhausting but rewarding and enjoyable and I was pleased to note I had gotten over Una. I appreciated Judith's fecund body and her enthusiasm for strenuous sex and in our brief conversations I learn some interesting snippets of information about the goings on in England. It appeared that Tostig was not popular in Northumbria, especially in the far north, Bernicia. Tostig was inclined to stay too long in the south with the King's court leaving the administration of the northern lands to his favourite thugs. One of them Copsig seemed to be virtual ruler of York during the earl's absence. Neither the Danes in Deira nor the Angles in Bernicia were happy with Tostig and the Scots had started to raid across the border again.

Further south my brother Aelfgar was surrounded by Godwinsons. Earl Harald ruled Wessex and controlled the Hwicce, his brother Gyrth Godwinson was now Earl of the East Angles and of course Tostig was north of the Humber. Aelfgar was not as close to the Jarls in the Danelagh has his father had been, which only left his ally King Gryffudd in Wales as his supporter. It was also rumoured that Aelfgar had been unwell and the rule of Mercia was being undertaken by his two sons, Edwin and Morcar, my nephews. The king, Edward the Mild, had retreated into his ecclesiastical works, the building of his favoured abbey at Westminster, and of other establishments throughout Wessex. He paid due courtesy to his wife, Edith, Harald Godwinson's sister but it was well known he did not sleep with her and no heir of his body would ever rule England. I was concerned about my brother's health, he was much older than I, but not an old man. My nephews were only boys, slightly younger than me, finding their way in the world. However, there was nothing I could do about events in England.

After Tostig and Judith rode out of the gates of Lille I started to frame my campaign in Scheldtmerland, although I knew the area vaguely, I needed a guide who was intimate with the area. It occurred to me that I might recruit one of Jan the farmer's sons from Tonnekreek, where Martin and I had stayed over on our first journey to Flanders. Tonnekreek was not far from Scheldtmerland and being fishermen, they may well know the area well. After a month in Lille, I freed myself from both the Baldwins, father and son, leaving their advice and instructions to fly in the wind and headed for Bruges.

Spring 1059 - Dedda

I arrived in Bruges as spring flowered and the sea lanes opened for serious trade, I hoped that my ship and crew would be either already beached or returning from England shortly so that I could begin my little war.

I was informed by the castellan that my crew had not yet appeared and so I accepted his invitation to bed down in his town stronghold. He was an entertaining old man who had a propensity to fall asleep in the evenings after a few goblets of wine and it was no surprise to me that I was soon swiving his beautiful young wife. Dedda was as different as could be from Countess Judith, smaller, darker, more vivacious, narrow waisted, pointed breasts, dark extended nipples, more interesting physically but also more mentally stimulating. We could generally have an assignation mid-evening quite safely and after a physically exhausting bout of lovemaking we could return to the hall and have a stimulating conversation about just anything and everything. She had a greater insight into the world of European politics than I, so our conversations benefited me greatly.

Her ancestry, as she related, was in southern France; Visigothic she called it, which probably explained her dark mysterious appearance. She greatly admired the Duke of Normandy and another person who I had never heard of called Rodrigo de Vivar from Spain, a great champion but she never actually mentioned her own family and I suspected it was not respectable. How she ended up in Flanders was never explained. One thing she told me surprised me considerably and that was that Duke William of Normandy considered himself to be the legitimate heir to the throne of England.

"Why ever would you think that?" Was all I could say to such an outrageous belief.

"It is well known in Normandy that the English King, Edward, looks upon William like a son or nephew, which in a way he is, as Edward is the son of Emma of Normandy, William's great aunt. Edward grew up in exile in Normandy and is more Norman in his outlook than English, is he not?" Dedda explained biting into an apple with her tiny white teeth, vivacious always.

"I do not know King Edward well, I have only met him once when he exiled me from England, but he seemed, well 'English' to me. He was not severe like the Norman nobles I have met, he wore his hair long and flowing, like mine; and anyway, he does not have the right to select his successor without consultation with the Witanagemot." I stopped realising that I was expounding the same argument I had made to Duke William himself not so long before. The conversation went on a different course but I could not push the thought of Duke William coveting the English throne. The concept of hundreds of mailed horsemen sweeping the untrained fyrd away was too frightening to contemplate and I eventually dismissed it from my mind.

After I had been dallying in Bruges for a couple of weeks Martin appeared. He looked well, sleek even, which was not what I was used to. He had two leather satchels, which he deposited on my bed before he squatted down before me, like the old Martin used to.

"Well, Martin, it is good to see you, how was your journeying?" I enquired.

"Prosperous master, prosperous. I have a full tally of our transaction here." He patted the satchels, "But first I must partake of some sad news."

"Sad, how sad?" I tensed unsure of what was to follow; thoughts of my mother and uncle Brand flew through my head and I cursed for not being able to see them for so long.

"Your brother, Earl Aelfgar has died this month past, he died of a wasting sickness from what I have heard and there was no mention of foul play." Martin explained quietly.

"Aelfgar, my brother; how can this be? He was no longer young but nowhere near as old as father."

"Fate is inexorable master."

I sat silently for a while contemplating the situation. I loved my brother dearly and, if truth be told, I had spent most of the years of my outlawry fighting his cause. I felt cut adrift, while my brother lived there was always hope that my outlawry would be rescinded in some way, but I had the honesty to acknowledge that I did not want to be just a thegn in Mercia anyway.

Nevertheless, his ambitions did give me some sense of purpose ensuring that I did not become a complete mercenary for foreign rulers. Pulling myself out of my reverie, I leaned towards Martin and said, "And Mercia, what of Mercia?"

"The Mercian thegns immediately proclaimed Aelfgar's eldest son Edwin as their new earl, your nephew master."

"Good, and what of Harald Godwinson?" Martin realised that I did not query Edward the Mild's response to the elevation of my nephew to the midlands earldom.

"He acceded to the decision, and there seems to be harmony on the surface."

I had two nephews Edwin and Morcar, sons of my brother, they were both very young, younger than me and I was still only twenty-two years of age. They must be about five or six years younger, still untried, and vulnerable; I should be there to support them; never had my exile been so bitter.

"Well, I cannot help my nephews, Edwin and Morcar both, and there are good men in Mercia who will be able to assist them and look out for the wiles of Harald Godwinson and Tostig Godwinson both. Tell me of the trade expedition?"

Martin extracted sheaves of parchment from his leather satchel and laid them on the only table my small room provided.

"These are the records of our trading trip, Master." Martin sounded laced with satisfaction.

"Spare me the inventory, a brief summary will do." I responded, in no mood for a lecture on trading economics.

"Following your instruction Egil decided to sail north-east to Denmark and we made landfall at Ribe a trading emporium of the Danes. At Ribe we were able to purchase a knarr suitable for trading purposes, which Egil chose to name *Hilda* after his wife. Egil took the helm of the knarr and Eystein now skippers the *Ottar,* saving your final decision, of course, Master."

I nodded, "Go on."

"We split the crew, lost a couple of lads to the taverns of Ribe but gained ten more young Danes who were looking for adventure. With *Ottar* guarding *Hilda* like an old sheepdog we made for the German port of Hamburg, far down the River Elbe. There we bought a cargo of mostly Rhenish wines, which Egil and I agreed should be sold in London for a handsome profit.

With the wind in our favour, we crossed to the Thames mouth within days and Egil took the *Hilda* up river to the wharves of London. So as not to draw attention to our enterprise Eystein took *Ottar* into a creek to the north side of the Thames at a place called Canvey to wait out the trade. We felt that the Reeve of London would not look kindly upon a snekkja full of Danes and Dubliners sailing into port.

Egil and I traded the wine for wool and tin which we brought back to Flanders. We off-loaded our cargo at Boulogne, where we felt we would get the best price and then returned here, master. It was here that we were met by Beornwulf who informed us of our next employment and by that time it was too late to acquire another ship or more men. Master, we have enough silver to buy several ships or have them built."

"That was well done, what about the payment to the men?" I enquired.

"Egil and I have apportioned the profits fairly but have saved the rewards for your distribution, as is right. We allotted an extra portion to Gautrek who prevented a thief stealing from the cargo whilst it was on the jetty awaiting loading. The thief knifed Gautrek but was disembowelled for his temerity and is at the bottom of the river weighed down by stones; Gautrek will be alright, it was only a minor wound."

"Good, it is time I left Bruges." I stated, I was mindful of the fact that I could not keep my liaison with the castellan's wife a secret forever.

The next morning after a formal farewell to the castellan and his wife I rode out of Bruges and back down to my ship. The muddy village of Bruges by the Sea seemed to be more prosperous than I remembered it and this was probably because of my crew being in semi-residence. Martin informed me that at least two of the crew had formed more or less permanent relationships with girls in the village and I was sure that their fishermen fathers would welcome the extra wealth coming into their families. Nether sides of these partnerships expected the relationships to last but they all made the best of it, as sailors tended to do everywhere. The tavern was certainly busier and I noticed several of my crew sitting outside in the pale spring sunshine enjoying a flagon of ale. When they saw me, they quickly terminated their drink and made their way back down to the beach.

Ottar was pulled up onto the soft white sand above the tide line with wooden chocks holding it upright. Most of the crew were working diligently scaping the hull and repacking the strakes to reinforce the snekkja's water tightness. The ship's cauldron had been set up on the beach and I could smell the aroma of bubbling fish stew. Eystein was standing by the cauldron with a wooden bowl in his hands carefully sipping at its contents. I dismounted and walked over to the cauldron.

"That smells like shit, have you an extra bowl?" I queried. One of the crew handed be another wooden bowl and I ladled a generous helping of the stew into it.

"Greetings, Lord Hereward; how was Lille, entertaining?" Eystein smiled obviously pleased to see me back. I liked that.

"Food wasn't as good as this fish stew, but the ladies were cleaner than the doxies up at the tavern, I'll avow." Eystein laughed at that, Martin looked quizzical. It was true that after many years of being uncomfortable around women, since Una I had found a release in intimacy with certain types of women.

"Where is your father?" I asked. Eystein looked out at the knarr lying off shore.

"He is on *Hilda*; I think he enjoys sailing a trading ship more these days."

"Is that so? Well, there is no reason why he cannot continue skippering the knarr but for the time being I need that boat to ferry men and supplies to our base in Zealand." I responded thoughtfully. "I need the men to gather around so that I can distribute our gains and explain our next employment."

"Right, I'll send a man out to father." Eystein walked away. While the men were gathering, I asked Martin to brief me on the portions that each crew man was to receive so that when the men were finally assembled, I was fully briefed.

I stood on a wooden crate so that all could see me and addressed them.

"Men, good Danes and Irish and whatever other tribes and clans I have missed, now is the time to distribute the wealth and profits of our trading. Egil and Martin have allotted the portions and as most of the cargoes have been sold it will be paid to you in mostly hack silver, which I know is your preference." The men cheered, hack silver was easily transferable anywhere a ship landed, into women, food, weapons, or any other worldly goods a sailor might need. I duly shared out the portions as agreed and I could tell that the men were generally well pleased with their shares. They cheered Gautrek when I gave him his double share, he grinned and showed off his bandaged ribs.

"Right lads, Egil, Eystein and Martin also receive double shares as the leaders of your expedition and I notice that there is a large share for me." They all cheered again, so there was no animosity towards me having a share even though I had not accompanied them; I raised my voice again. "While you were sailing the winter seas, risking your lives, I was in the royal court at Lille, humping Flemish noble ladies." They laughed again wondering where I was leading. "I dined on fresh meat every day supplemented with fine French wines. I hunted with counts and dukes; who among you would not have wished to be in my place." There was laughter now and some puzzlement, was I insulting them?

"It is for this reason that I must forgo my share of the profits from the trading expedition. I have an extra ship, called *Hilda* no less, with a broad beam as wide as Egil's wife. No wonder he is besotted of her." Again, the laughter. "My share of the profit will be shared out between you equally and I thank you all for agreeing to be my crew, I couldn't wish for a better set of reivers." This time the crew cheered even more wildly as my largess had nearly doubled each one's profits from the enterprise.

"Now listen and I will tell you what my next undertaking will be." They all quietened. "This time it will be war not trading, but war the way vikings prefer. I have been employed by the Count of Flanders to wage a war against Scheldtmerland and if you do not know where that is you may know it as Zealand; and for those of you who are none the wiser it consists of those islands in the estuary of the River Scheldt, not more than thirty miles north of where we are right now. The Count of Flanders has already waged war against these recalcitrant rebels many times with little success but that was because he took an army of foot and horse to fight men living on a dozen or so islands. I will not do that, I intend to raid the islands and plunder them, a 'somerleding', I do not need an army, all I need is a shipload of warriors to raid farms and villages and live in a defensive camp the way our ancestors did when they raided England and France all those years ago when the sons of Ragnar Lodbrog led the Great Army. Are you with me?" The crew roared their approval, nothing appeals more than raiding to take other people's wealth and women. I waved them quiet. "Good, and the best of it is that the Count of Flanders is going to pay us to do it."

After the crew dispersed, mainly to the tavern I drew my closest confidents together, Egil, Eystein and Martin. "We need more men and another snekkja to achieve my objectives and at the moment I have no idea where to get them from, any suggestion?"

"I have no doubt that you would be able to buy a snekkja in Denmark, but it wouldn't be a new one and with the fighting that is habitually taking place between the king of Norway and the king of Denmark, Sweyn Estridson needs all the warships he can hold on to." Egil expounded.

"We won't find any snekkjas in Flanders, or Normandy for that matter." Martin interjected.

"There are some Frisian pirates we could look to recruit, they have longships." Eystein suggested.

"What about the Zealanders themselves. They must have some shipping or how could they live successfully on the islands?" Martin added thoughtfully.

"That is an interesting thought, Martin, however, I suspect most of the Zealander's boats are fishing vessels, skiffs, and the like, I hardly see them having snekkjas. I quite like the idea of recruiting Frisian pirates though." I suggested.

"I have decided on a preliminary plan." I finalised. "Egil, you take *Hilda* north to Ribe again and see if you can recruit men for our campaign. Once we have a beachhead with ramparts on some small island in the Scheldt delta it does not matter if we do not have sufficient ships for all the men who defend it. We will take *Ottar* and scout the islands to find a suitable base for our island fortress, one of the smaller islands where we can either beach the ships of keep them at anchor on a lee shore away from the open sea. We will meet back here in two months, the start of summer and then we will begin raiding."

Summer 1059 – Roggen

Eystein Egilson steered *Ottar* into the mouth of what I considered to be the northern branch of the Scheldt estuary but which the locals called the eastern Scheldt apparently. I stood at the prow next to Gauti who was peering over the bow, scanning the waters for shallows upon which we could so easily run aground. Our sail was furled and the lads were at the oars pulling lustily against the ebbing tide and current. Ahead of us and nearing rapidly was a small low island lying centrally between the large islands of Walcheran to the south and Schouwen to the north, although there were enumerable smaller islands dotted about, this one looked the most promising. I looked aft and saw my prisoner Radbod tied to the mast. I had captured Radbod in the spring on my first reconnaissance of the islands. He was a fisherman, but also something more, perhaps the headman of his village. He was fishing in the river with four other companions and a young girl, his daughter, when we pounced. My men killed his men and kept him and the girl. I had gleaned the names of most of the islands and headlands of the Scheldt islands from him.

Apparently, there were no towns, as such, just villages, the largest one being the middle burg on the centre of the largest island, of which the peninsula of Walcheran was part. There was a jarl, of sorts, but Radbod claimed he did not know his name, I did not believe him. I had decided that the small island that we were approaching would be our base for raiding the isles. Radbod said it was called Roggen but I doubted that such a small insignificant sand bar had a name. It was only about two hundred strides long, low, and flat; no trees, no water but a nice beach on the east side of the island protected from the wind by slightly rising sand dunes and gorse bushes to the seaward side. I intended to beach the snekkja and keep the knarr anchored in shallow water. Looking further aft I could see the *Hilda* following in our wake on half sail, she was too unwieldy to row with what oars she had available. The knarr was piled high with wooden stakes intended for a palisade that would eventually encircle the island. The knarr was low in the water for in addition to the stakes there were twenty Frisian recruits, to my band, looking for plunder, an untrustworthy bunch if ever I saw any, but beggars cannot be choosers, I needed the man power. Fortunately, the Danes, Frisians and Flemings I had in my crews spoke a sufficiently similar language to make themselves understood to each other without difficulty, and the dialect in the English Danelagh was also similar, so although it was a motley group there was some synergy between them.

Behind the *Hilda* two smaller boats, karvis, was being rowed by eight oarsmen apiece, more Frisians. I was intrigued by these small boats they were unsuitable for the open sea but I could see their merit for riverine raiding in the low-lying wetlands of Frisia and of the Scheldt both. They just might prove more valuable than my snekkja for what I wanted to achieve. In total I now had one hundred and twenty men under my command, of these thirty-four were Frisians upon whom I had scant reliance at the present, sixty-four, the bulk of my crew were Irish and Hebridean Norse, eight Flemings had joined me and I assumed at least one of these was a spy for Baldwin of Hainhaut or his father, and finally thirteen Danes from Ribe and of course Martin. I realised that I had to appoint at least one Frisian to my inner circle of captains and possibly one Dane.

I noticed that Eystein had shoved the young girl into the stern and covered her with a sealskin cloak so that she was almost unnoticeable. I could just see hair like golden straw and startled blue eyes. My crew suggested that I should torture the Zealander to make him reveal more but I was not sure I would achieve much by that. I was still unsure who or what he was, when captured he had a half decent dagger that I did not think the average fisherman would own.

Eystein brought *Ottar* around the south side of the island and the small but smooth sand bar spread out before us. With Gauti calling the depth Egil swung the longship into the beach and the rowers bent their backs and pulled her smoothly up onto the sand. Within a few heartbeats the two Frisian boats slid up onto the beach beside *Ottar* and their crews jumped out.

"Secure *Ottar*." I cried and threw some chocks overboard so that they could hold the longship upright.

I jumped off the prow strake onto the soft but quite firm white sand; just as I remembered it from three months past. I could see that Egil had brought *Hilda* in close but well clear of the ships pulled up on the sand. I could hear him shouting to get the wooden stakes overboard and floated into shore. There were no sand dunes on this side of the island but I could see across the flat expanse to the sand dunes facing the open sea and they rose maybe five or six feet above the water level. We had enough stakes to build a wall right around the eastern side of the island from north to south some twenty-five paces from the high tide line. This would leave a very narrow space for any attackers to muster and well within missiles range of my wall. Of course, the west side of the island was still wide open and unprotected but I intended to send Egil back to Bruges for more stakes so that I could enclose the entire island.

I had all the crews hammering the stakes into the sand immediately, I had no doubt that we would be observed from the surrounding larger islands within days if not hours and intended to be ready for any measures taken against us. When a stake was hammered in securely it was about four feet high, easily defended by archers and spearmen from an attack. Many of the crew off-loaded their wooden sea chests and rammed them up tight against the inside of the walls to give greater strength to the walls and provide a higher platform on which to stand to repel any would be attackers. It also marked their section of the wall, which they took personal responsibility for; I liked that attitude. The stakes were lashed together with ropes at the top and bottom and I was confident that the wall could not be pushed over without a concerted effort that would be impossible whilst being assailed by the defenders.

All these preparations aside I had no intention of being trapped on the island and had every reason to carry the attack to the islanders. After the stakes had been secured, which took most of the day the men looked to make shelters from spare canvas sheets brought along for that very purpose. The tented accommodation all tended to face one way as the crews instinctively new which way the prevailing winds swept the island. They piled sand up on the west side of their canvas homes to ensure they were as snug as they could possibly make them. I had the foresight to bring extra wood for cooking fires as I was sure the flotsam washed up on the island would be insufficient for our purposes. By the evening the crews were exhausted and after a makeshift meal consisting of cold meat, mostly sausages, bread, and cheese they all turned in; that is all except the sentries posted at each end of the island, locations that could sweep the horizons both up river and out to sea.

The following morning Egil took the *Hilda* back to Bruges to load more wooden stakes and supplies. He only needed ten crewmen to achieve this, which left me with the bulk of my small raiding force. I intended to make a start immediately. I decided to leave twenty men on Roggen island to protect our equipment under Martin's command, together with our captives, Radbod and his daughter. I manned *Ottar* and the two Frisian karvis for the raid and before we left, I noticed Eystein speaking to Martin and gesturing towards our captives. My intention was to sweep the southern shores of the four islands lying immediately to the north of Roggen and take, or destroy all the shipping I could find afloat or on the beaches. I explained to the men I was not too bothered about pillaging villages at this point and that I merely wanted to blunt any opportunity the islanders may have to counter-attack us over the summer.

These four islands were all close together with small shallow channels separating them, to the undiscerning eye they appeared as one island. I was pretty sure that *Ottar* could not penetrate the creeks that separated the islands as even its shallow draft was too much for the sand bars and shallows. I therefore decided that the two Frisian karvis were to row up the creeks and smash any boats they could find, whilst I took *Ottar* around the outer rim of the islands searching for larger boats to capture. Although I had specifically ordered that the objective of the raids was to eliminate shipping, I knew that without my immediate control the Frisians would not stop at that.

Shortly after Egil had sailed south my little flotilla rowed north. It was less than a mile to the southern tip of Schouwen and I directed the ships west along the south coast. There was a sandbank to our steer board side and we were obviously rowing along a deeper water channel with the main island's beach to our left. I could see a small village up ahead and directed Eystein to steer towards it. There was a slight rise in the sand dunes with a palisaded stockade taking advantage of the height. The size of the village indicated that there could not be more than five or six families living there so the stockade was either for the headman or a refuge place for the whole village if attacked. As we neared the beach, I could see five small fishing boats pulled up on the sand with a series of shacks or bothies presumably for storing nets and gutting fish. There were a few men around the boats presumably readying for that day's fishing expedition. As we approached and they noticed us they stood and stared, there was no apprehension or feeling of danger in their attitude.

Turning to the men crouching behind me I gave instructions. "They do not look like they will run, to start with. I want the boats, when we ground, leap ashore and kill a few; then they will run. I want the boats pulled into the water and tied to our stern so that we can tow them back to Roggen. Understood." They all nodded. I strung my war bow, this was in clear sight of the villagers and still they did not run, they were either brave or stupid. I noticed one of the men had a harpoon of sorts, so they were clearly game to take on a small whale. I drew my bow to the nock sighted and loosed; the missile arced over the water and pierced the villager with the harpoon in the neck, it must have sliced through some tendons, his head slumped to one side and the impact of the arrow carried him backwards several paced so that he toppled off the wooden jetty into the water.

Eystein neatly brought the *Ottar* gliding into the end of the jetty ordering the oarsmen to first hold their oars into the water to slow the longship and then to lift the oars upright before they collided with the wooden jetty. Gautrek was first over the side leaping onto the wooden gangway. The fishermen, still in shock, scattered but not before Gautrek had thrown a javelin into the back of another of them. I clambered over the side more sedately.

"Untie the boats and float them, Gautrek, stop chasing the fishermen and see if there is anything in those sheds of any use to us."

I examined the five boats that were being tied in a line onto the *Ottar's* stern post. Four were in good shape and not dissimilar to our Frisian karvis, the fifth was clearly rotting but I decided to take it with us as we needed the wood on our fortified island.

Gautrek returned, "Lord, the huts are filled with nets mostly but I have these 'ere harpoons." He hefted four very heavy wooden staves with long metal shanks and barbed heads.

"Good, we will take the harpoons and nets. We can supplement our diet with fish and I have a hankering to hunt a whale before the summer is out." I ordered.

Several of the crew dragged out the nets and dumped them in the fishing boats. We all re-boarded the *Ottar* and Eystein carefully turned the ship in its own length and the rowers slowly pulled away from the village. The snekkja shuddered as it took the weight of the fishing boats and the stern post creaked somewhat causing me some concern but all was well as we got under way. I needed to get the boats back to Roggen, which was going to curtail my raid almost before it had begun so I called for the Frisian karvis to come alongside.

The skippers of these two boats were called Hartman and Sibald. "Listen, when we clear this channel, I am taking these boats back to Roggen, I want you two to proceed as planned. Turn east and make for the creeks that separate Schouwen from Duiveland. Row up them and find any boats you can find and sink them, stove in their bottoms but make sure they are sunk in the channels not in shallow water, I do not want repairs to be easily achieved. Do not take risks. Oh! And keep a tally of boats sunk." I directed them and was pleased to see their enthusiasm. "Don't take risks." I reminded them again.

My small group of ships separated as we cleared the channel and the two Frisian karvis darted off eastwards whilst my crew rowed the two miles or so back to Roggen. The rest of the morning was spent dragging the fishing boats up onto the sand in front of the stockade. Martin and the ships carpenter, Njal had been busy erecting a gateway access from the stockade to the beach. He was trying to make it as strong as possible using ships nails to secure cross beams to the uprights. The hinges were strips of leather hide, which was clearly the weak points but Martin was cleverly encasing the leather hinges in wooden covers to prevent attackers slicing them apart. Several of the more enterprising men had dragged the rotting fishing boat into the stockade and overturned it to make one of the more comfortable shelters, which they then proudly presented to me as my headquarters. I thanked them and made a mental note to use more of the captured boats in this way.

Past noon I promptly ordered the crew back onto the *Ottar* to resume our raiding. I followed the earlier route to the raided village but rowed past the inward channel and on along the coast. The coast narrowed into a vee shaped bay and I could discern the entrance to the creek that separated Schouwen island from Duiveland. The two Frisian karvis should have entered this low-lying swamp and lagoon area and I was disinclined to follow with *Ottar* as I was sure the sea bottom would shelve, hiding sandbanks.

The coastline curved south and we rowed along the bleak sand-dune shore looking for habitation. We came upon a couple of huts nestled in the dunes and one had a boat staked to the shore on a rope. I ordered Eystein to steer towards this boat, which he did most carefully. Fortunately, the bottom shelved quite steeply here and we were able to bring *Ottar* in to the floating stern of the fishing boat. This was the smallest boat we had found so far and would only accommodate four men when crowded. Two of my crew clambered down into the boat and cut the tether rope. The oars were on board and they started the long three-mile row back to Roggen.

We rowed on, and where the dunes flattened out, I could see cattle grazing and I made a mental note to return and steal the cattle to bolster our larder. After another mile or so we came to a low headland and beyond the coast bent north again into another bay. I suspected that this was where another creek separated the islands. Most important I could see another village, larger than the last one, and I directed Eystein to steer directly towards it. The village was certainly at the mouth of a river or creek and had wattle and daub cottages on both sides of the river mouth. I counted twenty dwellings, none large so I calculated that there could not be more than thirty able-bodied men available to protect the place. We probably outnumbered the villagers two to one, and fishermen against warriors did not give the villagers much of a chance. This village did not have a jetty and all their boats, that is the boats that were not out fishing were beached. I counted ten small fishing craft. I instructed the crew that we would take the two smallest boats and destroy the rest. I

300

instructed Gautrek to secure the best two smallest boats and I led the party to destroy the rest of the fishing boats.

Eystein slid the bow of *Ottar* gently onto the shelving sand and I leaped over the sheer strake. I carried my shield as a precaution but did not draw my sword. The crew all held small axes and they spread out along the beach and in groups of four rolled the fishing boats and started hacking at the bottom strakes. As anticipated the villagers came running down from the village shouting for us to stop. Initially they did not realise their danger. Leading the villagers was a lousy old dog, easily outrunning the men, growling, and barking excitedly. It reminded me of Boy, the dog I lost when Godgifu had it drowned, but I steeled myself, rather a dead dog than massacring the villagers at this stage of the campaign. I drew my sword and as it ran up to me, I swung my sword and brained the animal. It whimpered pitifully and sank down with its brains spilling out onto the sand. The villagers were stopped in their tracks, total silence, surprisingly they did not flee but just stood there watching as we destroyed their boats. After we had completely reduced their fishing boats to matchwood, we leisurely loaded the splintered planks onto the snekkja, clambered on board and backed water, clearing the beach. I decided that we had done enough for one day and Eystein steered for Roggen, dragging the two small fishing boats astern.

Back at our stockade camp I had the two extra boats dragged through the completed gates and upturned to make two more sheltered sleeping compartments. Dusk was falling and the two Frisian karvis had not returned, however, there was still time before I needed to be worried. Martin had arranged for several cauldrons of stew to be simmering and the first proper meal on the island was fast developing into a boisterous affair when the Frisian karvis were sighted. They were low in the water and I knew they had exceeded their orders. The karvis beached and Sibald was the first Frisian through the gate. I beckoned him over.

"Report."

Sibald smiled easily, rubbing a small scar on his cheek, which I had noticed earlier; it bothered him a lot. "Hartman and I entered the creek between the islands as you commanded, after a quarter of a mile or so we came upon a cluster of villages around a small lagoon or lake. The lake was fringed with huge bullrushes so our approach was masked and the villagers only knew of our presence when we burst out of cover and bumped against the wooden jetties they had built. The villages were quite large and Hartman and I decided to stay together so that we would not be outnumbered. The first village had four boats which we sank by stoving in their bottoms. Several of the villagers tried to stop us but we speared a couple and the rest ran off. We did the same at the next village and destroyed six small boats. Finally, we came to the last village in the lagoon; this one had a church, a small wooden affair; whilst half of the crew destroyed their boats, six boats this time, the rest of us rushed the church to see if there were any valuables."

I was becoming increasingly annoyed; it was obvious they had started to loot the village and I did not want to terrify the islanders before I had demolished their means of escape or send out warnings. Destroying boats was far more important at this stage of the campaign. As Sibald was still speaking Hartman came through the gate dragging a woman whose hands had been tied.

"Stop!" I held up my hand. "I specifically ordered that no looting was to take place until we had crippled their sea power. I see a woman captive and I am sure you have more loot in your boats."

"What of it? We have destroyed their boats as you required of us, the plunder was there for the taking."

Sibald looked annoyed and insolent. Hartman came over. "What's to do?"

"You have exceeded your orders and I will not have men under my command that act independently. You two can leave in one of the small fishing boats and I will appoint men I can trust to skipper the Frisian karvis."

"The hell you will, these karvis are ours not yours." Sibald stepped back placing his hand on his axe handle wedged in his belt.

"We had an agreement made when I employed you and at the first opportunity you have broken that agreement. In recompense for my loss and your bad faith I am taking your karvis. You can fight me or leave. The choice is yours."

I placed my hand on my sword hilt, a move designed to deceive. Sibald ran at me pulling his axe free but I had already gripped the scramaseax strapped to the back of my waist belt and before he could raise his axe to strike me, I stepped forward and whipped the scramaseax out with my left hand and around slicing his throat cleanly. His look of shock was immediately followed by a fountain of blood from the left side of his neck where the artery had been severed. Hartman was much slower, he dropped the rope tethering the girl and reached for his dagger only to gasp, wide eyed as a spear protruded from his chest. Eystein stood at his back grasping the spear handle.

"I don't think you will pull that out without help." I commented. The rest of the Frisians stood huddled behind the bodies of their two dead leaders.

"Now listen to me." I shouted. "All under my command are treated equally as long as they obey my orders. You Frisians are good men but you were badly led." I indicated to the bodies. "These two, did not follow my orders and may have jeopardised my little war. You Frisians will still be treated equally with all the other warriors here. It is my rule that all plunder is shared equally and no loot is to be kept back from the common pot; Martin will keep the tally. The two Frisian karvis will be returned to you after the campaign is over. Now I ask you, is there any amongst you who are kin to these two, if there is to be a blood feud, I would settle it now with a holmgang?" None of the Frisians stood forth and I hoped that would be the end of it.

The Frisians, together with some of my Dublin men off-loaded the karvis. Most of the loot was poor stuff, hardly worth disobeying my orders for, certainly not dying for. There was a crucifix and two brass candles from the church, a poor altar cloth and a clay cup, presumably used for the eucharist, but I doubt the priest had any wine. I had to acknowledge that the three dead geese, a squealing pig and several coils of smoked sausage was most welcome but the three captives would be problematic; they were all women. At least they could not escape from the small island, that is, unless they could swim. The issue, of course, was that the men would eventually fight over them. I asked Martin to

303

secure the prisoners and ensure that they worked for their keep, not whoring but cooking and mending.

After a while Martin came back to me, whilst I was checking the condition of the boats we had captured "Master, there is a problem you should know about." I stood and stretched my back, looking at the bottom strakes diligently was uncomfortable work. I looked at Martin questioningly.

"The three women from the plundered village are all of an age to work, none are particularly attractive and eventually they will be used by the crews like whores; if this does not happen there will be trouble so I will arrange a rota, which will appease the men somewhat and hopefully there will be no fights over them. You were right not to want women on the island yet but what has happened cannot be undone."

"So, what is the problem?" I asked cutting to the nub.

"It is Radbod's daughter, no one has had a good look at her but Eystein and to say he is smitten would be an understatement. She is only twelve but apparently, and I am not a judge of these things, she is a beauty. Eystein has been shielding her since their capture and I can see blood being spilt if any of the men take an interest in her."

"I see, I will think on this." Eystein was my best man, leaving aside Martin who was like an extension of my arm, Eystein had become my lieutenant, the skipper and helmsman of *Ottar* and together with his father contained the wealth of seamanship I needed to sail my two ships, in fact, the snekkja and knarr felt more like their ships that mine. I concluded that I owed Eystein and if he wanted this girl, he should have her. Her father and the girl had been held captive for just over a month and whilst we were in Bruges, I had kept them locked up in a hut near the beach and had them reasonably well looked after, I did not really have a need to keep the girl other than to make sure her father remained compliant. On reflection I should have left her in Burges but she was not a person I had given much consideration to.

Later in the evening I called Eystein over to sit by my fire in front of my upturned boat home. "Eystein, sit." I offered him a mug of ale to ease the tension, he kept looking over to where the girl was tied next to her father.

"Eystein, there is something I want you to do for me." I eased him into the conversation hoping he was listening. "Your father will be back tomorrow, or the day after if all goes well. The men will then spend the next day completing our fortifications before resuming our raiding. I have decided that we can be more effective in the smaller boats, the karvis, and we will continue raiding using them rather than *Ottar*." As soon as *Ottar* became the topic of the conversation he was all ears. "I want you to return to Bruges with Egil and see if you can acquire another boat, I would prefer a snekkja, but a knarr would do. Sooner or later, I expect the Zealanders to try and attack us here and I need larger boats to repel them. Can you do this for me?" I would not normally ask but I wanted him to know I valued him. I could see the concern in his eyes as yet again he furtively looked across to the girl. "I would have you do something else for me." His attention returned to me. "I would have you take Radbod's daughter to Bruges. The island is no place for her and I would ensure she is a hostage for Radbod's compliance. She can be placed in the care of the Lady Dedda, the castellan's wife, she will be safe there." This had him hooked I could see.

"Lord Hereward, I will carry out your orders to the letter." Eystein appeared relieved confirming everything Martin had told me.

"Good, and as you and your father will be my link with Bruges and the castellan you can keep an eye on the girl for me, by the way, what is her name?"

"Marieke, her name is Marieke Radbodsdottar. Her father is the chieftain on the island we raided, Walcheren."

"He is a chieftain; how do you know this, has he told you?" I became alert to the situation.

"No Marieke told me, she let it slip actually." Eystein admitted.

"You should have told me this sooner." I was thoughtful but did not mean the comment as an admonition.

"I'm truly sorry Hereward, I wasn't thinking." Eystein sounded despondent.

"No matter, you are not the first man to be distracted by a pair of beautiful eyes." I smiled and Eystein, who was very fair anyway, coloured up. I laughed.

That was how I resolved the issue of Marieke, the next day I gathered the men around and explained how I was going to continue the raiding in future.

"I have decided that raiding these low-lying fenlands is not a suitable job for *Ottar* and that the Frisian karvis and the fishing boats we have captured are far more suitable for sneaking up the creeks and wicks. We have nine fishing vessels in total, the smallest can only accommodate four men so we will use that one as our fishing boat to maintain our stock of fish food. The two Frisian karvis can hold up to twelve warriors each at a push, and each of the other fishing boats can manage eight to ten overloaded; that means we can raid the coast and creeks with eighty or so men, which should be enough to overwhelm most villages. I intend Eystein Egilson to sail *Ottar* into the main channels of the Scheldt estuary and attack any trading or fishing vessels that belong to the Zealanders, which is clearly a more suitable role for a longship. Any questions?"

The men shuffled about and eventually one of the Frisians spoke up. "Who will skipper the boats?" he hesitated, "Lord."

I gave him a hard look, there was upwards of a third of my men who hailed from Frisia and they had got off to a bad start with me. "Know this, I hold no man responsible for another's mistakes. The two men who skippered the karvis disobeyed my instructions and held me in contempt; they have paid the price." I looked around at the Frisians who had naturally grouped together. "You Frisians will be split up into different boats but you will be treated with honour until proved otherwise. I have decided who will skipper the boats. Martin read the list of skippers and crews."

Martin came to the fore and cleared his throat. "Men, the skippers, and leaders for each boat will be these eight men. Hereward our chief, Eric the Dubliner with the bearded Dane axe, Gauti from Islay, Beornwulf the Manxman, Magnus from Ribe, Coll from Veðrafjǫrðr, Folkar the Frisian and finally Wighard the Frisian. I will inform each captain of his crew so that he can get to know them before you sally out. Eystein Whaleleg and I will command the camp."

I could see many of the Frisians visibly relax when they heard that two of their number were to captain boats. I had consulted with Gauti, Beornwulf and Martin regarding the Frisians who seemed best suited to lead and they had all come up with the same two men. Both men were older than Hartman and Sibald and less inclined to recklessness. I trusted their opinion and the choice was made. I had considered Gautrek as a skipper but he tended to go berserk in battle and I needed cooler heads in control. The Frisians were split up so that about a third of each boat was made up of Frisian mercenaries. I was counting on successful raiding to form a bond within each crew.

My little fleet sallied out before midday and my intention was to complete the circumvallation of Schouwen island as we had already scoured the southern coast line. With small leather sails we made our way north west around the island's round headland that pointed out to sea. Once north of the point, the north coast of the island developed into one long sandy beach with sand dunes protecting any villages; but the sand dunes did not protect the fishing boats, which were dotted along the coast half a mile out, we swooped on them with oars and sail and as each Zealand fishing boat only contained four or five crew, we easily overcame them. Most were killed with arrows, some jumped overboard and tried to swim for the shore. My crews hunted them down and harpooned them, none survived. We scuttled twenty fishing boats that were sunk in water deep enough for them to be permanently lost. By mid-afternoon we had cleared the creek separating Schouwen from the next island, I assumed to be Duiveland. Fishing boats were still out in the centre of the estuary, although some had already started to make for the shore. My little fleet hunted them like a pack of wolves, first surrounding them and closing in for the kill. By this time my archers were running low on missiles and we had to close quicker using javelins and small throwing axes. My men were cautious as they did not want to waste valuable weapons to the deep.

Trial and error found that by bringing our boat alongside the fishing boats we could shoot down into the well of each boat and kill their crews without losing any arrows or javelins. All the crews were killed and a further fourteen fishing boats had been consigned to a watery grave. I ordered a return to Roggen by the way we had come. I did not want to run into any trouble at this early stage. We had severely damaged the livelihoods of the

307

inhabitants of Schouwen and Duiveland and it was inevitable that the villagers on these two islands would be taking their complaints to the local chiefs.

On the following day I turned my attention to the larger island to our immediate south, this was the main island of the Scheldt delta and went by the name of Walcheren or Zealand. Again, we caught the fishing fleets out on the water. The weather was calm so I chose to go west about the island facing the open sea. I hoped that this tactic would confuse any chieftain trying to track us as it would place us on the opposite side of the island from our base. We passed a village I knew was called Domburg and I could see out on the water as many as twenty fishing boats; as on the previous day we cut them off from the coast and the safe haven of Domburg and hunted them down as a pack. We killed all of the crews and scuttled their boats. From Domburg we sailed further west passed the west cape of the island and then turned into the southern arm of the river Scheldt. I had to take care in this channel of the river as it eventually flowed upstream to Antwerp a major trading port in Flanders. There would be many merchant ships in the river and I had no intention of disrupting Flemish trade.

Sailing south-east, we identified more fishing vessels from the villages dotted along the shore of Walcheren and we eliminated them in the same manner as before. By the time I ordered a return to Roggen I estimated we had sunk at least thirty-five fishing boats and killed upwards of one hundred and forty men, young and old. Coupled with the fishing boats sunk the previous day it meant we had destroyed nearly seventy boats and three hundred men. This was a fearful loss of manpower and the ability to feed the islanders and with no loss to ourselves. I was pleased with the way my campaign was developing.

After the long row back to Roggen I saw that *Hilda* had returned and was anchored in the lee of our fort. My men were already off-loading the second cargo of stakes to complete the fortifications on the island. With my small fleet beached I went to find Egil, he was sitting with Martin near my boat turned house sipping ale.

"Ho! Egil, well met. I see you have brought the rest of the wooden palisade. How are things in Bruges by the Sea?" I hailed him as I walked over.

"Well, my lord. Bruges by the Sea is what it always is, awash with whores and men seeking their fortune by sailing with the Bearslayer."

"What have you brought more men?" I asked pleased with the prospect.

"No, I have not." He sounded apologetic, but I was already one step ahead.

"Tell me they are recruited to sail the new boat Egil is requisitioning for me?"

"Indeed, I have signed on thirty Flemish sailors who are camped in Bruges by the Sea until my son arrives with another larger boat." Egil explained, relieved that I had worked out his logic without him having to justify his actions.

"Good that is as it should be, the more of the smaller boats I can place on the water the more damage I can inflict on the Zealanders."

I explained to Egil our progress over the two days he had been away, which I was pleased with. One more day was to be spent completing our fortifications and then I wanted to continue our sweep of the islands to take out the fishing craft and cripple the economy. After that we would start to raid the villages in earnest. Egil felt comfortable being the supply master for our campaign as he was getting too old to be a raider but as he was an experienced trader and viking I wanted to have his opinion on my strategy. He well understood my emulation of the old viking raiding techniques and approved but was more concerned on protecting *Ottar* and *Hilda* when the inevitable Zealander counter attacks developed.

I agreed that the two larger ships must be protected and assured him that when the counter-attacks developed I wanted *Ottar* and *Hilda* off the beach and counter raiding elsewhere.

"And what of your son, where is he?" I asked.

"Well, we knew that he would not be able to acquire a suitable boat at Bruges so we thought he may have better prospects further south at the mouth of the Seine." Egil again looked for my approval and I nodded. Most of the longships were in the service of the Godwinsons along the south coast of Wessex and we were not going to have any luck acquiring a ship in that direction.

The next day all the crews worked on completing the stockade defences, rather than raiding and later that day we had an attempt at a feast to celebrate our success so far. One of the Hebridean Norse was something of a skald and recited several of the northern saga stories and a young lad from Flanders had a fine voice for singing but unfortunately only knew some psalms. Martin's rota held good and those warriors that were inclined took turns with the captive women who mostly suffered the abuse stoically all night. I circulated around talking to as many of my warriors as possible, especially those I did not know well. I explained my ideas for the campaign and how my intention was to bring the Zealanders to the idea that it would be in their interest to submit to the Flemish count and stop a bunch of vikings from destroying their way of life. I felt that the makings of a cohesive force was developing and that several more days raiding would make them formidable. I retired for the night feeling progress was being made.

In the early morning Egil took the *Hilda* back, yet again, to Bruges, now that my army had a defensive stronghold, I wanted to ensure they were all well equipped to fight in a shield wall. Egil was instructed to acquire superior weapons and mail to create a more uniformed force and of course a further supply of drinking water.

I took my small fleet out again to Walcheren with the intention of attacking boats on the north side of the island. It became immediately obvious that there were no fishing boats out on the water and that someone had taken charge and kept the fishing boats ashore. As we sailed along the coast it was also clear that the fishing boats had not been left at the high tide line but pulled further up the beach or up the many small streams and creeks out of sight. It was not until we crossed over to the island of Tholen that we again started seeing fishing boats on the water and on the beaches and we immediately attacked. Over the day we destroyed a further fifteen fishing boat crews, but this time we kept five more of the fishing boats, the best and largest, to supplement our raiding fleet. The crews, all men, and boys, were killed, contributing a further sixty-odd to our tally of murders.

On our return to Roggen, I was informed by Martin that a party of men had been seen watching the island from Schouwen, which after all was only half a mile away. This was not unexpected; our activities must have caused alarm by now and some fishermen must have worked out where we were operating from. I decided that I must put into place measures to ensure we were not surprised and attacked by the Zealanders. In discussion with Martin, Egil and the boat skippers it was agreed that several boats must, at all times, be posted about a mile out from Roggen and placed so that we would be forewarned of any naval attacks. Martin drew up a rota and this project was implemented immediately.

We also decided to put the next stage of our campaign into effect, this was to start raiding the villages in earnest the objective being to instil terror. Slayings, rape, plundering were the order of the day. I decided to lead a raid the following day into the creek between Walcheren and Beveland. This raid would be the riskiest adventure yet as it would take us near to the largest settlement in Zealand, aptly named Middleburg.

Starting before dawn it was only a couple of miles to the mouth of the large wide creek that separated Beveland from the larger island of Walcheren. The banks were covered in high reeds with heavy bullrushes and flooded gorse bushes abounding. Our approach was masked by the heavy vegetation and there were no lookouts that we could see. We came upon a large village about a mile and half up the creek, there were at least twenty fishing boats moored in the creek and I silently detailed off two of our karvis to destroy them. The rest of my crews pulled our boats up alongside the wooden jetty and disembarked. The village was still asleep and unprepared for our assault. Not surprisingly the first indication of our presence was several dogs that started barking; but by this time, it was too late and my men had spread out, several men to a hut. Sleepy heads poked out of doors and windows promptly to be crushed with axe heads, whether men or women. Doors were kicked in and my men rushed into the huts to deal death and destruction. Soon screams were being heard, dogs were yelping as they were silenced by a thrust of a spear.

Within a very short time the groans of the dying had stopped and were being replaced by the screams of the abused women. I knew this would happen and it gave me some concerns.

My men would now be distracted and not alert to any counter-attack. I had deliberately kept my crew back from the plundering to ensure that the perimeter of the village was monitored. After about half a watch the crews started to debouch from the huts carrying all sorts of goods; obviously food was a priority but many men carried what, in my opinion, were useless items; women's dresses, pot and pans, bedding and worst of all children.

I shouted, "Remember men, there is only so much we can take back in our boats. We cannot take children, only one woman a boat, we need all the food you can find." By the time I had herded all the crew members back to the boats, we had wasted more time than I wanted. Many children were left crying on the river bank, at least my men did not have the heart to kill them, but I thought they would die of starvation anyway. I was annoyed, we had lost one man who had been stabbed whilst raping a woman, he should have been more careful.

"Come on, we need to find more villages. Remember we fire them on the way back." I shouted.

Three smaller villages were attacked by mid-afternoon. The inhabitants were more alert as they had risen and were about their business when we struck. Many of the villagers fled, some of the men were foolish enough to try and resist with pitch forks and wood axes; they died. Again, we destroyed more boats, I was losing count.

At the third village, which would have to be the last, after we had killed most of the inhabitants, we fired the thatched cottages. They went up in a plume of billowing smoke that I knew would be seen for miles. My small fleet of boats then retraced our route and torched the previous two villages we had raided. At the last and largest village, the first we had attacked, some men had arrived, possibly from Middleburg. There was about twenty men, most had spears and some had axes, none were armoured and they had no shields. I quickly formed a line of archers and within a hundred heartbeats ten of the Zealanders had been shot, the rest ran away. The last village took time to fire, there were many cottages and the subsequent column of smoke may have been visible in Bruges?

When we arrived back at our fortified island the crews were in good heart. They had a lot of plunder to add to the communal treasure and a significant amount of fresh food, including three pigs and some geese. The island now had to accommodate six more young women and I knew that eventually there would be trouble as a result.

I decided that I probably had one more day's grace before the islanders responded and decided upon another raid but this time on an area that we had not visited before. The next morning, we raised our heavy leather sails and headed out towards the sea, north-west to round Schouwen, my target being the island of Goeree, north of Schouwen. Technically Goeree was in the County of Holland, not Flanders but the area was in dispute anyway and was definitely inhabited by Zealanders. Our raiding pattern was the same, we spotted villages along the coast and landed to take anything we could, making sure men died. The plunder was sparse but it satisfied the crews. Continual success gives confidence and I wanted my men to be confident for any confrontations to come. After this raid I decided that all the crews needed a respite to recuperate and enjoy the women and looted provisions. I expected a visit from the Zealander's leaders.

I was not to be disappointed, early the next day a boat was spied exiting the creek we had raided two days before. Between Roggen and the main island of Walcheren was another flat, low sandbar. The Zealander's boat headed for the sandbar and several men alighted and walked across to face us waving a white flag, an action I interpreted as wishing to parley.

I took a Frisian karvi and manned it with Danes and they rowed me over to the low island. I took Egil and Gauti from Islay, both of who could not be mistaken for anything other than Norse. I splashed out of the boat onto the sandbar, fully armoured in my mail sleeved coat, viking baggy trousers, reinforced sea boots and my white polar bear fur shoulder cape. I had combed my blond locks until they shone, and tumbled down to my shoulders and trimmed my drooping moustache and freshly shaved my chin. I intended to relay the picture of a true viking. I carried my bearded Dane axe and had my father's sword gift strapped to my side. Fixed to the back of my leather waist belt was my scramaseax. I did not wear my helmet but carried it in the crook of my elbow so that the engraving around the nasal guard was visible.

The men before me were clearly not farmers or fishermen. There were two reasonably well clad huscarls with shields and spears, no mail, and the leaders, two of them were alike as two peas in a pod; brothers, if not twins. They were tall and ruddy men, like me without helmets, so displaying their wheat gold hair plaited down both sides of their heads and entwined with ribbons. They wore studded leather jerkins over thick woven trousers tied at the calf. There boots were heavy and serviceable and eminently suited for the marshy landscape. They both also wore woollen cloaks pinned by round silver brooch pins. Both men carried swords sheathed and attached to their waist belts. All four men presented a picture of greyness, there was no colour between any of them.

"Good day to you, and how may I help you?" I tried to make my accent sound as broad Norse as possible.

"Who are you, what do you want here, why are you camped on our island?" One of the 'twins' asked angrily.

"So many questions, but I am a reasonable man and I will answer you." I smiled. "I am named Hjorvard Bjornbana and these are my men, we are vikings and take what we want, when we want and from whom we want." I smiled again. "We like your island, Roggen, I think. We like your food and we like your women."

"We will not let you take any more, you must leave or we will destroy you." One of the 'twins' shouted.

This time I laughed. "One of my ancestors Rurik, Jarl of the Great Heathen Army took these islands a hundred and fifty years ago and you Zealander peasants could not do anything about it then and you will not be able to do anything about us staying here now. What are you but fishermen and farmers, you have no Flemish or Norman horsed warriors here and we have already destroyed most of your boats? No, we will stay here for the summer and you will pay us gelt not to raid you."

"We will get the counts of Flanders and Holland to come to our aid, they will slaughter you all."

314

"I understand you do not bend the knee to either of these counts, so why should they assist you. If you have nothing to offer me and my men but idle threats I will return to my island and fuck another of your women."

I turned to leave and instinctively felt one of the Zealanders rushing towards me. Without a pause I continued my turn to a full circle and lashed out with the side of my axe connecting with one of the 'twins' on the side of his head. He dropped the sword he was holding and collapsed in a heap unconscious.

"Hold, if you don't all want to die." I shouted, holding my axe above the prone man. The Zealanders all hesitated. "I see you are faithless and do not recognise the sanctity of a truce." I stated in a calmer voice. "Now all of you, get into your boat and row away." The other 'twin' moved forward towards the unconscious man.

"Stay back." I ordered. "This man broke faith and he is coming with me as a hostage. Now go." My axe hovered over the prone Zealander. The other 'twin' and the two huscarls reluctantly backed off and returned to their boat. Gauti grasped the ankle of the unconscious Zealander and dragged him across the sand to our boat. We returned to Roggen.

The captive women were cleaning up the remains of the early morning meal and Eystein was training and exercising some of the men to keep them sharp. Gauti and two of the karvi crew carried the Zealander, who had now started to groan, to my upturned boat home and dumped him on the floor.

Martin came over looking quizzical. "What have you here?"

"Not sure but I will find out soon, Gauti lash his feet together and halter him to a stake." Gauti was swift to comply. The Zealander was coming round, his eyes were open and he was shaking his head gently.

"You will have a splitting headache because of your foolishness." I observed.

He looked towards me his eyes unfocussed. "My, my brother?"

"Oh! He is safe and gone. Obviously not as foolish as you."

"Where am I?"

"You are on my island, Roggen, and here you will stay until I decide to let you go, or kill you." I explained. "Gauti, give him some water."

When I felt he was sufficiently lucid I interrogated him; "What is your name and your brother's name?"

He thought for a moment and decided to answer, "I am called Liudger and my brother is named Renhard, we are the sons of Hrodhard the Lord of Middleburg. My brother is older than I but we are often mistaken for twins, he is heir to my father, I am nothing."

"Did your father send you to parley?"

"No, he would have come himself but he is in the east meeting the other Zealander chiefs. If he had been here, he would have attacked you and killed you all. He is a great warlord."

"Really, if there is a great warlord in Zealand I have yet to hear of him." I replied sarcastically. "So, when will your father return?"

"Soon." Liudger sneered.

"Does your father command the whole of Walcheren or just Middleburg?" I asked, wondering how much this idiot was prepared to tell me before I needed to apply torture.

"He is the greatest chief in Walcheren, all the other village elders follow him."

"And, how many men can he muster to fight off an enemy?"

Liudger reddened, realising that he had said too much. "I will not tell you that."

"Yes, you will. I have men in my crew who can make a blind man see and a dumb man talk and you will scream when they hurt you. Why not just tell me what I want to know. It will be much easier for all of us."

"No, I will not betray my people."

I sighed, "Gauti, go and fetch Gautrek the Berserker I have a task for him."

Gautrek came and dragged Liudger away. I had learnt much from our brief conversation, the Lord of Middleburg, the largest settlement on Walcheren was away east so there was unlikely to be a concerted attack on my fortress for at least one or two days. I felt I could safely raid Walcheren again before any serious confrontation. Although this lord, Hrodhard was likely to have his best huscarls with him the two I saw with his sons were not formidable and my men clearly outmatched them.

I decided I would go and visit the Jansen's, a family I had stayed with when I first made my way to Flanders. They were fishermen and not technically in Zealand so may be of use to me as information gatherers in eastern Zealand and south Holland. I would travel with Egil in *Hilda* and double the voyage by trading in Dordrecht. I anticipated that the whole project would take no more than two or three days at the most. I decided to leave Martin in charge of the camp and the next day's raid to be led by Magnus the Dane from Ribe who had shown remarkable aplomb in his ability to raid. I would have preferred to sail up river in *Ottar* but I did not expect Eystein to return for some days yet.

Egil, of course, would not be separated from *Hilda* and he certainly was not going to let me navigate a knarr up stream through the shoals and sandbanks that littered the river. Obviously, we waited until the flood tide to sail up river; we swept inland with Schouwen and Duiveland on our larboard side and Walcheren on our steer board side, the sun rising weakly in the south-east behind the Duiveland mist. There was an off-shore wind, not strong, so we did not raise the sail relying solely on the tide. We swung north passed Duiveland and another island I had not learned the name of yet to join the main channel of the estuary of the rivers Maas and Waal. We now had the island of Goeree to our larboard and the mainland, I think, to our steer board side. Hoeksche island lay ahead and Egil neatly steered *Hilda* into a channel leading east into the interior through a maze of low treacherous sandbanks, whilst the crew stood ready with the long oars to pole us away from any sandbanks we drifted too near to. I knew we were now in the channel where Tonnekreek lay and Jan Jansen's farm on the mainland, that is the south bank of the river. It was not long before the farm came into view; our knarr caused no concern as shipping must pass up and down the river all the time from Dordrecht and beyond. However, activity markedly increased when Egil brought the knarr as close into the shore as possible and we lowered the small lighter and I rowed it to shore. By the time I had reached the shore Jan Jansen and his sons had walked down to the shoreline. I clambered out of the boat and one of the smaller children grabbed the anchor line. I looked up and smiled, Jan recognised me.

"Hereward the Bearslayer from England, this is an unlooked-for surprise, welcome." Jan boomed his voice friendly.

"Master Jansen, it is good to see you again. I would stay the night with you, if possible, I have six crew but do not be alarmed there are ample provisions on boards for all and gifts for you and yours."

"You are most welcome, and your crew, I will inform my wife and a feast will be provided." I waved to Egil and knew he would arrange for the gifts I had prepared for the Jansens to be brought ashore.

"How is Buttercup?" the small boy who had previously told me the old nags name stood looking up at me enquiringly.

"Well, I left him with a prince of the church in Ghent and he now has the best grain to eat every day and wears a golden bridle. Buttercup is very happy." I explained. The boy gave a toothy grin and ran off. Jan's wife came to the door and welcomed me over the threshold; she did not appear at all fazed that seven unlooked for men were staying the night and might eat her out of house and home. Shortly afterwards my crew came up to the farm carrying the gifts I had selected for Jan and his family.

"Master Jan, seeking you out has given me the opportunity to return your previous hospitality with some of my own." A crew member set down a small casket of hack silver. "Some portable wealth so that your wife can visit the nearest market and buy some things for herself." Another crew member set down a couple of squealing piglets. "These two little squeakers will grow and mate providing your family with much needed pork to supplement your diet of fish." Another crew member dropped a bundle of wood axes and knives that had been looted from our recent raids, but of course Jan did not know their origin. "Some useful tools and finally if you will row us back to the knarr tomorrow you can keep the lighter." Jan stood bewildered.

"This is most generous I don't merit such a bounty." Jan flustered.

"Of course, you do; you could have turned Martin and I away but you were hospitable. Over there." I directed the crew to deposit the haunches of beef, bacon and freshly plucked geese on the wooden trestle table outside of the Jansen's cottage, and don't break the ale flagons." We all feasted royally that evening; Jan sat at the head of the table like a lord and his wife fussed like only a farmer's hausfrau can. After the food we all settled down to drink the ale, and having regained his composure, Jan searched my face quizzically and finally posed the question.

"Lord Hereward, I appreciate this largesse but if I am not amiss you are here for a reason, other than to shower me and mine with untold wealth?"

I smiled, "Master Jan, you are not wrong." I explained what my small army and I had been up to for the past week. He looked grave.

"You are visiting war and devastation on my neighbours. The Zealanders are a wild bunch, proud and surly and I can see why they will not bend the knee to the count of Flanders, those parts, aye, and these parts are remote and seldom visited by the lords down south or the Frisian lords up north, they don't like the mud you see. It is true I pay some taxes to the nearest lord but I can see why the Zealanders will not. What do you want from me?"

"All I want is the benefit of your eyes and eyes. I need to know what is happening at this end of the isles. In truth I need you to spy for me. Knowledge is power, the Zealanders know of your farm and do not suspect you may be aiding me, whereas if I posted one of my karvis in these waters permanently it would be spotted almost immediately. I had hoped one of your sons would row down the creeks at night and warn me if anything was happening, I needed to know about."

I could see the concern for his children in his eyes. "Let me think on this and discuss it with my eldest."

"That is all I can ask. Let us drink as friends should." The rest of our small feast went well, Jan's family was happy and content. My men were relaxed, that is all except the one I sent out to sit by the river bank as our night sentry. It was well known to my men that I was ever wakeful.

Like all good farmers and fisherfolk the Jansen's were up early the next morning, which was fortunate as Egil wished to continue to Dordrecht on the early flood tide. "We must take our leave of you now, Master Jan, what say you to my proposal?"

"My second eldest, Dietrich has already threatened to run away and join some lord's mesnie and is gagging at the opportunity for adventure. I figure if I give him this opportunity it may get the itch out of him, either that or at least he will be with as great a lord as yourself." I smiled; I anticipated that at least one of his sons wanted a taste of adventure.

"Dietrich, come here." A large gangling youth, maybe five years younger than I ambled over, looking sheepish.

"Well Dietrich, I hear you are willing to help me?" I smiled at him and he nervously grinned back.

"Yes, my lord; I will serve faithfully as my father has taught me."

"Then I can ask no more. I am for Dordrecht and I suggest Dietrich accompany me so that I can brief him. Dietrich, speak to your mother and ask her if she wants you to acquire anything from the market."

Jan rowed us to the knarr himself, returning to the river bank in his newly acquired boat.

Egil up anchored and we drifted off upstream towards the side creek leading to Dordrecht. I took the opportunity to explain to Dietrich what I needed from him by way of monitoring the river traffic or large movements of men towards my island fortress. Using the lighter, I left with his father he was to row, sail, or drift downstream and warn me. I concluded that Dietrich was an innocent who had no knowledge of the outside world, he was eager to please and he would probably risk his life unwittingly to impress me, and his parents. He was strong, no doubt about that and willingly took a sweep to guide the boat. The river Dortrecht was situated upon was called the Thure, I would have called it a creek, nevertheless Dortrecht was a bustling town with lots of river traffic and a large market stretching along the river bank. The town was firmly in Holland and I was not at war with the count of Holland and neither was Flanders, to the best of my knowledge. It was vitally important that my little war did not interrupt the trade from Holland or any of the numerous German states in the interior. I explained this to Dietrich hoping he would understand the convoluted nature of my campaign in Zealand.

Egil found a birth for the *Hilda* and it was only moments before the port reeve was at the gangplank to demand the

320

berthing dues. Without a cargo he was flummoxed to know what to charge and said he would return and assess our export cargo. I instructed Egil to negotiate a cargo that would be useful on the island, whilst I wandered around taking stock of the place. I strolled away from the jetty towards what I could clearly identify as a stone tower, probably attached to a church. I spied a large bronze bell suspended in an arched opening at the top of the tower. A nice touch. The streets were muddy, which was not surprising given the low-lying location of the town and at various points my boots sunk up to my ankles. I realised that each building, whether cottage or shop had laid down planking outside their doors and that with a bit of judicial hopping and striding out I could make my way along the street on these boards, like the locals were doing.

I reached the church square and entered the smartest inn I could see, sat down at a trestle table, and beckoned over the landlord.

"Good day to you, landlord; may I have a cup of your best ale and whatever is being served as breakfast today." I handed over some Flemish coins that would more than cover the cost and observed the broad smile it elicited on his rotund face. Very soon the landlord placed a large flagon of ale on the table with a platter of fresh crusty bread, hard cheese, and sliced pork, all together with a large reddish apple.

"And how are things in Dortrecht, landlord, is trade good? I hail from England with a cargo of wool and look to make a tidy profit." I smiled and offered him a drink of his own ale; it must have been reasonably good or he would not have agreed to share it with me.

"Ah! Captain, trade is good with the interior at the moment there are no petty wars ongoing, both the counts of Holland and Flanders are behaving themselves. Although I have recently heard of some viking activity in Zealand, did you see anything when you entered the mouth of the Scheldt?"

I answered in the negative, "No, narry a thing."

"Oh, good, maybe the rumours are not true then, no other trading ships seem to have been affected. As for trade, the German states make fine swords and pikes, the Dutch towns make beautiful clay ware, see these plates." He indicated some colourful platters lining the shelves. "There is wood aplenty, but I doubt England is short of timber."

"And who does the port taxes go to?" I asked innocently.

"The port reeve pays some to the count at the Haag but we also have a local lord who pockets most of the profits."

"Does he defend the town?" I asked.

"He says he does, but from whom, I have never ascertained." The landlord sounded disgruntled.

I laughed, "Tis the same the whole world over my friend and now I must see how my business partner is faring." I took my leave and returned to the docks.

Egil was seeing to the loading of livestock, pigs, geese and even some rabbits in cages. He also had purchased some sacks of grain and root vegetables and finally a cow for milk and cheese.

"Cast off as soon as we can, I'll be damned if we are paying a port tax for this lot." I instructed Egil tersely.

As soon as the cow was manoeuvred on board, my lads pulled up the gang plank and cast off. I saw the port reeve running down to the quayside with a couple of guards trailing along behind.

"Stop, stop, you have to pay your dues." The reeve shouted in a shrill voice. We had only moved a few paces from the wharf but he was helpless to do anything about us leaving. I calmly strung my powerful Dane bow and nocked an arrow. Drawing the iron tip to the stave I pointed the missile straight at the reeve who blanched in terror. At the last moment I raise the bow and sited on the church tower and released. The arrow arched over the town, almost disappearing from sight before the church bell emitted a dull clang as the arrow point glanced off its round surface.

"Mark my visit Reeve, when next I call, your miserable town will go up in flames." An idle boast as I had no intention of returning, but fate is inexorable.

The tide soon turned, which assisted our return down river. I anticipated that we would make Roggen in time for the evening meal. The return journey was uneventful and not surprisingly there were no fishing boats on the water. My few days of raiding had put an end to that source of food for the Zealanders, whose fishing activities would have to be limited to rod and line fishing in the creeks and smaller areas of water inland. Food would become scarcer, which was part of my plan.

Egil anchored *Hilda* off the beach where all the smaller craft were pulled up on the sand and Martin sent several of the smaller boats to carry us and our cargo off. The cow was made to swim rather ungainly to the beach. It struggled and I had to admit I had no knowledge of bovine swimming ability; nevertheless, it made it to the shore and was soon tethered and dragged into the fortified area.

I introduced Dietrich to my captains. "This is Dietrich Jansen who will be our eyes and ears upriver, so if any of you see him rowing our way in a boat do not kill him, pick him up and bring him in. Dietrich, you remember Martin." I indicated my friend and Dietrich nodded. "Good, when I am not present you must always seek Martin out and report to him. Now go and find something to eat."

"How are things, Martin? I see there is still no sign of Eystein and *Ottar.*"

"No, no sign of Eystein yet. I have sent for Magnus, who I believe is taking his turn with one of the slave women, so that he can report on his raid, which I might add was very successful." Martin smiled. "Also, while you were away, we have noticed a group of Walcheren Zealanders have been posted across the water to watch us. They have been there for a day and half now."

"Interesting, the hand of chief Hrodhard taking control." I mused.

"Yes, and since this morning a similar number of Zealanders are spying on us from Schouwen." Martin added.

Magnus, the Dane from Ribe walked up and saluted me. "Good day, lord. You summoned me?"

"No Martin requested your company I hope we didn't disturb your business with the slave?"

"In truth, I would have liked it to have lasted longer, but as I don't get the opportunity every day I don't last as long as I would like." He smiled, I laughed.

"Well, that is unfortunate, I am sure we can acquire some more women but not too many or we will turn into a whore house rather than a viking encampment."

"Is there a difference?" Magnus asked with a look of innocence on his face. I burst out laughing again. Even Martin laughed at that sharp quip.

"To business, Martin tells me your raid was successful, tell me more."

"After you left, I decide that I would raid an area we had not covered before, so I took the boats passed Goeree to the next island along called Overflakkee. We rowed north around the island down the Haringvliet; incidentally there was lots of merchant shipping in this channel so I assumed this must be the favoured route to the open sea from the interior. Naturally we left the trading ships alone. We found several large villages less than two miles away from each other with a creek lying in between. I directed the boats into the creek and we attacked what appeared to be the smallest of the villages, the one furthest west. I left the boats well-guarded but we still outnumbered the villagers. We surrounded the village and went in on an arrow signal. The villagers were having some kind of a meeting and we easily surrounded them. First, we killed all the men and boys and rounded up the women and girls. There were thirty or so, all told. We killed the elderly women leaving about twenty women and girls. I left two men in the deserted village and we returned the prisoners to the boats. By mid-day we had approached a larger village. This was a more organised village they even had a wooden look-out tower with a sentry in it. We surrounded the village again and the signal to attack was when I shot the sentry. The village was twice the size of the first one, maybe twenty or thirty cottages and a small church. The villagers were not gathered so we had to take the men in scattered bands. Some managed to arm themselves but we took these men down with spears and arrows. Gautrek the berserk was with me and he went wild and started killing anything that moved. We dare not go near him and so he killed a lot of women and children wastefully. He even started on the animals, pigs, a goat, and an old horse. Eventually he curled up on the ground and fell asleep and that allowed us to sort out the mess. We took a further ten young women captive and brought all the dead livestock. We then fired the village and the church; when the men I had left in the first village saw this they fired that village and met us back at the boats. We also found another four useful fishing boats that could be used as raiding craft and destroyed another eight boats in the creek. I lost one man who was stabbed in the back by a woman and Gautrek cut the hand off another of my crewmen when he rather foolishly tried to calm Gautrek down."

I interrupted, "Where is the berserker now?"

"He is asleep somewhere. We bundled him back in the boat, many of my men wanted to leave him." Magnus explained.

"I will deal with him." I decided. "We seem to have a lot of women on the island, too many." I mused.

"May I make a suggestion." Magnus interrupted. "You know I hale from Ribe, well Ribe is one of the main Danish ports to sell on slaves. Rather than sailing *Hilda* to Bruges for supplies next time we could take twenty or more of the women and girls to Ribe and sell them for a tidy profit."

I raised my eyebrows, we had become slavers now just like the Dubliners, but I really had no choice, they could not stay on the island and I did not want *Hilda* to be anchored here when the Zealanders decided to attack. "I agree, Egil is to take *Hilda* to Ribe tomorrow, Magnus, you accompany him. Oh! And look out for Eystein he may be trying to acquire a snekkja in Ribe. Magnus, you have done well and will receive a double share of the profits from the sale of the slaves."

I took a stroll around the camp with Martin and Dietrich. The stake palisade was in good order and each crew member had placed his sea chest against the inside of the stakes so that he could stand on it like a parapet to a real fortified wall. This spread the men out naturally around the perimeter of the stockade. The live animals were kept in a compound at the north end of the island, the goats, pigs, and cows roped off from each other. The geese tended to roam free. The supplies such as grain, root vegetable and cheese were kept in the middle and the slaves were kept in a compound at the south end of the island. There was a continuous toing and froing from the slave compound as my followers came to claim a woman to seed. The rutting was usually done under canvas or the up-turned boats for privacy but some men were quite happy to couple with the women out in the open for all to see. There was generally an air of distress about the women's compound. I noticed that all the women were relatively clean, presentable even. Martin noticed.

"I ensure all the slaves are washed every day and I have given strict instructions for none of them to be mutilated in any way."

Finally, I saw that Radbod was still staked to a post rammed into the earth where he could see the degradation of his womenfolk, beside him he had been recently joined by Liutger who looked the worse for wear. He was minus an ear and the tip of his nose and I noticed that all his fingers on his right hand had been severed at the middle knuckle.

"Well, well, Liutger if I am not mistaken. Gautrek the Berserker did not kill you then. I assume he had elicited all worthwhile information from you?"

"Leave him alone, you bloody butcher, he is only a boy and you have ruined his life forever." Radbod spat at me. I walked away laughing.

Dietrich was all agog at what the men were doing to the captive women.

"Tell me Dietrich, have you ever had a woman?" I queried.

He coloured up in embarrassment. "No, my lord. I saw my mother naked once, is all."

Thinking immediately of the beautiful Lady Godgifu, my stepmother, I responded, "I wish I had, not your mother Dietrich, I think of another."

"Martin, you had better place Dietrich on the women's roster before he goes home."

That evening after our meal, I called a meeting of my boat captains and invited as many who wanted to sit around and listen. "Men, we have achieved our first goal, and that was to establish a safe camp in the Zealand islands. From the first days we have ravaged the lands destroying boats and attacking some of the villages to bring fear and apprehension. We have accumulated some plunder and over time this will increase, either by raiding or receiving gelt as in the old days. I notice since my return there has been a marked increase of women in the camp." The men all laughed. "This is acceptable within limits, too many and the camp will become less secure and so I propose that most of them will be sold in Ribe. The profits will be shared amongst you as it was done in the olden days, equal shares." The men cheered. "I am sure other women will find their way into our camp over the coming months." I added.

"Now, hear my plans. I expect there will be some attempt by the Zealanders to drive us away. We will resist this. I intend to stay on Roggen for the rest of the summer, maybe even the winter. We will raid intermittently, maybe once or twice a month to keep the islanders guessing and afraid. Because of the infrequency of our raids, they will find it difficult to anticipate our next move. Remember, my real objective is to drive the Zealanders back into the arms of the count of Flanders, not wipe them out; but best of all not only do we get to keep our plunder but the count of Flanders is paying us to do this." The men cheered again.

The men settled in for the night but I noticed Dietrich was sent off to the women's compound. I found that amusing and wondered if I had lost some humanity since Una left me, I had no wish to take a woman by force but equally their abuse by other men left me unmoved.

Egil set off yet again the next morning after herding thirty women and young girls tied by a long rope tether on to the knarr. I looked around for Dietrich, expecting him to be ready to row back to his family farm but I could not find him. Martin eventually dragged him in to my presence; he was still tying up his breeches. "I found him at the compound, he has used three women this morning and two last night."

"In that case it is well that you leave this morning or the rest of the men will take your balls, through sheer jealousy." I grimaced.

Martin directed Dietrich to the smallest boat and instructed him to row. Dietrich waved goodbye and manfully set off east, rowing with the flood tide. For the rest of the day, I had the men drag our raiding boats into the stockade, safe from destruction.

Two more days elapsed, days of weapons training and enforced inactivity before signs of movement. Early on the third day a flotilla of small boats vomited from the mouth of the creek separating Walcheren from the smaller island of Kamperland. They only had a two or two and half miles to row to reach Roggen and sensibly they skirted the intervening sandbanks on the steer board side; as they approached, I counted upwards of thirty fishing craft all crammed with men. I calculated that there must be upwards of three hundred Zealanders. With *Ottar's* and *Hilda's* crews absent I had ninety men to defend the stockade, they were all well-armed, experienced fighters and I was sure they would repel a bunch of fisher folk without any problem but I was interested to see how many trained warriors the chieftain who led them could bring against me. The boats were brought around in a line, up against the narrow sandy beach. My men had a clear line of fire with no obstructions. All the Dubliners and Hebrideans had long Dane bows, as did the Danes themselves. The Zealanders would be walking into an arrow storm the moment they tried to disembark.

However, before the boats drove into the sand, one lone boat rowed forward and three men climbed out. One held out a hazel branch as a sign of their wish to talk.

"Approach, fear not, we honour discussions under truce." I shouted.

The three men trudged forward, I recognised one of the 'twins', Renhard, I remembered his name. The older man was clearly his father, a grizzled man with a salt and pepper beard and shaggy eyebrows under a leather arming cap. He was stocky and broad and wore a leather studded jacket and woollen trews. He had a sword hanging from his belt and a leather faced shield slung cross his back. This must be Hrodhard, chief of Middleburg and possibly all of Walcheren. The third man was a huscarl, by all accounts. He wore a long leather coat reaching down to mid-calf. This coat looked to have metal plates sewn inside. His helmet was of sectioned bronze plates with iron rimmed banding with an attached nasal guard. He had an axe slung on his back. Could be formidable I mused.

"Good morning, and how can we help you?" I boomed.

"I am Hrodhard Renhardson, Chief of Middleburg and leader of the Walcheren settlements. I want you gone and I want my son and nephew released. I am prepared to pay a ransom for them."

"As I told your son there," I pointed towards Renhard, "I am Hjorvard Bjornbana leader of the Roggen vikings and we are very comfortable here. Your son is very comfortable here too and has no wish to leave just yet. As to your nephew, I am not sure we have him, unless he answers to the name Radbod."

"He does, that is my nephew and he has not wronged you."

"I tell you what, as an act of conciliation I will release one of them for ten pounds of silver, the other I will hold as surety for your good behaviour."

Angrily Hrodhard shouted back. "You play with me; I have the means to kill you all." He swept his arm out to indicate his fleet.

"Not before your son and nephew die." I smiled tauntingly at him.

After all the death and destruction, we had visited on the islanders, I doubted he had the strength and authority to call off the impending attack anyway but enraging an enemy was always a preferable tactic before a battle.

"You have chosen your path you will not live to regret it." Hrodhard thundered as he swung around and marched back to the waterline.

"With his back towards us he stretched out his arms like a cross and shouted loudly, "Disembark Zealanders."

I was not prepared to oblige them and no sooner had the huscarl cast down his hazel rod than I shouted, "Loose." Thirty or more arrow shafts sped across the narrow beach towards the boats. The huscarl was struck twice but his reinforced coat saved him. Three arrows impacted into Hrodhard's wood and leather reinforced shield that protected his back, they all penetrated through to his leather jacket and I suspected that they pierced his back, wounds but none fatal. However, my arrow took his son Renhard in the neck, and was fatal. The boy swayed and toppled forward into the gentle surf.

Many of the other arrows found a mark. The Zealanders howled in fury and pushed and scrambled to disembark from their boats but they were not clear of them before my archers had sent two flights of arrows into their array. Few of the Zealanders had shields and I could see that there was perhaps only a dozen trained warriors crowding around Hrodhard. The arrow storm counted for more than thirty of our assailants dying or wounded before they lined up for a charge. Hrodhard was temporarily distracted kneeling beside his dying elder son; this gave my archers the opportunity of releasing another volley of arrows that took down a dozen more of our opponents.

I shouted, "Come on, what are you waiting for you snivelling peasants." Without waiting for an instruction from their leader the Zealanders surged forward, it was less than thirty paces to the stockade wall and they ran at it in a line fifty men wide, six men deep; no planning. The west side of our stockade was virtually unmanned, most of my men stood on their sea chests looking over the stockade covering their heads and shoulders with their shields. The Zealanders ran through the arrow storm only to be assailed by a flight of spears and throwing axes at ten paces. Within moments a third of their men had fallen and of course when they reached the wall, they did not know what to do. My men leant over the parapet and stabbed down with their spears inflicting terrible wounds. Some of the Zealanders tried to pull down the wooden palings, which held in the ground better than I had hoped. Others climbed upon their colleague's backs reaching for the top of the stakes, only to have their hands chopped off, or their heads smashed in.

The assault on the stockade was like the crest of a wave dashing onto a cliff, it smashed at the wooden palings and ebbed back broken. There was not to be a second wave. The Zealanders ran back to their boats despite the exhortations of the professional huscarls. Although we still had many arrows my men let them run without a sting in the tail. The Zealanders had lost upwards of a hundred men in the assault and did not have the manpower to row all their boats away; five valuable boats were left on the beach enhancing our little fleet. The repelled enemy rowed off the beach with difficulty and it was fortunate for them that they had not far to row to reach the haven of their islands.

The beach fronting our stockade was littered with the dead and dying their screams, groans, and pleas for God to help them were pitiful. I sent a party out of the stockade gate to end their suffering. Gautrek suggested that we take their heads and impale them on our stockade palings. Initially I rejected this idea as too gruesome and I certainly did not want the smell of their rotting heads creating a miasma around the camp. However, on second thoughts I realised the terror it would instil in the Zealanders so I instructed Gautrek and several of the more bloodthirsty crewmen to raise spare stakes at the shoreline away from the stockade and there impale as many heads as they could without hindering the ingress and egress of our boats. Later I found he had clustered the heads on stakes at either end of the beach in two forests of pure horror. Dead men's faces in a rictus of pain, mouths open in silent screams, eye sockets soon to be empty as the seagulls soared and swooped in anticipation of the forthcoming feast.

My small army celebrated that evening; only three men had been killed more by ill-fortune than our assailants' skill. Several men had been injured but none seriously, it had been almost a bloodless victory.

After the feast and loud acclamations by the skalds who I was informed were vying to create another praise song about the Roggen vikings, the drunken men lined up at the women's compound and the slaves were roughly used. It is a hard world for the weak and helpless I mused.

I discussed the situation with my skippers and Martin. I was sure that we would not be attacked again for many days but when an attack did come it would be better organised than the first. I did not want to provoke another attack immediately so I decided there would be no more raids for a month to let matters settle down and that when we resumed raiding it would not be on Walcheren so that Hrodhard of Middleburg would not feel directly threatened.

I decided that when either Egil or Eystein returned it would be a good time for me to visit Lille, or wherever the Count of Flanders court was at the time to update my paymaster on our progress. The camp settled down to days of training to stay combat sharp; there was plenty of food and ale but water was always an issue on an island without any natural fresh water. Whilst Egil and Eystein were away I had to arrange a routine water supply from Blankenberge, the nearest point in Flanders, which was a good thirty-mile sail in the largest karvi we had. The route was around the headland of Walcheren, which was risky for a small boat that would be vulnerable to attack, but without the larger boats I had no choice.

The sentinels on the headland of Walcheren and Schouwen had resumed their surveillance of us and I had to assume that they would notice the regular movements of the water supply craft.

However, after two weeks of relative inactivity the *Hilda* and *Ottar* were sighted turning the headland of Schouwen and I was pleased to see a third boat following in their wake, another snekkja. The three boats rounded Roggen and dropped anchor along the beach and soon three smaller boats were lowered and I could see Egil, Eystein and Magnus being rowed to the shore by their crewmen. I was eager for news and we all assembled in front of my boat hut with ale and bread and cheese.

"Ah! Dry food." Exclaimed Egil, "Weather was a bit rough along the Frisian coast."

"I see you have another snekkja with you." I started enthusiastically.

Eystein took up the tale. "My father found me in Ribe, I had negotiated for the snekkja out there, it is an eighteen-oar longship, as you can see. Not quite as big as *Ottar* but more able to access the shallow waters around the islands here."

Eighteen oars, I mused, thirty-six rowers, a steersman and skipper and half a dozen additional warriors giving a complement of forty-four, not counting ship's boys of which we had none, at the moment.

"That is excellent, how does she sail?" I asked.

"She is nimbler that *Ottar* but not as powerful through the water with a stern wind. She does not flex as much as *Ottar* either and would not sail as well in rough seas. Nevertheless, she is only ten years old, I am told, and seems very seaworthy." Eystein explained and I noticed Egil nodding in affirmation of Eystein's analysis.

"Does she have a name?" I asked.

"Well, the previous owner called the boat *Little Runa*, God knows why." Eystein responded.

"*Little Runa*, a strange name, sounds a bit pagan but I am reluctant to change the name of a ship, don't want to offend it's spirits." I grinned realising I was sounding superstitious and 'pagan'.

"I agree." Egil put in, "changing a ships name is always bad luck, unless there is a good reason."

"I need to collect the crew from Bruges by the Sea, they have been hanging around too long and I suspect we have lost some by now." Eystein interjected. I could see the eagerness in his eyes and knew that the girl Marieke was uppermost, rather than the ship's crew.

"I agree with you Eystein, when your father and the crew of *Hilda* are rested, I want Egil to take the knarr to Bruges by the Sea to fetch water so that we do not have to rely on the small karvi going back and forth to Blankenberge; you will take *Little Runa* and pick up the crew. Magnus and I will travel with you as I wish to see the count, Robert his younger son and the castellan of Bruges. I may need *Little Runa* to sail down the Flemish coast to drop me off and wait for me." Eystein grinned at my pronouncement, clearly the possibility of seeing the object of his desire was within his reach.

Two days later, I left Martin, Beornwulf and Eystein Whaleleg in charge of the stockade and sailed on the *Little Runa* south to Bruges by the Sea. The weather was good and the winds were kind and we made land by mid-afternoon. It seemed to me that Bruges by the Sea was thriving, and growing. I noticed that there was a small compliment of the castellan's men housed next to the inn and I suspected a port reeve was soon to be appointed. I would make a point of suggesting to the castellan that my ships should be exempt.

By the end of the day Egil had managed to round up most of the men he had initially signed up to join my small army, twenty-eight men in all and after asking around he supplemented those men with a further five young Flemings looking for adventure. Thirty-three rowers would be enough to sail the *Little Runa* most anywhere and with the skeleton crew Eystein had brought from Roggen he made a full complement. I left Egil sorting out the fresh water and Magnus training the new crew to row *Little Runa* up and down the coast. Eystein and I borrowed two old nags and rode to Bruges with the intention of arriving for an evening meal, hopefully at the castellan's expense.

We were allowed to enter the castellan's hall and was met by my lover Dedda. She smiled at me lavisciously and I knew my previous dalliance was renewable. She wore her usual alluring gown, low cut, leaving little to the imagination, her hair loose and tumbling around her shoulders, her eyes sparkling blue, challenging. Beside her stood little Marieke, as fair as Dedda was dark. This was the first time I had properly seen her and I had to admit she was a beauty, a bit young, but she would blossom. Her hair had been meticulously washed and combed, platted in two thick ropes of golden sunshine, tied with blue ribbons to set off her blue gown. Obviously one of Dedda's old gowns as it was far too revealing for a girl so young. Nevertheless, she presented as pretty a picture as one could hope for and I could see why young Eystein was besotted. Marieke smiled demurely at Eystein but gave a startled and frightened glance at me when she realised who I was.

"Lady Dedda, how wonderful to see you again." I started. Dedda interrupted.

"My dear, Hereward, you are most welcome, but I am sad to inform you that my husband is not here at the moment and will not be returning for several days. He has travelled to Ghent where the count is currently in residence to discuss business." The fire in her eyes told me that the last place she wanted her husband was here in Bruges.

"My lady, that is excellent news for I am off to see the count and his current location suits me very well. I was hoping I could stay the night, or possibly two, here before I ride on?"

"Why of course, I will arrange for your sleeping quarters. Please take a seat and Marieke here will send for food and drink."

I introduced Eystein, but of course he had delivered Marieke to Dedda so they knew each other already, we all sat whilst Dedda devoured me with her eyes. I could not imagine why she found me so attractive, everyone else found my parti-coloured eyes off putting, apparently giving my face an unbalanced look. I knew my body was reasonably pleasing, I was well muscled and only had a moderate number of scars, to date. Perhaps I was just a convenience and an excitement measured against her elderly and frankly boring husband. I probably had more stamina than the castellan, as well? We made desultory conversation whilst we awaited Marieke but eventually, she arrived with a couple of servants carrying trays of cold meats, cheese, and bread. We ate and talked, mostly about local issues. Since the small war with Guines the county had been mostly settled and quiet. Dedda smiled when she mentioned that there was a rumour than vikings were raiding in the mouth of the Scheldt. Marieke blanched at this aside, Eystein placed his large hand on Marieke's tiny hand by way of comfort, Marieke hardly noticed. When the repast was over, it was clearly time to retire; early!

"Marieke please show Eystein to the bedroom above the stables, Lord Hereward will be staying in the guest room at the foot of the watch tower. Before I retire, as my husband is away, I must check the guards and door ward first, as is my duty." Dedda smiled at me.

"Permit me to accompany you, my lady. I have an abiding interest in fortifications." I responded.

"Surely you are not considering storming the walls of Bruges castle, Lord Hereward." Dedda purred.

"I may wish to penetrate your fortifications someday." I smiled in return.

"Lah! How terrifying, an assault on Bruges' virtue."

"Battering down walls is a speciality of mine." I undressed her with my eyes. My hand stroked her buttocks as she ascended the stairs to the parapet. The round of the sentries was achieved in double quick time and we were virtually ripping each other's clothes off by the time we had reached the chamber I had been allotted, adjacent to her own. Although I needed to rest before I continued on my journey the night was long and energetic.

We made love, no we had sex with abandon; it occurred to me that I might impregnate her but as long as any child did not have parti-coloured eyes and blonde hair the castellan would probably be happy to have an heir. Alternatively, there was something of the witch about Dedda and if anyone could prevent an unwanted pregnancy, she would be the one. After an exhausting night we lay together between sweat soaked furs as the dawn light filtered through the window shutters. Dedda lay languid, curled across my side with a possessive leg laying across my groin. She was smiling that witch smile, all knowing.

"What? What is it that amuses you.?" I asked.

"That boy, Eystein; he is besotted with the Zealand girl, Marieke."

"So?"

"She does not even know he exists. She is terrified for her father, what was is name. Oh, Radbod, that's it. As far as she is concerned, he is just another bloodthirsty viking, like you."

335

"Like me. He is not at all like me." I harrumphed.

"No, he is not, but she cannot see that. He will not have her unless he takes her the viking way." Her tongue slid across her tiny white teeth in anticipation.

I reached across and cupped her vulva. "Like this?" The conversation ended for a while.

Later, as we were dressing, I returned to the subject of Marieke. "I want to oblige Eystein, he is a companion of mine and he wants her. I want you to suggest to her that her father will be saved if she submits to him."

"And will he, be saved?" she prompted.

"He and Marieke are the only Zealanders who know that the Roggen vikings are working for the Count of Flanders. The count can hardly ride to their rescue if they find out he is the hand behind the sword. No Radbod will not live and I am not sure the Marieke can either but I want him to slake his manhood on her before she is killed."

"I like that, for a young girl submitting her maidenhead for her father's life is poetic, and evil." Dedda smiled wickedly.

"Good, I'll leave him here; work your wiles." I left Bruges at mid-day and rode on to Ghent. Eystein was all smiles when I told him to stay in Bruges and did not even query why I would order such a thing. I informed him I would be back within four or five days and to send a message back to Magnus, to that effect.

I timed my arrival in Ghent for the early evening and before the evening meal. I was closeted with Gilbert of Ghent first as castellan of the town for the count. Baldwin of Hainhault as usual was affable but to the point. He was concerned for his wool trade with England, specifically Norfolk and Lincolnshire and was keen to identify his shipping that sailed in and out of the Scheldt. I assured him I had taken steps to protect the interior trading ships and was only raiding the Zealander islands. I explained that if he needed to contact me getting a message through via Bruges by the Sea or Tonnekreek with the help of the Jensons would achieve this. Next Gilbert of Ghent took me to the chamber of Robert, Count Baldwin's son and my friend.

"Hereward! My viking, I have heard something of your doings. You have conquered?" He enthused.

"Not conquered, my lord, but I have softened them up a bit for you." I grinned gripping his hand.

I explained what I had been up to, the raids, the island fortress, and the brief battle on Roggen.

"I wish I could join you, real viking raids, just like Hardrada of Norway." Robert opined.

"You will get your chance of glory, my lord." I assured him. Strife was endemic and if he lived Robert would get his fill of wars.

"I will take you to see my father, he needs to know that the Zealanders may approach him sometime this year for help." Robert nodded to Gilbert of Ghent who escorted us to the count's chambers.

Count Baldwin sat in a carved chair next to a roaring fire, it was not particularly cold outside but the castle certainly was chillier than outside and the count was elderly. He was wrapped in a fur mantle.

"Ah! Hereward Leofricson, what of our campaign in Zealand?"

I recounted the events of the expedition, yet again, but this time I explained in detail what I intended as the outcome of the year's events. "My lord Count, it is hoped that by the autumn and with no signs of the Roggen vikings leaving the Scheldt the Zealanders will request assistance from you to rid them of the heathen scourge. Of course, the price for your assistance will be a return to fealty and the payment of gelt. The Flemish host will then march on Zealand and the show of such overwhelming force will persuade the vikings to set sail and leave."

The Count laughed, "You're a rogue, Leofricson, and no mistake, remind me not to lock horns with you."

"There is a possibility of my plan failing, my lord." I said, pouring water on the count's enthusiasm.

"How so?"

"Well, the Zealanders have vague allegiances; it is my understanding that some of the islanders, obviously the northern ones, see themselves within the sphere of the count of Holland rather than owing fealty to Flanders. So, in their desperation they may seek succour from him rather than you."

"Ah! I see, Floris, first of his name, Count of Holland, he is old like me but unlike me he has no adult, male heir and would have to find a military leader to lead his army and I know just the man, Dirk Hammerhand, his bastard nephew, a real troublemaker. Have you a plan?"

"The truth is my lord that if both the hosts of Flanders and Holland marched into Zealand, without ships neither host could dislodge me from Roggen. If they choose Holland over Flanders then my men and I will winter over on Roggen inflicting the occasional raid, The Zealanders would then see that their reliance on the count of Holland is misplaced and then they will eventually turn to you for assistance."

"You sound confident and one year or two makes little difference to me; how are your funds?"

"Plenty, my lord count, but Zealand, or Scheldtmerland, as you call it will be the poorer for accommodating the Roggen vikings."

"No matter, the whole will become the lordship of my younger son Robert who will be the noble Flemish prince who expels the evil vikings from their territory." We all laughed.

It was important that I was not seen abroad in Ghent with the Flemish leaders and so I informed them I would return to Bruges the next day and be back on Roggen shortly. I asked the castellan of Bruges if I could convey any messages to his lady wife, Dedda and he informed me that he would return within days. I left early the next day. I had the opportunity to have a further dalliance with Dedda, that afternoon, but as I explained the last development, we needed was for her husband to burst in on us that evening and she reluctantly agreed. I summoned Eystein, who not surprisingly was with Marieke, he did not seem too disappointed or down, which suggested to me that he had made some progress in wooing the girl of his dreams.

Magnus had the new snekkja beached ready for our departure when we reached Bruges by the Sea. I informed him that we would sail first thing in the morning weather permitting; it had been a fine summer so far with benign winds. I took the opportunity to meet the new crew in the inn that evening to take their measure. They were the usual bunch of innocent youths and older miscreants who were one step ahead of the town reeve.

None showed any remarkable martial skills and they would have to be taken in hand by my more experienced warriors before they would be reliable in a shield wall. Most of the new crew slept where they sat in the inn, I preferred to bed down on the new snekkja, using my old polar bear skin to keep the chill off, Magnus was also on board and I liked the idea that he already had an attachment to the *Little Runa*.

"How does she handle?" I nodded to Magnus.

"She is a good boat, nimble and answers to the helm well. The crew are shaping up too, a week working the oars and sail and they will pass muster." Magnus smiled and then rather hesitantly, "Who are you considering appointing as her master?"

I looked suitably solemn. "Why I am not considering anybody I have already chosen the boats skipper, you."

Magnus' grin almost split his face in half. "Lord Hereward, you have no idea how long I have wanted to be the master of a sea going ship, snekkja or knarr, no matter."

"You are a reliable man Magnus and you deserve this opportunity. It was your idea to sell the women in Ribe as the best place to buy a ship so your contribution was important. I hope you will consider sailing my ships for many years to come. Now let us sleep."

At first light the new crew manhandled the *Little Runa* into the surf and we all climbed aboard. Magnus turned her north into the wind and the crew bent to the oars. It was only half a day's row to the mouth of the Scheldt, which was a good examination of the new crew's ability to work as a team. They did well and there was friendly banter, as well, which suggested they were bonding together as a unit. Whilst sliding along the coast of Flanders I dwelt on the lack of foresight that hampered the Flemish and indeed the Normans, descendants of the Norse invaders of Neustria two hundred years before, in not maintaining a fleet; that a small island archipelago at the mouth of the Scheldt, not many miles from the centre of the County of Flanders could defy the count and his cavalry and infantry because of a few miles of water separating them demonstrated that vulnerability. Just such a situation had hampered the Angle and Saxon kingdoms of England when the great heathen army had invaded some two hundred years ago, that is until the Wessex king, Alfred had built a fleet and successfully reclaimed the English Channel.

Our arrival back at Roggen caused much interest in our new acquisition and I think some jealousy towards the new crew, as many of my existing band would have preferred to be assigned to a snekkja, rather than one of the smaller karvis. Gautrek was mightily pleased with the name of the ship and he roundly confirmed that it was named for Alruna, one of the Valkyries, that chose the slaughtered warriors from battlefields to abide in Odin's hall until the day of Ragnarok. After this many of the Christian warriors made the sign of the evil-eye and one of them, Christofer wanted me to change its name, which I would not do. There was almost a fight when Christofer caught Gautrek smearing chicken blood on *Little Runa's* stern post by way of some pagan sacrifice; as most of my men were nominally Christian, I could see that Gautrek was becoming a liability.

I noticed that Eystein had gone over to Radbod shortly after our return and I presume he was giving him an account of Marieke's wellbeing. I made a note that this development needed watching although I had no reason to doubt Eystein's loyalty, women make men do strange things. I held a council of the boat masters that evening to discuss our next moves. I was informed by Martin that while I was away the watchers on the shoreline had remained there throughout and that small fishing boats had taken station east of the island, some half a mile off mid-river. I decided that another raid was required to demonstrate how vulnerable the islanders were. The raid would be for supplies, slaves, and devastation, we would burn any villages of farmsteads we came across. After a lengthy discussion we decided our objective would be the island of Tholen, an island we had not raided yet. The fishing boat watching us from the river would lie right in our path and if we did not want it to raise the alarm then it had to be eliminated, which suggested a night attack on the boat and an early dawn raid on the island. The raid was set for three days' time.

My little armada set out two hours before dawn with muffled oars. I had decided to give *Little Runa* a run and station her in the river channel while the raids were underway. I took six karvis and left a sizable force back at the stockade as I did not want to lose my base through negligence.

Little Runa swept forward outpacing the karvis with the intention of bearing down on the fishing boat before any warning could be raised. Approaching from the west we were still in the shadow of night whilst the fishing boat was slightly illuminated by the dawn light creeping over the eastern horizon. We saw the boat stationary in the water and it looked as though the crew were hunkered down, asleep. *Little Runa* swept up alongside and the bodies in the boat were riddled with arrows. For good measure two of my stronger men hurled large ballast stones into the well of the boat and I heard at least one of the boat's ribs crack; the boat would settle in the water and eventually sink.

Magnus gave orders to rest on the oars and we slowed down to wait for the karvis to come up. One of the karvis manoeuvred alongside the fishing boat and for good measure the Zealanders were speared. We regrouped our formation and continued our fifteen-mile row to Tholen, which took us to mid-morning, as the early morning off-shore wind prevented the use of sails. The headland of the island loomed ahead and a small village could be seen behind the sand dunes. Smoke trailed lazily into the sky; it was going to be a beautiful day.

Undoubtably we would have been spotted by now by any watchers on Walcheren, but unless they had a smoke signalling system there would be no way of knowing that we were swooping down on Tholen. I hoped this raid would be a repeat of the previous raids. I indicated that we should steer north of the headland out of sight of any watchers on Walcheran. We passed the low-lying headland and swung in to the flat muddy bank. Magnus spotted a narrow creek, too narrow for *Little Runa* to negotiate. I called to Wighard on the nearest karvi to come alongside and I jumped down. It was cramped on the karvi, with ten men, the helmsman and I but I did not wish the raid to go ahead without my presence; especially as there were a majority of Frisians in the raiding party and the unpredictable Gautrek. The karvis entered the narrow creek in single file; I led the boats in, my force numbered about sixty men, which should be more than enough for the task in hand. Small trees hung over the creek, willow and oak, large rushes, and a profusion of wild flowers.

The creek opened up and suddenly there were about twenty boats moored up along the west side of the creek. This was a sizeable community and I anticipated that there could be as many as eighty men living in the village and probably an equal number of women and children. We were outnumbered but the non-martial quality of the villagers would be their undoing.

I told Wighard to pull our karvi all the way along the line of the moored boats so that our following boats had room to tie up along the sterns of the moored fishing boats. Some of the villagers had already noticed our approach and there were cries of alarm.

"Stay together until we have beaten the resistance, if you wander off alone you will be surrounded and killed. Stay together." I shouted. We clambered across the moored fishing boats and assembled on a rickety wooden jetty.

"On me." I shouted and stepped off into the village through a maze of timber-built cottages, some hovels, some quite substantial. I could see a slightly larger cottage, a small hall, and headed for that. So far, we had met with no resistance, in fact, we had met no one. As we neared the hall, I could see people assembling ahead. None wore armour but many had spears and pitchforks, both men and women. Standing on a stone slab upon which a large cross had been erected was a man who was armoured, He had on a mail shirt falling to just below his waist, tied tight with a leather belt in which an axe was thrust. He carried a spear and a shield and wore an old battered helmet, metals strengtheners over a leather cap. He had a long white beard, flowing down across the upper part of his chest. I could hear him shouting.

"Stavenisse, hold fast, repel the raiders. Show them how we resisted the Flemish." The crowd shouted, as one. "Stavenisse!" I assumed that this was the name of the settlement.

I shouted to my men. "Archers to the fore, bring down some of those unarmoured men." I had two archers in each boat so in all twelve archers stepped forward and let fly in a ragged volley. At a hundred paces they could hardly miss the tightly packed crowd so every arrow found a mark, but not always a fatal strike. Nevertheless, the missiles incapacitated a dozen of the villagers and gave the rest pause. Instinctively they started to scatter to reduce the risk of being hit by another volley.

The old bearded leader shouted, "Don't scatter, stand firm, we must charge the vikings. With me!" He shouldered his way to the front of the crowd and it was then I could see that he had at least six other, younger men, armoured in mail surrounding him. They all had spears and axes in their belts in the same manner. I could see that the mail shirts were old but serviceable, heirlooms, no doubt.

The old man turned to his companions and the villagers and screamed again. "Charge!" He waved his axe high and down towards us; he was courageous.

"Shield wall, on me." I shouted in return. My crews bunched together and the clack, clack, clack, of their shields overlapping to form a tight shield wall was reassuring. We formed a thirty-man wide shield wall, two men deep between two sturdy cottages so that we could not be immediately flanked. My archers were in the second row, giving them time to release two more volleys of arrows before the impact. The rest of the second line held spears overhead ready to thrust over the heads of the front line when any of our assailants exposed themselves. My front-line men were armed with large Dane axes that could spilt a shield in two, but as the villagers had no shields the slaughter would be fearful.

"Ut! Ut! Ut!" I raised the war cry of the Mercians, my personal battle shout and my men joined in, the front rank beating their shields with their axe handles. With the desperate cries of the villagers and the rhythmic chant of my men, the volume from such a small number of combatants was potent. The villagers swiftly crossed the intervening space between the cottages to our line and with bravery born from fear they crashed into our shields thrusting out with their spears. The impact made us all step back a pace and then brace, to hold the pressure. Our shields prevented casualties and then as one we pushed back swinging our axes in overhead slashes. Most of our blows found a mark. Sharp heavy steel tempered axe edges sheared into brain pans, shoulders or raised arms and the first row of the villages crashed to the ground in writhing agony; blood sprayed everywhere. I noticed some were women; but in a melee no lives are sacrosanct. Instinctively after delivering an axe blow my front-line men crouched down behind their shields whilst the second rank men leaned forward and rammed home the points of their spears into more unarmoured bodies. Within a few heartbeats nearly fifty of the villagers had been killed or wounded, men and women. Untrained villagers could not sustain this sort of courage and almost immediately the unharmed and walking wounded started to stream away. The less courageous of the villagers that had hung back immediately turned and ran. However, the old warrior and his six young supporters tried to rally the fleeing mob. It was time for me to intervene.

"Wighard, take half the men and pursue the villagers, try and capture the women and boys." I turned to the old warrior. "Gauti, bring up the archers and the rest of the men." I strode over the bloodstained path between the cottages right up to the old man. Only one of his men was injured; an arrow through his forearm.

"Was this your village, old man?" I called out.

"No, but they are neighbours of mine and I and my sons stand with them."

"These are your sons?" He nodded. "You are fecund, six strong strapping boys, you must be proud of them; surely you don't want to see them die?"

"We do not fear you, viking scum. We have beaten the Flemings and will beat you."

I looked back at my men and could see only one man down and several minor injuries. "Well, you and the villagers have not done all that well so far and I can see no reason why we should fear you. While we talk my men are enslaving the villagers, killing the men and no doubt raping the women, Oh! And boys probably; they are a heathen lot mostly. I like your style, old man and would let you and your sons go, leave if you have any sense."

I could see the old man seething with anger but I could see he was also a realist and knew he could do little to stop us. "We will go, but remember me, I am Hagen of Bierren and we will meet again, my wife is from this village and will take this hard."

I laughed, "A married man must be subservient to his wife to survive in this world, which is why I am not married. I am Hjorvard Bjornbana and I lead the Roggen vikings and to ensure we meet again I will take one of your sons as a hostage of intent.

Come for him and me, when you are ready." I nodded to Gauti. "Take the wounded son."

I could see Hagen was thinking about fighting so I signalled to the archers to draw to the nock. Hagen and his sons hesitated in the face of certain death and Gauti pulled the wounded boy away from his brethren.

"Now go." I ordered. Hagen and his sons left the village and I instructed my men to scour the cottages for plunder.

The men under Wighard returned to the village with two score of women and children, tethered by their necks with a thick rope. The village was systematically plundered for food and useful goods.

"Gauti, I want to take six boats back to Roggen with us, get Wighard's men to tie the slaves in the boats so they cannot jump overboard, it will be a hard row if the wind is against us but it will be worth it. The rest are to be destroyed and the village burnt. We ended up with such a good haul of plunder from the village that it was not possible to contemplate continuing the raid.

"Burn the village." I ordered.

We pulled away from the jetty and returned to the main river as plumes of white, billowing smoke spiralled into the blue sky. Once out in the main river channel we linked up again with the *Little Runa* and I transferred back onto the snekkja along with the principal prisoner, Hagen's son. The wind had turned and there was a steady off-shore wind that would carry us down the river to Roggen. One by one the tiny leather sails of the following karvis were hoisted.

"Half sail, Magnus, we don't want to outpace the karvis, we are supposed to be guarding our plunder." Magnus smiled, the urge to break out a full sail and speed down the river was always in a skipper's mindset. The whole expanse of the Scheldt estuary lay before us and I could see the watchers on the sand dunes on both sides of the river following our progress. I smiled at the impotency of the islanders who could not concentrate their forces at any particular point to repel us. I could choose my targets with impunity knowing that the Zealanders could not concentrate their forces at that point in advance. The only way they could dislodge us was to attack our defences on Roggen and I had severely weakened their ability to do that by capturing or destroying their boats.

We made a leisurely return to Roggen; the rowers were exhausted towing the additional weight of the full captured fishing vessels but they were happy knowing that there would be an increase of our food stocks and that every one of them had the opportunity to take a new woman tonight, if they so wished. I had decided that I would not lead any more of the raids on the islands; my captains were well into the routine of raiding and understood the precautions they had to take to stay alive. I wanted to use my snekkjas on the high sea against merchant shipping, particularly the Godwinson's and King Edward of Wessex's shipping. I considered that it would be many months before the Zealanders could mount a coherent counter-attack.

After we had off-loaded our plunder and turned the provisions over to Martin and placed the women in the slave compound, I called another meeting of my captains prior to our evening meal. I turned the captive son over to Gautrek to interrogate making it clear I did not want him overly damaged, yet. We all had a horn of ale and settled down outside my boat hut.

"Men, everything is still going to plan, our raids are still being met by poor or little opposition because they cannot second guess our raiding pattern and where we will strike next. I have decided that I will no longer accompany the raids on the islands as you are all adept at this task. I have also decided that the raids will be divided into small raids on individual farmsteads by two or three raiding boats and the occasional larger raids on villages by all the boats. Martin will make a roster and I will stipulate which of the boat captains on the raids is in overall charge. Let all captains remember, follow the commands, and do not break ranks, lose discipline or loot until the order is given." I took a large swallow of ale. "Any questions?" There was no response and from the nods and grunts I perceived that this had gone down well.

"Whilst the raids are being carried out, I intend to take *Ottar* and *Little Runa* out into the Channel and along the English south coast, the Wessex coast and raid merchant shipping." I paused, everyone looked interested, Magnus captain of the *Little Runa* more so than Eystein. "I have reasons for this; first I believe the raids on the Zealanders will not provide the supplies we need to maintain our position here. I do not wish to waste our plundered gains on buying supplies at Bruges by the Sea or elsewhere if I can help it, after all we are all here to make a profit. Second, as some of you already know, I have a feud of sorts with the Earl of Wessex, Harald Godwinson and the English King, Edward the Mild who outlawed me from my homeland. I intend to remind them of my existence." I looked around and all seemed satisfied with this arrangement. None of my men were English, of any persuasion, and probably did not care one way or the other who they raided.

Whilst I was talking Gautrek ambled over dragging the limping hostage. "Well?" I queried as he pulled the boy into the circle and pushed him down onto his knees in front of me.

"He will talk now." Gautrek smiled, a foul evil smirk. I noticed Gautrek had blood on his hands but I could see none on the prisoner. I decided I did not want to know Gautrek's methods of interrogation. I studied the boy he was probably no older than fifteen and after having been stripped of his mail shirt he looked puny and thin.

"What is your name, boy?" I asked.

"Haki Hagenson of Bierren."

"And you are the youngest son of Hagen of Bierren?"

"Yes."

"Is Hagen the lord of all Tholen?"

"No"

"If he is not the lord of Tholen and only the chief of Bierren, what was he doing in Stavenisse?"

"He was meeting with the villagers when you came raiding, he was trying to get them to act with him and the men of Bierren and the other villages on Tholen to fight you as one." The boy looked really sullen after admitting this development.

"So, your father is a chief who will try and unite the Zealanders on Tholen against us. Does he also talk with others from the other islands?" The boy was clearly reluctant to admit to this, but a prod from Gautrek, elicited a nod. So, I thought, in due course a more concerted attack on our island would materialise, but our fortuitous attack on Stavenisse probably will have delayed this. "How many men can your father muster from Tholen?"

The boy was quick to answer this question and so I assumed he was lying and probably inflating the number at least twofold. "Six hundred men, all armed with spears and axes."

Of course, the problem for Hagen of Bierren was that he did not have enough boats to bring even three hundred men to Roggen. "Martin, see to the boy's wound, I don't want him to die of the fever, yet." I waved the boy away.

We all settled down for the night and I was pleased to see that the posted sentries were all vigilant still. I walked the perimeter of the camp I did not want the men to become lax with unremitting success. I checked the food stocks with Martin and was assured we had sufficient food stocks to last a few weeks. I saw the rows of smoking fish and the pens full of pigs and goats and our solitary milch cow. The men were like flies around the women's compound where the men took turns, some led the woman away to the privacy of a tent or hut, whilst others openly copulated on the ground. The women had long since ceased to scream and plead and the air was punctuated by dull groans, the sound of hopeless submission to fate. I made a mental note to have some of the more saleable women sold on in Ribe by Egil within a few days.

Early the next morning just as dawn broke, Dietrich was seen rowing up to the east beach manoeuvring his way through the anchored boats and fishing boats. I was pleased to see that the watchmen were still alert at first light. The boy was brought straight to me and he looked full of news.

"Well, young Dietrich, what have you to tell us?" I asked.

"The day before yesterday several boats were rowed passed the farm heading east. They were obviously Zealanders so I followed them on our old nag and after four miles of so they turned up the creek to Dordrecht. They came back yesterday and I could clearly see a big armoured man in one of the boats who definitely was not on board when the boats went upriver." Dietrich looked pleased with himself but the information he relayed was only half the story.

"Was there any way of knowing from which island the boats came from?" I asked.

Dietrich looked crestfallen. "My father would not let me follow them and said I was not to set out until after dark as I would alert them to our role as lookouts."

"Your father was right, don't worry." I mused. "Go and get some breakfast."

So, it seemed that some of the islanders were seeking assistance from Dordrecht, or to be more precise the Count of Holland. It was most unlikely that Count Floris of Holland was in residence at Dordrecht and whoever was in control in the port would need to send word to the count. The whereabouts of the Count of Holland would not necessarily be known for sure as like most rulers he perambulated his county staying with one lord or another; or in one merchant town or another. I did know that his favourite lodge was a place called Graven Hage, which was a sort of hunting lodge near the coast, perhaps thirty miles of so north of Dordrecht.

The Reeve or Castellan of Dordrecht would not send for help from the count without firmer information and that is why he would have sent a retainer, someone like a huscarl, a trusted warrior, to have a look at Roggen and the alleged devastation. So, even as I considered the situation this warrior would be examining the villages we had devastated and looking at our encampment from the shores of either Walcheren or Schouwen. I sent for Magnus.

"Magnus, I have decided to take *Little Runa* up the Scheldt and try and intercept the warrior who has been sent to check on us from Dordrecht. I anticipate he will be returning up river in the next few days and if I can capture him then we will delay the confrontation with the Count of Holland's men. Have the snekkja ready before first light as I do not want to alert the watchers that we are moving up river."

Magnus hurried off to make preparations.

Martin came over and squatted down next to me. "Are you taking Dietrich back with you?"

"I haven't given it much thought, I can why?"

"Well, if you do not, I am not sure the women in the compound will survive. He has tupped ten already and he seems in no way worn out. The men are laying bets he can fuck the lot

349

before the morning, the lad is insatiable and what is worse the women seem to like him."

I laughed, "I am not sure his mother will appreciate that we have ruined him, he'll not want to become a farmer's boy after this."

Martin looked serious, "This is no joke, it could lead to jealousy and fights."

"Oh! Alright, we will tow his boat and take him home on the *Little Runa*." I smiled, "You had better haul him off the latest woman he is covering and tell him to get some sleep ready for an early start."

Almost as routine the *Little Runa* slipped its mooring line, a line that had been set up across part of the beach front for the larger vessels to tie up to. Dietrich's small boat bobbed along in the larger ship's wake while Dietrich himself was put to the oars to toughen him up a bit, an exercise that I was not above submitting to myself. It is good for the men to know you are not above their station. It was still pitch dark, a sickle moon, low on the horizon providing little in the way of illumination. There was no need to muffle the oars for although sound travels far across water, we were still too far away from the watchers on the adjacent islands to hear us. Magnus ordered a brisk pace up river and we had rounded the island of Tholen and turned into the northern channel before dawn started to illuminate our surroundings. Before long we had entered the main channel that led up to Dortrecht and Tonnecreek. I indicated to Magnus that both Dietrich and I should be relieved from rowing and then I told Dietrich to come to the tiller.

"Dietrich, I intend to wait, hidden for the returning Zealander boats. I need a suitable hiding place to lay up this snekkja so we will not be seen until the smaller boats near us. You are the local, do you know of any such places?"

Dietrich thought for a time and then grinned. "I know of three places that may be suitable. One is about a quarter of a mile this side of home, sorry my home, Tonnecreek. It is a small creek that you could probably back your boat up but there is not much in the way of tree cover and your stem and stern posts and of course your mast would be clearly visible. The other two places are the other side of Tonnecreek, one is on the south side of the river and is a sort of natural pond that joins the river and has trees around it giving excellent cover, the other is on the Dordrecht side of the river and is another creek joining the main river; I think cover is sparse there too."

"Good, we will examine the two places further up the river passed your home, you will show us." I ordered. Dietrich went to the stem post and gazed out at the river.

"He's a good lad, make his father proud." Observed Magnus.

"Not if he knew about is sexual escapades." I observed laconically.

Magnus laughed, "I'm jealous." We coasted past Tonnecreek with Dietrich frantically waving to his siblings who lined the bank. It was not long before we came to the natural pond on the south bank, which Dietrich named as Noordschans, it was practically perfect except that there was a long sand bank in the river dividing the main channel that would hinder our approach to any boats in the other, principal channel. I instructed Magnus to continue up stream and almost immediately a creek on the north side of the river appeared but not until we had rowed passed it. It ran into the main river at an angle west to east and was hidden by small trees.

"Magnus, take us about, I want to examine that rivulet over there."

Magnus put the helm hard over and performed a neat circle that brought the snekkja's stern first into the creek. It was shallow but took *Little Runa's* draught. The oarsmen had to shorten oars so as not to foul the banks but the whole length of the longship was enclosed within the stream and hidden behind the small tress and foliage.

"Perfect, couldn't be better." I sighed.

"The Zealanders might see our mast, lord." One of the rowers suggested.

"No, we will un-step the mast, we don't need it for this fight." Magnus asserted. I nodded.

"I want two men a quarter mile along the bank, east of here to warn us of any approaching boats; Dietrich, you go with them as you may recognise the boats and even the warrior who went downstream. Make sure you take provisions for at least three days, no make it four days. Magnus, I want another two men to scout north of here, I do not want to find we are just over the horizon from a village or military fort; we need to be in the wilderness."

The chosen men set forth and the rest settled down for a boring and probably long wait. Later that day the scouts sent into the interior returned and reported that there were no settlements within half a day's walk from our hiding place. I still kept scouts out so as not to be surprised. For three days I had time to contemplate my current state and future. I am not usually introspective, living for the moment, but enforced idleness leads one's mind through convoluted ways. By my reckoning I was about twenty-one or twenty-two years of age and I seemed to have been fighting all my life. Until recently I had nothing but a reputation as a fighter, a warrior of some renown. It was what I had sought after and I had achieved it. After a slow start I had taken to women, but I was not obsessed with them. Not true, I had been obsessed with my step-mother, Godgifu, and I still unconsciously measured all women against her. I had now acquired a following, a nucleus of a comitatus, as the Romans would have named them and a small fleet; I jest, three ships, two snekkja and one knarr. I decided I wanted more. I had rejected the possibility of lands in England although if my outlawry was ever lifted, I technically could lay claim to land near Bourne that my father had left me, but under the care of my brother Aelfgar. I wondered if my nephews would honour such a commitment? Perhaps I could acquire lands in Flanders, or even Zealand, a land so like the part of the Danelagh where I was born. I could become a lord of a town, or shire commensurate to my birthright? I could achieve this through military service or marriage, the usual route.

Such thoughts played on my mind for the next three days. Eventually I was jolted out of my reverie by one of the scouts leaping over the sheer strake of the boat. "They are coming." He was excited.

"Slow down, give me the details?" I demanded.

"There are just two boats, not overloaded, maybe six men in each boat. I saw a man in mail sitting near the stern of the lead boat. Dietrich was positive it was the man who he had seen going down stream. They are rowing down this side of the river and will be here in short order."

"Where is Dietrich?" I asked.

"He is running behind and Egil, the other scout, is watching the boats.

"Right, Magnus get everyone to the oars." I raised my voice. "Men we will be in action soon, make ready, arm yourselves; archers to the prow post. Remember, shoot the rowers not the mailed warrior, I want him alive if possible."

We settled to wait; Dietrich came panting over the side. "Too much fucking boy, swiving women won't keep you fighting fit, remind me to train you." He grinned back, happily.

"Get a weapon from my sea chest, a scramaseax is best." I ordered. The rowers braced their oars against the creek banks on either side ready for a mighty push off. I strung my Danish long bow and made my way to the stem post. Dietrich followed me, "Go to the stern, Dietrich, I do not want to explain to your mother that I got you killed." I dismissed him.

After a long wait the second scout ran along the bank and jumped in. "They are coming!" Moments later the two fishing boats sailed past the mouth of the creek under sail taking advantage of a mild easterly breeze. Fortunately, the wind was not strong enough for the small boats to in any way out sail our snekkja rowed at pace.

I chopped my hand down as the signal for the rowers to push us out of the creek. The oars bent as the rowers pushed them against the banks to give the *Little Runa* movement. One oar, weaker than the rest, gave a load crack and split in half. The rower cursed and threw away the broken shaft into the water. All the heads on the fishing vessels spun around in our direction, startled by the unusual noise. At the same time, like an arrow released from the bow, *Little Runa* shot forward out of the creek mouth like a cork from a bottle. The fishing boats had been sailing as near as safely possible to the north bank of the river and were only some fifty paces out and now slightly ahead of us. They were clearly surprised and had lost rhythm and way somewhat. It took us some time to clear the creek and river bank before our oars could be fully extended by which time the helmsmen had the fishing boats in hand and were trying to make full headway. A few oars came out to assist their speed but that would be to no avail against an eighteen aside oared longship.

Little Runa shuddered under the force as the oarsmen strained until her speed matched their efforts. My snekkja sprang forward against the current heading straight towards the Zealander boats. There was no way they could escape us; we had effectively cut them off from the river bank and they could not out run us or reach the south bank. Predictably the two boats split, the one carrying the mailed warrior continued east up river and the other boat turned across stream towards the south bank.

"Follow that one." I yelled and indicated to Magnus the boat sailing on up stream. The second boat may well escape us but I cared nothing for that, it was the warrior I wanted. After a short while we came within twenty paces of the fishing boat. I nocked my arrow and sighted the helmsman; releasing my arrow, it took him squarely in the back and he slumped down dragging the rudder arm to the larboard side. The boat wallowed in the water athwart our path. I did not want to ram her so I called for my crew to hold water; they braced the oars against their bodies and dropped the blades into the river. The ship slowed sufficiently for Magnus to bump the prow into the fishing boat whilst my archers peppered the Zealanders, within moments all but the mailed warrior were dead.

The mailed warrior stood foursquare in the belly of the fishing boat, sword drawn and with his round shield held before him. His face was obscured by the nasal bar of his helmet but I could see that he was clean shaven apart from a curling moustache, a beautiful ginger affair. I stood high on *Little Runa's* stem post and looked down upon him.

"Good day to you sir; will you not join me. It would be prudent as your boat will shortly be sinking and with all that mail on, I am afraid you would very soon be at the bottom of the river."

The warrior hesitated but realising the futility of his situation he nodded assent. Magnus had let our snekkja drift sideways on to the fishing boat; the warrior sheathed his sword, slung his shield onto his back and climbed on board.

"Dietrich, come here." I shouted down the length of the ship." The boy sloped down the walkway and presented himself to me.

"Your job is done here for today. Get in the fishing boat and drift it down stream to your father's farm. It is a gift from me.

You have done well, keep a sharp look out for other movements I may be interested in knowing about. You can keep the scramaseax, but I would advise you not to let your mother see it." I ruffled his hair and the boy gleefully clambered over into the boat. "Egil, help Dietrich throw those bodies over the side." I ordered. "Magnus, follow the other fishing boat."

I turned to the warrior. "Well now, I am interested in your business; who are you?"

"Why should I tell you anything? I do not know you or why you have attacked the fishing boats." The warrior replied in an angry and surly voice.

"Come now, let us not beat about the bush. You know I am one of the Roggen vikings and I know you have visited the islands after they sent for help to Dordrecht. We could play games for a long time and I would still find out what I need to know."

I looked forward and I could see the other fishing boat nearing the south bank of the river; I doubted we would catch them before they ran off into the hinterland. It would be days before they returned from whence, they came.

"Let us start again, I am Hjorvard Bjornbana, leader of the Roggen vikings and all these islands are mine to do with as I please and until such time as I am inclined to sail away and terrorise someplace else. There I have told you my name and my business, good manners require you to reciprocate." I suspected my taunt would open him up somewhat and I was right.

"I am Dagling Herbrandson, a retainer of Dirk Hammerhand, Lord of the Gouwe and close relative of Floris Count of Holland. I was in Dordrecht at the time the deputation from Tholen arrived. The Port Reeve referred them to me and I agreed to return to Tholen on a fact-finding mission."

It was clear to me that neither the Count of Holland nor is nephew, this Dirk Hammerhand, had any idea what was transpiring in Zealand and that representation would have to be sent again from the Zealanders to make them aware of my raiding. It was unlikely that the Port Reeve in Dordrecht would be overly concerned if Dagling Herbrandson failed to return from his 'mission' as long as shipping into and from Dordrecht remained unmolested.

"There, that was not so hard, was it? A little politeness between captive and capturer. You will be entertained royally on my island until I decide to leave and then I will let you go."

Dagling looked troubled. "I don't suppose you will consider a holmgang, you and me on that sandbank yonder." He challenged.

I laughed, "Under other circumstances I would oblige you, but I am under no obligation to fight a captive. I have been courteous but now you must surrender your weapons." Two spear points suddenly prodded him in the back initiated by some of my men you had gathered around. Reluctantly Dagling divested himself of his sword and dagger and for good measure his hands and feet were bound and he was thrown into the belly of the ship.

Magnus had brought *Little Runa* gently into the bank of the river where the now empty fishing boat had been abandoned by the Zealanders.

"Magnus, get some of the crew to break it up." I ordered. Dietrich had disappeared down-stream and the Zealanders were also out of sight. The men smashed up the bottom of the fishing boat.

"Time to go home." I said to no one in particular but suddenly realising that I had spent as much time on Roggen as I had spent anywhere since my outlawry. As the crew gently rowed back down stream letting the current take the strain, I sat next to Magnus at the stern contemplating my next move. I had bought time by preventing Dagling's report on matters in Zealand to his masters. To send another deputation for help and achieve an organised response would take two maybe three months, well into the autumn. I would clearly have to winter over on Roggen and complete my objectives in the next year. Our raids on the islands would continue and I would develop my idea of raiding shipping in the channel between England and Flanders. Very likely I would receive an attack on our camp in the autumn. I would need to report the situation to the Count of Flanders so he could stand down any force he may have set aside for the relief of Zealand this year. We returned to Roggen after five days away, Dagling joined the other male prisoners in their compound and I immediately sought a report from Martin and the other boat captains. We had the usual assembly in front of my boat hut.

First, I informed them of what had been achieved up-river and the capture of Dagling. I made it clear that come the autumn we would have to face a major battle with the Count of Holland's men supported by the Zealanders, or at least some of them. I stressed the need of continuing to destroy the boats available to the Zealanders and harrying the villagers to destroy their morale.

Whilst I had been away one raid had been undertaken on Walcheren that had burned a farm but had to rapidly retreat when large numbers of islanders had been seen approaching the burning farm. Clearly the Zealanders were becoming more organised but it did not prevent the raid making off with light goods and the three women from the farm. The farmer and his labourers were all killed.

"Eystein, I want you to go with your father on the next supply run to Bruges by the Sea and travel on to the Count of Flanders to deliver a message from me. I will take over *Ottar* temporarily. I intend to take *Ottar* and *Little Runa* out into the channel and raid sea going shipping over the rest of the summer months.; the objective for this move is one of pure gain and to keep our people on Roggen living comfortably; Eystein, the count is not to know this. Martin is to remain in charge of the camp, he is doing a good job of this and we must all be appreciative. There has been no reported trouble caused by the slave women and no disagreement over supplies. I do not want to share out the loot until we leave here and leaving the silver and other treasures in a common pile under guard seems to be acceptable for now. Egil, another snekkja would be useful so keep your ears open when in Bruges by the Sea, similarly I hope my raiding in the channel may acquire extra keels of one sort or another."

My announcements invited questions and the situation was discussed in depth. One of the concerns was to ensure that all the men were utilised fully and that there was no idleness in camp. I listened carefully and decided on further guidance.

"The raids upon the islands are to also continue but with less frequency as we now want the Zealanders to be unsure of the need to bring in the Count of Holland into this business. Any of the men who do not have specific tasks at any time must take part

357

in fighting exercises. Axe work, spear work will be most important. Those with bows must practice daily. Anything else?" Martin raised his hand tentatively. "Go on Martin." I prompted.

"Lord Hereward, it has occurred to me that there is more we can do to make our island fortress more impregnable. The use of stakes quickly made the island a stockade but we do not always have sufficient men in the stockade to defend the whole perimeter, for example when the crews of *Ottar*, *Little Runa* and *Hilda* are all away together." Martin paused and the silence suggested everyone was listening at carefully. "After the palisade was completed, we had some stakes left; most of these have been utilised as parts of the men's shelters. However, it has occurred to me that we could use these stakes placed submerged off the beaches surrounding the island as snares to breach boat hulls, those of the enemy as they try to make landfall. There would be an added value in that those parts of the palisade circumference covered by the submerged stakes could be lightly manned meaning we could concentrate our defenders at more vulnerable places along the palisade." Martin stopped talking and this was followed by a collective exhalation of breath from the captains.

"What a brilliant idea." I was not sure who said that but I could see that there was collective agreement with the idea.

"Well done, Martin. What would we do without you? This will be done; the stakes will be retrieved from the shelters and more stakes can be fetched from Bruges and additionally some of the captured boats can be scuttled off the beach making the area even more hazardous. Martin and the other camp captains can organise this." I was pleased by this development. It occurred to me that sinking stakes under water would not be easy especially on the sea side of the island but I was also sure that Martin would overcome the issues. The meeting broke up with an exhortation from me that the captains talk to all their crews so that everyone was aware of what was happening and why.

Egil and Eystein set sail for Bruges by the Sea two days later, Eystein to travel on to Bruges itself and after to wherever the Count of Flanders may be in residence. It would obviously give him the chance to meet Marieke again so I did not expect him to hurry back. It would be interesting to see who he was in love with more, Marieke or *Ottar*.

There was fierce competition to be included with the crews of the *Ottar* and *Little Runa* and I had decided to take a heavy complement to ensure any ships we attacked on the sea would be heavily outnumbered. The two snekkjas rowers were already established but I had some flexibility with the additional warriors and archers. I wanted to give the impression that we were Danish raiders so all the Ribe men were enrolled but no Flemings. In all, between the two longships, I had some one hundred and ten men. Although I had indicated to Eystein that I would skipper the *Ottar*, I did not consider myself a consummate sailor and I invited Coll from Veðrafjǫrðr to take the helm. He was a colleague of Egil who approved of my choice. Our venture was delayed a couple of days by inclement weather but eventually the skies cleared and a good south-easterly wind set in that was likely to blow for at least two or three days. It meant that we would have to initially row in the teeth of the wind on our way out into the channel between the Kent coast and Flanders but it would enable us to return to our roost quickly in case of pursuit.

We rowed south along the Flemish coast and put into Bruges by the Sea on the first night. On the second day we rowed further along the coast and pulled our ships up on the beach just north of Calais for the night. On the third morning we raised our sails and slowly tacked across the narrowest part of the strait between the Kent coast and Calais. By mid-day we were standing off the white cliffs maybe a couple of miles out trying to hold our position; the strong tidal currents and prevailing wind did not help and I prayed for the sight of some shipping to release my sea dogs upon. By mid-afternoon my prayers were answered when we spotted a merchant ship, an English version of a knarr with a fore and aft platform and a swollen fat belly, sailing north-east under full sail. It was sailing about a mile out from the shore, for safety, and passed between us and the shore heading towards the Thames estuary or further north. I signalled to Magnus on the *Little Runa* that we would intercept and both snekkjas hoisted their spars and unfurled their sails in unison. With the wind to our stern, we flew across the water and closed on the merchant ship gaining over half a mile before we were spotted. The captain considered running for shore but the Kent coast north of Dover was treacherous and there was no way the wind would allow him to make Dover harbour. As we closed the merchant ship heaved to and dropped its sail. My pair of sea wolves swept up to the merchant ship furling our sails and sliding up to the high sides of our prey, either side. I put an arrow into the merchant ships mast to give notice of intent. Grapple ropes were thrown out and the three ships were held fast together drifting north-east in the fast-flowing current. Two of my warriors hastened to climb up the side of the merchant ship before I had the opportunity, possibly to protect me. I followed, still with my sword sheathed and my Dane axe slung across my back. On deck I came face to face with the ship's captain, standing wringing his hands in some distress.

"Good day to you." I began pleasantly. "What ship are you, where bound and what goods do you carry?" Straight to the point.

"This is Earl Harald's ship, the *Gabriel* out of Bosham, I am her captain and we are carrying trade goods north to Norwich. We have wine, grain, glassware, and pots. Nothing anyone needs to die for."

"Die! Who said anything about dying?" I was quietly elated; a Godwinson ship, it could not be better.

"How many crewmen have you?" I asked.

"Six and the helmsman." The captain replied.

I turned to the rail and shouted down to Coll. "I want four men to escort this boat to Roggen." I turned back to the captain. "You will be going elsewhere with your cargo, four of my men will accompany you, if you try and resist, they will kill you and your men. I will be taking four of your men as rowers for my snekkja. Their life will be more interesting, for a while." Crew men from the Ottar clambered aboard and I gave them instructions, I noticed one of them was Gautrek. "Not you Gautrek, go back and send someone else." I walked over to the opposite side of the merchant ship and shouted down to Magnus telling him to sheer off and I would join him shortly.

The merchant ship was released from the grapples and raised it sail once more steering towards the mouth of the Scheldt. Magnus on *Little Runa* and I on the *Ottar* slowly made our way north along the Kent coast resisting the current, our sails furled and the oars dead in the water. It was most unlikely that any more shipping would come up behind us but we were now able to intercept shipping exiting the River Thames. Wool was the main export commodity to Flanders from England and I intended to make a gift of several ship loads of the stuff to Count Baldwin. As anticipated, two more merchant ships were spotted later that day appearing from the wide river mouth, I executed the same tactics and laid alongside each one after a show of force. The only down side was that I was now another eight fighting men short and gained a further eight slaves to row at the oars. Captives rowing at the oars is quite unsatisfactory, they are not likely to think and cooperate and invariably do not exert themselves as a freeman would. When one of the captives fouled the oars, deliberately, in my opinion, I made an example of him and decapitated him with my sword and threw his body over the side. The other captives were more demonstrative after that but I still did not want them.

By late afternoon we had drifted from our station at the mouth of the Thames along the Essex coast. I knew there were numerous creeks and rivers all along the Essex shoreline and I had decided to slip into one of them overnight. I headed for the most obvious river mouth north of the Thames as the light faded. I was cautious and wary of sandbanks, but as my two ships neared the estuary the river appeared deep and wide enough. I thought it might be the River Blackwater where Olaf Tryggvasson and Thorkell the Tall defeated the English at Maldon three generations past, I knew at least one of my father's kin had died there on the English side. We pulled gently into the river mouth, the land was low lying and marshy to the south side, ideal for us to hide there as the land would discourage movement. A small stream opened on our larboard and I indicated to Coll to steer into it. Magnus followed us in and both snekkjas did an ungainly full turn in the river before tying up side by side.

I climbed over into *Little Runa* to consult with Magnus and we agreed to share out the captive rowers.

"We are not in the Blackwater, I have been there before, years ago, it is a bigger river than this and further north, I think." Magnus expounded. "I am not sure what this river is but it is a better place to hide than the Blackwater, which has more open banks and is less marshy." Coll joined us.

"Everyone is eating the evening meal, cold, no fires." Coll explained. "So far this has been like taking a rattle from a baby." Magnus grinned in the half light.

"True," I agreed, "but sooner or later our luck will run out and we will be spotted by one of the king's patrol boats. Ever since the Godwinson's rebellion and my brother's raids the king has kept up a coastal patrol."

"The English will not know of their missing merchant ships for several days." Coll observed.

"I think that we will have been spotted from the cliff tops above Dover, there is a fort there. I would not be surprised if there are warships out looking for us tomorrow and the day after for sure." I concluded. "Eat, rest."

The next morning, we exited the mouth of the river, which one of the captives named the Crouch, with the area where we had laid up overnight going by the ubiquitous name of the Foul Ness, the bites on my exposed forearms and face vouching for the efficiency of the ferocious insects. The wind was still from the south-east so we idled in the mouth of the river waiting for shipping to sail from south to north along the coast. By mid-day nothing had materialised out at sea, whereas several fishing boat drifting down the River Crouch had turned back whence they came when they saw us. The men were getting restless when, shortly after mid-day a large knarr, similar to *Hilda* but bigger came around the headland to the south, heading north. I indicated to Magnus that we would attack and Coll gave the orders to give way and the *Ottar* slowly moved out of the estuary mouth. As soon as we had cleared the mouth of the river the wind could be felt on our steer board side and we raised the sail. I had deliberately ensured that there was no identifiable insignia on the sail, I would have liked to display the Mercian knot but now was not the time or place. Magnus' snekkja *Little Runa* had a sail that had a large black raven painted on it and that image was perfect for our Danish viking persona. As before, we swooped down on the merchant ship but this time the knarr did not slow or veer away. I could see as we closed a line of archers along the sheer strake. Magnus took the *Little Runa* over to the off-shore side of the knarr and I shouted to Coll to bring *Ottar* up to the knarr stern on, to minimise us as a target.

My archers crowded into the prow trying to get a clear shot at the knarr's helmsman but he was hidden by the stern post of the merchant ship and a well-placed shield held up by an obviously warlike crew member. All my crew were ready and waiting to board, as we approached the timing had to be right before we furled the sail, otherwise we might over shoot the side of the knarr. Coll executed the manoeuvre perfectly; the sail was pulled up and *Ottar* slide alongside the knarr. Grapple lines snaked out and the momentum of our snekkja was reined in by the weight of the leashed knarr. Heads appeared over the side above us, and bows were lifted over the sheer strake to shoot down into my ship. At the same time my archers let fly and their arrows caught the defending archers in their faces; they either ducked or died. Ten of my men went up and over the side in unison and I followed in the second wave carrying a short axe and my scramaseax, ideal for close combat.

My men had cleared an area on the deck of the knarr midship but one of them was down from a spear thrust in his gut. He was writhing in agony and the blood from the wound was making the deck around slippery. I had the opportunity to look around and was surprised to see far more defenders on the knarr's deck than there should have been. Apart from the crew, who seemed to be the fellows with the bows, there were at least six huscarls, mailed and carrying swords. Neither side had shields, as they were usually an encumbrance on a ship's deck. The conclusion was still predictable as I had now been joined by a further dozen of my own warriors meaning that each huscarl was outnumbered two or three to one; it would be bloody though. The huscarls swords were getting in each other's way and none could give a telling swing at my baying men. Sensibly, the huscarls had bunched up to defend each other. A couple of my archers climbed into the knarr and started to shoot down the unarmoured knarr crewmen.

The huscarls were beginning to feel secure when the crew of the *Little Runa* clambered over the sheer strake behind them and took them in the rear. Before any of the huscarls could turn and defend themselves two were cut down with stabs with scramaseax' in their backs that burst through their mail hauberks. Another huscarl was stabbed in the neck as he glanced behind, by a stout fellow next to me who was immediately cutdown by one of the last three remaining huscarls. This huscarl stepped forward with the intention of killing another of my men so I stepped forward and blocked his sword thrust with my scramaseax and chopped at his sword arm with my small axe. The axe blade sliced his arm below his mail sleeve and he dropped his sword. I kicked his sword aside just as another huscarl came at me, sword swinging in towards my left side. I blocked this slash with my scramaseax but the power of the blow pushed the flat of my short sword into my left side ribs. The position of my scramaseax saved my life but I felt a rib crack. In fury I lifted my axe and smashed it into his face. His helmet did not have a nasal guard and his face exploded in blood; my second chop went into his neck above his mail shirt and severed an artery and blood fountained out across the deck and my crew man to my right; the huscarl collapsed. The last huscarl was chopped down by a rain of blows front and back. The deck before me was complete carnage. I had lost six men to the huscarls and that made me angry as I considered it my fault.

I looked around in pain and discomfort and saw that the captain of the knarr was standing at the tiller together with four others. They were elaborately dressed and were clearly the group who the huscarls were desperately trying to protect. The captain only had a dagger and he was elderly as well. There were two men and two women passengers. Both men were young and armed with swords and daggers but had no mail or other means of protection. The two women were young and attractive, finely dressed, one more than the other. The principal of the two women wore a fine silk robe with ermine trim, her hair was fair and was enclosed in a pearl net. Her complexion was clear and I noticed her eyebrows were darker than the hair on her head. She had gold rings on her fingers and the shoes peeping out from under the hem of her dress were embroidered; she could not have been more than fourteen summers old and her breasts were just budding. Her female companion was more plainly dressed and had her hair bound up in a cap. Sensible dress but a fine figure, brown hair, slightly sun-kissed complexion; the other's maid, for sure, and at least eight years older, near my age.

I ordered my men to clean the mess up and I walked over to the group. "Good day. May I know who I have the privilege of addressing?" I hoped the pain in my side did not translate to my voice.

The captain of the knarr spoke up first. "These noble persons are under my care and I am conveying them to Northumbria. They are under the protection of King Edward; this noble lady is the king's ward and is to be married to Gospatrick, Earl of Northumbria. These two noble youths are of the younger branch of the royal family of Scotland. They should not be harmed."

I smiled, "I know Earl Gospatrick, he ran before my sword at Dunsinane and I helped him become earl by slaying his predecessor; but I have a score to settle with Malcolm Mac Duncan, as MacBeth was a dear friend of mine. For the time being you will all come with me, you will be hostages and treated with respect." I spoke to my crew men behind me. "Bind the boys, kill the captain."

I turned towards my own ship, when the girl called. "Wait!" I turned.

"Please do not kill him, he is my uncle and I am sure a suitable ransom can be provided. Please"

I stopped and turned back. "Who are you and who is he?" I enquired.

"My name is Alftruda and I am a niece of the King; that is King Edward of England. This is my uncle Aethelweard, my mother's brother. We are from Wiltshire and my father's brother is ealdorman there, we can pay."

As the girl pleaded one of my men came up and whispered in my ear. "Lord, ships masts, three, south on the horizon."

I became cautious. "Quickly, ransack the boat and stove in the hull. Get the captives onto *Ottar*, all of them; Magnus sheer away and run for the mouth of the Scheldt." I shouted my concern. My lads threw bundles and chests over into the *Ottar* and then leaped down after them.

"Cut the lines and make sail." Coll yelled. The oars came out and he yelled the stroke. At the same time the sail was unfurled from the yardarm and as *Ottar* made way Coll ordered the oars in and the crew hunkered down to manipulate the sheets to coax as much speed out of the snekkja as possible. We settled into

Little Runa's wake; we could probably out run *Little Runa* but I wanted us to stay together in case we were caught.

I walked to the stern of the snekkja and climbed up the strakes attached to the top of the stern post behind Coll. I could clearly see the three sails maybe two miles astern. The little white sails clearly displayed crosses emblazoned thereon; King Edward's patrol ships. These longships would be larger than mine, maybe thirty benches with up to eighty men on each ship but they probably could not out pace us.

We sped away due east; I calculated that the mouth of the River Scheldt was exactly due east but it was much further away than when we crossed the narrows between Calais and Dover. It was probably a little over a hundred miles to Roggen, which would mean that we would have to sail through the night to reach safety. As the pursuing longships did not know our destination, they would lose us as night fell; equally they were unlikely to follow us as far as the Scheldt. I watched the pursuing ships for some time and eventually was satisfied they were not gaining on my two ships. The wind held and we scudded across the sea towards the mainland and safety. I was not ready yet to take on King Edward or Harald Godwinson head on but I intended to harry them and I would probably try my luck against one coastal guard ship if the opportunity arose.

The dusk crept across the face of the world from the east and it appeared we were steering into a wall of darkness. I suspected that we were already invisible to the pursuing longships who, if they were sensible would soon call off the chase. It occurred to me that it would have been a good idea to have a beacon burning on Roggen to guide shipping during the hours of darkness. The night fully enveloped us, I signalled to Magnus on *Little Runa* to heave to so that we could come alongside. I intended the two drakkers to be lashed together and continue to sail east on half sail. I had no intention of going aground on the Frisian or Flemish coasts, such an event would be a godsend to the Zealanders.

We gradually drifted across the sea, which was fortunately quite calm, through the night with extra lookouts at both the stem and stern of both boats. It was a long night and I took the opportunity to sleep. When dawn broke a cloud bank could be observed ahead of us, a sure indication of land. We uncoupled the boats and raised our sails. There were no other sails across the horizon and I was sure that the English longships had abandoned the pursuit. By mid-morning the low-lying dunes of either Frisia or Flanders were discernible ahead.

"Coll, we must get some boat boys, someone athwart the yardarm would be invaluable; where do you think we are?" I mused.

"Water colour suggests we are entering the estuary of a big river, which must be one of the Rhine outlets or the Scheldt; the wind has been trying to push us north and although Magnus and I have been trying to counter the drift I suspect we are off the mouth of one of the northern entrances to the Rhine." Coll suggested.

"Yes, I suspect your right, we are in for a long pull against a head wind to reach Roggen."

Over the days my small army had been ensconced on Roggen we had become quite familiar with the coastlines both north and south of our base it was no surprise, therefore, when one of the crew shouted that ahead was the coast of Goeree the next island above Schouwen we all cheered, we were much nearer to Roggen than we hoped. Both Coll and Magnus turned the tillers to bear away from the wind and head south-east, adjusting the sail accordingly. The wind started to push us south and east in the direction we wanted to go, we would probably only have to row round Roggen to beach. By mid-day we had entered the mouth of the Scheldt approaching Roggen; I could clearly see the masts of the knarrs we had apprehended off Kent on the far side of the island. We rounded the island and beached the snekkjas.

As I trudged up the sand from the shore towards the gate, I could hear a heated debate taking place. I was surprised to see Martin and Beornwulf arguing.

"What is the issue here?" I demanded abruptly, in a voice that cut the argument dead.

Startled they both looked round, my approach had been unnoticed. Martin gathered his wits. "We were just discussing the fate of the three captured merchant ships. I am of the view that they should be scuttled around our little island fortress, Beornwulf believes they should be sold on, for profit."

"I see, this decision will be discussed in our captains' council and the final decision will be mine." I asserted. I looked at both pointedly and they nodded in acceptance.

"We will all meet this evening, as we usually do. Martin, can you assemble an inventory of what our piracy has achieved." I walked away.

Everything else in the camp was on a normal footing, many of the men were weapons training and I made a note to join them later, to loosen up my bruised ribs that had stiffened noticeably. I directed the prisoners to the captives' compound but did not place the two women with the sex slaves. I instructed Gautrek to interrogate the prisoners but not to physically harm them at this point. My attempt at exercise proved abortive as it aggravated my obviously broken rib more than I had anticipated. I had my torso tightly bound and realised I would have to take my time for a few days. The evening meal was a delicious fish stew with lots of root vegetables and my favourites, mushrooms, and onions. I was in a good mood by the time the captains assembled.

"Men, our piracy in the channel has ended sooner than I had anticipated. I had expected to be out for several more days but circumstances determined that we should run for home sooner. Nevertheless, the raid has been a success, once we were stationed off Kent, we quickly took three merchant vessels, the ones you see moored off the beach here. No one was hurt, sorry, no one of ours were hurt, and the crews were mostly captured, some died. I believe about a dozen merchant sailors are prisoners in our captive men's compound. All three ships were English merchant ships as I had intended and all three ships were full of goods, plunder." I looked around everyone was listening intently. "Yesterday, off the mouth of a river called the Crouch, north of the Thames we intercepted a larger knarr and to our surprise it put up a fight. The reason for this was because it was carrying important passengers who were protected by huscarls. The huscarls are dead as are some of ours, the huscarls were courageous. The passengers are now our prisoners. You may well be wondering where is the knarr they were on? Well, we had to scuttle it with most of its cargo. As we were looting the ship three English longships appeared and closed upon us, so we were forced to run before them. I would remind you we are being paid to do a job for the Count of Flanders and raiding English shipping is not part of that task, however lucrative that may be."

"Who are these important prisoners?" Beornwulf asked.

"I know that the most important is a young woman by the name of Alftruda, a ward of King Edward himself and the betrothed of Earl Gospatrick of Northumbria whence she was heading when we waylaid her ship. Her uncle, called Aethelweard was captaining the ship and he has much less worth. There are also two youths, relatives of Malcolm, King of Scots, Gautrek can you enlighten us?"

Gautrek shouldered his way to the front of our circle; he was stroking his dagger hilt, as he was want to do, and he looked unhappy. "Well, they were happy to divulge their names and their position and as I was not allowed to touch them, I cannot vouch for their truthfulness. They say that they are bastard sons of Donald Bane, the brother of King Malcolm apparently, they do not want to go to King Malcolm, who may well shorten their lives somewhat. Their names are Duncan and Aedh for what that is worth."

"Thank you, Gautrek." I looked around the group. "Any comments, suggestions." I looked at Beornwulf and arched my eyebrow.

Beornwulf cleared his throat. "Lord Hereward, the captives are yours to do with as you please. The plunder from the merchant ships will either go as additional supplies for our stay here or to be shared from the common pile in due course. I am particularly concerned about the merchant ships you have captured. They are very valuable and would fetch a good price in any port. Martin wants to scuttle them around this island and I understand his reasons but these are valuable ships to waste like that."

Magnus interrupted, "These merchant ships have probably been trading in these waters for many years and would be well known. Questions would be asked if we tried to sell them around these parts." Several captains nodded at this comment. A lively debate took place between the captains, I noted that few were in favour of scuttling them. Martin's face grew longer.

After a lengthy discussion I held my hand up. "Captains, I have listened. This is my decision. First, the prisoners. I intend to send Aethelweard to King Edward's court and demand a ransom for the girl, Alftruda. Her maid can go into the women's compound to comfort the men. The two bastard Scots may be useful but at the moment I cannot see my way so they will remain in the men's compound. The ship's cargoes, that is those parts that are of little use to us here will be taken to Ribe on the *Hilda* and sold. Now the merchant ships, Egil will examine them and decide if any of them are not pristine and more suitable to scuttle. Any of the merchant ships that are in particularly good order will be sold, but not locally, even Ribe is too near. They will be sailed to Norway and sold in the Trondelag and I want to ensure that another snekkja is acquired as part of any transaction, or better still two smaller snekkjas." I looked around, "Can we agree on that?" Everyone nodded, Beornwulf beamed, Martin looked unhappy.

As the group dispersed, I asked Magnus and Martin to stay behind.

"Magnus, I want you to take *Little Runa* and drop this Aethelweard off on the English coast, do not get caught. Magnus nodded and left.

"Martin, I want to explain my decision. The merchant ships would not make good underwater barriers, in my opinion, they are two large and would probably be spotted. Smaller boats and stakes are better and Egil will hopefully acquire as many stakes as we need from Bruges. Additionally, it is important to meet the men's aspirations. They are not here for any other reason than plunder. If I fail to continually increase their wealth, they will seek employment elsewhere so I must balance our long-term objectives with keeping the men content. I am sorry to go counter to your wishes but defending Roggen is not my long-term objective. I want a powerful fleet of snekkjas so that I can be an influential independent sea lord and the value of the merchant ships will assist in this."

"I understand, master." Martin smiled ruefully, "It is just that I find the minds of these pirates stultifying and frustrating."

I laughed, "Is that all, I doubt you will find an intellectual viking, I will have to capture some priests so that you can have some stimulating conversation." We both laughed and the tension eased.

"You had better get this Aethelweard over here." Shortly afterwards Gautrek led the led captive over.

"Sit." I ordered. Aethelweard sat, his hands were still tied and I made no offer to untie him. "Listen well, you will be taken to England and landed I know not where. You will make your way to King Edward the Mild's court and give him this message. I Hjorvard Bjornbana hold his ward, Alftruda hostage; as yet she is unharmed and will remain so if I receive five hundred pounds of silver, either in coin or hacksilver, within a month of days. The payment to be delivered here on a single ship, a knarr, if Harald Godwinson tries to trick me, I will rape the girl and hang her from one of my ships' yardarm. Now you will be returned to your prison compound. Go."

In the next few days, I arranged for the merchant ships to be manned by sufficient crew members to be able to man any longships acquired in Norway. I decided Beornwulf would lead the expedition as he was the captain most enthusiastic about selling on the boats. Egil returned in the *Hilda* with a supply of stakes and additional water; Eystein was not with him and I assumed that either the Count of Flanders was as far south as Lille or he could not drag himself away from Marieke. Egil examined the knarrs and announced that they were all in good condition, far too good to scuttle. He wanted to keep them but I pointed out that my ambition did not run towards being a merchant prince. Egil was by nature a Norse Irish trader. I sent the merchant ships off; the crews were mainly Flemings and Frisians as I still wanted to display a mainly Danish persona to the surrounding islanders.

Magnus sailed *Little Runa* to England with Aethelwaerd on board; he was back on Roggen in three days and informed me that he had dropped Aethelweard off on the Isle of Sheppey, south of the Thames and that Aethelweard could be in London in less than a week.

I anticipated that the reeve at Dordrecht would have realised by now that Dirk Hammerhand's huscarl had gone missing and send others to find out what was happening; however, I received no notification from the Jansen's of movement on the river and we were still being observed daily from the river banks. I had to assume that we had been observed by another representative of the Count of Holland and that some sort of action had been instigated. I hoped that the absent crews would return before the crisis came to a head; I had to assume that the force the Count of Holland would commit would be in the hundreds possibly up to a thousand men. We had been on the island for nearly three months and summer was on the wane. I did not think that Beornwulf and his crews would return for at least two months; late autumn., the onset of winter. On the positive side the Count of Holland would not be able to assemble a force until after the harvest had been brought in; a close-run thing, maybe Martin was right and we should have scuttled the merchant ships?

Martin ensured that the laying of stakes in the water around the island went on apace, he became less truculent when he realised that he had sufficient stakes to cover the west side of the island and the merchant ships were not needed.

I approved two more raids on the surrounding islands; one raid went as far down the estuary as the island of Rilland and plundered and burnt two farms before a group of islanders came and dislodged them. One man was lost to a spear thrust but the raid did return with two more valuable women and six children, potential slaves for the Ribe market. On the downside no boats were destroyed and there was no sign of any boats on the riverbanks. The second raid was on the north side of Duiveland, a long sail but worth it to create uncertainty about where we would strike next. This time three farms were raided, plenty of supplies were acquired but no slaves. Apparently, the boats were seen by the farmers and they fled into the interior leaving the farms deserted.; again, it was observed that there were no fishing boats along the river banks. I concluded that what fishing vessels we had not destroyed were being assembled somewhere ready for an assault on our fort. I was sure that the severe disruption of the fishing around the islands caused by our depredations was causing concern. The accumulation of smoked and dried fish that would normally be put aside for the winter months had been severely depleted and famine was a possibility.

Life went on as normal in the camp for several weeks, the weather turned bad and storms swirled in from the west. Sea traffic would be severely disrupted and it would be likely that Beornwulf would be delayed. I kept *Hilda* and *Ottar* on the lee side of the island for safety. The bad weather would also damage the harvest and the islanders would be increasingly desperate.

Dietrich was spotted rowing towards the island in a downpour that restricted vision to an area around the island, just the weather that I would contemplate using for an assault. Like everyone else on Roggen who was not on guard I was sheltering. The interior of the camp had turned to a sandy sludge and I wondered how much rain was needed to return the low-lying sandbank to the surrounding waters. Martin came splashing over with Dietrich and we all hunkered down in my upturned boat.

"Well, what has made you turn out in weather like this?" I asked him. Dietrich sat on a barrel looking like a merman rising from the sea, he was covered in seaweed that had clung to his body when he dropped into the sea to drag his boat up onto the beach. I had noticed that the river had washed copious amounts of the stuff up against the island's shore in the last few days. Water was dripping from the end of his nose and there was a pooling of water beneath him as the water dripped from his saturated clothes. I threw him a cloth, "Here, dry yourself."

"Thank you, lord. That was a stiff row." Dietrich grinned totally unsubdued. After Dietrich had wiped the cloth around his face and hair, he looked less bedraggled. Martin picked the weeds from the lad's clothing.

"Well now, tell your tale." I prompted.

"Lord, nothing was to be seen at the farm and I kept a good watch for days. Finally, my father decided to row to Dordrecht to sell fish. There has been a dearth of fish in the markets and they are fetching high prices. My father took two of my brothers to row and me to watch for sandbanks; we didn't sail down the main channel in case larger ships capsized us." Martin gave Dietrich a jug of ale and he took a long draft and licked his lips. "Everything was in uproar along the riverbank at Dordrecht, we tied up and I went with my father to see the port maister. He agreed to take a payment of fish and directed us to where we could sell our wares. However, that was when my brother arrived running. He told my father that there were men down by the boat saying they were impounding it, whatever that meant. We hurried back to the river and there were armed men. They told my father they were taking the boat on the orders of the Count of

Holland. My father protested and said we were no Hollanders but from the Flemish bank of the river and we had come to sell fish. The men said they did not care what or who we were they were taking the boat and that if we complained further, they would take our fish as well. We off-loaded the boat and they took it. My father and my brothers took the fish and sold them in town for a good price but I followed the men who took the boat. They rowed it up the River Maas about half a mile where I saw a great fleet of small boats assembled, I thought, maybe a hundred but there were too many to count anyway, and right in the middle was a huge dragon ship, a snekkja as you call them. On its stem post it had a carved head, at first, I thought it was a dragon but when it swung around in the current, I could see it was a horse's head. I returned to find my father and because it was late, we had to stay overnight in an inn. The next day we had to get home; my father knew there was a ferry further east across the River Waal so we had to walk nearly forty miles to get home. As soon as we arrived at Tonnecreek my father insisted I come and warn you."

"You thought there was maybe a hundred fishing boats; how sure are you?" I pressed.

Dietrich looked flustered. "In truth, lord, I cannot count overmuch but there was a lot. More than any boats I have ever seen at one time and more than twice as many as you have."

"And the snekkja; how big was it, bigger than *Ottar*?"

"It was longer than both your dragon ships, maybe the length of *Ottar* and a further fishing boat length added on." Dietrich tried hard to articulate what he had seen.

"Did you see any armed men camped about the river side?" Martin interjected.

"No, my lord Martin, there did not seem to be any men about, just lots of boats."

"Alright Dietrich, that is enough for now, go and get warm, get something to eat." I dismissed him.

"I am sure there will be a woman that will warm him." Martin predicted.

"Well, we have the news we were expecting. The Count of Holland's men are assembling to assault us. If what Dietrich says if half true then we can expect upwards of six hundred to a thousand men pouring onto the island." Martin added.

I laughed and Martin looked at me puzzled. "What so funny?"

"Can you imagine over six hundred men trying to crowd on to the beach here, it will be chaos."

Martin listened, thought about it, and laughed with me. "I see your point, master."

"The whole of the might of France could not dislodge the viking armies on the Seine or the Loire, so I cannot see the Count of Holland shifting us from here."

Martin and I discussed tactics. We agreed that we needed a day to pull all our raiding boats into the compound and that the larger ships would need to be taken to safety at Bruges by the Sea.

"We need to place our own scout boats out to give us warning and we need to infiltrate Dordrecht, and we need more archers. I want the east beach to be a killing ground."

"We won't have time to fetch bow staves from Ribe and I doubt the Flemish will have any." Martin calculated.

I thought about it, "Arbalests."

"What crossbows?" Martin frowned.

"I am sure they have some in the armoury in Bruges. I seem to remember seeing some when I was shown around by Lady Dedda."

"It might work, arbalests are easy to work and learn to use, the Pope in Rome has tried to ban them but I am sure that is of no matter." Martin grinned.

"Arbalests shoot flat and are as powerful as a Norse longbow at short range, perfect for our east beach. They will penetrate mail and even smash through a shield. I must send Egil back to Bruges to get them. I will not have time to go myself and Egil can round his son Eystein up, he has been away too long."

The next morning, on my instruction, Wighard and two of his chosen crew, all Frisians, set off in the smallest karvi we had to set up a scouting post. It was Wighard's task to infiltrate Dordrecht to give us advanced warning. Their first port of call was to be the Jansen's farm and I had decided that the karvi could hide in the same creek where I had hidden *Little Runa* when we captured the huscarl, Dagling. Wighard would then infiltrate Dordrecht and spy on the Count of Holland's preparations. Dietrich delayed his return to his father's farm and I am sure the females in the women's compound was the main cause; he seemed insatiable and inexhaustible.

I instructed Egil to return to Bruges by the Sea and acquire the arbalests from the Lady Dedda in Bruges as a matter of urgency. I took stock of our situation, I had one hundred and forty-six men, in total, but currently nearly half of them were away selling knarrs and collecting arbalests. I had acquired twenty-four small fishing boats that I chose to refer to as karvis, shallow skiffs useful for raiding in shallow creeks, too many to crew. I had made a mistake, if the Count of Holland's army attacked before my absent crews returned, I would not be able to hold the stockade. Additionally, the response from England with regards to the blackmail for Alftruda was overdue and if Harald Godwinson sent a fleet of English longships instead, I would be caught in a pincer movement, an attack from both sides, however uncoordinated.

My concerns were relieved somewhat when, after a week Egil sailed the *Hilda* around the island and dropped the anchor stone against the lee shore. Within the hour his crew were off-loading fifty arbalests and nine hundred bolts, at two arbalests per man, twenty-five men could discharge fifty bolts, in two waves within ten heartbeats, from prepared and loaded arbalests. Together with my twenty longbow men that would be nearly a hundred missiles before the enemy could run up the beach. Along with the arbalests and extra supplies, Egil had dragged back his son, Eystein from wherever he had been dallying, but best of all Eystein had an additional twenty-two recruits to enhance our forces. He had promised them pay and it was clear that they were mainly churls but I immediately earmarked them as arbalesters; easily trained in the short time I had available.

Prior to the usual evening captains' meeting I quizzed Eystein, he seemed buzzing with news and was definitely a happy man. "Did you deliver my message to the Count of Flanders?" I started the discussion with the pertinent question, the reason for Eystein's journey.

"Yes, my lord. I had to travel to Lille, which took some time. The count was sanguine about your report, apparently, he has some difficulties with the German Emperor over some lands in the east and it would be inconvenient for him to spare an army this year."

"That is good news, I did not want to disappoint him overmuch." I responded, I found that I was quite relieved that one issue and been temporarily shelved. "Where did you get the recruits?"

"The lady Dedda forced several of her peasants to volunteer on the promise of freedom from servitude, that was their so-called payment, but I told them that if they fought well, they would receive a small part of the plunder. I am sorry if I promised them too much."

"You said well, in the forthcoming fight we will lose men and we will be able to pay extra to the survivors. "What other news do you have?" I prompted.

"I heard that the Duke of Normandy had to supress a rebellion, which he did with his usual brutality. No news from England." Eystein shuffled about nervously.

"Well, I can see you have other news, what is it?"

"Marieke has agreed to become my wife." He desperately searched my face for approval that was not there.

"Marieke is my prisoner, not some free maiden to give her hand to whom she pleases. More, her father is also my prisoner and an enemy. How has she agreed to become betrothed to an enemy warrior?" I remained stern.

Eystein struggled with a reply. "I love her and she loves me. I had hoped that you would agree to our union." He paused and took a deep breath. "I had hoped that you would agree to the release of her father after all this is over."

I remained stony faced. "Radbod is an important hostage and he is Hrodhard of Middleburg's nephew. I cannot make such a promise. If Hrodhard attacks, along with the Count of Holland's men I will impale Radbod on a stake above the gate along with is cousin Liudger Hrodhardson." Eystein looked ashen, I could see he was speechless. "Look Eystein, I value your friendship and your father's; I want you to have the girl and if I can I will not kill her father but I cannot make promises. Can I count on your continued loyalty, I must ask?"

Eystein looked horrified, "Of course I am loyal, till death. I will give the girl up if you ask."

"No, you will not, I know, love tests all loyalties. When next I am in Bruges, I will tell her myself that I will not kill her father as a favour to you. If I am foresworn then I will be accountable, not you. Small comfort I know but that is the best I can do."

Eystein looked relieved and went away presumably to speak with Radbod and convey the news in some way, how I could not comprehend. I wondered if Marieke had promised herself to Eystein to save her father?

I immediately set to organising the training of the new Flemish thralls on how to use the arbalests. Of course, one of the problems was that I had no idea how to use one either. I made enquiries in the camp and found a Dane who claimed he had been to Aquitaine in France where he had seen Moors using these simple crossbows. All the crossbows were of the same simple construction, a wooden stave and a wooden bow about a yard span fitted at one end. The cord was pulled back manually to be held by a peg attached to a long wooden trigger through a hole in the stock. Each crossbow had a rope loop attached to the front of the stave so that the archer could place a foot into it when pulling back the cord to the peg nock. The stock had a groove cut into it in which the bolt was placed against the cord when stretched back. The archer then sighted the arbalest and pulled the trigger. I was astonished when I realised that such a deadly weapon could be mastered in a few hours, unlike a sword, axe or longbow that took many years of practice to perfect.

The new recruits were lined up and issued the arbalests, Eystein Whaleleg was placed in charge of them primarily because he was not agile and an arbalest would suit him well. I drafted in a couple of the least effective Flemings that had been with us for a while to make up the full complement. I was not particularly concerned with absolute accuracy, a hit, any hit could disable an enemy, which would be just as useful. I therefore had large bundles of wood erected the height and width of a man. Each Fleming was shown how to use the crossbow and all he was required to do was hit his wooden target, anywhere. After a couple of days, they had learnt not to shoot high and most of them could hit the mark, somewhere; how they would perform under pressure of conflict remained to be seen.

The weather remained poor but significantly the wind was still blowing from the north-east, a precursor to the onset of autumn gales and eventually winter storms. The attack would come soon, I knew it, but with the winds as they were there was still a chance of Beornwulf returning. What was not going to happen was any news from England, but that was a secondary consideration.

We were as ready as we could be, but I desperately needed the return of Beornwulf, Magnus and the *Little Runa*. What a fool I was for splitting my forces. My tension was conflated further by the arrival of one of Wighard's men who rowed in as dusk was falling. He was brought straight to me. Wet and bedraggled he touched his forehead with his fingers as a sign of respect.

"Fenn, my lord. Wighard sent me."

"Sit Fenn, drink and speak." I instructed.

Fenn took a long draught of ale from the jug I proffered. "Wighard came from Dordrecht yesterday with the following news. The army of the Count of Flanders has assembled, Wighard counted one hundred mailed warriors, huscarls, all with shields, spears swords or axes. There are a further six hundred town dwellers and farmers assembled; of these maybe half are from the islands and led by Hagen of Bierren. The men of the islands come from Tholen, Schouwen, Duiveland and Goeree. The rest are townsmen from Dordrecht. All the farmers and townsmen have been given wooden shields and spears, no mail, no helmets. The huscarls have been training them to fight in a shield wall."

"Interesting." I mused. "Who leads?"

"Dirk Hammerhand, a blood relative of the Count of Holland, albeit a bastard. He has a longship with a horse head stem post. And most of the huscarls are his crew. It is a twenty-five bench snekkja, absolutely magnificent, Wighard says." Fenn added.

"When does Wighard think they will come?" I prompted.

"Within the next few days, he thinks they are hoping for the weather to improve." Fenn related.

"Good, Wighard has done well, return and tell him to get out of Dordrecht now."

Fenn left before dawn. Timing was now critical. I had a karvi out on the river watching the eastern approach to Roggen and

379

warned the camp guards to be extra alert. After two days the weather improved, the wind remained from the north-east but had dropped to a stiff breeze; ideal sailing weather. I prayed to all the sea gods for Beornwulf and Magnus to come. For some idle reason I wondered if I should suggest to Christofer to build a small Christian church for men of that persuasion. Whether it was my nod to the higher powers or just luck but by mid-day on the following day my snekkja appeared over the horizon out from the headland of Schouwen island and a sweet as an apple in *Little Runa's* wake was another snekkja. All my men were now assembled and I became confident we could repel the forthcoming assault.

The snekkjas dropped their anchor stones along the lee shore, alongside *Ottar* and I saw Magnus coming ashore in the longships small boat. Such was my enthusiasm I strolled down to the shore to meet him.

"Magnus, it is good to see you back." Magnus clambered out of the small boat and I noticed he had a young boy right behind him.

"It is good to be back, lord. I was worried we would be too late; we had many delays but we prevailed."

I looked out towards the other snekkja, a smart little longship the same size as *Little Runa*. "Where is Beornwulf, I expected to see him rowing to the beach by now?" I asked.

Magnus looked pained. "Beornwulf is dead."

I realised this was a story to be heard in privacy. "Come up to my hut when your men have been settled in."

Later Martin and I sat with Magnus, Eystein and Egil before the usual captains meeting. "Magnus, tell us what has happened?"

"My lord, we sailed around the Skagen and straight into the port and berg of the Geats, three days sail with friendly winds. The merchant ships attracted much interest and Beornwulf negotiated with several local magnates to inflate their price. A deal was struck with two of these local merchant princes and a great deal of silver changed hands. It was then that I perceived a problem, Beornwulf had suborned some of the men and it became clear he expected the crews to join him, take the silver and not return here. His men secretly circulated around the crews trying to gain support and this was when the treachery was reported to me. I took twenty loyal men and confronted Beornwulf, in short there was a fight and men fell on both sides, but I killed Beornwulf and confiscated the silver." Magnus paused for breath.

"Go on." Martin urged.

"All this did not go unnoticed by the authorities in the town and not surprisingly the port reeve came down to the berth where *Little Runa* was tied up. He insisted that we were to remain berthed until the king's men could investigate the incident. I was concerned that the merchants might see this as an opportunity to retrieve their silver and still keep the merchant ships Beornwulf had sold; it was clear Beornwulf had painted himself as the leader of the expedition and that his murder was to steal the silver from him. Just as at Dordrecht, I ignored the reeve but better, I pushed him into the water and put out to sea. We fled north and hauled up in the Vik, part of Norway."

"What of the men, the men from the merchant ships?" I started to worry that I had lost a lot of men.

"Lord, Beornwulf had a dozen followers and they were all killed or fled. The crew of *Little Runa* were, are loyal and the crew of one of the merchant ships was not involved. We have lost twelve men."

"What about this new longboat?" Egil interjected, boats always being his first concern.

"We bought this new snekkja in the Vik for a good price and we have much silver left on *Little Runa*; apparently the King of Norway has laid an embargo on selling warships out of Norway but the jarl who sold us the boat hates Hardrada and did not want the king to get his hands on it. We manned the new snekkja with the crew from the merchant ships and some of *Little Runa's* crew and as soon as the wind became favourable, we sailed for Roggen." Magnus paused for response.

"I never suspected Beornwulf was going to betray us." Eystein commented.

"He was vehement in his belief that the merchant ships should be sold and not scuttled." Martin added.

"It is a salutary lesson for us to learn, all the men with us are here for profit, not loyalty. The treasure we hold in common binds them together and they will fight to keep it but if any one of them see a better profit elsewhere they will take it and when this is over the army will disintegrate into individuals once more." I observed.

After some deliberation I decided to gloss over Beornwulf's treachery to ensure we had a united front for the forthcoming battle.

"Who is the boy, Magnus?" Martin asked.

"Oh! Him; his name is Grub." Everyone laughed. "Well, that is what we call him. I found him grubbing around on the wharf for food. He is my boat boy and he has learnt to cling on to the yard arm in pretty brisk weather and he has eyes like an eagle."

"Right, Martin, call the captains meeting." I ordered.

When all the captains had assembled, I related the circumstances around the trip to Sweden and Norway giving a sanitised version of Beornwulf and his adherents demise. I praised Magnus for his loyalty to the Roggen vikings and assured them that there had been a significant addition to the army's wealth. I asked them to particularly emphasize this to the men.

"Magnus, how is the new snekkja named?"

"The old jarl in the Vik referred to the longship as *Wave Rider*, which seems like a good name to me."

"*Wave Rider* it will remain then." I confirmed, "But, she will not berth here long. It is clear that the Count of Holland's forces will be here within days and I want to safeguard our sea-going ships. To that end all four boats, *Ottar*, *Little Runa*, *Wave Rider* and *Hilda* will be sailed to Bruges by the Sea for safety. They will be manned with skeleton crews under Egil's command and then they will return to Roggen by rowing boat to take part in the forthcoming fight. Only Egil, the boy Grub and two of the older warriors will remain to guard the boats. Meanwhile, the remaining karvis, fishing boats and smaller craft that we have will all be hauled up the beach into the fortification so that they cannot be destroyed. We currently have twenty-four such boats and we cannot possibly man all these boats at one time so we will take the least seaworthy, say eight of them and scuttle them where we normally beach them so there is a ring of underwater wooden hazards around the island." I paused for comments and when none came, I continued.

"All the men have trained hard throughout the summer months in preparation for this confrontation and we are as ready as we can be, I am confident in your skills and ability. It has been confirmed that the army coming against us is in the order of seven hundred men, I say men because Wighard has informed us that there are about one hundred skilled warriors, and six hundred farmers, fisher folk and townsmen. This six hundred are followers that will run towards us or run away as the success or failure of their warlike leaders becomes apparent. So, in real terms our army of just over one hundred and sixty warriors outnumbers their one hundred warriors." At this the captains laughed; they appreciated such imaginative counting. "Finally, Wighard has also confirmed that the farmers and fisher folk have been drawn from the northern islands of the Scheldt estuary, that is mostly those who identify with South Holland rather than Flanders. The islands that associate most with Flanders do not seem to be part of this alliance at the present. They are being led by Hagen of Bierren whose son we hold captive. The day that their boats appear over the horizon Haki Hagenson will be impaled on a stake over the gate of our stockade." I paused. "Any questions?"

As usual there were a few questions designed to clarify specific groups roles, and in this case specifically the role of the arbalesters. I concluded the meeting with what I hoped was a comforting observation.

"It is common military wisdom since the Romans that a smaller number of defenders can successfully repel an army many times their numbers if the defenders are behind a wall, a fort. We can be outnumbered five to one, as we will be, and easily repel our attackers. We will prevail." The captains cheered.

The next day the larger ships were sailed away to Bruges by the Sea and the arduous job of hauling the smaller boats inside the stockade began. Shortly after mid-day Wighard and his two crewmen rowed up to the beach followed by the scout boat and they were guided through the narrow channel that had been left to access the beach.

"They will be leaving Dordrecht tomorrow." Wighard confirmed.

I anticipated that the leader of the expedition against us would not wish to arrive at our beach at any other time than dawn, this probably meant that they would attack the day after tomorrow. However, there was an outside chance that they would sail at midnight and arrive on our beach in the morning. I would not do this as the army would be tired before the attack, but I did not know how rash this Dirk Hammerhand might be. We would be ready whatever.

The enemy did not appear the next morning and I ordered my men to stand down. There was a marked rush to the women's compound with the men satiating their fears through their manhood. I had a last meeting with the captains to ensure there was no misunderstanding regarding our tactics. Christofer the Christian, held an impromptu service, obviously there was no priest to hear confessions, but as I suspected most of the men were semi-pagan and believed equally in the white Christ and Odin. I had the stockade heavily guarded that night and I slept poorly, as I usually did before a battle, not because I was afraid to fight but because I feared that my decisions may be wrong. I noticed many others were restless.

An hour before dawn I had the men assemble along the east side of the barricade with just a token of men on the west side towards the open sea. The archers and arbalesters were to the fore and behind them was a line of spear men. The dawn broke to a mist on a very calm sea; ideal for the attackers. I called for silence and we all listened intently. The mist swirled and suggested shapes looming from the blank whiteness, all mirages. The waves lapped gently on the shore line mimicking oar splashes; the men were becoming agitated. We stood to arms for a third of a watch and gradually the mist lifted twice a man's height, and there they were. Two hundred paces out from the beach a long line of small boats, crowded with men. Dirk Hammerhand had assembled nearly a hundred small boats that came towards the island in three waves. The attacker's problems were exactly as I had envisaged. To attack the east side of the island only, the small boats were pressed together and could not all land at the same time and bring their numbers to bear at a strategic point. Coasting behind the smaller boats was the great longship of their leader, it was a magnificent sight, even with its sail furled. The oars dipped in unison and the horses head on the stem post stood proud. Two men clung to the stem post gazing at our defences, obviously one of them would be Dirk Hammerhand but I could see neither of them clearly.

Gautrek the Berserker pushed up next to me, he carried a javelin and dragged the young, naked Haki Hagenson by his hair; and I could see the javelin's point was covered in blood and had a pair of black bird's wings attached to the shaft beneath the blade. He grimaced at me showing bloodied teeth and held out the weapon and grunted.

"Odin!"

I nodded and took the javelin; it was along cast but I was sure I could reach the boats.

"I give thee to Odin." I shouted. I hurled the javelin with all my strength and watched it fly up over the first line of boats approaching the island. The javelin dipped and hit one of the boats, I could not see if it had struck anybody or just slammed into the wooden hull but that did not matter. The Hollanders and Zealander, whether Christian of pagan knew what the gesture meant; no quarter, no retreat, no plunder, to the death.

My men roared in unison, "Odin."

I turned to Gautrek and nodded, he grinned evilly. Two of his henchmen, Odin's men all, came up with a stake sharpened at both ends; they laid it on the ground with one of its ends braced against the wall. Gautrek hurled the boy captive to the ground and his two henchmen grasped his ankles. Gautrek lined the sharpened stake up between Haki's legs in line with the boy's anus. By now the boy was screaming in terror and thrashing about but the two men were powerful and held him firm whilst Gautrek shoved the sharpened stake up with a powerful thrust. The boy's shriek was almost girlish, high, and shrill. In his fear he voided his bowels over Gautrek's hands and the stake.

"Good boy." Gautrek crooned, "Nothing like shit to lubricate an impaling. Hoist him up lads." The stake was longer than the stakes used for the fortifications and Haki's thrashing torso stood proud of the wall for all to see. Gautrek clung on to the boy's ankles and pulled as the other sharpened end of the stake sunk into the sand. His henchmen lashed the stake to the wall so that it would not fall. I was sure the howls of anguish that emitted from the on-coming boats was Hagen and his sons witnessing the inhuman treatment to his youngest son and a beloved sibling. Blood started to dribble down the stake from the poor boy's back passage.

I set up the chant, the Mercian battle cry, "Ut! Ut! Ut" and started banging the face of my shield with my axe, the men followed suit and the thunderous noise rolled across the water to unnerve our foes. A horn sounded from the longship and the first line of boats increased their blade rate to hit the beach at pace.

I held up my hand and shouted, "Hold! Hold."

As one, the line of boats shuddered to a halt, stopped by an invisible force. Standing men tumbled from the boats into the water, the sound of splintering wood reverberated along the line. Startled rowers looked around them and saw water rushing into their boats around wicked fire hardened points. The wooden stakes had achieved their purpose, at least half of the boats were sinking, men were standing and looking around for a safe means to jump from the boats and wade to the shore.

"Now! Fire!" I yelled and the archers and arbalesters released. The distance was such that any hit could be fatal but most would be just debilitating. Within a few moments the archers had released three volleys of arrows and many of the men on the boats were hit and fell into the water. In the same time the arbalesters had reloaded and sent their second volley with similar results. Of the thirty or so boats in the first wave over half were sinking the rest were milling about trying to find their way through the line of stakes. One boat, by luck, had found its way through the channel that had been left free to access the beach. They rowed nearer to the beach and they stood preparing to disembark. My archers concentrated their fire upon this boat and cleared the deck, none survived the arrow storm. It was obvious that the first wave of boats was manned by unarmoured farmers and townsmen with no professional warriors amongst them. I scanned the water seeing dozens of floating corpses riddled with arrows and the foam had a distinct pink tinge. I estimated that we had killed or wounded half of the men before the rest of the boats pulled back, away from the underwater stakes. Maybe a hundred of the enemy had been effectively eliminated. My men cheered at the confusion of the enemy; it was clear from the horns sounding from the longship that the leadership was pulling back to reconsider their tactics.

I watched as several of the smaller boats clustered about the large snekkja and I could see an exchange of men. After this eight of the smaller boats approached the hidden stakes, the helmsmen swung them in unison broadside to the beach and shields were lifted in what could only be described as a line of small shield walls; ingenious. The boats gently drifted up to the stakes and I could see hands reach down from beneath the shields feeling for the stake points. I knew that hands alone would not be able to remove the stakes but eventually ropes would be brought and the stakes would be removed by rowing them out. This would take time. Meanwhile I saw two more smaller boats, again with shields raised cautiously feeling their way around the stake line, their intention was clearly to circumnavigate the island to see if there was a weak point in the defences. Martin watched them make their way around the island.

For the rest of the day the enemy laboured to remove and float away the stakes to the east beach. I ordered the men not to waste their missiles as with shields covering the work it was unlikely that many would be injured and I did not want to waste ammunition.

My men stood down in shifts to eat and rest while our opponents clustered uncomfortably around on their small boats. I ruminated on the many times such enemies had tried to eject viking raiders from fortification like this, mostly unsuccessfully. By late afternoon the enemy had managed to clear an area about thirty paces wide before they came up against submerged wrecks that were almost impossible to remove. I calculated that this space would allow for maybe ten small boats to paddle, not row in line to the beach. I concentrated the archers and arbalesters on this narrow front. Although most of the day had gone there was still enough daylight to launch one more attack and this was what the enemy leadership obviously intended. This time the small boats were assembled in four lines of ten boats but each boat contained at least one mailed huscarl to lead the less martial men. On the sound of a horn from the longship the lines of small ships paddled forward, shields to the fore and along the sides.

"Hold, don't shoot until they start to disembark when there is more chance of a hit." I shouted. The first line of boats flew forward at speed onto the beach. The huscarls yelled for the men to disembark and for shields to be kept up. Inevitably in the confusion of disembarkment, gaps appeared in the shield walls. "Shoot!" I shouted. The order was repeated along the stake wall.

Arrows and bolts flew across the narrow beach and inevitably found some marks. Some of the crossbow bolts, at this range, burst through flimsy wooden shields and impaled the unarmoured bodies beyond. Men fell, leaving greater gaps between shields.

"Javelins." I yelled. A line of javelins looped over the wooden stake wall and several found their mark. Of the hundred or so men in the first wave fully a third fell at the water line. I admired the huscarls' efforts to keep the farmers and fisherfolk together without them the first wave would certainly have bolted and run. Whilst the huscarls attempted to form the first wave of attackers into a shield wall the second wave of boats banged up against the first row.

To reach the beach the men had to clamber over the boats, already beached across the narrow attack zone. My archers and arbalesters saw their opportunity and directed their missiles on the unprotected bodies of the scrambling men; many more fell. The first line had now formed into a solid shield wall and the huscarls shouted the advance. The line of men advanced steadily towards the stockade wall sixty odd men wide. I wondered how they had worked out they could scale the walls without ladders or break in the gate or walls without a ram. At this point there seemed to be no organised thinking behind the assault.

"Spears to the front." I shouted.

The archers fell back and were replaced by a line of spearmen standing on the rowing chests. When the shield wall reached the stockade wall they were forced to stop, they thrust up with their spears, which were easily deflected by my warriors' shields and then they returned spear thrust for spear thrust. Not many men died, it was all very much prod and slap. The second line of boats had now debouched their men onto the beach and a second shield wall marched across the sand to join the first. There was now upwards of one hundred and sixty enemies clustered against the stockade wall but this did not avail the enemy any gain. I knew I needed to break this group and I had planned for just such a situation. I signalled to a small group of my best axe fighters, twenty-five in all, and we split from the defence and ran to the north end of the stockade where I had earlier had a small gate installed. We slipped through and formed up in a swine array with Gautrek and myself at the apex.

"Odin" I yelled.

We swept around the stockade wall and smashed into the unshielded side of the attackers. Our large Dane axes rose and fell and carved great wounds in the men totally surprised by our attack. The impetus of our charge carried Gautrek and I deep into the melee before us onto attackers totally unaware of our presence. Gautrek screamed and swept his axe in great swaths lopping limbs and slicing through spear shafts like twigs. His mouth was foaming and his eyes bulged with madness, his very appearance terrified the farmers and fishermen who shrank away from him. I was obliged to move away from him as there was every prospect of being decapitated by one of his wild swings, although my move disbanded the head of the swine array the damage had been done. The attackers were streaming away in front of us and others had turned to us to see what was transpiring; thus, they became vulnerable to the archers and arbalesters within the stockade who returned to the wall and rained missiles down at point blank range. Dozens of men fell transfixed, and the untrained farmers and fisherfolk fled regardless of the remonstrances of the huscarls. The scramble to regain their boats left their backs exposed and the archers and arbalesters inflicted terrible retribution upon them. My men held back, not wishing to be hit by our own projectiles.

"Open the gate. Archers out." I shouted.

The third wave of boats had now crowded behind the mass of boats congested two deep against the shore. Men were clambering back onto the boats and screaming for the latest arrivals to get out of the way. My archers ran down to the shore line and whilst protected by my warriors they poured missiles into the backs of the desperate enemy. Interestingly the dozen or so huscarls who had led the first two lines failed to run. My men streamed out of the stockade and surrounded these professionals with a hedge of spears. I ordered up six arbalesters and went over to where the huscarls were clustered, at bay.

"Remember men, these men have been dedicated to Odin and they must die." I nodded to the arbalesters and six heavy bolts were released at point blank range. They burst through the wooden shields and into the bodies of the foremost warriors. The rest, perceiving they had no option, ran forward onto the waiting spears, and died transfixed. The third line of boats withdrew more or less intact but of the first two lines of boats that attacked the island, few survived.

It was now mid-evening and the light would fail soon, too late for another assault. After a short while the flotilla of small craft pulled back and started to row back up-river. The large snekkja turned in its own length and expertly pulled away from the rest of the fleet. I found Gautrek curled up in one of the small boats with bodies all around him. He was covered in blood and his axe was smeared thick with blood clots from blade to stock. I saw he was breathing so I left him, I decided disturbing him was dangerous.

Magnus joined me and I explained what I wanted. "Magnus, these men and all their weapons and clothing have been dedicated to Odin. I want them piled up, use the boats for fire wood. Everything is to be burned or destroyed. Make sure Christofer and any other ardent Christians do not oppose this." He nodded and went to gather men for the task. Later in the evening, in the dark, Magnus came to me. "The bodies have been gathered and a pyre has been raised higher than the stockade wall."

"How many dead?" I asked.

"Of the enemy, one hundred and eighty-two." Magnus proclaimed.

"And ours?" I asked, not really wishing to hear the answer.

"Two dead, ten wounded, they will all live." Magnus grinned in the dark I could see the flash of his white teeth.

"Two!" I gasped astonished.

"You were right about their inability to attack into a funnel allowing only a small number of their men that could be brought to bear."

"Burn them."

The pyre was lit and after an initial struggle to take hold the flames licked up towards the top of the mountain of wood and bodies. Shortly the fire exploded into a huge fireball, coupled with billowing dark and acrid smoke from the wet wood. I was sure the fire could be seen for miles, across all the neighbouring islands and surely to where the much-reduced fleet of Dirk Hammerhand lay licking its wounds. We had to retreat into the fortifications due to the extreme heat, the fire raged all night, the smell of burning bodies gave a sicky sweet smell reminiscent of roast pork. I walked up to Haki Hagenson still impaled on his stake near the gate. He was groaning and hissing in obvious pain, still alive. I picked up a nearby spear and thrust it through his stomach up into his heart. He spasmed and slumped forward; as he rotted, I assumed the stake point would exit from his back.

Gautrek stumbled up, still covered in blood and gore, it was obvious he had just woken. "Bloody soft, you are." He staggered passed me, grumbling. "I need a drink."

We rested the following day, euphoric with our success, but I was actually disappointed with the outcome of the battle, it was not decisive enough. I sent out a scouting boat, which was duly dragged out of the fort and rowed up the river. The men sated their lust on the women in the compound and I called for a meeting of the captains. Ale flowed freely and congratulation were given, all round. I stood to address them.

"I congratulate you all for yesterday's stramash. You all performed as I anticipated you would, a more organised army I could not wish for, even the Flemish peasants." They all laughed. "However, I am disappointed that we have not settled affairs with the Count of Holland and his commander, Dirk Hammerhand. I promised the Count of Flanders that the Zealanders would come 'cap in hand' next year for him to march on us heathen vikings. We need to nail these Hollanders to the mast before the winter closes in."

"More raids then." Grinned Folkar, a noted raider and looter. Everyone looked pleased with that prospect.

"No." I stated emphatically. The smiles faded from everyone's faces; they look confused. I explained. "I do not want to reduce the islanders to complete destitution, I only want to humble them. There must be something left for my friend Robert

391

the future lord of these islands, but to do this they must lose all faith in the Hollanders for aid."

The more thoughtful Coll prompted. "What do you propose, you obviously have a plan that has not occurred to any of us?"

It was my turn to smile. "We are going to raid Dordrecht and destroy it." The faces surrounding me looked stunned, I went on. "Think, the army that attacked us will undoubtably disperse for the winter and Dirk Hammerhand will contemplate a further assault on us in the spring, if we are still here." I pulled them all in. "That just leaves the one hundred or so huscarls that led the assault, or anyway the eighty or so that survived and even some of them will leave for their homes. I have thought on this all night and this is what I propose; we recover our longships and sail into Dordrecht undercover of the dark. Wighard, Dietrich and a few more of our men know the ways into the stream to Dordrecht intimately. We run up against the wharfs and clear them, killing everyone. We must penetrate Dordrecht nearly as far as the church and then fire the town, half of the men must loot the wharfs of plunder because *Hilda* will follow us in and will need filling." At the mention of plunder, I had them hook line and sinker. "If we can do this the Zealanders will lose all faith in the Count of Holland and approach the Count of Flanders next year."

Winter 1059 – Dordrecht

It took a week to assemble the longships back at Roggen, the weather visibly worsened and I was glad that I had the fleet back in the sheltered river mouth. A week of overcast clouds and cold rain crept in from the north and I felt it was imperative to attack soon. I was encouraged to see that the watchers on the islands had disappeared, the inclement weather driving them indoors. I decided it was now or never and assembled everyone before the sun set.

"Men, this is the final battle, we are going to raid Dordrecht and take their wealth. Obey your captains and do not loot until ordered. We are leaving within half a watch."

As usual Eystein would be skippering the *Ottar*, Magnus the *Little Runa* and I gave Coll the *Wave Rider*. Egil would follow on with the *Hilda*, All the boats were fully manned and I had only left the Flemish peasants manning the stockade with Martin. I hoped that the islanders from Walcheren would not take advantage of the fact that the stockade was lightly occupied.

The three snekkjas swept up-river, the helmsmen confident even in the half-light. The dim outline of the islands guiding us into the northern channel passed Tonnecreek and on towards the stream leading up to Dordrecht. We were in the northern channel half a watch passed midnight. I anticipated a short row to the wharves of Dordrecht and slowed the stroke pace. Our arrival was perfect and we glided up against the boats tied along the wooden jetty whilst it was till dark. We went over the side onto the moored craft and then onwards onto the wooden jetty. There was absolutely no one about, no guards, no one working. I split our forces, half stayed at the wharves with Magnus and Eystein and I took the rest with us silently through the streets towards the church square.

The first man we met was a baker who was making is way to his bakery carrying a sack of flour. Gautrek gutted him with his scramaseax and the baker crumpled silently to the muddy street. The next opposition was a young boy who slid out of a window with his pants around his ankles, at least he had a satisfactory illicit liaison before he was speared in the back. I was annoyed because he cried out and this prompted a young girl with tangled blonde hair to look out of the window. Gautrek reached up and grabbed her by the hair and cut her throat, she did die silently and predictably Gautrek was already sheeted in blood. We hurried on and neared the church square and I signalled to the men to spread out and start the fires they had come prepared to start. The thatches were damp and hard to ignite but eventually the steaming smoke turned to small tongues of flame, at the same time cries started to be heard throughout the town. Time to start a panic.

"Kick the doors in and throw in the brands, nothing like a hall burning," yelled Gautrek. The crash of doors being kicked open woke the town with a vengeance. Like bees spilling from a hive people started tumbling out into the streets only to be cut down by sword and axe. The torches thrown into the houses had more effect than the slow burning thatches and within a short while two or three houses went up in flames with a 'whoosh'!

"Stay in the streets!" I yelled; we could not afford to be entangled in the houses. One man rushed out of a nearby house, his mouth a round wet hole silently screaming, wild eyes, his hair smoking. He had a wood axe in his right hand and what looked like a poker in his left. He ran at me but I am not sure he saw me. I sidestepped and punched my scramaseax into his side. He continued running until he bounced off the wall opposite his home and slid on to the floor.

Horns were sounding further into the town and it was time to pull back.

"Fall back." I yelled.

The men around me formed a shield wall across the street, five wide and we stepped back keeping our faces to the church. The men behind me continued to ignite the cottage roofs and anything else that would catch alight. Very soon we were fleeing from a wall of flames; looking down side alleys I could see others of my assault team also slowly retreating towards the wharves. I could now clearly hear the screams of the dying from within the burning houses, Occasionally, a woman or child would run into the street, clothes burning only to die on the point of a sword or scramaseax. By now I was sure that any real opposition could not penetrate the fiery furnace behind us.

I turned and hurried back to the wharves leaving my men to make a slow withdrawal, killing along the way. Back at the wharf Magnus and Eystein's men had broken open the warehouses and were removing the contents. There was plenty of sacks of grain and root vegetables, perfect to see us through the winter; even the piles of wood were useful for fires. Coll had found some barrels of salted dried fish; we took it although I was sure there would be plenty fresh fish around the island throughout the winter months. Surprisingly Coll found a dozen adolescent boys chained up in one warehouse, clearly earmarked for the slave markets further east. He herded them out and onto the plank over the sheer strake of the *Hilda*, I hesitated, we would not have the opportunity to sell them on before winter closed in but, perhaps we could adopt them as boat boys and eventual warriors, who knows; I decided to let Coll take them. Another warehouse had bundles of wool, obviously brought from England, they were little use for us so I had an idea.

"Place a bale of wool in each boat along the wharves and fire them." I instructed.

Before long flames were licking up the masts of the merchant shipping along the river, there was no opposition as my warriors had already killed all the sleepy boat watchmen.

"Back on the boats and pull clear." I yelled, pushing, and ordering a quick retreat. The last disaster I wanted was for my ships to catch alight in the general conflagration.

"Back water, pull." Egil yelled as his small crew worked the long knarr sweeps. My snekkjas slid back out into midstream and waited for the knarr to join us. Looking across the line of the wharves the whole of Dordrecht looked to be aflame but this was misleading as I was sure that the fire was only confined to the area around the dockside streets and warehouses; nevertheless, the damage being done to one of Hollands main trading ports was immense. I was sure that there would be no pursuit as the authorities would be concentrating on fighting the fires, in fact I suspected that many people in the interior of the town and beyond may not even realise the town had been attacked.

The weak morning light had painted the river in low mist as we rowed away. It was still early morning and I intended to make one more strike against the Zealanders before returning to Roggen. Hagen of Bierren had called in the Count of Holland's men to chastise us; he had witnessed his son's impalement before the stockade on Roggen but he still needed to be convinced that no material help would be forthcoming from Holland. The island of Tholen was at the halfway point on the way back to Roggen and I intended to raid it again, but this time my objective would be Bierren itself. I understood from the information extracted from Hagen's son by Gautrek that Tholen was a chieftain's hall some way up Krabbenkreek the water that separated Tholen from the island to its north, by midday I ordered *Ottar* and *Little Runa* to turn east into the Krabbenkreek channel, whilst *Wave Rider* escorted *Hilda* back to Roggen. My two snekkjas with combined crews of a hundred warriors would be more than enough to take on Hagen.

Looking north-east, from whence we had come, I could clearly see the smoke billowing up into the heavens from Dordrecht, I smiled, this would be a warning signal to half of the islands. I was jolted out of my reverie by Eystein at the tiller.

"Hereward, look!" He was looking dead ahead and there it was beating up the channel, blades flashing, Dirk Hammerhand's snekkja.

"Dirk Hammerhand, no less; he must have been with Hagen of Bierren and having seen the smoke he is rushing to Dordrecht." I surmised.

"Stand to!" I yelled. "Eystein, pass on the steer board side." I climbed up on the stern post and yelled across the water to Magnus on *Little Runa*. "Magnus, go larboard, we'll grapple."

Magnus waved back in acknowledgement. We were probably about a quarter of a mile apart but closing fast. The opposing longship did not slow or swerve and was clearly intending to accept our challenge. A snekkja of twenty-five benches would have a full complement of fifty rowers, maybe a dozen to fifteen warriors, the helmsman and captain, sixty-seven fighters in all so we outnumbered them by maybe twenty men, good odds. However, the crew of the approaching longship were professional warriors, well-armed and unafraid, this would be a stark fight. I reached to my bundle of belonging, those that would not fit in my sea chest and pulled my Danish longbow and arrow case out of their seal skin wrapping.

"Archers to the fore; warriors, shields up, protect the archers. First, tenth and twentieth oars ready the grapples. Eystein shield the helm." I made my way casually to the stem post and held my bow high for Magnus to see my intent. Nothing to do now but wait. Eystein would calculate when the oars should be pulled in, it would be a catastrophe if the enemy vessel was able to sheer off our oars and injury a whole side of oarsmen.

The three longships raced towards each other, none wishing to give way. At one hundred paces I decided I would try a shot. The helmsman was masked by the stem post and those men clustered around it so I sighted on the man who appeared to have the least armour. I raised my bow and drew to the stave and realised. At that moment I released, that the other man was an archer as well, he was nocking an arrow as my shaft took him in the neck and he fell back into the belly of the snekkja. I nocked another shaft and waited for an opportunity to shoot the helmsman.

"Steer board oars." Yelled Eystein.

I looked aft and saw that Eystein had two arrows protruding from his shield. I was annoyed because I did not see where they had come from. Within moments we slid alongside the opposing snekkja, I caught a glimpse of the helmsman crouched behind a shield. I drew and released without thought, some of my best shots were made that way. The arrow sped across the rapidly shrinking space between the boats and pinned the helmsman's arm to the tiller. The force of the projectile pushed the helmsman back causing the tiller to swing wildly after him. The enemy snekkja shuddered as it lost way and the stern swung into the path of the *Ottar*.

"Grapples!" I screamed and simultaneously three grapples shot across the intervening space between our snekkja and theirs.

My steer board rowers were now armed and had their shields up ready to attack or repel boarders. The enemy were not slow either, their steer board rowers were also armed and ready. Arrows flew across the intervening space to little avail and I yelled for them to get out of the way. As the grapples held and the two boats became locked together my larboard rowers joined the steer board rowers; two lines of warriors ready to board. From my vantage point at the stem post I could see *Little Runa* glide up alongside the opposite side of the enemy longship. Dirk Hammerhand's men were now at a severe disadvantage. I could see the larboard side crew preparing to receive boarders from *Little Runa*, all with their backs to me. I rapidly nocked and drew another arrow and shot it into the back of a warrior facing Magnus' men. I rapidly shot four more warriors in this way. Someone on the enemy ship saw the damage I was doing and ordered a charge across the sheer strakes. Brave men placed their feet on the sheer strakes and leapt across. Many were met by spear points, several lost their support leg in the traditional viking manner, lopped off by axe or sword. I laid my bow down.

"Archers, shoot at the backs of the men facing *Little Runa*." I yelled. The few archers I had nodded, they clambered on the rowers' sea chests so they could shoot over the heads of their crew mates, I hoped the small number of archers on *Little Runa* were mirroring this tactic.

My crew were repelling the attackers who were finding it hard to gain a footing and it was clear to the enemy command that this deadlock could not be allowed to continue. I had drawn my scramaseax, a good weapon for use in close-quarter fighting, with the intention of leaping onto the enemy foredeck when I saw a giant of a warrior pushing through the Hollanders. He had his shield slung on his back, there was already several arrows embedded in it. He wore over-lapping plate armour; a heavy suit from collar to below his knees, amazingly his head was uncovered, no helmet, very rash I thought. His face was broad and fleshy and he wore a full red beard that covered his chest. The plate coat had half sleeves leaving his forearms bare except for metal plated wrist guards. In his right hand he held a giant hammer, that is the head of the hammer was enormous, brutally heavy but the shaft was shorter than you would expect. My immediate thought was he wielded Mjolnir, Thor's magic hammer. In his right hand he held a javelin. This must be Dirk Hammerhand, I decided, who else would dare accoutre himself in this way.

The giant took a short run and leaped across the intervening gap and crashed into my line of warriors. He slammed forward his hammer and bowled over two men who did not look like they would get up again. Several spears and axes rained down upon him but he skilfully deflected the axes with his javelin haft and the spears glanced off his plate armour suit. He steadied his stance and then swung his hammer in a wide arc connecting with four of my men. It mattered not where he connected with the head of his hammer the sheer power of the blow bowled them over and cast them down; broken shields, broken arms. If the hammer connected with someone's head, he was a dead man. My crew scattered before him and this allowed several of Hammerhand's men to follow him onto the deck of the *Ottar*.

I had to stem this attack; I leapt down from the prow post yelling.

"Make space, give me room."

The giant turned on me, eyes blazing in fury. I had to be quick if he hit me once with the hammer it would be all over. I was glad I did not carry a shield it would have been no use. He was a lot taller than I was, which was not an unusual occurrence for me and for him to, probably. There were no preliminaries, whilst holding his javelin out at me, to hold me at the right distance, he swung up his hammer overhead and brought it down with blistering speed and power. I had no intention of being at the receiving end of the hammer and slid to his right. The hammer slammed down into the wooden planking in the belly of my snekkja splintering the planks. I quickly grabbed the haft of his javelin just behind the iron head and pulled it aside, I then leant in and sliced his exposed arm above his wrist guard. The slice I inflicted with my razor sharp scramaseax went down to the bone, but it was on the back of his arm and did not sever any of the vital arteries. Still there was a satisfactory flow of blood. It must have stung but it did not slow him. He brought his hammer around in a sideway sweep, little power but it brushed me off and flung me into the side strakes of the boat, right under the feet of his supporting huscarls. They were as surprised as I was but I recovered faster and stabbed the nearest Hollander in the groin. He gave a high scream and clutched his abdomen. Fortunately, he screened me from the other attackers and I climbed to my feet just as Dirk Hammerhand came at me again. His tactics did not vary, once again he advanced with the javelin to the fore intending to hold me away so he could crush me with his hammer. This time, however, he swung is hammer at me in a wide arc from his right side towards my left side torso. I either had to jump back or duck. I chose to duck, actually I went down on one knee. The hammer flew over my head; I had to get within the range of the javelin or he could extend it and skewer me. I literally rolled forward and slashed at his legs below his armoured skirt. I connected but felt the impact of iron bracers stitched into his boots. I continued to roll away knowing he would try and stab me with his javelin. I felt a sharp stab of pain as the javelin head caught in my mail skirt, broke the links, and raked my hip. I squirmed away slashing backwards with my scramaseax and as luck would have it severed the haft of the javelin, leaving the point embedded in the planks of the boat. The hammer came after me like a living beast and I had to scramble back pushing away on my backside. My free left hand connected with an axe laying on the bottom planks and I gripped at it. Dirk brought the hammer down in a massive overhead sweep designed to flatten me against the bottom of the boat. I rolled again and the head of the hammer splintered the planks to my right, several splinters peppering my face and pinging off my helmet. The hammer wedged in the deck slightly and this gave me the time to stand up and resume my guard. I exchanged my weapons, preferring the axe in my right hand, the scramaseax in my left.

I needed to end this I was tiring and he did not seem to slow at all. He seemed invulnerable apart from his exposed forearms and his uncovered head. Striking his forearms was not going to kill him, so it had to be his head. I needed him to strike the planking below his feet again but his stance suggested another slantwise blow was coming. I crouched low again, a position unsuitable for a side swipe and he changed his stance to deliver a two-handed overhead blow. As the hammer head was propelled forward, I jumped back, the hammer head crashed into the planking with a resounding crack; being prepared I stepped in and placed my right foot on the hammer head. It was my turn now, quickly I raised my axe and buried the blade deep into Dirk Hammerhand's brain pan.

The giant's eyes rolled up into his head and blood gushed from his nose and mouth, amazingly this did not stop him pushing me backwards and raising his hammer high above his head. He was probably already dead but I knew that if the hammer came down and hit me, I would be dead too. I stepped away and everyone around looked on horrified as the giant swayed and bled out. From somewhere within this giant corpse there was generated a superhuman burst of strength, the hammer flew downwards for the final time and buried itself in the planking in the belly of my snekkja. The planks cracked and splintered and a jet of water shot up into the air.

"Odin's eye! He has sunk my longship." I muttered.

I looked around and Dirk Hammerhand's crew were looking on in horror, their leader was dead. I could see that the crew of *Little Runa* had pushed their way onto the enemy's longship and the mailed Hollanders were fighting on two fronts; many men on both sides had fallen.

"Take the longship." I yelled. "Eystein, get over into that snekkja, *Ottar* is sinking." The bilge underneath the planking was filling with water rapidly and little could be done to save the boat while fighting was ongoing.

I took a run up and launched myself into the late Dirk Hammerhand's beautiful snekkja, As I landed, I managed to bring my axe down on a huscarl's shoulder breaking his collarbone, he reeled away. I swept my scramaseax around to make room but the huscarls were already backing away. I took a chance and shouted.

"Hollanders, you do not need to die, we have no quarrel with you. Stop now and you will not die uselessly for a fallen lord." I hoped they did not have the old Scandinavian and Angle ethic of dying with and for their lord.

A huscarl near me threw down his sword. "I am not one of his sworn men." Suddenly swords were being laid on the decks and sheepish men were stepping away. It would seem that the majority of these huscarls were not Dirk Hammerhand's sworn men; my lips curled with distaste.

Everyone on *Ottar* had clambered over into Dirk Hammerhand's snekkja; no! My snekkja. There were thirty men from its crew still alive, some wounded. Those who would not survive their wounds I allowed their fellow crewmen to send to which ever god them believed in. I had lost twenty-two of my crew and Magnus informed me that he had lost ten of *Little Runa's* crew. These deaths were a significant loss to my small army and was a matter of concern; I did not want the islanders or the Count of Holland to know this so I could not let the Hollanders go free. My men herded the prisoners into two groups, ten were taken onboard *Little Runa* and put to the oars. The rest were split up around the front rowing benches on their own snekkja.

Eystein was looking down at *Ottar*, it had sunk to the sheer strakes and seemed to have found its own level in the water, perhaps it would not sink entirely.

"What do you think, Eystein, can we save her?" I asked. Eystein turned a face streaked with tears; like his father sailing was in his blood and the loss of the snekkja he had sailed for so long was heart breaking.

"I doubt we could tow it as far as Roggen." He lamented.

I thought about it; the situation had not turned out as I had expected but possibly for the best. Dirk Hammerhand had been removed and by all accounts the Count of Holland, himself, was far from warlike and aged. It was now too late in the day and my men to worn and battered to attack Hagen of Bierren and this would have to be delayed to a later day.

"I have an idea. We will tow *Ottar* into shallow water and on to one of the numerous sandbanks around here. I still want to attack Hagen of Bierren soon, when we return to do that, we will try and effect temporary repairs and take her back to Roggen where she can be made as good as new over winter."

Eystein nodded, wiping the tears from his face. Whilst we were talking several of the men had gone over the side and swum the short distance to the mostly submerged *Ottar*. These men grabbed the floating sea chests, which fortunately were constrained within the boat by the sheer strakes that were still proud of the water. These sea chests were floated over to our new snekkja and hoisted aboard. Possessions had not been lost, although most of our plunder was held in trust on Roggen each of the men had some private items, an ivory comb, a silver belt clasp, an armband, these could be dried out and saved. One of the men came over to me with my long bow and sealskin arrow bag, unfortunately all the arrows were missing but they could be replaced. I was sincerely grateful; the bow meant a lot to me and I rewarded the crew man with an arm ring.

Others of my men lined our dead in the centre of our new snekkja, the enemy dead were cast overboard. Eystein was organising ropes around the stern post of the *Ottar* so that the boat could be pulled across the river to the shallows north of Tholen. My men were sorting out their rowing places, a sopping Gautrek clambered over the sheer strake into our new snekkja gripping Dirk Hammerhand's hammer. He looked at me wild eyed with froth and spittle still framing his mouth as he came down from his berserker fury.

"Mjolnir." He mumbled and he scuttled off clutching the hammer like a baby. I wondered, yet again, if Gautrek was worth the trouble, he could break a shield wall, yes, but he was equally dangerous to friend and foe alike and unlike myself he really believed in the old gods. I looked across at the first of the Holland huscarls to throw down his weapons.

"You," I pointed at him, "I would talk with you, come here."

The man rose from his seat and stumbled over, he looked afraid.

"What is your name?" I demanded.

"Finn, my lord."

"This boat, do you know what Hammerhand called it, its name?"

"He called it his mare, *Mare Swallow*."

"What! What sort of a name is that?" I laughed incredulously.

"Apparently Lord Dirk had a horse, a mare called Swallow that was the fasted horse in Holland and in honour of this horse, which died of old age a couple of years ago, he named the snekkja after her; that is why it bears a horse head on the prow post."

"*Mare Swallow*, well I don't like to change ship names, bad luck; I am not much of a horse rider myself but I intend to ride this one." I indicated for the man to return to his place. Eystein was ready and the crew took their places and my new snekkja slowly circumnavigated the sunken boat and took up the slack on the rope. The rope tautened and the rowers took the strain and pulled. *Ottar* came around slowly, laying astern of *Mare Swallow* and gradually the sunken boat moved steadily along behind us. It was only a short row across the sound, especially as the sandbanks soon loomed beneath the surface.

Magnus in *Little Runa* shouted across the water. "Look, an old tree stump, clear of the water surface, over there." He indicated an old withered branch standing proud of the water. "If we put a rope around that stump, we could pull *Ottar* in and onto the sandbank without risking our ships. *Little Runa* has the shallowest draft, I will take her in and put a rope around it." I nodded my agreement.

Little Runa edged into the sand bank and one of Eystein's men threw a rope around the stump; it took a further quarter of a watch to ease *Ottar* onto the sandbank and secure her to the wooden stump. "That will have to do, let's go home." I sighed for the sad fate of *Ottar* and preyed we could return and raise her from the dead.

We reached Roggen in the fading light and if it was not for *Little Runa* accompanying us the arrival of our new longship would have caused consternation. The Flemish peasants had been kept busy whilst we were away and some of the wrecks and stakes had been pulled out of the way allowing for the ships small boats to pass through. *Little Runa* and *Mare Swallow* were tied up against the outer wrecks, next to *Hilda* and *Wave Rider*.

I immediately called a meeting of the captains, large and small boats and gave them a detailed description of the events since *Hilda* and *Wave Rider* separated from *Ottar* and *Little Runa*.

"It is still important that I deal with Hagen of Bierren and I would like to raise *Ottar* from her watery grave, but winter is coming and the raiding season is almost over." I concluded; I looked around for comment.

"Winter will last roughly four months and we have sufficient supplies to winter over without shortages; plus, there is the fishing in the river." Martin explained.

Wighard cleared his throat, "We need more women if we have to winter over here for so long with the men inactive."

"The men will not be inactive," I assured them.

"The few women that we have kept are jaded though, each one gets used a dozen times a day and although most of the men are not cruel, they are suffering." Christofer explained.

"We could pay for some whores from Bruges by the Sea to come over." Gauti suggested.

"A hall burning." Magnus interjected into the discussion.

"Explain." I prompted.

"All the famous hall burnings, Thorfinn at Jarlshof, Burnt Njal, the surrounding men allowed the women to come out before the hall was destroyed by the fire. If we commit a hall burning at Bierren we could take all the women as slaves and still kill Hagen and his sons."

"Does anyone know how large Bierren is? Hagen has five more sons; I doubt they all live in the one hall." I posed the question.

"We lost men in the fight with Dirk Hammerhand, how many men would we need to take Bierren?" Coll asked.

"I had intended to raid it with two snekkja crews, a hundred men, to be sure we could take all three snekkjas but that would leave the fort seriously weakened and we have already taken that risk once." I explained.

"I doubt it would be a major risk if we waited until mid-winter to raid Bierren." Martin suggested.

"That would be too late for *Ottar* to be rescued." Eystein interjected worriedly.

"Retrieving *Ottar* and attacking Bierren need not be simultaneous, if we save *Ottar* now it may suggest to the men of Tholen we are not interested in raiding them over winter." Egil suggested.

"I will think on this." I stated. "Martin, how have the Flemish peasants that the Lady Dedda sent us performed?

"Well, as you know they were resolute in repelling the attack on the fort here; their arbalest skills made a significant impact and they probably killed as many of the attackers as anyone else. Whilst you raided Dordrecht they have worked hard. I fed them well but denied them access to the women. There only fault was an accident of birth, given the opportunity and training they will become effective warriors."

I looked around the group," What say you?" Some of them looked uncomfortable but none spoke up.

"Good, I intend to raise them up from thraldom and offer them full membership to our viking band."

Christofer nodded enthusiastically. I continued.

"They will receive a reduced part of the plunder commensurate with their contribution and will be trained." I hesitated, "Christofer. Call all the men after the evening meal, I know it is late but I need to explain my plans to them."

The men assembled by torchlight and I stood on a barrel to address them.

"Men! Roggen vikings." They cheered, all of them. "We have had a great victory." They cheered again. "We repelled the Count of Holland's forces and gave them a bloody nose. We have raided Dordrecht and burned half of the town, a deed worthy of our viking ancestors. Finally, we took Dirk Hammerhand's snekkja and killed the bastard." More cheers. I paused. "We lost good men across the longships' boards and we mourn them." Silence, they did not like being reminded of this. "But we have gained stark comrades who stood with us against our enemies. The Flemish peasants sent to work for us have become formidable arbalesters, I offer them their freedom from their thrall status and invite them to become full brothers." This time the Flemings cheered vociferously but it seemed that the decision was popular with all. "Men! We are moving into winter and our raiding will be reduced severely, it will be boring for the next few months but you will fish, train, and waste your seed on women." Some groaned, some laughed but the announcement did not elicit dismay. "Eystein has been distraught since *Ottar* left him to go swimming but I have promised him that we will return her to his loving care before full winter sets in." More cheers, Eystein was popular. "Finally, I believe that in the spring the need for the Roggen vikings to be here on this island will come to an end. I hope some of you will stay with me on my next adventure, but then will be the time when our plunder will be apportioned and you will all be rich men." The cheering broke out again, all was well. Our dead were then burned on the beach where they had been piled upon a wooden stack.

A great deal of repair work had to be undertaken both to the stockade and the ships. The smaller boats were dragged out of the stockade and beached; at least half a dozen went out into the river each day fishing and our food stocks were replenished accordingly. The stakes in the front of the stockade where the assault had taken place were reset and embedded firmly. Eystein and Egil worked on the retrieval of *Ottar*, their thinking was that they would take a sail and tie it around the hull of the foundered boat pack the fractured planking from the inside and then bail the boat out until it gained some floatation. With continuous baling this would allow the boat to be towed to Roggen and beached for repair.

"The water is cold and getting colder, the sooner this is done the better." I observed.

Martin came to me and suggested we should talk about our prisoners. We currently had our original prisoner Radbod Gewerson the nephew of Hrodhard Chief of Middleburg, his daughter, Eystein's betrothed, Marieke was in Bruges, his cousin Luidgar Hrodbardson, these three were still valuable and would be preserved. Haki Hagenson was still rotting, impaled on his stake above the gate. Dagling the huscarl from Dordrecht did not seem to have any value now that Dordrecht had been burned and his master Dirk Hammerhand slain. Then there were the three prisoners awaiting ransom, Alftruda, Duncan and Aedh; it was now obvious that a ransom would not be forthcoming before spring. Finally, there was the group of Hollander huscarls, I had promised them life but they were now an inconvenience unless they could be persuaded to join us.

"Well Martin what do you suggest?"

"If winter wasn't coming, I would recommend they all be taken to the slave pens in Ribe, but winter is imminent and rescuing *Ottar* from the shallows takes priority. They are a burden upon our food stocks but we cannot let them go because if they have not worked it out yet they will soon realise we are colluding with the Flemish and are not the independent viking force we have been at pains to present to the islanders."

I could see that a hard decision needed to be made and it fell upon my shoulders to make it. "I will give them the opportunity to join us, any that do will be released from the compound but remain unarmed until they prove themselves. Those that refuse I will have executed."

"Now what about the two Scots and Alftruda, the Saxon girl?" Martin asked.

I had thought on this, "Martin, as I understand it these two boys are the sons of Donald Ban, the brother of King Malcolm of Alba, but they are in rebellion as their father had made a bid for the Alban throne and failed. I want to release them as they may cause more trouble to King Malcolm than can I, but they will have to wait for an opportunity to return to Alba, so for the time being they stay with us. The girl Alftruda is clearly not worth a ransom, either that or Harald Godwinson has been unable to send it to us because of inclement weather or other circumstances. I am inclined to hand her over to the Count of Flanders, he may be able to use her."

I sent Martin off to get men to bring the Hollanders to me, the bedraggled group were eventually brought before me all with hands tied and roped together in a line.

"Listen to me and listen well. Your lord is dead, you have no lord to protect you. I give you a choice, join us, share in our good fortune. Serve me well and you will be at liberty. When we sail away from here in the spring you can sail with us and live a free life. The alternative is not certain, you are prisoners, less than thralls, who live a life unbound. Who knows what fate could dole out to you if you choose not to join us? Think on this, if you want to be free you can swear homage to me as Dirk Hammerhand neglected to have you swear to him." I left them with Martin and went to take my ease, a leisure I had not had recently. After a long wait Martin eventually came to me.

"Better than I had hoped, two thirds of these men will join us, many through fear, some because they had no allegiance to the Count of Holland or Dirk Hammerhand. In fact, most of them are not from Holland but further north in Frisia. The ten men that have refused to swear fealty to you are from Dordrecht and believe that they owe Holland their service. They do believe that you will not kill them." Martin looked grave.

"I have little choice Martin; I know I told them they would not die but I did not promise them freedom. I have decided that they will be blinded and have their tongues cut out. Most will die, those that survive will be the most miserable of slaves. Get Gautrek, he no doubt has a pagan ritual for this sort of butchery." I returned to the shackled men and sat on a barrel before them.

"You men who have agreed to join us, know this, I am Hereward Leofricson, called the Bearslayer. I am an earl's son from England and friend of Robert the son of the Count of Flanders and I am here to chastise the Zealanders. It is right you know who I am if you are to swear loyalty to me, we are not viking raiders. Each of you will kneel before me and place your hands within mine and swear homage. If you foreswear me, it will mean death, your death."

Each man who had chosen to swear loyalty to me and mine, led by Finn, came forward and knelt before me. I placed my hands around each of their hands held in prayer and they repeated the oath of allegiance as Martin recited. After each oath taking the prisoner was cut free and taken to a large cauldron of stew, given a hunk of fresh bread. They were to receive better clothing than their own ruined apparel.

I was left facing the ten men that defiantly refused to come over to us. "I promised you that you would not die when you surrendered and I will keep my word but I cannot release you. You now know who we are and why we are here, this fact cannot be spread from this island and here you will remain. Know this, I do not intend my men to spend their time shepherding you so you must be neutered. You will be blinded and have your tongues removed and you will work as the meanest slaves until your miserable lives end." I finished to a chorus of groans and protests, cries of alarm and fear. I turned and nodded to the grim Gautrek, who with several savage henchmen moved forward and grappled with the prisoners. They were hustled away to a fierce fire that Gautrek had engineered, several daggers were already molten hot buried within the flames. I had no wish to watch the terrible tortures that were going to be administered by my order but a judge should be prepared to witness his decisions so I walked over and with a stony face watched as Gautrek applied the white-hot blades across each of the struggling prisoners' eyes. The screams were feral, animalistic and I noted that Gautrek blinded the poor souls before he severed their tongues from their roots. The screams obviously satisfied his bloodthirsty demeanour.

I heard Gautrek mutter, "Odin gave an eye for wisdom, how wise will these men be now."

The new recruits who had just joined my band of vikings blanched at the tortures meted out on their erstwhile brethren. I hoped it would make them wary of betraying me. I indicated to Eystein I would speak to him in private, we wandered out of the gate to where the small raiding boats were being cleaned and checked for leaks.

"Eystein, yet again I need someone to travel to the Count of Flanders and appraise him of the situation, you he knows well now, will you do this for me?" Eystein nodded enthusiastically, he saw Marieke in his mind's eye. "Eystein, the count may not be overjoyed about what we did to Dordrecht so your task is not without risk. You must explain to him it was necessary to eliminate Dirk Hammerhand and Dordrecht as a centre of resistance to achieve his objective." I explained; this did dampen Eystein's enthusiasm somewhat. I went on. "I also want you to impress upon your Marieke that by marrying you, you will bring about a solution to this conflict." Now Eystein looked genuinely puzzled. "Consider, if you marry Marieke, you are changing the course of your life forever. Your home, if you have one is in Ireland, Vedrafjiord. With Marieke your home will now be Flanders, probably Zealand. You will have to reach an accommodation with Marieke's father and Hrodhard. I cannot, I have already killed one of Marieke's uncles and hold the other prisoner. You will go to Radbod before you leave and offer to betray me, you will tell him that for his blessing and agreement for you to marry Marieke you will go to the Count of Flanders and persuade him to rescue Zealand from the Roggen vikings. I am sure he will agree, when you have achieved this, you must go to Middleberg and win over Hrodhard. Return here in the spring, you will be a great thegn in Zealand and owe homage and fealty to the Count of Flanders. The future of the islands is what you can make of it. Now go and speak to your father about this."

Eystein stumbled away, struggling with the burden I had placed upon him. I was asking much of him to appear as a traitor to his brethren but in truth I could see no other way for him to gain his desires. Later that evening Egil came to me and we discussed the situation frankly. He was clearly not happy that Eystein was set on marrying Marieke and realised that it would lead to a long road of heartache and pain.

"Why could he not have married a good Norwegian girl like my Hilda, she was stout and merry, never refused me and accepted the good times and bad equally stoically. A wife fit for a Norseman, not some silly, unskilled Flemish girl."

"Egil, he will become a great lord in Zealand, own a large hall and several farms. He will not be a sea rover like you but he will put down roots and men will not even know of what we have planned."

"So be it." Egil went to sit on *Hilda* and thought about his dead wife.

Eystein went off on one of the smaller fishing boats to be dropped off on the coast of Flanders; he took the unsullied girl Alftruda with him. Within days I set out east on *Mare Swallow* with *Little Runa* and *Wave Rider* in our wake; Egil accompanied me as he had no intention of anyone other than himself coaxing *Ottar* back to the surface of the river. Only the crew of *Little Runa* rowed armed and ready for war, Magnus was to be our guard against unexpected attack whilst the crews of *Mare Swallow* and *Wave Rider* worked on raising *Ottar*. It was a comfortable row up-river for the seasoned crews. I scanned the banks of the surrounding islands but could see no watchers, but I knew they would be there.

Ottar was still marooned in its watery grave and did not appear to have moved or been tampered with. Probably the nearby islanders assumed that it was sunk and useless and maybe it was but we were here to find out. *Wave Rider* edged up alongside the fore post of the submerged boat and lashed it fast to their stern post. Egil brought *Mare Swallow* along *Wave Rider's* open side and tied on fore and aft. My crew climbed across *Wave Rider* and both crews lowered themselves across into *Ottar* clinging to the sheer strake. Many leather buckets were then passed down ready for bailing. Finally, Egil and his chosen swimmers manhandled an old rolled up sail across the boats and into the water alongside where I indicated the damage to the bottom planks was; part of *Ottar's* keel was aground but I hoped that there was sufficient keel length that was not grounded under which the sail could be dragged. The swimmers lashed the length of the sail to the oar holes, unfurled and rolled down the sail under the water. The other side of the sail already had ropes attached, which were to be pushed under the keel to the opposite side of the boat. Another line of swimmers spread out waiting for the word to swim down and locate the protruding ropes. The swimmers went down and there was a good deal of kicking and churned water.

The floor of the river was muddy and black and the silt was soon swirling about, reducing visibility. After several attempt the swimmers needed to rest and let the water clear. After a while they tried again, and again. Exhaustion was setting in so Egil rotated the men. Eventually they were satisfied they had forced the ropes under the keel far enough to be grabbed from the other side and brought to the surface. The second part of the process went much easier, the ropes were located by the swimmers and brought up to eager hands. All along the line of the sail the men pulled on the ropes and eventually the heavy wet sail appeared above the water. It was pulled taut and lashed to the oar holes again, the whole sail was like a cradle that *Ottar* rested in and although wet, the sail would prevent the water seeping into the hull faster than it could be bailed.

All the men of the crews now bailed with a will using the leather buckets and anything else they had to hand. With sixty or more willing hands a noticeable difference had occurred after a whole watch bailing. After the first initial enthusiasm had waned, Egil sorted the men int two groups who took turns to bail or rest and in this manner, progress was made. Eventually the belly of the snekkja became visible and the loose planking was removed, exposing the ballast stones. These were hastily thrown over the side exposing the damage to the bottom strakes. Two strakes to the larboard of the keel were broken in two and the men set to pack the cracks with sacking. Once the ballast had been removed the bailing went on a pace.

I yelled down to Egil. "We should be towing *Ottar* away now, or we will lose the light before we make Roggen; leave ten men aboard to keep bailing." Egil nodded and the men made their soggy way back to their posts. The ropes holding *Ottar* to *Wave*

Rider were realigned and rigged so that *Mare Swallow* and *Wave Rider* pulled upon *Ottar's* stern post equally. The reduced number of rowers on *Mare Swallow* meant that the two longships would pull evenly making *Ottar* run true with the minimum of wallowing. It was a long row back to Roggen and *Little Runa* idled along behind on quarter sail. As we eventually approached Roggen several of the smaller boats were rowed out to bring the *Ottar* up to the beach whilst the larger ships threw the anchor stones and tied up to some of the stakes. Ropes were passed around the stern post from the beach and after we had disembarked lines of men were assembled to drag *Ottar* up onto the beach and careened, exposing the damaged strakes. The sail was cut away revealing the damage that one iron hammer wielded by a maniac had inflicted.

Egil went down on his knees and examined the hull meticulously. I stood awaiting his verdict. "The two strakes will have to be replaced and all the clinkers repacked as they have sprung in several places. We do not have wood long enough for two bottom strakes so we will have to take shorter ones from one of the fishing boats and patch them in, it will not be perfect but it will serve. Fortunately, we have all winter to repair her and make a good job of it." Egil explained.

I was satisfied with this solution and left Egil to select a team of our best carpenters, men from Ireland and the Hebrides. The Flemish and Frisians were useless when it came to boat building and repairs. Winter crept in upon us, iron grey skies, blustery cold winds freezing rain. Apparently, it rarely snowed along the coast of Zealand and the tidal reaches of the river certainly would not freeze over. I was concerned if storms blew in from the north or west and overwhelm the island. I was confident that the boats were sufficiently sheltered to be safe.

For days on end the men practiced their skill at arms and I with them. Egil and his team laboured on *Ottar*. Food was plentiful and fishing in the river was bountiful and entertaining, there were multiple varieties of fish, all salt water as the tide penetrated far inland up the Scheldt. Water still had to be imported from Flanders and sometimes it was in short supply when the weather was particularly bad and preventing the short row being risked. The one cow we had did not provide sufficient milk but although I liked a cup of milk, I was amused to learn that not many of my colleagues were keen. We had plenty of hard cheese but none soft so the milk was used mainly for that purpose.

It was observed that gradually fishing boats were seen on the river further up-steam, desperation taking the place of fear of us. The lack of food in the farms and villages where our raids had taken place in the summer must be acute, which of course is what I intended. The weather became steadily worse and most of the men were reluctant to crawl out of their makeshift houses. Finally, as Yule approached a light smattering of snow cloaked the island and the surrounding islands. I called the captains together.

"Now is the time for us to raid Tholen. Hagen of Bierren will be preparing for the Yule celebration, food, drink, and ale will be gathered in, friends and neighbours will be invited. Hagen will deliberately wish to raise the hearts of the islanders and fortify them to continue the resistance against us. We must strike just before the Yule feast." I announced.

"That is good." Magnus added. "The snow will be worse inland and most people will be indoors, our approach, if executed properly, will go unnoticed.

"I figure we have two weeks before the Yule gatherings, so we need to plan now." I added.

"Will we take the snekkjas or small boats?" Egil asked, his concern was always for the ships.

"I am undecided." I announced. "The smaller boats will be easier to conceal but will take longer to reach Tholen. We must travel after dark and surround Bierren after everyone has bedded down for the night. It is twenty or so miles to Tholen, half a watch in the longships, up to a full watch in the smaller boats."

"The longships then; I will stay and guard them with a few chosen men." Egil suggested.

"Fetch Finn." I ordered Coll. The Hollander was brought into the circle looking frightened. "Finn, you have been to Bierren with Dirk Hammerhand." I stated. "How far up the inlet where we encountered you does Bierren lay?"

"Only about five miles." Finn responded clearly eager to please.

"Describe Bierren to me." I demanded.

"There is a large hall, maybe a hundred strides long. There are also several smaller cottages surrounding it that accommodate some of his sons and their families. There are also several barns for pigs, cattle and goats, his thralls also sleep in the barns. The settlement also has a windmill for grinding wheat that apparently is grown on the island further east. All the buildings are thatched." Finn outlined in detail the layout of the settlement.

"How many men does Hagen have that he could call upon to fight?" I queried.

"In truth lord, I am not sure. I saw his sons, five I think, they certainly would not have children old enough to fight. I think he may have up to thirty thralls and a dozen freemen." Finn trailed off.

"Good, thank you Finn you may go now." I dismissed him and turned to the captains.

"In twelve days from now we will leave in the three snekkjas well after dark, say half a watch. We will beach a mile away from Bierren, Finn will guide us, and approach stealthily and surround the settlement. We will approach in the dark and on my signal set light to the hall. Men will be detached to deal with the smaller cottages, the barns, windmill, and thralls will be ignored until later." I paused.

"We will need to take combustibles to stack against the hall doors and walls, best soaked in seal oil." Egil added.

"Can we trust Finn?" Folkar expressed the fear most of them felt about the cowardly Hollander.

"A coward is unlikely to betray us." Magnus commented grimly.

"I agree." I said with a note of finality.

Since their mutilation, of the ten Hollanders subjected to the torture, six had died of wound fever and shock. Now the plan had been determined upon everything became bustle and purpose. We still had several woollen bales stored that could be used as flammables and they were duly soaked in seal oil. Many of the wood timbers that we had were chopped down to kindling size and bundled. Every warrior would be responsible for carrying a

415

bundle of firewood. All the wood was placed next to fires to help them dry out; we needed the wood to ignite quickly.

On the day of our departure, we loaded the snekkjas throughout the day and saw to our weapons and mail. Martin expressed a wish to accompany the expedition and so Eystein Whaleleg was left in command of the camp. The mutilated slaves were shackled and the comfort females confined. I left the Flemish peasants with Whaleleg but I did not anticipate an attack on the island in mid-winter. The men consumed a hearty fish stew laced with onions, turnips, and carrots, it was heavily laced with salt as sea fish stew is wont to be, but this enhanced the taste. Some fresh bread had been baked on stones that morning and chunks of bread were dipped in the juices as a further filling. I was pleased to note most drank sparingly.

Near the middle of the first night watch, I led the men down onto the beach and we embarked. I had placed a few of the newly acquired Hollanders of doubtful loyalty on each snekkja, Finn accompanied me on *Mare Swallow*.

"Cast off." I instructed Gauti who was skippering *Mare Swallow* and he ordered men to untie the snekkja from the stakes and haul up the anchor stone. The steer board rowers backed oars and the larboard rowers pulled and *Mare Swallow* swung around pointing its horse's head stem post east into the darkness. Although there was no wind Gauti ordered the sail raised to provide a pale off-white marker for the following snekkjas to follow. Magnus duly brought *Little Runa* into line astern and unfurled his sail, I was sure that Coll mimicked Magnus' manoeuvre with *Wave Rider*.

We rowed due east for well over a quarter of a watch at a steady stroke, Egil stood with Gauti and suggested that we slow down as we approached the inlet leading up to Bierren. I had the crewmen with the sharpest eyes at the prow scanning for the first sight of Tholen. Fortunately, the river did not harbour any hidden rocks, just sand banks that we could easily push off from, if we ran aground at a slow speed. Ref the sharp-eyed, held up his hand, I walked forwards and joined him of the foredeck. He was leaning out holding the prow post.

"What do you see Ref?"

"I see the faint line of the island ahead, two maybe three hundred paces." Ref stated in a quiet voice. Sound travelled far over water in the quiet of the night.

"Can you see the way up to Bierren?" I urged.

"The land drops away to the larboard, Lord. I think that might be the way in." Ref did not sound sure.

I made a gesture back up the ship to Gauti to put the helm over to larboard and I saw him lean into the rudder arm gently over to the steer board to bring her round. *Mare Swallow* edged around until the prow was three points to the larboard of where I believed the entrance to the sound leading up to Bierren to be. We continued slowly and I checked to see if *Little Runa* and *Wave Rider* had turned in our wake and was reassured to see both helmsmen making the adjustment to their course. *Mare Swallow* glided silently across the water at a very slow pace until the land slipped away. I walked back to the stern and joined Gauti.

"Turn into the down-stream current."

Gauti put the steering board hard over and the snekkja turned due east into the current. The rowers would feel the increased resistance and would need to pull slightly harder to maintain way, but I was in no hurry. The bank of the river, hopefully the sound leading up to Bierren, was now visible on our steer board side about two hundred paces away, the stars indicated due south. Magnus and Coll brought their snekkjas up close to the *Mare Swallow*. I indicated to Finn to stop rowing and join me at the prow, one of the additional crew took his place without fouling the oars and Finn walked up the centre planks and stood next to me looking out into the gloom.

"How far have we to go before we near Bierren?" I queried. Finn looked back at the mouth of the inlet we had entered, he was obviously calculating the distance, speed of the boats and scanning the shoreline.

"You need to row another two or three miles up this inlet and then look for a flat bank to tie up to, I think that you will then have a walk of maybe one to two miles to the hall." Finn responded.

"Not just us Finn. You will be with us all the way and at the first sign of treachery." I placed my hand on the hilt of my sword and smiled beatifically. Finn blanched.

My three snekkjas rowed on through the night keeping well clear of the shallows. Eventually Finn indicated that the snekkjas needed to be run up the bank at the first convenient place. I signalled to Gauti to bring *Mare Swallow* in closer to the bank, by this time only three rowers were pulling each side of the boat, I grabbed a spare oar and prodded the water at the prow of the boat seeking the bottom, the river bottom shelves quickly and very soon I was prodding the river bottom at a depth that was marginally deeper than the keel of the boat.

"Steady, back oars, Gauti, bring her around bow into the river bank." *Mare Swallow* swung around as Gauti pushed the helm hard over. "Pull now." I ordered the oarsmen and the snekkja nosed into the river bank, its keel digging into the river bottom until *Mare Swallow* came to rest six long paces from the river bank.

"Reef the sail." Gauti ordered in a measured voice, no time for shouting now. I signalled to Magnus on *Little Runa* to run in alongside us and shortly after the three snekkjas lay side by side wedged into the river bank.

"Egil tie up all three boats to the bank. Our gang plank should just about reach the bank so that we can disembark without getting our feet wet."

All three snekkja crews ran out their planks from their bow sheer strake and lashed them in position; carefully balancing in the dark I stepped down the plank fully armed with my shield slung on my back, sword sheathed at my side, scramaseax strapped at the back of my waist belt and carrying my large Dane axe. I wore my mail with my ventail hanging loose and my helmet tied to my belt by its chin strap.

Gauti came right behind me dragging Finn along. Finn of course not armoured or armed, I would have respected him more if he had begged me for a sword. Magnus and Coll led their men off the ships and the inflammables were thrown overboard by Egil's team. Each man picked up a bundle, which he had to carry to Bierren; it was going to be an uncomfortable night march. It took a while for everyone to form up, we were to march in pairs and the man behind had to be up close to the man in front so as no one became lost.

My crew went first, then Magnus and the crew of *Little Runa* with Coll and the crew of *Wave Rider* last. Finn was next to me at the front and we set off at a steady pace, I calculated that it was about midnight and that any feasting at Bierren would be winding down by now. Tholen, like most of the islands in the Scheldt delta was devoid of large trees, there were large bushes that thrived on wet and waterlogged ground and plenty of reeds and flora that did well in water and thankfully there was wide meadow land, wet but easy to cross if you did not put your foot in the icy puddles. A line of large shrubs and small willow trees marked the line of the riverbank and we marched parallel to the water making steady progress. The white blanket of snow illuminated our way and made the walking easier. Ice sparkled on the bushes giving an ethereal aura to the landscape. It took a quarter watch to walk the two miles to a wide path that showed up like a silver ribbon in the moonlight that ran from the water's edge into the interior.

"This is the path from the wooden jetty that we tied up to when I came here with Lord Dirk, it leads directly to Bierren, maybe a quarter mile south." Finn confirmed.

"Good, we move on Bierren up the path, until we see it. Gautrek, take two men up ahead of us and eliminate any guards, silently. You understand, silently." I gave the berserker a meaningful look.

He passed his bundle of inflammables to another warrior who staggered under the weight of two bundles. He chose two other men who also divested themselves of their burdens and all three went off ahead, disappearing into the gloom. I went over to the man Gautrek had given his bundle to and took it off him. "One lot of firewood is enough for any man." I smiled at him.

"Thank you, lord, but I can manage."

"I know you can, but that does not make it fair. I will carry the bundle."

We moved off walking down the path that was quite clear in the moonlight. We had not walked far when Gautrek returned along the path, we all stumbled to a halt.

"The hall is up ahead, it is big and there is a lot of buildings around it, some are clearly barns and one is a smithy, I can see embers burning. No guards." Gautrek grinned mirthlessly. "Probably dogs though."

"Gauti, fetch Magnus and Coll up here." I instructed. "Martin is the flint still dry?"

Martin dug in his wallet and pulled out the bundle of flints and dry wool fleeces. "Yes, master."

"Good." Magnus and Coll came up to the head of the column with Gauti. Gautrek explained the layout of the settlement.

"Right, this is what we do. Gauti and I will proceed down this path with our men, we will surround the main hall and lay the bundles of wood against the doors and walls. Magnus, you will direct your men to surround the other cottages and lay your bundles against them. Coll your men will follow my crew in and lay your firewood bundles around the main hall and then move back to act as a reserve force to move on any unforeseen development. Martin, you, and Gauti are to go to the forge, kill anyone there and bring some shovels of embers to the main hall, they will ignite the firewood quicker than flints. Before we move off, Martin hand around the flints to Magnus and Coll." I looked around at the faces of each captain, they all appeared confident. "Any questions?" None. "Right, we go."

I moved off at the head of the column and very soon the outline of the hall came into view. It was a big hall and I could see the shape of carvings on the apex of the roof. There was no stockade, only a water filled ditch with a wooden plank bridge across it. I led the men across the bridge as silently as possible. I could hear snoring emanating from the hall, I spread my arms as a signal to spread out and the men silently filed passed me right and left. Inevitably someone tripped over a tool or something in the yard making a racket. At once a couple of dogs started barking from within the hall.

I signalled the men to rush in to the walls and lay the faggots.

"Gautrek, hold the door." Someone from inside the hall shouted for the dogs to be quiet, and the dogs stopped barking momentarily. However, as soon as the click, clack, of the wooden faggots being laid along the hall walls began the dogs started barking again and this time more frantically. Martin came up with a metal bucket full of glowing embers.

"Cast them on the faggots, Martin." I ordered.

I could hear movement in the hall now, grumbling beneath the manic barking and growling being emitted by more than two dogs now. The embers fell on the oiled faggots and caught remarkably quickly. Martin ran along the length of the hall dropping embers as he went. The large door of the hall creaked open, pushing the already burning faggots away. I man stood silhouetted by a dim light burning somewhere behind him. Gautrek stepped up and shoved his sword straight into the man's stomach. The Zealander did not even cry out in pain, he just folded up clutching his stomach and collapsed on the floor. Almost immediately two large hounds jumped over the dying man straight at Gautrek. They both jumped at him simultaneously and such was their weight and ferocity that they bowled him over. He fell under his shield and the dogs scrabbled with their claws on the wooden boards, the dogs snarled and growled, teeth bared trying to get round the shield edges. Meanwhile several of my men ran up and started hacking at the dogs with their swords. I took my Dane axe and pushed aside the men and brought the axe blade down on the nearest dog severing its spine. Meanwhile the other dog was speared and tried to crawl away only to be hacked to pieces. The dogs' yelps and whines were piteous. I looked around and took in the scene. The settlement was illuminated like day now. Fire roared up the sides of the hall and I could see several of the other cottages catching alight. I went to the main hall door.

"Hagen! Hagen of Bierren. Do you hear me?" I kept shouting until a man armed with a sword and shield burst out of the door, before he reached me two of my men took him in the sides with spears, he fell in front of me and I brained him with my axe.

"Hagen, do you hear me, was that one of your sons I have just slain?" I looked at the roof of the hall and could see a mixture of steam and smoke curling around the eaves. The roof was drying out and would soon ignite.

"Hagen, you are going to die and so are your sons, as a sacrifice to Odin. I have sworn it."

Gautrek screamed in ecstasy "Odinnnn!"

Another opponent burst from the door and then a second, they both only made two or three paces before they were hacked down.

"Listen Hagen. Your women folk and children, they do not have to burn. I will let them come out; I will not harm them." The blood from the slain men was pooling on the boards before the door and started to bubble and sizzle in the heat. My men consciously pulled back from the inferno. I could hear women screaming inside and children crying, I hoped Hagen did not leave it too late or they would all burn.

"Men are breaking out of the thatch on the far side of the hall." Martin reported. I ran around the hall in time to see one of Coll's men throw a spear that transfixed an escaper on the roof. The spear took the man in the side and he fell back through the hole he had made. Smoke billowed from the gap in the thatch, it must be very unpleasant now inside I thought.

Gauti shouted around the hall corner. "Hagen wants to parley."

I ran back around to the main door, I could barely see him but the old warrior, Hagen stood to the fore with several of his family behind him; his beard was already smouldering.

"If it is just me you want, you can have me." He shouted. "Let my family go free."

I laughed. "You are in no position to bargain, Hagen. I have said your women and children can come out, you and your men will die, one way or another." I could see the slump of his shoulders; the walls of the hall were now a sheet of flame and the roof was likely to collapse in at any moment.

"They are coming out." Hagen called.

"No tricks or they all die." I called.

One by one a string of women exited from the hall door, they held the hands of children who could walk and they held in their arms babes of all ages from infants to toddlers. The children were crying and so were several of the women. Their clothing had been flung on hastily, they were in their night shifts with shawls wrapped around them. They kept coming ten, fifteen, twenty; my men hustled them away from the hall. Coll's men guarded them. As one tall woman came out of the hall Gautrek stepped up and thrust his sword through her back.

"Gautrek, what are you doing. I promised they would not be harmed."

422

Gautrek kicked the heavy boots the woman was wearing. "Would you bed a woman who wore boots like that?"

I walked over and hooked the body over with the beard of my axe. It was a man.

"Well spotted." I turned to the hall. "That's it; no more. Anyone who comes out now dies." I yelled. "Get ready, they will rush out any moment now." I called to the men around me.

Twenty men rushed out swords in hand, some with shields, all smouldering and scorched. They were met by a tight shield wall, which they hit and rebounded from.

"Push them back." I shouted. The men without shields soon died, the rest could not guard their backs or sides and one by one they we cut down. I did lose some men, wounded mostly. The roof of the hall collapsed in a shower of sparks and a tower of smoke. Without the roof the walls collapsed in and the hall turned into a giant bonfire immolating anyone left within.

Coll came over. "Hagen's wife is not with the prisoners; I think she is inside with Hagen."

"Good." I said with a note of finality. I walked away to find Magnus to see what else had transpired in the settlement while I eradicated Hagen.

I found Magnus in the smithy, he was holding the wrist of a young man and he was pushing the youth's hand into the glowing embers of the forge. The youth was screaming in pain and mortal terror.

"What are you doing?" I queried, although it would be a wonder if Magnus could hear me speak over the cries of agony.

Magnus turned and saw me and pulled the lad's hand from the fire. "Ah! Lord, this boy's sister accidently let on that their father, Hagen, has a hoard of silver buried hereabouts and I have been trying to convince them to tell me where it is."

I laughed, "Get Gautrek to sort this out, he is far more adept at extracting information by torture than you or me. What I need from you is a report."

"Yes, sorry lord. There were five large cottages and as you can see, we burned them all down. We persuaded everyone to surrender. None of my men were killed but one Fleming has been badly mauled by a dog. We have ten women and six children as prisoners; we have killed all the men, three of them were Hagen's sons. My men are combing the outhouses and barns now."

I turned and saw Martin. "Martin, can you organise two dozen men to go back to the boats, as soon as it is light, they need to be moved down to the jetty, which Finn indicated was at the end of the path we came down. We do not want to have to carry all the plunder back across the fields."

Almost everything in the cottages and the hall had been destroyed, there would be some melted silver in the ashes but that was about it. The livestock in the barns would be a bonus through the rest of the winter, as would the tack. Nothing much could be done until dawn; Magnus corralled all the prisoners in the largest barn and set a watch. I instructed several men to scout the perimeter of the settlement, half a mile out. I did not think it was likely that we would be surprised by a large armed party rushing to investigate the blaze, the island was not that heavily populated and now that Hagen was dead, lacked leadership. Nevertheless, better safe than sorry. Martin found some mead, delicious and unexpected.

We sat in the smith's bothy, with Magnus, Coll and Gauti and shared the contents of a large jug of the drink around a warm fire.

"Have you counted the prisoners yet?" I indicated to Magnus.

"Yes, no details, but we have thirty-two women and fourteen children younger than ten and three babes in arms. Two or three of the women are old crones but may be of some use."

"The barns, Coll, what livestock." I added.

"Ah! A fine bull that I would gladly keep if I was a farmer and four cows who are certainly carrying calves. A goat, a boar, and a sow, again probably pregnant, couple of dozen geese, and four fine horses, although where that bastard Hagen rode to on this island I cannot imagine." Coll looked pleased.

Martin chipped in. "There are also several dozen sacks of root vegetables and grain; there are some tubs of soft cheese as well."

"That is a good haul and will make the rest of the winter very comfortable, we do need the extra food to feed our new prisoners. The bull is a problem, we cannot take it on a snekkja too dangerous. Get Gautrek to sacrifice it, he will enjoy that and we can all have steak at our celebration feast. When we reach Roggen, we will select some of the women for the men and in

424

the spring, as soon as the sea lanes are open, the children and women will be sold as slaves at Ribe."

There was little else to do before dawn and everyone was beyond the ability to relax and sleep, so we sat in the smithy discussing trivia. One of the subjects was, of course, the famous hall burnings of the past. Everyone agreed that the burning of Njal on Iceland in recent history was the most infamous but that burning enemies was quite legitimate.

"I also remember Thorfinn MacBeth, the Jarl of Orkney and sometime King of Alba, he was badly burnt in a hall burning when his nephew Ragnvald Brusison tried to kill him but he burst through the burning wall of the hall and escaped; later he killed Ragnvald."

"Thorfinn was a great Jarl, he should never have tried to be King of Scotland as well." Magnus observed.

I had often thought that myself, but I had great respect for Thorfinn and being the son of Bethoc, daughter of King Malcolm he had a fair claim to the Scots throne.

Dawn eventually creeped stealthily over the horizon and I went outside to view the destruction we had wrought. The large hall was just a heap of charred timbers and ash. Smoke tendrils wafted upwards into the sky. The cottages were, likewise, heaps of ash. Here and there were burnt bodies, twisted violently in spasms of death, their mouths agape as the tendons shrivelled into a tormented rictus. Several of the men were sifting through the mess looking for melted silver, miraculously one of Hagen's carved chair arms was almost intact the rest of the chair, gone.

There were two sturdy carts in the barns and the horses were harnessed up to them. The plunder, sacks of food, utensils were loaded on them and some of my men set off with them along the path to the river.

"Fire the barns and the rest of the buildings." I ordered and set off along the path following the carts and prisoners. Gautrek waddled up holding a grubby looking wooden chest, which had clearly just been dug up.

"What have you there, Gautrek?" I asked, although I had already guessed.

"Hagen's treasure, lord." He placed the chest on the ground and flung open the lid. It was full of silver coins.

425

"Coin, who would have thought that." I bent and dug my hands into the pile and brought up half a dozen silver coins. I stared at them carefully. "These are from Lincoln and they are pennies from the reign of King Knut Sweynson. This I know because my great-grandfather, Outi was moneyer for the Lincoln mint and his men made these. How on earth did they come to be here in Hagen's treasure trove?"

Gautrek smiled happily, "Well if your great-grandfather made them your claim is better than Hagen's."

"Put the chest on the back of a horse and lead it down to the river. Oh! Where is the boy?"

"He is in the hole that the chest came from." Gautrek's face twitched, he was never far from the edge of sanity.

It was less than half a mile to the river and Egil had brought the ships upriver to the wooden jetty. By the time I arrived the plunder was being loaded on the ships. The snekkjas were not designed to carry enormous additional loads and the distribution of the live animals and prisoners presented some logistical problems. Nothing that Egil was not up to but I did hear him muttering under his breath about the merits of bringing *Hilda,* a trading knarr, along on this expedition.

Before we left the jetty, I ordered the men to push the carts into the river and smash up the six fishing boats that swung lazily against their hawser lines. Eventually with very overloaded boats and the sheer strakes ominously near the water line we pushed off. I intended the current to take the strain returning down river but there was an off-shore wind and the skippers of all three ships opted for half sail. The rest of the morning was taken drifting down steam towards the sea and Roggen. The men were relaxed and laughing, they felt they had achieved another famous victory with little risk. Ale was passed around and there was an obvious celebratory mood, I wondered how many of them realised that the campaign was effectively over and that if all went to plan my little army could be disbanded within three of four months.

Our arrival at Roggen was treated as a celebration by those that had been left behind with Eystein Whaleleg. It took the rest of the day and half of the following day to off-load the snekkjas. Egil was disgusted with the cattle dung and the droppings left by the other animals within the snekkjas and insisted that priority was given to cleaning and scrubbing them down. When he was satisfied with their condition and seaworthiness, he marched off to resume work on *Ottar*.

I discussed the prisoners with Martin and Eystein Whaleleg and it was decided to build another compound. The women without young children would join the other women that provided sexual services to the men, the women with infants and babes to be held separately and left unmolested. This compound would also accommodate the children without parents. Such was the number of animals on the island that it was necessary to corral them and a plan to manage this was left with Whaleleg. Martin took control of the food and mentioned as an aside that we now had to find fodder for burgeoning livestock and what on earth was he to do with the horses. My response to this comment was that the objective was not to keep the animals alive, but to eat them.

Martin was kept very busy organising the camp and for once I found myself at a loose end. I went down to see Egil working on *Ottar* and to my surprise I found that the repairs had already been achieved. What was really animating Egil was the carving of an elaborate prow head. I could see immediately that the carving was the likeness of an otter's head. It was designed to slot over the stem post and sit either side of the keel plank with holes for two wooden pins to be knocked through so that it could be removed when sailing on peaceful voyages. The carving was only three feet tall and would not make the prow of the longship look top-heavy; it had beautifully carved teeth, little pointed fangs. Egil looked slightly embarrassed.

"I have been thinking for some time that *Ottar* needed embellishing and seeing *Mare Swallow's* figurehead, I decided that *Ottar* would surface from the deep greater than before."

"Egil, it is beautiful, it brings the snekkja alive, a living hunter, a sea otter. Peg it on." I begged.

"It is not ready yet, it needs painting, but I will set it on." Egil lifted the carving and climbed the ladder already propped up against the stem post. He lifted the carving and slotted in on the top, he lined up the peg holes with the two holes he had already drilled into the stem post. I handed him the wooden pegs, which he placed in the holes and taking his wooden mallet and banged them through. He climbed down and we both stood admiring the effect.

"*Ottar* is alive, ready to swim." I exalted. Tears formed in Egil's old rheumy eyes.

"She will be faster than before, faster and with a fiercer bite." Egil stated.

"When Gautrek sees this, he will insist on a witches head for *Little Runa*." Egil and I both laughed.

"You will need to increase the water runs, I was hoping that rainwater would supplement our water supply but with the new prisoners and the animals, we do not have enough." I took a serious note. Egil nodded acquiescence.

"It would be useful if you could also get news of your son and his doings. I am hoping that the Flemish host will march into Zealand in March, April at the latest, and for that to happen the islanders' leaders need to be sending for help sometime soon."

"I'll send Gauti; he has been to Lille and Bruges with you and should be able to locate Eystein." Egil suggested, I knew he did not wish to go himself and leave his beloved longships.

Yule celebrations began on the island without any prompting from me. This mainly took the form of feasting every night, singing festive songs with pagan connotations with some tortuous Christianised interpretations. How the Christians justified the sacrifice of the Yule Goat mystified me, but I was interested to see that Yule was associated with the birth of Christ. The celebrations did seem to degenerate into a bacchanalian orgy as the Romans would have defined it. The women from the compound were dragged out and abused, forced to dance lewdly naked and then gang raped. I noted that the women were becoming careworn and physically weak. Martin had been concerned that the women could spread disease and forced them to wash in the river every day. Realising the benefits of this practise I ordered the men to bathe daily as well. Good food and cleanliness had maintained the health of the men and most of the women. However, their sexual abuse and their mental humiliation had gradually worn down most of the women. I personally could not find anything attractive in these poor souls but I realised that most of my men seemed to have an overwhelming desire to humiliate and force women and had little regard for the attractiveness of the women. I noticed that the men I considered to be the most intelligent often abstained from this sexual abuse, and interestingly most of these men were practising Christians. I found their actions slightly preposterous considering that most Christian priest were well known for their lechery.

I had to be practical as I knew that I could not hold my force together without providing access to female diversion. I was not sure if I could extend my moral force to order the men to abstain from abusing the women for a period of time, to save lives. Probably most of the men would not understand such compassion and it would be construed as a sign of weakness on my part. I discussed this with Martin and although he agreed with me, he believed preventing the men from taking the women would lead to trouble. I prepared for the reality that the women would start to die through despair.

Coupled with this problem was the issue of pregnancy, several of the women had started to show signs of being with child. Martin had moved four of them into the mothers' compound in the hope that they would birth and increase their value in the slave market. Inevitably the abuse they had suffered did not benefit their forthcoming ordeal and one of the women had already miscarried and died through loss of blood. Gautrek wanted the foetus to sacrifice to Frigg, the goddess of marriage and childbirth, but I felt this was a step too far into paganism and refused. I anticipated more women would die before the winter was over and so I decided that after Yule I would remove most of the women who had been in the compound longest and leave just the Bierren women to bear the brunt of the men's lust.

I also assumed that now the raiding had stopped for the winter the men on such a small island would start to irritate each other. I therefore increased the training regime ensuring the tiredness would take the sting out of the men's aggression. For me the monotony was broken when Gauti arrived back on the island after more than a month away. Martin and I quickly convened a meeting to learn of any development on the mainland.

Magnus, Egil, Coll, Eystein Whaleleg, Martin and I sat in a circle under the awning before my boat house, Gauti sat before us.

"What news?" I asked.

"Good news, lord. I met Eystein in Bruges and together we went to Lille where the Count of Flanders is wintering. Eystein had already been to Middleberg and met Hrodhard the chief; he convinced Hrodhard that he would betray us if he was allowed to marry Marieke and stay in Zealand. He would help to rescue Radbod and Luidgar. He told Hrodhard that he knew the Count of Flanders and he was sure he could persuade the count to assist the Zealanders to liberate themselves from the vikings. Apparently Hrodhard baulked at the idea of seeking assistance from the count as it would mean bending the knee and subjecting the islanders to Flemish rule. Eystein told me that at that moment the news of the burning of Hagen of Bierren and his kin filtered through from the north east, shocking everyone. This changed his mind and he accepted Eystein's offer.

Eystein and I went on to Lille where we met the count and his sons. As you had previously planned Count Baldwin appointed his son Robert to liberate the islands, Scheldtmerland he called them. He intends to raise a force of four thousand Flemings, at least two hundred horsed warriors and the rest spearmen. They will assemble at Ghent and march to Terneuzen on the river where they will be ferried over to Walcheren in merchant ships. Quite what they will do when they arrive on the island I cannot guess."

I laughed, "They do not have to do anything. The mere sight of their enormous force will frighten us into leaving." The captains grinned all round. "Was there any indication when the Flemish army will appear on Walcheren?" I asked.

"Lord Robert confirmed that his army will assemble on the feast of Saint Ludger, which I understand is somewhere in mid-March." Gauti explained.

"If they are in Ghent in mid-March, they will be at Terneuzen by the end of the month and on Walcheren in early April. We must prepare for an evacuation of the island when the Flemish army appears along the Walcheren shoreline to the south, second week in April." All nodded at my prediction. "When we leave, we will initially sail for Ribe and sell the prisoners and any spare goods we wish to turn into hack silver. At that moment I will share out the plunder, I anticipate most of the Frisians will disband. After that I intend to discuss my future with the Count of Flanders and will keep my ships on the beach at Bruges by the Sea until my future is decided, those that wish to stay with me are welcome, as you know the future is unlikely to be tranquil. You will all be rich men and can determine your own futures. We have a month and a half to prepare for our departure let the men know as they may wish to make representation with regards the shares, I want no ill feeling." I dismissed the captains.

The weather turned bad again with bitingly cold winds, steel grey skies and occasional downpours. The first of my men to come and see me was Christofer.

"What can I do for you Christofer?" I asked.

"I wish to redeem a woman from the compound as part of my share of the treasures."

This surprised me as I knew Christofer had not abused the women. "Which of the women would that be?" I asked.

"Eleanor." Of course, the name meant nothing to me and Christofer could see that. "Eleanor was the Saxon woman, Alftruda's maid. She is young, was innocent and deeply religious, Christian of course. I have tried to comfort her in her distress and I would redeem her and marry her."

"My dear Christofer, your faith is a truly remarkable and noble, the girl is yours, take her from the compound now and keep her safe. I can only wonder why you joined us in the first place?" I added.

"Penury makes men do strange things, I am now rich but I will repent for the rest of my life what I have done to innocent villagers and fisherfolk." Christofer predicted.

The rest of the requests from various men were more predictable, several of the Frisians wanted a fishing boat as part of their profit and I was glad to agree to their requests. This meant that the fishing boats had to be towed to Frisia on the way to Ribe. The most poignant of the requests came from Magnus and Egil and both had the same requests, to remain skippers of the *Hilda* and *Little Runa*.

I spoke to them together

"Egil, Magnus, you are like a father and brother to me. I cannot imagine either boat being captained by any other than you two. I am selfish and wish to bind you to me, I freely give you half shares in your boats and trust that you stay with me for the foreseeable future. I don't know where my future will take me, on land or sea, but if you will become my trading partners in war and peace, I can ask for nothing better." We all clasped arms to seal the deal.

Egil spoke with a broken voice. "I know I am likely to lose my son to this Marieke and the Zealanders, know this Hereward, you are like a second son to me and I ask nothing more than to sail this knarr until my poor broken body is slipped over the sheer strake to join Manannan Mac Llyr, in the watery depths."

I laughed, "That is an Irish Norseman talking and I hope such an event is many years in the future."

Spring 1060 – Testerep

One morning in mid-April, with a mild wind blowing from the west, forcing billowy white clouds across the southern horizon the army of Robert Baldwin's son appeared. Rank upon rank of foot soldiers carrying kite shaped shields and spears across their shoulders marched across the low sand dunes from the east. More surprisingly an equal number of foot soldiers appeared on the south beach of Schouwen to the north of Roggen.

"Come on, Magnus, Martin, time to do some play acting." I chortled and there were grins all round.

All the men were lined up along the stockade walls, eager to see the confrontation. I strolled out of the gate and down to the shore. A boat was rowed up to the shore but stopped fifteen paces out on the water, a herald held up a bough of a willow tree, good enough I thought. I could see Eystein in the boat but no Robert.

A large mailed warrior with jet black hair cut in that strange Norman manner, a round mop with the back and sides shaved off making a man's hair look more like a cap. This warlord had a moustache, which drooped around his mouth in the Norse manner, he twisted his head around and spoke to Eystein; Eystein muttered something back.

"You are the viking called Hjorvard Bjornbana?" he called across the water.

"I am that." I shouted back. "Spokesman for the free Roggen vikings and we honour your call to parley, unlike some in your boat." I had spotted Hrodhard and at least one of his sons. "Who are you and what can I do for you?" I prompted.

"I am Gherbod, spokesman for Lord Robert, the Count of Flanders son, he leads the army you see assembled against you, all around." He gestured with a sweep of his arm across the horizon of upright spears. "We are here to protect Scheldtmerland from your depredations. The Count of Flanders has been asked to protect his subjects in the islands and he has responded in force. You are to leave this little spit of sand forthwith or face dire consequences."

433

"I can see no reason to do so, your men are standing over there on Walcheren and Schouwen and unless they can all swim how can they compel us to do anything?" I concluded.

Gherbod continued, "We have more than you can see, our men are all over the islands and if you try to land and raid on any of them you will be overwhelmed and destroyed. A fleet is sailing north from Flanders to close you in, we know landing on your little island is hazardous, but we do not intend to, we will enclose you and starve you into submission."

A pretended to be angry, "I suppose that traitor I see with you put this idea in your head." I pointed at Eystein, "Eystein, you are a dead man if our paths cross again." I turned to go.

"Wait! We would trade with you for some of your prisoners." Gherbod shouted. I paused, this was the perilous point, Hrodhard wanted Radbod and Luidgar, his nephew and son.

"Our prisoners are ours to do with as we will, why should we give them to you?" I responded.

"You have my nephew and son and I want them released to me." Hrodhard shouted. Eystein has rescued my niece from your adherents in Bruges and the traitor castellan there has been punished by the Count of Flanders for his deceit." Better and better, I thought, Radbod and Luidgar knew we were obtaining water and supplies from Bruges but the Count of Flanders had skilfully exonerated himself and his son from complicity.

"I will accept ten pounds of silver for each of them." I called back and this time I did walk away. Martin stayed to hear their reply.

I later saw the boat row back to Walcheren and Martin came through the gate.

"Well?" I questioned.

"They have agreed, the silver will be delivered in the morning." Martin confirmed, but added. "We must be prepared for treachery tonight."

"Robert will not play me false but I agree Hrodhard may try something. The silver will come from the Count of Flanders coffers and I do not want to take silver from my paymaster in this way so we will set sail tonight and shelter beyond Schouwen until first light."

As soon as night fell and our activities on Roggen could no longer be seen from the larger islands, the prisoners were taken on board the boats. The treasure had already been placed aboard along with the supplies we had left. I ordered Radbod Gewarson and Liudger Hrodbardson to be tied to the stockade gates so that they could be found easily enough.

I looked into the eyes of Radbod. "Tell that traitor, whoreson, Eystein Egilson he is a dead man when next we meet, and your daughter, Marieke, is it? I will give her to my men, you know what that means."

The karvis were manned by the Frisians or towed along behind the longships. We did not have far to row, maybe ten or fifteen miles but I wanted the flotilla to reach well into the estuary north of Schouwen before we dropped the anchor stones. When we reached the open sea going was a bit rough so I had a light lit at the stern of *Mare Swallow* to guide the way and I hoped that the skippers of *Ottar, Little Runa, Wave Rider* and Egil on *Hilda* did the same. This was *Ottar's* first outing since her repair and I had placed Eystein Whaleleg in command as a trusted helmsman. It was not desperately dark, there was a large crescent moon shining through a clear sky and I could dimly see the boats in a line following in our wake.

The moonlight lit up the white crests of the waves beating on the beaches of Schouwen to the east. I could see we were far enough out to be safe from sandbanks but knew that when we turned east into the next channel inland, we would have to take great care. It took the best part of one full watch before we were on station behind two small low-lying islands, nothing much more than sandbanks really, like Roggen. We cast the larger ships anchor stones and then lashed all the crafts together; a stable sheltered platform. I set the guards and went to sleep, a more relaxed sleep than I had slept in weeks.

As soon as it was light enough to navigate safely, I ordered the sails set to take advantage of an offshore wind coupled with the prevailing wind blowing up from the south west. The result a turbulent but following wind that tempted the longships to stretch out ahead of the small boats. It was necessary to proceed on a quarter sail to let the smaller boats keep up. Nevertheless, my flotilla sailed north-north-east at a fair clip, sitting far out from the coast of Frisia, we continued in this way for the whole day, maybe seventy to eighty miles before the low-lying land fell away to the south and I signalled that we should turn due east along the low-lying islands. The off-shore wind had died away earlier in the day and we adjusted the sail yard accordingly to run before the wind. After another half watch I decided that it would be wise to find shelter for the night in the islands to our south.

I directed the flotilla to edge towards the islands and then indicated to Whaleleg to an obvious gap between the island line. One of the Frisians informed me that the island on our steer board side was called Texel and the island on our larboard side was called Vlieland. He was sure that by passing between the islands the waters behind would be sheltered from the open seas. I directed Whaleleg to steer us through between the two islands, I stood at the prow searching for unseen, shallow sand bars but *Mare Swallow* passed through the gap safely, which meant all the other boats would also be safe in the passage. I decided that the smaller island Vlieland looked ideal to beach on and signalled the boats behind to come into line and beach on the pale white sands.

Everyone disembarked and staked the ships fast to the beach; for good measure the larger ships laid their anchor stones on the sand. The men bustled about using fire wood we had brought with us along with some useful driftwood to make fires and cook food. The Frisians seemed most happy to be ashore on their home ground, particularly as several of them came from the islands rather than the mainland.

I realised that it would be sensible to leave the smaller boats on Vlieland, which was virtually uninhabited, rather than sail them to Denmark and back. I decided that most of the supplies should be off-loaded onto the beach and the prisoners for sale should be loaded onto two drakkers. *Hilda*, *Mare Swallow* and *Wave Rider* would also stay on Vlieland and only *Little Runa* and *Ottar* would continue. I left enough trusted men behind to guard my ships and what treasure was in their bellies. The English prisoners were left on Vlieland as well, they still had possible ransom value.

I left the next morning with my two snekkjas lightly manned, the wind held good, a fine north-easterly, which allowed us to set sail with a following wind away from the coast and set a direct course for Ribe some two hundred miles away. If the wind held and the weather remained clement, I intended to sail through the night and make landfall sometime the following day. I went on *Little Runa*, the men lounged around and played dice or hnefatafl and only leapt up to adjust the sheets as instructed by Magnus. Both *Little Runa* and *Ottar* raced along and I felt *Ottar* had the edge, which pleased me greatly, but clearly annoyed Magnus who started playing with the sheets to force every bit of speed from his longship. This soon disgruntled his crew and I told him to desist. The next day even earlier than I anticipated the shore of Denmark crept over the horizon under a white cloud bank. Magnus, who was a Ribe local declared we would almost hit Ribe harbour dead on. He smiled with the sheer pleasure at his ability to navigate so precisely. He informed me that Ribe lay near the sea behind a row of islands that gave Ribe a sheltered approach. The waters were shallow and needed to be navigated with care. It also informed me that the slave market was much nearer the sea than the town.

Apparently, Ribe was the oldest town in Denmark. As we neared the coast we passed south of an island and turned into a sheltered channel, Magnus directed our snekkja towards a small river outlet and I could immediately see several large barns, which Magnus informed me were where the slave pens and auction blocks were sited. I also noticed that there were dozens of snekkjas pulled up along the beaches either side of the river outlet and even one or two drakkars.

"I think maybe the king is in Ribe today." Magnus suggested. That could be a complication I did not need and I would really like to sell the prisoners and go, as soon as possible.

"Magnus, pull the snekkjas up on the beach, do not enter the river." I responded cautiously.

Both snekkjas were drawn up onto the beach at the end of a line of other longships. Magnus was very much in charge as he had done this before. The prisoners were off-loaded and roped together. Not being professional slavers like the Dublin Norse, we did not possess iron chains and collars. In fact, I found the whole process of selling slaves distasteful and could not imagine permanently owning any slaves, although I accepted that prisoners that could not be allowed to be released needed to be disposed of. Magnus lined up all the prisoners, there were fifty women and girls in all, of these eleven had young children held by the hand, four had infants at the breast and six were pregnant. We also had two male prisoners left after liberating Eystein's new relatives. This was Dagling of Dordrecht who had refused to join me, especially after he learnt of Dirk Hammerhand's slaying and young Haki Hagenson of Bierren the last of Hagen's brood, I knew I should kill both as they may bring blood feud against me if they ever gained their freedom but my men's greed persuaded me not to, so they were to be sold along with the women.

Magnus and his crew led them off to the slave auction and Martin went along as well, I decided that I did not wish to watch this spectacle and decided to walk into the town with Gauti and Gautrek. Ribe was a wooden construct with most houses two-storey affairs, wedged in between warehouses and traders' shops. Blacksmiths, tanners, clothiers were plying their trades from shops and workplaces next to inns and food stalls. It was obviously a thriving place, I could see a church, which appeared to be made partially of stone. Centrally there were several large halls, presumably where the town reeve dwelt and one might well be a king's hall. A market had been set up in the square before the church and there were innumerable stalls selling everything that anyone could want, it suddenly occurred to me that I wanted very little but I had to admit my boots were becoming quite worn. I had a problem though my boots had been made especially with vertical iron plates stitched on the outside and any boots I decided to purchase would have to be adapted. This did not stop me browsing the shoemakers' stalls and while I was doing this, I was nudged by Gautrek, I looked up and saw a line of heavily armed huscarls walking down the line of market stalls towards us. I hoped they would walk on and cursed myself for my inquisitiveness, I should have remained with the ships.

The line of huscarls reached me and stopped, four mail clad warriors girt with swords and carrying Dane axes. They parted, two to either side of the lane revealing a tall stout man with very fair hair, blue eyes, and sparse beard. He was a fine-looking man, handsome as some women would have it but he also had a softness about him. He was richly dressed with mail that appeared to have been washed with gold, a gem studded sword belt and a gold chain around his shoulders and across his chest. Around his forehead he had a thin band of gold, was it a crown? I guessed he was a foot taller than me, and towered over his huscarls. I noticed he walked with a slight limp.

He smiled, brilliant white, even teeth beneath a fine moustache. "Greetings, cousin."

Cousin! That threw me, how could I be a cousin to this man I had never met. I searched my knowledge of my genealogy. He could not be a relative on my father's side who were English ealdorman all, mainly from the Hwicce in the south-west. My mother's family descended from that renowned Jomsviking Palna-Toki who was related to the Danish royal family through marriage, I took a guess.

"It is an honour to meet you King Sweyn, I am surprised you know of me." I responded.

"How can anyone not know of the hero Hereward Bearslayer, your exploits are proclaimed by skalds throughout the north. Besides how many warriors sport a white bear shoulder protector and have eyes of a different hue." Sweyn Estridson, King of Denmark responded jovially.

"I did not know you were in Ribe, lord, or I would have come and paid my respects." I added rather lamely.

Sweyn Estridson had been King of Denmark for a couple of dozen years, in right of his father's marriage to Estrid the sister of King Knut the Mighty, he was about forty years old and had the gravitas of a king. I had heard he was courageous in battle, but did not have much success as a military commander. He had a continuous and on-going war with the King of Norway, first King Magnus the Good and now King Harald Hardrada who also claimed to be king of Denmark. He had been beaten many times but had always managed to hang on in his kingdom. No one really gave him much of a chance against Harald Hardrada, a man who was considered to be the greatest warrior in the north.

"Tell me, Bearslayer, what brings you to Ribe?" This was a loaded question I knew but as yet I could not fathom his desires.

"I am trading, my lord. I have some items for sale and would revictual my ships before I sail on." I answered blandly.

"And what have you been up to since I last heard of your exploits in Scotland and Ireland." The king prompted.

"I have been employed by the Count of Flanders and have also been doing some raiding further south." I answered.

"Ha! You are here selling off your plunder, a respectable viking activity and to the benefit of my kingdom's wealth."

"I pay the port reeves dues, lord." I responded; I had no intention of being intimidated.

"Are you under employment at the moment?" the king answered innocently. With a wave of relief, I realised the king wanted to employ me, nothing more ominous.

"I am still contracted to the Count of Flanders but by the summer I may well be free to undertake another contract." I responded cautiously.

"I need seasoned warriors and men would flock to sail with you, you would be rewarded well with land and silver." The king dropped all pretence of camaraderie.

I pondered the offer, I was intrigued, there was definitely opportunities here and I could not dismiss the fact that this man had a right to be king of England and may well make a bid for that throne when Edward the Mild died.

"My lord, it would be an honour to serve you when I am free of my current commitment. I must admit I do not see myself the equal of Hardrada, who is a master of strategies and deceit, but it would be a challenge." I added.

Estridson smiled. "That is good, I look forward to you joining me sometime in the future. Your support would add to my prestige and even the odds, I think."

"Count on it, lord." I assured him, just wanting to get away. We shook hands and the king wandered away surrounded by his huscarls.

Obviously, my ships were spied upon as they beached and the king wisely knew everything that occurred in his town of Ribe. I immediately left the town and hurried back to the slave auction, I found Magnus in one of the large barns. A rough looking broker was standing on a wooden platform and one after another, slaves were brought up onto the platform to be sold. Magnus informed me that our captives would be up shortly. There was a large crowd of buyers, which was positive and likely to bring a good price. Some of the slaves being sold were of poor quality and against these our captives should bring a good price. Magnus assured me that women with children were sold together and that pregnant women often produced a premium as buyers viewed the purchase as two for the price of one and the unborn child was often earmarked for the wife of the buyer who was barren or longed for another child. Our women came up for sale and I was relieved to see that a few days without being molested had improved their looks. Obviously, they were terrified for their future but realistically they would not end up being constantly raped by a small army on a regular basis so their future was an improvement, if you could call thraldom an improvement.

The bidding was brisk and our profits mounted up and the women with children did gain us a premium. Interestingly the young girls fetched the most profit, I suppose the buyers considered they gave a longer return on their investment. The situation changed dramatically when Dagling and Haki Hagenson were brought to the block. They were offered as prime field hands but the obvious muscular torso of Dagling put off the buyers. Too dangerous to risk coin on. After some pleading by the salesman the deathly quiet of the crowd told him he was wasting his time and they were pushed off the block back to Magnus' care.

Magnus went to sort out the profits with the slave auctioneer, he obviously had to pay a selling fee and a gelt to the port reeve but even after that he returned with two of his crew men carrying three heavy wooden chests full of hack silver and coin. I walked outside the slave warehouse with Magnus.

"What do you wish to do with Dagling and Hagenson?" Magnus asked.

"We'll take them back to the ships and Gautrek can cut their throats, he will like that."

"Nothing like a splash of human blood of the prow post of a snekkja for good luck." Magnus smiled mirthlessly.

I should have killed them sooner as they would always be a risk for me if I let them live.

We now had to return to the Frisian islands and the north-easterly winds were still prevalent. Both Magnus and Coll believed we should sail early in the morning and hug the coast to take advantage of the morning off-shore breeze; that way we could travel under sail for some of the way but it would also be a long hard pull into a headwind for some of the day. Tacking would possibly drive us too near the coast or too far out into the sea towards England and would be of little value unless the wind veered. I gave the prisoners to Gautrek, who gleefully stripped off their meagre rags they had to cover their nakedness with. He lashed Dagling to *Ottar's* keel with his hands tied up above his head with a rope that looped around the prow stem and he repeated the process with the young Haki against the prow stem of the *Little Runa*. I thought that he was going to cut their throats, but no, he sat talking to them all night, or at least past the time I fell asleep.

Everyone was up early, ready to be off, by this time the rumour had swept around the crews that Sweyn Estridson had offered me employment and I cursed Gauti and Gautrek for their loose talk. The two snekkjas were pushed into the swell and the crews backed water to clear the beach. As predicted, there was a slight off-shore wind and the crews raised the sails to take advantage of this blessing. I walked up to the prow and looked over the side, Dagling was hanging there, still alive his body dangling half in, half out of the water, buffeted by the bow wave. He must have been freezing, I looked over at *Little Runa* sailing in our wake and could see Haki Hagenson enduring the same torture on the stem post. I thought it likely that Haki would die long before Dagling. Gautrek was leaning over the side crooning and clutching himself in a rocking motion but he did turn towards me smiling mirthlessly.

"Bearslayer, Ull and Odin will be appeased by this offering and will ask Njord to send us favourable winds." Gautrek mumbled.

I believed him quite mad. We sailed for half a watch on full sail with the sail braced against a larboard wind. I anticipated that we would lose the off-shore wind very soon but remarkably when it died away it was replaced by a wind out of the south. The wind had swung around from north-east to north and this enabled us to set full sail and tack south-west out to sea, the men had to constantly adjust the sheets and braces to keep the wind.

Gautrek looked smug and ambled up to the prow, leant over and cut the throat of Dagling; I was not sure if Dagling was dead already but it was immaterial. I was sure Haki would have perished as he was nowhere near as robust as Dagling.

I decided it would be easier to sail on in this manner towards the English coast and then turn into the wind and sail back to the Frisian coast. This in effect doubled the distance we had to sail but saved us having to row long distances. We were half way to East Anglia, by my calculation, before we changed our tack and reversed our braces and sailed back towards Frisia. This took an extra day but we hove-to next to *Hilda, Mare Swallow* and *Wave Rider* in good order to the cheers of our comrades ashore. There were some puzzled looks when Gautrek cut down the dead bodies from the prows of our snekkjas.

All the treasure we had accumulated was piled onto the beach. Martin spent a whole day auditing and cataloguing it, so I called for a full meeting of the army for the following morning. Our supplies were fast depleting so our fast was broken with a thick heavy porridge. The crews obviously could not wait for the distribution of our wealth.

I climbed up onto the prow of *Mare Swallow* and holding onto the horse head addressed the men. "Roggen vikings, you have triumphed." They all cheered. "I will now explain how the loot we have accumulated will be apportioned." They all went quiet. "Martin has counted the treasures, which amounts to four hundred pounds worth of silver. This I will distribute, in its entirety to you; my share of the treasure has gained me three snekkjas to add to my other boats *Ottar* and *Hilda,* and I have given half shares of *Hilda* and *Little Runa* to Egil and Magnus." The men cheered again, Egil and Magnus were well liked and their bonus was well earned.

"The captains of the snekkjas will receive double shares, the captains of the little karvis will receive a share and a half. Martin and Eystein Whaleleg for overseeing the camp will receive a share and a half, every other warrior, including the Flemish peasants, who are now warriors like the rest of us will receive a half a share. The men who swore fealty to me under duress will receive a quarter share." I could see that this was not received so well but I was determined to be fair. "The Frisians have expressed a wish to have the small karvis, two of which were theirs anyway. The value of these boats will be deducted from their shares of the silver." There were nods of agreement to this. "Finally, Christofer has asked to have the girl Eleanor and I have agreed to this, I do not intend to deduct anything from his share for this girl."

There were some smirks on the men's faces at this announcement, none of them would want, I was sure, a woman that so many men had used, so there was no objection to this.

"There is also the issue of your pay from the Count of Flanders for being allowed to ravage his lands. I have his coin and each of you will receive a pound of silver from this payment. Martin, announce what a single share of the treasure amounts to."

Martin came forward and stood on a barrel so all could see him. "A full single share amounts to ten pounds of silver." There were gasps all round, none of the men had ever had anywhere near such largesse. They were all rich men, they could buy a farm, an inn, or a small boat but I suspected many of them would spend it on frivolities, drink, and women. Martin spent the rest of the day distributing the silver to the men.

By the evening meal everything had been completed, I could visually see the Roggen vikings splitting up and disintegrating. Wighard and Folker came to see me and to inform me they intended to row to the mainland the following morning. They would be leaving with all the karvis and most of the Frisians, maybe a third of my force. I would be sailing back to Flanders with my five ships and half-crews; they thanked me effusively and wished me well and I reciprocated.

"We will meet again." I said prophetically.

The following day the wind was still from the north-west and much stronger, I decided we would wait out the inclement weather on our island, this did not prevent the Frisians rowing off to the mainland and my much-diminished force waved them off. Hagen's treasure that Gautrek had tortured out of Hagen's son was still hidden in my sea chest and had not been distributed with the rest of the plunder, there was probably in the order twenty pounds of silver coin in the chest making me as wealthy as any earl.

Three days later the wind veered around to the north-east bringing squalls of rain, but it did allow us to raise our sails and fly down the coast passed our old raiding ground of the Scheldt estuary and haul up on the beach at Bruges by the Sea.

I called a meeting of my captains, Egil the part owner of *Hilda*, Magnus the part owner of *Little Runa*, Coll skippering *Ottar* and Eystein Whaleleg the helmsman on my own longship *Mare Swallow*.

"Martin and I need to go to find the Count of Flanders to determine the direction of my contract. I do not think we should leave the ships on the beach here all summer, they need to work for us." They all nodded in agreement. "We do not have enough men to crew all our ships so this is what I propose. *Hilda* will trade all summer and *Little Runa* will accompany her to add security from pirates like us." Magnus laughed at the irony. "We can crew these two ships with a full crew each. Until I know where we can permanently berth *Mare Swallow, Wave Rider* and *Ottar* they will stay here under the hand of Whaleleg, Christofer and the older members of the crews who fancy an idle summer of whoring. I will take Gauti, and Coll and a retinue with me and we will all assemble here at the start of harvest. How say you?"

"That is fine by me as long as you take Gautrek." Whaleleg snorted.

"I wouldn't have it any other way, the day he oversteps the mark I will personally gut him." I emphasized. Martin passed ale around and we sat on our sea chests discussing our plans. "Any ideas where you will trade, Egil?" I queried. I was not a trader and would not know where to start such a business. Egil looked thoughtful, but Martin interrupted.

"Bordeaux."

"Bordeaux" I questioned, "Why there?"

"Wine, master some of the finest wines in the world." Martin affirmed.

"Tis true, wine from the south of France, the land of the Romans and Visigoths would sell for a big profit in the north, Flanders or the northern German cities." Magnus agreed.

"And what would you trade for the wine?" I asked.

"Wool, we could buy wool from Grimsby in Lindsey, that would be far enough away north from Harald Godwinson's Wessex and English wool is the best."

"That sounds like a good plan, I will fund the wool purchase with silver coin and we will share the profits." I concluded.

"Let us drink to a fair wind and foolish buyers." Egil announced and we all drank deep.

Two days later I left Bruges by the Sea and with Martin and a retinue of twenty men, mainly Flemings I walked off towards Bruges town. It was only a seven-mile stroll to Bruges so we entered the gate by noon. The guards recognised me but were wary of my men, I informed the guards I would want my men to be housed in the garrison barracks and that only Martin and I would be going to the castellan's hall; that reassured the guards and allowed them to keep an eye on so many unknown warriors within the town. Martin and I went up to the main hall and made our presence known.

Shortly afterwards we were ushered into the main hall. Dedda was waiting in all her splendour, vivacious mouth, flashing eyes provocative body. She held out her hand to me and I bowed over it and kissed her fingers.

"O lah! Hereward, here at long last, how I pined for your embrace." Her voice was husky and potent, an open invitation. Martin stared at the ceiling.

"Lady Dedda, what has it been, nearly a whole year and me stuck on a barren island, but not as desolate as I without your company." I flattered. She laughed.

"I hear you connived to have my husband implicated in your plots and he has been hauled off to Ghent so that those grubby islanders can see his punishment." She explained, making a point of stressing her husband was not present.

"Your husband will be well rewarded by Count Baldwin for playing the game of duplicity." I suggested.

"Yes, he knows and looks to have his patrimony increased accordingly." Dedda was completely and honestly avaricious.

Martin intervened, "Lady, you have intimated that the Zealanders, sorry Scheldtmerlanders, are at Ghent?"

"Yes, a chieftain called Hrodhard and your Eystein with his child of a wife Marieke. Eystein came and removed her from my care a week ago and good riddance she was so boring, although I did try and educate her. He also took the girl Alftruda; you do like to accumulate young nubile children, don't you Hereward?"

I wondered just what sort of education from Dedda could benefit Marieke and I ignored her comments about young nubile girls. "In that case we cannot go on to Ghent while they are there as it would unravel the deception." Martin looked at me discomforted.

"Then it will be necessary to remain in Bruges until the castellan returns and the Zealanders leave for their homes. I am sure the Lady Dedda will extend her hospitality to us for a few days?" I answered smoothly.

Dedda smiled wickedly, "Of course, my hospitality is always yours for the asking. We will dine and then I will escort you to your quarters."

I could see that Martin was distinctly uncomfortable and it did not surprise me when he found an excuse to leave and be with the men in the barracks. Dedda did nothing to dissuade him and within short order dining was forgotten and I found myself in her bed and she was all over me. Her love making was frenetic and I felt like I was being ravished, her demands were such that I felt more exhausted than after a battle; no, it was a battle, there was no affection only pure lust.

The following morning, I needed sustenance, I slipped out of her bedroom and went to find food in the barrack mess. Martin and my retinue were breaking fast and I joined them grabbing a hunk of fresh bread, cheese, onions, and heavily seasoned cold sausage. Martin had been talking to the captain of the castle's guard who glared at me and stalked away when I approached them.

"What have I done to upset him?" I asked between chews of the excellent sausage.

"Not so much as what you have done to him but to the Lady Dedda; I think your presence in her bed has supplanted his position." Martin surmised.

"Well, he can have it back; he must have more stamina than me." Martin expressed a twitch of a smile.

"Tiring of her attractions?" Martin looked quizzical but I did not answer.

After we had broken our fast, I brought every one of my men together and asked around to see if any of them thought they would not be identified as one of the Roggen vikings by the Zealanders at Ghent. None of them came forward and it was apparent that any one of them could be identified by Radbod Gewarson if he was present in Ghent.

"Well Martin, now you know why I have to keep in the Lady Dedda's good graces, I need her to send a messenger to Ghent to inform the count of my presence."

I made my excuses and made my way back to Dedda's chambers. Dedda was surrounded by her maids and she was bathing in a large copper tub, she made no effort to hide her nakedness from me in front of her attendants, which I found reckless as she only needed to cause resentment with any of her maids for her nefarious behaviour to get back to her husband. The bath was massive and must have required the whole castle guard to carry it into the chamber situated on the first floor. It occurred to me that Dedda was sexually promiscuous to such an extent that she likely not only cuckolding her husband with me and the captain of the guard but probably several others of the castle's male inhabitants. My ardour was distinctly diminishing.

I had kept a silver necklace from the plunder to gift to Dedda and I now produced it and I made my request and Dedda readily agreed to become involved in a little intrigue. She sent for Erembald, a man whose name I was not familiar with, but it turned out to be the captain of the castle guard who had glowered at me earlier.

"Dear Erembald, I need you to convey a message to our liege lord, no not my husband, to Count Baldwin. Tell him that Lord Hereward is here present. Take your fastest horse and return to me promptly and you will be well rewarded."

I could well imagine what Sir Erembald's reward would be and I could also see he was entirely under her spell. Nevertheless, I was comfortable with the situation as this retainer was the last man that would reveal the infidelities of his mistress. The messenger was duly sent off on a very fast and spirited horse that I would probably have fallen off and I spent the rest of the day politely avoiding Dedda's sexual advances. I assumed that Erembald would deliver the message later that day as it was only twenty or so miles to Ghent. He or the castellan could return by the following morning and I did not wish to be caught in the Lady Dedda's chamber so I informed the lady I would stay in the barracks that night. My prediction proved accurate as by early morning Bauldran, Castellan of Bruges and Erembald his captain rode through the castle gate. The castellan saw me emerge from the barracks followed by Martin; I saw the look of disappointment on Erembald's face.

"Ha! Lord Hereward," Bauldran's voice boomed across the courtyard over the iron shod hooves of the warhorses, striking sparks on the cobbled stones, "Come up to my hall, I have a message from the count." I made my way across the small stone flagged bailey avoiding the crush of dismounting horsemen, defecating stallions, and cursing stable hands to the familiar stone steps leading into the keep. I suspected Dedda would not be out of her bed by now, let alone dressed to receive her lord, however there were page boys and maids in the hall with wine and viands for their lord's retinue in case they had not broken their fast before they left Ghent. I was provided with ale and went over to join the castellan where he sat having his boots pulled off by a young page.

"Well! I have been branded a bad boy for being in league with a band of heathen vikings preying on my lord's vassals in Scheldtmerland. Of course, I expressed my incredulity at such an accusation as I believed I was dealing with honest merchants. I have been suitably chastised and received a chest of coin and another manor as punishment for my misdemeanour." Baudran was jovial finding the deception of the Zealanders amusing. "Now, to the point, you are to meet Count Baldwin and his sons at Drongen Abbey nearby to Ghent. It is a foundation much admired by the count who restored the monastery recently. You must be there by mid-morning tomorrow and you can be sure the count is well pleased with you. I will provide you and your men with horses and a guide, Erembald here." The castellan waved in the direction of his captain.

"Thank you, my lord. I am relieved that Count Baldwin still thinks well of you, resolving any suggestion that the count was in league with the Roggen vikings was a convoluted process and your cooperation was invaluable. I have here a token of my gratitude and regard."

I unwrapped a beautiful gold crucifix embellished with jewels looted from Dordrecht, which I had earmarked earlier as a gift to buy my way out of any difficult situation. Bauldran's face lit up, the crucifix was worth a king's ransom and would be useful to him to achieve future ambitions. There was the expected feast in my honour that evening and it was clear that Bauldran would wish to avail himself of his wife's conjugal services. Obviously neither Erembald nor I would have access to the Lady Dedda's favours that night and I for one was relieved.

My force was up early and in arms; Martin had ensured that they had burnished their mail and helmets until they shone. The castellan had lent several kite shaped shields and spears with pennons attached so that they resembled a typical Flemish retinue to, hopefully, a typical Flemish lord. We were joined by Erembald who led us out on the short ride to Ghent and the nearby abbey at Drongen. Erembald was clearly reluctant to hold any sort of conversation with me and addressed Martin when it was necessary. The land thereabouts was relatively flat, as was most of Flanders, and well wooded; between the stands of trees there were villages dotted around the countryside interspersed by tilled fields and pasture, a very prosperous land indeed. There were many peasants working in the fields, presumably fighting the never-ending battle with weeds that threatened to strangle their crops.

Eventually the church spires of Gwent could be seen ahead and Erembald veered off to the right through a small wood riding to the west of the town. Shortly, up ahead, I could see a low stone wall surrounding a sizeable area that was dominated by a stone abbey of some size with a low flat tower. The abbey church was surrounded by several buildings whose purpose I could only guess at. We rode through an open gate into a grassed area where sheep were grazing and where a wooden palisade separated a herb garden from the voracious beasts. The flock provided a beautifully manicured lawn for our horses to trot across and we congregated before a large hall, adjacent to the church, from which an elderly monk appeared.

"Good morning, sirs, I understand the count will be here shortly, if you will dismount and follow me within, drinks and refreshments are provided in the refectory. We duly dismounted and followed the monk into the large hall where several monks were laying out cheese, bread and fruit, apples, and pears.

The elderly monk added. "The Lord Abbot is with the count and will arrive in due course, I am Brother Dominic. We are very fortunate here at Drongen in that the count favours our order and has had the monastery rebuilt and re-founded. Drongen Abbey was originally founded in the seventh century by the sainted Amandus, the missionary who Christianised the Leie and Scheldt lands. Tragically the monastery was destroyed by the Norsemen in the year of our Lord eight hundred and fifty-three but the liberal endowments of the Count of Flanders has restored it.

I liked that, there was a certain irony in the leader of the Roggen vikings meeting the count in an abbey destroyed by vikings and rebuilt by him. He was now going to act as the saviour of the whole of Zealand in the same manner.

I heard the arrival of the count's party when a large horsed group cantered into the grassed courtyard shouting for monks to take their horses. I decided to stay in the refectory and let the count come to me. Within a short time, the count's armed retainers entered the hall, checking that everything was safe for the count to enter. I instructed my men to move to the far end of the room and sit peaceably. I nodded to the leader of the count's guard who acknowledged the move and reciprocated ordering his men to line the walls around the entrance door.

Baldwin, Count of Flanders, strolled into the refectory flanked by his two sons. Baldwin, his eldest and heir, and Robert. No mail here, clearly Baldwin's excuse to come to Drongen was to worship; a fitting excuse that would not arouse suspicion in the minds of the Zealanders waiting back in Gwent. They were all wearing magnificent tunics embroidered with gold and silver thread. The father and elder son wore felt caps adorned with pheasant feathers that threatened to poke out the eyes of any who came too near. These feathers were held in place by elaborate brooches with pearl drops and enamelled badges with lion rampant motifs. Robert on the other hand wore no head gear, letting his hair flow loose down to his shoulders, clearly scorning the fashion of having his hair shorn in the Norman manner. None carried serious weapons and confined themselves to wearing elaborate jewelled daggers hanging from their belts. Robert was swishing his riding whip and slapping it against his thigh. I had the distinct impression he would have liked to have struck his more bovine brother. I large number of courtiers followed the princes in to the refectory.

"Hereward, well met." The count raised his hand in greeting, his voice was frail and gravelly and I wondered how long he was for this world. His patient successor nodded to me and Robert grinned in delight and held out his hand for me to clasp in the Norse way.

"Good day, Lord Count it is good to be here, I trust our plans have concluded to your satisfaction." I responded.

"Satisfaction, it is better than I could hope; the people of Scheldtmerland are humbled and have agreed to pay the annual gelt I require of them. They are grateful to my son, Robert for seeing off those evil vikings, they were Danes you know." The count winked cheekily making me smile. "Hrodhard has accepted the Lordship of Middleberg and Walcheren a formulisation of his current status, his nephew, Radbod, I have elevated to the lordship of Reimerswaal, another island to the east of Walcheren and our double agent Eystein I have made the lord of Santflit a miserable place on the mainland where I have commissioned him to build a wooden bridge across the narrows to join the islands to the mainland. His baronial house is henceforth to have the appellation van der Bruges, of the bridge and he will ensure that the military gateway to Scheldtmerland remains open."

So Eystein had married his Marieke and become a lord within the nobility of Flanders, or Scheldtmerland, I was not sure which; equally I was bemused by what his father, Egil would make of this.

"Now Hereward, I would make you an offer, I have no wish to lose your talents and I am conscious that other kings and princes will wish to hire your services. Oh! I know that you will stray and become involved in other adventures but I would always wish to be able to call upon you. I therefore want to offer you a vicomte, a lordship in Flanders that you can call your

452

home. In due course you may marry and settle down somewhat, after all you cannot remain a viking forever."

I was stunned, I had anticipated silver and other largesse but not lands and title. Did I want such things, I had wrestled with this problem since I was outlawed; I had a sense of entitlement to certain lands in and around Bourne left to me by my father and supposedly held in trust by my nephews. I had always rejected trying to gain them, I did not want to fade into obscurity as a small land owner, now I was being offered the same thing but in another country.

"You look troubled, Hereward, hear me out. I am offering you the lordship of Testerep, in west Flanders. It is an island on the coast with a small fishing village. Your lordship would stretch into the interior for ten miles but stretch along the coast ten miles north and south of the island. It is an ideal place for a port, a trading centre, and a maritime stronghold. You can keep your boats berthed there safely and I would look to you to provide my coastal defence."

The way the count described it was tempting and was certainly more than I could hope for in England if ever my outlawry was rescinded. The key point was that it would give me a safe berth for my ships, the opportunity to gain more crafts and the ease to sail away if I ever tired of the position.

"My lord, your offer is more than generous and I would be churlish to refuse. You can be sure that the coast of Flanders will be safe under my hand." I responded positively.

"Excellent. I will be finishing up with the Scheldtmerlanders in a few days and will be returning to Lille. I will look for you there in say two months hence for your formal homage, meanwhile go straight to Testerep and organise it to your liking." As an afterthought the Count added. "Oh! Thank you for the gift of the girl Alftruda, she will be an honoured guest amongst the Flemings and may be a useful bargaining counter in negotiations with my son-in-law Tostig." The count slapped me on the back in a friendly manner and took his leave to strike up a conversation with the abbot.

I did not wish to delay my departure but inevitably Lord Robert wanted to discuss the recent campaign in Zealand in detail. He knew the details of his father's land grant to me and approved and was only sad that he could not provide land in his new lordship of Scheldtmerland. Robert's rather stuffy older brother Baldwin Count of Hainhault, known generally as Baldwin of Mons avoided me; I believe that he was jealous of my success in the Guines campaign as he wanted all the glory for himself. Eventually Baldwin announced he was going to enter the church for a thanksgiving service and the lords reformed into his train ready to follow. I signalled to my retinue it was time to leave. I rode back to Bruges in silence, I had a lot to consider.

On our return to Bruges, I requested an interview with the castellan. I was now going to be a near neighbour of his, with a shared border. I was particularly concerned regarding the fate of Bruges by the Sea, which inevitably would suffer by my removal of my crews and ships from its beaches. Bauldran was surprisingly unconcerned about the success or failure of Bruges by the Sea's economy and took it for granted that the trade would move to my new port at Testerep but would still pass-through Bruges. He may well have been right and Bruges' trade might not take a downturn, but I did get the impression that trade was the least of his interests. I did not stop in Bruges but immediately continued on to my beached ships. I called a meeting on the beach that evening, a warm balmy evening where too many midges assembled to join us. Martin arranged for tall torches to be lit to attract the flying wolves away from our bare skin.

I addressed all the men still with me, that is those that had not sailed with Egil and Magnus. "Brothers, I am an earl's son and as such I often unfairly receive the accolades that rightly should be awarded to you, the warriors who have achieved so much. It is for this very reason that I declined a share in the Roggen viking treasure hoard and confined myself to the longships I acquired. However, now I have been personally rewarded by the count of Flanders, he has elevated me to the rank of a viscount, a personal representative of the count, and awarded me the lordship of the village and manor of Testerep and land thereabouts. Testerep is an island on the coast south of Bruges by the Sea, I have accepted this reward and the role of protector of the Flemish coast; I intend to make this village a trade emporium, a trading stop-over between Scandinavia and the countries in the south. I need sailors, I need warriors and most of all I need you all to join me.

It will not be a peaceful life but this land will provide a haven to keep your belongings and allow you to have a home, a wife, and children if that is your inclination." There was a good deal of muttering but it sounded positive. "To assist you in this offer I propose this; I am assuming that the village of Testerep is desolate, what great lord ever gives anything worthwhile away." At this they all laughed. "I want you all to have your own farm and although I know you are all rich men, I will pay for half of the construction of any home you may desire. Alternatively, as I intend to build a great hall, any who wish will always have a place, a bed and hospitality in my hall." Again, they cheered, this was obviously to their taste. "Think on what I have proposed, I intend to move the ships down the coast to Testerep in the morning."

I had decided to sleep in the belly of *Mare Swallow* and was making my way there when I was approached by Christofer who, to my surprise, had stayed with me after Roggen. "I would speak with you, Lord Hereward." He begged.

"Feel free, every Roggen man can speak his mind to me, that is the Norse way." I responded.

"I would like to accompany you to Testerep and I would like to build a church in your new village, if you agree." He knew that my Christianity lay lightly upon me and that I oscillated between that and paganism. He clearly was not sure I would like this proposal.

"Christofer, I would be delighted to have a nascent church in my new lands, I would only reserve the right to choose the priest that officiates there." I responded, positively, I hoped. I had no intention of having an arrogant, dismissive priest like Herluin, my nemesis back in Mercia.

It was only fifteen miles south-west along the coast to the island of Testerep and I used the early morning off-shore winds to sail the three longships along the coast with skeleton crews. I was not familiar with the coast south of Bruges as I had never had the occasion to sail further south before. The coast was a long low sandy beach that stretched for miles. It was quite hard to spot the profile of the island of Testerep from the land either side, or behind; the only suggestion was a break in the low-lying sand dunes where the water surrounded the island, fjord, or river entrances at both ends. I ordered a reef in the sail and with three oars out aside I edged the longship in to the shallows. The two following longships swung into *Mare Swallow's* wake and we all crawled over the water into the river mouth, if river mouth it was? I could see on the steer board side that once we had cleared the sand dunes there was a muddy water course running parallel to the sea shore, which may have been the dividing water between the small island and the mainland. I would not have wanted to put the keel of any of the snekkja into this watercourse and certainly not a knarr like *Hilda*, nevertheless, the waterway we were in was ideal to keep a number of ships safely harboured. I decided to throw out the anchor stone and row ashore in the little rowing boat to explore the island. Martin and I went ashore alone, if the site turned out to be depressing, I did not want to disappoint the men too soon.

"We need to find some native farmers or fishing folk." I declared to Martin as we grounded the boat. I clambered out and climbed up the low sandy rise to view the flat island vista. The island must have been about a quarter of a mile long and apart from two settlements looked deserted. There was some low wooden hovels and Martin and I headed for the nearest, which was back along the waterway at the very east end of the island and very exposed. We could smell the fish before we reached the hovels and when we arrived at the four dilapidated huts, we could observe several women gutting fish on a log outside one of the dwellings. We strolled over and when they saw us, they were clearly startled.

"Ahoy there! No need to run, we only want to talk." I called to them and opened my arms wide to indicate my peaceful intentions.

The oldest woman stood her ground but ushered the younger ones into the hut. "What do you want?" she demanded displaying a brave exterior.

"I would have someone describe this place to me, the island and the land beyond." I waved my arm inland. "Where the farms are, how many people there are around here, where is fresh water?"

"You are very inquisitive, why do you want to know all these things?" the woman put her hands on her hips in a defiant stance, she clearly was not to be bullied.

"As to why, I am the new lord of the island and the land ten miles in either direction along the coast and ten miles inland." I swept my arms wide again. "You are and all within are now my vassals and owe me fealty, I intend to build a hall hereabouts and start a settlement and I need information." This statement left her looking bewildered, after a few moments she responded.

"Do you intend to throw my family off our land?" she bristled angrily, and I was becoming annoyed too.

"It is my land, not yours, but I have no intention of removing you but I will be pulling down this miserable hovel you live in and rehousing you in a dwelling that does not offend my eyes." I was nearly shouting; I had certainly raised my voice.

Martin interrupted, "Woman, do you have a husband who can talk some sense?"

Now she looked distressed and cowed. "My husband and sons are all dead, drowned in a storm at sea; my daughters and my dead sons' wives are all that are with me now." Just to emphasise this state an infant started wailing from inside the hovel.

I turned to Martin, "Martin, get the men ashore and set up a temporary camp. I am going to walk the island to see what sense I can make of it." I turned to the woman. "Come with me."

I walked the dunes along the beach south until I came to a dyke where water was trickling down through the dunes to the beach, this confirmed that Testerep was an island of sorts.

"What is the name of this water?" I asked her.

She thought about it for a moment and then responded, "Obekins Dyke"

I turned inland and walked along the edge of the dyke until I came to the muddy watercourse, the other end of which I had anchored the ships. I pointed at the land the other side of the muddy watercourse,

"What is that called?"

"Testerep, more of Testerep, main part of the island, seven farms." She responded.

"Is there fresh water?" I persisted.

457

"Yes, wells at Leffinge and Slype on main island and at Bredene and Oudenberg, on mainland." She indicated north-east on the other side of the watercourse my ships were in.

"Good, I can see the island stretches further south than the dyke; how far does the island reach that way?" I pointed south.

"To river, river called Ysera, maybe further seven miles." The woman replied.

"We will go back now." We traipsed back over the sandy heathland until we reached the almost derelict huts the women and her daughter and daughters-in-law lived in. I reflected as we walked that the island was about ten miles square, a sizeable area without the additional land north and south.

Using sail cloths my crews had fitted out woollen tents that looked a good deal drier and accommodating than the hovels.

"What is your name woman?" I asked.

"Gritta." She thought about it for a moment and then added, "Lord."

"Right Gritta, you and your womenfolk cook up a really good fish stew for my men, they need a hot meal to cheer them up. You will be paid for your labour and if you are short of anything, herbs, vegetables, see Martin there and he will provide them."

I gathered the men around me. "Right lads, this stinking arsehole of an island is what my lordship is called after, but apparently there are better locations to settle on the other part of the island." I indicated passed the muddy water course, "and on the mainland at a place called Oudenberg, we will move over there tomorrow. You can see that the inlet where our ships are moored is an ideal haven for shipping and so is the river on the other side of the island this spot is referred to as the Ostend, or east end of the island and is ideal for a watchtower, so I will be asking someone to live here. Now all get down to the river and get a wash, there are ladies present." They all laughed at that having assessed Gritta and been thoroughly repelled.

The men began to show more interest when the younger women cautiously exited the hovel. Their ages ranged between fifteen and thirty and although they were dressed poorly and needed a good wash my men, who were ever optimistic, saw potential. The fish stew was not half bad either.

The next morning, we re-embarked on our longships and poled them across the sound to the mainland side and again dropped the anchor stones. The farmstead at Bredene was just over the sand dunes and was much better situated than the Ostend. Martin informed the farmer and his family that I was their new lord and we moved on south following the shore line. There were several inlets, small creeks where fresh water ran sluggishly into the main waterway and would be suitable for future development.

Eventually, at the end of a much larger creek down which the longships may just about traverse we came across the larger homestead of Oudenberg, or the old fort. The old fort, I immediately recognised as the remains of a Roman legionary camp. There was a low row of stone that delineated the outer perimeter of the camp and the outline of various buildings within it. More importantly there was a well for fresh water inside this camp. The homestead itself was outside the Roman walls, which was not surprising as the early Franks and Saxons who invaded this part of Gaul were cautious of the Roman 'magic' and rarely attempted to live within the confines of Roman settlements. Nevertheless, over the years the current settlement had pilfered stones from the site and the main farm had Roman stones rising to knee height, before wooden walls took over. I intended to stop this practice as from now on I would be the one who would use the available stone for my own building plans.

My retinue followed Martin and I across the sandy soil to the farmstead. This time our reception was more in the manner I expected. I burly man strode into the cleared area before the largest building, the farmhouse itself and several men congregated around him all carrying farming implements that, at a push, could be used as weapons. The burly man carried an axe, but it was a wood axe, nevertheless it could be a formidable killing tool.

"What do you want?" he shouted as we approached. I walked right up to him and he raised his axe.

"If you move that axe one more finger width, I will kill you." I said menacingly, he hesitated. "I am Hereward Leofricson, Lord of Testerep, Oudenberg and all the lands around here. I have been given these lands for services to the Count of Flanders, our liege lord and you and yours are my tenants and owe me fealty. Lower your axe." The farmer did as he was bid. I turned to the crowd of gathered men.

"I am an Englishman and do not believe in the system of subservience that applies in Flanders and Normandy. To me you are all free men and your lands will be held in fee simple to me. You will pay me an annual gelt, part of which I will forward on to Count Baldwin but you will keep the largest share of the profits from your labour. However, unlike other settlements within my domain, I intend to settle here, over there." I indicated the Roman fort. "You may not like this and if you want to leave, I will help you resettle at other places within my land so that you do not overly lose thereby."

"We are subjects of the lord of Bruges." The leader of the group responded.

"Not anymore, Lord Bauldran at Bruges knows I am the new lord of this area and we have an understanding. Later in the year I will be travelling to Lille to swear my formal fealty to the Count of Flanders; before then I will require all the men between twelve and seventy within my territory to swear fealty to me, any that neglects or refuses to do so will be turned off their lands. My seneschal here," I indicated towards Martin, "will be visiting your dwellings to record who lives within my domain at Oudenberg." I turned from the group, effectively dismissing them, and trudged over to the crumbling walls of the Roman fort.

"Martin, we need to set up camp here until we can build a hall, I do not want ill feeling with my new subjects so I will not dispossess anyone. After the evening meal assemble the men for a meeting." I instructed.

The boat tents and spare sails went up within the flat grassed enclosure a cooking fire was constructed and two of the ships bronze cauldrons were suspended over it. Dried fish and root vegetables were thrown in with fresh water from the settlement well. Everybody's spirits seemed to have picked up from the crews' initial reaction. The size of the lordship impressed everyone and they were particularly struck by the potential of the anchorage. The snekkja's shallow draft enabled them to be moored beam on to the bank with access by a simple gangplank to the shore. I would need to survey the inlets to ascertain if a knarr could be moored in the same fashion anywhere, otherwise I may need to consider building a wooden jetty. My biggest problem was lack of men. I currently had just over one hundred men; to crew my four snekkjas and the one knarr with full crews I needed two hundred and twenty-three men. I was sure I could recruit another fifty odd men from within my new lands but that still left me nearly half short of the numbers I needed.

After the evening meal my crews crowded around and I sat on a half-height wall that raised my head above them all when they sat on the grass.

"Well lads, you have seen some of my patrimony and I agree with your thinking, it is pretty desolate." They chuckled at the accuracy of my statement. "Nevertheless, few of you will disagree with me when I describe the harbour here as good. Although shallow at the entrance, I estimate that the Brede water, in which our ships are anchored can hold up to two hundred craft comfortably and this site has the potential to be the best anchorage between the Scheldt and Calais. Properly prepared and presented this site can become a major emporium and trading centre. From here I intend to trade along the coast, north and south, and I want to ensure all the farms and villages are prosperous and wealthy." Everyone was listening carefully now, smelling gain. "I want all my followers, all of you, to benefit from my plans. Those of you who want a farm will receive one as a fee simple tenant, those that want to trade, say open a tavern or inn, I will support, those with a skill, blacksmith, leather worker, wood wright, I will set up in your own workshop. In return for lands and support I require the provision of one oarsman, whether it is yourself, your son, or a labourer so that I can crew my ships for several weeks each year." There was a lot of thoughtful faces after this announcement. I went on. "I will not be allocating lands straight away, like you, I need to become familiar with the area, calculating the potential; also, I need to wait for the crews of *Hilda* and *Little Runa* to find us. While we are waiting, we need a roof over our heads and to achieve this we are going to build a hall worthy of the Roggen vikings. This hall will be my home and the roof under which I will accommodate my unmarried huscarls. It will be built inside this old Roman fort and will sit on the stone foundations already set. Its walls will be built with stones, there are enough of those lying about. I have a mind to have the roof covered in wooden clinker-built strakes, like an upturned boat as my tiny boat house on Roggen proved to be drier than any thatched house. What say you?"

"Aye!" a resounding shout of approval suggested I was on the right course.

I instructed Martin to travel around the island and surrounding area to record the inhabitants and their wealth while I supervised the construction of the hall. The next morning Martin set off with half a dozen men to record our new found wealth, while I marshalled the rest of the men in collecting the most useful stone blocks and on improvised stretchers carrying them to the place I had chosen for the hall. I could clearly see the outline of a very large building in the grass and a few tentative digs, removing the shallow turf revealed long stone foundations. As this building lay centrally within the fort, I assumed it was probably the Praetorium or commander's office; that much was based on my limited knowledge of the Romans. Still, it was ideal for my purposes and after a whole day's toil we had assembled sufficient stones to lay four courses along the foundation perimeter.

I had no idea how the Roman's managed to fix the stone blocks together but as they were uniformly rectangular blocks, I decided they would serve if we just laid them together as a dry-stone construction. When Martin arrived back that evening, he informed me that stone churches like the one being built in London by Edward the Mild used a lime mortar to seal the stone blocks together and that he had heard that using sea shells could produce a similar paste. I had no idea where to obtain lime but I knew that I could acquire sea shells in large quantities as I had noticed whole heaps of them at the women's farm at East End.

At the evening meal; fish stew again, I asked Martin how he had progressed.

"It will take time, I started on the island of Testerep proper, which is about a mile in depth and ten miles long. Starting at the east end you already know of the women's farm, Gritta the head of the household and eight other women, all of child bearing age, all previously married and four with infants at the breast. Two cows, a dozen ducks with wings clipped and an old mangy dog. One small fishing boat that would hold four at a push. Moving south-west, we found nothing along the coast but inland a mile from the east end we found two small farms. No names, first farm, farmer Dolf, his wife and four children, none of adult estate. One cow, a dozen geese, a goat, and some arable farming. Dolf said he had a small boat hid in the dunes for fishing. Second farm, farmer Tegen, no wife but three pretty daughters, do not want to imagine what he gets up to there. Ten cows and a bull, three goats to many geese and ducks to count and a large vegetable plot. I then came to the dyke you reached yesterday and followed on to the south side of the island where we came to Oberkinsdyke. This was a small village, three hovels, no chief, three heads of households, Sveinn, Witta and Skuld all married with innumerable children of all ages some of the older boys and girls need to be married off soon or they will start interbreeding. In the village, one horse, four oxen used for ploughing, six goats."

"Stop, stop." I cried. "Spare me the details. "Give me a summary."

"Of course." Martin huffed; he liked detail. "We crossed the dyke and surveyed the rest of the island up to the west end. There were two sizable villages, Westend and Middlekirk, yes that is right, a church at that village. In total about twenty folk live at Westend and fifty folk live in Middlekirk, also dotted around the island are several farms, eighteen to be exact, all with sizable families, livestock, and crops. Both villages have several fishing boats. I will start with the rest of the island tomorrow, although I am not sure if the rest of the island is an island as it is separated from the mainland by a dyke only."

"Well, if the rest of my lordship is like this, I need to bring wealth into the area to make it prosper. We need horses, cattle, wood, and ship builders.

"May I suggest you need a port reeve; I know how much you detest such administrators but the waterway needs supervision. We also need to build some hostelries and whore houses if we want sailors to stop over. Bredene and Stene, either side of the widest part of the inlet are ideal places for such temptations." Martin suggested.

"Yes, you are right. We need someone to go to Bruges on a recruitment drive and they need to be some of the first buildings to be erected." I concluded; but who to send, ships captains and noted warriors were not the answer. "Martin, what about the head man in the village." I nodded my head in the direction of Oudenberg. "I could send him with one of my men, have we any Flemings left in the camp?"

"Well, Christofer is a Fleming but he is hardly going to want to be enticing whores and prostitutes here. Svart is a Fleming, he usually keeps himself to himself but he does not put a foot wrong on board or in the shield wall; seems astute." Martin thought.

"Right, fetch me Svart and I'll see the village head man tonight." I determined.

Svart was, as his name implied, swarthy and small, but he was wide and could pull an oar for two shifts without tiring. I had noticed him before and exchanged a few words but never singled him out. He looked stolid and unworried, a good thing I thought.

"Svart, sit, I would talk with you." I handed him a cup of ale. "Svart, you have been with me since last summer and acquitted yourself well. Is there anything you hope to attain from our venture?" I asked, prodded more like.

He was silent for a while and then began. "In truth lord, I had not given it any thought. Two years ago, I was a farmer when all my family were killed by German's raiding into Hainhault, far inland. I lost the will to live but could not bring myself to end it all. I fell in with your recruitment by accident and killed Zealanders instead of Germans. Since then, I no longer feel the urge to kill and I cannot even remember my wife's face. This torments me. I need a reason to live."

"Svart, I will give you a reason to live; I will give you work to test your mind. I will work you hard, you will have no time to dwell on your past life." I could see a moment of fear in Svart's eyes and then a hardening, a resolve.

"What would you ask of me, lord?"

"First, you will accompany the village headman to Bruges; you and he will purchase a number of items we need here, horses, cattle, carts, tools, many things. You are to try and recruit men, and a certain kind of women, we also need tradesmen, blacksmiths, leather workers, all sorts of artisans. Will you do this?"

"Yes, my lord, willingly, anything to occupy my mind." Svart responded.

"Good, I am trusting you, occupy your mind by all means but ensure the results are good. Come to me on the morrow after we break our fast and I will give you funds to achieve our aims." I dismissed Svart.

Later in the day I wandered down to the village below the Roman fort. I went fully armoured but without a shield or Dane axe. I carried my bow and a sheath of arrows and two large dead pheasants, which I had shot earlier that day. The villagers eyed me askance, which worried me not, none approached me. I strolled over to the head man's cottage and rapped on the door frame. The head man peered out and looked uneasy when he saw me standing there.

"I wish to talk with you, inside or out?" I demanded. He struggled with his obligation of hospitality until he was pushed aside by a stout, bold woman, wearing a large white apron and head cloth to conceal her blonde hair.

"Please enter, my lord, my husband, Odoacer is a bit slow when it comes to good manners but he is a solid farmer and husbandman and the people in the village respect him." She spoke out boldly.

"Thank you, goodwife. I have here two fine pheasants for your pot with the evening meal coming on, and all." I held out the pheasants and the goodwife beamed.

"These will go down a treat with vegetables, and you will be staying for the meal I trust." She responded with alacrity. The head man stood aside and gestured me to enter. Not being as tall as the farmer I barely had to stoop to pass under the lintel. I placed my bow and quiver against the interior of the door post. I noticed a young boy staring up at me, he must have been around eight years of age; his head had been shorn of hair, although I could see blonde wisps and I suspected an infestation of lice. The farm house was quite large and it was obvious from the crowd of children that Odoacer's reticence did not include activity in his bed. I unbuckled my sword and handed it to the boy.

"What is your name boy?" I asked him seriously.

"Erik, sir." He chirped.

"Well Erik you must look after my sword and not unsheathe it. It is a magic sword, named Serpent's Breath, and every time it is withdrawn from its scabbard it must take a life. You guard it carefully for me."

I turned to the headman. "You have a fine boy there; I would talk with you." Odoacer gestured to a carved wooden seat by the hearth, which I suspect was his own master's chair. "No, you sit there, as you are the master of this house; I will sit on this stool." I sat down on a three-legged stool, which probably doubled as a milking stool. "Odoacer, that is not a Frisian name, sound more Saxon to me?" I ventured.

"My forefathers came to this area many years ago when the Saxons were driven west by the Huns. The Saxons were led by a mighty chieftain called Odoacer and the name has been in my family for generations in honour of him." The head man explained.

I marvelled at how such a racial memory could survive so long in a backwater like Testerep and I suspected that the farmer had no idea that the Odoacer he revered became the first King of Italy after the Roman Empire had fallen.

"Well, Saxon or Frisian, it matters not, I want you to do something for me for which you will be well rewarded." Odoacer looked cautious but his wife looked enthusiastic, I wondered if it wouldn't be better if the good wife would not be a better choice of ambassador? "As you know I intend to build up this area to make it an emporium of sea trade, but I also want the land-based dwellers to benefit as well. I have started a survey of the area and I am disappointed that there is such poverty. I want to boost the economy by giving the farmers and villagers the means to increase their wealth and live in better dwellings. There is the need for many improvements and to achieve these I need someone to go to Bruges and purchase a list of animals and supplies to distribute around the island. I want someone to buy horses, oxen and cows, a good bull, goats, pigs. The island needs good carts, lots of wood to build newer and better dwellings. Carpenters, blacksmiths all sorts of artisans are needed. I need supplies of grain for brewing, and wine. The list is long. I need someone to recruit labourers, milkmaids, fisherfolk. The person I have chosen to go to Bruges is you."

There was a look of shock on Odoacer's face but is wife beamed with pleasure. For good measure, I added.

"I suggest you take your wife with you; she will enjoy the journey and will have the opportunity to buy some new clothes and such things that good wives appreciate. I take your silence as agreement. You will set off the day after tomorrow, I will be providing the funds for the purchases and you will be escorted by one of my captains, Svart Arkilson by name, a Frisian, and an escort of ten of my huscarls. I expect you all to be riding back."

Once Odoacer got over the shock, he started asking pertinent questions that began to reassure me that I had made a sensible choice. He was obviously a farmer and potential trader through and through and would not be wasting my money. The evening meal was duly presented by his wife and all fourteen of his brood joined in. After a shy start the children gathered around and I was asked the usual questions, why were my eyes two different colours, was my sword really magic, what animal fur was that around my shoulders? While this was on-going it helped Odoacer to fully understand who I was, what my relationship with the Count of Flanders and his sons was, and what benefits could be forthcoming from my appointment as the lord of Testerep. The evening ended convivially and I bid the family farewell on a friendly and positive note.

Two days later, Svart, Odoacer, his wife another Hilda, and my huscarls assembled. I gave Svart a chest of silver, about a tenth of my wealth. Svart's job was to acquire whores and warriors, Hilda, I knew would guide Odoacer with the rest. It was a major trust on my part but I felt good about both of them and even more so Odoacer's wife. I anticipated they would return in about a week.

Martin had delayed his surveying to show the men how to grind and mix seashells into a mortar that set hard. It was an unpleasant job and smelled vile but the paste that resulted from the process, set hard and sealed the joints of the stone walls. It worked so well I decided to raise the walls of the hall and extra six courses with buttresses to support the weight of the roof. The men groaned about this but in truth the walls went up quicker than a timber frame and the rare materials were much easier to acquire as they lay about our feet. A week of hard labour finished

467

the walls and we now had to acquire some major wooden beams for the roof frame and that meant a trip to the nearest wooded area inland. I was not sure who claimed the woods as they seemed to be outside of my lordship; there was a few stands of trees within the lordship but I did not want to denude the area of trees. The larger forested areas seemed to be to the south-west of Bruges and I assumed that I would have to reach an agreement with the castellan. The lack of wood meant that I might have to initially abandon my desire to have a wooden slatted roof and revert to the traditional thatch.

A week to the day Svart and Odoacer with an extensive convoy of carts trundled back into the village. Additional to the laden carts I could see a drove of cattle, leashed goats, and crated geese. Svart, Odoacer and all the huscarls were riding, some on horses and some on mules. I also could see a flock of sheep, too numerous to count. I had not identified sheep for purchase; interesting? Hilda was sitting upon the lead cart like a queen with a new shawl around her shoulders, heavily embroidered in reds and greens. Finally, there was a long trail of people, men, women and even some children. I waved to Hilda and strolled over.

"I will visit you this evening and your husband can report on your venture." She smiled a broad smile, clearly, she had enjoyed herself immensely; I had been told by Martin, I think, nothing gives a woman greater pleasure than spending other people's wealth.

Svart came over to me and dismounted; his horse was a fine-looking palfrey, chestnut with white socks and a white blaze on his nose. "Lord, I have brought this mare for your use so that you can ride your domains, as your status demands."

"It is a fine-looking beast and reminds me of one I left in Wales and never recovered." I said with thanks. "Come over to my tent and you can report on your progress, I am seeing Odoacer later and you can accompany me; but first, sort out this large group of people."

Later Svart and I sat outside my tent and we were joined by Martin who had returned from his days surveying. Svart collected himself and reported.

"My lord, I will leave Odoacer, or rather his wife to report on their successes. I will confine myself to what I have achieved.

First, I have twenty new recruits for the ship's crews and as potential warriors. They are nearly all young lads between twelve and twenty and are keen for adventure. Secondly, I have persuaded seven doxies from the stews of Bruges to accompany me on the promise they will be housed in a whorehouse protected by your lordship and to receive a larger percentage of their earnings than they were given in Bruges. I believe they had problems with bullying pimps. Thirdly, I have acquired the services of two blacksmiths who have armouring skills, they can mend mail, hammer an axe or a decent sword; not the quality of a lord's blade but a serviceable weapon. The rest of the purchases were within Odoacer's remit but I helped him with purchasing the horses and mules." Svart paused.

"Svart, you have exceeded my expectations. These young men will become part of my hearth companions as they are too young to be given their own farms. One of the blacksmiths will become my personal armourer and work on my projects, the other will be the island's general blacksmith and improve the farming utensils and settlements needs, generally. We will now go over to Odoacer's place and see what he has to say."

I was very pleased with the developments, so far. I armed and dressed myself in the manner becoming of a lord and Svart, Martin and I left the Roman fort and walked down towards the village of Oudenberg. Young Erik was waiting outside of his parent's house and bowed respectfully to me, as he had been clearly taught to do. I unbuckled my sword and handed him the scabbarded weapon, I looked meaningfully at him.

He grinned, "I know my lord, I am not to unsheathe it, it's magical."

Erik entered the dwelling and announced me in a loud voice. "The Lord Hereward and Master Svart. I entered after him through the low door and straightened up, in front of me Odoacer and Hilda stood with their children in a line, they all respectfully bowed or curtsied. I acknowledged their greeting.

"Welcome to my home Lord Hereward, come sit and take a cup of ale and Hilda has some refreshments." I had already identified a delicious aroma that suggested a bird pie. I sat on the stool, as before and Svart pulled up another stool. It was obvious that the children were going to be short of seats but they did not seem dismayed. "Lord Hereward, I would give you a complete tally of our transactions and agreements, I cannot read or write but I assure you my memory is faultless in these matters."

"Please continue, Master Odoacer." I responded.

"As you commanded, I went to the markets of Bruges and waited for market day to ensure of the best purchases and competitive prices. I purchased one bull that will be able to service the cows across the island, to compliment the bull a herd of fine Flemish and Frisian cows to the number of forty. Goats, one billy and six nanny goats. Geese thirty crated, a mixture of male and female, chickens, one rooster and twenty laying hens. Pigs, two boars and eight sows, all good quality. I am sure you saw a flock of sheep in our train, sheep can successfully graze on sandy soil and even on sand dunes so I bought a flock, not the best, they are in England, but a scraggy lot that will provide course fleeces, they came cheap. I am short of a ram but that can be rectified in the future." Odoacer paused and took a sip of his ale. Hilda was dying to intervene but bit her lip and let her husband have his time. "We have purchased eight carts all pulled by two oxen that are good for the plough. We have a blacksmith who can forge new ploughs so we can plough eight village strips at the same time. That will service most of the island. On the carts we have one iron plough, an array of farming tools, forks, hoes, mattocks and much more. We have also purchased ten large sacks of grain seed for sowing; twenty sacks of fleeces for clothing or sail sheets. More important for Testerep we have four carts full of lumber for building. We have also acquired twenty mules as beasts of burden. Lastly, the people, I know Svart has recruited young men as potential warriors and then there are those women." Odoacer looked sidelong at his wife who clearly was not amused. "But Hilda and I have recruited people as well, we have brought ten families, husbands, wives and children all hoping for farm land to work on, to make a living away from the town where people lord it over them."

Odoacer stopped and clearly, he had run out of steam. Hilda nudged him and he started again.

"Oh! Yes, I forgot; the lumber was a gift from the Lady Dedda, no charge. Hilda purchased one hundred and twenty ells of cloth mostly undyed that can be used to improve the clothing of your men and dress some of the women around here more decently." Odoacer looked at Hilda again for inspiration and Hilda could not stay silent any longer.

"Lord, when my husband met Lady Dedda, he also spoke to the castellan about wood for the new buildings. He agreed a price for each tree, which we felt was very fair. The woods to the west of Bruges have some fine oak and elm trees and they are under the castellan's hand."

That last piece of information pleased me more than anything and we now had the wherewithal to develop the area as I wished; still Odoacer looked uncomfortable.

"There is more?" I queried.

"We have spent more than two thirds of the silver you provided us with, I hope that was not too forward of us lord?"

I laughed, "I expected you to spend all of it; look treasure is no use in a box, it must be used for good. I want you to keep the rest and make Oudenberg a really vibrant village. I want shops, inns, a blacksmith's workshop, and artisan shops." I smiled at Odoacer and his wife and tried to put them at ease. "You have done well, all of you." I indicated Svart as well. "Odoacer you are now the village reeve and will receive a tenth of the revenue I will receive each year, and you will need a bigger, better house." Hilda beamed. "And Svart, I intend for you to be the port reeve for the whole of the Bredene Fjord, your house and tax office will be built at the water's edge you will collect the gelt and supervise the shipping. You will receive a tenth of the port revenue. How say you both?"

Svart looked stunned, "I am not worthy of such trust, my lord."

I responded with a smile and a reassuring hand on his arm. "I trust you and Martin trusts you and his judgement is the best I have ever known. I cannot rule my lordship directly as I know I will be called to war. You are the trusted man to do this for me, this will be more your legacy than mine." Svart's eyes filled but he held back the tears.

"I only wish my wife was alive to see my good fortune." He whispered.

Hilda leaned forward and said comfortingly, "She will surely know."

"Odoacer, I know you will accept this responsibility or I will give the post to your wife." I threatened. They both laughed and held hands reassuringly.

"Two more items then before we part, tomorrow, Martin I need a convoy sent to the woods near Bruges for I need some tall trees to craft beams for the hall, no beam length less than the width of the hall and secondly we will meet tomorrow to determine the distribution of farmland to my captains and huscarls and the allocation of the farming families to their plots." This will consider those of my men who are away, but I cannot wait for their return to start the distribution and work." I announced.

"Should I try and find out which of the men want lands?" Martin asked.

"Yes, it would be best." I concluded. I took my leave and returned to the camp in the Roman fort.

Before I retired, I thought of one last task. "Martin, tomorrow there is nothing much for the men to do on my hall, not until the roof beams are acquired. So, the men can start laying the stone foundations and walls of other buildings; storage barns, stables, a bakery, a laundry, and a chapel, I will think of more anon."

"Yes, of course, there are enough men to lay these buildings out within a couple of weeks." Martin responded.

"Good, then they can move on to the shipyard and whorehouse down by the waterside. See you in the morning." I went to retire.

The next day after all the men had been set to work, I asked the captains that were still with me and not with Magnus and Egil trading, to join me for breakfast and discuss the allocation of lands. Breakfast was quite a sumptuous affair with fresh bread and butter sent up from the village, eggs, cold smoked sausages, cheese, and milk.

We sat around in front of my makeshift tent, as usual. Those present were Martin, my right hand; Gauti, the skipper of *Mare Swallow*; Eric the Dubliner, master of the *Ottar*; Eystein Whaleleg, Eric, his son; Coll, master of *Wave Rider*; Christofer the Christian, he was not a ship's master but was influential with my Christian followers; Svart my new port reeve and I had also invited Odoacer my new village reeve.

472

"Good morning captains. The only captains not present are Egil and Magnus who, for the benefit of Odoacer, here." I indicated my new village reeve to them all, "are away trading this summer. Martin has surveyed most of the lordship that I have been awarded by the Count of Flanders and it is substantial. I want my captains to benefit from this good fortune but I do not want the people under my rule to suffer. I am going to allot lands to those who want it but you must build your own hall and not displace the land folk." I received nods of agreement from this statement and I could see that Odoacer and Christofer were especially pleased by this decision. "I have already made certain appointments, many of you may have been wondering why Odoacer and Svart are with us; well, I have appointed Odoacer the village reeve for Oudenberg and this appointment will eventually cover the new buildings within the Roman fort as well as the expanding village. Odoacer has proved himself more than capable of undertaking this role. Svart will be my new port reeve for the whole of the river estuary on the north-east side of Testerep; this will include the control of the intended wooden wharfs, the warehouses, the inns, and whorehouses to be built down by the waterside. Svart has also shown his ability and you may already have noticed the arrival of several doxies that will eventually inhabit the said whorehouses." They laughed at this, good naturedly, I continued.

"Christofer has asked me if he can build a church and I have agreed, but I have already set in place the building of a chapel within this Roman fort. I understand from Martin that there are already the ruins of a church at a place aptly called Middlekerke on Testerep and a small church still functioning at a place called Snaaskerke somewhere across the water from here. These two places I gift to Christofer in fee simple to me to build farms and reopen the delipidated church. Do you accept?"

"I do my lord." Christofer looked well pleased.

"Good, next I give the east end of the Testerep island proper to Eystein Whaleleg and his son Eric. Eystein, I know you are well past looking after a farm and you are permanently welcome in my hall without obligation. Eric, you will manage your father's and your patrimony. I know the women we met on our first landing here live in a mean hovel at Oostende, which is very exposed to the weather and passing raiders, I would advise you to build your farm at Oberkinsdyke on the south side of the island where it is more sheltered. This is, again, an award in fee simple from me to you, however, there is one other requirement of this tenure and that is to build and man a wooden tower on the inlet headland to give warning of passing raiders. I have no intention of having my lands ravaged by vikings." I waited for the laughter but everyone was too serious when it came to the distribution of wealth they had not expected in their wildest dreams.

"Eric the Dubliner, so called to distinguish you from Eric Whalelegson, I offer you the villages of Leffing and Slype that lay within the centre of my patrimony, two good villages with several families." Eric always taciturn, nodded.

"Gauti, I offer you the villages of Hunckevliete and Manekesvere in the south-west of my lands."

Gauti responded, "Thank you, lord."

"Coll, I offer you the village of Gistel at the head of the Waresvaart, or Ware Water and both sides of the Waresvaart until where it joins the Brede Ee." Coll nodded.

"Svart my port reeve will also hold Zandvoorde, where the whorehouse and wharf will be located to build his own hall as I am sure he would not wish to live in the warehouses; I do not know about the whorehouse?" This time everyone did laugh.

"Know, although they are absent, I can tell you that it is my intention to give Egil the place called Staina and the land around the Oude Creke, it is perfect for ship building and if we can acquire the wood, I would like him to oversee the building of some of our own knarrs as I foresee trade as the lifeline and wealth of this lordship. As to Magnus I intend to award him Bredene and all the east bank of the Brede Ee. Finally, although he is young, it is my intention in a year or two to give the desolate Westende of Testerep to Dietrich Jansen, who has served me well."

"Good, that will keep him far away from the whores at Zandvoorde, they will be worn out else." Gauti commented and everyone laughed again.

"I remind you that all these lands are held in fee simple, you owe me homage and gelt from them and must swear your oaths. Equally, within the week I must ride to Lille or wherever the count is, to swear homage to him for this lordship." I looked around at their serious faces. "Rest assured though we are not undertaking the lives of farmers. You will need to ensure your farms can be farmed without you; that means getting a good wife or land steward because I do not intend to stop fighting, it is my life and I am sure the count and his sons will be calling upon me, as I will be calling upon you to fight and sail; we are still the Roggen vikings."

"That's a relief." Coll blurted.

Later after the meeting I cornered Martin, who appeared to always be busy. "Martin, I have not included you in the distribution of largesse. I have been presumptuous and assumed that you would stay with me whatever; but this can be remedied if you wish it?"

"No master, my fate is with you and I will live and die by your side. I will serve as your steward either formally or informally."

"Words cannot express what your devotion means to me, Martin." I acknowledged.

Summer 1060 - Fealty

I was riding hard to Arras in Artois where the Count of Flanders has summoned me to do homage for my lands in and around Testerep. Artois was a French county but was controlled by the mighty Count of Flanders. The French king probably did not want Count Baldwin to hold Artois but there was little he could do about it at the moment. The French king was weak and had come off badly in several military engagements with Duke William of Normandy. I assumed that Count Baldwin regularly perambulated his lands and that it was just my misfortune that he was in Arras when he decided he wanted me to swear fealty.

Arras was a further thirty miles, or so, south of Lille, which was the furthest south I had been until summoned. I still only had six horses to my name, so I was taking five retainers, not a great retinue for someone of my current status but the best I could do without taking weeks to reach my destination and I was not begging any more horseflesh from Dedda and her husband in Bruges. In truth I was still fixated on sailing the swan's path, the North Sea as the Flemish referred to the waters between England and the mainland of Europe. I was not a particularly good horseman when compared to the Norman and Flemish nobles and so my ideal conveyance on land was a palfrey, not a destrier; a warhorse. We clattered through Lille without stopping and eventually reached Arras on the fourth day of our travels. I decided to take Eric the Dubliner, Coll, Gautrek the Berserker, Christofer, and young Dietrich Jensen with me as the least needed bodies in Testerep. Martin would not hear of accompanying me where riding was involved, in truth, none of us were competent horsemen with Dietrich adapting best to his mare and as Gautrek quipped Dietrich seemed to be good at riding any female.

The town of Arras was situated on a chalk plateau with a river winding through it. The town was an assemblage of houses, shops and hostelries clustered around the Abbey of Saint Vaast, whoever he was, and I was not going to ask Christofer. We found a relatively modest inn that could accommodate us in one room and I sent Christofer, as the politest of my retinue, off to announce my presence at court. Christofer returned whilst we were having our evening meal of rabbit pie, vegetable and rock-hard bread that had to be soaked in the juices to be at all edible.

"Well?" I asked as I shoved a plate over to him and indicated the pie in the centre of our table.

"The oath takings are to be held in the abbey on Sunday, three days hence, for the next couple of days there is hunting and feasting to which you are invited." Christofer explained.

"Is Robert Baldwin's son there?" I asked.

"Yes, he is." Christofer replied.

"Good I will go and see him tomorrow." I decided.

The beds were more comfortable than I expected, but then I could not remember when last, I had slept in anything but a tent or upturned boat; the only problem was Gautrek's snoring! The following morning, I went to find Lord Robert. I found him preparing for the hunt wearing a very gaudy green velvet doublet and tight leggings.

"Hereward, my viking, how is it with you in your sleepy part of Flanders, some island near Bruges isn't it.?" Robert exclaimed. Clearly the Flemings believed the count's gift of land to me was something of a joke, a sandy bit of land no one else would want or care for. None of them realised the potential of the area because none of them were bred to the sea.

"Well, my lord, well. It is a safe haven for my ships and I cannot ask for more than that." I replied; he looked puzzled but then shrugged it off.

"I am for the hunt; will you join me?" Robert's naturally cheerful demeanour reasserted itself.

"Only if I must, I prefer to kill my prey not chase them." I added belligerently.

"There is boar in the forest nearby, not as ferocious as a white bear but dangerous none the less."

"I will leave that to you, Lord Robert but be careful, I need you to start my wars for me." Robert laughed at that.

I did not learn anything from my brief conversation with Robert but as I was leaving the abbey grounds, I bumped into Gherbod, the warrior I had last seen leading the Flemish army in

Zealand. He saw me and came over with outstretched hand, another man accompanied him.

"Ah! The Bearslayer, himself; how are you? Oh! This is Drogo de Bonueir, a valiant Flemish soldier you may not have met yet."

"Indeed, I have not, good day to you." I took Gerbod's hand and shook it in the English way and extended the hand to Drogo likewise. "I am fine and will be swearing my oath of fealty to the count on Sunday."

"Ah! You are lucky." Exclaimed Drogo. "Land is scarce in these parts and adventurous men may have to travel far to gain such."

"I understood not everyone wanted such a barren spot as I was enfeoffed with." I responded.

"Tis true that the land granted to you was not greatly prized but there are a lot of land hungry men in Flanders, who may have to look further afield than home to gratify their needs." Gherbod added.

"And just where are land hungry men looking?" I asked.

"The Normans have done very well in Italy and are carving great dukedoms that need warriors to defend them. Likewise, the Spanish need warriors beyond the Pyrenees to throw back the Moors." Gherbod stated.

"I have heard that Duke William hopes to rule England one day and he will surely need men to achieve this." Drogo pronounced.

"William has no right to England and you are right he would need many men to conquer the English." I countered.

"Ah! Might is right, whatever; did you not prove that in Scheldtmerland, Bearslayer?" Gherbod exclaimed.

We parted but the conversation made me uneasy. Did others deem me unprincipled, as a captain of mercenaries, it would seem so. I wandered back towards the inn where my men were staying and absentmindedly bumped into an old man who I nearly bowled over. I grabbed him and hauled him upright.

"I am sorry, I was not looking where I was going." I said by way of an apology.

"My dear Lord Hereward, not many people look where they are going in life, fear not." The old man said in a familiar voice. I looked hard.

"Why it is the surgeon, Salman ben Isaac, the Jewish physician, how are you?" I said with some warmth as this was a person I greatly respected.

"I am well, and still in God's grace." Salman replied.

"And your daughter, Rebecca, is she well?" I could never forget those beautiful eyes and long dark tresses.

"She is well and residing with my cousin in Ghent where she is learning mathematics and calculus. My cousin is a truly wise and educated scholar, although a little unworldly." Salman mused.

"Well as I have absolutely no idea what mathematics and calculus are, I am sure he must be a paragon of the sciences and the intellectual capacity of your daughter must terrify any would be suitors and scare them away." I laughed.

"Ah! You may be right, she is past marriageable age and there are so few eligible Jewish men around, I despair for my line." Salman looked troubled.

"You mean that Jews only marry Jews then?" I asked intrigued.

"It is essential. Oh, there are parts of the world where good Jewish girls are taken forcibly as wives and their fathers dare not object. This happens mainly in the lands of the Arabs and Moors who do not denigrate the Jews like the Christians do. Here no self-respecting Christian would ever marry a Jew."

"Yes, I remember warning you about that when we first met, a Christian would more than likely steal her away and enslave her, so I am pleased to hear she is in a safe place." I responded. "I take it you are still serving the count as his physician as you are here?"

"Yes, I am, and I am needed for the count is in poor health." Salman stated.

"The count is in poor health? He did not seem unduly unwell the last time I saw him." I commented.

"He is plagued with stomach pains and I am sure he has ulcers; I have prescribed the drinking of milk to reduce the acidic content in his stomach but I cannot wean him from wine and if he does not abstain, he may eventually die." Salman explained.

"Well, I have no idea what an ulcer is but it does not sound good; I wish you well in your endeavours."

"Changing the subject, I hear you are a lord in Flanders now with land on the coast." I could see on Salman's face he had heard the land I had been given was poor.

"Yes, I am now Lord of Testerep an island near Bruges and an excellent port, which I intend to develop into a major trading emporium. These Flemings only understand its worth for agriculture and stock rearing but its real value can only be understood by seafarers." I explained.

Salman smiled, "I see, you have duped your paymasters but do not make them too jealous."

"Ah! There is a Jew speaking." I laughed and Salman laughed with me. I explained my business in Arras and suggested that we get together before I left and partake of a meal together with convivial conversation, to which he agreed.

I stayed out of the way for the next few days as I had no wish to draw attention to myself. I had little in common with the lords of Flanders except a mutual attraction to war and conflict. I duly presented myself on Sunday morning at the Abbey of Saint Vaast as the great and the good were entering to attend mass. I understood the oathtaking was to take place after the mass. The act of homage was frequently reaffirmed so I expected many of the lords within Artois would be required to swear their oaths again and the process would be long and tedious and I was not wrong. The abbey church was thronged with the lords of the counties of Artois and Flanders. The mass was surprisingly short and I suspected that the count conscious of the time the homage would take had requested it so, to a very compliant abbot. After the mass the count sat on the abbots carved chair before the altar. A chamberlain stood up and addressed the congregation.

"My lords, reverend abbot, your prince, Baldwin fifth of that name, Count of Flanders, Artois and Scheldtmerland has summoned you here today to renew your oaths of fealty and pay homage for your lands. Some of you will be giving homage for the first time; your oath will be sworn before the altar and, on the

Bible, and relics of Saint Vaast. I will call your name and you will kneel before your lord."

The chamberlain held a long scroll, which confirmed that I would be waiting most of the morning. The first noble to step forward without being summoned was the count's eldest son Baldwin, Count of Hainault, this was symbolic and it was lost on none that the next time the oathtaking was demanded it may well be to the son and not the father. Following Baldwin, Count of Hainhault, I expected Robert the second son, but not so, Baldwin of Hainhault turned and beckoned a young boy, maybe five years old at the most, forward. I surreptitiously asked my neighbour who the boy was and was informed it was Arnulf the son of the Count of Hainault and the Count of Flanders eldest grandson. The boy's voice was reedy and unintelligible from where I stood at the back of the church. The elderly count gave warm words to his grandson who skipped away. Robert, the counts second son came next and his voice rang throughout the church bold and forthright. From then on it was a long line of Flemish nobles and lords from Artois one after another. I was becoming noticeable irritated when my name was called at last.

I had noticed earlier in the morning that none of the lords had attended church in mail and armour, but as I had no other apparel, I was wearing my chainmail hauberk, steel wrist guards, which the Flemish call vambraces, my steel lined boots and my white bearskin shoulder protector. I had left my helmet on the floor at the door, together with my sword, scramaseax and Dane axe. I strode forward, shouldering my way through the crowd, many of the lords were curious as to who I was, some had heard of me, the buzz of conversation died as I reached the front and faced the Count.

I did not kneel, I had no intention of so doing; Baldwin knew the story of Gangu Hrolf, the first Duke of Normandy who had unceremoniously up-ended the King of France. There was a pause and Baldwin stood, I stepped forward and placed my hands together, as in prayer, Baldwin placed his hands around mine.

"I Hereward Leofricson, Lord of Testerep, promise on my faith that I will in the future be faithful to my lord, Baldwin, the fifth of his name, Count of Flanders, Artois and Scheldtmerland, never to cause him harm and will observe my homage for my lands in Flanders to him completely against all persons in good faith and without deceit, so help me God, I so swear."

Baldwin smiled and nodded and said quietly, "Rollo the Norman, Eh?"

I smiled in return and walked back to the rear of the church. Later that day the count's chamberlain found me and recited the details of the gelt that I was required to pay annually for my lands. There was no mention of port dues so I was well pleased with this arrangement, for clearly the count did not appreciate the value of Testerep as a port either. I intended to return to my island first thing on Monday morning so I decided to find Salman Ben Isaac and spend some time with him. I located him sitting in the abbey grounds on a stone seat he looked up recognised me and smiled.

"Ah! Hereward did you know that this Saint Vaast, or Vedast in French, he was a Frenchman you know, and is the saint one prays to when you have eyesight problems. As a physician I find it remarkable that Christians believe that a long dead holy man can intercede with God to repair the deterioration of bodily functions."

"Does not your Jewish God help the Jews? I seem to remember that he frequently smote the Israelite's enemies." I responded.

Salman laughed weakly, "So the Torah says but I doubt such claims." He stroked his beard, "All intercessions by God on the part of the Israelites are before recorded history; God certainly has not done the Jews any favours since records can be verified, the Egyptians, the Assyrians, the Babylonians, maybe not the Persians, the Greeks and especially the Romans all oppressed my countrymen. Self-rule has been denied us and we have been dispersed over the face of the earth."

"So, you believe that saints are frauds?" I enquired.

"Oh! I do not deny that they were holy men and that they cured illnesses, I have done such myself, but I am no saint." He mused. "It is possible, of course, that this Vedast had some success in curing cataracts or stigmas to the eyes; perhaps if you prey to him, he could change the colour of your eye, but which one?"

I smiled, "My eyes are my eyes and they make me distinctive and remind me who to hate." Salman smiled back.

"Come take the evening meal with me." I begged.

"Gladly, and I know a place that serves passable food that is acceptable to my race." Salman waved me to follow him and gathering up his robes he strode from the abbey grounds.

The rest of the evening was spent in pleasant discourse that ranged across a whole range of subjects but the one topic that fascinated me the most was the way the Jews kept their wealth safe. It had long concerned me that I kept all my wealth in strong boxes that went everywhere with me, that is until recently, when I have kept it guarded at Testerep. The Jews had resolved this problem; they had long ago realised they were vulnerable to attack and abuse on the road or even in towns and so they kept their wealth with people they called bankers. These bankers operated a network of interconnected banks where the wealth was kept secure. When a Jew wished to travel, he would deposit his wealth at the bank where he set out from and was given a token, which he could redeem for the same wealth he had banked at the start of his journey at another bank at the end of his journey. In this way a Jew could travel hundreds miles across the world. Salman assured me he could bank monies in Bruges and redeem the same amount in Rome, or even Jerusalem. I could not envisage ever using this system but who knows?

It was useless trying to stop a Jew talking about religion so I did not try, I did find Salman's discourse on the religions of the world fascinating. What this discussion did remind me to do was ask the count if he could speak to the relevant bishop about providing some priests and maybe some monks for my new lands.

I was up and ready to leave early in the morning but had to kick my heels waiting for the count to appear. When he finally arrived at the door of the abbey's guest accommodation, I had to admit he did not look well. Too much wine the night before was probably aggravating the ulcers Salman referred to. I approached and saluted.

"My lord count, permit me to leave and return to my new lands, there is much to do; and I would ask a boon."

483

Princes are always wary of nobles asking for favours and rarely commit themselves.

"If I can help you in any way, Lord Hereward, I will; what sort of request do you require of me? The count harrumphed and twisted his torso clearly discomforted by his internal organs.

"It is a simple request, sire; that you ask the bishop whose diocese Testerep is in, Bruges, no doubt, if he can provide my lands with a priest and possibly some monks who wish to found a new monastery."

The count smiled broadly. "That is good news, Hereward, perhaps you are not as heathen as I thought. Bruges falls within the diocese of Noyon and Tournai, whose current Bishop is Balduin, a far-out cousin of mine, he will assist you, I will ensure it." I explained to the count that I had at least three potential churches and a chapel site that needed recolonising. Like most of the coastal districts of northern France, Flanders and Frisia, the Norsemen had devastated the religious centres a hundred years or more ago. So, I took my leave and returned to Testerep with a blithe heart, almost like returning home.

Summer – 1060 Homage

I still sat on an old chair provided by Odoacer's wife, Hilda, but every day I went to the workshop to examine the woodcarver's work on my high seat. I had insisted that he leave the seat itself free of carving, I had seen Irish kings squirm on uncomfortable posteriors because the wood carver did not know when to stop. The arm rests were carved polar bears with snarling mouths at the hand rests; very me. The two back uprights were writhing serpents, representing the world serpent Thor had to fight at Ragnarok. The legs were representative of four bases of the world tree Yggdrasill with interlaced branches and leaves supporting the seat. On the back rest the carver wanted to represent the Christ on the cross, but I was not sure about that and we had been debating the alternatives for a week now.

My hall had been long completed. The roof was indeed constructed of clinker strakes but unlike a longship the strakes were straight. At two points along the apex of the roof there were holes that had been covered in thatch. This was to let the smoke from the fires escape. The gable ends of the hall had carved lintels depicting the waves of the sea and various sea monsters, seals, walrus, whales, and the kraken. At the apex of each gable end was a carving of a dragon's head to which was affixed large stag antlers, an amazing creation. Although the exterior walls were dressed stone, pilfered from the old Roman site, the interior walls had been plastered smooth so the whole edifice was weather proof. Hilda had organised the women of the village to weave woollen sheets that hung on the walls covering the bare walls. A local seamstress was working through them gradually introducing colourful depictions of viking ships and hunting scenes. The horizontal roof beams were long but sturdy with support struts between the beams and the roof. The wood carver wanted to carve into them but I did not deem it necessary as with the smoky ceiling they could barely be seen through the smoke haze when feasts were ongoing. The beams had been brought from the woods nearby Bruges and pulled by the oxen acquired

485

by Odoacer and his wife, they took a week to be hauled the short distance.

The floor of the hall was covered in thick woven rush mats of which there were plenty in the riverine creeks around Testerep and along both sides of the hall were long trestle tables and benches for the feasting. Along both sides of the hall about seven feet in from the walls there had been placed a row of upright tree supports for the roof beams and between each of these uprights and the wall they had been filled in with sheets to create cubicles, one for each of my young huscarls. At the south end of the hall a wooden cubicle had been constructed for my private quarters; this was quite small as I did not have a wife or family and basically housed my bed and the large polar bear skin that lay atop it.

In the centre of the hall was a series of open fires troughs for cooking and warmth. The hall could accommodate well over two hundred people at a push and was the largest building for miles around and there were few larger buildings in Bruges. I had decided to have a huge feast for all my people at Yule, which I was going to call a hall naming.

Of the other buildings in the old Roman fort the granary and stables were now complete. Stone walls and thatched roofs and the warehouses and barns were being roofed. I had decided to leave the hostelry to last, or until trade was established. The chapel had not been started either but as we had no priest there was no urgency for this either. Hilda had supervised the building of a laundry, slightly outside the Roman fort, in the village actually but butting up against the remains of the Roman wall. Three of the daughters of Gritta at Oostende had walked over to be the laundry maids and were now working a brisk trade under Hilda's supervision. The proposed smithy in the Roman fort had not been started because the smithy down by the waterside was deemed to be more important.

With the use of the carts Svart had conveyed hundreds of stones down to the waterside and laid the foundations of the whore house and inn. He deemed that these two building, which was actually one with a dividing wall, should be built first, primarily because the whores needed somewhere to ply their trade and quickly, and the young men needed somewhere to drink and congregate without causing trouble in the village. The layout of this joint establishment was quite unique, the inn was a large room where people could sit, eat, and drink, the whorehouse was a series of small cells where the women plied their trade all joined together by a long corridor. There was much debate about what the establishment should be called from both lewd to noble, so I announced that they would receive names at the hall naming feast as well.

As expected, the *Hilda* and *Little Runa* appeared as summer faded. The two ships cautiously entered the waterway not knowing what to expect until they saw my other three ships moored at Zandvoorde. When the gang planks were run out and Egil and Magnus came ashore I was there to welcome them.

"Well met, Egil, Magnus, you both look a bit weathered, how are your ships holding up?" I asked, delighted that they both appeared hale and hearty.

"Ah! I hear you are a great lord now, Bearslayer." Egil grasped my outstretched hand. I shook Magnus' hand as well.

"We are all landed men now, but leave that until later how went your summer trading?" It was then I noticed Magnus had a bandage around his upper left arm. "Trouble?" I enquired.

"Narry a bit." Magnus grinned. "The pirates that tried to take our goods came off a lot worse and had to swim ashore after their boat sank."

"Well come into the inn and tell me all about it, it has been boring here building and farming, I missed the swan's path." I lamented.

"This here is the prettiest bolthole for a viking longship I have ever seen south of the fjords; how come you acquired such a favourable lordship?" Egil enquired.

This started me off giggling. "That is the whole point, the Flemings thought this was the arse end of Flanders with no merit and that my lordship was undesirable. I intend to make this the main port of call along this coast"

"Why have you set up the landing here when there is a beautiful creek nearer to the open sea on the other side of the waterway." Egil queried.

I smiled, delighted. "You refer to the Oude Creke, which I deemed is the perfect ship building spot on Testerep. I have

gifted this creek to you with the village of Stene at its fjord end."
Egil looked shocked.

"And Magnus, for you I have reserved the village of Bredene and its land along the east side of the waterway." I pointed back to the entrance to the Brede Fjord.

We entered the inn, which still had an air of newness about it. The table and benches were clean and there was no smell of piss or vomit. I ordered three cups of ale, which was brought by the landlord, none other than Finn the cowardly Hollander who I had plucked from Dirk Hammerhand's crew; a suitable occupation I thought.

"Good day Finn, you are well and prospering?" I asked.

"Oh, yes lord. This 'ere inn will make a small fortune, it will." Finn smiled a row of broken teeth, I dismissed him.

"Tell me of your summer trading?" I enquired of Egil and Magnus, when they had slaked their thirsts.

Egil responded first. "We did as you commanded and took on board a full load of wool and oak wood and sailed south and west until we sighted the peninsula of the Cotentin in Normandy. We berthed on the isle of Jersey for a couple of days and then continued south and hove up on the rocky coast of Brittany, which is dangerous to get too close to. We weathered the peninsula of the Bretons and put in at a marvellous port called Brest before we sailed south along the coast passing hundreds of small islands and sandy beaches, which we could pull our boats up on without finding a harbour, we sailed south for many days until we came to the mouth of a great river called the Garonne. The city of Bordeaux lies thirty miles up this river and is the land of the vine and grapes. We sailed up the river, not without being challenged by the local count's men but we convinced them of our peaceful intent and they let us progress to the wharves of the city; and a great city it is. Mighty stone walls and palaces and fortresses. We sold our wool, not for a very great price and then we purchased the sweet white and red wines of the region. Hundreds of jars, which they called amphora, we bought and stowed into the hold with hay packed tightly around them to prevent breakages." Egil took a long draught of his ale and smacked his lips in appreciation.

Magnus took up the tale. "The journey back was a lot easier than the journey out. The winds were consistently in our favour until we reached the coast of Brittany when the weather took a decided turn for the worse. However, we weathered the storm well, *Hilda* better than *Little Runa* but we had to stop over at the island of Guernsey, the sister island to Jersey to effect repairs. We then crossed the channel between the coast of Normandy and the southern coast of England and hove up at the little port of Bosham in the earldom of Wessex."

Egil cackled. "The earl of Wessex, Harald Godwinson lives in great state, grander than the king he is. He bought all our wine at a very good price. We took on a cargo of wood and sailed on to Norway, they are always short of wood there, we sold the wood to Harald Hardrada's agent in Viken and loaded on a huge pile of otter and beaver pelt, fox skins and elk skins."

Magnus took up the story, "We then sailed south again, we did put in at Bruges by the Sea but you had gone. So, we sailed on back to Bordeaux and parted with the furs at a fabulous price, if we had sailed further south into the lands of the Moors, we would have got more for them but time was running out and the summer was drawing in. The Archbishop of Bordeaux, no less, a scheming robber called Andro was set to buy the lot at a knock down price with the proviso he would let us leave port when the duke himself, William Duke of Aquitaine, rode into town. The duke promptly sequestered the whole cargo as a gift unto himself and in return awarded us gifts far in excess of the furs and pelts worth, such is the way he does business. The archbishop slunk away and we were free to leave port without a fight, but we left without a cargo, so on our way north we sailed into the River Loire to a town called Nantes. I am not sure if Nantes is in Brittany or Anjou but they cultivate the vine and their wine is passable to good, so we bought up a cargo full and sailed north, into the Thames estuary and up to London. This time we sold to the London merchants who were hard-headed individuals and haggled the price but we still made a hefty profit." This time Magnus took a swig of his ale and Egil finished the tale.

"There was nothing in London we wanted so we sailed out of the Thames estuary and sailed north to the port of Ipswich where we loaded a good quality cargo of wool to sell in Bruges. We sailed back across the North Sea to Bruges by the Sea and sold the wool to a Bruges merchant for little more than we bought it for; we would have liked to sail up to Antwerp to sell but as that meant sailing into the Scheldt delta, we thought it prudent not to, the *Hilda* and *Little Runa* being so well known around those waters and all. It was at Bruges by the Sea that we learnt where you had moved to and so we sailed down the coast and here we are."

"So, tell me how did you get wounded?" I asked.

Magnus looked sheepish. "Egil was quicker away from the beach at Bruges and was about a mile ahead of us when a small raider attacked *Hilda*, I should have been up with her so it was my fault. By the time I brought *Little Runa* up alongside the raider, it was little more than a glorified karvi, with maybe twenty pirates on board, that had lashed itself to the *Hilda* and were trying to board her. Egil and his crew were fending them off with their long sweeps. I ran my boat up the other side of the karvi smashing the oars they had left laying outboard and we put some throwing axes and spears into the attacker's backs. I was so angry with myself I was careless; I went over the sheer strake with my sword and promptly received a spear through my bicep. That will teach me to carry a shield. We killed all the pirates who did not jump overboard and as we were not sure where we were heading to find you, we scuttled their karvi."

"Yes, if we had known you were so near, we would have towed the karvi into this haven." Added Egil.

I explained to Egil and Magnus what had happened since we had arrived at Testerep and what we had achieved so far. Egil was extremely enthusiastic about building boats, knarrs especially. Magnus was less enthusiastic until I explained that our military exploits would not be curtailed. Magnus was basically a raider and escorting trading knarrs was alright but a slow way to accumulate wealth. I suggested to Egil that we needed two additional knarrs and that I would prefer a trading fleet as an alternative to one knarr; Egil agreed. I had formed the opinion that Egil would not be making many more voyages and that he would busy himself at Stene making boats. I informed him that I had a supply of good wood suitable for strakes and keels waiting for him and, better than that, two skilled carpenters

490

to work under his instructions. Magnus and Egil would keep their crews in their halls at their new farms but, of course, they had to build their halls first.

Odoacer and his wife had seen to the distribution of farmland to the incoming peasants and allocated them a local lord who would supervise them, thus each one of my captains became a village headman, or bondi, of some standing and was responsible for improving the dwellings and agriculture on their lands; I had ensured they had the means to do this and my captains had the treasure to achieve it.

What I did need was more fishing boats and I wondered if I could buy them from the Frisians but that did not resolve how to bring them back to Testerep? Egil and Magnus were pleased to know that Svart had suggested that I send messengers to all the ports north and south as far as Norway and Brittany informing traders of the existence of the port at Testerep, freedom to anchor over and trade with miniscule berth fees. I sent out messengers, I agreed with Svart's logic as although I would not receive much by way of berth fees, the settlement would more than benefit from profits at the inns, whorehouse and trading warehouses and hence so would I. By the time Egil and Magnus had returned a few knarrs were already sailing into the sound to investigate the benefits of weathering over.

A conversation with Magnus aside covered the issues of raiding. Now that Zealand was out of bounds the areas where raiding could be undertaken were severely limited. I was not comfortable raiding southern England or the Danelagh as Harald Godwinson had a substantial fleet that patrolled the channel between England and France. Scotland was a legitimate target as I had nothing but animosity with Malcolm the current king and perhaps Northumbria could be raided as I was no friend of Tostig Godwinson and he had no significant fleet. Wales was out as I was a friend to King Gryffudd and I also had links with Ireland.

Magnus believed any meddling in the north was likely to bring us into conflict with Harald Hardrada, who was far too powerful to upset. This left the south; was I prepared to raid into France and Spain and was the Moorish kingdoms in the south of Spain too far? We did not have to decide until the spring but I considered that the first raids would be on the Scots as the least contentious target. Egil and Magnus went to explore their new patrimony and work across my lordship went on apace. Christofer came to see me to inform me that many of the men were coupling up with local women; I was delighted as this would lead to stability and integration between the incomers and the indigenous inhabitants. Christofer was concerned as there was still no priest to marry them. I considered that some of the men would not be interested in marrying before a church door, but declined saying so, the young women would be keen to wed men from outside, even in this remote part of Flanders women understood the dangers of inbreeding. The young men in the area might be jealous and rivalries may develop but this was inevitable, especially as my crews were richer than the natives. I promised Christofer that the Count of Flanders was certain to keep good on his promise and that churchmen would eventually come.

Hilda and the other women of the village were busy preparing for Yule and I wanted it to be special as the first one spent in Testerep. I thought of inviting the Castellan of Bruges but decided it was too risky to have Dedda in my hall; it was safer to keep the Yule feast for the locals.

Meanwhile I started training the new and very young huscarls; they were eager but raw and it was more a case of toughening them up and increasing their stamina. Fortunately, there was a lot of heavy stone to lift and haul and after a month all of them could swim across to Stene to assist Egil with his house and shipyard building. By the time I gave the novice huscarls weapons they were strong enough to handle them for long periods. Chopping logs was also a useful exercise in the use of a Dane axe, especially when I made them do it one handed with a shield in their other hand. Each novice did an hour's spear and javelin throwing at straw targets every day and they improved remarkably when I explained I wanted distance throwing rather than accuracy so that as Yule approached, they all became capable of throwing two javelins, first missile to thirty paces and the second to twenty paces. Last thing each day they all ran along the fjord to Bredene and back carrying their round wooden shields. The continuous exercise kept them out of mischief and as they improved, I could see a camaraderie developing.

A few late autumn ships came into our sheltered fjord and we made sure they were welcome and that their stay over comfortable. Egil was able to help any ship that needed repairs and I felt sure they all went away with a favourable impression. As the autumn turned to winter and Yule was less than two months away four monks came walking into the village. I knew they were Benedictine monks as they wore the same black robes as my nemesis, Herluin; I hoped they were not like him. I greeted them in my great hall sitting on my newly completed high seat with my sword held across my knees like any Norse Jarl.

"Greetings, Christ men, you are welcome in my hall and on my lands; my hospitality is yours for as long as you wish. The Count of Flanders has sent you?" I asked.

The oldest of the monks, a portly man with a cheerful rosy face and a bald head, no place for a tonsure, spoke.

"Lord Hereward, we have been sent by the Bishop of Noyon and Tournai, Father Balduin, but yes, we understand this was at the request of the count. I am Brother Thomas an ordained priest and these younger monks, Edwin, Francis and Edwy are lay-brothers."

"That is excellent, we have need of religious education and guidance. We have three or four derelict churches that we have been repairing and there is a chapel here within the bounds of my hall. We have many Christian folk here but I will not lie to you, I have people you would refer to as heathen." I explained.

"I have heard somewhat of your exploits, Lord Hereward and have no illusions of the task ahead of us, but with God's good grace we will show everyone that the Lord's truth and love shines on everyone." Brother Thomas smiled beatifically displaying yellow fangs that must give him many sleepless nights of toothache.

"Come, sit, eat, and drink with me, this is Martin my right-hand man who can help you with all you need and I would have you meet Christofer the leader of the devout Christians in this community. He has much to tell you. I note one of your brothers is called Edwy, an English name?"

493

"Yes, Brother Edwy hails from England and is a far out relative of King Edward, but of the illegitimate persuasion. Brother Edwin is also English but comes from Northumbria and is named for the sainted King Edwin of Northumbria, who was martyred many years ago and Francis here is from our school in Paris." Brother Thomas explained.

"I have differences with the English king and the Earl of Northumbria." I thought I should mention this.

"None of us are political but if it sets your mind at rest, Edwy does not even know the English king and has never lived in England since his fifth year. Edwin is a younger member of the Edulfings of Bamburgh who have been displaced by the Godwinson, Tostig, and as I said before Francis is French from Burgundy and I, for my sins am from Nimes in the south of France."

I smiled in acceptance. "Will you all stay together or will each of you choose a church?"

"Initially, we will all stay together, whilst I examine the land grants you are awarding the church. While we are doing this, we will re-activate the chapel here. When I am sure of our way, I will ordain the lay-brothers here and they will shepherd their flocks. Until then I will perform marriages, baptisms, and death rites."

"One other thing." I added, "My men and I are not peaceful, we are warriors and we fight for the count. His wars are not always righteous,"

"Even the chosen ones of God, Moses, Abraham, David, and Solomon were not always righteous and they fought wars. I can only give you advice and temper your worst excesses." Brother Thomas remained serene.

"Good then we can work together." I beckoned Christofer forward, who had been waiting patiently to be introduced. "This is Christofer who will show you your churches, my men will be available to assist in the building processes. Your churches will be stone, we have a lot of that." I dismissed them, hoping they would not be a thorn in my side.

"Martin, remind me to tell Gautrek not to kill them."

Winter 1060 - Hvitbjornhalla

Hilda came to see me; her feathers had been ruffled. "Lord Hereward, Brother Thomas wants me to alter the Yule festivities. He wants me to do away with the Yule Log, the Yule Boar and Yule Goat. How can it be Yule if we do not sacrifice to the old gods and if we do not wassail in the new year?"

I knew this would happen, since arriving Brother Thomas and his acolytes had been like a gale; Odin and the Wild Hunt could not have passed over my lordship with such an effect. The churches had been repaired in a fervour of religious activity supported by Christofer and his supporters. Christian marriages had been happening every few days at the church door and I was happy about this as it was binding the people in my lordship together. Unlike in many areas of Europe all the marriages were with mutual consent and a token dowry. My men could afford this and I would have helped them if they could not. However, there were some of my warriors who wanted nothing to do with the monks or the church, it did not mean they were not Christian just independent. Similarly, many of the original inhabitants of Testerep were actually pagan and wanted to resist Christianisation. This was where the problem had arisen, the monks were actively encouraging their Christian flock to shun and refuse to cooperate with the perceived non-Christians. This had come to a head recently in one of the villages I had gifted to Christofer, Middlekerke, where his Christian followers had driven out several of the original inhabitants and burned down their cottage. I had told Christofer that he must make restitution to this family, he still had not done so and retribution on my part was imminent.

"Hilda, you take your direction from me, when Brother Thomas comes to you again send him to me." I decided there must be a reckoning before Yule was upon us.

After a week of inaction, I sent for Christofer; I sat on my high seat in the hall with my young huscarls around me, none were married and none attended church. Christofer entered the hall with a dozen men, I noted they had not left their weapons outside, that alone condemned them to death. Christofer walked up to me but did not salute me.

"You wanted to see me?" He started in a belligerent tone. In one movement I stood and grasped a javelin propped against my high seat; the javelin pierced Christofer's chest before he realised what I had done.

"Kill the rest." I ordered and my huscarls closed in on the men who were standing shocked watching the life blood seep from their squirming leader on the floor. Most died before their swords and daggers were freed from their belts.

"Find Brother Thomas and bring him to me." I ordered.

In less than a quarter of a watch Brother Thomas walked into the hall surrounded by huscarls. I registered the look of horror and dismay on his face when he saw Christofer's body lying on the rushes and he had already seen the line of bodies outside the hall where some of my young huscarls were busy hacking the heads off to adorn stakes.

"My God, what have you done?" he gasped when he took in the scene.

"Brother Thomas, I have administered justice on this traitor who disobeyed me. He was my oath sworn man and rejected my authority." I stated calmly.

"But what did he do, that would merit this type of justice?" Brother Thomas looked bewildered.

"He did not protect my people, he allowed them to be harassed and thrown off their land. He failed in his duty and also refused to correct his errors when ordered to do so. He entered my hall with armed supporters, which is against all custom and decency. He was a nithing and died a nithing's death, his followers died because they broke their oath of fealty to me but worst of all they died because of your folly." I added.

"My folly."

"Yes, you persuaded him and the other Christians that the people on my lands, my people, were not to be treated with respect. You may think this is acceptable and a righteous action but that is a spiritual viewpoint and my lordship is governed by temporal laws. You have a choice; you can leave my lands or you can treat everyone here with respect and with equal dignity.

Christianity must win over people with justice and good intent on my lands." I concluded. I dismissed him.

Later I learnt that Brother Francis had left and I assumed he was the instigator of the trouble. I informed Hilda to carry on with the Yule celebration planning and ignore Brother Thomas. Martin did some investigations and it transpired that all the supporters of Christofer had come from Middlekerke and that there seemed to be no problems at Snaaskerke; Brother Francis had been at Middlekerke.

This time I requested the presence of all three remaining monks; they duly presented themselves promptly with an outward display of humility.

"Brothers," I began. "We have experienced a difficult start to your mission and it is partly my fault." Before they could spout false expressions of denial, I held up my hand and they subsided. "Monks and priests often find it very difficult to live side by side with people with less devotion than they and I erred in providing the church land as a dual patrimony between you and my village chief. I am therefore correcting that error. From now on each of you will hold land directly from me and everyone in your appenage will be your responsibility to treat fairly and justly. I will force none of my people to live in villages under your control. The people forced from their homes at Middlekerke do not wish to return and I have accommodated them in Oudenberg and they have been made welcome. Any other families who do not wish to live under your rule will also be welcome elsewhere. Brother Thomas you will receive Snaaskerke and also the responsibility of the chapel here. Brother Edwin you will receive Middlekerke and Brother Edwy you will receive a new site at a small village named Willekinsby, henceforth to be called Willekinskerke. Christian people will come to you for mass and other services and as you accumulate Christian communities you will become self-sufficient, I am sure. Do you have any issues with this decision.?"

Brother Thomas spoke, "A wise decision lord, it will teach us caution and humility."

I smiled, "Good, that will be interesting, I have never met a humble priest." Before they could protest, I continued. "One final challenge; Yule approaches, I am aware it is a much beloved pagan festival to welcome in the turn of the year and I do not want to see it performed clandestinely. However, in many places the Christian priests have very wisely tried to combine Christian festivities with the pagan rituals. They have done this very successfully in Ireland and I am charging you to achieve something similar here. The pagans amongst my people will not abandon their Yule Log, Yule Goat and Yule Boar but in truth most of them have completely forgotten what the religious symbolism they had. They enjoy the wassail but the church also encourages the singing of hymns and psalms and a cunning priest could assimilate these harmless but enjoyable activity. Yule is sufficiently near the date affixed for the birth of the Christ to join the celebrations together. I charge you with bringing the people of Testerep together in harmony and love." I sounded far more charitable than I was and if any of these monks had any inkling of my history with the church they would be horrified. Nevertheless, hopefully they went away with a spirit of reconciliation.

When next I spoke with Hilda, I was delighted in that she was fully supportive of the introduction of some of the more rousing psalms into the Yule celebrations and that Edwin was teaching a group of the children to sing the songs beautifully. Brother Thomas had agreed to bless the Yule Log, not the sacrifice of the Boar and Goat however but he had been persuaded to bless the roasted joints before they were consumed by the revellers.

A week before the Yule celebrations were due to begin a very bedraggled stranger came to the hall door. He was challenged by the huscarls on watch and brought in to me. I had been practicing with my young huscarls and was in something of a sweat and had stripped to my breeches and was towelling myself off when the man came up to the high seat.

"Good day stranger, you are welcome in my hall, drink, eat."

The stranger sat at one of the tables and was given a trencher of cold meats and bread by one of the huscarls. I allowed him to finish his food and drink two cups of ale before I enquired of him who he might be.

"Lord, I am named Eilif Gunnorson an Icelander by birth and a scald by profession. I was heading north to either Norway or Denmark to seek employment, hopefully with a king or jarl but I was delayed in Aquitaine and missed the autumn sailings. I have been making my way slowly through county after county and a hard time I have had of it. I went to the south of France because I heard that they had a new type of song that thrilled the ladies; I ever seek new modes of hexameter and stanza and indeed I found a different world of song and poetry and beautiful women, to boot. It was such a beautiful woman, wondrous fair that delayed me and I only fled north to preserve my life from the wrath of her husband." I laughed at his brazenness.

"Well, you are nearly back in the north but you will not reach Denmark by Yule so you are welcome to stay in my hall for the festivities." I added.

"That is a right noble offer and I accept, especially if I am addressing the renowned Bearslayer, for there is only one hero I know of with party-coloured eyes and a white bear collar."

"Well, no offer is given for nothing, Eilif Gunnorson, whether it is to bolster my own renown or material gain, but a skald has to sing for a living and if you lift the hearts of my people at Yule you will be well rewarded." I acknowledged.

Yule came upon us with benign weather and no snow or persistent rain. In fact, a watery sun shone on a pale-coloured countryside. This enabled my people to congregate at Oudenberg in large numbers, at least one family came from every village and settlement and everyone in the village of Oudenberg intended to be in the hall. All my crews and huscarls wanted to also be there but mindful of what I visited on Hagen of Bierren I informed my huscarls that at least half of them would have to be on watch at any one time.

The Yule celebrations started six days before the date of Christ's birth and would finish six days thereafter, this period comfortably encompassed the turning of the year when the sun reversed its movement across the heavens marking the sacred winter solstice. Hilda had decorated the whole village with winter colour, which mainly consisted of holly berries on the branch and the pale ivy pods. Coloured ribbons bedecked the stunted trees around the village perimeter and each cottage and house had plaited figures and animals outside; stallions, rams, bulls, and goats all with outrageously large, engorged, and erect members. Odoacer had adopted the guise of the green man, or was he impersonating Saint Nicholas? He went around the settlement handing out gifts to children; sugar sweets, little carved toys, and ribbons for the delighted girls.

In the afternoon of the first day everyone congregated at the front of the little chapel where Father Thomas stood on a large stone and led prayers and told the story of Jesus Christ's birth. He delivered his homily with much fervour and expression and looking around the crowd I could see that the children were enchanted by the story and that Eilif Gunnorson was impressed with his rhetoric.

"He's good." Martin murmured into my ear.

"Yes, he is. I do not remember the bit about the shepherds and kings." I muttered back.

"Oh! I think it changes and gets better with the retelling." Martin smiled. "Bit like the tales of your exploits." I suppressed a laugh; it would not do to be disrespectful in front of the chapel.

Later that day every one congregated in the hall, it was so cramped that there was no seating for the children who all sat around the hearth on the rush matting. Above the fire trenches newly wrought iron spits were decorated with pig, cow and sheep carcasses slowly being roast and basted by nominated boys and carefully supervised by one of Hilda's kitchen maids. No other food had yet been brought into the hall but there were large pot jugs of ale and hundreds of wooden and pottery cups. Most of the huscarls and my ships' crew members cradled drinking horns, much treasured items often heirlooms with silver mountings and carved horn finishes. Other maids went around the hall filling all the cups and horns ensuring no one lacked a drink.

I stood up from my high chair and held up my hands for silence, it took a while for the hall to quieten. "Welcome to my hall good people of Testerep, this evening's feast is to consecrate this hall to God and his saints. There will be a hall naming, a competition that even the children can participate in." They all cheered at this. "For twelve days we will celebrate Yule, the turning of the year. Next year will be our first with an increased crop and new life both human and beasts. Wealth will come from the sea and the world will sail here past Oostende." Again, the hall erupted in cheers.

"Before Brother Thomas blesses this hall, I ask you all to raise your cups, your horns and your hearts and give a hearty wassail to our future." I raised my cup and shouted, "Wassail!"

Over two hundred throats called forth, "Wassail!" and the drink flowed. After a short period of noisy celebration, I managed to quieten the throng down sufficiently for Brother Thomas to affect an entry, flanked by Brothers Edwin and Edwy both carrying crosses on poles, a dozen small boys followed on behind singing what I assumed was a psalm. The singing was ethereal, beautiful in its simplicity and cadence. The crowd quietened and listened intently to the song; the small procession walked around the fire pits to the high seat and I stepped down to allow Brother Thomas the platform.

Brother Thomas raised his voice, "O loving Lord and God, ever ready to listen to the prayers of thy servants, I most earnestly beseech thee to hearken to me. To thee do I pray, trusting to the help and merits of the blessed and glorious Mary, ever a Virgin, and of all the holy Angels, Archangels, and heavenly Powers, of the holy Patriarchs, Prophets, and Apostles, of the Evangelists, Martyrs, and Confessors, of the Virgins and Monks, and of all the citizens of heaven, that thou wouldst increase the faith of thy Holy Catholic Church: beseeching thee that thou wouldst give peace to the inhabitants of Testerep; that thou wouldst forgive us our sins; that thou wouldst restore health to the sick, and afford to the fallen the means to repair the error of their ways; that thy faithful servants who are travellers on sea or on land may have a prosperous voyage, and at length reach this haven of safety; that those who are in trouble may find consolation, and those who suffer oppression, comfort and relief; that thou wilt in thy love send thy holy Angel to be our guide and protector here, and wheresoever we may be; that thou wilt give the blessing of mutual charity to those that are at variance, and true faith to the unbelieving; and finally, that to the faithful departed you will give eternal rest. Amen"

"Amen!" shouted the throng. He had gone on a bit but had expressed mostly the right sentiments. Before he stood down, he announced several marriages that would take place in front of the chapel during Yule. I was surprised when I heard the name Dietrich, he was still young not having yet twenty years to him, but I was even more surprised that he was marrying Eleanor. At first the name did not register but then I remembered she was Alftruda's maid, the one who Christofer had asked for as part of his share in the Roggen viking plunder. The young girl he had married and who I had widowed not long since; I made a mental note to speak to him about this development.

I thanked Brother Thomas for his blessing and he returned to the well of the hall and sat with his two brethren.

I shouted, "Let the feast begin."

A long line of girls and young men who had obviously been waiting outside flowed into the hall directed hither and thither by Hilda. They all carried plates of cold meats, warm bread, cheeses, and the boys carried more large jugs of ale. Several of the men from the village with large fleshing knives started to carve generous slices of meat from the roasted carcasses. Beef, pork with crackling, mutton strips and placing them on platters on the tables. Other men brought into the hall large platters of cooked birds, partridges, duck, geese, and there were hot pies and pasties containing smaller birds, blackbirds, and thrushes. Some of the men had braved the winter seas offshore and had caught several large cod that had been basted in herbs and garnished with nuts and apples.

There was enough for all, I had specifically requested Hilda not to serve me first but to flatter the monks I had them served first and then approved a right royal free for all. Eilif Gunnorson surprised me by remaining abstemious, with one cup of ale he removed himself to the end of the fire pit, sat on a stool and drew forth a small harp from an otter skin bag. It was a beautiful instrument, carved and gilded, the Icelander drew his fingers across it emitting a soft melodic sound. He proceeded to play background music whilst the gathering ate and drank, although his music could barely be heard it created harmony and goodwill. Many children came and sat around him watching his fingers dance over the strings, they fell silent while they ate allowing parent to have time to themselves.

The feasting went on for nearly a full watch and my village guards changed twice during that period. As the eating subsided and the heavy drinking took over the skald was called up to sing or recite a poem or praise song.

With some dread I realised that Eilif would almost certainly choose to recite a praise song dedicated to me as the first of many that night and I was not wrong. Standing Eilif raised his voice.

"I will now tell the story of how 'Hereward slew the white bear.' Everyone in the hall quietened. Eilif's voice was deep and cultured, he could mimic dialects of several nations and his delivery was perfect for the local Flemish natives. However, I was astonished by the tale that unfolded. It told the story of a young maiden under the control of a strict and unscrupulous uncle who wanted to gain her wealth by having her slain be a ferocious white bear that was kept in a cage in the castle yard. The bear escaped supposedly by accident but actually by the design of the wicked uncle. The young maiden, a princess no less, was entrapped in the yard with the frenzied bear. Then, a youth, handsome and bold; I cringed he meant me, burst into the yard wielding a magic sword. He protected the princess and slew the bear, a great feat. When Eilif announced the youth was Hereward the Bearslayer the revellers burst into cheers and load acclamations. I acknowledged the applause, it would have been churlish not to; Eilif's praise song was good, a much better tale than the slaying of Asbjorn Siwardson told in rousing hexameter and well-balanced words. I did what was expected and offered a silver arm ring for his services; again, everyone cheered but this time for Eilif himself.

Eilif then started a round of riddles, an enjoyable northern pastime and one the children could join in with.

Eilif began, "One for the children this."

"Who are those twain
that on ten feet run,
three their eyes are
but only one tail?
This riddle ponder,
O children of Testerep."

The children gathered round calling out their guesses. "A spider.", "No."; "Two oxen pulling a cart and the driver.", "No." "I know, I know." Another girl shouted. "Odin riding his horse, Sleipnir." "Yes, correct." Eilif handed out some honey comb.

"Another, another!" chorused the children.

"Four are hanging,
Four are walking,
Two point the way out,
Two ward the dogs off,
One ever dirty
Dangles behind it?
This riddle ponder,
O children of Testerep."

This riddle took longer to unravel, until one parent whispered in his son's ear and the boy shouted, "Mother Hilda's cow." Everyone laughed at this identification being so specific, but Eilif confirmed that the boy was indeed correct.

The riddles moved on to more complicated and obtuse verse for the adults.

"I am wonderful help to women,
The hope of something to come. I harm
No citizen except my slayer.
Rooted I stand on a high bed.
I am shaggy below. Sometimes the beautiful
Peasant's daughter, an eager-armed,
Proud woman grabs my body,
Rushes my red skin, holds me hard,
Claims my head. The curly-haired
Woman who catches me fast will feel
Our meeting. Her eye will be wet.
This riddle ponder; O men of Testerep."

Everyone laughed as this was a well-known riddle with a double meaning. Inevitably someone shouted out, "A man's cock."

Eilif then added, "This riddle ponder, O women of Testerep."

All the women shouted together, "An onion!"

While the riddles were ongoing, Martin quietly went around the hall collecting the nominations for the hall naming. Martin was one of the few people who could write and he duly recorded all the proposed names and the proposers. He returned to me with the list and I was dismayed to find there were twenty suggestions, far more than I thought would be entered in the naming. It was intended that each person should speak on behalf of their proposal and this would take a long time so I determined that the naming would be put off until the next feast, the day before Yule. Martin suggested otherwise, he proposed that three should be heard each night up until Yule as it would help bond the people of Testerep; I agreed.

After the riddles had finished and most of the younger children had already fallen asleep on their parents' laps Eilif was asked to recite one of the great lays of old. Eilif rose and addressed the crowd.

"In honour of the Flemings and Frisians who are gathered here I will recite the 'Lay of Baldwin Ironarm' and 'The Fight at Finnsburg'. The crowd erupted in cheers for the compliment the skald paid them. Eilif shouted across the noise, "And tomorrow I will declaim poems in praise of the Danes and Norwegians." Eilif was no fool and knew how to placate an audience of diverse origins so that no one was demeaned or omitted. I had never heard the lay of Baldwin Ironarm but I knew of him. Baldwin rose to prominence when he eloped with Judith, daughter of Charles the Bald, king of West Francia. Judith had previously been married to Æthelwulf and then Æthelbald, kings of Wessex, but after the latter's death in 860, she returned to France. At the instigation of Baldwin and with her brother Louis's connivance, Judith escaped the custody into which she had been placed in the city of Senlis, after her return from England; she fled north with Baldwin. Charles had given no permission for a marriage and tried to capture Baldwin, sending letters to Rorik the Viking of Dorestad and Bishop Hungar, forbidding them to shelter the fugitive. After Baldwin and Judith had evaded his attempts to capture them, Charles had his bishops excommunicate the couple. Judith and Baldwin responded by travelling to Rome to plead their case with Pope Nicholas I. Their plea was successful and Charles was forced to accept the situation. The marriage took place on 13 December 862 in Auxerre. By 870, Baldwin had acquired the lay-abbacy of Saint Peter's Abbey in Ghent and is assumed to have also acquired the counties of Flanders and Waasland, or parts thereof by this time. Baldwin developed himself as a very faithful and stout supporter of Charles and played an important role in the continuing wars against the vikings. He is named in the year of our Lord 877 as one of those willing to support the emperor's son, Louis the Stammerer. During his life, Baldwin expanded his territory into one of the major principalities of Western Francia. He died in 879 and was buried in the Abbey of St-Bertin, near Saint-Omer.

Obviously Eilif's poetic account was highly stylised, a tail of unrequited love, the slaying of a dragon and the capture of a huge ferocious viking who had kidnapped the Princess Judith, before their triumphal marriage and Baldwin becoming the first Count of Flanders and the ancestor of the incumbent Flemish Count Baldwin, fifth of his name. Eilif performed the poem well and the Flemings amongst my people loved it. The cheering at the end was voluminous.

The" Fight at Finnsburg" was entirely different in tone, more doom laden and tragic but high prose nevertheless. I wondered how many of the local Frisians realised that Hengest was none other than the leader of the Frisians, Jutes and Danes who had invaded Britain after the Romans left. It was Finn son of Focwald, King of the Frisians who was the tragic hero of the lay, noble to the last.

"Hnaef proclaimed then, battle young king:
Not is this the eastern dawn, nor here a dragon flies,
nor here this hall's roofs burn.
but here bear forth; birds scream,
the grey wolf howls, battle-wood clashes,
shield answers shaft. Now shines this moon
full under the clouds. Now arises evil deeds
that this folk will suffer.
But awaken now my warriors
take your shields, have resolve and courage,
fight with spear, be high minded!"
Then arose many gold laden thegns, who secured his sword.
Then to the door went lordly champions,
Sigeferth and Eaha, their swords drawn,

and at the other door Ordlaf and Guthlaf,
and Hengest by himself behind them followed.
Then yet Guthere told Garulf
that his noble life he would lose if at first
he to the hall doors went,
but he asked over all openly
daring minded hero, who then held the doors.
"Sigeferth is my name," said he, "I am a Secgan prince,
warrior widely known; many misfortunes I have endured
at hard battle. There is yet here an appointed
task by yourself to me that I will attain."
Then there was in the hall a murderous noise;
round board shields called for hands,
bone helmet burst, fortress floor resounded,
until at battle Garulf fell,
first of the lordly land dwellers
Guthlaf's son, around him many good,
quick men's corpses. Raven wandered,
dark and shadowy. Sword light stood,
such that all of Finnsburh was burning.
Not heard I ever worthier at battle were
sixty warriors good bearing,
never was sweet mead so well repaid
than to Hnaef his servants gave.
They fought five days, so that none fell
lordly companions, but they the door held.
then knew he was wounded withdrew and
said that his chainmail broken was,
battle gear unready, and also was his helmet broken.
then he soon asked the folks' protector,
how many of the warriors their wounds survived."

The hall was deathly silent whilst Eilif delivered the word song. I thought of the burning of Hagen and his sons, the enslavement of his womenfolk and children. Would such a fate be mine in time? My mind returned to the hall as the lay ended with Finn tragically dead and Hengest, noble in his revenge, exiled to distance shores. Finnsburg in ruins.

The people in the hall sighed and then erupted into acclamation of the scald. "Hail to the song weaver, hail to the skald!" Eilif had indeed given the hall a good night's entertainment. I beckoned him up to the high seat and took off a heavy gold ring from my finger. I do not normally wear jewellery, especially on my hands as it gets in the way of a firm grip on a weapon, but tonight I knew I would have to hand out at least one gift.

"Eilif Gunnorson, you set yourself too low, you are a fine skald and word weaver. I have rarely heard Finnsburg spoken of with such passion and skill. Take this ring as a testament to your skill, you honour the people of Testerep and they honour you in return. Eilif took the gold ring and held it up for the people to admire, it was a princely gift and he knew it.

"Hail to the ring giver." Eilif's voice resounded through the hall and again the people erupted in cheers of delight. There would be many who would speak of the first feast in the hall of Hereward, Lord of Testerep. I announced that it was late and we would retire and hear the name givers three every night between tomorrow and Yule.

Brother Thomas, who quite remarkably was still sober gave a final benediction and the feast ended. I left the hall for the fresh cold air of the night; the sky was clear and there was a layer of hoare frost on the ground and bushes. The stars were brilliant and clear, a myriad of pinpricks in the dark mantle of the sky. The hunter was dominant in the sky chasing the stag.

I did a round of the watches to make sure they were vigilant; although late the maids were still washing the dishes and bowls in the trickle of a stream that wended its way down to the fjord. It was not wise to leave dirty food standing as it invariably led to food poisoning, vomiting and diarrhoea and I had learnt that Hilda was meticulous where hygiene was concerned.

I made a note that we needed some guard dogs for the hall, we had lots of slops for them to feed on and they would give an alarm if intruders approached in the night. I had always been fascinated by the Irish wolfhounds I saw in Leinster and two large hounds; a dog and bitch would be ideal. I went to my lonely bed.

The following days were one long round of merrymaking. In the daylight hours there were competitions, games of athleticism, running races, wrestling, swimming even though the water was bitterly cold, jumping and throwing the axe and hammer. The children also competed although there were few enough to make really interesting races, I hoped there would be many more children born by harvest in the new year. Every evening another feast was held in the hall, Eilif's contribution was limited or there would not be enough time to hear the acclamations of the hall naming. I can only remember the best and worst of the names suggested. Three children had submitted suggestions; these were, Stonehall, Oudenberg Hall and the most imaginative Roman Hall. I believed it would frequently be referred to has Oudenberg anyway and I quite liked Stonehall.

Obviously, many of the adult submissions were more sophisticated and the ones I felt were worth consideration were, Braidahall, named after the fjord that it lay at the head of; Herot, named after the famous Danish king's hall; Viking hall, in memory of the Roggen viking fraternity; Bjornbana Hall; the Norse name for Bearslayer's Hall; Testerep Hall, called after the area of my lordship, again a sensible choice; I really liked White Bear Hall but it did not slide off the tongue easily. The obvious choice for me was Bear Hall, my life had been affected by bears, not real bears but people with bear appellations and I was always referred to as the Bearslayer. Most of the rest of the names had little merit and Gautrek's suggestion of Odin's Gift was bound to alienate every Christian within miles. The most ludicrous name was Upside Down Boat Hall, no doubt suggested by the clinker strake roof, which did give it the appearance of a longship upside down; although I would never agree to such a name, I feared that the hall may be called that as a joke and the name stick.

On Yule Eve I held the biggest feast yet, as luck would have it the lookout at Oostende spotted the spouts of a pod of whales coasting south off-shore. Hurriedly three karvis were manned and rowed out of the fjord armed with long spears. I was on board one of these boats and the intention was to kill a whale for the Yule feast. Fortunately, the beasts seemed in no hurry to flee south and appeared to be slowly making their way in between diving for their food. I was not sure what type of whales they were but they were not overly big.

We raced south trying to estimate when and where they would surface. I stood in the brow with a long heavy spear, I would have preferred a harpoon but we did not have any. When the beasts surfaced to a fountain of spray from their blow holes the stench of fish was overwhelming. I shouted to Egil who was at the helm to go hard over starboard towards the nearest whale. I could see maybe seven whales, monsters about the length and a half of the karvi with great white blotches on their heads. Magnus was in another karvi to my steer board side and closing on the same beast. Fortunately, the whale did not seem to want to dive and was skimming along the surface in an undulating motion. I shouted for more speed and the oarsmen were straining against their foot braces to extract every ounce of motion from each stroke.

We gradually came up on the beast on its left side as near as we dared without fouling its fin motion. I had two spears, the first was unencumbered and the second had a rope attached to the angons. I watched Magnus, whose boat was abreast of ours waiting for him to cast; when I saw his motion, his arm braced back for the throw, I mirrored his movement and we cast together. Both spears pierced the hide of the whale and I swear I saw it shudder. The whale appeared to hesitate and then its head drove downwards propelled by its side flippers and the flukes rose in the air before our boats and it dove down into the depths. It was then I noticed that Magnus' first spear was attached to a rope that Magnus had wrapped around one of the boat cleats.

"Magnus, cut the rope." I screamed. It was too late and Magnus probably did not hear me anyway, as the whale dived the karvi suddenly bowed down and its stern rose up out of the water in a mimic of the whale's dive. The crew were tumbled into the freezing water and the karvi disappeared into the murky depths. The following karvi came up behind Magnus and his crew as they floundered in the boiling sea almost instantaneously and started to rescue the men from the turbulent waters. I was distracted because almost immediately the whale broke the surface and the flooded karvi came up, dragged along by the spear lodged in the beast side. I was surprised because I would have thought that the spear would have worked loose but such was not the case and there was no way the whale could dive with the boat attached.

I grabbed my second spear and yelled for Egil to bring our boat up alongside. The beast was definitely labouring and making slow headway. Egil brought our karvi right up to the side of the whale; I could have stepped onto its back I was so near. Rather than throw the spear I leant out and thrust the spear downwards with all my strength. I felt the point slide through the whale's blubber until it reached a more resilient layer of meat. I kept pushing, even leaning out of the boat, pushing down until the point entered what felt like a vital organ, maybe the lungs or the heart.

Two oarsmen grabbed my belt to prevent me falling overboard; I released the spear at the same moment the whale started thrashing the water. Egil steered the boat away. The whale was in its death throws, the karvi, which was still attached to the beast lay submerged behind it. I looked back and saw a very bedraggled Magnus being hauled from the water, everyone was saved and I thought even the karvi could be re-floated. Eventually the whale's convulsions ceased and it floated benignly on the surface, the three spears jutting out of its back with blood seeping from the wounds. Already the gulls were swarming, picking at the lacerations, and fighting each other.

"Tie the whale to our stern and we will row it back into the fjord." I commanded.

I shouted over to the third karvi, "Magnus are you and your crew alright?"

Magnus stood, dripping wet. "Yes, we'll tow my drowned karvi back and beach it; everybody is safe, just cold and wet."

It was a slow row back but everyone was exhilarated; the blubber from the whale would provide enough whale fat and soap to last Testerep the whole winter. The whale bones could be used to make bone utensils and the interior meat of the whale was a delicacy that would enhance the rest of Yule.

The whale was dragged up upon the shore near to the wooden jetty at Zandvoorde. Dozens of people came down to the beach and Egil, who had flensed whales before took charge and ordered the men to start cutting longs wide strips of whale skin, which would be used for ropes and weatherproofing. Once most of the skin was removed great junks of blubber were cut off the carcass to be melted down for oil and fats. The blubber was incredibly thick but once cut away it exposed the meat of the whale; this was cut away in big steaks. Several carts had been brought to the beach from Oudenberg and the bounty from the sea was conveyed back for Hilda to prepare and store. The last cart conveyed the edible whale offal, which was removed last, this included the whale's tongue, which was considered a delicacy. The bare skeleton was left with ribbons of flesh and the discarded offal for the gulls, skuas and crows who descended on the carcass in their hundreds, screaming and fighting.

The other karvi arrived later in the fjord towing Magnus' half submerged boat. Magnus and his crew were met with laughter and jeers. It was the opinion of the experienced boatmen that Magnus had made a fundamental mistake in casting a spear with a rope tied to it first, however, my confusion as to why Magnus' spear had not come free from the whale when it dived was answered when a crew man who was cutting away the blubber came to me with Magnus' spear; it turned out to be an old Frankish angon with a barbed head, nearly as effective as a harpoon. It had obviously deeply embedded itself in the whale's body and would not pull free. People started referring to Magnus as 'Sinking Magnus'; but fair enough Magnus took this with good grace. I made a note that we had to become more efficient at hunting and killing whales.

On the morning before the Yule feast Gautrek came to see me. He had been very quiet throughout the initial days of celebrations but I could see he wanted permission to do something.

"Speak, Gautrek."

"Lord, Yule is upon us and the Yule sacrifices need to be made, a boar and sow to Frey and Freya, a ram and ewe to Thor and Sif, a stallion and mare to Odin and Frigg. My brothers and I are asking you to allow this?" Gautrek explained.

"Brothers? How many of you are there?"

"Not as many as there should be, twenty or so and all sworn to secrecy."

"Do you have a godi?" A godi was the pagan equivalent of a Christian priest, although godi's were not full-time priests,
"We have no godi, the sacrifices should be performed by our jarl." Gautrek looked at me pointedly.

Pagan sacrifices would be frowned upon by most of my people, although Christianity lay lightly on most and there was perhaps only as many as fifty people who were truly religious, however an openly pagan sacrifice would unsettle some.

"Gautrek, I wish you and your people to take all the animals required after dark and take them north beyond Bredene. The animals are to be taken from my stock and from no one else. There is a well wooded copse about half a mile north of Bredene, I will meet you there after tonight's feast, at midnight and we will perform the sacrifices."

I found the evening feast a muted affair, the villagers of Testerep did not attend all the feasts and as they were certain to attend the Yule feast itself the next day, this feast was mainly my huscarls and a few people from Oudenberg; that together with the fact that there were some noted absences made for a quiet evening. Eilif played his harp, gentle background music, and the three priests were holding a special mass across the fjord at their church, very convenient. I had been invited to the church service but I was able to cry off because I was required to listen to the last three declamations for the hall naming. The feast finished early and I went into my cubicle to dress for the sacrifices. I decided that I needed to be in my war gear; I checked my scramaseax as it would certainly be the weapon I would need for the killings.

When my hall was being built, I decided to have extra doors included in case an emergency required a stealthy exit; one of these doors was within my cubicle and allowed me to leave the hall unobserved if I so wished. I unbarred this small wooden door and slipped out into the compound. It was dark and quiet and I made my way north. I clambered over the remains of the Roman perimeter wall and clambered down into the ditch, which was overgrown with nettles and briars. It was easy to slip out and I realised that even with the guards I had on watch anyone could enter the compound without being observed. I knew I had to change that situation but I did not have enough stone or wood to repair the perimeter defences.

I walked through the meadows north of Oudenberg directing my feet towards Bredene, or just north of Bredene. I anticipated it would take me about a quarter of a watch to reach the copse in the dark but fortunately it was another clear night and the stars illuminated the landscape and a three-quarter full moon cast shadows even in the gloom. I arrived at the copse early, therefore and was surprised by the numbers of people gathered there. In the centre of the small wood was a glade, round in shape, where the bracken and shrubs had been flattened down. Upwards of sixty people were assembled. Yes, there were twenty or so of my own crews, warriors from Denmark, Frisia and Ireland but there were also twice as many villagers, some of them older children.

The people were standing in a wide circle with the trees at their back. I could see that several offerings to the gods had been hung from the lower branches of the trees behind them. There were small animal offerings; I saw rabbits, mice, a small fox, some birds, probably pigeons and pheasants tied with coloured ribbons to the branches along with corn dollies in the shape of humans suggesting human sacrifice substitutes. I could think of a couple of people I would gladly sacrifice to Odin. In the centre of the glade Gautrek stood holding a boar and a sow. They had their trotters bound so that there was no struggle in them. I wondered if Gautrek had given them a drugged mash, but decided he had not, he would not wish to dilute the power of the sacrifice.

I walked to the centre of the glade and stood next to Gautrek ensuring I was well away from the boar's tusks. The boar was domesticated but it was still capable of inflicting a severe injury. I nodded to Gautrek and spoke clear and loud into the night.

"People of Testerep, brothers, sisters, we are here tonight, the eve of Yule, to honour the old gods of our fathers, the Aesir, and the Vanir our ancestors who came from the far east to make the tribes of Scandinavia and north Germany strong. We honour the lords of the Aesir, Odin the Allfather, Thor the Mighty, Frigg the Fecund, the mother, Sif of the golden hair. We honour the Vanir, Frey and Freya, the lord and lady, Njord the wise and all the lesser gods and goddesses. We give sacrifices in honour of their roles in aiding us the little people on the earth; we acknowledge their right to mistreat us, to raise us up and cast us down. Gods of old accept our offerings."

I turned to Gautrek and took hold of the boar's ears pulling its head to the side to expose its throat; Gautrek continued to hold the torso of the beast tight.

"Hail Frey, Lord of the fields!
Lord of the Vanir,
Golden of hair as the fields of wheat,
Bringing riches of heart and hearth
To noble and common folk alike,
We hail you with the corn that springs forth
And falls again to nourish us.
We hail you, mighty boar in flight,
Lord of the phallus that gives life,
Lord of Love that is bound to land,
Love that is bound with commitment,
Love that does not come easily,
As one must toil for the harvest.
Teach us that love is worth working for,
And that work is worth loving,
And that neither lives long without the other.
Lord Frey, Corn God,
Husband of Gerda the etin-bride,
You who can warm the cold heart,
Warrior without a weapon
Who gave your sword for love,
You who make the grain spring forth,
Show us faith in every springtime."

I drew my scramaseax and slashed the boar's throat deep, severing the arteries in its neck. The boar struggled in terror as its life's blood splashed out onto the grass. The people raised their hands in supplication and chanted.

"Frey, Frey, Frey."

Gautrek and I let the boar's carcass slump to the ground and turned to the sow who was now struggling desperately. Gautrek grabbed hold of the beast and hoisted it up, I grasped the sow's ears and intoned.

"Hail Freyja, Vanadis,
I ask for protection,
Under your falcon wings
And war-maiden's shield.
Help me to make peace among my enemies.
Give me the courage to fight again
For if I am battle-slain in truth
May my actions be worthy of your choosing.
Hail Freyja, Lady of Sessrúmnir
Help me to set boundaries for myself
So I can honour the boundaries of others,
For as your home, when locked,
Is protected by your will
Let me be also protected
And closed against trespasses,
Yet may my hospitality be true
And help me act in faith.
Help me to pay fairly
And to accept fairly what is my due.
Show me your just ways."

I repeated the killing of the sow in the same way as with the boar. The people chanted.

"Freya, Freya, Freya." The two carcasses were dragged out of the glade.

The next two animals brought into the glade were a ram and an ewe. They were a good deal easier to handle than the pigs; they were hobbled so they could not thrash and resist over much. I took the ram firmly by the horns and intoned a prayer to Thor.

"Thunder rolls, lightning strikes,
And the hammer flies across the sky.
God of the weather, chariot of the storm,
Master of rain and torrents,
Son of the strength of Mother Earth,
I ask you to grant us that strength for ourselves.

You who are so great that you cannot walk
Across the Rainbow Bridge without breaking it,
You whose tree is the mighty oak,
O Thor, grant us that unending sturdiness.
Let us not break beneath the blows of misfortune.
Keep us from being crushed when the powerful
Stomp their large feet on the smaller ones below.
You who are the guardian of the common man,
You who care for the farmers and workers,
Look upon us here in this place where we are
Only a few of many, and protect our steps.
Make us resilient and mighty as your own arm,
Make us unbreakable, you who are Friend of Man.
We ask for one small percentage of the vigour
Of the right arm of the Thunderer,
That we might brave the tempest
And stand firm in the gales.
Thunder rolls, lightning strikes,
And the hammer flies across the sky."

I drew the scramaseax across the shaggy neck of the ram ensuring the blade went deep into the flesh. The artery severed and the blood gushed out. The ram did not even bleat but bore its death stoically. The crowd chanted
"Thor, Thor, Thor."
I repeated the sacrifice of the ewe with a prayer to Sif of the golden hair.

"Bride of thunder and lightning
Who calms the terrible storm,
Bride of war and fighting
Who offers the peaceful horn,
Sleeping fool of Loki
Who let bygones stay that way,
Teach us how to grit our teeth
And soften what we say.
Teach us that all hating
Is poison to the mind,
That no attempt at peace making

517

Goes unnoticed by your kind,
That when we hold our hands out
You notice and you smile,
Even when we are rebuffed
We are your hands and eyes.
We thank you, golden lady
All unafraid of strife,
Spread your peace throughout our homes
And throughout all our lives."

The crowd moaned, "Sif, Sif, Sif."

The ram and ewe were duly dragged away and Gautrek brought the final sacrifice; the stallion and mare were blindfolded but the smell of all the blood made them skittish. I laid my hand upon the stallion's nostrils and whispered calming words. His ears pricked up to listen, then I spoke the invocation.

"Those of us owned by You,
who have trembled in delicious fear
at Your presence, praise Your name,
Odin, All-Father, Master of the Tree.
Oh! Son of Bestla. Son of Borr
born when the worlds were yet to be formed,
born of those first generations
to arise from Ymir's horde,
You with Your brothers,
forged a new race of Gods,
rising from violence,
shooting toward wisdom
like the fleetest of comets
shooting toward the earth.
You are called Gangleri,
Wandering God,
at home nowhere and everywhere;
You are called Sigtyr,
brilliant in Your battle-glory,
born to conquer, to possess the world;
You are called Grimnir,
and by vitki Yggr,

in honour of Your terrible time upon the Tree.
You are known by these and many other names,
and the paths to You are many.
We praise them all, that You may savour
in each of Your guises,
and by whichever name pleases You the most
the fermentation of our spirits.
May these words please You oh God,
and may You bestow upon us,
whose mouths overflow
with adoration and praise,
the terrible grace of Your blessing."

Quickly I slashed the scramaseax across the stallion's throat, cutting deep to the bone. He tried to rear but Gautrek pulled down on the rope around the beast's neck. Blood sheeted across both of us and we were red from head to foot. After some struggles the stallion collapsed onto the ground, twitching in its death throws. I stood clear of the thrashing hooves and beckoned for the mare.

The crowd intoned, "Odin Allfather, Odin Allfather, Odin Allfather."

The mare was thoroughly disturbed by now and was whinnying and pulling at her halter. It took Gautrek and two others to hold her still. I needed to hurry. I invoked Frigg.

"Fairest Frigg, Fensalir's Lady,
Friend of families, matron of marriage,
Most gracious of goddesses, hear our hailing.
We pray for ourselves and for those with whom
we are handfast,
We pray for peace between our bonds,
We pray for our love to last through the long years
And all the woes that the world can wish on us.
We pray for patience on all our parts,
That we may salve each other's sight,
Every time we return to the haven of home.
Yet most of all we ask for aid
When anger burns, and baleful words

Come forth to fire each other's false suspicions.
Help us to turn once again to trust,
And come with courtesy to the table,
And talk, and find a fairer road to walk.
O Frigg who keeps our knotted cord,
Show us the shared road through the thorns."

With a final slash I severed the mare's artery and more blood pooled the ground.

The crowed bayed. "Frigg, Frigg, Frigg."

They rushed forward and scooped dollops of blood from the ground and smeared their faces in honour of the sacrificed beasts. Gautrek and his helpers dragged the horse carcasses away, whilst everyone was congratulating each other in celebration of the turning of the year. All were wishing others good fortune for the coming year. The sacrifices were good, clean, consenting, the next year would be fruitful. Gautrek and his minions returned to the glade with the intestines of the sacrificed animals and tied them to the tree branches. I knew that somewhere nearby the heads of the beasts would be set on stakes.

"Gautrek, make sure that the carcasses are returned whole to Oudenberg so that they can be roasted for the Yule feast. The priests will bless them and all will be well for all our faiths." I ordered. Gautrek grunted assent, the sacrifices had been made according to custom and the carcasses would be eaten by the people, he and his heathen followers would be content.

I left the glade but did not return to Oudenberg immediately. I walked south-west towards the sea shore. In less than a mile I had crested the dunes and walked across the flat white sand, glimmering in the starlight. I walked straight into the sea mailed and all with my scramaseax still held in my hand. The sea floor was flat and clear of entanglements and I kept walking until I was up to my shoulders. I dipped my head under the water, the chill ran through my head but I stayed submerged until all the blood had been washed from my face and hair. I scrubbed my naked face with my hands to make sure none of the blood had encrusted in the crevices of my ears and nose. When I finally burst up to the fresh air, I could see a pool of blackness surrounding me before the tide swept it away. I waded out of the sea and shook myself of the excess water, I then walked back to my hall refreshed and alert. The sentry was shocked when I walked through the main gap between the Roman walls. Where had I come from? How did he not see me leave?

"Stay alert, warrior." I said as I walked past.

I did re-enter the hall via my small door into my cubicle without disturbing the slumbering residents and drunken feasters. I unharnessed and laid my weapons against the wall and my mail on a wooden frame I had had made especial. I did not clean them and I knew that they would start to rust from the salt water by morning.

I sat on my cot and wished for a woman, I had not had a woman in many weeks and after the sacrifices I felt an animal urge to mate, to rut. I missed Una but at this moment I would have settled for the voluptuous Countess Judith or even the insatiable Dedda, but as I laid out and stared at the ceiling it was my step-mother that filled my mind. I had not thought of her for weeks, months even but now all I could see was her naked, a vision of beauty, a sublime sexual animal, Frigg incarnate. Without any prompting or assistance, I involuntarily ejaculated relieving many days of abstinence. I fell asleep only to be tormented by my ethereal step-mother shredding my torso with a knife and sacrificing me to her God.

I awoke late and groggy thankful that I had not been sacrificed and gone the way of the Yule beasts. I stumbled from my cubicle to find Martin sitting outside scrubbing my mail with a sand cloth.

"I won't ask you what you have been up to." He muttered.

"I have been acting the good lord to his people, but you are right, do not ask more." I grumbled. "Cannot, Grub or one of the other boys do that?" I suggested.

"Not if you want it done properly." Martin responded.

I looked around, the hall was all bustle, Hilda's women had the carcasses of the Yule goats, the Yule sheep and the Yule horses turning on the spits above the fire trench, boys had not started to baste them yet.

"So, what is the hall to be called?" Martin asked.

"Hvitbjorn." I confirmed, the hall of the white bear.

"Good, that is as it should be."

521

"I need a fight." I said belligerently.

"Yes, for you a year without a war, or raiding is not good, others will steal your fame." Martin remarked.

This deflated me somewhat; did I have to fight continuously to remain the darling of battles? "I intend to raid Alba in the spring, maybe Northumbria as well." I decided.

"Not much wealth in Alba." Martin observed.

"It will have to be slaves then, sell them in Denmark." Martin nodded in agreement.

Folk started arriving for the Yule celebrations before noon and impromptu games were organised by Odoacer. By mid-afternoon I assembled a group of locals, including Odoacer; Hilda, who said she could ill afford the time; Father Thomas, and a large assortment of children and off we went to the nearest wooded area. I made sure that this was not the copse where the pagan sacrifices had been performed.

The children scattered looking for the largest oak tree they could find; young Erik Odoacerson came running back to say he had found an old gnarled oak tree with mistletoe growing on it. I was sure he already knew of the whereabouts of this tree well before Yule but I bade him show us the spot. The tree was indeed old and had clearly been coped before; I was sure its branches had contributed to previous Yule feasts.

"This is clearly a holy tree." Father Thomas declared, much to my relief he was entering into the spirit of the festive game. I long thick branch looped away from the main stem; a branch made for a hanging. Gautrek would have approved as it clearly replicated the branch on Yggdrasil that Odin hung himself upon for three days and three nights.

"Give me the axe." I held out my hand and Odoacer gave me a stout wood axe. I swung lustily at the branch and after dozens of blows the branch fell away. I then chose a two-foot section and hewed at it until I had fashioned a log.

"Children, let Father Thomas bless the Yule Log and convey it to the hall." The children crowded around shouting and laughing, they picked up the log and carried it to Father Thomas, who intoned a brief blessing.

"Oh! Lord Jesus, son of God, let this Yule Log take upon it all our sins and burn them away. Amen."

"Amen!" the children shouted together and carried the log back to the village.

I fell in beside Father Thomas. "I must thank you for bringing all the villagers together, heathen, and Christian alike. I believe your tolerance will bring all into the Christian fold within time."

"Yes, I understand. However, it would greatly help if they saw their lord attend church more often." Father Thomas looked at me pointedly; did he know?

"I have a problem with ordained priests, father. I appreciate you are not all the same and yet I have met far too many grasping, worldly men of God who use their authority, shall we say, poorly."

"I understand, Lord Hereward, there are far too many self-serving priests in the higher echelons of our order but I hope you will find that the lower ranks of the priesthood are mostly inhabited by righteous individuals who only wish to improve the lot of the people." Father Thomas was at his most earnest.

"We will see."

I moved clear and re-joined the celebrating children. When we re-entered the hall, the children gave the log to Hilda's maids to adorn with trimmings. Svart who was something of a wood carver had fashioned small wooden mice and a squirrel to attach to the log. Twigs of holly berries and ivy pods would also be attached. I noticed that Gautrek took the log and shooed the children away and went to the kitchen; the children were deflated for a time, that is until Odoacer produced an inflated pig's bladder that they all kicked around the area in front of the hall whooping with laughter. As dusk descended everyone assembled for the Yule feast. This was the largest assembly of my people since I had come to Testerep and there were, maybe three hundred and fifty people, men, women, and children.

Everyone gathered in the hall, the children were still basting the Yule carcasses over the fire trench and the aromas were truly mouth-watering, as previously, ale was available for everyone. Martin called for order, banging the table furiously several times before the hall was sufficiently quiet to be heard.

"Father Thomas will bless the hall." Martin announced.

"All glory and praise are Yours, Lord God,

523

Creator of the universe and Father of all:
we thank You for calling us in Jesus
to be Your beloved people
and temples of Your Holy Spirit.

Remember the promises of the Lord Jesus
and listen to the prayer we offer in His Name.
Bless us in all our actions,
and bless this meeting place of Your people.
Help us to recognize Your presence among us,
fill us with Your joy,
and guide us at all times.

We give You praise and thanks, heavenly Father,
through Jesus Christ Your Son
in the love of Your Holy Spirit,
now and always and for ever.
Amen!

After Father Thomas had made the sign of the cross everyone shouted, vigorously, "Amen!"

I stood so everyone could see me. "Father Thomas has blessed this hall; hence forth this hall will be called Hvitbjorn, the hall of the white bear." I held up my ale cup and shouted loudly, "Wassail, Hvitbjornhalla."

The crown shouted back holding their cups and drinking horns high, "Hail, Hvitbjornhalla!"

Martin had disappeared into my cubicle and at that point reappeared with my white polar bear skin, which he hung up on a prepared frame behind my high chair.

"The white bear." My huscarls chanted. "Bearslayer!"

I held out my hands for silence, "Let the feast begin; where is the Yule log?" Egil and Odoacer together came through the hall entrance holding the Yule log up on two spear points. The log had been beautifully decorated but now was the time for the children to pretend that the log was actually Trickster Loki in disguise.

"Logi, Logi, Logi." They chanted, "Fire! Fire! Fire!" and then they changed the name from fire to. "Loki, Loki, Loki, burn,

burn, burn." Egil and Odoacer cast the log into the fire trench and it burst into flames immediately. I realised that Gautrek had been soaking the log in the animal fats of the Yule sacrificial beasts to ensure it caught fire and burned well to bring fortune to the new year. Everyone cheered and wassailed the Yule log, there was plenty of kissing and embracing and fumbling under outer garments. I was sure there would be plenty of new year babies in the offing after tonight. Hilda's girls brought in the food on great platters and the Yule carcasses were carved and the feast was underway.

Spring 1061 - Fenella

Three months after Yule the weather turned and spring started to show. The first tiny wild flowers started to peep out of the coarse grass on the sand dunes masking Testerep from the wild sea. The wind had turned from the frosty north until it blew more from the south-west suggesting that Norse minds should turn to the spring raiding season. I had made it known a month before that after the seeds had been planted, I intended to lead an expedition in my longships. This year Egil had decided to stay at Staina building a second knarr, so the trading ship, *Hilda*, would be skippered by Eric Whalelegson and sail south to Bordeaux on the wine trade route protected by Coll and *Wave Rider*. I intended to take the three other snekkjas to Alba and I needed three full crews, upwards of one hundred and sixty warriors, to crew them. I was short of at least fifty men and I hoped that I could recruit that number from the adventurous amongst the locals. I need not have worried; men came drifting in from all quarters when they heard I was looking for men, and that there would be profit. Most were younger sons of farmers but some were mercenaries with ill reputations but handy in a fight.

Svart, Eystein Whaleleg and Odoacer would stay behind to supervise the lordship in my name. Young Erik Odoacerson had badgered his mother and father long and loud to be allowed to go as a ship's boy and they reluctantly agreed. They had great hopes of him becoming a ship's captain in due course and the only way for that to happen was for him to learn the trade from a young age. I was also surprised when Dietrich signed up as a rower; I had recently given him the farm at Westende, young as he was, and with him being newly married I thought he would be content to stay at home. However, when I asked him about his decision, he was most adamant that he too was going to become a ship's captain and could not afford to miss the opportunity to learn the trade. I did not ask him how his marriage was working out.

Everyone put their backs into the sowing season, singing the songs of rebirth and secretly rutting in the furrows to ensure fertility. The stockmen made sure our bull covered as many cows as possible and that the chosen ram visited all the farms; the cockerel and drakes saw to themselves. We had few enough horses but each mare was covered by the few stallions we had.

When the time came everyone came down to the fjord to see our longships sail. Even Father Thomas came to bless our voyage. I found it strange that the Christ men could condone slavers and raiders when we were to all pretence and purposes Christian and yet would condemn heathens for the same practices; for slavery still existed and thrived in all Christian countries and when I questioned Father Thomas about this, he pointed out that God condoned slavery and there were many instances in the Bible that demonstrated this fact. He clearly did not approve of slavery but it said it was the way of the world. Eilif the Icelandic poet came down to the shore and asked for permission to sail with me; he wanted to reach Iceland this year. I informed him that the best I could offer was to drop him off somewhere in Alba and he was content with that.

We sailed on a morning tide with a strong wind blowing from the south west, as we hit the swell of the open sea some of the new recruits started to turn decidedly green to the amusement of the old salts. I knew that it would be several days before they found their sea legs and by then we would be well up the funnel of the North Sea. We sailed in line with *Mare Swallow* leading and *Little Runa* and *Ottar* in our wake; we were under full sail and stood well out from the coast of England as we did not wish to run in with any of Harald Godwinson's coastal patrols. I could feel my spirits lifting, to be free again from the responsibility of a lordship, anchored to the soil, flying across the swan's path with our longship monsters pegged to the prow strakes declaring our warlike purpose.

All three snekkjas had new sails that had been woven by the women of Oudenberg, the sails consisted of red and white strips sown together, a typical viking, Norse sail. *Mare Swallow's* sail also had a Mercian knot embroidered in the centre that could be displayed when the longship was under full sail. We sighted the coast of England where the large convex coast of Norfolk juts out into the North Sea. The undulating sand dunes mirrored the Flemish coast we had just departed from. The coast fell away to our stern as we cleared East Anglia looking for the Lindsey coastline. I decided we would shelter in the Wash for the night and so I signalled to the following snekkjas to follow *Mare Swallow* into the deep-water current that was the outpouring from the rivers that fed the Wash from all over the Danelagh; the Ouse, the Nene, the Welland and the Witham.

Most of the Wash was very shallow and the deep channels had been long ago staked to show the deeper drafted traders where to sail. I did not want to meet any English traders out from the ports of Lynn or Saint Botolph's town so as soon as we were deep enough into the wide but sheltered waters of the Wash, I ordered a turn to the steer board and glided out over the shallow beds of seaweed and mud. A few hundred paces off the main channel was sufficient for us to be unobservable from passing traders in the dark so we hove-to and the three longships were lashed together and stone anchors thrown overboard. We were safe for the night.

The night passed peaceably enough and we sailed on with the dawn light. There were a few ships masts on the horizon but they ignored us, presumably hoping we would ignore them and pass by. We stood well out from the coast again and sailed north under full sail at a rapid clip. We now had a choice of heading for the Humber and its wide sheltered estuary and anchor for the night behind the Spur of sail on and find ourselves somewhere along the long, rugged coast of Deira with no friendly sheltered ports as night fell. Although the wind was in our favour I decided on caution and by mid-afternoon we shortened sail and coasted into the wide estuary of the Humber. There were many ships sailing west up the estuary, fishing boats from Grimsby and Kings Town and traders heading for the northern River Ouse and the quays of Yorvik, or York. I had no intention of attacking any of these boats on our journey north, but some would be fair game on our return if we had any room left on our longships for additional plunder. Clearly, they were all wary of our low, sleek snekkjas but we were not aggressive so they went on their way without evasive action such as running for shore. For our second night at sea, we ran our longships up onto the shallow beach on the southwest side of the Raven's Spur; this was the land of the Holdr's Ness that had been in the Holdr's family for generations. They were of Danish stock and were ambivalent towards raiding ships, as long as the Ness was left un-molested.

The crews were free to stretch their legs and build fires for hot food; this put them in good spirits. Eilif played some sailors' rowing songs and some of the crews joined in the choruses. Just before we were about to bed down the sentries called in that a host of horsemen were closing on the camp. I immediately ordered a shield wall across the sterns of the boats. I could hear the thunder of hooves as the group closed upon us.

"Hold the line and do not cast a spear or axe unless I give the order." I bellowed. I could see beams of light arcing over the sand hills.

"They are riding with torches; their night vision will be ruined; do not look at the torch flames." Horses breasted the tops of the sand dunes, one, two, ten, no maybe twenty. If that was all nothing to fear.

"Hold!" I shouted. A middle-aged man on a mettlesome bay stallion jerked his reins and his horse swerved to the side and pulled up on his haunches. The following riders rode left and right to avoid their leader. The lead rider held up his hand; he wore mail but his sword was sheathed and he was bare headed.

"I am Somerled Carlson, grandson of the Holdr and lord of this land, who are you that trespasses on the Ness?"

"A trespasser with more men than you." I responded just to make sure he knew what was what. "Somerled Carlson, I like you am of Danish descent and I have no quarrel with the men of Holdr's Ness. I am Hereward Leofricson the outlaw and I am on my way to raid in Alba. I tell you this knowing you are no friend to Tostig Godwinson, so-called Earl of Northumbria, although I met your older brother Gamel in the earl's company a few years back."

"Ha! The Bearslayer no less, you are welcome on my lands. My brothers and I are no friends of the earl but we tried when he was appointed. A raid on Alba, in that case you will want my news." Somerled hoisted himself from his horse and tossed the reins to one of his huscarls and trudged over to me offering his hand. I reached out and gave him a salutation with a firm grasp.

"I would invite you to my hall but it is too far if you intend to sail at dawn."

"We do, but come sit and share a horn of ale." I invited him over to the fire. "You mentioned news?" I prompted.

"Tostig Godwinson is on his way to Rome via London. Northumbria has been suffering raids from that bastard Malcolm King of Scots and Tostig has brokered a truce. The truce was sealed in London and sanctioned by King Edward. Tostig has gone on to Rome with his wife and a gaggle of bishops and Malcolm has returned to Scotland. I cannot believe how stupid the King and Tostig are, as soon as Tostig is out of the way Malcolm will start raiding again, it is in his nature, he is a wolf."

"So Tostig has abandoned you to the Scots." I summarised.

"Yes, but I doubt they will come this far south, Malcolm wants Cumbria and Bernicia."

"What about the Edulfings of Bamburgh, Gospatric, now isn't it?"

"Ha! Tostig as taken Gospatric as a hostage with him to Rome. He has left his chief huscarl, Copsic in control of Yorvik." Somerled looked sour. I had met Copsic, he was only a minor lord far below Somerled, I could see there was an insult here.

"So, if I raid Alba, Malcolm and his army may very well be absent raiding in to England?" I mused.

"I wish I could come with you." Somerled opined.

"You are welcome to accompany us, but I could only take a dozen or so of your huscarls."

I could see Somerled struggling with his desire to strike at the Scots but eventually his obligations to his people overrode his personal desires.

"No, I must stay and protect my people."

"I understand; myself, I have good men to protect my lands while I raid and Flanders is not in turmoil." Somerled and his men exchanged friendly conversation and a few jars of ale before they parted.

The following morning, we rowed out from behind the Raven's Spur into the Humber channel and beat around the headland against the prevailing winds. We made the open sea and turned north with a following wind, raised the sails, and continued north along the Northumbrian coast. The weather still held good and the wind could not have been sweeter; by late morning we sailed passed the beetling cliffs of Flamborough and the Scar. There was only one suitable place to shelter for the night and that was the mouth of the River Tyne, after that we would be sailing passed Edulfing country and even with their lord a hostage and away with Tostig it was not a place friendly to Norsemen. I decided to sail on through the night, preying the weather held and this should place my flotilla north of Bamburgh and the Farnes and off the Lothians, fair raiding territory. Nevertheless, I did not want to raid so far south in Alban territory, I had my mind set on the kingdom of Fife where the MacDubh ruled.

I had come up against MacDubh when I had fought for Thorfinn MacBeth and I liked to pay back old scores. If Malcolm was indeed intending to raid in Northumbria, then there would be scant resistance for us further north. The night's sailing went without mishap; my innate caution placed my longships further out in the North Sea than was necessary for there was no way I intended to founder on the Bass Rock or the cliffs of Lothian. Most of the crews had slept throughout the night and only came fully awake at dawn as we passed the wide estuary of the Myrkvifiörd, or the Forth fjord, with Fife along its northern shore. My target was the Tay fjord where I had fought for Thorfinn MacBeth. There were settlements on both sides of the fjord and some Culdee monasteries. The town at Perth was too big a nut to crack but I could loot all the settlements east of the river itself. I gave strict instructions that the villages were not to be fired; I wanted no warning given to other villages that death and destruction was on its way to them.

We coasted down the southern shore of the fjord, that is the north coast of Fife until it narrowed into the River Tay proper; I saw a settlement on a bluff above the river and signalled to the following snekkjas to follow us in. Coll pushed hard on the helm and heeled *Mare Swallow* over to larboard and we headed straight in towards the narrow beach. There were a few fishing boats pulled up on the shore but we ignored them especially as I was intent of scanning the waters ahead of the snekkja to ensure we did not breach on any underwater rocks or obstructions. We ran up onto the narrow shingle beach without any difficulty and moments later *Ottar* and *Little Runa* ran in alongside us. I shouted across.

"Magnus, take your men and go east about the village, no one to escape." Magnus acknowledged and his men started jumping from the bow strakes onto the beach. I turned to *Ottar*.

"Eystein, take your men west about and ensure no one escapes to warn the villages further up the fjord."

I jumped down from the prow and my men followed; it had already been decided that each helmsman would stay with the longships with ten men a ship and the ships' boys. I strode up the rise from the river through heavy tussocked and coarse grass followed by upwards of forty men along with Eilif Gunnorson and Gautrek. We all carried our shields and swords or axes, spears are often an encumbrance on a ship and we were mailed and helmeted. I did not expect trouble but the surprise appearance of a warlike force can never be ruled out.

The settlement was in a shallow dip in the landscape indicating a pond or stream around which the village nestled. All appeared quiet and it was just possible we had not been seen sailing down the sound. However, as we reached the outskirts of the settlement I heard shouts and screams from the west suggesting that the villagers were fleeing and had run into *Ottar's* crew. My men spread out and we entered the village in an extended line. At the same time, I saw Magnus and his men entering the settlement from the east.

"Search the cottages, take anything of value. Gautrek check if there is a church." I ordered; as I spoke several villagers burst back between the houses obviously being chased by *Ottar's* crew. They all skidded to a halt not knowing what to do.

"Round them up." I yelled.

Most were women, old and young with crying and screaming children. There were some men and some were armed with wood axes and hay forks with wicked tines.

"Be careful, kill those men." I directed men towards the armed men who were at the back of the other villagers presumably to protect their kin from the pursuing raiders. I noticed one villager had a sword so I set myself and offered combat; he ran at me swinging his sword wildly. He may have been a thegn, but I doubted it, his lack of proficiency with his weapon suggested he was less, a village head man? He swung his sword at my head, I raised my shield and deflected the blow leaving my opponent's chest wide open to my riposte, my scramaseax ripped through his stomach just below his sternum and slanted upwards entered his heart. His face barely registered shock before he crumbled on to the ground sliding off my blade. Several men threw down their tools and weapons hoping to live. Magnus jogged over, "That wasn't too hard."

"No, it was not; but we do not want this rabble; we need to select the choicest women and children for the slave block, kill the men, leave the old they will not reach any other settlement before we do."

The villagers were rounded up and six women and three young children were selected and roped together, the rest were released. They were obviously very unattractive as my men did not even bother to rape them. We returned to the ships and pushed off; the captives being placed in the well of the *Ottar*. I asked one of the women what the village was called and she informed me that it was named Balmerino. We executed the same raiding technique at the next three settlements along the south bank of the River Tay. There was little of no resistance and we increased the number of captives bound in the well of each ship. There was an island in the river a few miles further upstream and I decided to camp overnight there. I knew this island from when I fought Asbjorn, he and the Fife men had crossed the river somewhere here. I assumed that some of the villagers had escaped and made their way to Perth by now and that a strong force would be sent out in the morning to confront us. They would probably be sent along the south bank of the river towards the villages we had raided, but on the morrow, I intended to sail back towards the open sea along the north bank. I knew the north bank reasonably well from my previous stay in Alba, the mormaer of Angus had sided with Thorfinn MacBeth but had gone over to Malcolm Canmore after Dunsinane. I considered any settlement on the north bank fair game.

The following morning before daylight we set off rowing in line along the north side of the Tay. The stronghold of Erroll was about a mile away from the riverbank and I decided to raid the outlying village. I left the crew of *Little Runa* with the three grounded snekkjas and marched inland with two ship's crews heavily armed. The stockade of Erroll was prepared and all the villages were within, not what I wanted. Worse when we approached, we were met by a flight of arrows; these did little damage as they were short hunting bows, not the powerful Norse longbows. One of my crew received an arrow through his bicep. I held up my hand to halt the host; it was not part of the plan to assault defended fortifications.

"Back to the ships; I have no fight with walls." I commanded. I turned to Gautrek, "I made a mess of that, then." He smiled mirthlessly. "Cannot get it right all the time, lord; better to retreat and fight when Odin favours you." We returned to our ships and launched, rowing eastwards back towards the sea; I decided to bypass several villages that may well be prepared for us, as was Erroll. I decided to attack a small hamlet just before the town of Dundee, a place called Caenn Gaothach, it was only a smattering of hovels but I needed something positive. I took one ship's crew, *Mare Swallow's,* and surrounded the settlement. We rushed in and found, nothing, all the inhabitants had fled towards Dundee.

"Fire the place, lets worry the constable of Dundee." I ordered. As we retreated to the ships the hovels burned slowly, the roofs made of grass sods burned poorly, billowing acrid smoke floated away north, a beacon of intent.

I decided to sail on past Dundee, a large town we were not strong enough to raid, and sail on to Monifieth. I knew that Monifieth was an ecclesiastical centre of the Cele De, the Gaelic Christians. I felt sure there would be valuables to be taken, gold, silver, precious artefacts, and monks made good slaves.

It was just past midday and the weather had changed from a clear sky with high billowy white clouds to a greyer sky with drizzly rain when we approached Monifieth. The wind had shifted to the west blowing straight down the fjord to the sea. I considered our luck had turned as the visibility had diminished and any bonfire warnings from Dundee might not be observable from our target. There was a nice stretch of white sand to run the ships up on and we rowed in at some speed intending to disembark quickly to prevent any organised resistance as we had experienced at Erroll. This time I decided to take all the crews, just leaving a skeleton force to protect the longships under Martin. The landscape was relatively flat ahead with rising ground to the west hiding Dundee. The settlement was quite large, maybe thirty or forty cottages and a small stone chapel or church surrounded by stone cells for the hermits and monks.

We scraped up onto the sand, I jumped from the prow sheer strake and landed ankle deep in the loose shingle that formed a line just above the water line. I carried a small hand axe, a francisca in my left hand and steadied myself with my right hand on the beach. I forced myself to move knowing an avalanche of warriors would be following me. I ran up the beach to the coarse grass line and turned to watch the warriors debauching from my three longships. I drew my sword and signalled for the crews to spread out and envelope the settlement.

"We go in fast, kill all the men, take women and children and as much loot as we can carry." I instructed. I jogged forward towards the village, as we breasted the grass lip of the beach we were exposed to view from the village, maybe a hundred paces away. I kept on straight towards the small chapel and as I did so I could see Gaelic monks exiting their little stone cells. They all wore long grey gowns, totally unsuitable for running even though they had stout leather sandals. They all displayed that curious Gaelic tonsure, so different from the Catholic priests and monks. Instead of shaving a bald patch on top of their head they completely shaved the front part of their head hair leaving long straggly tresses falling down and covering their necks behind.

As one, they all ran to the chapel, maybe a dozen or more of them; they slammed the stout oak door shut and I heard a bar drop into place.

"Surround the chapel, there may be another way out and I don't want any of them to escape." I instructed.

My men spread around the chapel, whilst others searched the hermit cells for valuables, of which there was none, of course. I could now hear screams and the sound of fighting in the village, so at least some of the inhabitants were fighting back. I looked around but could see nothing suitable for a ram to smash the door in. The chapel was built of stone with white mortar holding the stones in place. The roof was thatched but was at some height.

"Men, search and find a ladder, we can pull the thatch aside and hurl stones down on the monks until they come out." I shouted.

A couple of old rickety ladders were eventually found that were long enough to reach the eves of the roof. Meanwhile, some of my men had started to pick at the mortar between the stones; it was hard but once one or two stones were prised loose the whole edifice would be materially weakened. I could now hear chanting from within, I thought it might be the prayer of Saint Patrick, which was well known amongst the western seaboard of the British Isles. Once the men had gone up the ladders the straw thatch soon started showering down; other men stood at the base of the ladders holding stones ready.

Another two of my men with large Dane axes had started to hack at the oak door, but with little result. I stood at the door hinges and shouted through the crack in my best Gaelic.

"You in there, as you can see, we will soon gain entrance, but in doing so we will destroy the chapel. Our entrance is inevitable so save the chapel and open the door and I promise we will not kill you." I stood back waiting for a response. The chanting had stopped and I could envisage a heated debate around my suggestion. When the first three of four stones clattered down into the interior of the chapel, I heard the door brace being lifted.

"Stand back." I commanded and my men stood around in an arc swords and axes at the ready.

The door creaked open, clearly it was seldom closed. An elderly monk emerged holding a crozier, a simple wooden staff with a carved hooked end; a shepherd's staff, no gold, no silver. The cross around his neck was wooden as well, held around his neck by a simple leather thong.

"I am abbot Cellach and these are my brethren, we surrender to you in good faith, are you Christians or pagans?"

I could feel Gautrek at my elbow start to grunt and hiss and I held my arm across his chest.

"Steady, steady Gautrek." I cautioned.

"I am Hereward Bearslayer and I gave you my word, you will not be killed, but you will be enslaved. As to whether we are Christian or pagan is an irrelevance to your future, the slave markets in Ribe know no ideologies but the god profit, bind them."

I pushed passed the monks into the chapel, the altar was bare and there were no candlesticks or other interior adornments but I knew they had no time to hide their treasures properly. I walked up to the altar, it was a stone slab on a square stone base, which looked very much like an old Roman ossuary, in fact there was carving along the sides, depictions of shells and doves, typical Roman symbolism. I grasped the altar top and heaved, it slid backwards and eventually tipped over and fell onto the floor revealing an open interior. It was an old Roman ossuary and it was full of silver ornaments; a massive silver and jewelled crucifix, chalices, candlesticks, even spoons and silver candle snuffers. There were some old bones at the bottom peeping out from a silken cloth, which presumably belonged to the founder monk who was revered as a saint, whoever he was? I tipped the bones out and wrapped the plunder into the silk cloth.

"Here," I gestured to one of my warriors, "Take this lot back to the ships, they do not want to be martyred this day."

Emerging from the chapel I could see that the raid was well in progress. All the dead men laying around the small gardens and lanes testified to the thoroughness of my men. I could hear screams and sobs from inside the cottages as some of my warriors sated their lust on the unfortunate women. I could never understand how men could be so easily distracted from their own safety by the prospect of imminent rape. A large rescue force could be descending upon us from Dundee and whilst humping a woman these warriors would be totally unprepared. I sent a group of my men west of the village to keep a watch. The monks were being led back to the snekkjas and other men were rounding up livestock and carrying portable loot, mainly utensils, tools, crockery, and cloth.

I looked around and checked we had been thorough, "Alright, burn the village but not the chapel." I instructed. "Call the men in and let's go."

Embarkation took time, especially getting the livestock aboard. Martin came over.

"What have you brought the monks for?" I looked across at the miserable monks roped together in the well of *Mare Swallow.*

"A moment of weakness, I just did not want to kill anymore defenceless holy men."

Martin grimaced. "Holy men! I do not remember meeting any holy men in the churches in England or Flanders for that matter."

I smiled at him. "Maybe these Cele De are different, who knows?" I responded.

As we pushed our snekkjas off the beach and back into the deeper water a group of horsemen timely appeared riding along the shore from the direction of Dundee. They shouted angrily at us waving their spears, which made my men laugh.

Gautrek standing beside me hissed. "They arrived just in time to wave goodbye they must have planned that very carefully."

"Not carefully enough." I said; I reached for my long Norse bow and strung it. The horsemen on the shore may have considered themselves out of range for an arrow kill. I nocked and sited an arrow and let fly; the missile arced across the water and disappeared from sight but almost immediately the lead rider threw his arms up and toppled from his horse. My men cheered; the horsemen scattered.

I had to decide now if I should continue raiding up the Angus coast or turn south and raid Northumbria. The longships were already quite full of captives and treasure, the haul at Monifieth exceeding our expectations. In the end the weather decided for me; the wind slewed around and a mild wind came from the east requiring my tiny fleet to sail beam across the wind south. I aimed for the Eye Water, a small river debouching into the North Sea and about twenty miles north of Berwick, I knew there was a small harbour at the mouth of the river and a fishing settlement; I decided that we would strandhog from within the small bay and stay overnight. I counted on most of the fighting men from the area being with Malcolm Canmore further south in Cumbria.

My little fleet enjoyed a beautiful day's sail with the full sails taut towards the distant coast on our steer board side. Anyone on the cliffs may have seen our emblems stitched proud against the red and white striped sail, although I doubted anyone would recognise my Mercian knot for what it was. The crews played dice or hnefatafl, some just dozed enjoying the warm summer weather. We were even joined by a school of dolphins, who playfully skimmed the bow wave of my snekkja.

By late afternoon we closed on the coast of Lothian and espied several fishing vessels making their slow way back towards the Eye mouth. I ordered some of my men to string their bows and as we coasted passed each fishing boat the small crews were riddled with arrows. There must have been upwards of twenty men and boys who died in the fishing boats, which meant that there would be that many less in the Eye settlement to oppose us. I clambered over to Eilif Gunnorson who was sitting in the prow of the ship.

"Eilif, I should have dropped you off on the north bank of the Tay River, now you will have much further to go to reach Caithness and your Norse kind. I am sorry about that but the wind stays for no man."

"No matter." Eilif smiled, "It has been an interesting interlude staying with you and the opportunity to meet and see one of today's heroes of song and rhyme and is not to be missed."

I laughed, "Well, I am not sure I am a hero but Martin will be delighted for me to be referred to as such, as that is what he aspires to make me. You take care and make sure the Albans do not take you for a viking and kill you."

I also called the two miserable looking Scottish youths to me, they had to be relieved of their oars as I had made them row. Do them good I thought, toughen them up. I spoke to Aedh as I could not remember the other one's name.

"Well, you have had an uncomfortable time living on my hospitality. Now I have decided to release you. If you are lucky, you can steal a couple of horses when I raid the community at the mouth of the Eye River and ride west where I understand the clans are still opposing Malcolm Canmore. I do not particularly like the King of Scots so if releasing you two irritates him, even a little, that will please me." They had nothing to say and presumably they could not believe their luck after seeing so many barbaric killings and tortures of others of my prisoners; I dismissed them.

We reefed our sails and rowed straight into the small bay at the mouth of the river. There was a small defensive tower on the headland and no doubt we were observed as we approached. Horns would have been sounded and the villagers would be fleeing. We ran our longships up onto the small sheltered beach and I jumped off the stem sheer strake followed by my warriors. There were still people trying to collect their valuables before running, big mistake. My warrior crews rolled over them, killing those inhabitants who they deemed of no worth and anyone who was so presumptuous as to show resistance. There were few males as most had already been slain out on the fishing boats. All the women and children that had not already escaped were rounded up. The cottages and storehouses were ransacked and very soon a stream of goods and captives were being loaded onto the ships.

I had kept several of my best men together in the eventuality of any warriors attacking us from the tower; I could see several heads peeping over the palisade wall but I suspected that those inside were too fearful to try and rescue their people from the village; besides there could not be more than a dozen watchers in the tower. However, as the captives were being led away a small door at the base of the tower was thrown open and a young man sprinted out towards us. He was screaming someone's name and eventually I registered the word 'mother'. One of the women turned and saw the Scot running towards his certain death, she started screaming and begging him to turn back but he took no notice and within a few heartbeats he was pierced through with several arrows. The woman was dragged away screaming and crying. Embarkation resumed and the woman was thrown onto *Mare Swallow;* the longships were now over full with captives and plunder and it was time to return home. My men had found a small herd of ponies on the hillside above the village and had brought them down to the ships, a valuable asset. I selected two of these sturdy ponies and handed them over to the Alban youths and pointed in the direction they needed to go to find their fellow rebels. They left without a word, in a hurry; I suspected they did not believe that they would be freed.

Now the ships were heavily laden, a good strandhog, a good summer's raiding, all we had to do now was get back to Testerep in one piece. Although we had been at the Eye mouth most of the day, I decided that it would probably be safe to remain in the bay overnight before we sailed on. It was a calm night, weather wise that is; the boats were disturbed by my crews molesting the women taken from the village, the weeping, the groans of pain permeated the gloom. The night was balmy and warm, unusual for the coast of Alba. I was thinking that I would have liked to raid Northumbria again but now that my ships were strake board heavy that was now out of the question.

I was looking across the beam of *Mare Swallow* at the woman whose son had been killed in the village; she was no longer young but had clearly been handsome in her maidenhood. She had been left alone in her grief perhaps my men pitied her but it did not seem likely.

"What is your name woman?" I asked none to gently. She focussed on me a confused and disoriented face.

"Me? You mean me?" she mumbled.

"Yes, you."

"I am, I am Fenella. My son is dead."

"Yes, he should have stayed in the tower, he would be still alive."

"My daughter-in-law is over there being raped by several of your men." She looked furtively down towards the stern of the longship.

"Yes, it is the way of the world; if she is as handsome as you, they will not mistreat her over much."

"What do you intend to do with us, I mean after the rapes?"

"Most will be sold for profit who knows what will happen to them. However, I am setting up a new lordship in Flanders and I was hoping that some of you women will be claimed by my men as wives."

"How can you expect a woman to be the wife of any of your ruffians, men who rape and murder?"

"Because the alternative is definitely worse. My port has a brothel that needs whores." She blanched at this.

"Please, I will do anything to prevent my daughter-in-law suffering that fate."

"That indeed may be required of you." I answered solemnly.

There was something of my beloved Una about her and although she was nearly old enough to be my mother, I decided she would be my concubine until I could find someone more suitable. Her hair was still a glossy chestnut although it was now straggly and unkempt. She had green eyes and a freckled face with careworn lines at the sides of her generous mouth. Her stance was still strong, I could see that her arms and calves were muscled from hard work.

"What about your husband?" I asked.

541

"What is that to you?" She retorted angrily. The look on my face cowed her. "He is dead, a fever took him the winter before last." She had indeed had an overflowing cup of grief.

"I have decided that you will be my woman, for the time being. No one else will harm you, you are under my protection." I stood and walked away and informed Martin that she was not to be molested by the men. The night was calm and I did not feel like sleep, the moon was so bright I could see the outline of the hills to the west and a hint of the wavering colours of Bifrost the wonderful bridge to Valhalla. It was not usual to see them this far south but I had seen them clearly in the Orkneys where Thorfinn MacBeth had told me they were caused by the starlight rebounding from the shining armour of the Valkyries. Whatever the cause they were the harbinger of good luck. I tucked myself into the stern, beside the tiller and fell asleep watching the wavering lights.

It was a beautiful morning, a clear sky and gentle offshore breeze; I kicked everyone awake, eager to sail. I called in the sentries that I had posted above the village by sounding the bull's horn that hung on a peg on the stern post. As soon as they had hurried down to the shore and climbed aboard the ship that they belonged to, I shouted for the anchor stones to be hauled in. The men manned their oars and *Mare Swallow* pulled free of the small bay heading due east. The other two snekkjas followed in our wake forming a line. When we were clear of the headlands Coll ordered the sail raised and the off shore breeze carried us away from the shore; the oars were shipped and everyone sat waiting in anticipation for the prevailing wind to reveal itself. The day before the wind had been a mild easterly, which meant that if it continued, we would be required to row directly into it, or tack a long way south. I knew that Ribe must lay almost directly east of the Eye mouth so a south-easterly wind would be magical and I knew it was too early in the year to expect a northern or north-westerly blow. The crew raised their faces to the wind waiting for the off-shore breeze to die and be superseded by whatever wind the god Ull saw fit to send us; but the sail did not slacken, it was not taut but the wind kept on from the west until we all realised that the prevailing wind was indeed a westerly that would blow us straight to Ribe; the crew cheered, Bifrost had been a lucky sign after all.

It was about a two hundred miles sail east to Ribe and although the wind was not strong, we achieved about eight miles each quarter shift, which meant that if the wind held, we could reach the coast of Denmark in a full day's sail or sometime around dawn tomorrow. I intended to sell those captives that were of less use to me, at Ribe, especially the monks but I intended to keep most of the younger women as wives or concubines for my crews on the farmlands they had been allotted. As we would be sailing throughout the night, I arranged for a stern light to be lit in an iron casing to prevent fire reaching any of the wooden planking. Fire on any boat is hazardous but has its uses; this contrivance together with the light night minimised the chances of my tiny fleet separating. The crew was in high spirits now they were heading home with some useful plunder and I could see they were eyeing the women and I knew it would be difficult to apportion the them when we reached landfall. If anything causes more disputes and fighting it is the ownership of women and I did not want them to be the cause of friction in my nascent community. I asked Coll to find out which of the women had children on board the boats as I did not wish to separate them if possible; a man would have to take on the child with the mother. Any male children without a mother would be sold, they would not fetch much but it would be risky to keep them as they would harbour resentment as they grew and could seek vengeance, so they could not be trusted.

The voyage was uneventful and we spied the islands masking Ribe harbour shortly after dawn. This time the strand of Ribe was less crowded indicating that King Sweyn Estridson was not present, which was good. After we had beached the ships, I asked Magnus to sell the slaves as he had proved much more adept at this sort of thing than I.

After Martin had sorted out the wheat from the chaff, thirteen monks, five young boys and seven women considered to be unlikely to be desirable as a wife were roped together and marched off to the slave pens. Martin informed me that there was now thirty young women and girls left not counting Fenella.

"Good, they will be a useful contribution to my lordship and will mean more contented crewmen. How many women have children?" I queried.

"Five women have girl children, none of the boys being sold on have mothers here. All the girls are too young to be married off yet." The sale of the captives took most of the morning and gave my captains the opportunity to take on fresh water and for the crews to break their fast with hard cheese and flat bread baked over hot stones on the beach.

Magnus returned at mid-day with a pile of hack silver that would reward the crews. I had no intention of staying in Danish waters as the on-going war between the Norwegians and the Danes could envelope us at any time. It meant a long row against the prevailing winds but every mile south took us towards home waters and safety; as long as we kept near the Frisian coastal islands, we were unlikely to be intercepted by Harald Godwinson's Wessex fleet, which was the only naval military force that might stray into the North Sea. It was over five hundred miles home from Ribe and we had to row all the way against a steady westerly, by rowing into the wind we were able to tack south and although it increased the distance home it was worth it to give the rowers intermittent rests. We averaged only sixteen miles each watch and at the most thirty miles each day.

The Frisian islands were ideal places to pull our longships up onto the flat low-lying sand each night, allowing us to build fires and eat hot food, mostly barley gruel. In this way we brought our ships home to Testerep in two weeks without any undue mishap. The welcome sight of the watch tower on the sand dunes at Oostende was only improved upon when we sailed into the fjord and beheld the shipping anchored around, with the crews sampling the delights of our stop over haven. I counted twenty trading vessels mostly knarrs but some Frankish and English boats also; each ship paid a modest port fee for a safe night's shelter and the opportunity to use the services provided at the tavern and whorehouse.

We steered our ships past the trading vessels deeper into the fjord and nearer to Oudenberg before we berthed. It was my intention to disembark the plunder and convey it up to my hall, Hvitbjornhalla, before distributing it to the crews. My young huscarls that had accompanied me would receive hacksilver but other members of the crews would receive women and farming utensils, grain, and furnishings for their farms. The religious items would be kept as my share of the plunder to be sold off at Bruges. I would hold a feast for my crews before they dispersed and at the same time bring together those trusted captains' I had left to manage my lordship and receive reports of their activities.

The feast was a riotous affair as everyone considered the raid a success but I was astonished to find that the port fees collected by Svart far surpassed the value of our plunder. Odoacer and his wife Hilda also informed me that the harvest was ripening well and it looked to be an exceptional crop this year; I took their word on that as I knew relatively nothing about farming. The cream on the cake was supplied by Egil who informed me that his first knarr was nearing completion and would be larger than his *Hilda*. The evening ended for me when I took the captive Fenella, who had been sitting in a corner quiet and submissive through the whole feast, into my cubicle. She was much older than I, nearly old enough to be my mother, but I did not care for any of that; she had something about her that reminded me of Una, her face was careworn but I suspected her body was still desirable. I removed my mail and weapons and placed them in a corner on a wooden 'T' cross designed to display them. I then removed my tunic and trousers until I was entirely naked; I preferred to sleep this way and completely lacked any self-consciousness. I could see Fenella's eyes were drawn to my dormant manhood which hung limp between my thighs and this action alone made my member rise proud and hard.

"You are my woman now and you well know what that entails," I informed her. "Those clothes you are wearing are totally unsuitable for your new status as the lord of Testerep's leman so divest them and I will provide you with more suitable clothing in the morning."

Fenella shrugged out of her ragged gown and unsurprisingly she had no underwear to speak off but she was clean. She was a good height that suited me, nearly as tall as me. Her body was strong and muscular representing years of hard work in the fields, but the toil had not broken her. Her thighs were strong and sleek and her calf muscle looked hard, her ankles trim. I could see the

545

stetch marks across her slightly rounded abdomen, the tell-tale emblems of motherhood. Her Venus mons was raised and provocative and surprisingly hairless, reminding me of the fair-haired Countess Judith. Her breasts were large and rounded with little droop for her age, her nipples were large and long, well-used by her bairns. She had washed her hair since I first saw her and the chestnut tresses shone in the light of the cubicle candles. Although her face had a manly aspect at times and care-lined I still found her womanly and attractive.

"You have a body that is pleasing to me, come lay down, I will take you now." I ordered.

She lay down on my white bearskin and raised her knees and spread her legs wide displaying her vagina, she looked at the ceiling as if her mind was in a faraway place. I am not having that, I thought. I lay beside her and pushed her legs down and turned her towards me. I caressed her body, delighting in the shape of her breasts the unwilling hardness of her nipples. I kissed her neck and stroked her taut buttocks. I knew she was not ready to kiss my lips so I kissed and nipped her ears and neck, her shoulders and eventually her breasts. I could feel her shuddering and trembling beneath me; I reached for her woman's parts and stroked the lips of her inner sanctum. I inserted my fingers into her slowly easing her open feeling her lubrication spreading across her pink outer walls. I then surprised her; I suspect her former husband had never contemplated cunnilingus; I slid down the bed and pushed my face into her womanhood. I gently kissed her opening, licking it to moisten my intended entry. My tongue searched around to find her sensitive spot and she jumped with shock as my tongue glided over it. I could feel it quite clearly, it was round and bulbous, a miniature penis. I sucked it into my mouth and proceeded to suck it ferociously. She could not fend off her reactions any longer and cried out as she grabbed my head pushing it further into her body, which was now dripping wet. It was fortunate that I did not wear a beard like most men as it would be most uncomfortable by now. I moved back up the bed and she made a grab at my penis and missed.

"I want it." She hissed huskily, "Put it in me, boy."

I laughed, to her I was a boy, but a big boy nevertheless. I took hold of my penis and rubbed it around her opening, lubricating its bulbous head. Her eyes locked on mine she was crying softly, I pushed and my rock-hard member slid deep into her. She gave a contented sigh.

"Fuck your mother, fuck me good."

When she called herself my mother I nearly came there and then in shock; I had visions, not of my real mother but of my step-mother the lady Godgifu. I attacked her inner sanctum like a demon. I had never been so hard, so excited, so pleasured; but at the same time, I wanted these feelings to last forever. She now held me close, trying to pull me to the furthest extent of her vagina into her womb, if that were possible. She caressed me with hard calloused palms and worked her groin against me as only a peasant woman could.

"Do it in me! Do it in me now! Rape your mother."

Her words drove me to a frenzy, I surged in and out of her and felt the fluid build-up in my ball sack, my testicles became heavy, ready to explode, my mind fogged over, my being centred on my groin. I became so sensitive but continued, relentless, unstoppable. Then, I spasmed, keep going! I came in huge spurts of intense desire. I could feel my hard member filling her up, again, and again. I shuddered to a slow perambulation, I did not want to withdraw, it felt too good. Fenella's face was streaked with tears but she smiled and whispered.

"I want it again, fuck me again, boy."

Later, exhausted, and exhilarated, I walked down to the fjord, waded in, and swam over to the far bank. The water was cool and cleared my mind; I scrambled up onto the muddy bank and lay back and gazed at the stars. A myriad of sparkling pinpoints winked back at me and my mind drifted, contemplating my present circumstances.

Was this to be my future? A lordship in a foreign land, a viking warlord, an international maritime trader, what? The weight of responsibility hit me; I had a responsibility to so many people and I was no longer the itinerant warrior hero Martin envisaged I would be. The success and continuity of my lordship required that I marry and beget sons to follow me. Sons who would not be English but Flemish in outlook. The thought of a wife returned my thoughts to Fenella and my recent coupling. She had introduced another dimension to my life but I was realistic; she was a peasant woman from Alba and would be totally unacceptable to the Count of Flanders and his nobles as anything but a leman, a mistress. Besides, despite my current infatuation with Fenella I knew that it was not love and that I was ultimately looking for something more than good sex. She was submitting to me partly because I had not whored her daughter out.

Then there was England. It was years since I had seen my mother and my uncle Brand and I did miss them but did I have any feelings for England and my once home? Over the years I had fought the Wessex Saxons in the south of England and I had fought against the Northumbrians in Alba. I was realistic enough to admit I only had any allegiance to my mother's family in the Danelagh, in Kesteven. I was barred from entering England by the king and the Godwinsons, and of course, my evil step-mother Godgifu, instinctively I knew my business with England was unfinished.

My time would come and I would know my way.

END

Read how Hereward the Exile contends with William the Bastard and his Norman invaders of England in the second book of the Bearslayer trilogy.

Explanatory Notes

1. The family and descent of Hereward the Outlaw. (including analysis of Gestae Herewardi and Chronicles)

The records relating to the life of Hereward, latterly called by the Wake baronial family "The Wake" exist within the various Anglo-Saxon Chronicles. He is recorded as leading a rebellion in the Fens of south Lincolnshire and Cambridgeshire against the local oppression of the Normans after the Conquest. In AD1070 the Anglo-Saxon Chronicle relates *"then the monks of Peterborough heard say, that their own men would plunder the minister; namely Hereward and his gang"* and later in AD1071 *"When King William heard that, then ordered he out a naval force and land force and beset the land all about, and wrought a bridge, and went in; and the naval force at the same time on the sea side. And the outlaws then all surrendered; that was Bishop Aylwine and Earl Morkar; except Hereward alone, and all those that would join him, whom he led out triumphantly."* In these records he is not identified as a lord, thegn or earl and is simply referred to by name. This suggests that he was known as something of a celebrity and that he needed no further identification. This notoriety is somewhat confirmed by the written record of a Gestae or Saga in his name, which suggests that prior to its record his story circulated in verbal heroic verse from shortly after his death.

Now it is a singular fact that in the early medieval period and before that, in the so-called Dark Ages, there is no one person named, other than nobility, and such was the social structure before the feudal system and during the period of the feudal system that it is highly unlikely that any leader would be accepted unless he was of lordly status.

During Hereward's resistance in the Fens, he was joined by many eminent Anglo-Saxon nobles, earls, thegns and even at one point Edgar Aetheling, the rightful King of England. All these nobles accepted Hereward's leadership, which would be inconceivable unless he was of equal status to them, at the very least a legitimate earl's son.

The *Gestae Herewardi*, put down in writing circa AD1170, approximately one hundred years after Hereward's insurrection, identify Hereward as the son of Leofric Lord of Bourne and his wife Aediva. Based on this statement historians have generally believed that Hereward was not the son of the eminent Leofric, Earl of Mercia who was married to the famous Lady Godiva of naked horse-riding fame, but a lowly thegn with few lands. Why? Because Aediva is not Godiva. The family described in the *Gestae* also does not show any relationship to the known genealogy of Earl Leofric.

Nevertheless, when Charles Kingsley wrote his novel *'Hereward the Wake: Last of the English'* he had no hesitation is naming his hero as the son of the said Earl and his wife Godiva despite the evidence to the contrary. Other than that, his novel's narrative did tend to follow the *Gestae* however fabulous the stories about Hereward were.

It was the translation of the *Gestae Herewardi* by S H Miller and Rev W D Sweeting and their comments regarding the identity of Hereward that, to my mind, clarified and confirmed the true identity of Hereward Leofricson. It was not unusual in the early medieval period, especially in the northern, semi-pagan lands for men to have more than one wife at a time. A specific and relative example is Knut Sweynson, King of England, and Denmark. He had what was sometimes referred to as a hand-fast wife Elfgiva of Northampton, and a second Christian wed wife, Emma of Normandy, and widow to Aethelread II, King of England. Two wives, two sons, one who became King of England and one who became King of Denmark.

Leofric was a close confident of Knut the Mighty and the new Danish king wanted an English supporter in control of Mercia, a key central sub-kingdom of England. To confirm Leofric's hold on Mercia it was necessary for him to undergo a political marriage with the undoubted heiress of Mercia, Godiva/Godgifu. Most political marriages are devoid of love and thus leman, mistresses, or hand-fast wives, call them what you will, appear.

I accept the identification of Leofric, Lord of Bourne as Earl Leofric of Mercia and that his lands in Bourne were his by right of his marriage to Aediva. The family of Hereward, as described in the *Gestae* are those of his maternal ancestors from the

Danelagh. I have constructed a likely family tree of his ancestors at the front of the book. It should be pointed out that in the 11th century the Danelagh was not specifically part of Mercia, although part of it had been in earlier times and that Earl Leofric had only nominal control of it.

In his lifetime Hereward was never referred to as the 'Wake' but always as the 'Outlaw' or 'Exile'. These epithets describe his standing and life perfectly. However, it is interesting that the term 'Wake' does reflect Hereward's given name, i.e. The Army Warden. The man whose responsibility was to 'ward' the army should be ever 'Watchful'. How the Bourne family of Wake came by their name and link with Hereward is lost to history, but it is clear they believed in a relationship. The premier ducal family of Great Britain, the Howards, claim descent from Hereward's son Hereward and this descent is listed in Burke's Landed Gentry.

2. The milieu of Hereward the Outlaw

The only historical record in existence confirms that Hereward led the resistance to the Normans in the Fens, which was initially successful and recorded one of the few defeats that William the Bastard was personally subjected to, but it led to ultimate defeat.

The rest of the detail about the life of Hereward the Outlaw is related in the *Gestae* and the one kernel of history that can be extracted is that he had a long military career in Flanders before and after his Fenland resistance. Nothing is really known of his career after AD1071. Unfortunately, like all good oral stories this tale was embellished and added to. Some of these tales were later attributed to Robin Hood and just for good measure there had to be a fair share of giants, ogres, a monstrous bear, magical armour, and a wondrous horse.

Nevertheless, within the *Gestae* there was a core of truth that could be extracted that related to actual events in the eleventh century in north-west Europe and this I have sought to rescue. A wondrous horse would be of little use in the Fens; thus, *Mare Swallow* transforms into a longship. The slaying of a huge polar bear becomes the holmgang between Asbjorn Siwardson, prince of Northumbria and descendent of the fairy bear and Hereward's dual with the giant ogre is transferred from Cornwall to Ireland where something such must have taken place. My novel is colonised by real people in real places and events that actually happened.

3. The identity of MacBeth, King of Alba

Perhaps the most astonishing claim in my novel is that the celebrated MacBeth, King of Alba was, in fact, Thorfinn Sigurdson, Jarl of Orkney. This identification is based on the research by Dorothy Dunnett for her novel *King Hereafter*, which I would recommend to everyone who reads historical novels. In short, both MacBeth and Thorfinn were sons of the daughter of the King of Alba, born at the same time, died at the same time, ruled the same areas of Scotland and both went on pilgrimage to Rome in the same year; this person was just known by different names in the territories he ruled and were never mentioned together in any document of the time.

4. Viking longships

There were many types of sea-going ships built by the northern peoples of Europe that developed over hundreds of years into unique vessels capable of travelling over great distances with a better than average chance of surviving storms and mishaps. The most common types of ships were: the drakkar, the snekkja, the knarr and the karvi. All of these vessels were generally, clinker built and nailed together with a steer oar, or board, placed at the stern of the right side of the ship (the steer board side). The keel and lower ribs of the ships were boarded over and the seamen's sea chests were usually used as seats for rowers. All types had a single sail, usually made of woven wool and often displaying emblems such a raven, a lion or cross in later times.

a. The drakkar, or dragon, was the supreme viking ship of its time and the largest of all the long ships. It had at least thirty rowing benches indicating a rowing crew of sixty plus. These were usually owned by kings and jarls and were highly decorated. The most renown drakkar being the *Long Serpent* built for Olaf Trygvasson, King of Norway, which was approximately forty-eight metres long.

b. The snekkja, or snake, was the commonest viking raiding ship of the age with anywhere between eighteen and thirty rowing benches indicating a rowing crew of between thirty-two and sixty rowers. Jarls, wealthy bondis and farmers would use snekkjas for raiding and limited trading. Very few nobles could afford to build and man a longship larger than a snekkja.

c. The knarr, the Norse merchant ship used by the vikings for long sea voyages and during the viking expansion. The knarr was a cargo ship; the hull was wider, deeper, and shorter than a longship, and could take more cargo and be operated by smaller crews. It was primarily used to transport trading goods like walrus ivory, wool, timber, wheat, furs and pelts, armour, slaves, honey, and weapons. It was also used to supply food, drink, weapons and armour to warriors and traders along their journeys across the Baltic, the Mediterranean and other seas. Knarrs routinely crossed the North Atlantic carrying livestock such as sheep and horses, and stores to Norse settlements. The knarr was constructed using the same clinker-built method as longships. It was later replaced by the cog.

5. Flanders and the Holy Roman Empire

The count of Flanders had possessions on both sides of the frontier between the kingdom of France and the Holy Roman Empire. The vast majority of his county lay within the borders of France. "Imperial Flanders," as the portion within the borders of the Holy Roman Empire was known, was much smaller. Between 1055–1071 the count of Flanders was also count of Hainault, a separate feudal principality within the Holy Roman Empire. From this confusion much conflict ensued.

6. Angles, Saxons, Mercians and the Danelagh.

The various Anglo-Saxon Chronicles and Bede's History all suggest that the islands of Britain were invaded by Angles, Saxons, and Jutes from the 5th century through to the 7th century. Of course, the immigration of Nordic and Germanic tribes into the islands was a lot more complicated than that and the in-coming peoples who were invited and invaded certainly included Franks, Frisians, Alemanni, Geats etc. What is clear is that the majority of the immigrants identified most closely with the

Angles from the base of the Jutland peninsula and that apart from the royal family of Essex who claimed some sort of descent from the continental Saxons all the royal families north of the Thames claimed Angle descent; these included the Mercians, East Angles and Northumbrians. It is an uncontroversial fact these peoples came from the same place as the later Danes and in cultural terms were very similar and DNA cannot distinguish between the two tribes.

During most of the period prior to the Norman invasion the paramountcy of England was wielded by first Northumbria, then Mercia and finally the West Saxons. The peoples of Anglian descent north of the Thames by no means accepted Saxon paramountcy even up to AD1066. In fact, the later incursions of the Danes into what became the Danelagh and Kingdon of York was no more objectionable to the Angles than rule by the Saxons in the south based in Winchester. By the 11th century Northumbria, York and the Danelagh had been ruled by Danish and Norwegians leaders for at least two hundred and fifty years with only intermittent interference by the West Saxon kings.

It is with this mindset that Hereward's actions and beliefs, a half-Mercian, half-Danish noble, should be judged.

7. Paganism and Christianity in the 11th century.

Although Christianity was introduced into the British Isles by the Romans and in Ireland by the 5th century of this era, this by no means meant that pagan beliefs died out. This coupled with the fact that Christianity was only established in Scandinavia between the 9th and 11th centuries it is inevitable that the heathen religions survived particularly with noble families who claimed descent from Odin/Woden or Frey. Ultimately, the pagan religions revered these northern gods as ancestors and therefore found no difficulty in accepting the Christian beliefs alongside their existing reverence for their forefathers. Gods or human heroes.

8. Slavery in the Viking world.

There is no doubt that slavery existed and flourished in the viking world and there is plenty of physical evidence by way of slave manacles excavated in the viking entrepots of Dublin and

York. The various northern sagas detail slavery as a norm in Iceland, Norway, Sweden and Russia and the peoples of that milieu saw nothing immoral in this practice.

Slaves or thralls were commonplace throughout the north and in England in the eleventh century of this era. However, slaves tended to be dispersed in small numbers, ones, and twos, throughout families and villages and not used in large numbers for menial economies such as mining and heavy tasks. In essence the northern realms were not slave societies but understood the demands of societies that were. Scandinavians, as traders, pandered to the needs of the traditional slave economies of the Mediterranean; Roman, Byzantine, and Arab.

In such savage times slavery was relative, a brutal existence in a rath in Ireland could be transformed into a life of luxury in an Andalusian harem but if slavery as a condition is ultimately a matter of having one's own freedom of choice, slavery existed and continues to exist in the present.

Hereward was a child of his time and must be judged accordingly.

9. The passing of time

It would have been much easier to refer to the passing of time in hours in the book, but this is a modern concept even though intellectuals, such as Alfred the Great, divided the day into hours. The accepted divisions of the day in the 11th century, apart from the obvious ones i.e. morning, noon, afternoon, evening, and night, were the divisions of the day between the church's prayers.

The monastic rule drawn up by Benedict of Nursia (c. 480 – c. 547) distinguishes between the seven daytime canonical hours of lauds (dawn), prime (sunrise), terce (mid-morning), sext (midday), none (mid-afternoon), vespers (sunset), compline (retiring) and the night time canonical hour of vigil.

However, Scandinavian sailors and their Danelagh cousins were hardly likely to use such religious terminology and so I chose to identify time by the system of 'watches' that have been used on ships since time immemorial. A watch is generally about a modern four-hour period for a lookout/sentry.

About the Author

Dennis Freeman-Wright is a native of Lincolnshire, England with DNA that is Anglo-Danish. A family man with two beautiful daughters and four grandchildren, he currently lives in Charnwood Forest, Leicestershire with his very supportive and lovely wife, Ann.

Dennis has had several careers: initially an exciting period in the police force (yes it was a force then, not a service) in uniform and CID. Secondly, a successful career in sport and recreation management, managing large leisure centres, swimming pools, and theatres. Finally, he was employed as a senior consultant for a National Governing Body for Sport, becoming something of an expert in his field.

A prolific writer of technical guidance documents and historical papers, Dennis has embarked on writing historical and crime novels.

9 781917 425575